Michael Marshall is a novelist and screen-writer. Before writing the bestselling *The Straw Men* he had already established a successful writing career under the name Michael Marshall Smith. His groundbreaking first novel, *Only Forward*, won the Philip K. Dick and August Derleth awards; its critically acclaimed successors, *Spares* and *One of Us*, have both been optioned by major Hollywood studios. He lives in North London with his wife.

THE LONELY DEAD

A guilty man walks alone into the cold mountain forests of Washington State, aiming never to return. What he finds there starts a chain of events that will quickly spiral out of control. Meanwhile, in Los Angeles, a woman's body is discovered, sitting bolt upright in a motel bedroom. She is dead, and her killer has left his mark. It soon becomes clear he has something to say, and a lot more work to do. And Ward Hopkins, an ex-CIA agent recovering from the recent shocking death of his parents, is on the trail of his past, tracking down the men who destroyed everything he once held dear, and the murderer whose face he sees every time he looks in the mirror.

Books by Michael Marshall
Published by The House of Ulverscroft:

THE STRAW MEN

MICHAEL MARSHALL

THE
LONELY DEAD

Complete and Unabridged

CHARNWOOD
Leicester

First published in Great Britain in 2004 by
HarperCollins Publishers
London

First Charnwood Edition
published 2005
by arrangement with
HarperCollins Publishers Limited
London

British Library CIP Data

Marshall, Michael, *1965* –
    The lonely dead.—Large print ed.—
Charnwood library series
1. Suspense fiction
2. Large type books
I. Title
823.9′14 [F]

ISBN 1–84395–665–9

Published by
F. A. Thorpe (Publishing)
Anstey, Leicestershire
Set by Words & Graphics Ltd.
Anstey, Leicestershire
Printed and bound in Great Britain by
T. J. International Ltd., Padstow, Cornwall

This book is printed on acid-free paper

For my father

Acknowledgements

A big thank you to my editors, Jane Johnson and Susan Allison, for their patience and guidance, and to my literary agents Jonny Geller and Ralph Vicinanza. Thanks to my publishers, in particular Sarah Hodgson, Kelly Edgson-Wright, Fiona McIntosh, Jane Harris and Amanda Ridout for their amazing support; to Lavie and Ariel for hard work on the net; to Nick Marston and Bob Bookman in film; and to Phyllis Siefker, Frank Joseph, Melanie Nixon and Ella Clark, whose non-fiction provided snippets of background (apologies for what I've done with it).

Finally, as always, love and thanks to Paula for putting up with me while I'm writing. And also when I'm not.

Yakima

We met in the parking lot of the Yakima mall. Yakima is a small city in central Washington State. It's a city in the sense that it calls itself one; it has a mall in that you can go indoors and shop without views of the outside reminding you where you are. In three hours only two people had entered the mall. Both were teenagers wearing football shirts. Neither looked as if they had the hard cash to turn the place's fortunes around. They came out later, carrying nothing. Huge canvas signs around the third storey advertised retail space at knock-down rates. The big corner spot at street level was vacant, which is never a good sign.

I sat in the car drinking Americanos I fetched from a Seattle's Best across the way. The coffee shop was the only business on the Avenue that appeared to believe in itself: the rest looked like they'd stashed their For Lease sign in a safe place, looking to save a few bucks come the inevitable. I could almost hear the sound of a mayor sitting behind a big shiny desk, drumming his fingers, quietly losing his mind as he felt the town snooze around him. It would survive — even this dead zone needed somewhere to host a Les Schwab and make up the national Burger King quota — but it was unlikely to make anyone rich again. If that was what you had in mind, you'd go up to Seattle, or down to

Portland. What you did in Yakima I had no idea.

When John Zandt arrived he was driving a big red GMC, dirty and none too new. The passenger side looked like a bunch of cows had rammed it and nearly won. He pulled around the lot until he was level with my pristine Ford Generic. We wound our windows down. The air was cold.

'Hey, Ward. You ask them for that at the desk?' he said. 'Should've got them to spray 'Not From Around Here' across the hood.'

'You're unbelievably late,' I said. 'So fuck you. My place wasn't running a shit-kicker's special. Evidently you got lucky.'

'Stole it from the airport lot,' he admitted. 'So let's go.'

I got out of my car, leaving the keys in the ignition. I figured Hertz could absorb the loss. They had before. Neither they nor anyone else could trace me from the ID I had used in Spokane. When I climbed in the pickup I saw two handguns lying on the floor. I picked one up, looked it over, put it in a pocket.

'How far is it?'

'About an hour,' Zandt said. 'And then we have to walk.'

He pulled out of the lot and down the Avenue, past the grey new mall which had helped put the curse on the one I'd been watching without looking any too prosperous itself. Took a right to follow 82 down through the sprawl that became Union Gap, then buildings by a road, and then just a road. At Toppenish he took 97's abrupt swerve to the south west. There were no more towns now until an eight-point burg called Goldendale, fifty miles away. Below that, it was another twenty miles to one of the Columbia River's least attractive stretches, upstream of The Dalles dam. I'd spent time with a talkative barman the night before as I sat drinking in Rooney's Lounge, the excuse for a bar offered by Yakima's biggest hotel. I knew we were now in the Yakama Reservation and that there was nothing for eighty miles either side of the truck, the indigenous population having clumped together in a couple of small, battered settlements in the north. I knew that the place called Union Gap had once been called Yakima instead, until the rail company forced the Indians to move their capital a few miles north, reluctance worn down by the offer of free land, bribes dividing the tribe in a way hunger or cold winters never had. I knew also that just upriver from The Dalles was a spot where once had thundered the Celilo Falls, a raging, sacred shelf of water where men had harvested salmon for ten thousand years. It was now silent, buried beneath the bloated waters of the dam. Money had changed hands, some time before, but the Yakama were still waiting for their loss to be recognized in more meaningful ways. It seemed likely they'd be waiting a while longer, possibly until the end of time.

Like most people, I didn't really know what to do with this information. The barman was Native American but had short blond hair spiked like a 1980s pop star, and was wearing quite a lot

3

of make-up. I hadn't known what to make of that either.

Zandt had a map taped to the dashboard. The edges were ragged and there were smears of grease down the front. It looked like it had spent a long time in pockets and grimy hands. A small cross had been marked in the centre of a big empty patch, near a wandering blue line called Dry Creek.

'Where did this come from?'

'A call logged on one of the Rat-On-A-Friend lines. The note was heading straight for the trash — the guy was very drunk and didn't make much sense — but Nina grabbed it out of the slush pile.'

'Why?'

'Because it sounded a long way outside normal and she knows that doesn't mean it's not true.'

'So how'd you find the guy?'

'Those 800 numbers aren't quite as anonymous as the FBI make out. Nina had the call reverse-tracked to a bar in South Dakota. I went there and waited until he showed up again. It was not sudden.'

'And?'

'The informant's name is Joseph. Grew up in Harrah, a bump a few miles west of Yakima. You know this is Reservation land?'

'Too bleak to be anything else. We were so generous to these guys, it's weird they don't love us to bits.'

'This is where they lived, Ward. Not our fault it looks like the moon. Joseph was visiting family

4

and took a walk in the wilds here a week ago. A long walk. He ended up being out a few nights. I should note that his appearance suggests Joseph drinks a great deal on a regular basis. The insides of his arms look bad too. But he was definite about where he'd been.'

'Why didn't he tell the regular law?'

'I don't think he's had a good time with the local police. That's why he was in South Dakota.'

'But he saw your cute new goatee and decided to trust you right there and then?'

Zandt looked away. 'Hoped you hadn't noticed.'

'Man, I noticed. And I haven't even *begun* ripping the piss out of it.'

'Nina likes it.'

'Probably likes leather purses, too. Doesn't mean you got to wear one on your head. So where is this Joseph guy now?'

'Gone. He has two hundred dollars in his pocket and I don't think he'll be talking to anyone. He was spooked enough already. He thought he'd seen a spirit or something.' Zandt shook his head, as if he found that kind of thing too stupid for words.

I looked away before he could see the expression on my face.

$\star$ $\star$ $\star$

Half an hour out of Toppenish we could indeed have been on another planet. Maybe once there had been a reason to come here. There wasn't now. No trees; only sharp hills and shallow

5

canyons and small shrubs and grasses pale amongst the remnants of last week's snow. The rocks were grey and flat brown and looked like an icy watercolour hung in someone else's hallway. The sky had gone a deeper grey and clouds lay on the hills and in valleys like white moss. The only thing that drew the eye was the road.

Zandt kept his eyes on the clock. After another ten miles he started driving more slowly and watching along the side. Eventually he saw what he was looking for and pulled over.

'This is as close as we're going to get.'

He drove straight over the hard shoulder and down onto a track I hadn't even noticed. We bumped along this as it led down the side of a hill until it was beneath the level of the road, and then climbed around the side of an outcrop. It didn't look like anyone had come this way in a very long time. Within half a mile the grade was getting steep in all directions and I was hanging onto my seat with both hands.

Zandt checked we weren't visible from the road and stopped the truck. He got out, and I did too. It was very quiet.

I looked around. 'This is it?'

'No, but we're going to have to walk the rest.'

'Never been much of a hiker.'

'Why am I not surprised?' He pulled something out of his jacket that looked like a personal organizer with a fat slug lying on the top.

'GPS?'

He nodded. 'I want to be able to find our way back.'

He logged the car's position and pointed up the rise. The view was the same as we'd had all afternoon, except now there was no road. 'Let's get going.'

We followed the remainder of the track until it petered out around the back of the hill, and then walked out into nothing. Behind the hill was another, the far slope of which led down into a shallow canyon. We made our way down, mist settling around us, and up out the other side. Then it was pretty flat for quite a while. There were no trees. The ground was hard and rocky and bare except for tufts of the yellowish grass and more of the pale blue-green ground shrubs. Walking made a sound like someone eating Doritos with their mouth shut.

Zandt kicked at a plant. 'What is this stuff?'

'Sagebrush, I'm assuming. Though to be honest I know shit about high plains flora.'

'Fucking pain in the ass to walk through.'

'It surely is.'

We kept on walking, cloud gathering around us until we couldn't see more than thirty yards in any direction. John consulted his satellite positioning gadget every now and then, but this didn't feel like a place that had destinations. It was dry and cold, not bitter, but with the kind of steady chill that makes it hard to remember being any other way. I tried to imagine people living out here once, and couldn't. It must have been long ago. The land felt like it didn't want anyone bothering it any more.

After a good while I looked at my watch. It was after four o'clock, and the light was beginning to turn. A sly wind began to pick up. The sun was a silver coin in the mist, hazy and starting to tarnish.

'I know,' John said, before I'd even spoken. 'The mark on the map is all I have. We're there, or thereabouts.'

'We're not anywhere,' I said. 'I've never seen a place that is so not somewhere in my entire life.'

We kept on walking nonetheless. The mist got thicker, sometimes a grey blanket, every now and then suddenly hollowing out to form a hidden inner channel that caused the sun to make it glow from within like a golden vision. We found ourselves walking along a low crest, the foot of another hill rising like a grey-green sand dune ten yards to the right, the lip of a canyon over on the left.

We didn't seem to be making much progress but I didn't say anything. I didn't have anywhere else to be.

★　★　★

Finally it was John who stopped.

'This is bullshit,' he said. He was pissed. I didn't blame him, but he seemed edgy too, restlessly angry beneath the surface. The dark smudges under his eyes suggested he hadn't been sleeping well. I hoped his contact had the sense not to go back to the bar in South Dakota for a while.

'Your gizmo got a backlight?'

'Of course.'

'So we've got some more time.' I started off again.

He stayed put. 'Ward, I don't think it's worth it. Even in a straight line we're forty minutes off the road, maybe more. We've circled around the entire area covered by the mark.'

I turned. 'And where did he make that cross? Where was he?'

'In the bar.' From only a few yards away, Zandt's voice sounded as if it had to fight its way through the mist.

'Right. A week and many hundred miles from when he was here, in other words. How drunk was he at the time?'

'He said he was sure.'

'He's probably sure he can handle his drink too. You take a witness's word for anything back when you were a cop?'

'Of course not,' he snapped. He pulled out his cell phone and glared at it. 'No signal. We're a long way off the map out here, Ward.'

'In every possible way. But . . . ' I stopped talking, as the world seemed to take a side step. 'What the fuck is that?'

He came level with me and we stood shoulder to shoulder for a moment. Then he saw it. 'Holy shit.'

There was a man a little way ahead of us, just far enough that his edges were blurred by the mist. He was dressed in a grey business suit and black office shoes inappropriate for the environment. I could hear the sound of his jacket flapping in the wind. The set of his stride was

9

purposeful. Despite this, he wasn't moving.

I took a step forward, stopped. Reached for my gun, and then left it. Thought again, and got it out anyway.

Separating slightly, we approached the walking man.

He looked to be in his late fifties. He had grey hair that had recently been well cut, but it was now plastered down over his head. His hands and face were an unattractive colour. Once white, now a variable palette of blue and harsh pink, shading in places towards some purple-brown hue that had no name. A jagged cut gouged across his neck as far up as his left ear: the knife had taken off a section, giving him a curiously lopsided appearance. His upper lip was also missing. There was a smell coming off him, but it wasn't unbearable. It had been very cold, and dry.

Now that we were closer, it became a little more prosaic. No longer a ghost. Just a body. Nobody likes to see a body, but it's better than seeing a ghost. Bodies just make you doubt the world and the people in it. Ghosts make you doubt everything, and to doubt it in a part of the mind that has no words to answer the question, where the comforting promises you make yourself are neither believed nor even really understood.

Zandt headed around the back. He held his PDA up towards the man's face and started taking pictures. 'Look,' he said.

I circled, unconsciously keeping well clear, as if I feared the body would start moving,

10

resuming some progress across the plain. A metal pole, about five feet high and maybe two inches thick, had been driven into the ground behind him. He had been tied to it, his body held upright in a way that happened to make him look like he was walking. In time the body would fall and the clothes fade, and the pole would rust away.

'Christ,' I said. Zandt just nodded, apparently fresh out of other points of view. He put his hands in the man's jacket and trouser pockets, and came up empty.

I stood back. If you waited a while, as the mist ebbed and shifted, you could see that the positioning of the body had been carefully chosen. He was sheltered from view by the hill. You wouldn't see him unless you were actually out here, some place there was absolutely no reason to be.

Zandt looked out over what he could see of the plain. 'He said there were two.'

'Excellent. That gives us something to look forward to.'

'He didn't say where.'

I nodded at the walking man. 'I'd guess he was supposed to be going someplace.'

We walked in the direction that the man was pointed. After fifty yards we began to sense, rather than see, the lip of another canyon. Then we saw something else.

She was sitting right on the edge. She was about the same age as the walking man, but with her skin in its current condition it wasn't easy to be precise. Her elbows rested on her knees, and her hands were brought together to cup her face. The pose was natural, presumably achieved before the body stiffened. The only wrong note was her hair. This was wild and stood up in grey clumps. It looked as if crows had discovered her and started to do their work, and then stopped. Perhaps even they had their limits. Now, she just sat and stared with hollow, sunken eyes.

She looked like . . . I don't know what she looked like. I didn't really have a comparison. I turned away before she could turn and see me. If she did there would be no leaving this place.

Zandt took only two pictures, then logged the position. 'Okay,' he said quietly. 'Let's get out of here.'

I followed him as he walked away from the woman. I didn't know what I was feeling, wasn't sure what you were supposed to make of such a thing.

I stopped and looked back at her. Something about the way she was positioned was niggling at me.

'Ward, let's move out. It's going to get dark soon.'

I ignored him and walked back to her. Squatted down as close as I felt willing, and looked where she was looking. Her head was tilted slightly forward, as if she was gazing down into the canyon.

I wanted to be back in the car as much as Zandt did. Rooney's Lounge seemed like a good place to be at that moment. Even the Yakima mall, at a pinch. But something compelled me.

It wasn't easy getting into the canyon. I started

to go down facing forward, but soon turned around and used my hands. I heard Zandt swear from above, and then start after me, thankfully having the sense to pick a line a good few yards to the side. The rocks he dislodged fell well clear.

When I got to the bottom I couldn't see much at first. The same as up above, only rockier, with a little more vegetation and a few stubby trees. The mist was clearing now, drifting off somewhere else as the sky turned a darker blue.

Then I saw that there was another inlet up ahead, the memory of a smaller stream. I walked up it for a short distance, and was surprised to find it turning into a wider, open area. I was still standing at the entrance to this when Zandt arrived, looking at a bulky shape hidden under an outcrop.

At first it was hard to make out what it was.

Then we saw that it was the corner of a small building, flush up against the side of the canyon.

We got our guns out again.

We approached the building walking a few feet apart. It became clear that it was very old, a functional one-room cabin, pioneer style. It was made from big chunks of wood that had weathered well, still brown in places amongst the grey. Battered planks of more recent vintage had been nailed across the windows from the inside. The door was shut, held by a padlock that didn't look old at all. Someone had gone at the door with an axe or shovel, but not recently. Shapes that looked like letters were visible amongst the scars. I saw something that looked like a big 'R'.

Holding his gun ready, Zandt used his other

13

hand to click a few pictures onto his little machine. The windows. The walls. The door.

Then he pocketed it, and looked at me. I nodded.

I walked straight ahead and kicked the door in and swung the hell back out of the way. Zandt was right behind me, gun held straight out in front of him.

I slipped in and turned full right, getting behind the door. With the windows blocked it was dark but the door gave more than enough light. My scalp tried to crawl backwards off my head.

The cabin was full of dead people.

Three sat in a line on a bench, slumped against the back wall. One was little more than a skeleton, the other two dark and vile. One had no arms; the other's abdomen had burst some time before. Other bodies were gathered in a small deliberate heap on the other side, and at least two more lay along the front wall, heads opposed. The state of these indicated none had died recently. A few had scraps and tangles of skin and jerky-like flesh hanging from scaffolding bones. One skull had the upper half of a plastic doll protruding from a hole in its crown. Dust had turned the doll's hair grey.

As my eyes got used to the gloom, I began to see more and more desiccated body parts: a small, orderly pile against the wall on the left. I moved part of it with my foot, and saw a layer of bones underneath. A thick layer, some of it little more than dust.

14

We dropped our arms. Nobody here could do us harm.

Zandt cleared his throat. 'Did they do this?'

'The Straw Men? Could be. But some of this has been here a long, long time.'

Zandt wanted to take the cabin apart but one glance told me there was nothing for us to find. If you killed someone in this cabin you could take your time. Plus, I just didn't want to be there. At all. I wanted to be outside. The longer you stood in that place, the more it felt like the cabin was breathing, slowly, a palpable exhalation of rancid air.

I backed out over the threshold. I was less surprised now that some of the wood remained brown. It was as if many, many bad things had been absorbed into the walls, keeping it moist, keeping it alive. Whatever had happened here had taken place over an extended period of time. It had to be the work of more than one person, perhaps even more than one generation. Was it just a place to dump bodies, or was their silent presence, their positioning, supposed to achieve something more nebulous? I thought about the country as a whole, with all its wide, dead spaces. Was this the only one of these?

Zandt came out too, but then he stopped suddenly, and stared at something over my shoulder.

I turned and saw what he was looking at. It was twenty feet away, on the other side of the canyon, positioned where you would see it when you came out of the cabin.

I took a few steps towards it. This body was far

15

more recent. It had not been arranged like the couple up on the plain, but merely thrown on the ground, arms outstretched, legs bent. Something brown had been nailed to his chest, in the centre. It looked like nothing I'd ever seen, but the unnatural emptiness of the man's gaping mouth told me what it was.

When my stomach had stopped retching, I said, 'Is that the guy? Is that Joseph?'

Zandt didn't have to answer.

★　★　★

It was a long walk back to the car. We drove in silence, following the Columbia down towards Portland.

At the airport we got flights in different directions. We didn't meet again for another month, by which time everything had changed.

16

1: Cold Harbours

I do believe
Though I have found them not,
That there may be
Words which are things.

Lord Byron,
Childe Harold's Pilgrimage

1

There's never a pull-off when you need one. You're belting along, forest on both sides, making light work of shallow rises and swooping dips, ranks of paper birch framing a series of flicker-lit views so snowy beautiful you can't even see them, and you keep thinking that just around the next bend there must be a place to stop and park but for some reason there isn't. It's a cloudy Tuesday afternoon in mid-January, a fact that has already seemed odd to you, a strange time to be doing what you're doing, and you've got the road to yourself for probably five miles in both directions. You could just dump the car on the side of the road, but that doesn't seem right. Though it's only a rental and you have no attachment to it other than it being the last car you're ever going to drive, you don't want to abandon it. You're not being sentimental. It's not even that you don't want someone to see it, wonder if something untoward is taking place, and come investigating — though you don't. It's just a neatness thing. You want the car to be parked. To be at rest. Right at this moment this seems very important to you, but there's never anywhere to stop. That's the whole problem, you realize, suddenly hot-eyed: that's life in a goddamned nutshell. There's never anywhere to rest, not when you really need it.

Sometimes you don't need a vista point. You just want to be able to . . .

Shit — there's one.

Tom slammed his foot down three seconds late and far too hard. The car skidded thirty feet, back end swinging out gracefully until he came to rest straddling both lanes. He sat for a moment, neck tingling. Through the window came cold air and the sound of a bird cawing with maniacal persistence. Otherwise, silence, thank God. Anyone else on the road and it would have gone badly, which would be ironic as all hell, but again, not something he wanted. He was unpopular enough.

He straightened the car up and then slowly backed past the pull-off. Sarah would have been able to reverse right in, but he didn't feel confident of doing so, so he didn't try. That had always been his way. Hide your faults. Keep your secrets. Never run the risk of looking a fool even if that means you look a fool, and a cowardly one at that.

He pulled forward into the small parking area, crunching over a six-inch line of snow ploughed off the road. The lot evidently belonged to the head of some lesser-known hiking trail, firmly shut for the off-season. Only when the car was stationary again did Tom realize his hands were shaking badly. He reached to the passenger seat for the bottle and took a long swallow. Looking in the rear-view mirror he saw only the pale skin, brown hair, baggy eyes and incipient double chin he expected. Middle-age camouflage.

He opened the door and dropped the keys into

the side pocket. No sense making it too obvious. He hauled himself out, slipped immediately on a rock, and fell full length on the ground.

When he pushed himself to his knees he saw there were small wet cuts on one of his palms, and his forehead and right cheek were dripping. His right ankle hurt too. Face pricked with tiny pieces of flint, stunned into a winded moment of sobriety, he knew finally that what he was doing was the right thing.

He got his rucksack out of the trunk and shut it. He made sure the car was locked, then stepped over the low barrier made of logs and set off between the trees, in the opposite direction to the trail.

The bird, or another very like it, was still making its rasping noise. Tom tried shouting at it, first words, and then mere sounds. The bird went silent, then started up again. Tom got the message. In here he was just another noisy animal, not in any position to issue commands.

He let the bird be, and concentrated on not falling down.

★ ★ ★

The going was hard and steep. He soon understood why there'd been no rest areas: this forest wasn't a restful place. It wasn't here for anyone's benefit: there were no roped paths, restrooms or snack stops, none of the traditional mediators between the cooked and the raw. That was okay. His needs were few, and catered for. The rucksack had almost nothing in it except

21

alcohol, and he'd paused to repack the bottles so they didn't clink. He had nothing inside him except alcohol either. He was already doubting vodka as a way of life. It wasn't for the faint of heart, that was for sure. Feeling like shit took a high level of tolerance. His wasn't actually that high, but he was being quite brave about it.

After two hours he estimated he'd only travelled three miles, though he'd climbed enough to leave the birches and fiery dogwood behind and be alone with spruce and cedars. Up here the ground was mainly clear of snow, but it was choked with fallen branches and aggressive bushes that grabbed at his jeans and coat. The trees were tall and quiet and grew wherever the hell they liked. Occasionally he came across a stream. The first one he jumped, but as his ankle began to ache more he made detours to find places where it was easier to cross. Sometimes he muttered to himself. Mainly he kept quiet, saving his breath. The faster he went, the less he had to be aware. When he finished the bottle he dropped it and kept on going. A hundred yards on he realized this had been boorish, and reeled back to find it. He couldn't, which suggested he was doing his job: becoming both profoundly drunk and very lost. He kept walking steadily. Time spent with Green Trails sheets had shown that even logging roads were scarce in the area, but he knew from experience — albeit in cities — that his sense of direction was pretty good. He also knew how weak he was, how impulse could come and take his hand and lead him places he didn't want to go, then suddenly vanish, leaving him with blood on his hands. That's why being lost was crucial. Otherwise he'd change his mind. He'd cop out and procrastinate and fail, and surely there was nothing more pathetic than screwing up your own suicide.

Tom Kozelek had come to the Pacific North West with no plan except a desire to be somewhere other than Los Angeles. He had stood in LAX, a little drunk, and picked Seattle because he'd been there on business recently and knew a good hotel. He stayed there a single night and then drove east, into the Cascade Mountains. It's a strange area. There are peaks and vertiginous valleys, jagged rocks in every shade of grey. There's even a small amount of history, of an 'And then they cut down a bunch more trees' kind. But there aren't many roads, and the mountains pretty much keep themselves to themselves: unless you know where you're going — which Tom didn't — it would be easy to think there wasn't anything much to find. He moved vaguely between small, cold towns for two days, spent evenings sitting in motel rooms with the television off. He phoned what had been his home. The call was answered, which made it worse. The conversation with his wife and children was short and involved no shouting. Worse still. There are times when reasonableness is the worst cut of all, because if everyone's being adult and yet the world is still broken, where do you go from there?

In the end he found a town called Sheffer and dug in. Sheffer was little more than a main drag and five cross-streets that quickly petered out into steep fir-choked foothills; but a pair of snooty mini-hotels and a hippy café with good oatmeal cookies and five pristine secondhand copies of *The Bridges of Madison County* suggested people came there on purpose. There was a small railroad museum (closed) and a stretch of disused track alongside the main drag, home to picturesquely rusting hulks of rolling stock. It was out of season and the town was kicking back, locals moving forward out of the background, combing the moss out of their hair.

Four days before his walk in the woods Tom sat at the counter in Big Frank's, the least anodyne of its three bars, staring at television coverage of a foreign sport whose rules he didn't understand. He felt agitatedly becalmed, way out in Injun territory. He was forty-three years old and a grown-up. He had charge cards. He had a car at his disposal. He was not limited by anybody's expectations or prior knowledge: he could pretend his name was Lance if he had a mind to, claim to be an ex-fighter pilot turned dotcom millionaire; or a cult jazz-fusion choreographer called Bewildergob. Nobody would know otherwise, or care. He could do anything he wanted. But with this came the realization there was nothing he wanted to do. Nothing at all.

Nothing would make a difference now. He had crossed the line.

He drank until his brain was empty and cold. The idea, when it came, arrived in his head as if shot there by a distant archer. He realized there *was* a way of making things, if not better, then at least manageable. Of making the problems go away. He got another beer and took it to a table in a darker corner to consider the idea more carefully.

He'd thought of suicide before, like most people, but never seriously: an occasional glance to check the idea remained ridiculous. This felt different. This wasn't a gesture. It was entirely rational. His situation wasn't yet irrevocable, after all. His marriage was over, but not all his friendships. He could get a new job, design corporate web for somebody else. Find an apartment. Do his laundry. Buy a microwave oven of his own. A year from now it might all feel different. So what? He'd still be the same Tom, a procrastinating man of indifferent talents, slowly expanded by the metabolic cycle pump of age. The choices he wanted to make existed solely in the past.

So why not just have done with it? Draw the line. Swallow the loss. Hope reincarnation was true and try to make a better job of it next time.

Why not? After all — why not?

He drank until the bar shut, then tried to chat to the two young bartenders as they guided him towards the door. One radiated boredom, the other mild distaste. Tom realized he was probably not much younger than their fathers, most likely square-jawed mountain types who took a nip of bourbon or sour mash or whatever the fuck about once a month. The door was shut firmly behind him. As he staggered back towards his motel it occurred to him that he didn't have to care what they thought about him any more.

25

His new course put him on a higher plane. He got so cross that he turned around and reeled back to the bar, intending to explain to Chip and Dale that while these were great times for boys in their twenties, men in middle age weren't having it quite so smooth; that one day their own abs might sag and they'd forget how to love and have no clue who they were. He felt this would be a valuable insight for them. It was the only one he had, in any event, and he was willing to share it around. By the time he got back to the bar it was locked and dark. He hammered on the door for a while, telling himself they might still be inside but mainly just because he wanted to hammer on something. It wasn't more than five minutes before he was suddenly quite well lit. He turned to see a car from the sheriff's department parked on the street behind him. A youngish guy in a uniform was leaning back on the bonnet, his arms folded.

'Believe it's shut, sir,' he said.

Tom opened his mouth but realized there was too much to say and none of it made any sense. He raised his arms, not in surrender, but in a kind of mute entreaty. Strangely, the deputy seemed to understand. He nodded, got back in his car and drove away. Tom walked home, padding slowly down the middle of the main street through the steady, meditative blink of traffic lights with no cars to direct.

Next morning he thought it through. His options were limited. There was no gun store in town, and he didn't want to drive until he found one. Even assuming they let him have one, guns

26

were scary. Jumping off a cliff, supposing he could find one, was also out. The idea was self-evidently counter-evolutionary. Even if his mind was determined his body could simply over-rule — in which case he'd have a long walk back to the car feeling the world's biggest fool. *Yes, I was going to throw myself off, that's right. No, it didn't happen. Sorry. Nice view, though. Mind your step.* Besides which, he didn't want to end up as something distended or smashed or half dead, something to be found, photographed, and shipped home. He didn't want to be broken, he wanted to be *erased.*

On Sunday he was picking at a huge Reuben in Henry's, the town's more friendly diner, when he heard something that put the final piece in place. A local old-timer was taking delight in worrying a pair of Winnebago retirees about the scope and impenetrability of the woods. Tom's attention was drawn by the repetition of a number. Seventy-three. The local said it several times in a row. Seventy-three — how about that?

His audience were looking at each other and nodding as if impressed. Then the male of the pair turned to the local, with the air of a man who had spotted a flaw in another's argument.

'Big ones, or little ones?' he asked. 'The planes? What kind of size were they?'

His wife nodded. No flies on her husband. She'd always said so.

'All sizes,' the old geezer said, somewhat tetchily. 'Big ones, little ones, civilian, military. Planes go down all the time — matter of fact, many *more* than that have ditched around here.

27

My point is that of all the planes gone down in the Pacific North West since the war, *seventy-three have never even been found.*'

Is that right? Tom thought.

He pushed his sandwich away, paid his tab, and went to buy as much alcohol as he could carry.

★   ★   ★

He wasn't prepared for how quickly it got dark. He was stumbling more than walking, the muscles in his thighs and calves turned to lead. He'd still only gone maybe eight miles, ten at most, but he was exhausted. It occurred to him that if he'd spent more time in the gym he'd be in better shape to die. This made him laugh until his mouth filled with warm saliva and he had to stop walking and breathe deeply to avoid vomiting.

He was now about as drunk as he'd ever been. As he rested, bent over with hands on knees, watching the floating spots before his eyes, he considered what to do next. He was already very lost. Getting lost could be ticked off the schedule of tasks. The ground had been getting more mountainous all afternoon, steep and slip-slidy and treacherous. When it got properly night, it was going to be very dark indeed, the kind of darkness that would swallow up and deafen a city boy. He took the rucksack off and felt for the flashlight. When he flicked it on he realized it wasn't just the quality of the light that was changing. A mist was gathering. It was also

28

unbelievably cold. For the moment it was just sweat turning to frigid water on his skin, but when it got into his bones it would be hard to bear. Which meant he had to keep moving.

He rotated his ankle to warm it up a little, made a slight turn and kept ploughing onwards. The forest was very quiet now, noisy birds having cawed their fill and gone off home to roost. He wasn't sure about other animals. He'd already spent time not thinking about bears. He didn't think there were any around — or the old timer in the diner would surely have brought them up, he'd most definitely been the type — but you never knew. Tom didn't think he looked like a threat to any large mammal he might chance upon, and he had no food to attract them, but maybe that was all crap. Maybe they lay in wait and attacked people for the fun of it. Anyway, he didn't want to think about that, so he didn't. He kept not thinking about it at regular intervals. The flashlight had two settings, bright and not so bright, and he soon stuck to the latter. As the mist thickened it bounced more of the light back in his face, making his head whirl. Also, the light made the shadows worse. Forests in the day are friendly places. They remind you of Sunday walks, swooshing leaves, holding a parent's big, warm hand, or providing that hand yourself. At night the woods take the gloves off and remind you why you're nervous in the dark. Night forests say, 'Go find a cave, monkey-boy, this place is not for you.'

So he kept himself mist-blind and smacked his brain with vodka and kept moving. All of the crunches and rustlings he could hear were of his own making, he was sure. There were no shapes in the mist, only the movement of the moisture itself — that was also certain. You could take all of it to the bank, leave it there, and keep on walking in utter safety and only moderate discomfort: walking until it was totally dark and time itself seemed to flatten out, until each thought became hard to distinguish from the next, until fear twisted back on itself and swelled and he started moving faster and faster to escape from something he carried within himself.

★   ★   ★

He had no warning of the fall. He'd been shoving aggressively through a long trench of mid-level bushes, yielding to a third bout of head-snapping hiccups, when all at once his leading foot had nothing to come down upon. His body was tilted forward, the better to shove branches aside, there was no way back.

He was suddenly skidding down a sharp incline, legs apart, arms thrashing. Acceleration was halted by a full-body collision with a smallish tree, at which point he lost the flashlight and his bottle and was twisted and spun onto his side to slide the rest of the way via every rock in the ground. It was over quickly, and ended with him landing hard on his face with a crunch that knocked every last breath out of him.

He groaned, a low and desperate sound. At last, he shrugged off the rucksack and rolled over onto his back. The pain in his chest was so intense he let out an involuntary whistle. His right side felt as if someone had poked a spear in it and was encouraging a child to swing off the end. His balls ached too, pain rising to a hot little hollow in his lower abdomen.

After a little longer, he sat up. He ran a tentative hand down his side, not looking, just in case, but didn't find anything sticking out. He saw the flashlight was lying ten feet away, glowing dimly in undergrowth, and crawled through cold mud to retrieve it. His vision was slightly doubled, but this had been the case for the last couple of hours so he wasn't unduly worried.

Retrieving his light source felt like a step in the right direction. It seemed he'd fallen into a wide rocky gully, designed to hold a decent spring-thaw stream but now home to a thin trickle which he could hear from ten feet away. Otherwise it was quiet. Very quiet, and very cold.

He decided he'd gone far enough. Tonight would do. There didn't have to be a tomorrow after all. School was out a little early, that was all.

He pushed himself backwards until his back was against rock. Then pulled the rucksack up between his knees and opened it. One of the remaining bottles had smashed — the bottom of the bag was soaking and sharp and the smell smoked up around his face. Shining the light, he saw there was no way he could just shove his hand in so he upended most of the bag out onto the ground instead. It took a while, but he found the packs of sleeping pills.

As he laboriously pushed each pill out of its

individual foil pimple, laying them in a pile on a useful nearby leaf, he swam through an internal checklist.

Lost, check. Drunk, check. Christ yes. Great big check, in red.

He'd paid his motel bill, mentioning in passing that he was heading back up to Seattle. Check.

Anyone out hiking when it was this cold would have to be out of their fucking mind, and it was mid-week, out of season, and he'd headed away from known trails. Check.

Push, another pill. Push, another pill. He peered at the pile. Was that enough? Better make sure. He kept pushing. An overdose wasn't weak if done the way he was doing it. It was manly. And being way out in the middle of nowhere meant he would never be found, even if it went wrong. He was the man in control.

Oh yeah.

The car would be spotted tomorrow, perhaps, and in a day or two someone would investigate. Not on foot but from the air, most likely, a desultory grid pass at best. On his last day in Sheffer Tom had bought clothes and back-pack in autumnal colours, to make it even less likely that some passing plane or helicopter would be able to spot him. If he'd shelled out for some proper hiking boots too then his ankle wouldn't hurt so much, but it hadn't seemed worth it. Just went to show. Always get the proper equipment.

Anyway, a check in general. Checkety check.

As the pile of pills grew, he was surprised to find that he didn't feel afraid. He'd thought he might, that the proximity of the act itself might make him panic, that he would fight death as she had. He found he merely felt very, very tired. Somewhere in the journey from the car to this random gully he'd lost any remaining sense of his life as a process. It had become simply an event; this event, in this place, now. It was dark, and getting late. It was for the best. It was okay.

He was already very cold, his fingers thin and unmanageable. He started taking the pills, a couple at a time, washed down with more alcohol. He fumbled a few, but there were plenty. He took a lot, muttering in the dark. *Bye bye Sarah, go find someone else. Bye bye William, bye bye Lucy. You'll hate me for this, I know, but you would have come to hate me soon enough.*

At some point he seemed to accept he was into the realms of fatal dose, after which it all became more relaxed. Everything seemed easy, in fact. The forest got a little warmer too, though it was possible he just wasn't feeling his extremities any more. Everything went fuzzy and liquid as he sat and swayed in perfect darkness. He was cold and not cold, bone weary and awake. Fear circled in the bushes but stayed just out of reach, until he was barely aware of anything and didn't bother to keep putting things in his mouth. He sobbed briefly, then couldn't remember what he'd been thinking about. Trying to follow thoughts was like walking alone down a deserted street where the stores were closing one by one.

When his eyelids began to flutter he tried to keep them open, not with any sense of

33

desperation, but as a child might push away the sleep he knew could not be fought. When they finally closed it seemed lighter in his head for a moment, and then began to fade into slate grey and beyond. He expected, in so far as he had any expectations left, that this process would continue until everything became black and silent. A brief dreaming moment, as if tilting slowly backwards, and then not even that. Goodbye.

He wasn't expecting to wake up in the middle of the night, still drunk, racked with whole-body shivers. He wasn't expecting to be alive, and in thirty kinds of pain. He certainly wasn't expecting to see something standing over him, something big, something that smelled like the scent of rotted meat carried on a cold, cold wind.

2

The restaurant was a big room split up into different areas, a section of tables in the centre and booths around three sides. Small lanterns hung at the entrance to each booth, but they didn't work. The walls had been done out in big retro-style murals, lots of powder blue and pale pink and scratchy black lines. The scalloped double-height windows at the entrance showed a parking lot blown drab with old leaves, and I watched as a cold wind played with them a while. I was in my usual spot, one of the booths in the back of the room. I liked it there. The bench wasn't too close in to the table, so you didn't feel hemmed in. The menu was riddled with cunning puns and full of stuff like burgers, burritos, big old chef salads and chilli (Cincinnati- or Texas-style, 'Hot, Hotter or W-W-Watch Out!'), which is very much my kind of thing.

All in all it was a perfect place for dinner, aside from one thing. The service sucked. I'd been waiting a long time now and no one had bid me welcome, reassured me I was in the system, or given me ice water I wouldn't drink. And actually, it wasn't just the waiting staff who were slacking. When I first arrived I saw someone had knocked over most of the chairs in the central portion of the room, which looked messy. I'd put them back up, tucking them neatly under the tables, but that wasn't really my job. It wasn't my job to replace the light bulbs either. I considered going back into the kitchen, but I knew it would be pointless. It was even quieter back there, and darker, with nothing but spatulas for company.

I leaned forward on the table, wondering what the hell I was doing there. Three days is too long to wait for a bowl of chilli, no matter how damned good it is.

★　★　★

I sat for another couple of hours, until it was dark outside. A little after seven a pair of headlights swept into the lot, paused, then floated back out again. Cops, presumably. They evidently didn't feel their job extended to getting out of the car and checking the building's back doors and access hatches, otherwise they might have found evidence of how I'd forced the back way into the kitchen. The fact the place wasn't on fire was good enough. I could understand why they weren't too worried. The restaurant seemed to have a force field around it. None of the windows were broken. The chairs and tables remained in situ, along with pans and spatulas in the kitchen and maybe a hundred menus strewn over tables and the floor. Neither exterior nor interior walls had been tagged, and the smell of stale urine was notably absent. An empty *USA Today* dispenser stood outside the main doors, surely a clarion call for the moronic to explore what sounds it might make if hurled through the plate glass beside it. That call had gone unheeded. It was eerie. Vandalism evidently wasn't a huge problem in Relent, Idaho. It wasn't clear whether this said the town's youth were too refined or too apathetic for nihilistic self-expression, but brief acquaintance with the settlement suggested the latter. Evidence for refinement was scarce. Doubtless somewhere in town there were people living valuable and important lives, but from the outside it looked like a kid's trike left outside to rust.

I knew a lot about towns like Relent because that's where I'd spent most of my time in recent months, wandering directionless across many miles of backwoods and prairie in the country's least glamorous states. Initially I'd stayed in motels, then one afternoon I'd gone to an ATM and found there was no more money. It's amazing the difference a little brightly coloured rectangle makes to your well-being, to your sense of identity and belonging. You only really understand the card's importance when the machine coughs it back out again and tells you 'No,' and that word means not now, not later, not ever; when you are suddenly reminded the card was never some magical gold-producing chalice but just a piece of plastic you didn't even legally own. I stood in a parking lot in New Jersey turning mine over in my hands until a woman with an SUV and three fat kids told me to get the hell out of the way. She had her own card ready and every confidence it would perform its function. I envied her for that. Though not for her kids, who were ugly as sin.

I walked back to my car and climbed in. Sat

and looked out through the windshield for a while. I had eighteen dollars and change, plus less than half a tank of gas. Nothing else. At all.

'So, Bobby, what are we going to do now?'

Bobby didn't answer, because he was dead. He'd been my best friend, one of the few people whose long-term fate I'd cared about. He'd died up at a place called The Halls, as we tried to catch a psychopath who called himself the Upright Man. The Halls had been blown to kingdom come, vaporizing Bobby's body along with it. He'd become an unpredictable conversationalist since. Sometimes he said what I needed him to, telling me: yes, Ward, this is a good town to stay the night, or yes, you do need another beer — and yes, we did our best to find the people who murdered your parents and it would be stupid of you to feel guilty about everything that went wrong, up to and including the fact that I am dead.

Then he'd go silent for a long while. I don't know where he went during these periods, what change took place in my mind that meant I didn't hear him. And it *was* only in my own head that I heard him. I knew that. Really, I did.

In the end I drove out of the bank parking lot and found myself a job washing dishes and cutting potatoes three towns away. The Ecuadorian fry cook let me sleep on his floor for two days, after which I had enough cash to get a room of my own provided I didn't mind sharing it with bugs and dust and noise, and that I didn't eat. Working in kitchens is good for people in that position, though you become heartily sick of the cheaper food groups. Relations between the Ecuadorian and myself broke down a week later when I tried to get him to share the small coke-dealing business he had going amongst the other staff and a few young and not-so-young locals who'd turn up round the back some nights. I wound up driving the hell out of town in the small hours, bleeding profusely and feeling a fool.

The next morning I was taking a rest outside a Burger King in West Virginia, still bleeding, though less steadily, when a voice finally spoke and answered a question from nine days before. I cleaned myself up in the BK's wash-rooms, treated myself to a globalized breakfast of food-like materials and drove straight down to Arizona. Once there I located a residence in Flagstaff, which took a while because I'd been there only once, somewhat drunk, and had since lost the address. I watched the place carefully for twenty-four hours before getting out my otherwise useless rectangle of plastic, which I used to break in.

And so for five days I lived in Bobby Nygard's house.

★   ★   ★

First thing I did, once I'd had a look around and established that if anyone had robbed the place they'd done so very tidily and without being tempted by tens of thousands of dollars of computers and surveillance equipment, was get online. I hadn't done this in a while. I was semi-convinced that any attempt to trace personal information would be noticed somewhere and have people coming after me. Among the things Bobby had been expert in was the obfuscation of internet trails. I knew that if I used his home system I'd be safe, at least for a little while.

Bank accounts were my first stop. I soon established that my primary account had been closed, its contents AWOL. Not closed, but empty, was another account with a different bank. This was where the money from my parents' estate had been transferred. Someone had cleared it out, leaving credit of a single cent.

I logged out and sat back, light-headed. I wasn't surprised, but it still qualified as very bad news, and the leaving of the penny made me want to find someone and hurt them. I went through to the kitchen and found a saucer to use as an ashtray and stood looking out on the street. I heard Bobby talking then all right. He'd always been on at me to quit smoking, and in my head had evidently retained the opinion. I finished the cigarette anyway. It was nice to hear someone's voice, even if it was bugging me, and even if it was my own.

I stayed in the house. It seemed safe there, and I was tired of moving. I lived on the cans in the cupboards so I didn't have to go out. I spent a lot of time reading Bobby's notes and manuals, and I searched the house from top to bottom as respectfully as I could. I found a cache of false identities and took them, knowing Bobby would have bought them from someone he trusted. I also came across a little under six thousand dollars in cash, hidden in a computer box in the basement. I sat and looked at it for a while, feeling bad for finding it and even worse for what I was going to do. Bobby had a mother. I'd tracked her down a month before to pass on the news that he was dead. She had been drunk, and had thrown things at me, though it was not clear whether this was in response to the news — they had been far from close — or just a general policy. Probably the money should go to her, but that wasn't going to happen. It was highly likely it was dirty and I believed in my heart that Bobby would approve of me taking it.

A few days later I left the house wearing some clothes of his that more or less fit, and carrying a small bag with the money. I also had one of his laptops, having pawned my own some time before. Halfway across the street I turned and looked back at the property, wondering how long a house could go on, empty, unvisited. Weeks, certainly. So long as the bills got paid direct, and something didn't pop or burn itself out and start a fire, probably far longer. It made me wonder how many rooms and houses across the country were like that; their people disappeared, the machines in them still ticking and sighing with no one left to tend them.

★   ★   ★

After that it was places of that nature I tended to hang my hat. Occasionally I dipped into Bobby's stash to stay somewhere that reminded me I'd

41

once had a life, some big city downtown chain where you had to ring reception in the morning to be reminded which state you were in. Otherwise I took what I could find. Boarded-up motels just outside the limits; commercial zone office blocks where the glass had gone grey; anywhere forgotten and overlooked that had a sign saying KEEP OUT, because usually those two words were the only deterrent in place bar the fear of running into someone who might try to use violence to defend their temporary home. Luckily I was one of those people myself, so the prospect didn't overly bother me. There were a few confrontations, but people who have nothing are easily cowed, providing you keep your nerve and maintain the pretence you're somehow different. It's surprising just how much abandoned space there is; these places we once wanted, now home merely to emptiness and mattresses folded in odd ways and smelling of unnameable things.

I thought that maybe after I'd been to Bobby's house he wouldn't be with me any more, that he'd wanted to be taken home and would stay there when I left. But it wasn't like that. He followed me north to Montana, coming to Dyersburg when I decided to take the risk and visit the remains of my parents' house. By then it was a month after their death and the explosion up in the mountains, and I hoped life had moved on or at least that no one realized I was stupid enough to do such a thing. I passed the Best Western, where I'd stayed in the days before and after my parents' funeral and first watched a videotape which entirely dismantled what I thought I'd known about my childhood. Finally I doubled back and drove up to the mountainside residential streets where their house had been. I parked a hundred yards down the street and walked the rest of the way. On the first pass I walked right by, doing nothing but noting little had been done to protect the interior from the damage that a pipe bomb had done. On the way back I pushed the gate open and walked confidently up to the house. I was ready to be a loss adjuster, cop, or extremely optimistic Jehovah's Witness, whichever seemed most likely to make someone back off. None proved necessary. I looked around the house for a little while, picking up a few small items that reminded me of them, and then left. It was not their real house. That was in Hunter's Rock, the town where I grew up and thought I had been born. Walking around this shell brought little but out-of-kilter sadness, as if I had missed a train which wasn't even the one I'd planned on taking.

John Zandt called me one night and we went out to Yakima. Our friend Nina pulled the original tip out of the slush pile and re-forwarded it to the Yakima bureau, but it seemed to die the moment it left her desk. That was when we knew we were alone in the wilds, that the conspiracy we had uncovered had longer fingers than we'd realized. Not only did they kill people, both individually and en masse, they evidently did so with little fear of retribution.

After that I ran out of steam. My progress,

such as it was, grew slower and slower until I washed up in Relent. I had a cell phone registered in a false name. I had a dead man's laptop and a dwindling supply of bad money. My ribs still hurt from where I'd been knifed by a drug dealer.

My parents would have been so proud.

★   ★   ★

In the end I left the abandoned restaurant and walked into what passed for Relent's main drag. The menu's promises had made me hungry, and all I had in my pockets were some geriatric Teriyaki beef sticks I didn't even remember buying. I found a bar called The Cambridge, run by a middle-aged couple called Bob and Sue, him bearded and affable, her whip-thin and scarily efficient. They were nice but their menu was less enticing than the one in the dead restaurant, and I wound up concentrating on scotch and some local brew that looked like it had been squeezed out of the walls of old buildings but tasted okay after the first three or four. I kept meaning to leave but it started raining outside, a concerted downpour that gusted against the bar's glass frontage like someone throwing handfuls of gravel. So I stayed put, slumped over a seat at the bar and eating snack olives at a slow but consistent rate until I began to feel bilious and my fingers had turned faintly green.

By nine o'clock I was pretty drunk. An hour later nothing had improved. The room was sparsely occupied by knots of locals drinking with steady dedication. An intense young woman with frizzy hair sat on a small stage singing songs whose meaning I could no longer follow. I sensed the world had done her wrong and I sympathized up to a point but her voice was making my head ache. It was time to go somewhere else but there was nowhere in particular to go and it was still raining outside. Every now and then someone would come into the bar looking as if they'd just stepped fully clothed out of the ocean.

After a while one of these people caught my eye. He was tall and thin and went to sit by himself at a table in the back. I found I was keeping an eye on the table's reflection in the glass behind the bar. The Cambridge's lighting was subdued to the point of murky and I couldn't see the guy's face clearly, but a tickling in my scalp told me he was looking my way more often than randomly. I got up and took an unnecessary trip to the john but when I passed near that end of the room his head was turned away, ostensibly to look out into the night.

In the john I ran water until it was cold and splashed it over my face. I knew something was wrong about the man, but I wasn't sure what to do about it. Could be he was just noticing a stranger. But I thought it was more than that. There was a window high up on one side but nothing to stand on except a sink that didn't look like it would take the weight, and little chance my shoulders would make it through.

I decided I was just going to have to confront

him. If it was going to happen, then a public place would be best.

When I went back out the table was empty.

Cursing myself for paranoia, I returned to the bar and took a swallow from a beer that was getting warm. The singing woman had been joined by a friend whose hair was even worse. Their combined voices made the veins in my legs vibrate. I signalled at the barman and the owner brought me a bill that didn't seem anywhere near big enough. I chatted with him for another few minutes, and tipped high. My father brought me up well.

It was even colder than I expected when I stepped outside. I was tempted to turn straight around again, see if they'd maybe adopt me or let me sleep at the bar, but once a door is shut behind me it never feels like I can go back. I headed along the street, staying close to the store fronts, trying to keep out of the rain. The street was deserted. I could have driven back with my eyes shut and endangered no one other than myself.

It took a minute or two before I realized a tightness across my back was trying to tell me something.

I stopped. Turned. It wasn't easy to see back down the street, but I could see someone was standing in a doorway about halfway back to the bar. I still couldn't see his face, and he wasn't moving, but no one was out in a night like this for the view.

'Can I help you?'

There was no answer. I put my hand inside my

coat. I had left my gun in the car, of course. Who's going to need a gun in Relent, Idaho?'

'Who sent you?'

The guy stepped out. Stood on the pavement. He said something but the rain took it away.

I was tired and drunk and scared. Everything told me to turn around and take off. But I didn't. If they'd caught me here they could catch me anywhere. This was what my life was now. This was going to happen, somewhere or other, sooner or later. Suddenly everything I didn't have and didn't know was in front of me, and I felt light-headed and cold inside.

I started running towards him.

He took a couple of hurried steps backwards but not fast or directed enough. I was on top of him before he knew what was happening and I just started hitting him. I knew I ought to stop, that he might know things that I should know, but I didn't care. I used both hands and my head and we fell together out onto the street. I pushed him away to stand and kick and then bent back down to grab his head, hauling it up ready to hammer it down and up and down until this was over. I was dimly aware of noise in the background but didn't connect with it until I was being pulled back and I realized how stupid I'd been to assume they'd send someone on their own, that there wouldn't be a bunch of them and the only thing I had left to be surprised about was that one of them didn't just shoot and get it over with.

Someone grabbed me. I was held back, locked around each arm. Someone was knelt down next to the guy I'd been hitting, trying to keep his head off the wet street. His face was covered with blood but I saw he was a lot younger than I'd thought, mid-twenties at the most. I realized the person with him was a woman. She looked up at me, and I saw it was Sue, the woman from The Cambridge.

'You asshole,' she said.

'Big man, are you?' This voice came from behind my right ear, and I wrenched my neck around to see it was her husband.

'What the fuck?' I saw a couple people from the bar were standing around me. 'He was watching me in the bar,' I said. 'He was standing out here waiting for me.'

The woman straightened up. 'Ricky's gay,' she said.

I was panting, my face burning hot. 'What?'

Her husband let go my arm. 'You think you'd teach him a lesson? You got a problem with people like Rick?' He stepped away from me as if I was contagious.

'Listen,' I said, but they weren't going to. The frizzy-haired singers had helped the boy to his feet and were leading him back to the bar. The woman shot me one more look, started to say something and then just shook her head instead. No one I hadn't slept with had ever made me feel so small. She went back to the bar with the others, one hand protectively on the boy's back, and I realized

48

way too late that Ricky was her son.

Then I was alone with her husband.

'I didn't know,' I said.

'Could have asked him.'

'You have no idea what my life is like.'

'No.' He shook his head. 'I don't. Don't want to know. Don't know where you're staying, either. But you should move on. You're not welcome here.'

He walked back to the bar. As he opened the door, he turned. 'I'd be surprised if you're welcome anywhere.'

The sound of the door shutting behind him left just the rain.

⋆ ⋆ ⋆

Nietzsche said that men and women of character have typical experiences, patterns of events they seem destined to undergo time and again: things of which you have to say, 'Yes, I'm like that.' I think it was him, anyway: it could have been Homer Simpson. Whichever, they probably had something more positive in mind than fights in places no one had ever heard of, taking paranoia out on people who didn't deserve it. I'd done the same thing the night of my parents' funeral, unbelievably, pulling a gun in a hotel bar and scaring a bunch of corporate types and also myself.

Relent finally showed me this was no way to live. As a girl had told me three months before — a girl who had first-hand experience of what the Upright Man was capable of — there was only one person for the job I had to do. I had to stop running. I had to turn around, and chase.

By four o'clock the next day I was in San Francisco, and by the end of the evening I finally had a trail.

3

Dawn found Tom crouched at the bottom of a tree, wild-eyed and frozen solid. It found him and tried to put him back, but he was awake and couldn't be returned. He wasn't going to be denied a morning now, even if this was a day he hadn't expected to see.

When he'd woken in the night everything happened fast. His back brain found the flight pedal and stamped with all its weight. It didn't allow for rampant malfunction in all other quarters, and Tom was sprawling before he was even on his feet. With awareness came a terrible understanding of how badly messed up he was, but then the smell cut through again and the naming part of his mind woke up like a siren — BEAR! BEAR! BEAR! — and he was moving.

At first he was on hands and knees more than his feet, but claw-fear got him upright fast. He ricocheted off the sides of the gully until it came up to reach the forest floor, and then scrambled up over the muddy lip and was good to go. He went.

Not looking back was easy. He didn't want to see. Reports came in from distant outposts — head messed up, ankle screaming, don't have the flashlight — but he over-rode them and went twisting into the darkness. All pains and disappointments were as nothing to what it would be like to be caught by the BEAR, and he ran in a way that short-circuited everything his species had learned since the ice age before last. He ran like an animal, driven by pure body magic. He ran like a fit. He ran like diarrhoea. He pinballed through bushes and over logs, tripping and running, eventually bursting out into an area where the trees were more widely spread.

As he scrabbled towards higher ground he noticed it had snowed again, long after the information had filtered to him through the loud crunching of his feet. This combined with the whacks of thin branches and the wailing in his lungs to make such a cacophony of panic that it took him a while to realize these were the only sounds he could hear. He slipped, crashed down on hands and one knee. Struggled up but slipped again, momentum lost. He stopped, turned around. He was near the top of a small rise in the forest floor. Ready to run again, or die, whichever came first.

No BEAR.

He quick-panned his eyes back and forth across the low hill. Thin moonlight, blue-white reflections, no depth of field. He couldn't see anything. Couldn't hear anything, either, even when he held his breath to stop the panting. His chest hurt like fire.

He backed up a little, into the proximity of a large tree. He knew trying to climb it wouldn't help. The BEAR would be far more adept than he, not least because it probably wouldn't be so close to passing out. But being near the tree felt better.

He waited. It stayed quiet.

Then he thought he heard something.

Something down at the bottom of the rise, deep in the inky darkness and frosty shadows. A cracking of twigs.

His body went frigid with dismay, but he couldn't move. He'd run out of panic and had only terror left. Terror didn't know how to work his limbs.

He just stood, absolutely still, and didn't hear the noise again.

Finally he turned, making a full circle, staring and listening. Nothing. All he could see was snow and shadows. All he heard were dripping sounds, a soft nearby *whoosh* as a handful of snow sloughed off a branch. He didn't know what to do.

So he stayed where he was.

★　★　★

By six a.m. he felt appalling. He could have balled up all the other hangovers in his life and dropped them into this without touching the sides. A bump on his right temple — presumably a result of the second fall — added its own whirling note. Parts of his body ached shrilly whenever he shifted his weight: the ribs on his right side were mouth-open painful whether he moved or not. The cold squared the whole effect up into the unquantifiable. He realized he'd never been truly cold before. He would have liked it to have stayed that way. At one point in the night he had gotten to the point where it felt

53

like every inch of his skin was covered with bugs, and he'd spent much of the next few hours trying to keep moving, shifting silently and in what he hoped was a very small and invisible way. He wriggled his toes, or tried to. The response was increasingly hard to gauge. He kept his hands wedged into his armpits, occasionally removing them to rub meagre warmth over his face and ears. He drowsed off a few times, but never for long. He was in far too much scared discomfort to realize that at some point he'd stopped trying to die.

He felt nauseous too, dry-retching through the night, and was visited by half-memories that failed pill suicides left you with some key part of your innards badly screwed up. Was it the liver? Kidneys? He couldn't recall. Neither sounded a good state of affairs. Quite early into his vigil he'd worked out the reason he was still alive. It was stuck to the front of his coat, an icy substance with pill-shaped deposits. He'd thrown up in his sleep. He'd been too drunk, after all that. His body had jettisoned some of what was ailing it, and a lot of the drugs had come up before having a chance for effect. His upright position had prevented him from choking in the process. Perhaps the sickness had stopped the pills from having enough time to mess him up. Perhaps.

As the air around him gradually seemed to deepen, to allow shades of colour back into the monochrome flatness of night, Tom began slowly to accept that he was going to survive into another day. He didn't know what came after that. He was scared, pissed at himself, pissed at life, and most of all, he was *monumentally* pissed at the old fool in Henry's. If you were trying to scare people, and bears were likely, surely you mentioned them? What kind of rancid old scaremonger didn't tell about the bears? Impenetrable woods are one thing. The same woods plus huge carnivores famous for intractability are something else entirely. You owe it to your audience, especially the suicidal ones, to *bring up the fucking bears.*

As he lurched out from behind the tree Tom realized something. The idea of going back and slapping the old codger was the first he'd been excited by in a long while.

$$\star \quad \star \quad \star$$

The snow wasn't thick, but it was easy to retrace his progress down the hill. At the bottom he was confronted with tangled and frosty bushes. He turned, favouring his swollen ankle, and looked up the rise. He dimly remembered swerving right to bank up it. So he now needed to turn left. This would take him through the thickest section of the undergrowth. No thanks. Instead he took a detour up around higher ground, stepping over rocks and clambering unsteadily over nursery logs, until he could rejoin the right direction.

He didn't have any clear idea of how far he'd run. In the cold, beautiful light of A Good Day To Die + 1, he wasn't even sure why he was going back. Walking was warmer than standing, and if he was going to walk, it felt better to have a destination: a real one for the moment, not the dark, vague place he'd been stumbling towards the day before. That place was still out there, and there was probably enough left in his backpack to bring it closer still. He was no longer sure what he felt about the prospect, but finding the pack was something to do.

He walked for twenty minutes. The cold helped meld his myriad aches into one giant super-pain, a humanoid discomfort trudging between the trees. He spent some of the time muttering to himself about how cold it was, which was pointless but oddly comforting. He stopped frequently, turning his head in hope of recognizing something and to reassure himself that his environment remained BEAR-free. He'd just about given up when he heard something that sounded like running water.

He abandoned the path of least resistance and pushed his way through the undergrowth, very carefully. One more fall and he would not be walking anywhere any more.

On the other side of the bushes was a clearer area, and then a gully. *The* gully, he hoped, though it didn't look at all as he remembered it. He'd only been there in darkness, of course, and had no time to observe its appearance before finding himself at the bottom. His glimpses with the flashlight had shown it to be fairly wide, however, and about fifteen feet deep at the point where he'd holed up. What was in front of him could only be about twelve feet across, but was a lot deeper. The sides were extremely steep — far too steep and rocky for him to consider climbing down.

He must have overshot his position of the night before.

He glanced right, the direction he'd have to go. Tough-looking trees and bushes grew right up to the side of the drop. He could go back around the long way, but it was a long way. Hence the name. Left looked more clear, but was going in the wrong direction. And it was steep.

Christ, he thought, wearily. His stomach was full of razor blades. His head felt like an avalanche of glass. Did he even need the bag? Maybe it was the smell of alcohol which attracted the bear. Maybe it was still there, waiting. And drunk. He stood irresolute.

Get the fucking bag, he thought. What else are you going to do?

He trudged up along the edge of the gully. It began to narrow, but not enough that jumping it was a possibility. Then he hit a bank of trees and had to dodge left for a little while before skirting back around to the gully.

He stopped. A tree lay across the gap. It had fallen there from the other side, chance bringing it down neatly so there was plenty of trunk either side of the void it spanned.

Tom limped up to it. The trunk was fairly large, perhaps two feet in diameter. The wood looked to be in good shape. He gave an experimental tug on a branch, and it rebounded crisply back, suggesting the tree hadn't been down for long. So it wouldn't be rotten. Maybe. It went from the side where he was to the side

57

where he wanted to be. He could walk nine, ten feet, instead of many hundred.

Right — but nine feet during which there'd be nothing underneath him but empty space, and beneath that a lot of sharp rocks. Nine feet across a trunk that wasn't superwide, might be slippery, and which certainly had snow on it: nine feet which would be hard even if he didn't have a bad ankle.

Tom looked away, knowing he'd be taking the long way around.

Don't be a wanker all your life.

The voice which popped into Tom's head surprised him. Partly because it deployed a term (WANKER: orig. 'one who masturbates'; now vernacular for 'a weak and useless individual' [vulg.]) which he had only ever heard in the grim British indie movies Sarah liked to rent and which he thought should come with subtitles and a Valium and something to read while they were on. But mainly it surprised him because the voice sounded so impatient, as if he was making a big deal out of something very simple.

'My ankle's hurt,' he said, petulantly.

The response was instantaneous. *It's hurt whichever way you go. This is shorter.*

'It's dangerous.'

Five paces? Six? You can't take five steps in a straight line?

'If I fall on level ground, I won't break my back or pelvis or skull.'

So don't fall.

Tom's head swirled for a moment, as if some hidden deposit of alcohol had tardily arrived in his brain. When the world stopped moving, he stepped up to the log and put his good foot on it. The trunk didn't seem to move. It was big and solid. It would take his weight. His mind was the only thing which would make it harder to cross than a stretch of icy pavement.

He slid his foot a little further along, accidentally brushing some snow off in the process. Interesting, he thought, immediately seeing the possibilities: don't walk it — slide it. That way you don't have to lift your feet (less scary), and clearing the snow will make the next step less slippery too. He poised his weight and lifted the other foot up onto the trunk, so that he was standing sideways on it.

He stood there a moment, testing his balance, looking like the world's loneliest and coldest surfer.

Then he started out along the trunk.

He slid his left foot out, tested, put his weight on it. Then the right. Left foot right on the edge now. He slid it out about nine inches.

The more steps it takes, the more likely you'll fall.

Aloud, Tom said, 'Who made you the boss of me?' Nonetheless, he pushed his left foot out six inches, pulled the right along to match. He was now officially standing in mid-air, though a dive would take him back to solid ground. He wasn't sure where to look. Not down, obviously. Not up. So straight ahead, presumably. Out over the gully. Yi — no, not out there. Shit no.

To the left. To where you're going.

He turned his head. Good move — the other

59

side really wasn't that far away. He slid his left foot again. Then his right. Left, then right. He was now nearly in the middle of the trunk.

He slid out again. His foot hit a knot in the trunk, jarring up his leg. He thought he was okay but then realized he wasn't. His left leg was fine, but the rest of him was suddenly unsure. His torso felt three feet deep and heavily weighted towards the back. He sensed the mass of the planet beneath, willing him to join it.

Left. Look left. He felt weightless for a moment, but he wasn't falling. He found himself again, and was still. He stared at the end of the trunk, half hidden in the white-topped bushes, and made it the centre of everything that was flat. He kept going.

Slid and pulled once more. He was over halfway. He slid again, feeling a strange kind of exhilaration. A lot of the time he felt like a character in a video game controlled by someone's mother, allowed a turn for comedy value on Christmas Day. But just for once . . .

He slid and pulled. He slid and pulled, and he didn't fall.

He shuffled sideways a final time, and then he was standing on the trunk still, but over land. He paused, suddenly incapable of falling. He looked out over the gully, feeling as if he was hanging in the air, then he stepped off onto the ground.

For a moment the earth too felt insubstantial, as if it could sway and tip and fade. He took another step away from the gully, and it settled. He'd made it.

Looking back and forth along the other side

confirmed what he'd suspected: hard going in both directions. Whereas on this side it was going to be a relative stroll.

Nine feet, instead of hundreds.

'Thank you,' he said, into the silence.

The voice said nothing. Up above, the sky was turning grey.

★ ★ ★

He walked for ten minutes, straying recklessly close to the edge. For the moment, in his own small world out here in the trees, things were good. It seemed to be getting colder, unbelievably, but he could take it. He could do stuff, it turned out. He could walk on air. He wasn't surprised when he spotted his backpack below, even though it was largely covered in snow and would have been easy to miss. His luck had rebooted, that's all. The world was looking after him, for once. He held onto a small tree, leaned forward and beamed down at it. It was surrounded by disturbances in the snow, no doubt caused by his feet and hands as he tried to take flight.

But no BEAR.

He moved on, keeping to the lip of the gully until he came to a place where he could scramble down. He noticed some broken branches and, using his newly acquired bush sense, guessed that was probably where he'd fallen the night before. The second descent went much better, with only a slightly hectic slide at the end. He at least reached the bottom on his feet. Feeling as if he was completing some kind of circle, he limped over towards the bag.

It lay open, glass glinting inside. Next to it was a bottle, empty. There were a few scattered packets and a handful of the pills themselves, unnaturally blue. All in a little nest, a clear patch with the wall behind, the stream a way in front, bushes on either side. Tom stared down at it all, feeling like a ghost.

All at once his mouth filled with water, and his stomach lurched.

He took a hurried step backwards, not wanting to be too close to the backpack for fear of it pulling him back into the night, and then suddenly he was sitting down, the impact juddering up through his spine, the bushes flickering and wavering in front of his eyes.

After a few minutes' deep breathing the pain abated a little. Could be hangover. Could be the sight of the pills eliciting a DON'T DO THAT AGAIN response from the brain in his guts. It could actually just be violent hunger. It was hard to tell. His body had turned into a tower of Babel. Everything below his throat felt as if it had been replaced by the operational but incompatible gastrointestinal tract of an alien species: it was saying things, and saying them loud, but he didn't know what they were.

Oh, he felt bad.

He hunched forward involuntarily. He was shivering now, too. Shivering hard. With a twist of real fear he realized he felt broken, damaged somewhere deep inside the core. He looked up at the sky and saw it was now darker still, a

62

speckled and leaden grey. It looked like it was going to snow again, this time seriously.

What was he going to do?

Even if there were enough pills left, he didn't believe he'd be able to take them. He didn't think he'd be able to do anything, ever. There was no way forward. Nothing to do except sit, but how could he sit when he felt this bad? Vodka would at least make his insides feel warm. The prospect was not in the least appealing — in the light of relative sobriety he was prepared to admit that he preferred his vodka with tonic water and a slice of lime, in moderate quantities, and drunk *somewhere warm* — but it was all he had.

He pushed himself forward onto his knees, and reached out to the backpack with a hand that was shaking badly. Just the shivers. Just the plain old been-out-all-night shivers. Nothing worse. Please. Not a sign that his whole system was fizzing and sparking like a cut electric cable.

He touched the lip of the bag, and then stopped.

He pulled his hand back. There was something that didn't look right. Spots of something on the broken glass at the opening to the bag. It had a once-bright but now dull quality that he recognized. There were quite a few instances of it on the back of his hand.

Blood?

He pulled himself closer, wincing. It certainly looked like dried blood. A couple of splashes. He turned his hand palm up: no new cuts. He'd have felt it, even this cold. He was pretty sure he

63

hadn't done it the night before either. He'd had no need to put his hand near the broken glass.

He carefully lifted the lip of the bag between two fingers, and peered in. Inside he saw broken glass iced together. A whole pack of pills he hadn't gotten to. Bits of plant, presumably accumulated by the previous day's stumblings. Aha — a last half-bottle, unbroken.

And a couple more red-brown spots on a piece of glass.

Tom carefully picked up the shard. It was blood, and he was certain it wasn't his. He'd upended the bag the night before to get what he needed. He hadn't stuck his hand in there.

But the BEAR evidently had.

It couldn't have smelt food — there wasn't any in the bag, never had been — but the scent of alcohol must have been overpowering. Maybe it knew the odour already, from rootling through bins round the back of small towns. And that's why, presumably, it hadn't chased him. Too busy trying to get a drink.

Tom hurriedly put the piece of glass back down. The reality of what had happened in the night had previously been sealed behind hangover and darkness and a few molten snatches of sleep. This wasn't. This right here in front of him.

He'd very, very nearly been attacked by a bear.

Christ.

He levered himself to his feet. This wasn't a good place to be. He didn't want to be here when something big got the scent again and decided to come back for a second look. He grabbed the unbroken half-bottle out of the mess, put it in the backpack. As he prepared to go he noticed something stuck in the bush to his right.

It took a moment for him to work out that it was hair. Quite long hair, dark brown. A few thick strands, caught in the sharp upper twigs of the bush.

He tried to picture a bear. He knew they didn't have short fur, like a cat or something, a pelt, but these hairs were a good six to nine inches long. Could that be right? Were bears that shaggy?

Tom suddenly had a very strong desire to be somewhere else, regardless of how hard it was getting there. His body would just have to make the best of it.

He limped quickly out of his nest of the night before, and looked around for the flashlight. Then he saw the footprints in the snow and realized it hadn't been a bear after all.

4

At just after eight a.m. in North Hollywood,
Officer Steve Ryan was sitting in the patrol
vehicle waiting for Chris Peterson to come back
across the street with coffee. Officer Peterson
was taking a while because he'd been grabbing a
quick bite to eat while he was at the stand, which
he thought Ryan didn't know about but after two
years you understood an awful lot about the
person you shared a car with. Chris had done
this sneak-eat thing pretty much every morning
for six weeks because his wife was into some
complex health magic which meant that there
had to be effectively no edible food in the house
at all. He was being stand-up over it and more or
less sticking to it with her — can eat this, can't
eat that, can't eat much in fact and none of it at
the same time — even though being a cop on a
diet made you feel an ass (and was an invitation
for other cops to rip the piss out of you). So if he
was sneaking some jump-start carbs by wolfing a
pastry before his shift — and he was, because he
always came back looking down the street and
wiping sticky fingers on the back of his pants,
plus he volunteered to get the coffees every
morning now whereas in the past he had to be
kicked out the car with both feet — then Ryan
wasn't going to make a big deal of it. He knew
how it was with wives. As he sat there waiting,
eyes squinting against the slanting light coming

in through the windshield, he was secretly grateful for an extra five minutes to get his head in gear. He felt tired and his eyes were dry and his shoulders ached. He had been up talking with Monica until three. It had been the usual subject, discussed in the usual way, reaching the usual lack of conclusion. It wasn't that he didn't want kids: he absolutely did. It's just they had been trying for over two years (month in, month out, in, out, no pun intended) and the process was beginning to pall. Don't matter how much you love your wife, or how attractive you found her still, being required to perform at very specific times — then and only then, the urgency of the need retreating to about nil for the rest of the month — it soon stopped being something you thought of as recreation. It became a job, and he already had one of those. True, hadn't been much upward progress there either, but at least he had hopes, wasn't debarred from success by brute biology. He was getting pally with some of the detectives. Not pushy. Just listening, trying to understand what they did. Just because it never worked out for his old man didn't mean it was going to be the same for him. Right place at the right time, a pair of hands in a trophy arrest, could be you're seconded onto a team. Suddenly you're not just a stiff in a car out checking windows and breaking up domestic disputes (Ryan knew about wives, of all kinds, and he'd learned a great deal about husbands too) and chasing crackheads down alleys while their friends hooted and jeered and threw bottles at you. It was all a matter of hard work and luck, and Ryan didn't mind either of those. No, the stuff that wore you down was where no amount of work seemed to make a difference, where the luck simply wasn't there and you couldn't seem to explain that to someone who had their heart set on the world being the way it was supposed to be, instead of the way it was. Monica got very upset when they talked about it and he didn't blame her. It made him sad too, sad and tired and depressed. He wanted to be a father. Always had. Man, he'd even consider that shit with the test tubes, assuming they could afford it. He'd said so last night, that they should look into it, and that helped a little though then they went into a discussion of how they couldn't possibly afford it and so the whole thing was still a swirling vortex of despair. He said maybe they *could* afford it, if they saved, didn't take a vacation for a couple years, if he made the squad. She said no, they couldn't. He said yes, maybe. She said no, and started crying . . . and so it went, until he didn't know what was left for him to say and it was three a.m. and nobody had been made any happier and he *really* had to go to bed. She'd been a little quiet when he left that morning. Probably just wiped out. He'd give her a call in a little while, check she was okay. Assuming he ever moved from this spot: what the fuck was taking Chris so long? In the time he'd been gone, he could have gone to a Denny's and sneaked a whole breakfast complete with home fries and French toast. Ryan leaned across the passenger seat, caught a glimpse of his partner up at the counter, shoving something in

68

his mouth. He smiled, sat back. Whatever. Let the man eat. The radio was quiet, for the moment. It wasn't like the city would run out of crime and they'd be sent home without pay. That didn't seem likely at all.

'Good morning,' said a voice.

Ryan turned to see a guy standing on the pavement by the car. He was wearing worn green combat pants and a dusty grey vest. The sun was behind his head. He was tan and his hair was cropped short and he wore small round glasses. He looked the kind of guy you might see busking on a street corner, or running a Pilates course down on Venice beach. He didn't look the kind of guy to do what he did next, which was pull out a big handgun from behind his back and shoot Steve Ryan twice in the head.

* * *

By the time Nina got there the road was cordoned and a decent crowd had already gathered. A lot of civilians but a lot of cops too. They were standing in clumps, looking angry and impotent, largely staying away from the bench where a tall red-headed cop was sitting staring down at the pavement. Other officers, one male, one female, stood on either side of this man. The woman had a hand on his shoulder. The male was saying something. It seemed unlikely that either of these well-meant gestures would be making Patrolman Peterson feel any better about the fact his partner had been shot dead while he was across the street feeding his face.

She parked up and walked quickly across the road, seeing Monroe was already present, getting harangued. A couple of cops put their hands up as she approached, but she had her card ready.

'Nina Baynam,' she said. 'Feds.'

Sometimes she said Feds or Feebs rather than FBI, and sometimes it made a difference, heartily using a more casual term or one they might employ themselves. Not this morning, evidently, and those three letters had not been a passport to respect even before Waco and allied screw-ups had given everybody new angles from which to bust their balls. On every body-language wavelength the cops broadcast a single question: what the *fuck* are you doing here?

Nina was wondering the same thing. She walked over to Monroe, who turned away from two other cops and started talking hard and fast without preamble.

'Two witnesses. One saw it from a third-storey room in there — ' he pointed across the street at a battered-looking building with bleached-out signs offering weekly lets at suspiciously low rates ' — and the other was at the coffee stand. Ryan and Peterson arrived about seven thirty, Peterson goes across the street leaving Ryan in the car. Ryan has his eyes shut some of the time. He doesn't see a short-haired white male in glasses, trim build, dressed in either green and brown or brown and grey, coming down from there and approaching the vehicle with a hand behind his back.'

70

Her boss pointed again, this time up the shallow rise of parking lot which led to the entrance to The Knights, a two-storey courtyard motel. 'Guy walks straight down here and stands next to the patrol car. He says something and then takes his shots. Bam, bam. Then he's gone.'

'Gone how?' Nina said, turning to look around. 'The guy's partner is like thirty feet away.'

Monroe nodded towards an alley a little further along the street. 'At the speed of sound. Found the gun up there. By the time Peterson's heard the shots, checked Ryan, started running, it's too late. The shooter's vanished.'

He started walking towards the motel. Nina kept pace.

'Nobody knows anything about Ryan except he's a decent cop. Not the brightest, uniform for life, but doing a good job. No one has anything about him being on the pad or dirty in any way. So it looked like they just have a random psycho cop-killing until someone talks to the manager up here.'

The entrance to The Knights was wide enough to drive a car through. There would be no reason to do this, however, because the inside held only a small and scrubby courtyard with the long-dead remains of a small concrete fountain. A few plants were trying to prove life could triumph anywhere. They looked dispirited. On the right was a grey cinder block addition holding ice and coke machines. Cops were milling all around the other side, stepping back reluctantly as Monroe led Nina into the

71

glass-fronted office. They had the air of people who'd been stopped from doing a job they thought was theirs. There were four more cops inside the office, along with a fat guy in baggy jeans and a clean white tee shirt.

'Tell us what you told them,' Monroe said. Tall, hair cropped around a receding line and with the shoulders of a long-ago college boxer, people tended to speak up when he asked a question.

'I don't know anything,' the guy whined, for nothing like the first time. 'Just what the chick in twelve told me when she checked out. Said there'd been noise from next door, this was a couple days ago. I only mentioned it to the officer because they said the guy who shot the cop had short hair and glasses and I thought, you know, that's kind of what the guy in room eleven looked like, in fact.'

Nina nodded. Her eyes were on a magazine half hidden under the counter. The manager saw her looking, and seemed to find it kind of a thrill. 'I just adore that stuff,' she said, looking back up at him. 'Makes me want to fuck every guy on the planet. You want to get on it right here, right now?'

The guy looked away. 'As I thought,' Nina said. 'So meantime give us the keys to rooms ten, eleven, twelve.'

Monroe took the keys and pointed at three of the cops. They followed the agents as they left the office and stepped into the courtyard. Room eleven was four doors down on the right-hand side. The drapes were still drawn. Two of the policemen were given the keys to the doors either side.

They drew their weapons, opened the doors quietly. Pulled them wide and then slipped inside the rooms.

A minute later both came out. One shook his head. The other said, 'I could hear something. Could be someone talking.'

'Three areas,' the other cop observed, quietly. 'Sitting room, bedroom in back, bathroom.'

'Okay,' Monroe said. For just a second Nina thought she saw him thinking about handing the remaining key to one of the cops, then realizing how it would look. That kind of thing — plus just turning away from people like they didn't matter, the way he had when she'd arrived — was precisely why the street cops didn't love them like brothers. She got her own gun out, holding it with both hands and clear of her body. She was careful not to let anyone see a small wince. Three months now, and her right arm still gave her trouble. Two doctors and three physiotherapists had told her there was nothing wrong with it any more. Nina thought maybe it was the small round scar on the upper right side of her chest talking, saying it knew all about guns now and wanted nothing to do with them. Tough, in that case. FBI agents are constrained to have their weapon with them at all times. She slept with hers under the bed.

Monroe squared up to the door, Nina just behind. He told the cops to be ready to follow, but to give them time. They nodded. They looked more up for this than she felt, but that was part of being a guy, she knew. Any one of them looked wobbly in front of a colleague, no one would want them at their back again.

Monroe slipped the key in the lock. Turned it. Waited a second, then pushed it. The door opened to a dark room. The drapes on the other side were drawn too. It was warm.

'This is the FBI,' Monroe said. His voice was steady. 'Put down any weapons and come out with your hands up. This will be your only warning.'

They waited. No one said anything. No one appeared. The old conundrum, polarizing options for the near future: either there was no one in the room and everything was cool and after-the-fact, or there was a very bad man inside and he had in mind shooting him some cop.

Nina was in position. She stepped into the room.

Leathery dark. Heavy air. Really, really warm, like someone turned the aircon off twenty-four hours before. Room a square, holding battered sofa, two chairs, desk, big old prehistoric television. No personal effects evident. Flicker-light from doorway in corner on courtyard side. Door partially ajar.

Also a low sound. Very likely television.

Who's watching it?

Nina side-stepped across into the body of the room, making space for Monroe. He came in silently, hand held back to signal the cops to stay where they were. Once he was positioned on the door to the other room she turned, moved silently to the cupboard. Held her gun short arm while she eased it open.

Empty but for the smell of dust. Left it open. Turned on her right foot to face back to the room, nodded to Monroe. The cops at the doorway stood quiet and ready. Monroe moved towards the door to the second room. Nina came up, a yard and a half behind. Stopped.

Everything flattens out into *now*.

Monroe pushes the door gently with his left hand. It swings. Reveals more of the side wall of the bedroom, a grey-blue shifting light, and a little more sound. The sound has that rustling, high-pitched note above the low rumble. It's television for sure. Sometimes people leave them on. It's company. They forget when they leave. They figure who cares, it's not my electric buck.

Monroe takes another step. This puts him on the threshold. A beat. He takes one more and turns quickly, gun pointed past the door into an area Nina cannot yet see.

But she sees Monroe's upper back do a kind of thud, as if his leading foot found itself two inches lower than he expected.

Another long beat. 'Ma'am?'

Nina's stomach goes cold. She hears Monroe swallow with his mouth open, a dry click. He is staring. He is wired. He is ready to shoot. He takes another half pace forward, seemed to bend down and look upwards. Then he side-steps out of sight. There is silence for a moment, then a quiet swishing sound. Silence again.

'Nina,' he says, finally. 'Come in here.'

She knew that meant just her, so she raised a

hand to signal the other guys to hold position. She allowed her other arm to drop a little, but wasn't yet ready to let go of the gun.

The bedroom seemed even hotter than the other room. There was a strong odour. The television was a low burble up high to the left, fixed to the wall with a metal bracket. Monroe stood the other side of a queen-size bed.

A woman sat in the bed. She was in her late twenties. She had long brown hair. She didn't move when Nina entered, because she was dead. She was sitting bolt upright in bed, her head flopping slightly forward. She was dressed in well-worn blue cotton night clothes with a floral motif. Her stomach had begun to distend. Her face looked like painted putty. Her eyes were open. So was her mouth. Something had been put inside it.

'Jesus,' Nina said.

She leaned forward. The object in the woman's mouth was about the size of a waitress's notepad, about a quarter of an inch thick, two inches wide, and probably a little over three inches long, though it was difficult to be sure without removing it. It seemed to be made of shiny metal. A very narrow label along the protruding end had a string of numbers and short lines on it.

'What the hell is that?' Monroe said. He was breathing hard, and a line of sweat glinted on one temple.

Nina shook her head. 'I don't know.'

★   ★   ★

Thirty minutes later Nina stepped outside. The first wave of forensic geeks had arrived. With the drapes still drawn and the heat still trapped, it was like milling around in a crowded, hellish cupboard. Nina made sure to take a thorough look around the suite, which was always easier when it had been established you weren't going to be shot at, and then left. Monroe was still inside. It would take the arrival of cameras to flush him out.

There were no other bodies in the room. The swish Nina had heard was the sound of Monroe checking the bathroom. It was devoid of personal possessions. There was no sign of the clothes the woman must have been wearing when she arrived. You can't wander into a motel dressed in pyjamas. Even at a place like The Knights. You would normally think to bring some toiletries, too, a handbag. There would be identification of some kind, somewhere, however accidental. Cops were already canvassing missing persons reports, but something told Nina news wouldn't arrive soon.

She walked out through a sunny courtyard which was full of yet more cops and the quickly moving bodies of civilians who thought they were going to be able to check out of this death block quickly and get back to their anonymous lives, but who were about to spend a large number of hours being asked a small number of questions. That evening they would see, on television, the place they'd spent the night before, as the media repeated its name again and again to make it one of those venues the mention

77

of which would tug at the memory for years and possibly decades to come. Nobody involved was going to forget today in a hurry, least of all the woman Nina saw when she left the courtyard and walked back out into the lot. Patrolman Peterson was still sitting on the bench. Two of his colleagues were trying to restrain this woman, whose name was Monica, who had arrived to find her husband's remains had already been taken to the morgue and who was screaming at his ex-partner because there was nothing else to do.

Only when Nina was clear of the entrance and standing some distance from anyone else did she get out her cell phone. She walked to where she couldn't be overheard, and hit John Zandt's number on speed-dial. He didn't answer after twelve rings, and she was put through to the phone's answering service.

'Hi, it's me,' she said to the machine. 'I know you don't want to talk about this kind of thing any more. But I could do with your help.' She hesitated, not knowing what else to say, then added: 'Hope you're okay.'

Then cut the connection, and stood irresolute. For just a moment she felt odd, fluttery at the back of the neck, as if someone was watching her.

She turned, but there was no one. No one she could see, anyhow.

★   ★   ★

At just after two she sat stirring a coffee while her boss talked on the phone. They were perched outside a scruffy café half a block from The Knights. All but one of the squad cars had now moved on to other things, but from where she sat she could see four unmarked vehicles that were part of the investigation. She sipped her coffee and watched as further pieces of Room 11 were hauled out to be analysed in depth. It had been established that the room had been rented five days before, cash in advance. Nina hoped he was being grilled, yet again, and she hoped it was somewhere airless and hot and that they took their time.

Monroe closed his phone. 'It's done,' he said, with evident satisfaction. 'Olbrich is assembling a task force: RHD of course, us, FD&D, the whole Serious Crime Cluster Fuck. This needs to be kept tight. There's a lot of angry officers around.'

'Clipping a cop in broad daylight. Even by wacko standards, that's extreme.'

'Wacko?'

'Come on, Charles.' Nina had lost patience with official nomenclature round about the time she assisted with the extrication of a young black kid from a trash can. The kid had been there a week, in weather as warm as today's. His mother ID'd the body, then killed herself three weeks later by walking off the Palisades. That had been a few years ago. Monroe still went through the motions of using impersonal and uninflected terminology for people whose deeds shredded whole families and histories in their grubby hands. 'What would *you* call him? Inadequately socialized?'

'This is going to happen fast,' Monroe said,

ignoring her. 'A cop-killing in broad daylight. This is not a man who has control of himself any more. We're going to have to hit the ground fast.'

Nina rolled her eyes. Out of control, begging to be caught. And yet nowhere to be seen. The most high-profile investigation she had yet been involved in — officially at least — had been the Delivery Boy murders back in 1999/2000. Again, here in Los Angeles, and also working under Charles Monroe. He'd made similar assumptions then, about a man who'd taken the lives of three bright and worldly young women without leaving a trace. He had killed again, more than once, and then disappeared, and had never been caught. Monroe had floated on to the next job, onwards and upwards. The girls' parents still took the world one day at a time. 'Question is, will there be others?'

'There may be, yes. That's what I'm saying. Unless we . . . '

'No. I mean *have* there been any before this? If this is the end, as you think, where is the beginning? What got him to here? What's this guy spiralling out *from*?'

'People are on it. LAPD are cross-checking as we speak.'

'And we still have no idea who she is.'

'No purse, no possessions apart from old pjs, dickhead behind the desk says he never saw her before she was dead. A photo will be prepared once they've cleaned her up a little: people will be on the street with it by the end of the afternoon. You know what that thing in her face was?'

Nina shook her head, a coppery taste in her own mouth. She had seen many dead bodies, some of them in states around which she'd had to build a wall in her head, so she didn't come upon the memory unexpectedly. But there was something about the ones where they did things to the victims' mouths. Sexual mutilation you almost took for granted. The mangling of a public part of the body, like the eyes or mouth or hands, somehow seemed a more social desecration. Sexual was private, a personal assault; public said LOOK, UNIVERSE, AT WHAT I HAVE DONE. It was outward-directed, some statement designed to change the world. Or so it seemed to her.

'A hard disk,' Monroe said. 'A small one, like in a laptop. One of the techs recognized it before it was even out of her head.'

'No prints?'

He shook his head. 'Clean. But someone in a lab is finding what else it can give us. There's a serial number, for a start. It came from somewhere, was bought somewhere. And there may be something left on it, of course. We'll know tonight.'

He caught the expression on Nina's face this time. 'He left it there for a reason, Nina. Let's get back to work.'

He stood up, thumb already dialling another number on his cell. Thunk, thunk, thunk. She wouldn't want to be Charles Monroe's phone, Nina thought. That was a job for a phone with tough abs.

She drained the rest of her coffee, aware of his

81

eyes on her, critical. 'What, Charles?'

'How's your arm holding out?'

'Fine,' she said, irritably. He wasn't asking about her arm. He was reminding her of unfinished business and of why their professional relationship had taken its second turn for the worse. She got the message. 'Good as new.'

He looked like he was going to say something else but then got an answer on his cell, and turned and strode away, already in mid-flow. Someone was learning just what a damn fine SAC Monroe was; how in control, how just *right on top of things*.

As she followed him, Nina checked her own phone for something like the twentieth time. She saw there was a text message from Zandt, at last, and quickly called it up.

It said: I'M IN FLORIDA.

'Oh for fuck's sake,' she muttered, stuffed the phone back in her bag, and walked back out into the heat.

5

I checked into the Armada on Powell, in San Francisco downtown not far from Union Square. It was appealingly expensive and had a guy dressed as a Spanish soldier standing on the pavement outside. Passing tourists were taking photographs of each other with him, presumably so that back home they could tell their friends that here they were, with a guy in a costume, outside a hotel they weren't staying in. By the time I was settled it was too late to do the big thing on my agenda, so I went for a walk instead.

As I walked I thought about what I knew, which boiled down to this: I had been wrong about just about everything to do with my life. I had believed I'd been born to Don and Beth Hopkins in Northern California, where they had been living well-tempered lives of average tedium. They mowed the yard and kept the car clean and they bought enough material goods to keep the gods of commerce smiling upon them. My father built up a realty business and, after I'd left home, this led to them moving to Dyersburg. He had continued to enjoy some success as a broker of luxury houses until a car crash had taken both of their lives. But on the day after their funeral, when I'd gone to their house to try to understand what I was supposed to do about it, I'd found a message. It had been hidden in such a way as to draw the attention only of someone who knew my father very well.

The message had said, simply, that they weren't dead.

This is the news everyone wants to hear — everyone, that is, whose relationship to their parents is marred merely by distance — and it was enough to make me spend the afternoon searching their house. I found the videotape my father had sealed into a VCR in his study, and this ultimately led to my discovering just how wrong I had been about my life. Wrong — or deliberately misled.

I had thought I was an only child. A section in the video showed me with a brother of the same age, a brother deliberately abandoned on a city street, somewhere back in the late 1960s.

I had thought my parents' death had been an accident. They weren't my parents and it wasn't. They had been murdered by the group my natural father had belonged to, thirty-five years earlier. This group was called the Straw Men, and believed themselves the only portion of humanity uninfected by a virus promoting social conscience above the cold-hearted individualism they believed inherent to our species. Whether they genuinely thought this, or it was just a convenient cover for acts of violence and depravity, was not clear. What *was* clear was that the group was wealthy and well connected. It was also evident that their point man, a person who called himself the Upright Man but could more accurately be designated as Paul, my lost brother, was about as dangerous an individual as could be imagined. The night before Bobby

Nygard died we watched a government tape together, a compilation of the world's atrocities over the previous two decades. Shootings, explosions, mass killings. We saw the Upright Man in the background of a number of these events, mutely claiming the glory. In addition he had been acting as a procurer for the occupants of The Halls, a group of men — and, for all I knew, women — involved in considered and repeated acts of serial murder.

The first steps had been easy. I did my initial research a hundred miles down the road from Relent, sitting in a wired coffee bar with a laptop. I hated the idea that someone might think I was writing a novel, and kept glaring at people who smiled encouragingly at me, but I needed the net access. What I had to do first was confirm the city in which my sibling had been abandoned. Paul had sent me a message in which he claimed he had been left in San Francisco, but I was not inclined to believe anything he said without evidence. I had nothing else to go on except the short section at the end of the videotape my father had left me, which I had converted to a DVD.

The last section was in three parts. The first showed a train journey. There was no locating information — but I knew my father well enough to be confident he would not have included it just for background colour. So my guess was the first section was to signal a journey had been undertaken — and that it was far enough from our house to make sense by rail, but not far enough to take a plane. This gave me a choice of

85

maybe thirty or forty cities and towns in or around Northern California or Oregon.

The tape cut then to a wide street in a downtown area. The camera followed my mother as she walked down a sidewalk, hands down and out of sight: holding, as the final section would make clear, the hands of two young boys. There was not much else to see except passing examples of the fashions of the late 1960s, in the shapes of suits and cars; and understated store fronts of the kind that made you wonder what made anyone buy anything in those days. Nothing remarkable, except . . .

I froze the image. Over on the right side of the road was a small department store, opposite a grassy square. I could just about make out a name — Hannington's.

Ten minutes on the web told me there were no department stores by that name still in operation in the US, or at least none who'd made their existence known to the internet. So I had to let scientific detection methods go hang, and work back from the conclusion.

I tracked down a selection of 'San Francisco of Yesteryear' sites and spent a while dredging through evocations of the city's days of yore. My eyeballs were beginning to melt by the time I found a reference to a Saturday morning ritual for one little girl, now grown old, whose long-dead mother used to take her to look at fancy haberdashery in a store called Harrington's. They couldn't afford any of it. They just went to look.

I flipped back to the freeze frame. I had

misread the sign. The angle wasn't good, and sun was hazing out the film in a way that would have been difficult to predict when it was being shot. A quick check said there was no Harrington's still in business either, on the West Coast or anywhere else. Further web-mining with the new spelling established that the store had once sat on Fenwick Street, and been a big deal in its day. Big enough of a deal, probably, that my father might have assumed it would be there forever.

So. San Francisco was confirmed. My brother was evidently capable of telling the truth.

★   ★   ★

Fenwick was ten minutes' walk from the hotel. The streets were crowded, flocks of end-of-the-afternoon strollers and shoppers casting long shadows on clean grey pavements. Though the road had been widened, and just about every ground-level aspect of the architecture had been altered, it wasn't hard to see I was in the right area.

When I drew opposite to the huge building that had once housed Harrington's, I ground to a halt. People cruised around me like leaves skirting a rock in a steady stream. The old store front had been split into two, and now held a Gap and a vast make-up emporium from which women of all ages were emerging with expressions of glee and very, very small bags in each hand. The floors above appeared home to the lairs of attorneys.

I found my eyes drawn to the sidewalk in front

of my feet. I didn't remember having trodden this precise spot, but I had. I had walked here holding my mother's hand. My father had filmed us. They were gone but the place was still here, and me along with it. I was older now than they had been then, but at the time I had been about the same age as a toddler I saw being pushed past me in a stroller, a small being so different from me that I found it hard to believe I had once been one.

Time is strange.

'You in a fucking coma, man?'

I turned round to see a shithead in a suit standing behind me, unable or unwilling to do as everyone else had and step around me. I was about to explain how stupid this was but then realized I didn't want to get into another fight, even a verbal one.

I apologized, moved aside. 'Asshole,' he said.

A woman's voice said, 'Oh grow up.'

I turned and saw it was the woman with the stroller, who had stopped to deliver this advice to the other man.

He glared at her, then stormed off up the street. The woman winked at me and went her own way. In the trivial way cities sometimes do to you, I felt I had been taken inside.

I glanced across once more at the corpse of Harrington's, then set off up around the other side of the square and headed west. I had a print-out of several frames from the final part of this section of the video, which showed the area where the child had been abandoned. I didn't have much hope of finding the actual spot, or even the street. But Chinatown lay in that direction, and somewhere in there was a big bowl of food with my name on it.

Sometimes you have to keep your goals to a manageable size.

* * *

Next morning I was on the phone at five after nine. By ten thirty all I had established was that you didn't get information out of social services in a hurry. After a while I had spent so long pushing buttons in menu systems that I began to be afraid I might eventually be put back through to myself, which I knew would freak me out. So I got onto the street and walked over there instead.

Within five minutes I wished I'd stuck with the phone. There's nothing like the waiting room of any office of the government or its allies to remind you how lucky you are. You enter a non-place, non-time. You sit on battered chairs in murky blues and greens that nobody ever names as their favourite colour. You stare at signs that have no bearing on you, non-specific communiqués from the land that punctuation forgot. You wait until the waiting loses all sense of direction or purpose, until you become like a stone deposited in a field millennia ago by a careless glacier. You are here. This is all you have ever known. In the meantime you are stripped of any sense of individuality, of the idea that you might be different from anyone else in the room except by virtue of your particular problem; and so you become that problem, defensively, accepting it as identity, until it swells and suppurates and becomes all you are. As a species we'll tolerate being close to others, but not so close, and not in those circumstances and when we feel so small: we become rows of dry, fretting eyes, hating everyone around us and sincerely wishing our neighbour dead so we can move up one place in the line.

Or maybe that's just me.

I spent a long time waiting before I could even delineate my basic needs to someone. It then took us a while to get around the fact I didn't have a proper address, and for him to accept the Armada's details instead. I explained I had a brother who I thought had been taken into care in San Francisco in the mid to late 1960s, probably around 1967; that I believed his first name to be Paul, that I was trying to trace him, and that I had no other information whatsoever except that he might have been found wearing a sweater with his name stitched into it. The man wrote down what I said but the looks he gave me suggested it was going to be a long day. Finally he handed me a number, and I was released back into the milling, coughing herd of problems, psychoses and whines.

Two hundred thousand years later, my number came up. I was invited down a long corridor and into a room in the far back of the floor, where a middle-aged black woman was sitting behind a desk covered in paper. A sign said she was called Mrs Muriel Dupree. The wall behind her was covered with posters in which one word in three was underlined and confidentiality was usually guaranteed.

'I can't help you,' she said, before I'd even sat down.

I sat down anyway. 'Why?'

'It's too long ago, that's why.' She referred to a piece of paper in front of her. 'Says here it's about a brother, and you think it was around 1967. That's before my time. It was also before a lot of other big things happened. Those, for a start.' She nodded towards a computer so old I wouldn't trust it to hold my laptop's coat. 'Only about twenty years ago all this stuff started going on computer, and then we had a bad fire in 1982 that took out the tapes and files in the basement, so we lost most of the information prior to that date anyhow. Even if something *was* written down about it the old-fashioned way, and it wasn't burned, it wouldn't have been a whole lot and you'd have a better chance of finding God than finding it now. I don't mean that personally. You may know Him already, in which case, good for you.'

She read the disappointment in my face, and shrugged. 'Things were different then. Today no one gets 'put up for adoption': the mother makes an adoption *plan*, there's legally binding contact arrangements and everybody gets that a blank canvas isn't the best thing for the child, that she or he needs to own the information about their own past, da da da. But back then it was 'Okay, you been fostered or adopted or whatever. Welcome to your new life. Don't look back, because there ain't nothing happy there to be found.' People would change the kids' names, birthdays, whatever. You know how they say the expression 'Put up for adoption' came about?'

I shook my head. I didn't know. I didn't care, either, but Mrs Dupree was evidently viewing me as a welcome five-minute break from people who would shout at her.

'Way, way back they would take the orphaned children out of the cities on the coasts, put them on trains. They'd take them out into the country and stop at the itty-bitty stations and the kids would literally be 'put up' onto the platforms in the hope that some farmer with a bit of room — and a need for some more labour — would take one or two in. Here's the kid. Feed it. That's that. Everything prior is dead and gone. Things weren't quite like that in the sixties, but in some ways they kind of were. Half the time the kids wouldn't get told they were adopted ever. Most of the rest, the parents would wait until they thought the children were old enough, which meant probably they'd been voting for a few years and were spaced out to all hell to find out mom and dad could have been hundreds of miles away at the moment they were born. It was not a good system and we know that now, but at the time it was thought to be for the best — and a whole lot of those children grew up to have happy and productive lives. Honey, you okay?'

'Yeah,' I said, looking back up at her from my hands, which I had been inspecting while wondering if I would ever have a happy and productive life myself. 'I didn't expect to get so stopped, so soon. And . . . this is very important.'

'I know it is. I understand.'

I shook my head, wanting to be somewhere else. 'You don't, I'm afraid, but thank you for your time.'

I got up and headed towards the door. My hand was on the handle when she asked: 'You sick?'

I looked back at her, confused and caught unawares. For a moment I thought she was suggesting something in particular.

'What do you mean?'

She raised an eyebrow. 'I mean is this about you having discovered that you have a medical condition which someone else needs to know about, because they might have it too?'

I looked her in the eyes and considered lying.

'No,' I said. 'There's nothing wrong with me. But there's something very wrong with him.'

I left her sitting behind her desk, and walked the long corridor back towards the outside world, where I could smoke, and breathe first-hand air, and where my problems were only part of what I was.

★　★　★

'So what now, Bobby?'

Silence. He was AWOL again. Off somewhere in the spirit world with a beer and a grin, freaking out the other ghosts.

It was late afternoon and I had a beer of my own and was sitting at a table outside L'Espresso, a café-bar just on the corner up from the hotel. My feet felt aggrieved and full of bones. San Francisco is a pleasant enough place but frankly, it has too many hills.

In the face of the complete bust of the morning, I'd done the only other thing I could think of. Maybe, I thought, just maybe Paul hadn't even gotten into the system. Perhaps he'd been picked up by someone off the street, taken in by some kindly storekeeper's wife. I knew this was a fantasy born of Mrs Dupree's tale of baby trains in the Midwest, but I really didn't see any other avenue open to me and I had to do something to find him. I had drifted for too long. This was my job. No one else's.

In the absence of any useful visual reference, I tried another approach. I knew my parents weren't the people to just throw a child to the wolves. It was likely that they would have left the child somewhere they believed not to be openly dangerous, and where there would have been a decent flow of pedestrians. They were on foot. There is a limit to how far you want to walk with two-year-olds. Thus it was likely, or at least possible, that I was looking for a busy area within very easy walking distance of Union Square. Worst case, it would be somewhere that also matched that description, but on a tram line.

So I bought a map, and I walked areas like that, trying to find somewhere that matched my pictures. I found nothing, which meant I had nowhere else to go. I had tried, a couple of months back, responding to an email Paul had sent. The message was bounced back to me within the hour, his address unknown, unheard of, impossible to find. His messages were statements to me, not attempts at communication. There was no trail there either.

I finished my beer and walked the few yards back to the hotel. As I headed through the reception I heard someone call my name. I turned, slowly.

The fresh-faced young guy at the desk was holding up a piece of paper. 'There's a message for you.'

That sounded unlikely. Nobody knew where I was. The few people whose contact I might have welcomed would have called me on the cell phone. I walked over to the desk, feeling as if I had a target on my back.

I took the piece of paper, thanked him, and turned away. When I opened it I saw the following message:

'This lady might be able to help you. If she wants to.'

There was a phone number for this unnamed woman, and the name of the person who'd left me the message. Muriel Dupree.

★   ★   ★

A phone call, a visit to the web and a fast shower and then I went back downstairs and hailed a cab from outside the hotel. It took a while to find someone who was prepared to take me as far as I needed to go, which was over the Bay and then some, and then, it turned out, a good way more. The one I wound up with was intent on exacting a bonus through my providing an audience for a long series of diatribes. Luckily he was too wrapped up in his own dialectic for me to have to play a speaking role. I grunted and said 'Right,' and watched out of the window as city and then suburbs passed me by.

The phone call I'd made had been to social services, hoping to speak to Mrs Dupree. This turned out to be as vain a hope as it sounds. I'd have been better off trying to go back in time. The web had told me the telephone number belonged to a Mrs Campbell, and also where she lived. It's one of the things I know how to do. I didn't know who this person was, or what Muriel thought she might have to say to me, but experience told me you get closest to the truth by not giving it advance warning that you're coming. I do know what I'm talking about. Bobby and I met while working for the CIA.

Eventually the guy in front stopped talking and started glancing at a map. We pulled further and further from through routes and eventually hit some straggled blocks of residential streets. The neighbourhood was white semi rundown, no realtor's dream. We went back and forth through it for a little bit before I took hold of the map and guided us in. We stopped halfway up a street of small wooden houses each on their own very little plot.

I got out and paid. There was no one around.

'If you're looking to party, you've come to the wrong place,' the driver said, and then took off up the street.

I waited until he was out of sight, and then walked fifty yards back the way we'd come, having deliberately told him not quite the right address. Two turnings away was the road I actually wanted, and three minutes along it was the house I had come to visit.

I walked up a short path and two steps onto a porch area. It had been well painted in white, a few years before. It would soon need doing again. I looked for a bell and found none, so rapped on the door instead. I had no real doubt that the woman would be home.

After a few minutes I heard a sound behind the door, and then it was opened. In the shadows beyond was a small figure.

'Mrs Campbell?' I asked.

She said nothing, but slowly reached to the screen door and pushed it slightly ajar. Through the gap I saw a woman in her seventies, with hair that was still looked after, but a face that was grey and pouched; and also seemed to be in shock. She looked me in the eyes, then up and down, and then in the eyes again.

'My God,' she said, eventually, still staring. 'So it was true.'

6

When the phone rang Nina was on her so-called deck. Theoretically she was out there thinking; if the truth be told, she was asleep. Back at the field office you couldn't hear yourself think for the sound of men storming up and down, barking into phones, being brisk and professional. One of the big things about being a man, she'd noted, was that being good, doing the work, wasn't enough. It had to be generally acknowledged that here you were, damn well seeing to business. She found her deck much better for head work, better too than the rest of the house. She ought to move, she knew. Especially after things had gone wrong with John, the house felt awkward and tired of her and wanting in almost every regard. It was in the Malibu hills, which was great, but she could only afford to rent it because it was falling apart. The polished concrete of the living room floor was cracked across the middle, wide enough to slip three fingers down. The swimming pool had been melted in a bush fire long before she moved in. One good shake and the deck would end up in the Pacific; two shakes, and the house would follow. For some reason, the prospect had never unduly disquieted her. Some people smoked. Nina sat out on her deck.

She had spent the rest of the day on the streets and in offices, on the phones, sifting through non-information and being briefed on results from a slew of forensic investigations. None had turned up anything useful. The pyjamas had been nailed to Wal-Mart, never a happy thing when you're trying to trace an object's history. The disk out of the woman's mouth was still in analysis; a photo of her face was now being shown around town by detectives and patrol division. It could be forever before they got a match. A woman, once attractive, now dead. Lots of those.

She got back to the house to find a message on the machine. She jabbed the button, thinking it might be Zandt with a more constructive response to her message. Instead it had been Meredith, an old college friend, agreeing that yes, it was time they met up and had dinner and a good long *chat*. Nina didn't remember the matter being discussed, but she supposed it was time. It had been a year at least since her loose, small group of old friends had gotten together. Merry lived in the Valley and had acquired a husband and three young children, apparently effortlessly, as if by winning a weekly competition. She now cared a great deal about things Nina found either trivial or incomprehensible or simply irrelevant, and her hairstyle was becoming more and more irrevocable. Soon it would be impossible to look at the face beneath it and remember the times Nina had sprawled laughing next to her as she threw up in a variety of toilets in vague parties held in various professors' tiny, book-strewn homes. That girl had gone away somewhere, answering the call of happy hour in some far-away and long-ago bar, and had sent grown-up-mom Meredith Jackson to take her meetings instead. This woman was likely just as baffled by Nina's current incarnation, which kept looking like a woman without seeming to understand what the job entailed. Nina knew she ought to keep the friendship going, but often wondered why either of them bothered. Maybe Meredith liked knowing an FBI agent. Maybe Nina liked to believe she still had some kind of connection to real life, that on the other side of the ring of murderers and desks and men in suits and late nights that surrounded her, there was someone who wanted nothing more from Nina than gossip, affirmation, and a smile.

She hadn't been able to face making the call, and so went to think instead. She wound up wondering how much difference there had been between Merry, or herself, and the young woman who had been found in The Knights that morning; how much alteration in a life it would take to wind up dead in a motel, impregnated with the cigarette smoke of men who had come to document your final moments, your deaf ears party to much rambling discussion of recent sporting events and at least one observation regarding your tits. John Zandt — who had been a homicide cop in the city before the Delivery Boy had taken his daughter — had long ago observed to her how fast a teenager's life can go from A to B in Hollywood; then from B to Z, then the easy flip from Z to a Jane Doe toe tag. They don't know how fast and easy it's going to be. It's not years, it's months. It can be weeks. It can be virtually overnight. You start the evening somebody's much loved and pampered child, nicely lit; you see in the next grimy morning stripped of everything you hadn't yet learned to value about yourself. You think you're the star, but instead you're just cannon fodder waiting in line to have promises broken by friends, lovers and fate.

She went indoors and fetched a glass of wine. Fifteen minutes later she was asleep.

She woke up with a start. When the phone finally made it through to her she lurched out of the chair feeling late: it felt like it had been ringing a long time, at first powerless to haul her out of a dream in which an old man had crept around a dark room after her.

She ricocheted blearily off both the glass door and the kitchen counter on the way in, and was ready to give Zandt a very hard time. But it wasn't John.

It was Monroe. 'You'd better get back over here,' he said. 'We've found something.'

★ ★ ★

She met Monroe in Doug Olbrich's office. Olbrich was a Lieutenant in Special Section 1, the Robbery Homicide division responsible for high-profile and externally liaising murder cases. He was tall and rangy with hair buzz-cut short.

'Hey, Doug.'

'Nina. How's tricks?'

'Same old. I haven't actually spoken to John in

101

a while, but if I had, I'm sure he'd have sent his love.'

'Thanks. I'll smoke it later.'

In front of Olbrich was a small sheaf of paper and something in a clear plastic bag. Three cops were talking over a second desk in the background. Door-side of Olbrich's desk perched a thin black guy in shirtsleeves, whom Nina vaguely recognized.

'Nina, this is Vincent,' Olbrich said. Monroe meanwhile handed her a cup of coffee. She took it gratefully. He was good like that.

'I remember,' she said. 'Lab rat, right?'

Monroe frowned, but the tech grinned happily. 'Vince Walker, technological wunderkind.'

'My favourite kind,' she said, feeling very tired. 'So what do you have for us, Vince?'

'This,' Olbrich said, pushing the bag across the desk to her. 'And what was on it.'

Cleaned of blood and no longer stuck in someone's face, the object looked mundanely technical. Two inches by four and a half, a quarter inch thick. One end a row of gold-coloured connectors, the other flat. The top side was a metal plate with two stickers which had once been white but were now unevenly stained a pale brown. Underside, the spidery green tracks of a printed circuit board. A third of the way from the top was a small circle, presumably the point around which the internal disk spun while in use. A label here said, 'VOID WARRANTY IF SEAL BROKEN'. What if it was found in a dead woman's mouth, Nina wondered: where would you stand then?

'The disk,' she prompted, dutifully. The men were evidently building up to something, each trying to claim it as their own.

'Right,' Vince said. 'It's a Toshiba MK4309 drive. Capacity a little over four gigs, cramped by today's standards, and the serial confirms it was made nearly two years ago.'

'It also enabled us to nail the disk as factory-installed in a machine assembled in Japan and imported into the US in mid 2002,' Monroe interrupted. 'We're running that right now. It may tell us who the woman was, maybe not.'

'People are still on the street with the victim's photo,' Olbrich added. Nina had met him several times before, back when Zandt had been on Homicide, and he had impressed her as one of the least showy detectives she'd ever met. 'We know she didn't eat much the day she died, but she drank a whole lot. As of two hours ago I've got three detectives fanning back out from The Knights and hitting local bars and clubs again. Didn't get anything the first time, but . . . '

'And still nothing on the killer from the room?'

He shrugged. 'No prints, no fibres, nothing on the victim. This guy barely moved the air, by the look of it.'

'So what's with the disk?'

'It was blank,' Olbrich said. 'Except for two things.'

'Two things,' the tech repeated, determined not to lose his moment. 'The largest is a

103

seven-meg. MP3 file, a piece of music.'

'The Agnus Dei from Fauré's Requiem,' Monroe said. 'Quite a well-known piece, apparently. There are people trying to work out what particular recording it is, and of course we'll try to track recent CD purchases but I don't have much hope in that direction. It could have been downloaded off the internet, for all we know.'

'And?' she said, bored with prompting.

'You asked me earlier where he'd come from,' Monroe said. 'Said there might be something he was spiralling out from. It's looking like you might be right.'

He pushed the sheaf of papers towards her. 'Read this.'

She read:

'Sleep is lovely. Death is better still. Not to have been born is of course the miracle.'

His mother wouldn't let his grandmother smoke in the house. So there would be days when the old lady's temper was not good, and there would be other days when she would insist on being put out on the porch. She would be left there, no matter if it was too cold or if it rained down hard. His mother would not help her in: she would also forbid him from doing so. God help him if he went against her on that or anything else. Grandma stayed outside until her daughter was good and ready to take her back in. She did so none too gently.

On one of these days, an afternoon so cold that icicles hung from the roof, he asked her what it was it about this thing that made it worth being out there on the porch when it was warm and comfortable inside.

She looked out ahead for a while, until he was beginning to wonder if she'd heard.

'You know that joke,' she said, eventually. 'Why did the chicken cross the road?'

He said yes he did. To get to the other side.

'Well, that's what the cigarettes are like.'

'I don't get it.'

She thought again, for a moment. 'You end up living on the wrong side of the road. Best I can put it. Every night you have to walk across this road, in the dark, to get home. You can't tell if any cars are coming, but that's okay because it's not a very busy road. But the longer you cross back and forth, in the pitch dark, the more likely that sooner or later one of them cars is going to hit you. The cars are called cancer, and they're big and hard and they drive very fast, and if they get you, you die.'

'But . . . so why keep crossing the road?'

A dry smile. 'To get to the other side.' She shrugged. 'It's too late, you see. You made your bed, you got to lie in it. The only thing you can do is try to make sure you don't end up living on the wrong side of the road.'

She coughed for a while, then lit another cigarette. She took a long pull, held it to look at the glowing tip. 'Don't you ever start up with this crap, you hear?'

'I won't,' he said.

He did everything he could to take her advice. He was careful with alcohol, never used drugs, and he didn't let food or exercise or reassurance or pornography or collecting china dolls ever take his hand and pretend it was his friend.

And yet still, on a night only seven years later, he stood with blood on his hands and realized he'd found his own smoking road.

'Christ,' Nina said, eventually.

'He's killed before,' Monroe said.

'Or he wants us to think he has.'

Monroe smiled tightly. 'He's sure as hell capable of doing it again. Can we agree on that?'

'Yes,' she said. 'I'm with you there.' Her eyes felt dry. 'Who's the quote from?'

'We don't know yet.'

'You okay, Nina?' This was Olbrich.

She nodded, still staring at the note. 'I'm pissed off, that's all. A look-at-me note and a requiem, for God's sake. It's like a lunatic's serving suggestion.'

'This talking about himself in the third person,' Olbrich said. 'Isn't that strange?'

'Not especially,' Nina said. 'It's been observed in interrogation many times. Ted Bundy, for example. It can be a way of getting them to open out. The theory is that it makes it easier for them to describe crimes from which other parts of their mind wish to dissociate. In Bundy's case it also enabled him to describe hypotheticals — 'I imagine a killer would do such and such in this situation' — without technically admitting responsibility. Can we get anything from the nature of the text file itself?'

'Afraid not,' Vince said. 'The disk's standard PC format but the file has no OS signature: could have been written on anything from a

106

Supercomputer to a Palm V. Somebody downstairs is trawling through the directory structure but we don't have a whole lot of optimism on that either. The disk was securely wiped before these files were put on. This is someone who knows about computers.'

'Which could be useful information in itself,' Monroe said.

'Absolutely,' Nina said. 'It says he's under fifty and lives somewhere in the Western world.'

Monroe cocked his head and looked at her. Nina decided it would probably be a good idea if she went home again soon.

'A copy of this is with Profiling in Quantico now,' Monroe said. 'They should have some ideas soon.' His voice was a little louder than usual. He sounded serious, studious, professional, but there was a note of excitement too. That was to be expected: if you didn't get a big buzz out of going after bad guys, you wouldn't be in law enforcement. But ever since Nina had first worked with him, catching a killer called Gary Johnson who had murdered six seniors, all women, in Louisiana in the mid 1990s, Nina had been in no doubt that Monroe had other agendas. The crimes and their solutions were means to an end. She didn't understand quite what the end might be — politics? having the biggest corner office in the Continental USA? — but she knew it motivated him more than any need to look the relatives of victims in the eye and say, 'We got the guy, and he's going down for ever and a day.' Perhaps there was something not too stupid about this. On the few occasions

Nina had been able to do something along those lines, the dull expressions on the faces of her audience had not seemed to change a great deal. Six mothers and grandmothers died before their time and in sordid ways: the guy responsible is put in a concrete box for the rest of his life. As a medium of exchange, it didn't really seem to work. Nina didn't believe most of the killers felt the full force of incarceration, because they just didn't understand things the way the rest of us did. They ate, slept, took a dump. They watched television, read comic books. They took courses and meandered through endless appeals which wasted everybody's time and burned enough public money to build half a school. This was, of course, their right. What they didn't have to do was lie, by themselves, in a hole in the ground, with nothing but the slow sound of settling earth to keep them company. They didn't sleep, arms tight by their sides, in a box their children couldn't afford and which they can feel beginning to get damp, starting to rot.

So yes, maybe Monroe had it laid out sensibly. Fight the good fight. Climb the ladder. Then go home to the wife, grab a healthy supper in front of the late news. Who knows — you might even be on it, saving the world. Bottom line was the FBI weren't even directly mandated to investigate serial murder. Monroe got involved for reasons of career development. So what? What was *her* excuse?

'Go home again, Nina,' Monroe said. 'Get some sleep. I need you functioning early tomorrow morning.'

Nina looked up, surprised by his voice, and realized she'd just zoned out. Vince was looking at her a little curiously; Monroe without much affection. Only Olbrich had the grace to be looking elsewhere.

Monroe stood and started talking to Olbrich in a way that firmly suggested Nina's further input was not required. She waited until they wandered over to the cops in the back of the room. Then she turned to the self-proclaimed wunderkind and spoke in her quietest, most friendly and appealing voice.

'Vince,' she said. 'This is where I ask you a favour.'

Twenty minutes later she left the building with something in her bag. She stepped out onto the street and into an evening that was still very warm, and wondered if she was deliberately trying to screw up her career.

She needed to talk to someone, but John wasn't answering the phone and the truth was he was more screwed up than her. There was one other option. She thought about it. Then she drove home sedately. By the time she pulled into her drive she'd made her decision. In the kitchen she picked up the phone and dialled. It rang and rang, but he didn't answer.

She left a message, feeling like just another voice on just another machine.

7

The back of Mrs Campbell's house looked out over a small patch of yard that said everything the front of her house tried not to. I stood in her kitchen, waiting as patiently as I could while she clattered about. I remembered my mother once telling me that the day you refused a hot beverage from an old person was the day they learned their company was not worth the wait. I know shit about plants, however, and the view was not interesting me in the slightest. It took everything I had not to go through and grab the old lady by the throat.

'Muriel was adopted herself,' she said, when she eventually led me through into the sitting room. 'Did she tell you that?'

'No,' I said, stepping quickly forward to take the tray from her. I don't know what the protocol on that is, but the way I saw it, I had about ten seconds before it wound up on the floor and I just wasn't waiting for her to make a new batch. 'She told me she couldn't help me, and that was pretty much that.'

'She can be that way. I knew her when she first started working there. She had some bad years at the start. First husband left her, cleaned out the house when he went. Beat up on her some, too. But come what may, she turned up on time and she did what she was supposed to do and she helped a lot of people out. Lot of the public go

110

into a place like that big old department on Adams and forget the staff are human too, folk who got their own lives.'

'I understand it can be a difficult job,' I said. 'People can be hard to deal with.'

'Damn straight. Course, some of the folks work there are assholes, too.'

I laughed. She nodded approvingly. 'You should smile more,' she said. 'People look better that way. You especially. You don't smile, your face looks like you mean people harm.'

'I don't,' I said.

'So you say.'

'Mrs Campbell, I got the sense that . . . '

'Okay, I'm coming to it. You're looking for a brother, that's right? Muriel said you thought it would have been 1967. That would be correct. In fact, as I remember it was October. Though truth be told my memory really isn't what it was. I'm okay on *things*. Just not so good on pure facts.'

I nodded. My chest felt tight.

'A Chinese storekeeper found him on the street. A toddler. Don't know how long he'd been there, but he'd been crying a good while.'

'My parents had their reasons,' I said, feeling an absurd need to defend a decision which had not been my own, and which I barely understood. 'The background was complicated.'

'I'm sure. And they didn't dump him in the Tenderloin or the Mission District, which is something. Anyway, we knew he was called Paul because he had his name stitched right there on his sweater. Course a lot of times back then families would choose a new name anyhow, but

111

Paul's name stuck. We did the usual checks but we had no way of tracing where he might have come from, and so he went into care here in the city. Stayed a few years, too. Usually finding a home for one that's little and cute isn't so hard. But with this one, it seemed like they wouldn't take.'

I wanted to know what she meant, but didn't want to interrupt her flow.

'I lost track of him for a while. There are a lot of kids. Next time I heard about him was when he was becoming a problem.'

'What kind of problem?'

'He'd be with a foster family for a few months, and then he'd be back, well ahead of schedule. At first I didn't pay much attention. It happens. But it started to become a thing. *Hey, Paul's back.* The temporary family couldn't . . . well, I was going to say 'couldn't cope', but it never seemed to be that. Not exactly. It was just, here he is, back again. And you need to bear in mind these were families who'd looked after a *lot* of kids, who were good at taking children in and making them feel all right. We'd have him placed and mentally wave him goodbye, then five weeks later I'd go into the home and there he'd be, sitting on a windowsill, looking out. I'd ask him what had happened and Paul would say the same thing the families did: *it just didn't work out.*'

She paused and took a sip of her coffee, as if considering long-ago mistakes. 'Anyway, finally it's decided that we need to step up the search for an adoptive family, some longer-term solution. So I talked to Paul, and told him that's

112

what we were going to try to do. He nodded — he's about six, seven years old at this stage, bear in mind — and something tells me he's not agreeing with the idea, just recognizing it was what was going to happen and his role is just to let it roll on. So I asked him, didn't he want to find a permanent family? And he looked me right in the eyes and said, 'I had one. It's gone. When everything is in place, I'll get it back.''

I felt cold across the back of my neck. 'He remembered us?'

'Not necessarily. But he knew that once there'd been something else. You don't have to be the brightest firework in the box to realize his position wasn't natural, and he was a very smart kid. You could tell. That's all it was. Kids often get this feeling they've been abandoned, taken away from where they ought to be. Even the ones who *haven't* been adopted get it. The 'I should be a fairy princess' syndrome, or 'I am rightfully a king and when I cry the earth cries with me'. That's what I thought it was.'

I'd watched the abandonment part of the video many times without really confronting what it must have been like for the child who was left behind. In the last three months I hadn't really cared what he'd felt. I tried hard to do so now.

'Look,' I said, 'do you mind if I have a cigarette?'

'Go ahead,' she smiled. 'My husband used to smoke. I like the smell. You do know it will kill you, though?'

'Not going to happen,' I reassured her. 'Just a

113

rumour put around by the gym addicts and health nuts.'

She nodded, no longer smiling. 'Yes, that's what he thought too.'

Something about the way she said it meant that though I smoked the cigarette down, I didn't enjoy it very much. 'So what happened when you looked for a permanent family?'

'I'll tell you.' She was quiet for a moment, before continuing. 'You know, I did that kind of thing for a long time, and I thought about it a lot. Most of me believes that where we're born seeps up into us like water from the soil, that we have leaves like trees do; and where the seed that becomes us first lands, that's who we are and that will determine the colour of our leaves — even if some bird picks us up that same afternoon and moves us fifty, a hundred miles away. Another bit of me thinks well, we're all God's children, aren't we? We're all just human. Isn't that what the Bible says? Two hundred years ago there was barely anything on this spot but birds and some animals and every now and then one of the native people, out hunting in a land so big they called it the world. Now we've taken it and call it our home and go fight wars over it in places half of us can't even spell. So what does it matter if a child is brought up by someone who isn't its kin, or in some other part of the country? Give them a good home and it could be nothing ever happened. I've seen it work hundreds of times. It isn't always easy, but it works, and it's one of the things makes me think we humans aren't such a bad lot after all.'

114

She shook her head. 'Finding an adopter for Paul just wasn't that simple. He was placed with three families after that. First lasted a year, another foster arrangement. They had an older daughter of their own already. I was dealing with my own things at that time, my husband got sick. I got into work one Monday morning with stuff on my mind and I was told that Paul was in a room on another floor. When people had turned up that day, he was sitting on the step outside. He hadn't run away. His family had put him there. After that, he was back and forth for a few months, then we found him someone else. That one lasted two whole years, by which time he was coming up to nine. Then one day there's a knock on my office door, and the mother was standing there. She told me, politely, that they'd had enough. That it wasn't Paul, not at all, but she had a little baby girl of her own now and they'd just decided fostering wasn't for them any more. I was mad at her, I can tell you. I nearly chewed her head off. That's not the way it works. But . . . you can't leave a child with people who don't want them any more.'

She picked up her cup, found it was cold, and put it back down. 'Do you . . . '

'I'm fine,' I said. 'Please go on.'

'I saw Paul again at the home, soon after that. I was feeling sorry for the kid. I told him I thought he'd had a raw deal. He just shrugged. 'I already have a family,' he said, again. I was concerned to hear that he was still thinking that way, and I tried to point out that wasn't the case, not really, and he had to help us in finding him a new set of people to be with. He'd once had a birth mother and father, and that would always be true. But now he had to be with someone new. 'Not them,' he said. 'They weren't real. But I had a brother. He was real. He was just like me.' He put a big stress on the 'just': *just* like me, was what he said.'

She smiled, faintly. 'I didn't believe him, of course. Thought he was just conjuring; there was something about him by then that was a little . . . I don't know. But when you turned up at the door tonight, I saw he was right after all. He did have a brother, *just* like him.'

I nodded, because I had to, but I was thinking that she was wrong and he was wrong too. I resembled him physically, that was all. The idea that the similarity went any deeper made me feel sick inside. I was surprised she could see the resemblance, too, if Paul had been a child when she last saw him.

'Then finally we found one that took. We got him placed with a family here in the city, and he was there a year before they moved out of state and he went with them. Whatever had been wrong, it got right. This time it worked. That's it.'

I looked at her.

'What?' she said.

I just kept looking at her.

She looked down at her hands. Her voice was quiet. 'What has he done?'

'Mrs Campbell,' I said. 'Tell me what you haven't yet said. I really have to know.'

She looked back up at me and when she

spoke, she spoke fast and her eyes were flat. 'Few years later I ran into the husband from the couple who had been responsible for leaving him on the steps of the building. Hadn't seen anything of them since that day — you treat a child like that, you're off our books and going to court. Matter of fact, they nearly were, but the wife got sick, and so . . . it was let slide. I saw this guy across the street and deliberately looked away, but next thing I knew he was running towards me through the traffic. He came right up and stood in my way and he just started talking. He told me that his wife had a dog, back when Paul was with them. Said that most of the time the boy was good, very good, almost as if he had decided this was the way things were and he'd better make the most of it. Got along okay with their daughter most of the time. But this dog, Paul didn't get on with it, and he hated it when it barked, and said it looked at him funny. The dog was pretty old, his wife had had it since she was in college, and she loved it more than anything else in the world. Even more than him, her husband said, but that was okay: he liked the creature too. Big old dozy hound, didn't do much, just slept in the back yard and thumped his tail on the ground every now and then.'

She stopped, took a deep breath. 'Then one day Paul came running in the house and said the dog had an accident. They went running out back. The dog is lying half in the yard and half in the narrow road at the end. Its head is all messed up, like it got caught in a car's wheels. Paul's crying and stuff so the dog's quickly buried and

117

it was only later that night, when they were sitting in bed, that his wife said something. She didn't look at her husband and she talked quietly, as if speaking to the wall. She said that in all the years they'd lived in that house, the dog had never gone anywhere near the back road. She said how it would be odd for someone to be driving along it too quickly to stop. She said, too, how it was strange that it was only the head that had been so badly injured, that both eyes, and the mouth, should be so damaged.

'Her husband thought about this. Nothing more was said that night. They went to sleep, eventually. That was a week before they brought Paul back. The husband admitted that they didn't know *how* they knew, that they had no proof. It could still just have been an accident. But that week was enough. His wife couldn't have him there any more.'

Mrs Campbell held a finger up to stop me saying anything. 'Now listen, you. This is just something a man said. I thought it could just be some kind of overblown lie to make up for what they'd done, and that was probably there to read in my face. The guy just shook his head, and said that if I'd had to look in his wife's eyes all the years since, I'd know what was the truth and what was not. Then he walked away, and I never saw him again.'

'Jesus,' I said.

'Right,' she nodded. 'And the last thing is just me, and I'm going to tell you it, and then you're going to go. Six, seven years after *that*, not long before I retired, there was a fire. Muriel said

118

she'd told you. A lot of paperwork got lost.'

'Yes,' I said. 'She mentioned it.'

'Something she doesn't know about is this. I was late getting to work that morning — tram got fouled up, I had to walk the last six blocks. Time I got there, building was already up in smoke, people standing out on the street, everyone running back and forth. Could have been a very bad day. As it was, four people got killed and a lot more got burned. Fire went up when the building was full. And as I was standing there, trying to take it all in, I got a strange feeling in the back of my neck. I turned, and . . .'

Her throat clicked, dry as old bone. 'There he was. On the other side of the street, watching. Grown up a little now, a young man. Looked just like you do now, only thinner. I saw him just a second, and then he was gone. Or maybe I didn't see him at all. Sometimes I think I saw that face, and recognized it. Most of the time, I think it was just in my own head, which is why I never mentioned it to no one. Not even Muriel, and she was like a daughter to me. Still is, when she's got the time.'

'It was him,' I said, quietly. 'It was Paul.'

She gripped me by the arm, her fingers strong and sharp. 'What you *must not think* is this was anything to do with him being in care, with the people who fostered him, who tried so hard to give him a life. It was not. Those people helped bring up Muriel and thousands more like her.'

'I know,' I said. 'My parents weren't my real

119

parents either, and they gave me more love than I ever deserved.'

She was surprised, but gathered herself. She stood, and I understood my time was over.

At the door, as I stood on the porch, she put her hand on my arm again and said one final thing.

'I've spent all my life with young people, and on the whole I've enjoyed it a lot. But one thing about my view of the world changed in that time, and changed for good.'

'What was that?'

'I still believe we're all human,' she said, stepping back and closing the screen door. 'But I don't believe we're all God's children. No, I don't believe that at all.'

* * *

I went back to the hotel because I wasn't sure what else to do. I ran out of steam when I hit the lobby and ended up sitting in the bar, staring out at the street through tinted glass. Everyone has their typical experiences, as discussed. This is one of mine.

I was spaced out and ticked off. San Francisco was a dead end. Mrs Campbell didn't remember the name of the family which had taken Paul in for good. In any event, they'd moved, and she didn't know where to. Her colleagues from that time were either dead or scattered. The trail had been severed, not least by the fire. 'I believed Paul had come back and set that fire, and I knew Mrs Campbell did too: just as I believed she understood that the young boy who had been found on the street alone had merely tolerated being moved from pillar to post until he was old enough to leave and make his own way in the world: when he would become the person to 'put things in place.'

When I reached for my wallet to pay for the first beer, I remembered I'd turned off my cell. I had a missed call. It could only be one of two people, so I hit callback without bothering to listen to the message.

She answered quickly. 'John?'

'No,' I said. 'It's Ward. Your phone tells you who's calling, Nina. Just look at the display.'

'Right,' she said. 'Silly me. Where are you?'

'San Francisco,' I said.

'Oh. Why?'

'I left my heart here. Came to pick it up.'

'Good move. How's it looking?'

'Barely used,' I said, and she laughed briefly. 'What's up?'

'Nothing,' she said. 'Well, not true, things are going crazy. We had a double murder this morning; someone killed a Jane Doe in a nasty motel and then whacked a cop to underline his point. He left a hard disk in the woman.'

'Charming,' I said.

'Not very. It's LAPD's business, of course, but Monroe is all over it and thus so am I. Wondered if you would take a look at this disk. I had a copy done, unofficially. I know you used to do that kind of thing on a professional basis.'

'Sure,' I said. 'Though Bobby would have been a better bet for you. And even a byte-for-byte copy isn't going to be exactly the same as the original. But I'll take a look.'

'They've already found a note and a piece of music on it. This one has a real sense of theatre.'

'What's the music?'

'Fauré's Requiem.'

'Nice.'

'I haven't listened to it.'

'You should. Quite uplifting, given it's for dead people.'

She was silent for a little while. I didn't interrupt.

'Are you okay, Ward?'

'Sort of.' I told her, briefly, what I'd found out from Mrs Campbell. 'So that's weirded me out. Plus . . .'

I shrugged. She heard it. 'Yes,' she said, quietly. 'I know. I . . . I have this dream sometimes. I'm up at The Halls again, on the floor of the lobby building, after I'd been shot. You and John are out there in the houses, trying to find Sarah Becker. Bobby's gone, I don't know where. I'm on the floor, and I hurt bad, and somebody's coming to get me. And this time I think he might.'

'Shit,' I said. 'That sounds like no fun.'

'I had it again just three hours ago. It gets longer each time. I . . . sometimes I worry there will come a time when it doesn't end. Where he gets me, and I don't wake up.'

'Dreams last as long as you let them,' I said. 'Both good and bad.'

'Very deep, Ward-san.'

'Yeah. Sorry. I have no idea what I meant.'

She laughed, and it sounded a little more convincing this time.

'Okay, so, call when you've got the disk,' I said. 'I'll head down. There's nothing else for me up here.'

'It's sitting here on my table now,' she said.

I had been to Nina's house only once, and briefly, but I could picture it clearly. For just a moment, sitting on an uncomfortable stool with half a beer and the sound of generic chatter around me, I wished I was there now. There, or some other house. Something approximating a home.

'Don't let John meddle with it,' I said. 'I'll be there tomorrow evening. Can you put him on the phone?'

'He's out,' she said. 'I'll let him know you're coming.'

* * *

I went up to my room and smoked my head off. It didn't seem to help my mood much, though it at least shoved the nicotine monkey off my back. I pulled the room's armchair over to the window, yanked the sash up, and sat looking out for a while. I saw tall dark buildings, and lights. I heard sounds of life from outside and below. I felt like I was sitting on the edge of a huge continent by myself, without tribe or hearth or hunting ground.

Slowly my depth of focus pulled closer, until I was looking at my feet instead, propped on the windowsill. Must be a strange life these days, for toes. A simple twist of fate and they could have been the big boys, the much feted opposables, spending busy days carrying things and controlling machinery and touching interesting parts of people's bodies. They don't get to do any of that. Instead they just get pushed into small, dark leather places and forgotten about, and when they're let free they often seem little more than a strange fringe on the end of your feet.

In the end I fell asleep, and dreamed.

The place was some old town, a place of cobbled streets and teetering houses, with a compact square that held a farmer's market and stalls selling household things. I was young, teenaged, and I was in love with the gypsy queen of this market, a girl who was young, long-haired and beautiful, who glowed with the confidence of knowing every alley of this vibrant selling place, who had grown up in it and felt its forces and lives running through her: confident with beauty, unreachable but at the same time so gorgeous that she felt like everybody's love. There was a moment that felt like a real memory, a glimpse of her walking through the stalls with a couple of lesser girls in tow, her face the clearest thing in the world, surrounded by a tumble of dark hair shot with auburn lights.

Then later, I returned as a man, more confident but more dry, having lost in magic what I had gained in stature. The market had shrunk to a few stalls, revealing the streets — where before it seemed the market existed in a realm by itself, needing no such environment in which to live. I walked it, hearing echoes

124

where before there had been only the sound of bargaining and laughter.

And then I saw her. She was working at a stall selling offcuts of cloth, mixed buttons, things made of plastic. Her hair was cut short, and had gone prematurely grey. She still looked young in the face, but had thickened, and seemed shorter, more businesslike.

I passed by the stall and saw her pushing something into a plastic bag, some two dollar purchase for an old woman. I realized she was now just a woman who ran a market stall. The princess I was returning to see, to show that I was now a man, and thus worth something, worth her gaze, had gone: all the more so because there was someone who took up her place in the world. If I hadn't seen her, I could still have believed that somewhere she walked, still wreathed in magic and sex and smiles.

But now I had, and could do nothing but walk a little way from the market, and turn and look back at it, knowing that my youth, my core, the thing that had driven me all these years, was dead. Only then did it strike me that though she had glanced at me, she had not recognized me; that though she was now just a market stall holder, I was not — and had never been — anything at all.

When I woke I turned groggily to the clock by the bed and was astonished to see only an hour had passed.

My cell phone rang. I picked it up, recognized the number.

'You're back,' I said.

There was a pause. 'It's Zandt,' he said.

'I know,' I said, foggily. 'You were out earlier.'

There was another pause. 'Ward, I'm in Florida.'

This made no sense to me either, but I went with it. 'Okay, good for you. So?'

'Yakima,' he said.

I sat up straighter. 'What about it?'

'I've got some information. Maybe. It doesn't make a huge amount of sense.'

'Well, I told Nina I'd come down to see her in LA tomorrow. Why don't I see you there?'

'You spoke to Nina today? Why?'

'She's after some whack-job and she wants me to take a look at a disk.'

'So where are you now?'

'San Francisco.'

There was a pause. 'Why?'

'I've been trying to track the Upright Man. Without much success.'

'Stay there. I'll come to you.'

'John, I just told you: I'm supposed to go meet Nina.'

'I don't want to go to LA.'

There was something off about his voice. 'Okay,' I said. 'I'll see you here.'

'I'll call you when I get in.'

And with that, the phone went dead. I was pretty sure that what I'd heard in his voice was that he was drunk.

I thought about that a moment, then called Nina back and said it would be an extra day before I could get down to her. I didn't say why. She said she'd overnight the disk to me instead.

126

'Fine,' I said. Then: 'Is John back yet?'

'He was. He went out again.'

'He's hard to tie down.'

'You said it.'

We said goodbye.

I turned back to the window, and looked out at the city some more. It ignored my gaze, as cities do.

8

Nina was just heading into LAPD the next morning when the call came in: a cop in patrol division had gotten a strong hit on the photo of the dead girl. She swung a turn which had twenty drivers hammering on their horns, and headed for a bar called Jimmy's, over near where La Cienega hit the Boulevard.

There was a black and white and an unmarked with a flasher parked outside already. Nina added her car to the collection and hurried inside. The bar was dark and smelled of spilled beer: the air felt worn, as if it had passed through the lungs of too many people who couldn't sit up straight. She spotted Olbrich standing talking to a guy who had long hair and a glassy smile that said if he'd known this kind of heavy shit was going to break out, he wouldn't have had that huge joint before he left home.

'This is Agent Baynam,' Olbrich said as she approached. 'Don, why don't you tell her what you've told me.'

'Her name's Jessica,' the bartender said. 'That's for sure. And I know she lived in West Hollywood. I'm pretty sure also her second name is Jones, I think she said that a couple times and I know people here called her JJ, but . . . you know, not everyone . . . '

'Uses their real name. I got you,' Nina said. 'Jessica was a regular?'

128

'Yeah, then some. Lot of nights. Some afternoons.'

'She a hooker, Don?'

'No.' He shook his head vigorously. 'Absolutely not. She was going to be a singer or something once, I think. Think she said that one time. She was pretty enough, that's for sure. She's a waitress now. Or was, I guess, shit.'

Olbrich prompted him. 'And she was in here on Saturday night, you think?'

'Yeah. She came in around five with a girlfriend. Don't know her name, but I've seen her around before. Black, long straight hair. It was two for one pitcher night so, you know, they both got loaded pretty fast.' He coughed. 'The girlfriend's more of a full-on goodtime person, and I'm pretty sure she ended up at a table with some guys and took off with them. JJ just kind of hung out for a while, then she was sitting with this other guy.'

'What guy was that?' Nina's voice was even, but her chest suddenly felt tight. Olbrich was good, and kept out of it.

'I was telling the officer here. Don't know the guy. I only noticed because . . . ' He shrugged.

Because you were kind of sweet on Jessica, Nina thought. *I understand.* 'Did she often meet up with guys?'

'Pretty often,' the guy said. He looked away, apparently at the rows of battered tables and chairs he had to put in place.

Nina nodded, watching him. *And one night, maybe several nights, a wet kiss on your cheek bought another pitcher after the money had run*

129

out, yes? And do you still think about that sometimes, though for her it was a nothing, forgotten forever by the second swallow?

'Anything unusual about this one?'

He looked back at her. 'He was just a guy. He had short hair. Kind of good-looking, I think. That's all I can tell you. It all got busy after that, and next time I looked it was late and JJ was gone and someone else was in the booth. You could talk to the girls who were working the floor, they might have served them. But they won't be in until tonight. Except Lorna, she'll be on lunch.'

There was a shout from the doorway, and a uniform stuck his head in. 'Lieutenant?'

The policeman turned. 'You got it?'

'We do.'

Olbrich jerked towards the door with his head. 'We got an address, Nina. I'll go with you.'

'She really dead?' the bartender asked.

'Yes,' Nina said. 'She's really dead. I'm sorry.'

He nodded, and turned away.

When Nina got to the door she glanced back and saw the man slowly wiping a cloth over a table in a bar that he had to keep working in, and she thought: we never really know who we leave behind.

★ ★ ★

The address was Apartment 7, 3140 Gardiner. When Nina's car got there, Monroe was already outside with two cops.

'He moves fast, doesn't he?' Olbrich said.

130

'You better believe it.'

The building was three storeys high and dirty white. A staircase went up the outside of either end. Nina walked up to the second storey and waited with Monroe while one of the detectives tracked down the building's super.

Monroe looked at her. 'Feeling better this morning?'

'Fine,' she said. He spoke quietly, and so did she. 'And thank you for your concern, Charles, which is not at all beginning to bug me. Anything useful from Profiling on the note?'

'Not yet. And you don't think there will be. Why?'

'Profiling didn't really work for the Washington sniper, did it?'

'That's a completely different . . . '

'No it isn't. They decided it had to be a white guy because the perceived wisdom — based on a not-very-scientific study done a pretty long time ago — is that the majority of serial killers are white, and so any report phoned in about a black guy was ignored. Meanwhile a couple people said they saw white trucks, and so suddenly that's what everyone's looking for, despite the fact white trucks are the Starbucks of the highway and *not* seeing them would be unusual. The licence plate of the killer's *blue* car is run through the system half a dozen times because of suspicious behaviour, but no, it's not a white truck and he's not a white guy, so we're not interested. The profilers say killers never work with other people — except, um, this one did. We shouldn't have been listening to them anyway:

131

anyone with a brain knew from the start this was not a serial killer but a multiple murderer on a politico-religious mission, in which case anything profilers say is irrelevant. All it did was cloud the issue, and it could do the same here. I'm just not sure I believe in their shtick any more.'

'So why did you ask me if they'd come back with anything?'

'To try to steer you away from further solicitous enquiries.'

'Nina, when are you going to tell me what happened last year?'

'I already done told you, boss,' she said, smiling sweetly. In her head, however, she reminded herself to be careful. Monroe was many things, but he wasn't stupid.

At that moment Olbrich appeared at the stairs with a bunch of keys. 'Zinman's taking a statement,' he said, heading for the door to Apartment 7, 'but the guy's got nothing for us. Kept herself to herself, blah. And he's as dumb as a bag of rocks. We set?'

Guns now in hand, Nina and Monroe nodded.

Olbrich knocked on the door, waited, and received no response. So he unlocked the door and opened it slowly.

'This is the police,' he said. 'Please step into sight.'

Nothing happened. He opened the door a little further. This revealed a fairly large room, about twenty feet square. Electing to wait outside, this was all Nina saw until the two men had gone in and called an all-clear. Nobody home.

When she stepped into the apartment she saw a coffee table and a tired red couch in the middle, and a computer workstation under a window on the far side. The computer was grey and cheap-looking. There was a small red light at the bottom of the monitor, but the screen was black. A television sat to the side of the workstation, where it would be visible from the couch. For optimum viewing it would have been moved a couple of feet to the left, but there it would have blocked the door to the bedroom, where the two men were. A thin black cable was running in there across the floor from the computer workstation. Before following it Nina took a few steps the other side of the sofa, and peered into a small kitchen with a big window overlooking the street. It was tidy. As she turned back she noticed a battered-looking guitar propped up in the corner behind the sofa. It was dusty and missing a string.

In the room's remaining corner was a small desk. A couple of notepads. Nina carefully lifted the cover of one and glanced at a page. Doodles. Stuff that looked like lyrics. One sentence, 'Rain that never washes', had been written and then crossed out.

'Come look at this,' Monroe said.

The bedroom was small, enough space for a double bed, a small vanity and that was that. A tiny bathroom stood off the bottom end. The bed was unmade. The men were looking at a small object on a tripod to the side of the bed. It was to this that the black cable ran.

'Camera,' Olbrich said.

133

'Webcam,' she corrected. 'See where the cable goes?'

She followed it back into the main room and over to the workstation. Turning her hand over so her fingertips were out of the way, she gently moved the mouse.

The screen of the monitor flickered and woke up. In the centre of the screen was a window which took up about a third of its extent. It showed a picture of the side of the bed Monroe was still standing by.

'I'm not going to touch it,' she said, 'but you're going to find a cable modem feed out the back of this machine. Jessica had a website where people could watch her.'

'From where?' Olbrich asked.

'From anywhere in the world.' She stood back from the desk. 'Bad news. Our suspect list just jumped into the tens of millions.'

★   ★   ★

Three hours later she was back at Jimmy's and sitting in an upper room that belonged to the owner/manager, who wasn't called Jimmy.

'Sounds like a bar's name,' Mr Jablowski had said, when she asked. 'Whereas mine doesn't.' Alerted by Don the barman to the morning's visitors, he'd elected to be on site for once. He was strangely dapper for a man who owned what was basically a beer-pit for the afternoon alcoholic crowd, but there are a lot of drug dealers who don't jack the product either. Don meanwhile had gone home for a few hours, to 'chill out'. The investigators had his address, but she privately didn't think it was one they were going to visit. She was no profiler either, of course — which was why, on her suggestion, a plainclothes was following the barman home.

Another detective and an agent were out in the sparse lunchtime drinking crowd. One of the waitresses who'd been on duty the night of Jessica's last visit was due to arrive soon, and an eye was also being kept out for men who fitted an extremely generalized description. Things were going nowhere fast out there, in other words. Back at the girl's apartment, the opposite was true. It was being ripped apart, and investigating officers from three separate agencies were ploughing into anything they could find: reading, photographing, dusting.

Nina, meanwhile, was talking to a young black woman called Jean. Jean had come in looking for Jessica because they'd been due to hook up the night before and her friend had never showed. Also because she wanted a drink. Don had pointed her straight in the direction of the cops, and kept her heading that way even when she remembered she'd much prefer to be somewhere else.

'Cam whore?' Nina said, repeating what the girl had just said.

Jean shrugged. 'That's what it's called. Don't mean you do nothing like having sex or whatever. 'Cam girl' is okay too.'

'Jessica never entered into sex for payment, as far as you're aware?'

'Hell no. Nor me neither, lady, get yourself

135

straight about that.'

'Working girls are not allowed on the premises,' Jablowski said, smoothly. 'I'm very strict about that.'

'When you're here, which sounds like it isn't very often. Sir — I wonder if you could leave us alone for a moment?'

The owner left. Nina let a pause settle. 'And so, Jean, I take it you're a cam girl too?'

'Yeah. I, uh, I put Jessica onto it. But like I say, it's not like . . . '

Nina looked her straight in the face. 'I'm not suggesting it's like anything at all, Jean. Cam whoring is a field of which I'm almost entirely ignorant. I need to know about it, though, and I need to know right now. It could have a lot to do with why Jessica isn't around any more. So why don't you just tell me how it is?'

The girl sat back, lit up a cigarette, and talked.

Hooking was one thing, she said. Everybody knows where that's at. Putting up a cam, that was different. You never met no one, you took no risks, you encountered no bodily fluids. You never even *did* nothing, not really. Just took your clothes off. Do whatever you'd be doing normally, but naked. Watching TV. Cleaning the kitchen. If you had a boyfriend round, maybe you left the camera on, maybe you pointed it the other way. Whatever. Weird thing was that for some of the watchers, the less you did the better. Jean had a day one time when there was lots of shit going down and she didn't slop around in her underwear, just plain forgot about the camera and got on with her life like a normal person — and next morning she had a tray of sweaty emails wowing her for such 'great teasing'. Men were whacked out when it came to sex, Jean believed. Just when you thought you'd got them figured out, they did or said something made you realize you hadn't scratched the *surface* of how fucking weird they could be. She had a weird-ass impulse, every now and then, to fuck with their heads. To sit around looking fine and then hold up a piece of paper saying, 'I cooked some skanky vegetarian crap last night and the apartment still smells like a cow's insides'. To wander just out of the range of the camera's gaze and do something *really* rude and sexy, that would pop those guys' eyes out if they could only see it. Or to let rip with a life-changing fart and sit there and smile into the camera, knowing that no matter how big and flat their screen, it wasn't telling them everything there was to know about *her* world.

'You said you got Jessica into this,' Nina said. 'How did that come about?'

'I met a girl at a party, like eighteen months ago. She was doing it already and she gave me an email address for this guy who sets up sites. This dude calls himself the Webdaddy, and never mind how fucking creepy *that* is, but basically he knows the science bit. You email him a picture; he emails you back and you talk some about 'boundaries' — like how naked you will go, what else you'll do, if you got a boyfriend and if you'd do things together, if he's on for it, stuff like that. If Webdaddy likes you, he mails you a CD with some shit on how to set it up. You get yourself cable internet and go over to Circuit City and buy a webcam for fifty bucks. Everything else, he takes care of it. Your site, your billing, the works. End of the month, a cheque arrives. Simple as that.'

'Do you have a street address for this person?'

Jean shook her head. 'Email, is all. Jessica was the same. He's right there on the web. Why you going to meet him in real life?'

'But what if there was a problem with the system, or a payment didn't arrive?'

'You email him. This guy *lives* on the web, lady. You mail him, there's a reply before the SEND button has bounced back up.'

You set your webcam in position — basically a cheap, low resolution digital camera. A USB cable went from that into the back of your computer. Software there grabbed a picture of what was visible through the camera's lens and automatically uploaded it, via cable internet, onto a server on the web. A little while later that picture was replaced by a new one, and so on and on. Meanwhile, out there in the universe of men with time on their hands, the user had your web page loaded in his browser, the picture right there in the centre. A piece of code caused the page to refresh the picture regularly, uploading the new image from your webcam to replace the old one on the screen. An interaction of computers, software and telecoms that would have been science fiction twenty years ago; years of research and millions of dollars, and *voilà* — people in Kansas, Cardiff and Antwerp can desultorily jack off while you vacuum nekkid in

LA. Weird world? It surely is. But Jean didn't have to have sex with strangers or go shake her stuff with scary-ass strippers. Jean was all for it. Jean thought it was progress that worked for womankind.

'Jessica would have been making a few hundred a week from doing this?'

The girl shook her head. 'Nothing like. She only been doing it a few months, didn't have many subscribers. She didn't go out of her way to entertain, you know what I'm saying. Most the girls *perform*. She'd take her shirt off sometimes — you got to or you get dropped — but she didn't like doing it. And she didn't do no sexy stuff either, I don't think. She was going to stop doing it at all, she said, going to get back into writing songs. She kept it real secret. Nobody here knew about it. Only me.'

'The men who subscribe to your site. How much contact do you have with them?'

'Just emails,' Jean said.

'They have no way of finding your address?'

'Not unless you give it to them.'

'Did Jessica give any indication she might have done? That she was in special contact with any of her subscribers?'

'Like I said, she wasn't really into it at all. She needed money. But she was a proud person. She wasn't going to do nothing she was going to feel bad about. Leastways, not unless she was real drunk.'

'You guys were pretty drunk the other night, right?'

Jean gave a lopsided grin. 'Could be.'

139

'And you left Jessica when you went to party.'

'I met some guys. When I left, she was still here.'

'The barman said he later saw her sitting with a man. You know anything about that?'

'Like I said, I was gone.'

'She didn't have anyone in particular that you know about?'

'Not right now.'

'Any in the recent past?'

'She had boyfriends. But they were just guys.'

Nina sat in silence for a moment, and looked at the woman opposite. After the initial news of Jessica's death, she'd bounced back fast. Jessica was evidently an acceptable loss. Nina thought again about the speed of A — Z, and Z to Jane Doe. It was hard not to when confronted with a girl who was twenty-three and mostly having a good time and thought it would always be so, that self-belief and attitude would work as a magic cloak.

She said: 'You realize you're not invincible, don't you?'

Jean looked right back at her, cocked her head and smiled coldly. 'You neither, girl.'

★   ★   ★

'We're on it,' Monroe said. 'Soon as you called we got one of the techs into the machine. We have the physical location of the web server her site was on and we've also got an at for this Webdaddy person.'

'An 'at'?'

140

'Geek slang for 'email address', apparently.'

'You live and learn.'

They were standing on the balcony outside Jessica's apartment, which was still being taken apart. Monroe was sipping from a cup of ice water, but he looked unusually hot and crumpled.

'Nothing of interest in there?'

'Not aside from the computer. She kept the place pretty clean. There's not a lot of prints. LAPD will run what we have, but . . . There's some notebooks with scribbles and what looks like very bad poetry. No numbers or names yet. Forensics are in the bedroom now, but there's no sign she was killed here.'

'How soon before someone knocks on Webdaddy's door?'

'Not long. Email address was no direct help but we have a lead out of the registration information for the virtual server. Jessica and Jean were two of fifteen girls — here in town, two in San Diego, one in San Francisco, some out in the sticks. Barstow, for Christ's sake. The overall domain was called 'daddysgirls.net', incidentally.'

'Nice.'

'If it's here in LA then we'll go along,' he said. 'If not, it'll be whoever's local. Speed is going to be important.'

'So what do you want me to do now?'

Monroe shook his head. 'The guy you put on the barman said he just went home, smoked drugs while staring at the wall for three hours, and is now back heroically serving beer. From your impression plus what we're waiting for, I don't make him for it anyway. You could save me a phone call and bug Quantico over the note profile, but other than that . . . have you eaten today?'

'No.'

'I would go do that. Somewhere close. I hear anything, you'll know.'

Forty minutes later and halfway through a salad, she got the call. Swearing — it was a good Cobb, and her first meal in over twenty-four hours — she dropped money on the table and ran to the street.

By the time she was halfway to 4th Street in Venice, her phone rang again. She pulled over on the Boulevard and listened to a Monroe whose voice was flat.

'It's not him,' he said. 'His real name is Robert Klennert, and he's fifty-eight years old and significantly obese. He's basically a fetid sack of shit who sets up live porno sites. He knows tech, which is good for the hard disk, but I have a hard time buying him for being able to trap and kill a young woman or frankly a woman of any age or level of fitness whatsoever, not to mention he's way off the witness descriptions. File under 'pervert' and throw away.'

'So we're back to the 'one of millions' scenario.'

'A little better than that, maybe. LAPD have Klennert's records. Anyone who subscribed to or even guest-visited his sites will be logged. His computers are being carried past me as I speak.'

'On what charge?'

142

'None. He's co-operating fully. Weirdly, he appears to have genuinely paternal feelings towards 'his girls'. Which is either a big-time bluff, or . . . ' Monroe fell silent for a moment. 'Or more likely not. It isn't him. Meanwhile it looks as though the music on the disk is going to give us absolutely zilch. I can feel this drifting, Nina. Unless something happens, I think we may have lost it to the grunts.'

Right, Nina thought. Or you sense a slog through a bewilderingly vast virtual trail that you don't understand, and you don't see how it's generating plot for The Charles Monroe Story, HBO Special.

She said goodnight. On the other side of the street a car pulled into a driveway and a small family climbed out. Husband, wife, a little girl. The adults appeared to be having an argument.

Nina wound her window down a couple inches and listened, and heard the little girl laugh. The adults cracked up soon afterwards.

Nina realized the altercation had been fake, an impersonation of whomever the family had just visited. She thought for a moment of her own childhood, which in general had been straightforward but had also featured enough genuine male anger that she doubted she could ever have laughed as that little girl across the street just had.

She watched the child as she followed her parents up the path, thinking that if the girl was greeted by some cute little puppy bounding out of the house tied with a ribbon,

143

she might have to go thump the lucky little princess herself.

No dog. The girl lived to laugh another day.

Nina started up the car and drove towards the ocean.

9

The girl was quiet. Before she'd been wall to wall
— nice to meet you, hey great place, ooh that's
nice, oh yeah. Now, afterwards, she had nothing
to add. Maybe she thought that was the way he
wanted it (and she was right, for the moment);
perhaps she believed it was all over bar the
tipping (in which case, she was wrong). Could be
she'd had an embolism and was committing all
her energy to not keeling over. Pete Ferillo didn't
know. Pete didn't care. Not even a little bit. That
was what was so great about it. The not knowing.
The not having to know. The not having to give a
blue-eyed shit.

He reached to the table and got a cigar from
his case. Ran it under his nose. No reason to, he
knew what it would smell like, but he was feeling
sensual. It smelled good.

He clipped the end and stuck it in his mouth.
Lit it with a match — recently someone he
respected had told him that was the best way, so
that's how he did it now — and puffed it into
life. Thick smoke barfed out of the end. He
watched it go.

He was naked, lounging in an armchair with
his legs stuck out straight in front. He never sat
like that at home. He would be too aware of his
gut, the dimpled thighs, the harsh contrasts
between his sallow crotch, permatan forearms
and the blotched and scarred alabaster of the

rest. Here, this afternoon, he didn't have to care about any of this. Didn't have to feel it marked him down as ageing or unfit or undesirable. Didn't have to listen to its dismal messages about the passage of time or what it said about the likely state of his insides: didn't have to try to use this pudding mess to jump-start a wife who said she loved him but who used her endless sessions on the step machine as a taunt. Yes, Maria looked better than he did. A lot better. So what? Hitting the gym and the malls was all she had to do. That was his 'job', he'd look better too. He loved her, of course. He'd loved her twenty-five years. You learn to smile when you're mad, and stay your hand, and everyone gets along most of the time.

The apartment belonged to a very important customer at the Dining Room, someone with whom Pete had done business for quite some time and in other places. He was also a man who came to dine sometimes with a lady who wasn't the woman to whom he was married. Pete was discreet, could keep in his head who the guy had come with the last time. A friendly deal was struck, man to man, and now he had his own keys. A maid came in every day to keep the place spick and span and the fridge full of mineral water. The apartment was simple but well furnished. Bedroom, balcony, bathroom, living area. This last was a good-sized room, a section of it partitioned off with a little table for dining, also designed so you couldn't see the door when you sat in the main area of the suite, so the place felt bigger. Clever. The balcony was good for standing on in a robe, savouring late afternoon fun times while the proles of the city toiled and honked below. Maybe later.

For now, the chair was working for him. He watched the girl as she moved around at the counter in the bijou little kitchen area. He didn't know her last name. Didn't know her favourite colour, movie star or show. Didn't know the names of her previous boyfriends, hadn't heard about high old times with them or anyone else. He knew about her on a want-to-know basis only. He knew she was tall and tan and called Cherri, and he loved the fakeness of her name, the 'And now, on stage four'-ness of it. Her hair was every shade of blonde from strawberry to platinum and fell straight and thick down between her shoulder blades. She was slim (*young* slim, not watch-every-mouthful turkey neck scrawny) and she had big tits and a pretty face and a cute little tattoo of a black rose on her lower back, actually pretty well done. Pete didn't like tattoos, in general. Not on normal women. But on girls like this, he liked them. It was appropriate. It said here was a woman who was aware of her body; who owned it, used it as a resource. Pete knew of women, the girlfriends or wives of friends, who had tattoos done a year or two back, when everyone was doing it. Maria wanted one, can you believe it? Fucking cat, or something. He told her no, and he was right. Tattoos made you look like a stripper — which was fine if you *were* a stripper, but stupid otherwise. It was like pole-dancing, for Christ's sake. Couple years back there had been this fad

147

in the local yuppie class for the wife to 'learn' pole-dancing, or at least take one blushing class with some smug aerobics Amazon who knew she was onto a good thing. The stupidity of it made Pete's head want to explode. There's no point in wives doing pole-dancing. The whole fucking *point* of pole-dancers is *they're not your fucking wife*. Any woman who gets into such a thing thinking they're demonstrating some deep inner sexiness that sets them apart from the vanilla wives is more likely expressing the fact (a) they take themselves too seriously, which is very un-sexy — take note, Demi-fucking-Moore, (b) they think they're pretty hot for their age, which is boring even if it's true, or (c) they're not too happy at home and would like to be having sex with somebody else. Anybody else, probably. Case in point was Pete's former friend Johnny, guy who did his accounts for eleven years. Johnny was doing great, had the place in Incline Village, the works. Then Johnny's wife went to one of these classes. Said it was the new boxercise. Did it at home for him. First time it worked, kind of, then after that it's — right, but you're still my wife, and really, you could lose a few pounds. Four months later she was fucking one of the pimple-faced slackers who worked in the personal empowerment section of the Barnes & Noble. Somehow this turned out to be Johnny's fault, so goodbye marriage, hello child support. Soon he was spending his afternoons watching real dancers, ones with scars and children, and drinking way too much. Pete moved his business to another company. So did everyone else.

Pete took another big puff on the Don Thomas, enjoying the way the smoke fugged up the room. It wasn't Cuban, not even a particularly expensive Honduran — he didn't throw money away, never had — but it tasted good. Been three years since he'd been allowed to smoke indoors at home. It wasn't impossible, wasn't like Maria set up snipers in the living room to bring him down, but there'd be the Disappointment. The silent deterrent, the weapon of mute destruction: the look that said that, despite all her dreams, life had turned out much as she'd feared. For a while you thought avoiding the Disappointment was worth it, that you didn't mind. Then some day you realized you did, but you smoked outside anyway because who needs that kind of shit every night? You smoked outside, and you minded. Quietly.

Cherri finished cutting a slice of citrus — there were fresh lemons and limes in the little fridge, how's that for a cute touch — and dropped it into her drink. Gin and tonic. Pete could smell it. His nose was very good. Had to be, you were in the food trade. Maria drank a nice glass of Chardonnay, always had. The girl sensed him watching, turned around. 'You want something?'

Pete laughed. 'Oh yeah,' he said heartily. 'But give me a minute here. I'm still breathing hard.'

She smiled professionally. 'Not that. I meant to drink.'

149

'Oh. Vodka,' he said. 'Neat. No fruit. Lots of ice.' He winked. 'And there will be a second time, trust me.'

'Can't wait,' she said, and turned back to fix his drink.

Pete smiled. He heard a clank from out in the corridor — some job donkey getting back from work. He took another puff of the cigar, settled back. Savoured sitting there. Loved it, the full naked ugliness of it. Out there some spent management consultant with Tums breath, some exhausted attorney struggling home with an armful of files. And him, in here, balls in the wind and a big drink on the way. *Can't wait*. Sarcasm? Almost certainly. Didn't matter. She looked forward to it, or not. She found his body bearable, or not. She liked doing what he asked — nothing weird, he didn't need weird, just the usual from someone new and young and beautiful was enough — or not. None of it mattered. She had four hundred dollars of his already. At the end he'd most likely make it up to five. Maria could drop that much on some Manolos without blinking; and did, regularly. Meanwhile, that was all it took to get someone like Cherri to give it all up.

As she clattered about, pouring Stoly Black into a glass, then adding the ice, Pete considered booking her again. Though she was cute — really *very* cute, when she squatted to pick up a spilt cube, looking briefly unpoised — he knew he wouldn't. Having a new one each time was the point. He went with her again, there'd be the question of whether it was better or worse than

150

last time. She'd use his name, know what he wanted to drink, and familiarity would start to set in. He'd have time to notice things about her, to wonder why she didn't have the sense to put the ice in the glass first, or how she hadn't learned that gin went better with lime. And now, this afternoon, when they had sex again and this time he got only semi-hard and had to finish it off himself, that'd be just the way it was. He knew it would be that way, but she didn't. Next time, she would. Not knowing was the big thing. Not knowing, not having to care.

She was out of sight now, making some godawful noise with the ice box. What the fuck for? The glass was sitting there on the counter, full right to the top. Any more and it would be spilling out the . . . hey. Ice cube around the nipple. That was a thought.

He leaned across to the ashtray to rest out the cigar. Save it for later. 'Babe,' he said, indulgently. 'The ice is fine. You can bring it on through.' He turned back.

There was a man standing in the room.

'Who the fuck are you?' Pete said.

The man's smile said he had no intention of answering. Pete knew straight away that this wasn't some other guy with a key to the fuck pad. The girl stepped into sight behind him, putting on her shirt. 'I'm done, right?' she asked the man.

He didn't answer her either. Without taking his eyes off Pete he reached to the side and grabbed her by the hair. Before she'd had time to squawk he'd smacked her face into the partition wall. She grunted, went straight down.

Pete put it together quickly. The clank in the hallway; the rattling of the ice bucket to disguise her opening the door. He didn't know who the guy was, or what he wanted, but he could see now that he had a knife. It was a big knife, could be a cook's knife. Except it didn't look at all clean.

The room seemed cold suddenly, flat and full of stale smoke. The man stepped over the girl, glancing away for a moment. Pete dimly realized this was a chance, that he had to get up, move, get out of there. He couldn't seem to do any of these things. The man was only a little over average height, and trim. Pete outweighed him by many pounds and had long-term experience of smacking people's heads: he just wasn't convinced either would make a difference. He felt fat, naked and in no position to change anything about the world.

'You're Peter Ferillo, is that correct?' the man said, picking something up off the counter. When it glinted Pete saw it was the apartment's bottle opener, and when the man turned his face to him, all thoughts of movement seemed to fade away.

'Look,' Pete said. 'I don't know what the fuck's happening here. But I got money. With me. If that's what this is about, it's okay.'

'It's not about money,' the man said. His voice was soft, almost friendly. His eyes were not.

'Then what?' Pete said. 'What have I done?'

'This isn't about you,' the man said.

'Who the hell are you?'

'My name . . . is the Upright Man.'

The man watched Pete's face for a reaction. He rolled the bottle opener in his hand absent-mindedly, then nodded — as if, with sudden inspiration, he'd thought of a use for it. Pete didn't know what that might be.

Over the course of the next hour and a half, he found out.

2: The Smoking Road

This is what I intend to do,
but I do not know why.

Gerard Schaefer, serial killer,
Into the Mind of the Ghoul

10

When the guy first appeared Phil Banner was leaning against the car outside Izzy's eating a hot mushroom and eggs sandwich he hadn't paid for. Not his fault — he always offered, and Izzy always said no — but it still made him feel a little guilty. Not enough to stop him eating it, though, or to keep from going back most mornings. The sandwich was good and thick and not really designed to be eaten with fingers, and the guy with the blood was probably in view for a few minutes before Banner lifted his head and saw him. When he did he watched for a good five seconds, still chewing and not really sure what he was seeing, before he hurriedly put the food down.

The man was walking right down the middle of the street. The road was empty because it was eight thirty in the morning and very cold but it didn't look like traffic would have changed the guy's course. He looked like he barely knew where he was. He was wearing a backpack that looked both new and tattered. He was lurching like something out of a zombie movie, one leg dragging behind, and when Phil took a few cautious steps forward he saw he was also covered in blood. It was dried, or seemed to be, but there was a lot of it. There was a big bump and a nasty gash on the man's forehead, and innumerable other cuts and scrapes across his

157

face and hands. Dried mud covered most of the rest, and just about all of his clothes.

Phil took another step. 'Sir?'

The man kept on moving as though he hadn't heard. He was breathing hard but steadily, the exhales clouding up around his face. In, out, in, out, as if the rhythm had become important to him. As if it was that, or nothing. Then slowly his head turned. He kept on moving forward but looked at Phil. His eyes were bloodshot and he had a couple days' growth of beard. There was ice in it. It had been a long time since Phil had seen a man who looked so cold.

The guy stopped, finally. He blinked, opened his mouth. Shut it again, looked up the road for a moment. He seemed so interested in what was down there that Phil glanced that way himself, but saw only the short remaining stretch of town that he expected.

'Sir, are you okay?' He knew it was a stupid question. The guy evidently wasn't. But it was what you said. You came across a person with a knife embedded in his head — though in a town like this choking on a fish bone was far more likely — you asked if he was okay.

A slow, uneven change occurred across the man's features, and Phil realized it was probably intended to be a smile.

'This is Sheffer, isn't it?' he asked. The movements of his mouth were cramped, as if his face was almost frozen shut.

'Yes sir, it is.'

The smile broadened. 'No shit.'

'Sir?'

The guy shook his head, suddenly looking more together, as if the shambling had been some habit he'd gotten into to keep himself going past the point at which he thought he'd have to drop. Phil realized he looked slightly familiar.

'That's some sense of direction,' the man said. 'Say what you like.' His face crumpled.

Phil saw that Izzy and a couple of local customers were now standing outside the diner, and that a similar audience was assembling across the street in the market's small parking lot. It was time to take charge of the situation.

'Sir, have you been in an accident of some kind?'

The man looked at him. 'Bigfoot,' he said, nodded, and then slowly fell flat on his back.

★   ★   ★

Two hours later Tom Kozelek was sitting in the police station. He was wrapped in three blankets and holding a cup of chicken soup in both hands. He was in the room they normally used for interviewing, on the rare occasions the Sheffer Police had cause to interview anyone, and for storing coats and wet boots and has-no-other-home stuff the rest of the time. It had a desk and three chairs and a clock. It had previously been the kitchen area before that was moved upstairs to be next to the redone administrative space, and had a partially glassed wall that made it look a little like a room in some much larger and more urban law enforcement

159

facility. At least it would have done had the glass not been home to stickers celebrating the town's Halloween parade. The stickers had been designed each year by the school's most talented art student, which was the main thing that stopped the glass partition looking businesslike: either someone had blindfolded the kids before handing them the paints or Sheffer was never going to host any famous hometown museum. Phil Banner had occasionally expressed the opinion that they should get them done by someone who could draw a little. He had been assured that when he had kids he would feel differently. He was going to wait and see.

Phil was standing with Melissa Hoffman. Melissa lived thirty miles away over in Issaquah and worked at the small county hospital there. Sheffer's own doctor, Dr Dandridge, was well liked but older than God and significantly less infallible, and so lately Melissa's tended to be the number they called. She was in her late thirties, not at all bad-looking, and didn't seem to know it. She was happily married to a thick-set guy who owned a small second-hand bookstore and chain-smoked Marlboro Lite. Go figure.

She looked away from the glass window. 'He's fine,' she said. 'Ankle's a bit messed up. Banged around in general. Little bit of exposure, but no frostbite. He's vague on details but from what he said he got most of his big bumps a couple of days ago: if he was going to get concussion, he would have had it already and probably not be here now. He needs feeding and sleep and that's all, folks. He's a lucky guy.'

160

Phil nodded. He really wished the Chief was here, and not a hundred miles away visiting his sister. 'But the other stuff.'

She shrugged. 'Said he was okay physically. Mentally is another story.' She turned to the desk where the backpack the man had been wearing had thawed. Cold water covered the surface and had dripped through cracks to the floor. She took a pen from the pot on the corner and used it to poke around, holding the bag open gingerly with her other hand. 'This thing is laced with alcohol, and you say he'd been drinking before.'

Phil nodded. It hadn't taken him long to work out why the man's face seemed familiar. 'He was trying to break into Big Frank's late one night at the weekend. I had to request that he stop.'

Melissa looked at the man through the window. He appeared only dozily awake, and incapable of raising a rumpus of any kind. As she watched he blinked slowly, like an old dog on the verge of sleep. 'Did he seem dangerous? Psychotic?'

'No. More kind of sad. Happened to run into Joe and Zack next morning, and they said some guy had been in there all evening, drinking it up by himself. Sounded like the same person.'

'So four days of drinking, most likely nothing to eat, then a stomach full of sleeping pills. The signs for being in a happy place aren't great. Still, he doesn't come across like a crazy person.'

'They never do.' Phil hesitated. 'He said he saw Bigfoot.'

She laughed. 'Yeah, people do, from time to

time. What he actually saw was a bear. You know that.'

'I guess.'

Melissa looked at him hard for a moment, and Phil found himself blushing when she smiled. 'You do *know* that, right?'

'Of course,' he said, impatiently.

Now was not the time for a discussion of what Phil's uncle had once thought he'd seen — or *felt*, more accurately — in the deep forest way up over the ridge. No one had ever taken that seriously, except perhaps Phil himself, when he was small. His uncle eventually stopped telling the story. More than a handful of towns up in the Cascades had their own local legends and BF displays, and you could buy lattes and muffins from more than one roadside stall fashioned in the shape of a big hairy creature. Not in Sheffer. Around these parts, Bigfoot was bunk. Or, as the Chief liked to put it, BF was a pile of BS. A wellworn lure for a certain kind of tourist town, that was all, and Sheffer wasn't that kind of town. Sheffer was quiet, genteel, and had once been used in the background of a whimsical television series. It had the rail museum and rolling stock. There were nice restaurants, and only nice people came to eat in them. The town wanted to keep it that way. The Chief wanted it most of all.

But more than a handful of people had been standing out in the street when the Tom guy had said the word, and not all of them were locals. By the end of the day a few might pass on what had happened that morning to their friends and

162

relatives. Phil knew what the Chief thought about that kind of thing too, and he really wished he'd got the guy inside someplace before he could say the B word. When Phil had called him on his cell phone, the Chief said he would be back by early afternoon at the latest. Phil was glad about that.

'Going to see if that guy wants some more of Izzy's soup,' he said, and Melissa nodded.

She watched as he went into the room, sat at the end of the table, and spoke gently to the man. She believed Kozelek should really be examined for aftereffects of the sleeping pills he'd taken, but he was adamant that he didn't want to go to any hospital, and she had no power to make him. He'd survived three very cold days and nights in the woods, and walked a very long distance in hard terrain. Given that, he looked in good shape for a guy who'd been out there trying to die. There was a case for saying he should be talking to someone about that part of things, too, but again it wasn't something she could force. She privately thought that when his brain had thawed out properly, both that and talk of unknown species would gently fade away. Then they could just ship him back to LA or wherever it was, and life in Sheffer would go on as usual.

As she turned to go she noticed something in the bottom of the open backpack. She stopped and took a closer look. In amongst the shards of glass and sodden fragments of drug packet were a few things that looked like tiny bunches of dried flowers.

She took one of them out, and saw they weren't flowers after all; more like short, bedraggled stalks. It looked as though it must have fallen into the man's bag as he careered through the forest, knocked off passing bushes and trees.

Either that, or as if it had been bought from a man on a street corner somewhere, and had fallen out of its baggie.

Here was a man who said he'd seen things, and tried to break into bars by all accounts, and in his bag was a little bunch of natural-looking matter. How about that? Partly out of professional concern, but mainly from good, old-fashioned curiosity, Melissa slipped the tiny bunch in her bag and then went outside to drive back to the hospital where, she was fairly confident, not much of interest would be happening.

★ ★ ★

At about lunch time, his head began to really ache. It had been hurting a little before. Had hurt for a significant proportion of His Time Away, in fact. But this was different. This was worse.

The headache was a slow, rolling affair and had an expensive, professional quality to it. This headache knew its trade. It had relevant experience. It covered his head like a cold counterpane, heavy and insistent, and had begun to maintain outposts in other parts of his body too. His guts, primarily. He had told the doctor he didn't want to go to the hospital at least partly to gauge her reaction. If she'd barked, 'Think again, moron, you're deeply, deeply fucked and we're going to drag you by the hair to a scary place with machines with green readouts and then you're going to *die*,' then he'd have gone quietly. She hadn't, which meant there was a chance he was okay. He felt okay, in general, apart from the headache, and the feeling in his guts, which he was inclined to see as a sub-division of the headache. He'd read somewhere that there was a mat of neural tissue spread around the stomach, actually the second largest collection of such tissue in the entire body (after the brain, of course). Hence gut reactions, gut feelings, blah blah blah. He could see this might make evolutionary sense: give the innards enough of a brain to enable it to send up signals saying, 'don't eat that rotten crap again, remember what happened last time', much as his own had done when he'd made it back to his bag, in the forest. He was hoping the way it felt now was merely a sign of it being in sympathy with his head. If it felt this way on its own account, it was possible he should have gone to the hospital after all.

He was also hoping that the painkillers the doctor had left would start to kick in any minute. His head was making his eyes go funny. He was still hanging onto the idea that at some point he was going to stand up, go walking out into town and find the ancient fucker who hadn't mentioned the bears, but just at this moment the plan didn't feel realistic. It seemed all too likely the old geezer could beat him up.

Just then, Tom suddenly smiled.

Of course bears weren't actually the issue. Not any more. One of the reasons he wanted to feel better very soon was that he had something interesting to tell people. Something very interesting indeed. A piece of information which had kept him alive, which had hauled his body out of the wilderness. He'd kept quiet about it so far, biding his time. But when the moment came . . .

Then, just as suddenly, his smile dropped. He had new information, yes. A life-saving datum. That didn't make it a life-changing one, however, big enough to blot out the dark light from what had come before. He was still compromised. Once you've done the thing, you've done it. Even if people don't know. The only difference was he now perhaps had something big enough to make it worth his while taking the risk it would never be found.

He watched blearily through the glass as the Sheffer sheriff's department (in the person of Phil, whom Tom increasingly thought he vaguely recognized from before His Time Away) went about its duties. Phil was young and slightly built for a cop: most city police seemed to spend their whole time in the gym, making sure their arms bulged nicely in those short-sleeve shirts. Basically, Phil was sometimes in the room, and then sometimes he went outside. That was about it. Presumably, apart from dealing with car wrecks and people skipping their tab in bars and the occasional recreational domestic in the long

166

winter nights, this was about as frenetic as it got: until someone came back out of the woods with a strange story to tell.

The deputy would come to check on him again soon, and then maybe he'd get into it. In the meantime, he sipped a little more soup. It had cooled, and could do with a little salt, but otherwise was very good. It was making him feel better.

His vision slowly went white.

★ ★ ★

The voice came from behind him.

'Sir?'

Tom shook his head, knowing that he wasn't going to be able to get away from this. But still, he shook his head. There was red on him. There was crunching underfoot. He finally turned, and he already knew what the news was going to be, but he did not know how it was going to fit in his head.

'Sir?'

Then everything was different. He jerked his head up woozily and saw he was still sitting in his chair in a police station, a very long way from LA. It was bright, and he was swaddled in blankets and there was a small heater sat on the floor about a yard away, shoving a thin stream of warm air at him. That was new, he thought. Don't remember that.

New too was the man standing on the other side of the table. Tom blinked at him. 'What time is it?'

167

'It's a little after three, sir,' the man said. He was much older than the one called Phil. He was taller, and broader. He was bigger in every way. He sat in one of the chairs opposite.

'Who are you?'

'My name is Connolly,' the man said. 'I work here.'

'Okay.' Tom's voice came out a little petulant, and he suddenly yawned massively. 'I'm actually kind of hot, now.'

'My deputy says the doctor said to keep you warm. So that's what we're going to do. That is, unless maybe you think it would be better for you to spend the night over in the hospital. Seems to me there's at least a couple reasons why that might be the case.'

'I'm fine,' Tom said.

The man leaned on the table and looked at him. 'You sure?'

Now that he was a little more awake, it was becoming clear to Tom that Connolly didn't seem to be in any hurry to be his friend. He was not treating him like someone who'd made a miraculous and welcome escape from a snowy wilderness.

'I'm sure,' he said, reaching for the voice he used in meetings, when a client needed convincing that the web design work they'd received was exactly what they wanted, despite its apparent lack of similarity to what had been discussed in the briefing. It felt a long time since he'd used this voice, but it was less than two weeks, and while rusty, it did come. 'Thank you for your concern.'

'Okay. So why don't you tell me your story?'

'Al, he's kind of been through that.' This was Phil, entering the room with two cups of coffee.

Connolly ignored his deputy, sat back in his chair, and kept looking at Tom.

'My name is Tom Kozelek,' the man in the chair said. 'I'm . . . on vacation. Three days ago, I guess it was, I went driving up into the mountains. I parked up at a trail head, I don't remember the name.'

'Howard's Point,' the policeman nodded. 'Your car was towed back from there yesterday afternoon. You turning up has solved that little mystery, at least.'

'Right. So I parked up there, and went for a hike.'

'A hike,' the man said, nodding to himself. 'What exactly did you take with you in the way of provisions?'

'I assume you know,' Tom muttered, coldly. 'I can see my bag out there on the table.'

'Yes. I know,' the cop said. 'Don't know whether you've had a chance to catch any TV while you've been here, but at this time of year there's an advertisement which runs every hour or so. It suggests that people stay the hell out of the mountains unless they know what they're doing and have the equipment to do it with. You not watch much television, Mr Kozelek?'

'I was in a confused state of mind.'

'Right.' The man nodded again. 'And so where have you been since?'

'Walking back here,' Tom said. 'I got lost. I had maps, but I left them in the car by mistake. I was

169

a little drunk when I started out, and usually my sense of direction is pretty good but it snowed and I fell down a gully and to be honest I just got really, really lost. I tried to find my way back to the road but by then I'd gotten turned around and evidently I just kept heading away from it. Then I found something that looked like a trail and followed it, but it didn't seem to go anywhere and kept cutting in and out.'

'Old logging track, probably,' Phil said. 'Could even have been a bit of the old mountain road itself. Most of it you can only tell something used to be there because there's a line of trees that are a little thinner.'

Connolly turned his head slowly to look at him. The deputy shut up. The sheriff looked back at Tom.

'Look, what's your problem?' Tom said.

'Me? I don't have one. Please continue.'

Tom deliberately took a long time over a sip of coffee. The guy was really beginning to piss him off. They were all like this, in the end. Every one of them so full of their special status, pretending they'd never been in a difficult situation in their own lives.

'So I just walked,' he said. 'I don't know where I was. Then last night I finally found a road. I stood by it for a while, thinking surely someone must come along and give me a ride, but it was snowing and nobody came. So I walked. And I got here early this morning.'

'Quite a little adventure, Mr Kozelek,' Connolly said. 'You must be glad it's over, and looking forward to going back home.'

'Not just yet,' Tom said, shrugging off the top two blankets. Not only was he too hot now, but he sensed the 'little boy lost' look wasn't helping the sheriff take him seriously. 'There's things I have to do here first.'

'What could those possibly be?'

Tom looked him in the eye. 'I'm going back into the forest.' He took a deep breath, and prepared to say something he knew he was going to remember for the rest of his life. 'I saw something when I was in there. Something pretty amazing.' He paused again, savouring the moment.

'This would be Bigfoot, right?'

Tom stared at him, side-swiped. 'How did you know?'

Connolly smiled, gently. 'You mentioned it a couple of times to my deputy when you first got here. To the doctor too, I believe. Matter of fact, from what I hear, it was the very first word you said when you came staggering into town. Before you fell down.'

Tom's mouth felt dry, his face red. He didn't remember telling them about it. Shit.

'Okay,' he said. 'I knew that. But I saw it. I saw Bigfoot. It was standing right over me. I *saw* it.'

'What you saw was a bear, Mr Kozelek.'

'No it *wasn't*. I thought so at the time, but it wasn't. It didn't look like one. And what do bears smell like?'

'Can't say as I've ever been close enough to find out. They're picky like that.'

'This one smelt awful. Really, really bad. Not only that, but I also saw footprints.'

171

'Is that so?'

'Yes it fucking well is so. You want to pretend it was a bear I saw, fine. But I saw footprints. A line of them, leading away from where I'd been.'

'They weren't your own? From when you ran from the bear?'

'No. I was scrabbling all over the place. The shape would have been all messed up. And also, you could see the fucking toes. Five big round toes, at the front. Look, I *saw* this.'

'Sure you did.' Connolly turned to Phil. 'You want to get Mrs Anders in here now?'

Confused, Tom watched the younger policeman as he went out to fetch a woman he now saw was sitting on the other side of the main room. Connolly meanwhile drank his own coffee in one long, slow swallow, looking coolly at Tom.

Phil returned with the woman. She was in her mid sixties, grey hair gathered in a loose ponytail. One hand was thrust down into the pocket of a yellow all-weather coat worn over a thick fleece. The other was clutching a large plastic bag. She looked apologetic and embarrassed.

Tom began to have a sinking feeling.

'This here is Patrice Anders,' Connolly said. 'Patrice lives out a few miles past Howard's Point. Don't know if you noticed it from your maps, but there's a little subdivision around from there, up off the next highway over the mountains. Was going to be the next big thing. Present time, Mrs Anders remains the only occupant.'

'It's nice to meet you,' Tom said. 'But I don't

172

understand what this is about.'

Connolly looked at the woman, and raised his brows.

'It was me, in the forest,' she said.

Tom stared at her. 'What do you mean?'

She shook her head. 'I'm so sorry about this. I go walking a great deal. I belong to a couple of national programmes that monitor wildlife, and I keep an informal tally of what's around at each time of year. I don't know whether it's of any real use in the long run, it's not very scientific, I don't suppose, but . . . ' She shrugged. 'Anyway, it's what I do. And the other morning I was out there, quite early, and I saw something lying down by the gully. It's actually not too far from the edge of my land, as the crow flies. Well, it's a distance, you know. I like to walk. Anyway, I went down there, and I saw it was a backpack. I didn't know whether someone was coming back for it, so I just left it there.'

Tom looked at Connolly. 'Okay. So what?'

'The footprints you saw belonged to Mrs Anders.'

'Bullshit. Are you not listening to a word I say? These were huge.'

'Give the sun an hour and the edges will melt. They're going to look much bigger than they ought to be.'

For a second Tom thought he was going to throw himself over the desk and grab the man by the throat. He knew it would be a bad idea, and not just because he was the law. So instead he kept his voice very level. He had the clincher, after all.

'Right. And the sun will also make footprints look like they've got five big toes, correct? Weird sun you've got around here, if so.'

There was quiet for a moment, and then a rustling. The woman called Patrice pulled something out of her bag.

For a moment Tom couldn't make out what he was seeing. Then the back of his neck started to buzz.

'You can buy them over in Cle Elum,' she said. 'Kind of stupid, I know. But, you know, kind of fun too. My husband bought me them for a joke.'

Tom kept staring at the pair of novelty boots, with their furry top halves, and their brown plastic feet, complete with five big toes.

★ ★ ★

Phil took the woman away. It might have been his imagination, but Tom thought he sensed that the deputy was feeling a little bad for him. He hoped so, anyway. There weren't going to be any other candidates for sympathy within driving distance.

Connolly glanced up at the clock on the wall. He reached into his shirt pocket, pulled out a battered pack of cigarettes, and lit up.

'Strange old day,' he said. 'More excitement than I was bargaining on when I got up, that's for damned sure.' He tapped a little ash onto the desk. 'Not a huge amount happens around here, as I'm sure you've guessed. Bet you've worked out I like it that way, too.'

Tom shook his head. 'I still know what I saw.'

'You saw jack shit, Mr Kozelek.' The policeman's grey eyes were cold. 'You went out into the woods with a bad purpose in mind, and I'm not even going to talk about how irresponsible that is when it's other men's jobs to come out and find you regardless of why you went. You got yourself screwed up with booze and pills and you either saw a bear or you hallucinated one or what the hell else.'

Tom just shook his head.

Connolly ground the cigarette out. 'Suit yourself. I'm not going to tell you to ship out tonight, because you've had a rough couple days and despite what you might think, I'm a reasonable person. You look like shit and you need to eat and get some sleep. So why don't you go do those things, and then maybe tomorrow morning think about sampling some of the other nice little towns we've got around here. Snohomish, for example, the antiques capital of the North West. Or maybe even Seattle. They have an airport there.'

'I'm not going anywhere.'

'Yeah, you are.' Connolly stood up, stretched. Bones cracked. 'Soon. You want my advice?'

'Not even a little bit.'

'Just be grateful you got away with it. Be happy you didn't get attacked by that big ole bear, and that you didn't die out there out on the mountain. Leave it at that. Because here's something else.'

He glanced out through the glass, and saw his deputy was putting his coat on at the door,

175

ready, as instructed, to help Kozelek find somewhere in town to stay for one night only. Still, he lowered his voice a fraction. 'On my way back here, I checked up on you.'

Tom stared at the man's back, suddenly realizing that while His Time Away might have changed him, it had made no difference to the outside world. There'd been no mid-season culling of the parts of his life he didn't like. Out here, the dreary, long-running series he lived was still going strong, despite the fact its primary audience — himself — believed it majorly sucked.

Connolly looked back at him. 'I know what you did.'

11

A package from Nina was waiting at the desk first thing. I told the restaurant to round up all the coffee they had and send it to my room, and headed back upstairs. I didn't have a lot of optimism that I'd be able to do anything for her — both LAPD and the FBI would have grown-ups on the case — but it was something to do while waiting for Zandt.

I laid my gear out on the table, and got to it. When I opened the package I found a small, shiny, semi-transparent plastic bag designed to combat static, which is the main way of screwing up delicate electronic equipment. Other than dropping it, of course. Inside was a small hard disk. Stuck to it was a note from Nina.

'Be VERY, VERY careful with this,' it said. *'It's the original. Find something on it for me, then get it the hell back.'*

Before I did anything else, I rang Nina's cell. She sounded hassled and distracted. 'I'm glad it arrived,' she said. 'But I don't think it's going to lead anywhere. LAPD just got done tracing the history. They found the guy who bought the original laptop, some movie industry bottom feeder called Nic Golson, but he has a receipt proving he sold it on to a second-hand store in Burbank in July last year. He thought he was going to get some big script job but then didn't so he couldn't afford to keep the machine. After that, someone bought it cash, then stripped this part and dumped the rest somewhere we'll never find it. The store's employees are being interviewed right now, but this killer strikes me as brighter than that.'

'So how come I've got the original disk?'

'I used my feminine wiles.'

'You have wiles?'

'You'd be surprised. Actually, so would I. Probably just rank.' She admitted she'd leaned on an LAPD lab rat after I'd made it clear a copy was only that. The guy was willing to cover for her, not least because they'd done everything they could with it. It had already been fingerprinted, so touching it was no problem. But . . .

I said I'd take good care of it.

Then I put the phone down, and looked at something I now knew had spent a while inside a dead woman's face. It was hard to work out whether it was that, or the risk Nina had taken, which was the more unnerving.

Coffee arrived. I drank some with a cigarette. This had the usual result of making the world's challenges seem more feasible. I pulled out a cable I owned which had a Firewire plug on one end and an Oxford Bridge on the other and carefully inserted the disk's connectors into the latter and the plug into the back of Bobby's laptop. The disk appeared on the desktop.

I opened it and confirmed what I'd been told. There were two files, a piece of music stored as an MP3 file and the message. Nina had told me that the quote at the beginning of the text had been nailed to a German writer called Heinrich Heine. The recording of the Fauré Requiem was from a well-respected issue of the early 1960s, which didn't necessarily mean anything either. There's a timelessness to classical music performance. Most recent is not necessarily best. The most I could take from the music was to note it had been digitized at 192 k/sec in joint stereo, a high-quality setting. Given that most people can't hear the difference between 192 and 160, that *maybe* suggested either it had been designed to be played through a quality audio system, which could reveal the deficiencies of a lower sample rate; or more simply — and more obviously — the music was of importance to the person who had put it there. So, big deal either way. I listened to it several times while getting on with the next part, and noted what sounded like a little channel hiss, and a fairly certain click or two. It was possible the MP3 had been recorded from a vinyl source. It seemed unlikely that someone computer literate would disdain CDs entirely, so this maybe suggested the person owned an LP of the music that had some kind of sentimental value. Big deal again.

I fired up a piece of industrial-strength scanning software, and waited while it went about its business. A lot of people seem to think computers are just machines, like vacuums or the VCR. They're wrong. Right from the start, from the jumped-up abacuses of the Amiga and Apple II, we've had a different relationship with computers. You knew right away that this was something that had rights. If your washing machine stops working or TV goes on the fritz then you get it repaired or take it to the dump. These are pieces of old, transparent tech. They have no magic any more. If a computer messes you around, however, you're never really sure whose fault it is. You're implicated. You feel vulnerable. It's like the difference between a pencil and a car. A pencil is a simple and predictable piece of technology. There's only one way of it working (it will function when it is sharp), and an obvious failure model (too short, too blunt, no lead). With a car, especially the kind of limp-along rustbucket most of us got for our first ride, it's more complex. There's coaxing involved, especially on cold mornings. There's that noise that never amounts to anything but never goes away, random stalls you begin to put down to the cast of the moon. None means it's broken, just that it requires friendly attention, that it has needs. Gradually you acquire a ritualized relationship to it, a bond forged by its unpredictability, by the fact it has to be *dealt with*. Which is how you come to know people, after all: not by the things they have in common with everyone else, but through learning your way around their eccentricities, their hard edges and unpredictable softnesses, the things that make them different from everybody else.

A computer comes in between: like a car, but magnified a thousandfold. It has fingernails wedged far deeper into your life. Your computer is a backup of your soul, a multi-layered, menu-driven representation of who you are, who you care about, and how you sin. If you spend an

180

evening skating around the web looking at naked ladies, your trail is there in the browser's history log and in the disk cache — not to mention all the sites that logged your IP address as you passed through, so they can spam you until the end of time. If you exchange the occasional flirtatious email with a co-worker but carefully throw them all away, you've still done wrong until you Hail Mary the command to actually *empty* your software's trash.

Even if you think you're being clever and throw everything away, emptying the trash or recycler, you aren't out of the woods. All that happens when you 'delete' a file is that the computer throws away the reference to it — like destroying the file card that refers to a library book on the shelves, telling the visitor where to go find it. The book itself is still there, and if you go looking you can come upon it or track it down. It's like a man writing notes in pencil on a huge piece of paper. If you blind him, the notes are still there. He can't put his finger on them, can't show you where each one is, but they remain. If he keeps making notes (if you keep saving new files, in other words), he will start writing over the originals. His new notes, his new experiences, extend over sections of the original files, making it impossible to return to what once was, to understand or even remember what happened first, what made his life like it is. Sections of these files remain, however, hidden and lost, but real — the computer's earlier experiences; severed from the outside world but still inhabiting portions of the disk like ghosts

181

and memories, mixed up with the here and now. We're like that.

It took half an hour for the software to do its pass. This brought up nothing, and merely proved what Nina's pet tech had already established: the disk had been very comprehensively wiped before the two files were copied onto it. Not only had the note-writing man been blinded, he'd then been taken out and shot.

The jug of coffee was cold. I set one of Bobby's proprietary pieces of pattern-matching software working on the disk. This would trawl over the surface looking at the junk which had been written over it, checking for any irregularities — or unexpected regularities — in the binary stew. Short of physically taking it apart and going in with tweezers, this was as deep as man could go into the shadowy childhood echoes of the digital mind. The past resists intrusion, even amongst the silicon-based.

A dialogue box popped up on the screen and told me the process would take a little over five hours. It's not very exciting to watch. I made sure the power was plugged in, and went for a walk.

★   ★   ★

At three o'clock Zandt called from the airport. I gave him directions to L'Espresso and headed back over there to wait. Forty minutes later his cab pulled up. John got out, glared at the guy in costume in front of the hotel, and walked up the street to me. He came at a moderate pace and

182

very steadily. I knew what that meant.

He told a passing waiter to bring him a beer, and sat down opposite me. 'Hello Ward. You're looking kind of lived in.'

'Me? You look like a crack house. How's Nina?'

'She's great,' he said.

He waited for his beer. The beard had gone. He didn't ask me how I was or what I'd been doing. In my limited experience of Zandt, I'd learned he didn't do small talk. He didn't do tiny talk or big talk either. He just said what he had to say and then either stopped or went away. He was drunk. You'd have to have spent time with a drinker to know — as I did, for a year, once — because there were few external signs. The bags under his eyes were darker, and he reached for his glass the moment it was put down; but his eyes were clear and his voice calm and measured.

'So what do you have on Yakima?'

'Like I said, not much. I went back to LA and told Nina what we'd found. She reported it, and nothing happened. I basically started looking into it because . . . '

He shrugged. I understood. There wasn't much else. He had been involved in the investigation of the Delivery Boy murders, as a result of which his daughter Karen had been abducted and never seen alive again. His marriage fell apart. He quit the force. I believed he had been a very good detective: it was he who had worked out the Upright Man was running a procuring ring for well-heeled psychopaths up at

183

The Halls, abducting people to order. But even if Zandt had wanted to go back to being a cop, which he didn't, LAPD weren't likely to be in the market. So what else was he going to do? Become a security guard? Go into business? As what? Zandt was as unemployable as I was.

'We could join the Feds.'

'Right. You were thrown out of the CIA. That's always impressive. Anyway. Do you remember the word on the door of the cabin we found?'

'Not really,' I said. 'I saw there were letters there, but they just looked like they were part of the general mess.'

He reached into a pocket and produced a small piece of glossy paper. 'One of the pictures I took,' he said. 'Printed at high contrast. You see it now?'

I looked closely. There certainly were letters hacked into the door. If you studied it hard, you could just make out the word or name 'CROATOAN'. It had been there a long while, too, and was partially obscured by later weathering and further marks. 'Meaning?'

'I thought it might be an old mining company name or something. But I can't find one. The only reference I could find to it is strange.'

He pushed a further thick sheaf of paper towards me. I saw a lot of words in a variety of very small typefaces, divided into sections, underneath the overall title 'Roanoke'.

'I'm hoping there's a précis.'

'You've heard of Roanoke, right? The one on the east coast?'

'Yes,' I said. 'Vaguely. Bunch of people

184

disappeared a long time ago. Or something.'

'They disappeared twice, in fact. Roanoke was England's first attempt to establish a colony in America. The Brit explorer Walter Raleigh was granted a stretch of land by Elizabeth I, in one of her charters to try to grab a chunk of this New World. In 1584 Raleigh sent an expedition to see what he'd got: specifically, they checked out an area called Roanoke Island, on the tidewater coast of what is now North Carolina. They took an initial look around, made contact with the local tribe — the Croatoan — and wound up heading back to England. In 1586 a second group of a hundred men went out. They didn't have it so good. Didn't take enough supplies, ran into trouble with the locals through not treating them well, and in the end all but fifteen were picked up by a passing ship and went home. But Raleigh was keen to establish a working colony, and so the next year a further party was sent to make sure this new 'Virginia' got consolidated. He appointed a man called John White to lead them and be their governor. One hundred and seventeen people went along. Men, women, children — the idea being that family groups would make it more permanent. They were specifically told not to head for Roanoke Island, but . . . that's where they ended up. They found the fortifications the previous group had built, but no sign of the fifteen men who'd been left to guard it. Just gone. Vanished. White re-established contact with the Croatoan, who said an 'enemy tribe' had attacked the fort and killed at least some of the soldiers. White was

185

ticked, obviously, and when one of the new colonists was found dead he decided to attack the local bad-boy tribe, the Powhatans. Except his men screwed it up and managed to kill some Croatoans instead, presumably on the time-honoured 'they all look the same to me' principle.'

I shook my head. 'Nice going.'

'So of course the Croatoans suddenly and reasonably retract all previous goodwill — and refuse to supply them with food. The colonists had arrived in summer, too late to plant crops, and what little they'd brought was going bad.'

'They were kind of stupid, the early settlers.'

'Stupid or brave. Or both. Either way, White decided to go back to England for supplies. There was no choice. It was agreed that if they ended up having to go inland, the colonists would leave markings showing which way they'd gone. Also, that if they'd left because of attack, they'd carve a cross somewhere prominent. Problem was, when White got back to England he found the country was at war with Spain — and he didn't make it back to Roanoke for *three whole years*.'

I thought about that for a moment. Abandoned in an alien land with neighbours who hate you, the food running out. The leader pops home for a take-out and stays gone from 1587 until 1590. 'And when he returned?'

'Gone. Every single one. Disappeared. Nobody living, no sign of bodies. Personal possessions left behind. No sign of a cross carved anywhere. There was the word

'Croatoan', however, carved on a gatepost.'

'Okay,' I said. 'That's kind of spooky. So what happened?'

He shrugged. 'That's the last sure thing anybody knows. White wanted to know what had happened to the people he'd left behind, but the captain and crew of his ship couldn't care less, so he was forced to go back to England. He tried to get another expedition out there in late 1590 but by this time Raleigh and his investors had lost interest. Since then lots of people have tried to put the thing together, starting with a guy called John Smith who was at the Jamestown settlement twenty years later.'

'And?'

'Smith talked to the locals and came up with a few ideas, and they're pretty much the ones still floating around. It turns out the word 'Croatoan' was applied not just to a tribe but also to a large and not very well defined geographical area. So it could have been carved to indicate a destination, as agreed with White. Alternatively it could have implied that the Croatoan themselves had a change of heart and started helping the hapless colonists. Or, if you choose to believe it meant the named tribe had started attacking, then you could theorize that the colonists were forced to head inland. Either idea leads to the possibility that some or all of the settlers (some theories have the male colonists being killed, leaving just the women and children) became assimilated into a local or not so local tribe, and there are a couple of native peoples — notably the Lumbee — who have long-term claims in

187

this direction, some of which sound pretty solid. This theory has been taken seriously since the mid-1800s at least, and speculated about since Jamestown. There's stories of a minister in the mid-1600s meeting friendly natives in the area who spoke English, and talk of some German explorer whose name I couldn't track down who claimed to have had meetings with 'a powerful nation of bearded men' — i.e. possible descendants of the settlers.'

I'd thought the carvings on the door of the cabin hadn't made much impact on me, but as John said this, I found myself suddenly cold, out in the middle of nowhere, in the company of the dead.

Zandt waved an arm to catch the waiter's attention. The waiter started to explain he was busy, caught the look in Zandt's eye, and went to get him another beer. 'The question is why it was carved on the cabin door we found.'

'A quote?' I said. 'Some reference to the Roanoke mystery? But what sense would that make?'

'He's trying to tell us something.'

'I really don't think that place had anything to do with Paul. There was nothing to tie him to it. And anyway — why would he care? Why would he want to tell us stuff?'

'He spent half of Sarah Becker's incarceration lecturing her. Then there's the piece you found on the web three months ago, the diatribe about how everyone except the Straw Men are infected with a social virus which made us start farming, and started the slide towards being civilized.

He's on a mission to inform.'

We paused, as drinks were put in front of us. 'The big thing about Paul,' I said, 'is that he doesn't think he's just another lunatic.'

'None of them do, Ward. None of these men get up in the morning and think 'I'm going to do something evil today'. They do what they do, and some of them understand that it's bad, and some don't, but either way it's not why they do it.'

'Yes,' I said, irritated at his tone. 'I understand.'

'They do it because *that's what they do*, just like addicts jack themselves with smack. They're not trying to kill themselves. They're not trying to fuck up their lives. They just have to have some heroin, as you need a cigarette and some people need their shoes to be clean and others have to make sure they tape their daily shows or check the door's locked three times when they leave the house. Everyone's got their magic spell, their maintenance rituals, the private things they do that they believe make the world work.'

'What's yours these days — beer?'

'Fuck you.'

'What's the deal with you and Nina?'

'It's none of your fucking business.'

'Yes it is,' I said, angry now. 'There are three people in the world who know about the Straw Men. I've spent three months skulking around the country keeping out of the way. I beat the shit out of some poor guy in Idaho because I thought he'd come to clip me. I'm out on a very long limb with very few resources. You two are it.'

'What about the money from your folks?'

'Gone,' I said. 'Not spent. Wiped. They got to it.'

'Shit,' he said. 'I'm sorry to hear that.' He looked across the street for a moment. 'Things got fucked up,' he said eventually, apparently watching a man who was moving paintings around in a gallery window. 'I moved in. You know we'd been together before, back when I was married. I thought it might work. We both did. But . . . She's quite intense.'

'Right. Whereas you're just a big fluffy teddy bear.'

He turned his head back, his gaze ending on me as if I was by only a narrow margin the most interesting or relevant object in vision. 'I've always thought so.'

'What were you doing down in Florida?'

He just shook his head. He was beginning to really piss me off.

'Okay, so what else have you found out?'

'Nothing,' he said.

'That's *it*, for a month of looking? You came all the way over here to tell me this? That's your big news?'

'I haven't spent my entire time on it, Ward, and I don't report to you. I've been trying to have a life. There are other things that are important. The Straw Men aren't everything in the world. The Upright Man is just another killer.'

'Bullshit,' I said, loudly. 'He killed your daughter and my parents. He's not just another anything. And your investigative response is

190

some crap that happened four hundred years ago?'

'Sometimes you have to go back a long way to do what needs to get done.'

'And that means . . . what?'

He shrugged. He'd said all he had to say.

'So what are you going to do now?'

'Check into a hotel somewhere, I guess.'

'This one's not bad.' I felt exposed the moment I'd said this, and wished I'd kept my mouth shut.

He smiled. 'Too expensive for the likes of me, Ward.'

Digging myself deeper: 'So accept a loan.'

'A loan? I thought you were the guy with no resources.'

'John, why are you being such an asshole?'

He stood, and dropped ten bucks on the table. 'Because it's going to take more than this to do something about them,' he said.

He walked away, up the street, and didn't look back. I watched him until he had disappeared from sight, and then went upstairs to pack.

12

It was a little after six and Tom was standing on the balcony that ran along the entire front of the two-storey, L-shaped motel when the car pulled into the lot. He was feeling better in most ways, but worse in others. Getting out of the police station had helped. Also changing his clothes. The deputy had been patient about waiting while Tom picked up new jeans and a fleece jacket and everything that went underneath. What else he had owned prior to His Time Away was stowed in the trunk of the rental car, now sitting down in the lot.

A long hot shower and a sit in the room's single chair had got him to the point where he more or less felt able to go in search of food. His old clothes were stashed in the bag the new ones had come in. Though it seemed hard to believe they'd be wearable again, he felt a superstitious bond with them. A part of his mind — the part that had kept every wallet he had ever owned — was prepared to impute power to the inanimate, to believe power lay lodged in *things*. Without those clothes, who knows what might have happened?

Though he would not quite have been able to admit it, even to himself, there was another aspect to it. The clothes were his witness. They had been there. They knew what he had seen, or felt. In all the time he'd been struggling through the wilderness, desperate for civilization, Tom had kept one thought in his mind. Not only did he now want to stay alive after all, he had a reason to. He knew something. He was bringing news.

The experience had not gone quite as he'd hoped.

He still believed in what he'd seen — or had felt. It was evident that no one else did. The sheriff's position had been starkly clear, and the deputy took his time from him. The fifteen minutes he had spent in the little clothes boutique across from the market had shown Tom that news travelled fast. He'd already guessed this from the fact that the Patrice woman had heard enough to come and drop her drab bombshell (she had spent five minutes afterwards apologizing profusely to Tom, which had somehow just made things worse). People quickly knew what he'd said he'd seen. And by the time he was handing over a credit card for his purchases, it had become evident to Tom that everyone now thought he was a crazy person.

He was drunk in Frank's, you know, couple nights before. Tried to kill himself in the forest, but not with a gun or something hunky like that. Pills, I believe. Passed out, thought he saw something. Then spent two days lost. How funny is that!

Funny, or sad. The girl behind the register didn't articulate any of this, but her very, very kind smile said it all. The man behind the motel's reception desk hadn't given him much eye contact either; but at the end, again there was a slanted smile. Tom got the message. He was one step away from laughing stock. And two steps away from something far worse. If Connolly said anything about what he'd found out, the kind smiles would stop. And Connolly didn't know the whole of it.

He had spent some of the time in the chair staring at the phone, wondering whether he should call home. It had been three, four days. He couldn't remember whether he'd called the night before His Time Away. He knew this didn't speak well of his state of mind. He didn't believe he'd done so, thought he'd wisely denied himself the temptation to say something big or portentous. He felt he owed Sarah a call now, to let her know he was all right, but knew she had no reason to suspect he wouldn't be. His radio silence would be nothing more than additional evidence for the 'Tom is an asshole' school of thought. He wanted to tell her his news. He had to tell someone, and one of his key insights in His Time Away had been that he still cared about Sarah very much. He wouldn't have to tell her why he was out in the woods in the first place (though she might find out later, so he'd have to leave room for that revelation): he could just say what he'd found. The problem was that, as he stood trying to hang onto the feeling he'd had in the forest, that of being in danger but being worthwhile, his news looked flawed.

Without it there was no reason to call 'home', and nothing new to say. And what did it amount to, after all?

That thing which everyone knows doesn't

really exist? The big silly furry one that always turned out to have been faked? I saw it. I was that close to a mythical beast. It stood over me and I smelt its terrible breath. At least . . . I think I did — while I was drunk out of my mind, and half asleep, and a retch away from death. And then I saw a footprint. Though maybe I didn't, and if the truth be told I was hearing voices at the time. That's my news. PS I love you.

Ought to win her respect right back. She'd probably leap straight down the phone, just to be with him again. My brave explorer. My . . . stupid fucking fool.

No. What she knew already was bad, but not as bad as what she might some day find out. For them to stand any chance against that, any chance at all, things had to be good from now. She would have to believe his word against that of others. He couldn't call her now sounding like a lunatic. Didn't want to even send her a text message. When he communicated with her again, it had to be the start of an upward track. But no matter how long he stood out on the balcony, he couldn't work out where one of those might start.

The car pulled around the lot in a smooth arc and came to rest right in the middle. The driver's side door opened almost immediately and a man got out. He was a little over medium height, had brown hair cut well, and was dressed like city folk.

He looked up at the balcony and gave a little wave. 'You wouldn't be Tom Kozelek, by any chance?'

Tom frowned at him for a moment. 'Yes,' he said, eventually. 'Who are you?'

The man grinned. 'How about that? Come a long way fast to talk to you, and there you are, just like that.'

'Okay,' Tom said. 'But who are you, exactly?'

The man pulled a card out of his wallet, and held it up. It was too far for Tom to read the words, but the logo looked familiar.

'I'm someone who wants to hear your story,' he said. 'Now — should I come up there, or are you going to let me buy you a beer?'

★   ★   ★

At quarter of seven Al Connolly was still sitting at his desk in the station. There was no real reason to be. Phil had gone off duty but his other deputy, Conrad, was killing time out in the front. Connolly could have been at home, but the truth was there wasn't a great deal to do there. Still, he was just about to get up and head on out when there was a knock on his door. He looked up to see Melissa Hoffman standing outside.

'Doctor,' Connolly said. 'What can I do for you?'

'Well,' she said, 'it's nothing really. Just . . . well, I found something out, and I thought I maybe should tell you.'

He looked towards the machine in the corner and saw it was half full. 'You want a coffee?'

She nodded, sat down diffidently. People always did. No matter how much they wanted to look at ease, all but a few looked as though they

196

wanted to have the cuffs clapped on right away, in case there was some sin they'd forgotten. The few who didn't look that way were always genuine criminals, who at some deep, deep level just didn't understand.

He fixed them both a cup, sat back at the desk, and said nothing.

'Okay,' she said. 'I did something naughty. When I was in here this morning, checking the mountain guy, on the way out I spotted something in his bag.'

'What kind of thing?'

'This,' she said, and put something on Connolly's desk. He picked it up, turned it over. It looked like a small clump of weeds. Old weeds. 'I probably shouldn't have taken it.'

'Probably,' he said. 'What is it?'

'That's just it,' she said. 'I saw it there — actually it was one of several in the bag — and I wondered what it was. Here you've got a guy who's making outlandish claims which we know aren't true.'

'That's all been squared away,' Connolly said, comfortably. 'Turned out there was a confusion.'

'Oh,' Melissa said, disappointed. 'Then maybe this isn't news after all. I just thought I should check it out. Didn't want to find it was some bad stuff he'd got locally, and we were going to have a rash of drug nuts popping up all over.'

'It was a good thought,' he said. 'So . . . '

'So I have a neighbour who knows about plants and herbs. I took it to her, see if she could tell me what it was.'

'Would this be Liz Jenkins?'

Melissa looked very slightly uncomfortable. 'Yes.'

'She understands a lot about herbs, I know. Matter of fact, you get a chance, you might want to find a way of hinting to her she might want to be a bit more discreet about her use of one of them. Her boyfriend, also.'

'I will,' Melissa said. 'And I know about all that, and it's part of the reason I went to her.'

'Oh yes?'

She flushed. '*Yes*. I thought she'd be able to recognize the kind of thing that people might want to smoke.'

Connolly smiled. 'Whereas you'd be at a complete loss.'

'Exactly.' Melissa cocked her head and smiled back, thinking not for the first time that Connolly was a better guy, and a little bit more subtle, than most people gave him credit for. 'Shall I go on?'

'I'm agog. Did she know what it was?'

'Actually, it's two things.' Melissa placed a piece of paper on the desk and smoothed it out so they both could read — or attempt to read — Liz's baroque handwriting. 'If you look closely you can see one stalk has the remains of some tiny flowers on it. I didn't see them at first. That one is called *Scutellaria lateriflora*, or skullcap or sometimes Quaker bonnet or hoodwort.'

She leaned forward to disentangle another of the scraggy strands, which to Connolly looked indistinguishable from the rest. 'And this other stuff in amongst it is *Valeriana officinalis*. Now.

198

Scutellaria grows all over the US and Southern Canada. It's not especially rare. But the interesting thing is Liz said a group called the Eclectics back in the nineteenth century used it as a tranquillizer or sedative, to treat insomnia and nervousness.'

Connolly nodded. He sensed there was more.

'And valerian is mentioned by a pre-Civil War herbalist called Thompson. He says the earliest colonists found several Indian tribes using it, and he called it, and Liz showed me the quote, 'the best nervine known' — by which he meant 'tranquillizer.' Complementary therapists use it today for anxiety and headache and (again) insomnia, and Liz claims it's been favourably tested against Valium.'

'That's real interesting,' Connolly said. 'Amazing what you can run across out there in the woods.'

'It is, isn't it?'

'So you're saying this stuff is just local flora, and it got brushed into the guy's bag as he was stumbling along in the night.'

'No, Al, I'm not saying that at all. I'm not saying that for three reasons.' She put her coffee down, and counted off on her fingers. 'The first is it would be a family-size coincidence that two known herbal remedies happened to fall into his bag, especially ones that sound perfect for the mental state of the guy at the time. The second is that if you look down at the lower end of the stems there, it looks a little like one of the stalks has been used to bind them all together.'

'Can't really see that,' Connolly said. 'Could

just be the way they were mushed together in his bag.'

'Okay,' Melissa said. 'Be that way. But here's the thing. *Scutellaria lateriflora* is a perennial. It dies back in the winter.'

Connolly said nothing.

'Al, that guy could have dragged his bag from here to Vancouver and none of that stuff is going to end up inside. Which means it was put there deliberately.'

Connolly looked at her for a long moment, then reached across and picked up the coffee pot again. He raised it at her, but she shook her head. He took his time pouring another cup for himself, quietly wishing he had gone home just a little earlier.

'I don't really see where this is leading,' he said, finally. 'Okay, so the guy went to a herb doctor recently. What's the big deal?'

'Maybe there is none,' Melissa said. 'But I don't see him doing that, getting these kind of dried remedies and taking them along on an admitted suicide jaunt. Does that make sense to you?'

'No, I guess it doesn't.' Connolly could have suggested that the plants were left there from some earlier time or trip, but he'd already noticed that backpacks just like the one Kozelek had were for sale right there in Sheffer. 'So where does that leave us, Mrs Fletcher?'

Melissa laughed attractively. 'Nowhere. Just thought I'd pass it on. We're having supper over at the Wilsons' tonight anyhow, so it was on our way. I left Jeff over in Frank's, and actually, unless I want to lose the Wilsons as friends and dining companions, I should go haul him out of there before he gets into another round.'

Connolly accompanied her out to the street, and stood watching as she walked the long diagonal across the wet road to Frank's double-lot spread of warm light and neon, treading carefully to avoid messing up her dinner party shoes. She was a good doctor, and it didn't matter to him if she and Liz Jenkins spent the occasional private evening not making much sense. Al had enjoyed some nights like that himself, back in the day. She'd most likely drop the stuff about the plants. Wasn't really anywhere it could go.

But he walked back to his office just the same, sat at his desk, and thought a while.

★ ★ ★

Tom and the journalist were just starting on their second beer in Frank's when the doctor lady came in to pick up a guy who was presumably her husband. This man had been sitting talking affably with the barman on the other side of the room. She calmly but firmly made him leave his drink on the counter, and led him back to the outside. Tom turned to watch them crossing the lot and saw her laughing hard at something her man had said. Tom had made women laugh sometimes, too. Suddenly he missed the sound very much.

'Anyone you know?' the journalist said.

Tom shook his head. 'Local doctor. The police

got her in to look me over.'

'Cute.'

'I guess so,' Tom said. 'Taken, though.'

'Everybody's taken these days, Tom. Including you, judging by the wedding bands you got there. Is there anything I need to know about that? About how come you're up here all on your own?'

'There was some difficulty back home,' Tom said. 'I came out here to clear my head.'

'Okay. That will do for now.'

Tom wondered how long it would be before the man decided he had to know more about that, and how he could keep him away from that information. He set his beer down and looked at him. From his neat shirt and suit alone you'd know this was a guy just up from the city, and who maybe wasn't quite as smart as he thought. As usual, he was smiling. Tom supposed that was a trait that came in handy when getting people to tell you things. The man — whose name was Jim Henrickson — worked for *Front Page*, whose red and white logo Tom had recognized from twenty yards. Fashion, fame, celebrities — along with Hitler's Hideout in Antarctica, Aliens Abducted My Pay Check, and Fish Boy Born To Idaho Beauty Queen. And now . . . Suicidal Designer Finds Bigfoot.

The difference being that *Front Page* headlines were never actually that bald, and the writers went to some trouble to look like they were proper journalists. Even if some of the stories wandered into the realms of the bizarre, they were soberly written and took an even-handed approach. Plus it was glossy. The entertainment world took it pretty seriously and their film and fashion people got invites to all the big parties. It was, as celebrity hack mags went, pretty classy. That made a difference. If Henrickson had been from the *Enquirer* or *World News*, Tom would be elsewhere by now. Eating, probably. But the news had to start somewhere, and in the last half-hour, Tom had gradually started to think that he might have an audience for his announcement after all.

'You believe me,' he said.

'Actually, I do.'

Tom felt exhausted, and strange, and tearful. The man saw this, and gently clapped him on the shoulder. 'It's okay, my friend.'

'Why?' Tom asked. 'Nobody else does.'

'Main reason is you just don't seem like a liar, and most of the nonsense I hear is lies rather than mistakes. Second thing is that this is not the first time I've been up around here on a story like this. Nine months ago three hunters fifty miles north east of here, up near Mazama, reported a very similar incident. Something appearing in their camp in the night. A pungent aroma. They heard strange noises, too, a kind of quiet wailing. You hear anything like that?'

'No. But . . . I was very firmly asleep, before I woke.'

'Right. Well, it freaked them out. These were three big ole boys, been going out in the woods since they were kids, and they came running scared out of their minds.'

'I don't remember hearing about that.'

'Read us every week, do you?'

'No,' Tom admitted. 'In waiting rooms, mainly. Sorry.'

'Your implication saddens me, Tom. Waiting rooms are an important environment. We get men and women through that pre-dental anxiety, more power to us. No, well, you didn't hear about the hunters because we didn't run with it. Hearsay from three beardy guys in plaid may be enough for our competitors, but it's no use to FP's sophisticated readership. Our whole USP is that though we'll cover the Weird Stuff, we won't even table it unless we think we've got a case.'

'Hitler's Hideout in Antarctica?'

'What can I tell you?' The man laughed, throwing his hands wide. 'It was a strange old rock formation and no mistake. Personally I wouldn't have run that one, I admit it freely, but I'm just a field grunt. Sold a shitload of copies, that's for sure. Hitler, the perennial bad boy. We miss him now he's gone. Anyway, my point is if BF's going to be found anywhere, it's going to be up here in the Pacific North West. You have literally hundreds of reports over the years, back to a guy called Elekah Walker in the 1800s — and there's deep background stuff too. All around this part of the US you can find ancient rock carvings of things that look pretty monkey-like, despite the fact you've got no native primates, or so They say.'

'Wasn't there some footage, too?'

The man shook his head. 'The Patterson film.

Turned out to be a fake, only recently in fact. All of it does, either fake or could-be-fake and nothing to prove otherwise. That's your biggest problem right there. There's lots of people who don't want the Truth to be known. You give Them the slightest opening and They're going to take you down. But we'll get there.'

Henrickson took a sip of his beer, eyes bright with good cheer. 'You want to know what else I think?'

'Okay,' Tom said. His own beer tasted good but was making him feel strange. It was probably a bad idea, but he didn't want to stop just yet. In the meantime, he was happy to let the other man talk.

'Conspiracy theories are bunk.'

'Right,' said Tom, nodding. 'Okay. Which one?'

'Not one. *All* of them. All conspiracy theories are false. They have been invented by the Authorities — to hide what's *really* going on.'

Tom laughed. 'Good one.'

'I'm not joking.'

'Oh.'

'The only theory which can be true is this one, because I know for sure it has not been put about by Them, because *it was invented by me.* The more bizarre it appears, the more likely a theory is to be true — because it only sounds weird in the context of the lies we've been trained to accept.'

'You've lost me,' Tom said. 'Could be the beer.'

'The authorities control all information — therefore they *must* have invented these

205

theories too. They plant 'conspiracy theories' because the real truth would be even worse for us to know. Example. You know this idea that we never really landed on the moon, right? That it was all a fake?'

'I saw a television show. Plus there was a movie . . . '

'Right. *Capricorn One*. And a bunch of books, dah dah dah. But the truth is that the idea we didn't go there is *itself* a fake conspiracy theory, invented to draw attention away from the real truth. There is no moon.'

'Excuse me?'

'*There's no moon*. No planets or stars either. Everyone's yakking about did we go there or not, and so they miss the real truth. There's no there, there. Galileo was on drugs. This is it, my friend; this ball of rock is *all she wrote*. Which also explains the 'The Government Knows About Aliens And Is Covering Them Up' theory, right? Fact is there *are* no aliens, because — see above — there is no rest of the universe. The idea was invented back when it got obvious we needed a new horizon, otherwise we'd kill each other by Tuesday. Gives us something to focus on. Who's going to get to the moon first, us or those super-bad Reds? Then we land there, but it's like we get bored immediately and don't bother any more. Isn't that kind of *weird*? We got there with forty-years-ago technology, but we don't do it now we could fit those computers on the head of a pin?'

'But there's the space shuttles.'

'Right. And every so often one of them blows

apart. 'So *that's* why we haven't made it to Mars yet, boys and girls — because space is *dangerous*'. It's all bullshit, and that's what the Little Green Men are for. We don't go out there, but it comes down to us, therefore it *must* exist. And it's not just far horizons crap, either. Tell me this: who killed John F. Kennedy?'

'I don't know. My impression is it's sort of a mystery.'

'Right. And why is that?'

'You're going to tell me, I suspect.'

'To cover up the fact that Kennedy isn't dead.'

'He's not?'

'Of *course* not, Tom. Actually kind of a sweet story. He was forced out by the people he and his family had pissed off, the mob, Cuban nationals, the CIA; and it's like, 'Go forth, or we're going to whack you'. So he struck a deal so he and his one true love (Marilyn, who else?) could disappear. Their deaths were faked and now they're living in Scotland together. They started an alpaca farm. One of the first in Europe, I believe. It's small stuff, but they do okay and, you know, they've got each other, right? That's why shit keeps happening to all the other Kennedys. Some of them know about JFK's secret love farm. They're supposed to keep quiet about it, otherwise the whole conspiracy base will come to light and people will think 'Shit, if they can do that, then what else isn't true?' The first sign a Kennedy's going to squeal, and splat! They're history. Discredited, dead, or both. There's a rumour Lady Diana got wind of it too, need I say more?'

'You don't really believe all that.'

The man smiled. 'No,' he admitted. 'That's not what happened to JFK. But that's the first thing you learn in my business. What's true is immaterial. It's what people *believe*. Belief is the truth.'

There was a soft clunk at Tom's elbow, and he saw a new beer had arrived. He didn't remember seeing it signalled for. Another skill that probably came in handy in a job like Henrickson's.

'Jim, you don't have to get me drunk,' he said.

'Tom, Tom, Tom,' Henrickson said, shaking his head. 'Jeez! And you think *I'm* paranoid. Trust me. I'm in the mood for some suds, and you're keeping me company. You're in the system now, and that means you're not going to get screwed around. We have a story here, I'm hoping, and that means you're going to get paid big time. Though I do want your word, right here and now, that you're going to talk to me only on this, not anybody else.'

'Sure,' Tom said, knowing no one else would listen.

'Excellent. Which means we only have one remaining thing we're to sort out.'

'Some kind of proof.'

'I'm not talking court-of-law proof, of course. We had that then I'd say screw *Front Page*, let's get talking to the BBC and CNN and NYT. But we need something. You got a description that sounds promisingly like the thing the hunters ran into, but you could have picked that up somewhere else.'

'But I hadn't heard . . . '

'I believe you. Others won't. You had a footprint, too, but that will be long gone, plus there's the inconvenient old woman with her stupid boots.'

'But that's it,' Tom said. 'That's all I had.'

'Actually no.' Henrickson shook his head. 'Not from what you said. You might have something you don't even realize. Tomorrow we'll go take a look.'

Tom just looked confused. 'Trust me,' the man said again, and winked.

★   ★   ★

Al Connolly was leaving the station for the night. A quick conversation with Patrice Anders had explained Melissa's find: she had put the herbs there. The situation was nice and tidy again. He considered heading over to Frank's for a soda and some wings, but decided it had been a long day and that a beer in front of the tube at home would do just as well. His house was big and empty, but it was quiet and the phone wouldn't ring.

That sounded good.

13

Ten minutes after her phone conversation with Sheriff Connolly, Patrice was still standing in the little kitchen area of her home. A scant four-by-six-foot corner of the main living space, it had a window that looked out into the trees. She was looking out through it now, though if the truth be told she wasn't seeing anything.

Not anything anyone else would see, anyhow.

★　★　★

For almost all their lives Bill and Patrice Anders had lived in Portland. When the kids left home in the mid 1980s the adults started tentatively to remind themselves how you spent free time: like staff from an abandoned zoo, released with the animals back into the wild. They began to go for weekends out of the city, enjoying themselves in a somewhat aimless way, but it wasn't until they discovered Verona that they had horizons once again.

Little more than a bump on 101, the coast road down the state's Pacific edge, Verona has a few streets, wooden houses, a grocery, not much else: chances were you'd be through and past without it occurring to you to stop. But if you were dawdling south, and kept your eyes open as you left town, then just after the bridge over the inlet there's a sign for the Redwood Lodgettes. A sign burned into an old log, pointing into trees. Patrice saw it, and they pulled in to have a look. That whim changed the rest of their lives.

The Lodgettes were a piece of fading history, the kind of old-school resort that used to mark the end of a morning's driving and the dawn of an afternoon's swimming and shrieking and padding to the sea and back with sand and pine needles underfoot; mom happy because the place was nice and had somewhere to wash clothes, father relieved a budget had been met; the children knowing these things, however vaguely, and basking in the warmth of a family bound in simple satisfaction for once. Fourteen cabins were dotted around a couple of wooded acres, bordered by rocky shoreline on one side and the inlet on another. On that first visit Bill insisted on sketching out the layout of their cabin (Number 2), so taken was he with the way it had been put together: sitting area, kitchenette, bedroom, bathroom and storage eking every spare inch of living space out of sturdy log constructions twenty feet square. A wood-burning stove in the sitting room made it the perfect place for chilly spring evenings; the bedroom was cosy on cold winter nights. The wraparound porch was where you lived in summer and autumn, listening to the birds and the distant sound of water, musing about what you might have for supper, keeping a book open on your lap to legitimate not doing anything, including reading it.

In the evening they wandered over the bridge back into the tiny town. They found a bar that stood on stilts in the bay and had pool tables and loud music they recognized, and further up the hill a restaurant as good as any in Portland. They drank local wine and local beer and were enchanted. It was a long time since that had happened. Enchantment isn't easy to come by, in this day and age. Verona pulled it off, in spades. Bill and Patrice found themselves breathing more slowly, holding hands on the beach and smiling at fellow walkers, looking out to sea and feeling the curvature of the earth. They chose the same appetizers three nights running. The old couple who ran the Lodgettes — the Willards — were calling them by first name by the second day. When it came time to leave Patrice had to be hauled away by a tractor, and extracted a promise from her husband that they were coming back as soon as they could.

It was decided there and then. When the world needed getting away from, this was where they'd come.

$$\star \quad \star \quad \star$$

Ten years passed, with twenty visits, maybe twenty-five. The Willards retired in 94, but nothing much changed: Patrice and Bill kept pulling in to the Lodgettes like seabirds bobbing up on a twice-yearly tide. They nearly brought their children, once, but the visit fell through. This was far from unusual. When discussing Josh and Nicole one time, Bill described the relationship they had with them as 'cordial', and that pretty much nailed it. Everyone loved each

212

other, there was no question of that, but they kept their heads about it. Nobody went berserk with affection. Phone contact was regular, visits friendly. They met for the major festivals, when well-chosen gifts were exchanged and everyone was helpful in the kitchen. Their children worked hard. If their careers were more important than visiting, there wasn't a great deal that could be said. They went down to Verona anyway. It was nice to have the place to themselves, not to have to worry whether others were finding it quite so comfortable as them. They didn't suggest a family trip again.

Then they happened to be in Verona for a weekend one late August and fell to talking to the new owners. It wasn't that they had a close relationship — unlike the Willards, Ralph and Becca seemed to forget them after each visit and affability had to be forged anew — but they soon picked up something was afoot. There was an air of non-renewal. They asked, and Ralph confirmed it without much evident regret: this was the Lodgettes' last summer.

On hearing this Patrice's heart was pierced, and her hand went up to her mouth. She barely heard as they were told the business wasn't making enough money, though the town was growing in popularity as Cannon Beach and Florence and Yachats got too expensive and people looked further down the coast for romantic minibreaks. This wasn't helping the Lodgettes. Young money didn't want rustic cabins. It wanted DVD players and organic

213

juices. Stone Therapy was a baseline requirement. The resort occupied a prime location and a spa hotel there would be a no-brainer for someone who knew the business. Bill later muttered to Patrice that if Ralph or Becca had mastered the art of remembering guests between stays then things might have gone differently, but that's the way it was. A developer up from San Francisco had made an offer they weren't prepared to refuse.

They sat on the deck of the bar before dinner, sipping their Verona drinks: a rare beer for him, an even rarer Sweet Manhattan for her. Patrice felt more glum than in a long, long time. Why did life have to be this way? It seemed as if with every passing year the world accepted into it more and more things that meant nothing to her, innovations that seemed trivial or confusing but were heralded like the dawn of a new age. She put up with all that stuff, did her best to understand the attractions of cell phones and Windows and Eminem: but why did the parts that mattered to her have to get shoved aside in the process? Bill was also quiet. There was a look on his face, the one he got when he was trying not to think about something. He was reserved during dinner, not even bothering to look through the wine list, something which — since more or less giving up beer — he'd tried to get in the habit of doing. Patrice put it down to him feeling the way she did, to asking himself the same questions, most of all a question she was too sad to put into words.

Would they still come to Verona?

With the Lodgettes gone, vanished beneath just another hotel of the kind you could find by the bushel in glossy books telling couples of a certain age where to go to rekindle their love (or have affairs with their brokers or neighbours, more likely), where would they stay? There was already a hotel further up 101, on the north side of town, but it was a characterless brick sprawl with a treeless lawn, nowhere you'd go on purpose or twice. They could try the new place after it was built, but it would be disloyal to something that mattered, unfaithful to the old place. She knew the paths between its trees. She couldn't take breakfast on a balcony over a parking lot where their cabin had once stood.

So what would they do? Find somewhere else? She didn't want to. She didn't want to have to start afresh. Having Verona meant they took far more breaks than they might otherwise. A decision was saved. They knew every mile of the drive, stopped at the same places for lunch there and back. They'd lose all of that, along with countless other rituals too small to have a name, down to the little joke by which they referred to the elderly gay couple they exchanged nods with on the beach as The Two Gentlemen of Verona. Of course there were other places along the coast, and it wasn't as if Verona was actually heaven on earth (the grocery store remained very functional, so they always stocked up in Cannon Beach), but you can't find another bolthole just by looking.

One of the walls of Patrice's inner house had been taken from her, and she couldn't find any way to feel good about it.

As they walked hand in hand down the road after dinner, still quiet, Bill surprised her by suggesting a nightcap. In the early years they'd always done this: people-watching the locals, a quiet cigarette for Bill out on the deck hanging over the bay. Gradually they'd found that dinner left them comfortably tired, and had taken to just wandering home.

Patrice smiled, said yes. She was glad. He was good like that. He didn't always talk about things out loud (which had driven her crazy on more than one occasion over the years), but he always understood. She sat out on the deck while he fetched the drinks. She could see lights in some of the cabins across the inlet, just as always. They were like stars to her, something by which to navigate through life. She realized that next time these lights would have been extinguished, and knew there and then this was their last visit. When she turned at the sound of Bill coming out with a drink in each hand, her eyes were wet.

'I know,' he said, sitting opposite her.

He put his hand on hers, looked out at the lights for a moment. Then he picked up his drink and held it for her to knock against. She shrugged. She didn't feel like it. There was nothing to toast.

He insisted, keeping his glass high. Stranger still, she saw he had a cigarette in his hand — and he hardly ever smoked by then. Patrice began to suspect his faraway look hadn't meant quite what she'd thought. She raised a quizzical eyebrow, and then her own glass.

'I've got an idea,' he said.

* * *

As she stood now, still looking out at the forest, Patrice could remember that evening with a clarity missing from almost all of her life since. The last big decision. The last thing that had felt like a step upwards rather than more standing in place, or worse, slipping sideways into some place she'd never been.

'We've talked about buying some land,' Bill said. 'Somewhere cheap, with trees.'

That was true. They had. Or Bill had, anyway. She'd listened and nodded and been vaguely positive, not thinking it would ever happen. They didn't need somewhere else. They had Verona.

Except . . . now they didn't.

She said: 'We don't really have enough . . . '

'Money. Yes we do. For the land.'

'But not to build a house.'

'Right. So how about tomorrow morning I go to Ralph and make him an offer on one of those cabins?'

She stared at him, willing him to say it.

'Cabin Two,' he said, and by then her eyes were wet again. 'We do a side deal with Ralph. Developer's not going to want them — they're just in the way. They don't have to knock it down, and we get it moved to wherever.'

'Can you *do* that?'

They talked about it for an hour, until both were wild-eyed and starting to gabble. Next morning Bill did as he'd said.

Ralph made a phone call and half an hour later the deal was done. The faraway look didn't quite leave Bill's eye, however: by the afternoon things had progressed and they were the owners of not one, but three of the cabins. Bill told her they could have one for them, one for an office/study, one for guests. The kids, perhaps. Patrice didn't really care. The main thing was that Cabin Two was safe. She still wished it could stay in Verona, that the Lodgettes would be there forever and nothing had to change, but if that wasn't the way it was going to be, then they weren't taking it lying down. She wanted to fix stickers over the cabin saying it was their property now. She wanted to lift it up onto the car's roof rack and take it right away. She wanted to set up a machine-gun post.

Once they had three cabins to find a home for, buying a piece of land changed from a vague notion into the thing they were doing next. They spent a few weekends looking for a spot and settled on the area just north of Sheffer, on the east side of the Cascades. It was an afternoon's drive from Portland, up 5 and over 90; a nice little town, charming without being fake, and land was still reasonably priced. Developers had staked out stretches on the roads out of town, but there hadn't been any takers so far and some of the For Sale signs were beginning to fade. They bought a forty-acre lot way out at the end of the access road, complete with a ton of trees and its own cold little lake. If you climbed over their back fence you were in National Forest, and no one was ever going to be able to change that. This time Cabin Two had a permanent home.

Most utilities were on site, and the rest didn't take long. They got the cabins moved, ritualistically following them up the coast in their car. One had to be virtually rebuilt at the other end, a cost they hadn't anticipated, but when she saw them in place Patrice stood and looked with tears running down her face. She didn't turn to Bill. She knew he didn't really like her to see him cry.

Cabin Two went near the lake, the 'office' a little further around, and the guest cabin right the other side. By the time they had been on their plot for a week, Bill and Patrice knew this was where they lived now. They sold the house back in Portland, got rid of most of their stuff, and committed themselves. He tweaked and customized the office and guest cabins, learning skills he'd never realized he wanted to have. She did a little landscaping around the cabins before the snows came down, and then sat by the fire with plant and seed catalogues, planning for the spring. They spent the Christmas up in Sheffer, getting to know the town, what it had, what it didn't. Both children called on Christmas Day, which was nice.

On January 1st, 2001, Patrice was led out of the cabin to see that Bill had built her a bench which went around the biggest tree by the lake — manhandling rustic chunks of wood down there by himself and in secret. They sat shivering on it together, drinking a big thermos of mulled wine, and she grew warm in his arms and believed she was about as happy as she could ever be.

In March it turned out Bill had lung cancer. When he died four months later, Patrice could have picked him up with one hand.

14

Somewhere, on a screen, a young woman sits crying on her couch, captured in the past. The couch is saggy and covered in a suede-like material in dark rust. The wall behind it is white and holds a mirror and a large painting of tulips which is not altogether bad. The woman is in pretty good shape and tan but for pale triangles over her breasts; she is naked apart from a pair of tight white pants. In her right hand she is holding a cigarette; the left is in her hair, which is long and brown. Her face is wet and crumpled, eyes open but turned inwards. In front of her is a coffee table on which sits a large glass ashtray, two remote controls and a half-empty coffee cup. It is early on a Sunday morning, and she looks badly hungover.

She smokes her cigarette down and stubs it out. You see this in jump cuts, because even though you have been a member of this website for three months, the software you are using to watch it — the cheerfully named CamFun, a $12.95 shareware value — is set to update the image only every two minutes. Most people simply log into the web page using a browser like Microsoft Explorer. You are using CamFun because it enables you to save the pictures more easily, storing them onto the hard disk as a movie file of sequential images which you can re-watch any time you choose — which is what you are doing now, in fact, watching something that happened several weeks before. The site itself hasn't been updated for a few days, which is weird. The other reason you use the software is that you can select the frequency with which the image you see is updated. You can take advantage of the members-only fifteen-second update, or choose instead to be updated every third image, or every sixth — thus, every minute or two. This might seem perverse when you are paying $19.99 a month for access to the quicker rate, which is supposed to make the experience seem more real. For you it has exactly the opposite effect. A scene updated every twenty seconds looks like something filmed by a security camera: the way it samples reality implies that what is missing is not important. But it *is* important. The reality of the original is lost in those infinitesimal omissions. If you cut the gaps back to a minute or two, however, something changes. What's missing seems to swell, giving the images more weight, making them pregnant with duration: a daisy chain of moments, stasis toppling into sudden movement, a dance to stuttering time.

The period through which you wait for an update charges the scene with anticipation. Two minutes is enough to hop someone from one end of the couch to the other, as if by magic, or to take a freshly lit cigarette and burn it halfway down, apparently in an instant. It's enough to make a woman disappear, to zap her from couch to kitchen. To the kitchen. Back to the couch again. There she is . . . blip — she's gone. Where?

Out of vision, off radar/the planet, and yet still within the apartment, one presumes. Blip — she's back again. Two minutes is real. Things can happen in it.

The fact that the woman is semi-naked is almost immaterial. Not completely, of course: the webcams of the fully clothed are a niche interest. They do exist, in droves, bright and intense young ladies with their weblogs full of Highly Individual Thoughts About, Like, Everything (how embarrassing if they ever got to read each other's, and discovered they'd had identical Highly Individual Thoughts), but they're of no interest to you. This woman is pretty. You like seeing her body once in a while. But you are not like all the other perverts, and ultimately it is *her* you are watching, not her breasts — which is just as well, because she does not reveal them often.

This woman, who has chosen to set up her life in this way, to have a window in her apartment through which people — men bathed in cathode glow or wreathed with flat-screen pallor, sitting in bedrooms and dens across the world — can peer. This woman, who has an acoustic guitar which she picks up every now and then, but not for long; who gets through a steady half-bottle of Jack Daniels a night when she's at home; who occasionally has noncommittal sex on this couch — encounters in which you are not very interested, hardly at all, though you do have some saved to disk and on those occasions you *did* increase the frame rate. She does not play to the camera during these events, and you half suspect that she has simply forgotten it is there.

This woman who was, for some reason, sitting crying alone on a Sunday morning four weeks ago. You have watched this movie before, and find it fascinating for reasons you cannot quite understand. She blips to invisibility, stays hidden for another two-minute beat, then is back on the couch. She has lit another cigarette in the meantime, and is wearing a blue towelling gown. Her hair has been pushed back to fall behind her ears. She is no longer crying, though her face looks drawn and glum. She is looking to the side, out of a window, you think, though you have never directly seen that wall of the apartment. Two minutes later her feet are on the coffee table and she is looking at her knees, the cigarette almost finished. She looks tired, and resigned to something or other.

How many thoughts have passed through her head in that time? What were they? You cannot tell. Somewhere between her and you that information has been lost, trimmed from reality by the processes of digitization and transfer and storage and re-transfer and projection in red, green and blue. It seems obvious that the loss occurred somewhere in that process, at least, but perhaps it did not: maybe it was only at the very last second, as the information tried to leap the gulf from the screen to another human's mind, that all was lost. All the differences in the world are as nothing compared to this: the difference between being you and being me. It makes the chasms between gods and men, between men and women, between dead and alive, seem almost trivial.

You are you. She is someone else. Between lie the stars.

You watch, and you speculate, and you think. You can do all this without knowing the answers, without having to engage with the mundane truth. It might be something trivial or boring: a broken nail, a bent fender, the sudden and vertiginous realization that she's approaching thirty and still doesn't have a child. It might be something else, something darker and sharper and outside of your world or understanding: a bad experience with a client (you vaguely assume she might be a whore); bad news about a friend (some predictable drug-fuelled auto-da-fé); some other bad bit of bad news of the kinds that this bad old world always has up its bad sleeve. It doesn't matter. That is the beauty of this webcam, of all webcams, of the internet itself — of our world as it has become. You can observe, and interpret, or just let the images welter there in front of your eyes, until you've had enough. Then you can quit the file and close the hidden folder where it rests, and get up and walk away. It is like the news, glimpses of Iraq or Rwanda. It is someone else's life, someone else's problem. You are safe from it.

Or so you think — until an hour and a half later, when two FBI agents turn up at your house while you and your wife are eating dinner. You realize then, far too late, that gaze is two-way even on the internet. You listen, hot-faced, in the final moments of the period in which your marriage is straightforward, as the female agent tells you the woman called Jessica is

225

dead, and that in the last three months the expensive computer in your study logged more watching time on her site than anyone else.

You have been her biggest fan, in other words, and the FBI want to talk about what happened to her, as do the policemen outside; and your wife looks like she was carved out of cold white marble; and you cannot Quit out of this, and there is no escape.

★   ★   ★

Forty minutes later Nina came out of the living room, leaving the Jessica fan — whose name was Greg McCain — sitting opposite Doug Olbrich. She joined Monroe, who had been listening from the hallway. McCain was bolt upright in a corner of the couple's nicely distressed leather couch. He was in his mid-thirties and had an expensive haircut of the kind Hugh Grant used to affect. He had requested that his lawyer be present. Maybe McCain should have been left to his own devices in the meantime, but Olbrich was sitting silently opposite. Sometimes that kind of thing worked.

Monroe turned to her. 'What do you think?'

'I don't know,' she said. 'His wife alibis him for around the time Ryan was shot. She says he left for work at about quarter of eight and she's so evidently pissed at him that it seems hard to believe she'd back him up out of loyalty.'

'Discovering your husband likes watching women on the web is not the same as dropping him for the murder of a policeman. Or believing

226

him capable of it. Either way, it's not impossible to get from their house to The Knights in a quarter-hour.'

'No, but it would be hard. And I've had another thought.'

'Which is?'

'We've been assuming the man who killed Jessica was also the man who killed Ryan.'

'Well of course. I don't think that's a useful . . . '

'Charles, listen. Jessica was dead maybe forty-eight hours when we found her; hard to pin it down because of the heat. The story we have is that a man murders a woman, in private, and then a day or so later comes out and kills a policeman as a 'look at me'. As I said at the time, this is extreme behaviour.'

'Explain it another way.'

'I can't. Yet. I'm just saying that the only link between the two events is proximity.'

Monroe shook his head. 'Hell of a coincidence, don't you think?'

'No. They could still be connected. Just not the same guy. Which means Jessica's killer could be in some other part of the country by now. Or he could be happily sitting at home, with an alibi for the wrong day.'

Monroe looked away then, and spoke unusually quietly. 'Why would someone else kill a policeman?'

'I'm just saying if we work with the idea then we have a different question to ask Mrs McCain.'

He nodded. 'Do it,' he said.

Gail McCain was in the kitchen. She was standing looking out of a window onto the yard, and her back was straight. Nina wondered what the woman had been assuming the evening would hold. The couple had no children, so their quiet, civilized meal would have most likely been followed by a little television or gentle work, two people sharing their affluent, child-unfriendly space.

'Is my husband under arrest?'

'No,' Nina said. 'Not yet.'

'So we don't have to entertain you here any longer.'

'You could refuse to, certainly. In which case the LAPD might have to arrest you so we could talk somewhere else. Knowing those guys they'd break out some of the extra big flashing lights, the ones that really shine into the neighbours' windows.'

'If they had reason to do that, you'd have done it already.'

'Are you an attorney, Mrs McCain?'

'No. I work in television.'

Something in the woman's voice or face heated one of Nina's brain cells half a degree. She turned to the policewoman who was standing by the door. The officer was short but stockily built and stared impassively across the corridor. Her hair was in a ponytail, pulled back so tight her forehead looked hard enough to flatten a nose like putty, or batter through walls.

'How about that?' Nina said. 'The lady works

in television. Pretty cool, huh?'

'Whatever,' the policewoman said, without moving her eyes.

Nina shrugged at Mrs McCain. 'Officer Whalen is notoriously hard to impress. Me, I think television's fabulous. So well *done*.'

'It's just a job.'

'But it's such an important one, isn't it? Friend of mine, guy called Ward, has a theory says producers are the new priests, and their job is to mediate between the common man and the heavenly realm the other side of the screen. Say the right thing, be the right way, and you'll put them in a reality show or a soap or the new *Friends*, zap them straight to the Emmys at the right hand of Whoopi Goldberg. You feel like a priest, ever?'

'I have no idea what you're talking about.'

'I don't blame you. I don't understand Ward half the time either. But my point here is that being a lawyer would be a lot more use to you, right at this moment. You sure you understand the situation?'

'I believe so.'

'You understand we are investigating the murder of a woman called Jessica Jones, found dead on Wednesday morning. You understand that Jessica was a web girl, and your husband was a member of her site. This entitled him to view a webcam in Jessica's apartment, which frequently showed her in the nude.'

The woman spoke through clenched teeth. 'I understand all of the above.'

'Good. Would you say your husband was

technically competent?'

'What do you mean?'

'Computers. I see there are several in his den. Is he good with them?'

'I think so. He fixes mine, if it goes wrong. But . . . '

'Thank you. Now, in general your husband doesn't look like a likely suspect. Which is why we're glad to have you both voluntarily assisting us, and why we're here quietly, without the big lights. For the moment. I just want to ask a few questions, and you're done. Okay? You told Lieutenant Olbrich that your husband left for work on Wednesday morning at around seven forty-five, is that correct?'

'No,' the woman said, coldly. 'I told him Greg left at *exactly* that time.'

'How can you be so sure?'

'Greg always leaves at quarter of eight. That's what time Greg leaves.'

'But presumably sometimes it's a little closer to eight, and sometimes it's a little earlier? Your husband's also in television, I understand? I'm assuming sometimes he has to make sure he's there early. It's not like punching a clock, right?'

'Yes, but . . . '

'So he must have early meetings, on occasion.'

'He does, of course.'

'And while he generally leaves at seven forty-five, there will be times when he could have left the house at quarter after, or even a little later. What makes you sure that on the morning in question he left at this default time?'

The woman looked irritable. 'Because I just

know. Look, Ms Baynam, are you married?'

'I'm not, no.' The brain cell heated up another half degree.

'It figures. If you were, you'd know what I was talking about. When you're married to someone, you know what's going on in their world. Too much, maybe. You get your own life and half of the other person's. I know when Greg's busy, when he's up against it at work, when something's going haywire and meetings start popping up all over the day. No, I don't carry his diary in my head and I can't always quote chapter and verse. But I know what's going on in his life.'

'So . . . I'm sorry: so you knew about the webcam thing? You knew he was spending time watching girls getting naked, having sex, live on the internet?'

'No I didn't, but that's . . . '

Nina cut in smoothly. 'Different. Of course. You know everything about Greg, apart from that, and that's perfectly reasonable. Men are sneaky about that kind of thing. You can't be expected to know about it. There's probably a detail or two he doesn't know about you either, right? That's also fine. That's married life, from what I understand — but, you know, I'm only guessing. Looking in, from the cold, dark wastes of spinsterhood.'

'I didn't mean . . . '

'Of course you didn't, Gail. But otherwise, apart from these little details, you'd say you have a solid understanding of Greg and his schedule and his life.'

'Yes. Yes I do.'

'Excellent. You've been very helpful.' Nina heard the doorbell ring from the other side of the house. 'Sounds like the cavalry has arrived. I think the Lieutenant is finishing up with your husband anyway, so we're going to be leaving very soon.'

Nina smiled warmly, and started to walk away. Then she turned back and asked, as if enquiring after the name of her interior designer; 'What was your husband doing on Monday evening?'

The woman stared at her. 'Excuse me?'

'What was your husband doing on Monday evening? From your understanding of his schedule?'

'He . . . '

Nina watched as the woman realized she had hesitated too long, that the question, dealt unexpectedly out of nowhere, had penetrated a weak defence she hadn't realized she had to build. 'Was he out, that evening?'

'Yes. He . . . he had a meeting. A late meeting.'

'How late would that have been?'

'I don't remember. It was late.'

'This was a meeting relating to his work?'

The woman saw Nina staring at her.

'Yes,' she said. 'I think.'

★   ★   ★

'We're going to go,' Olbrich said, quietly. He, Monroe and Nina were now alone in the kitchen. 'Two people at his company confirm he

232

was at or near his desk by the usual time on Wednesday. He was out late Monday evening, as you found, and it wasn't a meeting. What it was, he claims, is a strip club with a client. The alleged client is now back in England.' He looked at his watch. 'McCain has no personal address for this person, and so we're going to have to wait until UK business hours to chase that down. But frankly . . . '

He tailed off.

Nina yawned massively. 'We don't have shit to hold him on and he doesn't look like the guy Jessica was seen with in Jimmy's.'

'Right. Yes, he watched Jessica. Yes, he occasionally goes to strip clubs. When he 'has to'. Nice work if you can get it. Any more than that and he's a dead end. His lawyer's with them now and he's pumped up to fight, and he's got a point. We either have to make this serious or leave it alone for now.'

Monroe shook his head and stalked out into the hallway.

Olbrich looked at Nina. 'What's his problem?'

'Doesn't like leaving empty-handed when we came in this heavy.'

'It was his call. I told him it should be more subtle.'

'Monroe's more of an 'Advance straight to Go' kind of player.'

They followed her boss along the hallway and stopped outside the door to the living room. Nina was expecting sass from one or other, and most certainly the lawyer — it seemed like everyone in television or movies was forever

233

talking back to the police nowadays, and so everyone in real life felt they had to do it too, as if to stay in character — but there was none forthcoming.

Olbrich apologized without apologizing. Monroe asked that they take no out-of-town trips for a few days. Nina was going to just breeze on out without a backward glance, but then she heard her name being called in a female voice.

Go ahead, sister, she thought, as she turned. *Push a little harder and just see what happens.*

The McCains were standing together facing her. Their lawyer had faded to the back of the room and wasn't looking happy.

'My wife says I should give you this. My lawyer disagrees.'

The husband was holding something out to her. It was smaller than a paperback book but about as thick.

'What is it?'

'A portable hard drive. I, uh . . . '

His wife looked at the floor. 'Get on with it, Greg.'

'There are some pictures on it,' he said. 'Movies, too. Recorded from the site. I don't know whether it's any use but . . . '

His wife finished for him. 'We don't want it in the house.'

Nina took the disk. 'That's very helpful.'

Once it was out of his possession, the man's shoulders seemed to slump with relief. Nina realized that far from being an all-out disaster the evening might even work in his favour. A minor middle-class guilt, now blown into the open, fate taking the secret out of his hands. Sure, his wife would give him hell for it, and be hurt, and he was going to have to accept the role of house scumbag for a while. It would sure as hell Come Up In Conversation.

But it wasn't a secret any longer, and being able to throw open the windows of your dark private rooms can be worth quite a price. His wife wasn't going anywhere: they had this lovely life together and who the fuck wants to start dating again? A couple of months down the line this evening's embarrassment might even have been parlayed into a revivified sex life.

Some people just float.

'I didn't know she was dead,' he said. 'I'm sorry to hear about it.'

'The circumstances have not been widely reported, and we'd like to keep it that way.'

He nodded, looked away. His wife took a step back, as if unconsciously detaching herself from the evening, but then came forward with her husband to see Nina to the door: to see her off the premises, in effect — woman dealing direct with woman in a way men never really seemed to realize was going on. Saying things without saying, pushing without raising a hand.

As she walked down the path to the cars Nina made her own small side-step in her head, and slipped the disk into her pocket before it was visible to the men. Tomorrow it would join the rest of the evidence, such as it was.

Not tonight.

15

I got to Nina's mid-morning. The cab driver who dropped me off looked down at the house dubiously.

'You live here?'

'A friend of mine does.'

'Brave friend,' he said, and backed off up the road.

I walked down the vertiginous driveway that curved around to the front of the house. I had been to Nina's only once before, briefly and three months previously, sleeping on the sofa for a night after she, Zandt and I had returned Sarah Becker to her home and family. Nothing good seemed to have happened to the house's exterior since. The property was old school California Modern: a row of square rooms with a kink for the kitchen turning it into an L, like a very small motel. Possibly something of a big deal in the late 1950s, a kind of low-rent Case Study house, but from a stone's throw away you could tell its days were numbered.

I knocked on the door. 'It's open,' a voice said, from a distance. When I stepped inside I could see Nina out on her balcony, talking on the phone. She waved distractedly without looking at me.

I dropped my bag and hovered for a minute in the main living space. The space, anyway. It didn't look like much living had taken place there recently. It wasn't dusty, particularly, or markedly untidy, but that was because the room held virtually no personal possessions bar the racks of books and files on the long cases over on the other side. I walked into the kitchen area and opened the fridge: inside were two bottles of wine, a carton of orange juice and another of milk. Nothing else, and nothing in the cupboards either. Nina evidently subsisted on liquid fuel alone.

When I turned back to face the main area it somehow looked even quieter and more still. I had read once how in first millennium Britain the locals would use the long-abandoned remains of Roman villas and ruined churches for shelter on journeys across a land that was otherwise largely uninhabited. They called these places 'cold harbours', because while a night's protection from the elements could be found there, they harboured no other life or warmth. Nina's house felt like that, and I thought this as a man who had stayed nights in motels and factories with boarded-up windows and big demolition notices nailed to the walls.

'Hey, Ward.'

I looked over to see Nina was off the phone and standing in the doorway. Her hair was a little longer than it had been, and it seemed like she'd lost a few pounds from a frame that had always been slim. Something about her put me in mind of something, or someone, but I couldn't immediately work out what it was.

'Should call the cops,' I said. 'Someone's stolen all your food.'

'You didn't look hard enough. It's all stacked right where I need it. In the supermarket.'

'You have any coffee on site, at least? Or is Starbucks looking after that for you?'

It turned out she had lots.

★   ★   ★

'I've run most of the software I can,' I said, handing the disk back to her. 'And come up blank. There's a couple more pattern-searching things I can try, but they can leave traces, so I'll do them on the copy, if you've still got it. Bottom line is that whoever erased the disk did it well. It's very, very blank. I'm sorry. Sometimes there just isn't anything there.'

'Don't worry,' she said. She was leaning on the rail of her deck looking out across a hazy sea. 'I knew it was a long shot.'

'Are you any closer to finding the guy?' I had my chair as far back on the deck as I could, so as to marginally increase my chances of surviving when it all suddenly gave way.

'No. There are cops talking to the main users of her site. There aren't many, and none of them look good for it. We talked to the number one fan but I don't think there's anything there either. We have a very generic description of the guy she was seen with the night she died, we know now she waited tables sometimes and cops have talked to people where she worked, and that's it.'

'Who was she, anyway?'

Nina shook her head. 'Down from the Bay

238

Area. LAPD are still trying to trace family in Monterey. They have an address they believe is current but the parents seem to be on vacation. Her few known associates in LA seem to know nothing about her prior to meeting. You know what these people are like: yesterday was likely a bad day — so why not just have a beer and forget it? You should have met this Jean friend of Jessica's. They were big buddies, apparently — had the same first initial and everything, hung in the bar a lot, you know, like, super-best friends, rilly. Now she's dead, and with Jean it's like 'Bummer. Where's the next party?'' '

'Nice.'

'What do you expect? Jessica was a woman who lived in an apartment and got sad sometimes and drank too much and then died. That may be all we ever know.'

Her voice had died during the last few sentences, until it was barely more than a mumble.

'Nina, are you okay?'

She turned to me. Her eyes were green and bright. 'Sure I'm okay,' she said, more strongly. 'I just don't know the answer to your question. Who was she? You tell me. She had a name and a guitar. She lived, she died. Come Judgment Day, that's all that can be said of anyone.'

'A depressing world view, but anyway not what I meant. Was that John on the phone? You can drop the 'he's out buying groceries' line, by the way. I've already gathered you aren't an item any more.'

She opened her mouth, then closed it again.

239

I prompted. 'So where is he now?'

'I don't know,' she muttered. 'It took a day and a half of messages to get him to call me back, for which I get five minutes of evasion and then a dial tone. It's not like I'm fucking stalking him. We're over, and that's fine and dandy by me. I'm just worried. He's acting strange. Stranger than usual.'

'What happened with you guys?'

'You ask him the same question?'

'I did.'

'And he said?'

'Nothing intelligible.'

'Figures.' She looked resigned. 'It just didn't work out, Ward. Like the man said, maybe you can never go back, and it's not like we had so much to revisit. We had one thing in common — two, I guess: time spent together before Karen was murdered, and the fact neither of us are going to make the starting line-up for any All Star Relationship Squad.'

'Plus you're both kind of scary.'

She smiled properly for the first time since I'd turned up. 'Scary?'

'In a nice way.'

'Coming from a guy with scabs on his knuckles and a gun in his jacket, I'll take that as a compliment.'

I slipped my hands under the table. 'You're very observant. You should be in law enforcement or something.'

'Want to tell me about the fight?'

I didn't. Admitting to Nina what I'd done, or that I'd been nervous enough to do it, was not

240

something I wanted to get into right then. 'Guy kept asking me if I wanted fries. I just snapped. You know how it is.'

She shrugged. 'John was here for a few weeks. It kind of worked. We hung out, we took walks, we talked about my work — because, of course, he didn't have any. That's part of the problem. Maybe *the* problem. John was a very, very good detective. He has this insatiable urge to *find out*. But he couldn't go back to LAPD and he couldn't see anywhere else to go. Quite soon I started coming back from work and he wasn't here. He'd turn up after midnight. Wouldn't say what he'd been doing. Usually he'd been drinking, but that wasn't it. He just started shifting to the side. His head was somewhere else. Then suddenly he wasn't around for five days.'

'Where'd he go?'

'Florida. Where his ex-wife lives.'

I knew Zandt's marriage had broken up after the disappearance of their daughter. I also knew that he'd paid a visit to his wife after we'd found Karen's remains, eighteen months later; and I remembered him telling me the night before that killers weren't the only important things in life. 'He was there two days ago also.'

'I know. He sent me a text message.'

'You think he wants to get back with her?'

'I don't know. I don't think he does either. There's only one light in his head right now and that's finding the Upright Man. On everything else his wheels are spinning.'

'Funny. He told me exactly the opposite.'

'John lies.' She said this with a matter-of-fact bitterness, and thought better of it. 'Sometimes. He tells the truth sometimes too.'

'Well, his investigative skills are getting rusty, I'm afraid. All he has to show for his time since Yakima is some bizarre piece of non-information about the Roanoke colony in the late fifteen hundreds.'

'*What?*'

I filled her in on what I could remember of John's history lesson. She looked bleak by the time I was done, and we sat in silence for a while.

Eventually she stood. 'I have to get to work. You in a hurry to be elsewhere?'

I shrugged. 'I have nowhere in particular to go.'

'Good. I was going to ask you another favour.'

★   ★   ★

After she'd gone I made more coffee. It felt good to be in a house, even one as unhouselike as Nina's. In a house you don't have to be spending money or on your best behaviour the whole time. You can just sit around. It's not like that, out there in the world. But I found that having the opportunity to simply hang, unobserved and unbugged by other humans, made me feel a little weird. So I got onto Nina's request.

Before she left I'd copied all the files from the disk she'd been given by Greg McCain. The disk itself was now being taken into the care of the cops, along with the one from Jessica's head.

242

How she was going to explain the former's dog-legged journey I didn't know, and I didn't like the risks she was taking. She was the only one of us still latched into anything real world, and I got the sense she was drifting, like a plug slowly being drawn from a socket. I knew from experience that once this happens the shapes can subtly change, and you may find you don't fit back again. The huddled forms on every street corner and in each piss-reeking doorway show that the music of civilization stops often, and there are never quite enough chairs.

First thing I did was watch the movies. They weren't proper, full-motion video, but long sequences of stop frames blipping forward at intervals. There were six. Three showed Jessica having desultory, drunken sex with three different guys: twice on the couch that dominated her tiny living room, once on the bed. The frames were grainy and badly lit and in one case in almost total darkness. There was no attempt to play to the camera, the position of which remained static. It was like watching a Ken and a Barbie being banged together by a child who had no idea what the action was supposed to signify. Time-stamping on all three suggested they captured the very end of evenings spent in bars. One of the other videos showed a four-hour period in which the woman watched television, did some spring-cleaning, played the guitar briefly, and made a half-hearted attempt to put together a not very complicated shelving unit. For most of this period she was wearing a pair of orange shorts, and nothing else. Another

243

showed her sitting doing nothing, apparently in the aftermath of crying. The final video was stop motioned at much longer intervals, about five/ten minutes or so, and showed Jessica asleep on her couch, under a blanket, flicker-lit by the television out of frame. At the end she woke and sat watching it for a while with a cup of coffee. Nina had told me Jessica was in her late twenties. In the awake portion of this video, she looked about forty-five.

Then I worked through the stills. There were an awful lot of them. McCain had thrown them all into one big folder. I dropped this onto a graphics viewer and clicked through some examples at random. The images showed Jessica doing the same kind of things as the videos, but without the sex. Being naked or partially naked. Reading a magazine. Eating food. Sitting at a computer. Drinking coffee or Jack Daniel's. Sleeping. Smoking. Staring into space. The cumulative effect was strange, and I began to get a sense of Jessica's appeal to McCain. I was familiar with webcams myself, having spent some slow hours watching street corners in New Orleans, or the shore of Lake McDonald, or views out of computer stores on the main streets of nondescript towns in the Midwest. It had taken me a while to work out what I got from this. You didn't watch in the hope of seeing something exciting. Just the opposite. You watched because the very lack of discernible activity, of presented subject matter, made the view itself seem more real. If you watch something in particular, all you see is that thing

244

happening. You see the moment, the event, and you are distracted from the long, slow tide of eventlessness which it overlies. If you watch nothing, then you see everything. You see the thing as it is.

These myriad accidental views of Jessica achieved the same effect. Not a single image was composed. In many she was partly out of frame, or out of focus. The effect was to show nothing in particular, and thus to reveal everything. Your view of her life became similar to her own, an endless series of uninflected, unintended and ultimately quite tedious moments. McCain's Jessica collection brought home the reality of the woman more clearly than anything else I could imagine, capturing and celebritizing her in pixels. This was her fifteen megabytes of fame.

Having glimpsed her life before the event, only then did I look at the Polaroids Nina had left me. These showed Jessica's apartment on the day when the LAPD had found it. They too were flat, blank views, but they were not uninflected. Every square millimetre said something quite direct: their very existence announced that the girl who had lived in this place was dead, which is why I had wanted to see the others first.

I looked at them closely for a while. Then I went back to the beginning of the files on the hard disk, set the system to order them chronologically, and looked at them again.

It took a long time before I noticed something.

★   ★   ★

245

'See?'

Nina nodded. 'There's no picture that shows it better?'

'That's as good as it gets. I've blown it up but . . . ' I switched to a window I'd hidden behind the first. 'We don't live in a movie, and so the blow-up looks like shit.'

Nina leaned forward and stared at the picture on the screen. She was looking at a grainy and blocky picture that showed Jessica lying on her bed, from the chest up. A man's face was over hers.

Neither of us were interested in the man. LAPD moved fast: they already had print-outs of the three men featured in McCain's movies, and were showing them to Jessica's associates, starting in Jimmy's bar. The barman there had said none of them looked much like the guy he'd seen the girl with the night she died. These had been amongst the things Nina had achieved before returning to the house mid-afternoon. What we were looking at instead was Jessica's bedside table. This was visible in a gap between the blurred faces and chests of Jessica and her temporary new best friend. On the table was a lamp, a cheap-looking radio alarm, a small pile of books whose garish spines suggested they had self-help titles, three coffee cups, and a small picture frame.

Nina picked up the Polaroid which showed the bedroom, and peered at it. 'You're right,' she said. 'It's not there. And I didn't see anything like it in the apartment.' As soon as I'd noticed the discrepancy I'd called her with a description of the frame, and she'd stopped by Jessica's to look for it. 'When is this grab from?'

'Just less than a week before she died.'

'Assuming the date stamp is accurate.'

'It is. The creation date of the file confirms it.'

'A week. So she could have moved it somewhere herself in the meantime.'

'You couldn't find it. If a picture is important enough to keep by your bedside, you're not suddenly going to decide you don't want it in the house any more.'

'You could if it was an ex-boyfriend.'

'True. But look.' I switched to a third image, which showed only the frame on the bedside table. 'This is it blown up even more. I used interpolation software which basically looks at the colour value of each pixel, compares it to the ones surrounding it, and tries to make an intelligent guess at increasing the size of the image. It looks like shit when applied to a picture of this low quality, but it does show something interesting.' I pointed at the centre of the picture. 'You can't make out any features, but you've clearly got two heads there.'

'Exactly. Jessica plus a former guy.'

'I don't think so. What's the colour on top of both their heads?'

'Grey.'

'The hair colour of older people, in other words. Parents, perhaps.'

'You think?'

'Jessica may not have actually made it back home very often, but I'd have been very surprised if there wasn't a family picture in the

247

apartment somewhere. Nice photo of mom and dad, or if she had a problem with one or both, some idealized sibling or favourite niece. Some record of family. That's what girls are like.'

'Is that so? You found one here yet? Hidden amongst the sewing and the love letters to Justin Timberlake?'

'No,' I said. 'But I haven't looked hard. And you're not a girl.'

'Right. Just a scary woman.'

'Not just,' I said. 'But my point is that something is missing from Jessica's apartment.'

'You think the killer was there.'

'I do. And here's the proof.' I double-clicked on another file, one of the still images McCain had stored in the folder. It showed Jessica spark out on the couch in a somewhat inelegant pose. She was wearing floral pyjamas, pale blue, with little pink and white flowers. 'You said she was found . . . '

'That's them. Those are the pyjamas. Christ. You're right. He'd been there.'

'I think he had been closing in on her for a while — hunting her, as he probably thinks of it — and spent time in her space as part of the build-up to murdering her. He took the pyjamas and I think he also took a souvenir. He would have worked out that these were Jessica's family, and decided to take something that was close to her, something that mattered.'

'And she wouldn't have noticed?'

'Name me an object in this house that you look at every day. And look at the picture: the table is a mess. Also . . . '

'But what about the pjs? You'd notice if they were gone, surely.'

'Which is what I was about to say. He was most likely there during the day of the night before he killed her.'

'So why not just wait for her and kill her on home territory?'

'Because it was her home, not his. You know what these people are like. They want to sculpt the event. It has to happen on their terms.'

'Does this actually help us?'

'He found out where she lived. How? It means that on at least one occasion he could've been seen near her apartment. It means that he had to get in. Again, how?'

'LAPD have already canvassed the neighbourhood. Nobody saw anything.'

'But how did he find out where she lived?'

'Ward, you have very good eyes but you're not a cop. He probably just followed her home from a bar. I'm sorry, but even if you're right this doesn't give us anything more to go on. He took pyjamas and stole a picture. Maybe. Big deal. We'll put it right there on the warrant, just below the murder thing.'

I turned to her, irritable, but she looked tired and I put away what I'd been going to say. 'Funny you and John didn't make it work. What with you both being so reasonable and open-minded.'

She smiled. 'Look — I'll call it in.'

'Thank you,' I said. 'I feel validated beyond my wildest dreams. Now let's go liberate some of your food from the store.'

'Screw that. Let's go somewhere they'll cook it too.'

★   ★   ★

We ended up over in Santa Monica, eating at an Italian place on the Promenade. We ate for a short while, at least, and then moved back to the bar area for somewhat longer. Nina looked good with a glass of wine in her hand. It fitted like it was meant to be there. I told her what little I had done in the last few months, and as the wine kicked in I eventually told her how much I missed Bobby, and my parents, and she nodded and understood and didn't say anything to try to make it better. I realized I didn't know very much about her at all and found that she had grown up in Colorado, gone to college in LA, and not much else. She told me about some old girlfriend of hers who had called her and she was supposed to be meeting with, and we agreed that the past was another country and one which the movement of time's tectonic plates pulled further away every year. As it got to mid-evening the bar got more crowded, Nina glaring at people to keep them away from my seat during my occasional trips to smoke outside. With Nina, a glare is enough.

As I got more drunk the people around me seemed to get louder and more obnoxious. The chatter was of the movie business (of course), of money, of health and weight, of fashion. The more inconsequential the subject the louder they seemed to want to talk about it, an endless prayer to the gods of fate. I got more and more cranky until Nina was sitting silently while I ranted. Fashion makes me furious. It always has. This summer we're all going to be wearing vermilion, are we? Says *who*? When we see a bikini made of squares of brightly coloured plastic, why do we pretend anyone will wear it? *No one will ever wear it.* Ever. No one. So what was the point of the designer drawing it, showing it to other people, eliciting their ooh's and ah's? All of these activities took time and money, as did the marketing and the booking of hotels and equipment; all of it moved to and fro via the gas-guzzling limos and airports of the world until the action reached a beach somewhere exotic so an over-paid buffoon could photograph a skittish smack-head in a garment which *no one will ever actually wear.* The whole episode is a hypothetical. 'If you looked like this model (which you don't) and had the money to go on vacation to places like this (which you don't) and could further afford to pay a head-spinning amount for a swimsuit ($1000 — have you lost your fucking *mind*?) . . . then you might wear this — if it didn't look uncomfortable, modish and plain howling stupid (which it most certainly does).' This, I snarled at Nina, is what capitalism does to show off. It's our culture flopping out its dick. 'Hey, you shadows in the non-Western chaos — just *look* at our surplus capacity. If we can piss all this time and effort away on such useless, vacant crap, then just *imagine* the quantities of gold and guns and grain we must have stashed away, how well fed and happy the citizens of Our

251

World Inc. must be.'

Except they *aren't* all happy, and some of them aren't very well fed — and as time goes on, this fakery becomes all there is. But nobody knows or cares what happens behind the lifestyle billboards, because life for the people who matter just keeps getting better. The toddlers have taken over the asylum, and they're having everything made child-friendly to fit. They've turned smoky, cool coffee shops into places where the healthy go to iBook their Deep Thoughts; made fuggy, scary bars into places that look like airport lounges and feel like the Personnel Relaxation Facilities of futuristic megacorps. I was in a bar recently and it smelled of *incense*: how fucked up is that? Not smelling of smoke is bad enough, but *spiced lavender*? Inside is not supposed to be fresher than outside, can't they *see* that? The whole country is turning into a muffin-padded nest where the MBAs and soccer moms of America can sit reading books on how to love themselves more, as if that could be remotely *possible*. And they can't achieve this by setting up dedicated shrines for this ungodly self-absorption, they have to change all *my* places, the dirty and average and unexpected, so they're exactly the same.

Part of the problem, I went on — now easily as loud and obnoxious as the fashionistas and wannabe movie moguls — is that I could remember a world in which nobody ran. Can you imagine? Where the sight of average joes puffing along the street was bizarre and new and you wondered what on *earth* they thought they were doing. Now running is the new giving to charity. Running is the new wisdom, the absolute good: the modern ritual walkway to the gods' approval and beneficence. Run, and you will be successful; run and all will be well. If we were in charge of the Catholic Church then sainthood would be conferred strictly according to the time the candidate spent wearing Nikes. 'Yes, sure, Father Brian did good works and saved lives and stuff, but what were his splits on the mile? Father *Nate*? Forget it, dude. That guy never ran a half-marathon in his life.'

We have lost all sense of proportion, of what is important or reasonable or sane: while around the world the countries which don't have the time or luxury for this *bullshit* are getting ever more pissed at us for behaving like we own the whole playground. But who cares, right? Here's another dumb movie about wacky teens! A great new diet is racing up the charts! J-Lo got herself some new bling — just look how damned pretty it is! Who gives a crap what's happening in dusty shit-holes where they don't even speak American? Life's great! Crack open a decaf Zinfandel! I ran out of steam and drink at exactly the same time. Young people on nearby tables were staring at me as if I'd declared the three-act structure null and void.

'Fuck you,' I suggested, loudly. Everyone turned away.

Even Nina was looking at me, one eyebrow raised. 'The Prozac really just isn't cutting it, is it?'

'The world is fucked,' I muttered, embarrassed. 'Everyone in it is fucked too. Roll on Armageddon.'

'Yeah, I can remember what it was like being fifteen,' she said. 'Don't fret. It will pass.' She stood. 'Come on, Ward. I'm drunk. You're loaded. It's time to go home.'

I saw the credit slip on the table and realized that, somewhere in the last fifteen minutes, she'd paid our tab.

I slid off my stool and followed her out of the restaurant, feeling foolish. That, and something else.

★   ★   ★

By the time we'd located a cab and ridden it back to Nina's house the wine in my system had tipped over and started making me feel weary and worn out. Most of the journey had been in silence, though not an uncomfortable one. I made a big thing about paying for the ride and then stumbled wildly getting out of the car. Maybe Nina was right. Boys achieve a degree of timelessness: didn't matter how ancient my body sometimes felt, fifteen seemed a glass ceiling for my level of sophistication.

When we got inside I headed straight for the coffee machine. Doing so took me past Nina's answer phone.

'You got a message,' I said.

Nina touched a button and looked at the number it flashed up. 'It's Monroe.'

The message was short. A man's voice

brusquely told Nina to call him whatever time she got back. She rolled her eyes, but immediately hit a button that returned the call.

'Charles Monroe's office.' The voice came out of the speakerphone loud and clear.

'It's Nina Baynam,' Nina said, rubbing her eyes. 'I got a message.'

The person on the end didn't answer, but no more than three seconds later the voice of Nina's boss came on the line.

'Nina, where the hell have you been?'

'Out,' she said, evidently surprised at his tone. 'Why didn't you call my cell?'

'I did. Three times.'

'Oh. Well, I was somewhere loud.' She looked pointedly at me as she said this. 'What's the problem?'

'I've just had a phone call from the SAC in Portland.'

Nina immediately looked more serious. 'Another killing?'

'Yes, and no. Not another hard disk. Not another girl.'

'Well, then what?'

When Monroe spoke again, it was carefully and slowly. 'A prostitute named Denise Terrell — working name Cherri — walked into a police station there the night before last. She was disoriented. She claimed she'd been on an afternoon out-call and 'something happened'. Next thing she knew it was night and she woke up propped against a dumpster. Eventually they worked out she had serious concussion and took her to a hospital. The next morning she had

255

remembered some more and started saying she'd been booked to one of her agency's regular clients but had struck a deal with another man, who somehow knew they had dealings with this particular john. This man had contacted her direct and offered her money in exchange for her letting him know when and where the meeting was going to take place. Said the guy owed him a lot of money and he wanted to catch him somewhere private, when his guard was down. The girl agreed.'

'Charles, is there a bottom line here?'

'The Portland cops went to the address she supplied. They found a dead man. His name was Peter Ferillo. He owned a restaurant and used to have ties to organized crime down here in LA. He was naked and messed up and had been shot in the head and left sprawled in a chair. They dusted the room floor to ceiling but found nothing. But then a patrol officer found something in a flowerbed thirty yards up the street. It was a bottle opener, with traces of blood on it. Ferillo's blood. They got a print off it. A good, full print. They matched it.'

The wine in my system seemed to have disappeared. Nina and I were staring at each other.

'Nina,' Monroe said, 'the print belongs to John Zandt.'

16

As he drove, he was conscious of the web around him. The web of streets, of people, of places and of things. The other web, too, the new world. This parallel place, with its email address private driveways, its dotcom marketplaces. You could find out *so much* there, running reality through your hands like a god. Everything on the web is information; but everything is on the web, these days; so the world has become information. Everything has become an utterance of this thing, of this bank of words and images: everything is something it is saying, or has said. It's about buying, and looking, about our habits and desires, about contact with others, about voyeurism and aspiration and addiction. It is us boiled down; our essence, for better or worse. It is no longer passive. It is telling the story of us, and sometimes that story needs work. Sometimes things need to be taken out. Finding Jessica there had been the new beginning. Of course there are many Jessicas; but there was also only one. Once found, you could open the window into her life, confirm her existence; but you could shut it also. You could close the program down, make it unborn. You could quit and reboot, and then the past was gone and everything was clean. The DELETE key is there for a reason. Sometimes you just have to start fresh.

One of his favourite series of webcam pictures was of Pittsburgh, a city to which he had never been. The series consisted of three shots covering the period from 5.43 to 6.14, one morning in late May of 2003. All were taken from the same camera, though one which altered its direction and degree of zoom between shots, rather than giving one constant view. In the first picture the dawn sky took up the top half of the frame, all blue and red and swirled with epic cloud. Below, the Allegheny River curled up left from the centre, the 6th, 7th and 9th Street bridges and their lights reflected back up from the dark mirror water below. Everywhere, down the streets, along both sides of the river and in a circle around the fountain and pool at the end of Point State Park and the Gateway Center, there were more lights. Little points of white, made golden or rosy by the fading darkness and the limitations of the webcam. The second shot was much closer range, and in the intervening quarter-hour the camera had zoomed heavily and pivoted in an entirely different direction. It was impossible to tell how this little section fitted into the city as a whole. The frame was largely filled with trees, a glimpse of a curved highway cutting through them into the city, a few early birds on their way to work. In the final picture you were back out on the confluence of the rivers, and in wide shot. The angle was slightly different from the first. You were turned a little to the south and looking up the Monongahela just as it joined the Allegheny, the Fort Pitt Bridge still dark. There were no points of light anywhere now — either the city turned them off at six sharp, every single one, or dealing with a now brighter stretch of sky had caused the webcam to over-compensate in all the terrestrial areas.

He had spent time studying these images, understanding what the web was saying about the people it watched. It showed you could live in a city, be one of its inhabitants, without comprehending or being part of its wider picture. Like mice living in a human house: it was their address, but that didn't mean they had rights, that they had to be viewed with anything more than benign amusement, that they weren't fair game for cats or traps. Similarly, you could sit in a restaurant all day without ever becoming more than just some guy temporarily taking up space which belonged to someone else, space you hired by handing over money for coffee and burgers. Even if you had your nice house in the suburbs you paid tithes in every direction; you chipped away at the loan you took to buy the property, you hacked at the vig for your son's dentistry and the money pit of your daughter's someday wedding, you paid the insurance that might cover your parents' tumour care but wouldn't save their life. You took your days and handed them over to other people, who did things with them, who made stuff with your days, who sold their products with your life. Your days, your time, were their secret ingredient, their twelfth herb or spice; your life was given away free in the bottom of their packets like invisible jack-in-the-box treats. In return they helped you pay off some of your debts to the banks and the hospitals and fate: and so you went back and forth, every day, riding the rail between your house and your place of work, driving in a machine you were paying off in instalments and which someone would tow off your driveway, no matter how manicured, within days of a payment not being made.

You kept doing this until you got old and your life started running in reverse, and you went from having a whole house to just a room in one of your children's houses, assuming they'd take you; and finally to a stranger's building, some rest home, surrounded by old geezers you'd never met before and might not have liked even if you had: the young don't understand that the physical similarities of old people do not mean they're the same inside. They don't all got rhythm either, as it happens. Even more acutely than failing health, this progression makes it bluntly clear that life is going in very much the wrong direction. All that time spent owning a house, all those loans and aspirations, are erased, wiped off the disk of your life. It lifted gently out of your hands like a kitchen knife taken from someone too young. The things you acquired and which have helped define you are given or sold or thrown away, and you are squeezed again into a little room, as if you were twelve once more — but this time, instead of feeling at one with the outside world, by now the whole thing has long ago stopped making sense. You sit in quiet places and look out of windows and try not to panic as you notice both how much you are forgetting these days, and how little of value there is to forget. The layers of self you spent decades accreting are dissolved, reducing you once again to dependence, and there's no kidding yourself that this is a mere stage to be got through, that your time lies ahead. It doesn't. You've had your time. Your time has been and gone. Now you are merely colour in the background of someone else's time, and even that probably won't be for long.

Meanwhile other people now drive your freeway to and from work, and live in your old house, and repaint the walls and tear down your shelves, and the planet spins.

★ ★ ★

One day, after a particularly arduous trip to and from the john, when she was settled back in her chair and looking exhausted and small and ashamed, his grandmother had looked at the boy and said:

'It's a pity He puts the worst bit at the end.'

He hadn't understood immediately, but had done seven months later when he sat quietly behind one of the chairs in the living room, two hours after coming back from Grandma's funeral. He had been sitting there a while, thinking about the old lady, when his mother came into the room holding a record. She went over to the player, turned it on, and then sat in a chair and listened.

He was severely freaked. He didn't know what to do. He knew this was a private moment of his

261

mother's and she would not take at all well to finding she was not alone. He knew this especially when he heard something that might have been his mother crying. He had never heard his mother cry before. He never heard it again.

So he just sat, and listened.

His mother sat through the recording once, from start to finish. Then she got up, wrenched the record off the player and threw it viciously into a corner, where it smashed into many pieces.

She stormed out. The front door slammed.

When she was safely external he cautiously emerged from behind the chair. His body told him to get the hell gone from the room, go upstairs, go out, do something, but his mind said his mother was halfway to a bar already and it wanted to know what the music had been. The mind won.

He stepped over to the record player to look at the sleeve. It was Fauré's Requiem, and he recognized it from Grandma's room, one of the few possessions she'd brought to their house. The sleeve was old and battered, and it looked like the record had been pulled out and replaced a great many times, back in her real life, when she got to choose what music was played within her hearing. Perhaps it was this that made him go over to the corner, pick up one of the biggest fragments of the shattered disc, and take it with him back up to his bedroom: a realization that there would come a time when he would be controlled by others once more, and that the time in between was all he had.

He was twelve years old. Four years later, Fauré's Requiem was the first album he bought. By his late teens it was already something he played only privately. Fauré was one of those composers, he had learned, who was a little *too* well known. It was like putting on Vivaldi's Four Seasons, or Beethoven's Fifth or Bach's Air on a G String. You wound up looking ignorant no matter how much you actually liked it, because you were surrounded by people who valued ideas — including the idea that they were clever and unusual and not just part of the common mass — rather than experience. People who thought it was better to admire something than to actually like it, who either lived a life of constant fragility, or indulged themselves in private.

People who did not have the courage to realize that if they acted powerfully enough, they could tip the planet.

It was not long before he left those people, all people, far behind, when he found the smoking road. Listening to his mother, and hearing those strange, ugly/beautiful sounds coming from inside her, that had been real. That had been something that was *happening*, a real-time incident, a change in the world's colour as his grandmother's death scraped its indelible mark on reality. It had been like a glimpse of a distant lake or sleeping girl or grubby street corner, frank and vulnerable in its simple truth.

Death is real. Death changes things. Everything else is filler; merely a message from our sponsor.

The old woman's death said something,

especially as he knew the fall which had finally killed the old lady had not been purely accidental. She was being helped down the stairs, after all, and he had heard her say 'No' urgently, once, just before she fell.

But then everything was quiet for her, and she no longer cried out in the night or soiled herself, and her ragged breathing was no more. She was put in the ground and slept easily, and she must surely have known, in some way or another, that her daughter had cried for her after she was gone.

The worst bit didn't have to be at the end, that much was clear. It didn't have to be quiet and pointless. So long as there was someone there who cared, the end didn't have to be so bad at all.

So why wait?

★   ★   ★

When he got to the city he parked. He walked some distance to his destination. He kept on the move, because movement was best. Even now, this part of the process was strange and ungovernable, and a lesser man might have entertained the idea this was because the impulse was coming from somewhere other than his conscious mind. Not him. He knew it all made sense, that sometimes this was what we are for.

He walked. He waited for the night. He waited so that someone else special would no longer have to wait. He was actually doing it for his own reasons, of course, and for wider-reaching benefits, but that didn't stop it being the right thing for her too. Everything would be fresh, and all would be quiet.

It was truly a no-lose situation.

17

The elevator opened. Burt was standing inside. He grinned and stood back to let Katelyn in, then realized he had to get out with his big cart and that this had to happen first regardless of the dictates of his code of chivalry. He hesitated, went back and forward an inch or two, then rolled his eyes and shrugged. This, or something like it, happened pretty much every night.

He apologetically clanked his way out and then turned back to hold the doors open. 'Fetching the menus, Ma'am?'

'That's right, Burt. How's your night?'

'Getting it done.'

Burt was the Seattle Fairview's only black employee apart from the much celebrated Big Ron, the daytime concierge. Katelyn liked Burt. He was twice as old as anyone else on the payroll and worked twice as hard, even at gone three in the morning. If you saw Burt, he'd be doing something. The idea of him at rest was absurd.

Reassured that she was safely in the elevator, he winked and trundled off, on his way to fix something or re-attach something or scrape something off. Katelyn watched him as the doors closed. He was a night toiler too, and something told her he felt the same as she did, the same sense of being in a special position. She'd never asked because, well, you just didn't.

Or was that too simple? Did she believe such

an observation lay outside the terms of their working relationship, and if so, why? Did it say something bad about her? Was hierarchy more important to her than she'd thought? Or was she patronizing him without realizing it, not taking him seriously because he was old or . . .

Christ, it was too late now.

★   ★   ★

This was not a job for the night manager, she knew. Some hotels left it to the bell boy, a final errand before he knocked off; or, if there was 24/7 room service, sometimes the overnight cook would put the machine on in the dead zone around four a.m. and fetch them himself, most likely wandering the corridors with his pants down, judging by the night cooks she'd met. One place had asked for the menus to be hung on the door by six, rather than two, and there it had been the first job of the day for the service staff who'd later be running those same breakfasts upstairs. That seemed wrong to her. You might think breakfast was the first event of the new day, but it wasn't. Not for the guests. It was the last thing. They returned from evenings in an unfamiliar city, mid-evening and surly or late and politely shit-faced — guessing which was half of the fun. Katelyn liked to imagine them sprawled hiccupping across the bed, gripping a complimentary biro, brows furrowed with lonely concentration, ticking and annotating. When you were on vacation, or away on business, the arrival of breakfast was of existential significance.

It reminded you who you were — or who you'd thought you were, at least, at midnight and full up to the ears with wine.

So Katelyn believed. She'd tried explaining this to one of the guys on reception and he'd looked at her like she was speaking Mandarin. A few of them treated her like that whatever she said. Night managers were rarely women. Something to do with their responsibilities, maybe, the fact they had to deal with strange doings in the night — explaining to non-guests that you didn't run a cab service to the suburbs; dissuading goggle-eyed businessmen from bringing back women who were too obviously whores; finding someone to clear up the vomit in the middle elevator. (People always threw up in the middle one. Nobody knew why. Not even Burt.) Most night managers weren't on an upward track. They came on at nine, or whenever the particular hotel deemed the real action to have died down, installed themselves in the back office and drank coffee. If they were lucky, they'd continue doing that until the sun came up, taking a minute every now and then to check that the downtime maintenance and cleaning and restocking was getting done by people paid half as much as they were. If fire-fighting was required they'd boss people around until the problem had gone away, been forgotten or superseded, then go back to flipping through magazines. At dawn they faded like the dew, back to their apartment or little house, to sleep out the day like chubby vampires.

Katelyn was different. As the elevator rose in

the night, the reflection in its wraparound mirrors reassured her she was young, female and attractive. Okay, not young. Scrub that. She had good skin, though, and hair that needed little pampering. She looked businesslike in her charcoal suit. She didn't have to be here. Shouldn't be, perhaps. You could enter hotel management without any experience whatsoever, but she had worked for enough flip-chart generals to know that bullet points were no match for time spent on the ground. During the day a hotel seemed like a huge engine, driven by internal principle. Sure, as soon as you got the other side of the reception desk, once you'd stepped behind a few of those doors marked 'Private', you realized that wasn't quite the case. You understood that a hotel was the head-on collision of a zillion different 'To Do' lists getting done at variable rates; that it was a flesh-and-stone computer running seventeen competing pieces of software (some new and can-do, some old and bug-ridden and leaking memory all over the place), and that a full-scale crash was always just around the corner. There was a momentum, nonetheless, the sense of an ecosystem rubbing along together, a relay team running an endless race.

At night it was different. The software went to standby and you became more aware of the hard fixtures: the desks, the chairs, the wall lamps, providing rest and shedding light for no one but themselves. The elevators which might take it upon themselves to travel up and down, for no obvious reason, clanking and hissing in the small hours. Most of all, of the building itself, its long corridors and massive haunches, suffused with the white noise of downtime. Hotels see a lot of life. Hotels get kicked around. The action the average city hotel sees would give a normal house a nervous breakdown in a day. In the small hours the building has some time to itself, to think its big, slow thoughts. To wander the halls then was to sit down with some big brick animal in darkness and listen to it breathing at rest.

And maybe that's why most night managers weren't women. Katelyn knew she should have been at home, asleep, or listening to another human's breath. A cat didn't count, no matter how much she loved him. It needed to be a child's breathing, or at least a man's. You could listen all you liked in her apartment, but you wouldn't hear either. She should stop kidding herself.

That's why she was here.

★   ★   ★

The doors opened on the sixth floor and she strode out like a night manager should. Six wasn't so many floors, but it was all The Fairview had. Katelyn had been through this recently with a disgruntled guest, who'd been expecting the kind of vista he'd had at one of the sister hotels in the same small chain up in Vancouver. The Bayside there had twenty-two floors and superb views across Burrard Bay to the mountains — Katelyn knew this, having been there on an orientation course. There were hotels in Seattle with more extravagant views, but none with the same boutique attention to individual quality of service. The man glared at her, knowing he'd been volleyed with brochure-speak, but seemed happy enough when he left. Bit of a nut in any case: had the fruit plate with sausage patties on the side, both mornings, which spoke of conflicted desires.

The air was still and warm. She walked the silent, carpet-padded corridors, following three sides of a small square. Up, across, down. There weren't many menus. Weekends at this time of year were quiet. There was a tourist couple down on five — having seen them stagger home after midnight, Katelyn was interested to see what they'd ordered — but mostly it was business folk. These would be up early and sucking down the free Starbucks and croissants provided in the lobby between seven and half past eight. The whole floor yielded only twelve orders, mainly for the hotel's idiosyncratic version of a two-eggs breakfast. Nothing much of interest, though there was a request for the steel-cut oats which made her smile. The guest in question was a big guy. Oats wasn't what he wanted. He was being good. His wife would have been proud — assuming she believed him, assuming it ever even came up, which it wouldn't except in the context of a conversation he was destined to lose. He should just have had the big breakfast, like he wanted. Still, good for him.

At the end of the floor she glanced back to check she hadn't missed anything, and then opened the door to the stairs. The rich carpet

271

stopped just the other side of this door, a cost-cutting manoeuvre which she approved of.

She was making the stairs' halfway turn when she heard a noise above. She looked up, ready to smile, assuming it was Burt come to do something in the well.

There was no one there.

Odd. The sound couldn't be from below, because she could see the door to floor five. She peered over the rail. No movement down there either.

Whatever. Hotels made noises. Probably one of the cleaning staff coming on duty. Though — she checked her watch — at quarter after three, that couldn't be right.

She opened the door at the bottom of the flight, half expecting to see Burt clanking by and thinking maybe she'd say something to him. Something friendly, to show there would be no ageism, racism or hierarchy-dictated interaction on her watch.

The corridor was empty.

Oh well. Burt would never know what he missed.

Floor five was slow going too. A few toast and coffees, but — aha. Eggs, sausage, bacon, extra sausage(?), hash browns, oats, fruit, coffee *and* tea for what looks like, what, four? And a continental breakfast with toast. And an English muffin, probably. Could be *more* toast. Or bacon. And an orange juice. Delivered at seven thirty.

Katelyn smiled: that would be the drunk tourists. She pulled a pen out of her jacket pocket and made a few alterations, judiciously reducing their order to something that wouldn't scare the hell out of them when it arrived. She also nudged delivery back to seven forty-five. They'd thank her for it.

She walked on. More toast, more eggs. She tried to remember the last time she'd been on vacation herself. It had been a while, that was for sure, back before her parents died, which made it five years. Funny what you remembered. Snapshots of views. A favourite coffee place, reading a trashy novel. Some trinket lusted over, bought, now lying forgotten in a drawer. Vacation sex. Boys now men, just as she was now presumably a woman. Anyone over forty who thought of herself as a girl was kidding herself, whatever was implied by magazines that funded themselves through adverts for anti-wrinkle creams.

There was the sound of a door opening.

She turned. 'Burt?'

No reply. She'd kept her voice low — nobody wanted waking at this time — but he'd have heard, and responded.

A guest, maybe?

She added the tourists' menu to the bottom of her stack and walked back the way she'd come. When she passed the door to the stairs she noticed it was open. Not wide, but propped on the latch.

She hadn't left it that way. You had to close it. Fire regulations were strict on the subject, and there was a sign which said so very clearly. Burt knew about them too. Strange time to be using

273

the stairs, in any event.

She pushed the door further ajar, and said 'Hello?'

The sound echoed down the staircase, but didn't seem to meet anyone either going down or coming back. Just another sound in her own head. Except . . .

She turned quickly.

The corridor was empty behind her. Of course it was. But it felt like it hadn't been so a moment before.

That was kind of creepy. Burt wouldn't do that. A late guest wouldn't do it either.

There was only one way someone could have gone. Katelyn walked quickly back across the foyer, passing the elevators. A glance at the floor indicator showed they were all down in the basement. Which left . . .

She looked down the other corridor.

Empty. Pairs of doors, leading away. Silent as it should be.

But then she heard a click. Very quiet, from down the end.

So probably a *very* late guest. Came up the stairs for reasons of their own, let themselves into their room. Elevator phobic. That's it. No big drama.

Except . . . something didn't feel right.

The guest had to pass right behind her — which she'd felt. Wasn't it bizarre not to say hello, even if you were drunk, embarrassed at not being cool in front of the staff?

Unless you weren't supposed to be here at all.

It happened all the time. The hotel doors were

open all day and half the night. You walked in, nodded confidently at the desk, nobody gave you trouble. At the right time of afternoon or evening you could take as long as you liked to get into a few rooms.

Katelyn had two choices. Go downstairs, pick up the radio she should have had with her — damn it — and get hold of Burt, or else galvanize the useless security guy who spent the night lurking in the basement jerking off. Burt, preferably, who wouldn't look at her as if asking what she was doing being night manager if she needed her hand held after dark. He wouldn't say it, or possibly even think it. But other people would, if they heard about it.

Which led to choice two.

She turned from the elevators and set off down the corridor. Feeling very calm, business-like and relaxed, she picked up a couple of menus on the way. Continentals.

Behind her she heard the sound of one of the elevators in movement.

She stopped, looked back, hoping that it might halt at the floor and the doors open, that another employee would happen to arrive. If so, she'd call them over on some pretext or other.

The doors didn't open. She shook her head, irritated. This was her hotel. She wasn't going to be spooked.

Another menu. A few more blanks. Another menu.

She stopped in mid-stride, turned back.

Strange. The door of room 511 didn't have a

275

menu. But it did have a 'Please Make Up My Room Now' sign.

That didn't make sense. Who puts that up before they go to bed?

She gave the door a gentle push. It opened a couple of inches.

It was dark inside. Odd again. The door should have been locked, of course, self-locking doors being basic security in a modern hotel. Not to mention it having a latch, which at the very least should have kept it closed.

She rapped on it, quietly. There was no response.

She didn't know if the room was supposed to be occupied. Along with her radio she should have brought up a list. She'd never seen the point. People either wanted breakfast or they didn't. What was she going to do: wake them up to see if they'd forgotten?

She reached inside the door and flipped the light switch. Nothing happened. Ah. Suddenly this was looking more explicable. Obviously there was a problem with Room 511, circuits burned out or something. It happened. The sign was on the door was most likely there to remind someone to get on to fixing it.

But why hadn't she been told? This was exactly the kind of thing that should be on her schedule. If people didn't take her seriously how the hell was she supposed to do her job?

Katelyn's mouth set in a tight straight line. Not being taken seriously was something she absolutely couldn't bear.

She pushed the door open further and took a

step into the dark interior corridor. Stood and listened. Couldn't hear anything.

She walked into the room. It was stuffy. The air around her seemed to ebb and flow, stirred tidally with the breath of all those sleeping around her. Normally street and ambient light would have kept it light enough to make out shapes easily, but the drapes at the far end had been left drawn. She could make out that the bed was empty and unused, but little more than that.

She felt her way over to the desk and tried turning on the light.

It didn't work either. Okay, so the power was definitely screwed. She didn't really understand how that could happen in one room alone, but . . .

Suddenly the room seemed darker still, and there was a soft click. She turned. The rectangle of yellow light from the corridor had disappeared.

She heard something that might have been the sound of feet on carpet. She took a step back, banged into the edge of the desk.

She swallowed. 'Is someone there?'

He didn't answer, but there was. He stepped out of the deepest shadow, face a softness in the sparkling gloom.

Katelyn tried to move backwards, but there was nowhere to go. He took another smooth step towards her, and she caught a glint down by his hand.

She gathered herself to scream, but just then his face passed through a dim beam of filtered light, a cloud coming out from behind another, darker cloud. Something about his features stopped her mouth, and she stared at him.

'No,' he said firmly. 'You don't know me. Nobody does.'

And then he came at her, up through time, with a speed nothing could have stopped.

★ ★ ★

Nobody got their eggs or toast or steel-cut oats on time the next morning. There were a lot of complaints, especially from the top two floors, where the menus had inexplicably disappeared. It was early afternoon before a guest checked into Room 511 and found menus spread over the floor of a room that was otherwise empty, and where the lights didn't work.

The hotel kept the disappearance as quiet as it could. The police questioned Burt first, of course, but he was as bewildered as anyone and more upset than most. He'd liked Miss Katelyn. Last night he'd nearly said something when they met at the elevator, tried to say 'hi' in a way that was a bit more personal, case she thought he was being standoffish or something just 'cause she was the boss or white or something. Now she was gone. Most people seemed to think she'd just wigged out and would be back in a few days with her tail between her legs. A lady night manager meant 'no one back at home', so they said, and women like that were all one stop from the funny farm or Prozac Beach.

278

Burt knew Miss Katelyn wasn't like that, and when the elevator doors opened the following night and she wasn't standing there, he believed she was gone forever, and gone nowhere good.

18

When Nina woke at just before five she knew there was no point trying to sleep again. She and Ward had been up for two hours after Monroe's call, trying to work out what it meant and what it didn't mean. So far as she could see, it could be only one thing. Somehow, somewhere, Zandt had managed to tread heavily on the toes of someone close to the Straw Men. They hadn't been able to get to him direct, so they'd set him up. She'd tried throughout the night to get hold of him. His phone was turned off.

Ward had sobered up quickly, and in the end made a suggestion she knew she had to take seriously. She had to get Monroe somewhere private, and tell him some things. Not on the phone. Face to face. If she was going to try to convince him that there was a group of men and women operating behind the face of what most people understood as America, that they killed and lied and now had her ex-lover in their sights, they were going to have to be in the same room to do it. It probably should have been done three months ago, but — racked with paranoia and with several deaths on their hands — none of them had believed it the right thing to do.

Right now, that seemed like a mistake.

She drank five cups of coffee, working out what she was going to say. How much could be revealed about what had happened up at The

Halls, without putting any of them in jail. She waited until seven, when she knew that he would be awake and on his feet. If she could catch him before he left for work, perhaps they could meet. She was walking over to the phone when it rang.

It was Monroe. He was already in the office. He instructed her to meet him there immediately, and he didn't sound like someone she could tell anything at all.

★   ★   ★

He was waiting for her outside the elevator on the sixth floor. His face looked like stone.

'Charles,' she said, quickly. 'I need to talk to you.'

He shook his head curtly and turned to walk down the corridor. A little way along he threw open a door and stood back, waiting for her. She made up the distance hurriedly, stepped inside.

Room 623 was the kind of anonymous corporate space which exists in every good-sized company in America. Under business conditions it says 'Look: we can afford the best stuff out of the catalogue. We're not afraid of you.' What it was supposed to convey in law enforcement Nina had no idea. A large wooden table loomed in the middle, polished to a high reddish gloss and surrounded by the most expensive and least used chairs in the building. One wall of windows looked down over the back parking lot; the others were panelled to waist height but otherwise bare. There was a poorly framed

281

photograph of someone receiving a commendation, not recently, and nothing else.

A man in a dark suit sat in a chair that had been positioned so that it stuck out from the top left corner of the table. He was above average height and had the kind of skin which makes a man of a certain age look like he's been injection-moulded in very hard plastic. His hair was neatly cut. His eyes were a flat, pale blue. His lashes were long. He was not wearing a tie and everything about his shirt said this was because he didn't have to. He was in his mid fifties. Despite being put together with due regard for all the conventional aesthetic beats, Nina thought he was one of the most unmemorable-looking men she'd ever seen. Nothing specifically said he wasn't an agent, but he wasn't. He certainly wasn't the SAC from Portland, whom she'd met.

'Good morning,' she said, holding out her hand.

He didn't shake. He neither introduced himself nor smiled. Nina left her hand in place for five seconds, then dropped it. She stood her ground a few moments more, giving him the chance to stop being an asshole. He didn't take it. She held his gaze as long as felt necessary, then looked away.

She could play that game. 'Whatever,' she said.

'Sit down and be quiet,' Monroe snapped. 'You're here to listen. You're asked a direct question then you may and should answer it. Otherwise zip it. Understood?'

Nina knew then that something was badly

wrong. Monroe had faults. He had a tendency to think he was smarter than he was, and to believe that criminals — and other agents — would respond to the same management techniques as appliance salesmen. But he was above all else professional, and yet his tone spoke of anger and personal grievance.

He was still staring at her. 'Understood?'

'Sure,' she said, spreading her hands. 'What's . . . '

'The Sarah Becker case,' he said, and Nina's heart sank further. Even though this related to what she needed to tell him, this was not the way it could happen. Not in front of someone else, and especially not in front of the guy in the corner. Why not sit on one side or the other, incidentally? He had made himself impossible to ignore and yet Monroe had not introduced him. He seemed unwilling to even acknowledge his presence. It was as if there was a ghost at the end of the table, one Nina could see and he could not.

'Okay', she said. Monroe opened his folder. There were neat notes on the paper within, but he didn't refer to them.

'The Becker family claims their daughter simply turned up on their doorstep,' he said. 'Out of the blue, after being missing for a week. Says she was released near her abduction location, which she claims was in Santa Monica, and walked home by herself. A neighbour says otherwise, claims she saw the girl brought to the Beckers' doorstep by a man and a woman and that a car driven by a third man waited for them

283

across the street. This neighbour is elderly and I wouldn't normally be interested except that a teenage girl of Sarah's description and condition received emergency treatment at a hospital in Salt Lake City the night before. She was admitted at the same time as a woman who was suffering from a gunshot wound to the upper right side of her chest. Both patients disappeared early the next morning. And all this at pretty much exactly the time that you sustained just such an injury, apparently in a hunting accident in Montana.'

Nina's head hurt and her heart felt as heavy as stone. She shrugged, knowing she was not going to be able to tell Monroe anything at all. Not now, not ever.

'The hospital sighting engages my interest,' he continued, 'because between there and a town called Dyersburg in Montana — the town near to which you flew, only the night before — used to be a development called The Halls, now a hole in the ground that everyone from the local cops to the NSA would like to have explained. The cops are particularly interested because they have a missing officer, a dead realtor, and two other unexplained fatalities.'

Nina said nothing. Monroe stared at her. The man in the corner looked at her too. Finally it had begun to piss her off.

She turned to him and asked: 'Who are you, exactly?'

The man gazed back at her as if she was the vacation roster for a company he didn't work for.

When she looked back, Monroe's eyes were

cold. 'You think I'm an idiot, Nina? Is that what it is?'

'No, Charles, of course not,' she said. 'This is old ground. I don't know anything more about Sarah Becker's return than you do.' He kept silent, forcing her to continue. 'I was in Montana visiting John, as I said at the time and several times since.'

'Right,' he said, blankly affable, and Nina began to feel even more disconcerted. Something about his abrupt switch in tone made her understand there was more going on than she'd realized, and that she was about to find out what it was.

It wasn't Monroe who spoke next. It was Corner Man. His voice was dry and unaccented, somewhat nasal.

'This would be John Zandt, correct?'

'Yes.' Nina kept her eyes on Monroe, bleakly realizing that her boss might be more subtle than she'd thought. He'd just fed her to this guy. He didn't appear discomfited by her gaze.

'The former Los Angeles homicide detective now connected to a murder in Portland. Whose daughter was abducted in May 2000, and never found. Who left the police force and disappeared, before re-emerging three months ago as, I understand, your lover.'

'A situation which is no longer the case. And in what sense would this be any of your business?'

The pause she left before this question had been supposed to make her sound strong. Even she heard it as evasive. It didn't matter much

285

because she had evidently become inaudible. Neither of the men said anything.

She looked at Monroe, fighting to keep her voice calm. 'Is that what this is about? A slap on the wrist three years overdue? I kept John informed on the Delivery Boy case, which I shouldn't have done. You know this already. You know that I felt he deserved to know what we knew because his *daughter* was missing — and because he'd previously helped us nail a man who was killing black kids when we were getting nowhere at all and the media were kicking us all over town. You explained how my actions breached Bureau protocol and your own ideas of compartmentalization and you've never treated me quite the same since. I screwed up. I got the message. I thought we were done with it. Let's move on.'

Monroe glanced out of the window.

'We're not here to move on, Ms Baynam,' the Corner Man said. 'We're here to go back.'

'What the fuck are you talking about?'

'Nina . . . '

'Screw you, Charles. I'm tired of this. I don't know who the hell this guy is or why he thinks he's got the right to talk to me this way.'

Monroe pulled a briefcase onto the table, from which he slipped a standard-issue laptop. He opened it and angled the screen towards Nina. Neither he nor Corner Man made any attempt to move to a position where they could see, and Nina understood that they had already viewed whatever she was about to see.

The screen came on automatically, showing a

black window in the centre. Monroe hit a key combination and the window changed from black to show rapidly moving colours. It took a moment to make out that it was a view from a video camera, shot across a road.

The street was empty for a second, revealing the backs of a row of houses on the other side. The view then pulled sharply forward to focus on one in particular. A two-storey house, wooden, painted a sandy colour with white trim, none of it very recently. It was caught in three-quarter view, revealing windows on the back and one side, all with drapes drawn, and a door in the back.

Nothing happened for a few moments. Cars passed, one from right to left, two in the other direction. There was no sound, but Nina couldn't tell whether this was because the file lacked it or if the laptop's volume was turned down.

The camera zoomed forward. It took a second to see what the cameraman had noticed. It was the house's back door. It had opened a few inches, revealing darkness inside. It closed again, for a second, and then opened enough for a man to come out. He was a little over medium height, with broad shoulders. He closed the door and walked along the back of the house. He was moving in such a way that a casual observer would have seen nothing of his face, and probably not even noticed his presence at all.

The person operating the camera had evidently not been such an observer, however, and pulled in hard. Nina bit her lip.

The man was John Zandt.

He walked out onto the road and the camera followed him to a car Nina recognized, a car he no longer owned but which had spent a few afternoons parked outside her house. He opened the driver's side door and just before he climbed in the camera caught a full-on view of his face over the top of the car. It was pale, his eyes hooded. He looked like many men she had seen photographed, walking with their hands cuffed together in front. He didn't look much like the man she had briefly thought she loved.

The video slowly pulled out to its widest view yet, one that showed half the street, and then stopped abruptly.

Her face carefully neutral, Nina sat back in her chair. 'Where did this come from?'

'It was emailed to us,' Monroe said. 'It arrived in the early hours of this morning.'

'What a weird coincidence,' she said. 'Coming right after the body in Portland, too.'

The two men were watching her carefully. *Screw you*, she thought. *You want this, you're going to have to do it yourselves.* 'So what's your point?'

'Our point,' said the man in the corner, 'is that this video shows your boyfriend visiting the house of a man who was questioned in regard to the Delivery Boy abductions — an investigation you were intimately involved with. Stephen DeLong was interviewed, presented a tight alibi, and was eliminated from the investigation.'

'Circumstantial evidence from this scene

288

enables it to be dated to around the time of the case,' Monroe said.

'I'll just bet it does,' Nina said. 'Just like that big pullback at the end means any idiot could work out exactly where it was shot.'

Monroe blinked. Corner Man ignored her. 'About a week later, neighbours reported an offensive odour coming from the house we've just seen. DeLong was found in his bedroom, dead from a single gunshot wound. There was evidence of sustained physical violence to his person. The house featured the paraphernalia of small-scale narcotic distribution, which led the scene officers to assume the death was the result of a deal gone bad. DeLong was written up and forgotten. Nobody cared, and nobody put his death together with the ongoing investigation.'

'Why should they?'

'No reason, then. But as you've seen, there's a compelling reason to do so now. We really only need your input on one matter, Ms Baynam,' the man said. 'We'd like to talk to John Zandt.'

He leaned forward. 'Where is he?'

★   ★   ★

Fifteen minutes later Nina walked out of the building. Her back was straight and her strides were of equal length. She didn't turn to look up towards Room 623's window, though she strongly suspected Monroe would be standing watching her go. If she saw him there was a danger she would march back into the building, run straight up the stairs and attempt to do him

289

harm. She was strong. She might even manage it. It would feel good, but she might as well take her career and throw that out the window while she was there. This might effectively have happened already, but it wasn't going to be her who wrote it in stone.

Instead she got in her car and drove out of the lot. She took her time making the right turn and drove slowly for a while, not heading anywhere in particular. Within ten minutes she was both furious and a little frightened to see she was being tailed.

She pulled over at the next public phone box she saw. She walked over to it, feeling like an actress, and made two calls. When the first was answered she asked a favour, waited while someone explained why he couldn't do it, and then provided a brief but compelling reason why he could.

As she waited for the second call to be connected she watched the road and saw the nondescript sedan pull over twenty yards further along. The guy was either a beginner or he'd been told to make it obvious. Either pissed her off.

After about ten rings, the call was picked up.

'Things are badly fucked up,' she said to an answering service. 'Stay away and watch your back.'

She put the phone down and walked back to her car. As she passed the grey sedan she leaned across and flipped the driver the bird. He stared back impassively, but didn't follow. As she drove home she was dismayed to find that her eyes kept filling, until she realized it was fury that was causing it, as much as hurt. Fury was good. Anger led somewhere.

'You're going to rue the day, Charles,' she muttered, and felt a little better, but not for long. As an agent now suspended from duty, with an ex-boyfriend under investigation for two murders, and a boss who no longer trusted anything she said, it wasn't clear how she could make anyone rue anything at all.

⋆   ⋆   ⋆

'We're getting out of here,' Ward said.

He was stuffing pieces of computer equipment into the bag he'd come with. He had stood and watched while Nina screamed down the phone at Zandt's answering service for a second and third time, before finally taking the phone from her hand.

'It doesn't matter who the guy in the suit is,' he said. 'It's clear what his job is. He's part of the squeeze on John, and he's powerful enough to be able to walk into FBI field office and have the boss there do what he says. You sure he wasn't Bureau brass?'

'He just didn't come over like it.'

'Whatever. He's in security somewhere, and he's either one of the Straw Men or doing what they tell him. That means we're not safe in this house or this city.'

'But where are we going to go?'

'Somewhere else. Do you speak any Russian?'

'Ward, we've got to find John. He's in far more

291

danger than us. They're trying to nail him for something he didn't do.'

'Maybe. Maybe not.'

'What do you mean?'

'What I mean is we only know where he's been through what he's told us. He tells you he's in Florida, he tells me he's there too. He's got a previously established reason. Neither of us are going to run a trace on him, subpoena his cell company and demand to know exactly where the call is coming from.'

'But why would he have killed this Ferillo person?'

'Are you saying it's impossible? He killed the man he thought took his daughter. And back then he was still a cop.'

'I'm just saying he would have to have a very, very good reason.'

'Maybe he did. We're not going to know until he takes one of our calls. In the meantime is there any way you can get hold of his cell records? If we can do a point-of-origin trace we can confirm a wrong-state alibi for him.'

'I'm on it, Ward. I made a call on the way back here.'

'Fine. In the meantime, get your stuff together.'

'Ward, I'm not leaving my . . . '

He stopped packing, came and put a hand on each of her shoulders. He looked her in the eyes and she realized this was the closest they had ever stood. She realized also that this was a man who had spent three months on the road not for the fun of it, but because he'd known a moment like this would come.

'Yes, Nina, you are,' he said. 'We knew we only had so long before they came for us in earnest. This is it. It's begun.'

★ ★ ★

Two hours later they were on 99 passing Bakersfield heading north. Ward was driving fast and not saying anything. Nina's cell rang and she ripped a nail snatching it out of her bag. She swore when she looked at the screen.

Ward glanced at her. 'Is it John?'

'No. I don't recognize the number. It could be the call I'm waiting for. Or . . . '

'If it's Monroe, don't tell him anything, and cut it off fast.'

She hit connect. She listened to the voice of Doug Olbrich, who had done what she had asked. She asked him three questions she had already formulated in her head. When she'd heard the answers she severed the connection and sat with her head in her hands.

Ward gave her precisely twenty seconds. 'So?'

She didn't move her head. 'That was a guy I know in LAPD. He's heading the task force on the hard-disk killer.'

'And?'

'I asked him to chase some records fast. He has someone who's very good at it.' Suddenly, and with no warning, she punched the dashboard with all her strength. 'I've screwed up, Ward.'

'Why?'

'Olbrich got hold of John's T-Mobile account. He tracked some points of origin. He noted that three days ago John made a call to a number which I recognize as your cell.'

'Yes. Big deal. We arranged to meet in San Francisco. That's when he told me he was in Florida.'

She nodded, said nothing. Looked at her hands in her lap. The cuticle under her torn nail was bleeding.

'Tell me, Nina.'

'John lied,' she said. 'He hasn't been to Florida in six weeks. He was in Portland the day Ferillo died.'

3: The Falling of Rain

The meaning of life is that it ends.

Franz Kafka

19

She was found in some bushes. People are. They are found in woods, too, and in hot and cluttered bedrooms; they are found in back alleys and parking lots and the back row of movie theatres; they are found in swimming pools and in cars. You can be found dead almost anywhere, but bushes are often the worst. The bodies' condition and location leave little room for the comforting idea that they might just be asleep, drunk, passed out, unconscious in one way or another — but still capable of being led back to join the party of the living. Dead in the bushes is very dead indeed.

These particular bushes were around the back of the parking lot associated with Cutting Loose, a hair salon on the main drag through Snoqualmie. The body was discovered, as is often the case, by a man out walking his dog early in the day. Having kept it together for long enough to make a call on his cell phone, wait close to the spot — but far enough away to avoid attracting the curious — and finally point the way for the two cops from the sheriff's department, this man was now sitting on the other side of the street, back against a fence, head between his knees. His dog stood close by, confused by the smell of vomit, but loyal and game. When they got back to the house, the dog knew, he'd be confined to barracks for the long day while the human went out and did whatever it was he did when he wasn't there to hang out with the dog. The dog was therefore in no hurry to go home. If the price of a little extra freedom was sitting on rainwet asphalt near some regurgitation, that was fine by him. He licked his owner's hand, to show moral support. The hand flapped at him, feebly.

One of the policemen was now on the radio, putting out the word. The other stood a couple of yards away from the body, his hands on his hips. He had not seen a great many dead bodies, and there is something horribly transfixing about them. He was frankly glad that other policemen would soon arrive and take this situation off his hands, that it would not be his responsibility to spend the next several days, weeks or all eternity trying to work out what process had created this livid, could-not-be-deader thing out of someone living, how this woman had made the journey from some other place to here. He did not want to have to think overly much about the mind of a man — assuming it was a man, because it almost always was — who would think it right or even merely expedient to dump someone a few yards away from the side of the road like so much trash. Worse, perhaps, because people at least bothered to put their garbage in bags. This had been abandoned like it was less than that, as if it didn't even merit the temporary, above-ground burial people afforded to empty cans and cereal boxes.

He heard his colleague signing off, and decided he'd seen enough. As he was turning away, however, he noticed something glinting at the dead thing's head end. Against his better judgement, but feeling a little like a bona fide detective, he took a step closer to the body and bent down a little to get a closer look.

They had already informally decided that it would take neither long nor a genius to work out the cause of death. The woman was dressed in a smart suit, or the remains of one. Her body below the neck did not look like something you'd want to touch, but that was death's casual work, after the fact. It was above the neck that something had happened while she was still alive. There was something skewed about her head, and it was covered with brown, dried blood and other, blacker, material to such a degree that it was hard to make out the features. It was in the middle of this, just above the brow, that the weak morning sun was catching something.

'Careful, man,' his partner said. 'You screw up the scene and they'll pull your asshole out and wear it like a ring.'

'I know, I know,' he said.

Still he leaned in a little closer. This was as far as he was going to go, for sure. He tilted his head slightly, to reduce the glint. The smell was odd. The sight was bad. It was unpleasant all over.

In the mess that had been her forehead, something looked out of place.

He held his breath and moved forward another few inches. From here you couldn't avoid seeing the ants and other insects going about their duties, hurriedly, as if they knew someone was going to come and take this treasure away from them. You could also see that there was something stuck in the woman's forehead. The protruding edge was the width of a playing card, though it was much thicker — a quarter-inch, maybe slightly more. The glint came off the parts of this thing which weren't covered in dried blood. It seemed to be mainly made out of chrome, or some other kind of shiny metal. The lower edge of it looked to be black plastic.

Suddenly some of the remaining glare disappeared, as his partner leaned in to have a look and blocked out the sun. As a result the policeman could just make out something that looked like a very narrow label running along the end of the object.

'Fuck is that?' he said.

*　*　*

By a little after nine it had been established that the thing sticking out of the woman's forehead was a hard disk, a small one, the kind found in laptop computers. It wasn't long before this information reached the FBI field office in Everett, and then quickly down to Los Angeles. From there, everything went batshit.

Charles Monroe tried every number he had, but Nina Baynam wasn't answering. He kept trying anyway, at regular intervals. Something had gone wrong with Monroe's life in a way he didn't quite understand, and it was getting more and more wrong by the minute. He had looked away, lost concentration for just one second, and turned back to find his ducks were no longer in a row.

His ducks had always been in a row before. Not now. It was even beginning to look as if some of them were missing.

20

Henrickson switched the engine off and turned to Tom with a grin. It was, Tom estimated, approximately the man's fifteenth of the morning, and it was as yet only ten o'clock.

'You ready for this?'

Tom gripped the backpack on his lap. 'I guess so.'

Forty-eight hours had now passed since he came back to Sheffer. The previous morning he'd woken from a night's non-sleep to find he felt too ill to consider a walk in the woods that day. Whatever adrenaline had hauled him back to Sheffer had burned out, leaving him exhausted, in many kinds of pain, and deeply nauseous. He also realized he had to do some proper thinking.

Henrickson had been cool about the delay, and told him to rest up. This Tom had done, initially, sitting in the chair in his room wrapped up in all the bedding he could find; getting stuff straight in his head, working out things he could do. In the early afternoon he had gone for a long drive, coming back after dark. By then he'd felt well enough to go for another drink with the journalist. This morning he'd felt better, if not exactly on top form. Calmer, perhaps. More compartmentalized.

Pulling in to the lot at the head of the Howard's Point trail provoked a far stronger reaction than he anticipated. If returning to his nest down in the gully had made him feel like a spirit coming home, stepping out of Henrickson's Lexus made him feel like his own grandfather. The journalist had parked on the opposite side of the lot to where Tom had come to rest — and fallen, for the first time — but that somehow made the layering effect even more unsettling. When the clunk of his car door closing echoed tightly off the trees, the view seemed to have a shivery fragility, as if it had been quickly painted over some other scene. Some emotional charge had changed. Of course the last time he'd been here he'd been drunk, whereas now he was merely slightly hungover, and feeling a bit sick, and there was a lot more snow than before.

'Jim, you know it's going to be very hard to find the place.'

'Of course.' The reporter had ditched his suit and was wearing an old pair of jeans and a tough-looking jacket. His boots spoke of proper walking experience. He looked hale and fit and altogether more prepared than Tom felt. 'You were out of it, and it was nearly dark. Not the end of the world if you don't find the same exact spot. Just . . . it would be good if you could.'

'Can't you just tell me what we're looking for?'

Grin number sixteen. 'Don't you like a surprise?'

'Not so much.'

'Trust me. It'll be great for the book. 'Kozelek leads the way back to the spot that changes history and biology and what the hell else as we know it. His fearless scribe points out the final

303

proof. They share a manly hug.' It's a buddy thing. Hug's optional, of course.'

Tom nodded, wishing not for the first time that he hadn't mentioned the idea of writing a book. Henrickson had claimed not to be trying to get him drunk, again, and he believed him: yet by the end of the second evening Tom had spilled pretty much everything there was to know about himself. Pretty much.

'I just don't want to get lost again.'

'We won't. I've done hiking. I have a compass and I know how to use it. And if you didn't have a serious sense of direction, you'd be dead now.'

'I guess so.'

Tom swivelled his ankle gently. It still hurt, but the new boots seemed to help. He shrugged the backpack on. This time it held bottled water and a flask of sweet coffee and a couple of flapjacks. There was probably still glass at the bottom, too, but that was okay. He brought it along because it was from before. The glass was from before too. He had an idea that he might try to dump the bag in the forest somewhere, to try to leave behind everything it represented.

He walked over into the top corner, hesitated a moment, and then stepped over the thick log that formed a boundary to the parking area.

Henrickson waited until the man had made it a few yards up the trail, and then turned to look back across the lot. For just a moment he'd felt something in the back of his neck, almost as if he was being watched. He panned his eyes slowly around, but couldn't see anyone. Strange. He was usually right about that kind of thing.

He looked back to see Kozelek had stopped. Now that he was started, the man's enthusiasm for the trip was growing fast, as he had known it would.

'It's this way.'

Henrickson stepped over the log and followed him into the forest.

★ ★ ★

Though there was a bank of cloud over to the west, the sun was strong and bright. It cast attractive shadows in the undisturbed snow. The two men walked for a while, climbing slowly, without saying much. By this time the road was a good distance behind them, and there was no noise but for the sound of their breath and feet.

'You seem pretty confident, my friend. You remember coming up this way?'

'Not remember. Just . . . I recognize the shape. Sounds stupid, maybe, and I'm really not much of an outdoors person, but . . . '

He stopped, and indicated the layout of the trees and hillside around them. 'Which other way are you going to go?'

Henrickson nodded. 'Know what you're saying, Tom. Some people, they got no sense of direction at all. Like some kid's wind-up toy. Let them go, and they walk in a straight line until they hit a wall. Others, they *feel*. They just know where they are. Works with time, too, matter of fact. What time do you think it is? Take a second. Think about it. Actually, don't: feel it instead. What time does it *feel* like?'

Tom considered. It didn't feel like any time at all, but it was probably about a half-hour since they'd started out.

'Half past ten.'

The man shook his head. 'Closer to eleven. About five to, I'd say.' He stretched his wrist out of his jacket and looked at his watch. A grin, and then he held it out to Tom. 'How about that. Four minutes to.'

'You could have checked earlier.'

'Could have, but didn't.'

Tom stopped walking. They were coming to a ridge, and he was momentarily unsure of which way to go. Henrickson took a few steps back and looked the other way. Tom realized the man was giving him a chance to work things out, to feel the way, and felt an absurd rush of gratitude. It had been a while since someone had trusted him, had been willing to think of him as someone who knew things. William and Lucy had grown old enough to see him as someone with faults, rather than qualities. Sarah knew him all too well. He was a given. The curse of the middle-aged man was knowing — or believing — that he'd told all he had to tell. Soon as you suspected that, you started wanting something, anything, to prove it wasn't so: and that's where the mistakes started, when the bad things happened.

'It's this direction,' he said, turning right.

'Feel the force, Luke.'

The next twenty minutes were hard going, and it was a while before either had spare breath to talk. Then the ground started heading down the

306

other side of the ridge, with a much higher climb ahead. None of it looked familiar to him, but it seemed to be the way to go.

Tom glanced across at the reporter, who was walking alongside and matching him with easy strides. 'You've been looking for Bigfoot a long time, haven't you?'

'Surely have.'

'How come nobody believes in it?'

'Oh they do,' he said. 'Just, it's one of those things that's hard to make work, if you believe what we're supposed to believe. Nobody wants to look stupid, which is another way They work. You're prepared to look a little dumb once in a while, the world opens like an oyster.'

'So what is it?'

'What do you think?'

Tom shrugged. 'Some big ape, I guess. Something that lived here before humans arrived, then shrank back into the forests. There's plenty of space out here. Right?'

'Half right,' Henrickson said. 'Personally I believe they're the last surviving examples of Neanderthal man.'

Tom stopped, stared at him. 'What?'

Henrickson kept walking. 'Not a new theory, actually. Only problem is getting the detail to work. You know what archaeologists are like — or maybe you don't. Blah there's no evidence; blah the fossil record; blah my professor says it ain't so. Way I see it is this. You've got Neanderthal man, one of the best-adapted species the world has ever known. These guys had spears four hundred thousand years ago.

307

They spread out over half the world, including into Europe — when that's no place you want to live. The ice age is still frosty, there's animals with very big teeth, and there is nothing, repeat, nothing, to make life easy for them. Yet they survive for hundreds of thousands of years. They have burial rituals. They have dentistry, which must have been horrible without *Front Page* to ease the wait. They make ornaments and jewellery and they have trade ties which spread the stuff over Europe. Cro-Magnon man eventually turns up — that's us — and for a while the two species sort of co-exist. Then the Neanderthals die out, bang, leaving about enough bones to fill a handbag. And apparently that's all she wrote.'

'So what did happen? According to you?'

'They never died out. There were never that many of them. They just got good at hiding.'

'Hiding? Where?'

'Two kinds of places. First is deep forests and mountains, out in northeastern Europe, Finland, the Himalayas — but also here in the good old US of A. The prehistorians claim there's no way Neanderthals could have got to North America. Theory is that man got here via a high northern land bridge, and that it wouldn't have been possible earlier than say fifteen thousand BC. I think that's underestimating the Neanderthals. No reason they couldn't have had little boats. They could have hugged the coast from Russia, managed to get across the big icy water down to the Northern Territories, then kept coming down the coast until they found somewhere habitable.

Then, when we finally arrive in force, they head up into the forests. What better place? You've got thousands of square miles of wilderness that people still don't trouble much even *now*. Throughout Native American culture in this region there's some nice little hints. The Chinooks have tales about the 'ghost people' who lived in their own places, and who the tribe had a working relationship with. Then you got the 'animal people' of the Okanogans: the tribe lived right in these mountains and they believed there once were 'animals' that had culture before the 'people' — by which they meant humans — had got themselves together at all.'

'And the second place? The other place they hid?'

'Right under our noses. What's the most common type of legend all over Europe?'

'I don't know.' Tom also wasn't sure he was going the right way any more. They were past the bottom of the divide, and starting to head up again. The increasing harshness of the terrain was familiar, but nothing else, and the ground was getting steeper in most directions, so that didn't count for much. For the time being, he just kept going, and Henrickson kept on talking, with the smooth flow of someone who'd been over something many times in his head. And, if Tom was honest, with the confidence of someone who wasn't quite as bright as he thought.

'Fairies. Ogres. Elves. Trolls. All of which, according to me, are also examples of surviving Neanderthal man. Creatures that lived here

309

before we did, and had their own strange customs. Who were common at first but then got more and more rare — until hardly anyone saw them any more. But we remember them. Language works in strange ways. You must have heard stuff like, in legends, 'There were giants here in those days'? I think 'giant' didn't mean 'big in body'. It meant that incomers found a previously existing population that was powerful and accomplished, like the Okanogans' animal people: a species that was *culturally* big.'

'But they died out.'

'Not completely. What else do we hear a lot about, all over the world? Ghosts. Shadowy presences. And what else? Aliens. The greys. Who, incidentally, seem to land their ships in forests quite often, which is a weird approach to aviation, don't you think? Greys, fairies, spooks are all ways of explaining strange stuff that we see every now and then. Ways of explaining away a whole species They claim died out, but which just faded into the background — and creeps around us, keeping out of our way.'

'But none of those things look remotely like Neanderthal man,' Tom said.

'No, for two reasons. First is tales swelling in the telling. Over hundreds, thousands of years, the legends take on their own weight, their own rules and trappings. Fairies look like this or that, elves got their cool green clothes, ghosts always got some sad story behind them. Second is that Neanderthal man has a way of clouding our minds.'

'*What?*'

'They reckon the species' throat and mouth maybe wasn't up to fully articulated speech. Yet they managed to do all this stuff, so obviously they could communicate, and in a way that mere body language and a system of hoots and grunts ain't going to pull off. My theory is that they communicated at least partly through telepathy. They still do, and even we do, now and then. Telepathy is just empathy turned up a whole lot. When they're confronted by something they think is dangerous, like us, they throw shapes into our heads. We see pictures in our own minds. They reflect our imaginations right back at us.'

'This is all nonsense,' Tom said, distractedly. 'I'm sorry, but I don't buy a word of it.'

'Think about our current endeavour. If I'm right, and we're looking for a Neanderthal, why does everyone who's seen Bigfoot say it's eight feet tall? They make us *think* they're tall, because tall is scary. And why do so many people — like you, Tom — report a vile smell? Why should they or any other creature go around smelling bad? No reason. They just make us *think* they do. It's another protection mechanism, one of the simplest in the book. They hide by putting smoke in our minds. That's why they're so hard to find. Nearer to civilization, we think we've seen a ghost. In a forest you don't expect to see something like that — except on a lonely road, where you've got your 'hitchhiker who isn't in the back seat after all' formulation — which is why you get Bigfoot instead. You see something closer to their true shape, because part of us has

311

always known they're still out here.'

Tom stopped, and turned to look at the journalist. The man wasn't grinning, for once. He was deadly serious. Though Tom was pleased to have someone on his side, he'd have much preferred it if the man just thought there was a hitherto unknown primate on the loose, rather than a rationale involving elves and mind control.

But for the time being, that was a secondary concern. He had news of his own.

'I'm completely lost,' he said.

★ ★ ★

An hour later things were no better. Henrickson had been patient, often walking a little distance away to let Tom try to get his bearings, encouraging him to walk ahead and saying he'd catch him up if Tom shouted to say he was back on track. Tom wasn't on track, however. The further he walked the less he felt he knew where he was. In the end he came to a halt.

Henrickson called from behind. 'We getting warmer, good buddy?'

'No,' Tom said. 'I don't know where the hell we are.'

'Not a problem,' Henrickson said, when he came up level. He reached into his jacket pocket and pulled out a trail map. He unfolded it, consulted the compass attached on a string to his coat, and then made a small circle on the map. 'We're round about here.'

Tom looked. 'Here' was an area of white space

with some tightly grouped topographical lines — the last half-hour had been an up-and-down struggle. 'Middle of nowhere.'

'Not quite. This here is a stream,' the man said, indicating a wavering line. 'You reckon we're close enough that this could be your gully?'

'I really don't know. I guess we could look.'

'Let's do that.'

About twenty minutes later they began to hear a steady trickling sound. They came around a large rock formation to find a rocky stream, about five feet across, coursing hectically between shallow, mossy banks.

Tom shook his head. 'This isn't it. And my ankle is beginning to ache.'

Henrickson looked upstream. 'Could be steeper that way.'

'Maybe.' Tom felt foolish, though he'd known this was going to be hard to impossible, and had warned the reporter. 'I just don't know.'

Henrickson was looking as fit and hale as when they started, but hadn't produced a grin in quite a while. 'Know what you're thinking, my friend,' he said, however. 'And it's not a problem. Like you'll have gathered, I really want to find this critter. And hey — what else am I going to do? Go back to the city and sit in traffic? Rather be out here walking. Let's follow this one a little while. We know we're looking for something like it, and the map doesn't show any others real close. But first, I'm about ready for a java boost.'

Tom started to shrug the bag off his back, but Henrickson held up a hand. 'No need. I'll get it.'

He undid the fastenings, and Tom heard the

313

other man's hand rustling inside the top of the bag. 'Careful,' Tom said. 'There's glass in there.'

'Okay. But, um, why?'

'There's a couple of broken bottles from when I came out here the first time. I didn't clear it out properly. It should be down the bottom, but . . .'

He sensed the other man wasn't listening, and that his hands were no longer in his backpack. 'Are you okay?'

There was no reply. Tom turned to see Henrickson was holding something that wasn't the coffee flask, and looking at it.

'What's that?'

'You tell me. It was in your bag.'

Tom looked more closely, and saw a tiny bundle of bedraggled-looking plant matter. 'I have no idea.'

'Probably nothing. Must have just fallen in your bag, I guess.'

He looked up at Tom, and this time his grin split the man's face in two. 'Let's get going, what do you say? Upwards and onwards.' As they walked on, sipping hot, sweet coffee, Tom noticed that the other man seemed to have an extra swing in his stride.

Another forty minutes took them several hundred feet higher. They followed the stream through rises and falls, around outcrops. The banks didn't seem to be getting any higher. This time it was the reporter who stopped.

'Not liking the look of this,' he said. He pulled out his map again. 'We must be over here by now,' he pointed at another patch of white space, 'which is further east than I'd like to be.'

'What's that black line?'

'A road. It's possible that you just missed it when you were trying to find your way back, but . . . look at the topography lines. It's downhill to there, which you'd likely have been attracted to. Which case you wouldn't have taken two days to get home. So . . . what? You okay?'

Tom was standing with his mouth slightly open. He slowly shut it again. He spoke reluctantly. 'Yes. It's just . . . '

'I'm sensing inner turmoil here. Bad for the guts.'

'The woman. Patrice. The one who had the boots.'

'What about her?'

'She was there. She saw my pack and, according to her, left the footprints. Connolly said she lived up in a subdivision around here somewhere. Which means . . . ' He stopped.

'She'll know where the place was, and maybe be able to just walk right to it. That what you're saying, Tom?'

Tom nodded.

'You really didn't think of this earlier? Or perhaps you just didn't want someone else coming in on the story.'

'Honestly, it just didn't occur to me. I was very sick when she was in the station.'

'Shoot.' Henrickson stood with his hands on his hips and looked the other way for a moment. Then he shook his head. 'Okay, my friend. Should have put it together myself. And, yes, I can get that it would have been cooler to get there ourselves. But we're not getting there, are we?'

'Jim, I'm sorry.'

'That's okay. But I think what we're going to do now is walk back to the car, and go get us some reinforcements. This woman can take us there, it's going to save us a whole lot of time, and time is of the essence.'

Henrickson took out the map once more, and consulted his compass. 'We'll cut straight over there,' he said. 'Sense of direction is all very well. But let's go back the quick route, shall we?'

He strode off back the way they'd come, and Tom followed.

★   ★   ★

It took them a little over an hour to get back to the trail head, aided by a route that was more direct and largely downhill. By the time he stepped back over the log boundary of the lot, Tom knew something had changed. He was no longer leading, he was following. That wasn't the way things should be. If necessary, he'd have to do something to change it.

Henrickson backed out onto the road and went a couple of miles back towards Sheffer. He stopped at a roadside latte hut and asked a few questions while getting the flask refilled. When he got back in the car, he winked.

'Think we found what we're looking for,' he said. 'Few miles round up the other side. Development called Cascade Falls. Never took off. But there's one inhabitant for sure. The

316

stoner back there thinks the woman's name is Anders.'

'That's it,' Tom said. 'Patrice Anders. She's the one.'

'Hallelujah. We're back in business, my friend.'

It took nearly half an hour to take the road back over the highway, go north, then turn off into the mountains. The road soon began to narrow. Put in by the developer, it did nothing more than provide a way to get up to the land they'd been trying to sell. Soon there were thick trees on either side.

'Surely is the road less travelled,' Henrickson said, cheerfully.

Tom wondered what would make someone come and live in a place like this. Every now and then you saw a sign nailed to one of the trees nearest to the road. You could buy a piece of this, and come and live here. And then do what?

Eventually Henrickson pulled over and killed the engine. Just ahead on the left-hand side of the road was a gate. The name Anders was visible on a flat piece of wood nailed to it.

They got out, unlatched the gate, and walked down a track which wandered through the trees. After two hundred yards they saw a building up ahead. By the time they reached it, Tom was wondering if they were in the right place after all. The place looked small and cold and empty despite the light on over the door.

'Not much of a house,' he said. It looked like more of a cabin with a porch, just a square log building with a car port on one side. The entrance to the house was under there, looking

317

back up the track: a door with the number '2' burned in at waist height. There were four small glass panels in the upper half, the view of the interior obscured by a thick curtain.

Henrickson knocked. 'Compact, that's for damned sure.'

When, after a few moments, there was no answer, he knocked again. Tom meanwhile drifted up a little rise in front of the house. There was another small cabin twenty yards away in the trees, but it was dark and a little overgrown. When he walked a little further he could make out the faint glint of a small icy pond, also presumably on the property. The far side was a line of trees, apart from . . .

He walked a little further and thought he could see another cabin around the other side. He thought about calling out to Henrickson, but then, for some reason, didn't. Instead he walked back.

Henrickson was knocking for the fourth time. 'No one's home,' he said. 'She's probably back in Sheffer enjoying the bright lights and big-city ambiance. Which is kind of a pain. However . . . ' He looked at his watch. 'Time is moving on. You say she said the place where you were was a good walk out from her property. Maybe we're not going to make it there and back today anyhow.'

He stood back from the door and walked over to one of two small windows on the next side. This too was curtained, but with thinner material. Tom looked through it with him, but you couldn't make out much of the inside.

'We're done for the day,' Henrickson decided.

'We'll head ourselves to town and kick back. See if we can get hold of this woman's phone number, so we can do things properly tomorrow. For now, I'm as hungry as a bear. No offence.'

They peered back through the window a final time, and then set off back up the track towards the gate.

It wasn't until they were back in the car, and the noise of its departure had drifted down through the trees, that the curtain at the front door moved.

21

When she was sure the men had gone, Patrice unlocked the door and stepped outside. She stood a while, listening carefully, but heard only what she always heard on her property: nothing at all. She didn't count the fall wind, or birds in spring, or busy summer insects. They weren't noises.

Tracks in the snow showed the men had walked down the drive and then right around the cabin. She realized that it also suggested that one of them had . . .

She followed the shuffling marks which led up over the small ridge and down towards the lake. They stopped after a few yards. Patrice saw that, unless the man had been very unobservant, he should have been able to spot the other small building on the far side. Yet she had not heard him call out, or mention it to the other man. That didn't necessarily mean anything. He could simply have been cold or bored or hungry. Wouldn't have mattered anyway. There was nothing in that cabin except tools and damp and the memory of an unexpected bout of love-making that had swept her and Bill along with it one winter night when they were supposed to be patching up the roof.

She walked down to the quarter-acre pond that marked the start of the wilderness section of her property. She sat on the bench that hugged the big tree a few yards back from its edge, and looked out across the icy water.

'They're coming,' she said, quietly. 'What do I do?'

He didn't answer. He never did. He didn't even know what she was talking about. But she always asked, just in case. Men like to feel involved.

★　★　★

In the months after Bill's death, Patrice had found herself in a strange new world in which everything seemed to have been broken and put back together not quite right. She learned that a fridge looks cold if stocked only with what you need, unleavened by the unexpected that caught your partner's eye. She remembered that pieces of paper didn't actually come with doodles, that envelopes, bills and till receipts didn't spontaneously develop sketches of trees or cats or boats. They looked odd without them. One of the hardest things she learned was that there no longer existed homes for some kinds of information. She could pass the time of day with the mail man, and she could chat in line at the market: but she couldn't tell Ned his nose was weird, or turn to someone and sing the tune of some silly advertisement that made her smile. That's the kind of thing makes people think the poor old bitch is going batty, such a sad story, something should be done. An event happened and then was gone, like a drop of rain falling onto hot asphalt. Nobody watching but her, a

VCR that didn't work.

You got through a day and wondered what your reward was. It soon became evident the prize was you got to withstand tomorrow too. You got through it, hour by long hour, but at the end you looked up without much expectation. You had begun to understand the score. Sure enough: today's prize was the same. Outwardly calm, but with a scream building like the sound of a long-forgotten steam engine in the back corner of a basement, you got through that tomorrow too, and a flat hardpan of further tomorrows after that. You got through enough of them to realize you'd been had, that they aren't tomorrows after all but the wretched stretch of an endless today. What can you do? Rebellion gets you nowhere. If you're giving up smoking, and it all suddenly gets too much and you decide that the chance to not smoke tomorrow is *not* sufficient reward for having successfully not smoked today, then you can stomp furiously to the store and buy a pack and tear them open and make yourself feel happy and disappointed and defiant and guilty. No such triumphant failure exists with death. You can't say, 'Screw this. Bring my husband back'. People realize this, dimly. They don't put the world to the test because they understand that to finally articulate this demand, and have it denied, would drive them completely insane. They obliquely acquire the harsh intelligence that there's no way out, that they can't give up giving up, and go find the emergency packet of their loved one; can't retrieve him or her from where they've been hidden all along, on top of a cupboard in the kitchen or behind the bath upstairs; can't dust them off and run their fingers through their hair and kiss them gently on the lips to wake them and the world back to normality, as if the whole episode had been some bad dream or stupid idea.

After a lifetime of unconsciously doing and thinking the right thing, of being born on the liberal side of every debate, Patrice found herself prey to thoughts of the utmost political incorrectness. She looked at people clogging the lanes of the market, people who were old and cranky and a pain to be around. Six months before she would have asked herself what had made them so unhappy, and if there was anything she could do to help. Now she just thought how unfair it was they were still alive. When she saw an appeal on television for a children's hospital she asked herself why people went so misty-eyed over kids when they'd done so little for the world, when someone like Bill had so much longer to become a part of other people's lives. Hers, for example.

And when someone tried to put an AIDS pin on her in the street over in Snohomish one afternoon, she snapped at them and pushed the boy aside. The boy — who was doe-eyed and good-looking — turned to his co-worker, a strikingly pretty teenage girl fairly dripping with compassion, and made a remark.

Patrice fixed him with a look. 'Getting laid the caring way?'

The boy flushed. By the time she got to the

323

car Patrice was vermilion with self-dislike, but a voice inside was still jabbering. It just wasn't *fair*. Someone kills themselves skiing — after choosing to slide down a mountain on slippery sticks, in other words — and it's a tragedy. If someone gets lung cancer then it's 'Well it's your own fault, you me-murdering smoker shit.' Even his widow is implicated — she could have stopped him, surely? Did she just not *care* enough? — and the loss is compromised by shame. We search for fault because it lets God off the hook, and without Him we don't know where to turn.

Patrice knew all about fault. It was Patrice who had killed her husband, after all.

Five years before they came north, Bill buckled under the zeitgeist and gave up smoking. He found it hard, tough as hell in fact, but he stuck with it. Five months later they found themselves on the deck of the bar in Verona. They'd had a lovely day. A good meal was in prospect. As they sat with the balcony to themselves and the sun going down, everything was pretty perfect. They chatted, and they smiled, and they looked out over the inlet. Everything was fine, but it wasn't right, and Patrice watched Bill and knew he was dully accepting that some of his most pleasurable moments were now minor ordeals — the ordeal of missed pleasure, which is what we have in the West instead of pain.

And so she reached into her bag and pulled out something she'd bought at the market up in Cannon Beach that morning. It hadn't been a foregone conclusion, but now she'd watched his face she didn't know what else to do. She put the pack of cigarettes on the table.

He looked at the pack, and smiled wistfully, as if shown a photograph of a good friend who'd died eight months before.

He leaned forward, and kissed her.

He didn't have one that evening. But the next night, he did.

The pack lasted a whole month. There was no way of telling whether the cigarette which sparked off the cancer came from it, or the others which followed. But being human, you assume it came from the one she gave him, or at least could have done. We paint those lines, make those connections, open our hearts up to blame; we believe it rains because we are bad. In the remaining years he was never more than an occasional smoker, and he was certainly a lot happier. Maybe the cigarettes had nothing to do with it. Plenty of my-body-is-a-temple merchants get whacked with the tumour stick too. That's the thing with death: you just don't know. You never know what you should or shouldn't do or have done until it's too late — and actually, you don't know then either. It's all a great big game of truth or consequences, only there's no truth, only consequences. Truth is a fiction we backfill to make some circumstance seem less awful, more explicable, or someone's fault — even if it has to be our own.

She didn't think about that pack of cigarettes often, but when she did it wasn't long before another thought came to mind; came to ask her whether she'd bought that pack for Bill after all, or whether it had been more to do with her not wanting her precious Verona time to be spoilt by the knowledge that he wasn't as happy as he could be. The only thing that made those moments possible to bear was the certain knowledge that Bill wouldn't have minded even if the latter had been true. He had loved her that much. Then he'd died.

For a time, after a few months, it felt as if things were easing a bit. It soon became clear, however, that this was merely the calm before the storm. She started to slip, badly. Days began to get harder, longer.

Then, one long December night in 2002 as she approached her first Christmas without him, something burst in her head. She owned a CD of his favourite tracks, chosen by him to be played at his funeral back down in Portland. Songs she'd loved with him, classical pieces she'd never heard but which he evidently held dear in that part which was separate; that part that pre-dated them and had now gone on without her. She hadn't listened to the CD since the funeral. That night she put it on for the second time, listened right the way through. She found a huge bottle of scotch Bill had left behind, and drank it all. She had never done anything remotely like it in her entire life.

Midnight found her staggering in the trees outside, hair whipped by a cold gale, barefoot and nearly insensible. She had talked and she had screamed and snarled and she had cried. Her throat was torn and dry. She had left the door to the house open, and it was thwacking in the wind, way behind her. She didn't feel foolish. She felt like tearing out the eyes of everyone in the world. She felt like finding someone, anyone, and bashing their brains out with a rock. She was caught up in a whirling cloud of horror, and that night she knew she had cut through to the centre of everything. The centre, the truth, was this:

Hell is being alive, and being alive is all there is.

To kill herself would be to give in. Death's gang is bigger and tougher than anyone else's. Always has been, and always will be. Death's the man, there's no question, but she wasn't going to be on his side. So who else? It was impossible to take God seriously any more. She was sick of making excuses for the senile old shit, helping him out of his endless scrapes, patching and mending his appalling record of capriciousness. God was gone for her, but Death wasn't getting her for a sunbeam either.

Faced with this, she made a decision as she stood howling on the edge of a cold, cold lake, still swigging from the bottle of her dead husband's drink. She wasn't, in what she understood to be the popular parlance, going to be anyone's bitch no more. She would owe no allegiance to anyone or anything. No person, no god, no idea, no truth, no promise. Nothing was worth it, nothing could be trusted. There had been Bill. Now there was nothing.

But then two weeks later she had found something, something in the forest; or it had found her; and she changed her mind.

★ ★ ★

The sky was dark now, and the lake looked like a sheet of black marble. It was cold. It was time to go back inside. She sat a little longer, however, because she loved this view and she feared things were about to change. She feared that though the men had gone, they would come back, and that she might be forced to defend the only thing she really cared about.

So be it.

22

We had holed up in the Morisa, a hunk of faded grandeur near the centre of Fresno. The hotel looked like it had been built to withstand sustained bombing. We liked that about it. We arrived in town late the previous night and decided not to drive any further. Until we had a plan, and somewhere in particular to go, we could be heading in one of many wrong directions. We went to the desk separately and booked rooms on different floors and went upstairs and went to sleep. Early next day we walked out into the downtown. We walked and we walked but couldn't work out where to go or what to do. There's something very alienating about stores when you have no interest in shopping. Who are these people? What are they buying, and why? They seem no less weird and irrelevant than the boarded-up fronts or the graffiti-strewn alleyways between abandoned warehouses. Weirdly, I thought I saw some letters I recognized on a door down one of these, but closer inspection showed the second letter was a 'B', not an 'R'. I think. I'm not sure. I was feeling pretty paranoid.

Late morning had found us back in my hotel room. The room was not large and had not been decorated recently. I sat in the chair. She sat on the bed. We drank the coffee when it arrived.

Nina was regretting leaving LA. She wanted to

go back. I wouldn't let her. I understood that it felt like running away — it *was* running away. She had a job, too, even if she'd currently been asked not to do it. For her to be in this position because of a relationship to a man (and a relationship that was finished, moreover) was the kind of thing that would piss any woman off. Nina wasn't just any woman, either. She had ire in depth. She was so furious at Zandt having lied to her that she wouldn't turn her phone back on. I tried calling him, a few times, but never got anything more than the same old robotic voice telling me the phone was off. He could be anywhere in the country, doing God knows what — or in serious trouble. For all we knew, he could be dead.

It wasn't that either of us thought it was impossible that Zandt had killed Ferillo. We both knew that, during the initial search for his daughter, when he had still been on the force, he had privately cornered and killed the man he was convinced was responsible. The problem was that a further abduction had taken place after this event. We now had a name for that person — Stephen DeLong — and already knew he had been only one of several people abducting to order for the Straw Men, my brother being chief amongst them. The sudden arrival of a video file nailing John for DeLong's murder — and which had evidently been held in reserve for a long time — proved they were after him, and willing to do a great deal to send bigtime trouble his way. The question was whether the death of

Ferillo was an example of this, or part of the cause.

Nina had made two calls from the room's landline. These had established that Ferillo had a restaurant called the Dining Room on Stark Street in Portland. Four years previously he had been arrested as part of a racketeering investigation down in LA, and had been close to going away for a long time. He'd walked, and got himself from there into the position of owning a vaunted eatery patronized by the great and the good of northeast Oregon. From minor mob to wealthy restaurateur was a mighty bound, but said nothing about why Zandt might have decided to explode into his life — or why someone might choose to make it look that way.

After the calls we sat in silence for a while. The coffee got slowly colder, but we kept drinking it anyway, until my stomach felt bitter and curdled. I had the window open wide and was staring out over battered buildings as an angry sky dropped persistent rain. It felt absurd not to be doing something, but I couldn't think what it might be. We had no way of finding John, and no way of getting closer to the Ferillo investigation.

Then suddenly a very dim light went off in my head. It flickered, sputtered out for a second, then came back a little stronger.

'Call Monroe,' I said, slowly.

'No way.'

'See it from his point of view. He's not an idiot. He knows something major happened to you at the end of last year. You get shot, and Sarah Becker is back with her parents. But you tell him nothing, and now someone you're intimately tied to is going around doing very bad things.'

'Or looks like they are.'

'Whatever. Even if Monroe didn't have someone pushing him from behind, you'd be standing at the end of a long plank right now.'

'What are you not saying?'

'What do you mean?'

She looked at me squarely. 'What I mean is that there's something in your voice that I don't understand.'

'Tell me again about what happened when you went to The Knights motel. The day Jessica's body was found.'

'Ward . . . '

'Just tell me.'

'I got a call from Charles. On my cell. He said someone had just taken out a cop in a patrol car and then disappeared.'

'And then what?'

'Nothing. He told me where it was and said he wanted me down there.'

'For a cop-killing.'

She hesitated. 'Yes.'

'Which is nothing to do with the FBI, and of no interest to him. Unless . . . '

She was silent for a full twenty seconds while she thought it through. 'Oh Christ.'

'Yeah. Maybe.'

She blinked, rapidly. 'So why on earth would we talk to him?'

'Because we don't have anyone else. And because then you get to ask him this question and see what he says, and if he has no good answer, then . . . either we're in worse trouble than we thought, or we have something to work with.'

She'd evidently made the decision before I spoke. She got off the bed and pulled her phone from her bag, turning it on. Within a couple of seconds it chirped several times.

'Messages,' she said. She listened. Then pulled the phone from her ear and stood with a strange expression on her face.

'John?'

She shook her head. 'Monroe. Four times. No message, just 'call me.'

'So call him. Not his office number. Call his cell.'

'But if he does a point-of-origin he'll know where we are.'

'He'll know where we *were*. Come on, do it.'

She dialled. Listened to it ring, with her eyes on me.

Then: 'Charles, it's Nina.'

From six feet away I could hear the immediate torrent of speech. Nina listened for a moment.

'What are you . . . Oh Jesus. Charles, I'll call you back.'

She cut the connection. Seemed for a moment actually speechless.

'What? Nina — what?'

'They've found another woman with a hard disk.'

*　*　*

333

At half past five it was getting dark and we were sitting in the car fifty yards back from a place called the Daley Bread. We were there because it was a place I'd noticed on the way in the night before, big and anonymous, and we'd chosen it because it was on a big street, four turns off 99 and the open road north or south. Easy to find, easy to drive quickly away from. We were there early because we wanted to see if anyone was going to be put into position, whether calls might have been made to the local cops or field office, or . . . anyone else. Whether Monroe could be trusted even a little, in other words.

In half an hour we saw no one except a handful of bedraggled citizens shuffling past with tattered blankets around their shoulders, interspersed with small knots of the young and well-heeled. The two appeared utterly unrelated, and it was hard to understand how they inhabited parts of the same space, as if they were two separate species that just happened to look a little like each other. We watched each group approach and then walk away. Some peered into the car and doubtless wondered why a couple of people might be sitting there on a cold, dark evening. We stared back. We were about as paranoid as we could be. When no one was around we just watched the street in both directions.

At quarter past six, fifteen minutes ahead of the appointed meeting, I opened my door and got out.

'Be careful,' she said.

'I'll be fine. He doesn't know what I look like.'

'No. But other people do.'

I walked up the road at a moderate pace, trying to place myself somewhere between the derelicts and the young and cool. I waited a beat on the opposite side of the road to the diner, saw no one who looked like law enforcement outside, and very few people within.

As I walked across the road I realized that anyone with half a brain would have held the location of the meeting back until Monroe was actually in town, to make it harder for him to mobilize local agents, if he had a mind. More than ever before I wished Bobby was around. Or my mother. Without either, I knew there was some part of my back which was always going to feel uncovered.

I asked a question, quietly and without moving my lips.

'Is this a stupid idea?' There was no reply.

Inside the restaurant it was warmer and a little stuffy. A tired-looking girl in a uniform came straight over with a menu in her hand. 'I'm Britnee,' she said, unnecessarily. She had a badge the size of a plate. 'Will you be dining alone tonight?'

I said I would, and that I had my eye on one of the booths that ran either side of the central partition of the room. As there were only two other couples present in the entire place, she had no real choice but to sit me where I'd asked.

I ordered a chilli without looking at the menu. When she went off to wake up the cook, I got myself into the position Nina and I had agreed upon. I sat close up against the right-hand side

335

of the booth, with my back to the low wall which separated it from its twin on the other side. Neither table could be seen from the other side, but I should be able to hear.

I pulled out a free magazine that I'd picked up in the foyer of the hotel, got my head down, and started reading.

Five minutes later I heard the door of the restaurant open. A quick glance showed Nina entering. Britnee tried to send her to one of the window tables, presumably because of their fabulous view of the cold, wet street outside, but Nina insisted. I lost sight of her as the waitress led her around the other side, but a minute later heard the settling sound of someone sitting on old Naugahyde, the other side of the partition wall.

We sat in silence for a while. I heard another waitress shuffle over to Nina and ask if she wanted a drink, and I heard Nina's reply. Soundwise, it was going to work fine.

I kept running my eyes over advertisements for local stores I had no interest in, and for deeply historic, family-run restaurants which looked identical to what you'd find in any town in the country. It felt strange knowing that Nina was the other side of the divide, doing the same thing. Every now and then I watched the street outside for a while. Nothing happened.

Then finally I heard Nina's voice, quietly.

'He's here,' she said.

I glanced quickly at the door again and saw an athletically built man in his late forties. He was wearing a suit and a long buff overcoat. He came into the restaurant walking quickly, and was past Britnee before she could even suggest a nice seat out on the terrace. He'd evidently clocked Nina's position from the outside.

'Hello Charles,' I overheard, a moment later.

There was the sound of someone sitting down. 'Why couldn't we meet at your hotel?'

'How do you know I'm at a hotel?'

'Where else are you going to be?'

There was a long pause, and then Nina said: 'Charles — are you okay?'

'No,' he said. 'And neither are you. The video's been checked. It's John, and it's not faked. His thumbprint on the bottle opener in Portland isn't fake either, and there's now an eyewitness who saw a man leaving the building half carrying a woman. This man told the witness the girl was drunk and he was taking her home. The photo fit looks so like Zandt it's untrue, and the girl confirms the likeness. I also talked to Olbrich and I know what he found out for you. John was in Portland that night.'

'Thanks, Doug.'

'He's a policeman, not your personal fucking information service. Zandt killed Ferillo, Nina. Accept it. He also hit the girl hard enough to give her concussion. I don't know what the hell is going on in his head but protecting him is going to do you no good at all.'

'Going after him is not going to help you either. You're committed.'

'What do you mean?'

At that moment two things happened. The first was that the waitress arrived with my chilli and took about as long setting it down, and made about as much noise, as you would have believed possible. She also wanted to ask me a lot of questions. Where I was staying, how much I was enjoying being right here in historic Fresno, if I was sure I didn't want a side of onion rings, she could go back and rustle them right up? I answered these as quickly and monosyllabically as I could.

The second was that Nina dried.

I didn't have to see her to know she was staring down at the table, unable to take the next step. So I made a decision. It was a mistake. I stood up, left my food, and walked around the partition.

I pulled a chair over to the end of the booth where Nina and Monroe sat opposite each other with untouched sodas.

Monroe stared at me. 'Can I help you?'

'I hope so,' I said. 'I'm a friend of Nina's. I'm going to ask you the question she doesn't want to ask.'

'Nina, do you know this guy?'

'Yes.'

'Your name is Charles Monroe. My name is Ward Hopkins. I'm one of only two people who can back up what Nina's eventually going to tell you. Probably the only one you're going to listen to, as you're unlikely to take John Zandt's word for much.'

'I've no intention of listening to you either, whoever the hell you may be. Nina . . . '

'You will listen,' I said. 'After you've explained to us how you knew there was a body to be

338

found in The Knights.'

He wasn't expecting that. He tried to stare me down, but it's a funny thing: since my parents died, it's a lot harder to scare me. It was never that easy, and now it's pretty hard. It's like a part of me, right deep down, doesn't really give a shit any more.

Nina was watching him carefully. 'Are you going to answer him?'

He didn't say anything, and I saw the change in Nina's face, and realized she suddenly believed what I'd suggested.

'You bastard,' she said.

'Nina . . . I don't know what this guy's told you, but . . . '

'Really?' I said. 'Here it is in black and white. If a cop gets killed, it's LAPD's problem and job and business. It's not an FBI matter unless the cops choose to make it so, which they won't. The Feds are the big brother they never wanted: this isn't the X-Files, where you get called on parking offences or for spelling mistakes or just anything at all that looks juicy and like someone in a suit might help. Robbery Homicide has a special section dedicated to high-profile killings: they have entire *divisions* who'll drop everything to go after someone who killed one of their own. So what were you doing there? And so fast? How come you were on the scene before anyone went into the motel room? Before anyone knew there was something to be found?'

Monroe shook his head. 'This is ridiculous. Nina, this guy's crazy and we're in enough . . . '

'Charles, look at me and shut up.'

I didn't even recognize Nina's voice. It was a sound somewhere between a hiss and a ragged growl, like some large non-domesticated cat, long caged, finally tired of being screwed around.

Monroe looked at her. I did too.

'Charles, where are my hands?'

He stared at her. 'Under the table.'

'What do you think I'm holding?'

'Oh, Christ, Nina . . . '

'That's right. And I will shoot you right here and now unless you start saying things I can believe.'

'People know where I am.'

'No they don't,' she said. 'No way you're going to compromise your precious reputation by advertising you're coming upstate to talk to me, not with this crap about John floating around. Unless you've brought other people with you, of course, which so far it doesn't look like you have.'

'Of course I haven't,' Monroe said, momentarily looking so angry it was hard not to believe him. 'For God's sake — we've worked together for a long time. We owe each other.'

'Right. That's what I thought. Until I was suspended yesterday. By you.'

'I had no choice. You know that. Zandt has compromised you too much.'

'Compromised? Talk to me about being compromised, Charles. Start by answering Ward's question. My hands are still right where they were and I still mean exactly what I said.'

Monroe went quiet, staring down at his table mat. It held over-saturated pictures of high-fat

340

food, and I knew it wouldn't be able to hold his attention for long.

'Things are going wrong,' he said, in the end. His voice was quiet. 'And not just for you.' He looked up. 'But it's your fault. It's whatever personal mission you're on. Why wouldn't you just tell me what happened last year?'

'To protect you,' she said. 'There was nothing you could do to help, and we didn't know who we could trust. If anyone.'

'Sorry, that just sounds like paranoia.'

'It isn't,' we said, simultaneously.

Monroe looked at me properly for the first time. 'Who did you piss off? Who the *hell* were you dealing with?'

Nina looked at me. I nodded.

'They're called the Straw Men,' she said. 'We don't know how many there are, or even who they are. They used to own a big chunk of land up in Montana, which is the place that got blown up.'

'*You* did that?'

'They did. It was wired,' I said. 'It was a field of evidence. Bodies. Many bodies. These people kill for fun. They had a chain of victim supply using people like Stephen DeLong. The man you once called the Delivery Boy was another one of their procurers — the most important of them, a serial killer in his own right, and some part of the overall organization. He's also my brother. He calls himself the Upright Man. He was key to one of their other sidelines. You remember the explosion at the school in Evanston last year?'

'Yes. They got two kids for it.'

341

'It wasn't them. It was him. Also other events and shootings in Florida, England, Europe, going back twenty years. Maybe longer. The group already existed back in the mid-sixties. They do these things and set up other people to take the falls.'

Monroe looked bewildered. 'Nina — do you believe this?'

'Belief is irrelevant. This is all true. There is a group of people who live in the cracks of this country, and who have done so for a long time. They are powerful, and they kill. *That's* who we pissed off. And now, for the last time: tell me about Jessica.'

He only hesitated for a moment. His decision was made.

'I got a call,' he said, quietly.

Even though she'd known it was coming, I think she still nearly shot him. I think Monroe thought that too.

Then there was silence for a long time.

★   ★   ★

Monroe eventually opened his mouth to speak again. His voice clicked. He took a sip of soda, then changed it to a gulp.

'I got the call the evening before,' he said. 'To my cell — the personal one. Not many people have the number. I assumed it was you, in fact. I was at the theatre with Nancy. It was the intermission, we were in the bar, it was very noisy. A man's voice said something, but I couldn't really hear him properly and by the

342

time I was outside he'd rung off. I had no reason to . . . Then next morning I was on the way to work and I got a second call. Again it was a man, and he asked what the hell was wrong with me, was I not interested? I said I didn't know what he was talking about. He told me a cop had just been shot, and I should go to The Knights motel right away. It . . . '

'It would be good for you,' Nina said, as if Monroe had just admitted he wanted to feed crack to babies while beating off.

'Yes,' he said. 'That's exactly what he said.'

'The same number that called you the night before?'

'Yes. For all I knew it could have been someone in the department.'

'Without declaring their identity? Yeah, right.'

'If it was going to be good for me it would also be good for the bureau.'

'Talk to the hand, Charles. I don't believe you and I don't care. You went there because you were tipped off there was something worth your while, something good for your career, and you pulled me into something you knew was tainted. You told no one that you had prior knowledge. You manoeuvred Olbrich into assembling a task force and you worked it for a couple of days until it started looking like it wasn't going anywhere. When we were in the McCains' house and I asked if we were sure the cop-killer also murdered Jessica, you already *knew* the two could be different.'

'The fact they could be didn't mean they were.'

'Oh, come on. You even tried to push me away from the idea. Then the morning after John suddenly made the Most Wanted List for the Ferillo killing, you get another email. Untraceable again, I assume?'

'It doesn't matter how it came, Nina. It's real. And get off your horse, for God's sake. You knew. You *knew* that Zandt had killed DeLong and you withheld the evidence.'

'I didn't know at the time. He only told me late last year.'

'Whatever. The minute you heard you were an accessory after the fact, so don't . . . '

I interrupted. 'Who was that man with you when you showed Nina the film?'

'I don't know,' he said, bitterly. 'He arrived that morning and already knew all about it. About everything. He had NSA security clearance but yesterday I tried to trace him and they claim he doesn't exist. I pushed it and shouted at some people and . . . '

'And now things are getting shaky for you too,' Nina said.

'Only indirectly.' He breathed out heavily. 'The Gary Johnson file is being re-opened.'

'*What?*'

'Some attorney in Louisiana is suddenly claiming he has evidence we tampered with the forensic reports. Specifically, that you did, and I looked the other way. Someone wants you discredited, and as the senior agent on that case I'm going to share the ride. Satisfied?'

'You compromised yourself, Charles. Don't blame me.'

344

'And don't you claim any moral high ground either. You withheld knowledge of a homicide, lied about what happened last year — and do you really think I don't *know* you took Jessica's disk out of evidence for forty-eight hours? Either is enough to ruin you and both were your choice and your fault.'

'Now there's been another killing with a disk,' I said. 'Did you get a warning of that too?'

'No. And look — who the hell are you, anyhow?'

'Ward's parents were killed by the Straw Men,' Nina said. 'He helped us save Sarah Becker's life and he's the only person in the world that I trust right now. I think that's enough. Tell me about the new killing.'

'Nina . . . '

'You got pulled into this through Jessica. If this is another murder by the same man, then we have some small chance of solving them, which is the only outcome that stands a hope in hell of making your life right again.'

'And yours.'

'Mine's flushed already. That pisses me off. I want to find the people who've done it. Ward and I have business with them.'

'Her name was Katelyn Wallace,' Monroe said. 'She worked the night shift at the Fairview in Seattle. Someone came and snatched her out of a hotel full of guests and with a night janitor right there on duty with her. She was found forty miles east in some bushes in a small town called Snoqualmie. We have half a registration number for a car seen passing through late that night, but it's a rental and it's a vacation area. Katelyn's body was more messed up than Jessica's. The belief — and yes, it's a profilers' opinion, but the photos bear it out — is the killer is getting more out of control. He hadn't bothered to dress her for comfort and this time the disk wasn't just resting in the mouth. It had been shoved into a hole he'd made in her head. It had the same piece of music on it as Jessica's.'

'Was there a note?'

'No. Three long-distance landscape pictures, low quality. A webcam. Of Pittsburgh, believe it or not. So the bureau there is now on alert, but who knows what it means, if anything.'

'What do you know about the woman?' I asked.

'She was from San Francisco. Forty-two now, moved to Seattle twelve years ago. No partner, but plenty of friends and a cat, and nobody who can think of anyone who might have done it. So far as we can tell, she's a random victim.'

'I don't think so,' I said. 'Why travel halfway up the country to pick someone random, and then stamp yourself all over it with the same MO? There has to be a connection between them. Nina told you about the missing photograph in Jessica's apartment?'

'Yes. We tracked down all three of the men in the videos. Two were regulars at this bar called Jimmy's, the other was someone she met at a party in Venice Beach. None look good for it, though one did confirm she had a picture of her parents beside her bed; he seemed to get a kick out of the fact. But now this Webdaddy slimeball,

346

Robert Klennert, thinks he *might* have a recollection of someone trying to trace Jessica's location via an email to his main portal site, about two months ago. It happens all the time, apparently, all his girls get it. He just bounces them back. He didn't remember there was one for Jessica in particular until he started going through his files. It may not mean anything.'

'Or it could be the killer trying to find a way in. That's a long lead time, isn't it? Is there any sign that anything was taken from Katelyn Wallace's place?'

'How are we going to know? We don't have the lucky chance of a slew of images this time. Katelyn wasn't a web whore. She was a stable woman who worked hard.'

'They die too. But . . . We've been assuming that the killer took the picture as a random souvenir. Something personal, a way of getting his fingers into the life of a woman he was intending to kill. What if it was more than that?'

Nina was looking at me. 'What are you thinking?'

'They're trying to get the killer caught,' I said, talking slowly, trying not to get in the way of my thoughts. 'That's why they tipped Charles off. Obviously. But why? Who would the Straw Men want to get caught?'

I looked up, and that's when I saw him.

If I'd done what I was supposed to do, and stayed on the other side of the partition and kept watch while Nina did the talking, I would have seen him sooner. As it was I only got a quick impression of a slim man with short hair and

347

glasses, standing right outside the restaurant. Looking in, straight at us.

'Shit . . . ' was as far as I got — before there was a smashing sound, two claps, and the slapping thud of a bullet smacking into the padded wall behind us.

I threw myself out of the booth and went for my gun. I was fast but Nina was quicker because hers was already in her hand.

We were both firing before Monroe had the faintest idea what was happening. With my other hand I grabbed a chair and awkwardly threw it at the window, trying to give them enough time to get out from the booth.

The chair went wide but Nina was fast. The man kept firing through the hole in the glass. Measured shots, one after the other.

I scrabbled to try to get under his sight line, pulling Nina's arm and dragging her down behind a table. There was screaming around us. Britnee was lying on the ground, glass cuts over her face.

I saw the man running past the window, little more than a shadow, but he wasn't running away. He was heading around the front, to come into the restaurant.

'Oh Christ,' Nina said, and I turned to see that Monroe was slumped over the table. She started to head back to him but I grabbed her arm and yanked her down again.

'Leave him.' I heard the front door of the restaurant pulled open, screams of fresh intensity.

'Ward, he's been hit.'

'I know.'

Then the man came around and into our aisle. I think part of me had been expecting that it would be my brother, but it wasn't. He was younger, fit-looking but bulky in the chest. He was wearing combats and a dark coat. He stood at the end, apparently unafraid of what we might try to do, and took aim on Nina.

I shot him. I got him plumb in the chest.

He was thrown backwards, crashing into a table.

He stayed down for maybe five seconds, enough for me to start to straighten up, before suddenly standing again.

There was no blood coming out of him, and I realized he was wearing a vest. I backed away, trying to get behind something before he fired again. Nina fired past me, but missed. The man shot twice more and both came close. I fired again, aiming higher, but missed. Hitting a moving man's head is very hard. Just aiming for it isn't easy. You've got to really want someone dead. By now, I did.

The sound of a shot came from another angle and I thought *Oh Christ, there's another one of them* — but then I saw it was Monroe. His overcoat was covered in blood and he was wedged in the booth but had wrenched his upper body around and was emptying his gun at the man.

I took the opportunity, grabbed Nina again and pulled her around the back of the partition wall. My waitress was cowering there, breathlessly trying to scream but instead making a sound like a mouse being hit with a hammer.

On the back wall I saw a pair of half-height doors.

More shots suddenly, like the sound of slow hand clapping.

'Ward, we've got to get Charles . . . '

'It's too late.' I yanked her back towards the swing doors into the small kitchen. She fought at first but then followed me as I shoved past two terrified-looking men in whites and straight out the open back door. I slipped on the top of a short flight of stairs but grabbed the rail and made it down.

We ran down the side of the restaurant. The sound of shooting had stopped. I glanced in and saw the man standing over the booth where Monroe now lay face down on the table.

The man turned and saw us. Then he was running towards the door. Running fast.

'Get the car,' I shouted. Nina kept on running.

I turned and pointed my gun up the street, walking backwards as fast as I could. He'd fired his first shot before I even realized he was out on the street.

I shot and got him again, in the stomach, throwing him backwards once more. I turned and sprinted back to the car just as the lights flashed on and I heard the motor start.

Then it felt as if someone punched me on the shoulder. I was off balance and it threw me around and I fell and crashed onto the pavement. I pulled myself up, still unsure what had happened but feeling off-kilter and hot, and fired backwards.

The car jerked forward and the door flew open and I threw myself inside. My legs were still hanging out as Nina stood on the pedal and reversed down the street at forty miles an hour. When I was inside and had the door shut she whipped the car around in a tight turn and hammered off up the street.

'Where am I going?' She glanced across at me and the sudden widening of her eyes told me what I already suspected.

I put my hand up to my left shoulder. It was wet and warm.

'Just anywhere,' I said, as the pain suddenly cut in like a knife.

23

They stepped out of Henry's Diner into a drizzle that was light but insistent. Tom shivered massively as the cold hit him. He'd managed to eat only half his food, hunched with Henrickson over a table in the back corner. Tom saw a few locals glance his way. You could see they were thinking 'There's Bigfoot Boy' — or maybe 'Bullshit Boy' — and that hadn't helped his appetite much. Henrickson had been unusually quiet during the meal, and it had been a while since the last grin. It could be he was tired too, though he didn't seem it. His movements remained sharp and precise, and he ate quickly and methodically, making easy work of a chicken-fried steak. He'd asked for this to be done rare, which was a first for Tom — a first for the waitress, too, judging by the way she'd looked at him. When not eating, the man had looked out of the window as if wishing the darkness were over.

'Okay,' he said, as Tom tried to burrow deep in his coat against the wind. He looked away up the street. 'I guess I'll be heading back to the motel.'

Tom was surprised. He'd been assuming they'd be heading to the bar. It wasn't that he wanted a drink. He was exhausted from the day's walking, and the warm, stuffy diner had made him feel drowsy and dog-tired. Bed sounded good. But if he was alone in that room, he'd have to think about calling Sarah, and he still didn't have any proof.

'Buy you a beer?' The question made him feel gauche.

'Sure,' Henrickson said, slowly. 'Why not?'

There was something in his tone that made Tom wonder whether he was accepting for some reason of his own, one that had nothing to do with either a desire for a drink or Tom's company. But when they were sat at the counter of Big Frank's — which was otherwise stone-cold empty — the man clinked his glass against Tom's.

'Apologize if I seem kind of elsewhere,' he said. 'Just can't help feeling the time moving on. This is important to me.'

'I know,' Tom said. 'Tomorrow we'll find it. I promise.'

'Sounds good,' the man said, eyes on the door. 'But now let's see what's about to happen here.'

Tom turned to see a big man heading across the bar towards them. He wasn't coming fast, but there was purpose in his stride.

'Oh crap,' Tom said. 'That's the sheriff.'

Tom watched as Connolly and the reporter looked each other up and down. Then the policeman turned his attention to Tom.

'Mr Kozelek,' he said. 'See you just haven't been able to give up Sheffer's hospitality yet.'

'Who was it?' Tom asked. 'The waitress? One of the old boys in the corner booth?'

'Can't say I understand what you mean,' Connolly said.

'Think he's implying that someone let you

353

know he was still in town,' Henrickson said. 'I'm inclined to believe he's right.'

'This isn't Twin Peaks, son. I just happened to be coming up the way, saw you two coming in.'

Henrickson took a sip of his beer, and looked at the policeman over the top of his glass. 'Do you have some kind of problem with us, Sheriff?'

'Don't even know who you are.'

'I'm a writer.'

'And what would someone like you be doing up in Sheffer?'

'Big feature article. Charming vacation towns of the North West.'

'Mr Kozelek helping you out, is he?'

'You could say that.'

'Never really had much time for writers,' Connolly said. 'Most of them seem to be full of shit.'

Tom didn't like the way the two men were looking at each other. He tried to think of something to say, something so banal that it might defuse the atmosphere. Then he looked up at the sound of the bar door opening again. Two people came into the room, shaking rain out of their hair.

'Hello,' said one of them, a woman. Tom realized it was the doctor who'd examined him. She came over and joined the group.

'Melissa,' she said, helpfully. 'Don't worry — you were pretty zonked when we met. How are you feeling?'

'Fine,' Tom said. Her husband was behind her. He nodded at Connolly and headed around the other side of the bar, towards the pool table in

354

the far corner. He had the air of a man who didn't do polite conversation.

'That's good,' Melissa said, looking at Tom in that way doctors do: with bright, detached assessment, as if implying that his own opinion of his state of health, while mildly interesting, was of no diagnostic import whatsoever. 'No nausea? Headaches?'

'No,' he lied. 'I feel fine. Thank you.'

'Excellent. Oh — if I were you, I'd go easy on the herbal remedies for a while. You never know the effects of some of those things.'

Connolly seemed to stiffen slightly. 'That's been cleared up,' the policeman said. 'They didn't belong to Mr Kozelek.'

Henrickson cocked his head. 'Herbs?'

Melissa smiled tentatively, as if suddenly uncertain what she had wandered into. 'I found some,' she said. 'A little bunch. In Mr Kozelek's bag.'

'Melissa — do me a favour, would you?' Connolly said. 'Be glad to join you two in a moment. But there's something I need to discuss with these boys first.'

'Sure,' she said, stepping back affably. Normally she might have felt dismissed, but, as it happened, some of what Tom had seen in her eyes was not professional appraisal but the pleasantly lingering effects of a pretty major joint. 'You want a beer?'

'That would be great.'

The three men watched as she walked around the other side of the bar, and then turned to look at one another once more.

355

'So if these plants didn't belong to Tom,' Henrickson said, 'how did they get there, exactly?'

'Thought you didn't know what I was talking about.'

'I'm sorry if you got that impression. Actually, I believe you're talking about the valerian and skullcap Tom had in his bag.'

'What?' Tom said. He turned to the policeman. 'What is he talking about?'

'Beats me,' the cop said.

'I don't think so.' Henrickson reached into his jacket and pulled out a small plastic bag. He laid it on the counter. 'This the kind of stuff the doctor found?'

Connolly looked away. 'Plants mostly look the same to me.'

'Not to me. I know these are both medicinal herbs, and I know that both were used by a particular group of people.'

'The local Indians.'

'Little earlier than that, actually. So tell me, Sheriff. Judging by Tom's reaction when I found these earlier, I don't think he had anything to do with them winding up in his bag. But presumably you'll be able to tell me how that happened?'

'They were put there by a woman called Patrice Anders.'

Henrickson grinned. 'Is that right? This would be the woman with the boots.'

'When she came across Mr Kozelek's belongings in the forest it was clear to her that they belonged to someone in a poor state of mind. Mrs Anders has an interest in alternative therapies. She left these materials in his bag in the hope that, if he returned, he might recognize them and use them.'

This time Henrickson laughed outright. 'You're kidding, right?'

'That's what she told me.'

'Let me get this straight. She happens to be stomping around out there in her novelty footwear — kind of conveniently — and finds Tom's little camp. She divines from this that Tom's head is fucked up, and so she decides to leave some medicinal herbs in his bag on the off-chance he will work out that's what they are, and decide to take them? Herbs she just happened to be carrying around with her on a walk in the woods? And herbs that most modern people would dispense in a tincture, or at the very least in a tea?'

'People do strange things.'

'Yeah, they do. They surely do. Well, thank you, Sheriff. Those plants had been bothering me ever since I found them. I'm glad to have heard such a straightforward and credible explanation.' Henrickson stood, and grinned at Tom. 'Well, my friend, it's a shame we didn't run into this gentleman earlier. He seems to have all the answers. And now I'm kind of tired from our hike today, and so I think it's time to hit the sack.'

Connolly didn't move. 'I really would prefer it if you gentlemen would consider relocating to another charming North West town.'

'Maybe you would,' Henrickson said. 'And I'd

prefer it if you'd stop trying to bully my friend. He knows what he saw, and so do you. He saw a Bigfoot.'

'There isn't any such thing. He saw a bear.'

'Right. You keep believing that. But unless you're going to make an official deal out of hassling him, I'd say it's time you got out of his face.'

Henrickson winked, and headed for the door without looking back. Extremely confused, and not sure whether things had just gotten better or worse, Tom followed him.

As soon as they were outside the journalist started walking fast, heading back towards the motel through rain that was beginning to turn to sleet.

'Jim?' Tom said, struggling to keep up. 'What the hell was that all about?'

'I knew I was onto something when I found that stuff in your bag. I just wasn't expecting it to be handed to me on a plate.'

'Explain.'

'You've heard of herbal medicine, right?'

'Sure. People using plants to cure illnesses, instead of pharmaceuticals. Like, I don't know, aromatherapy.'

'No,' Henrickson said, as he stepped over the low fence into the motel parking lot. 'Different thing. People have been using plants for a long, *long* time. Medicine's nothing more than a specialized form of food, right? In the 1970s they found a Neanderthal burial in Northern Iraq. The body had been buried with eight different flowers, almost all of which are still used by

358

herbalists today. The Neanderthals knew about this stuff at least sixty thousand years ago, probably a lot longer. And that's why they're in your bag.'

'I don't get it. Why?'

'Because the creature you saw *did* come back. He came back and put this stuff where you might find it.'

Tom stopped walking. 'A Neanderthal man prescribed me herbs?'

'Got it in one.' Henrickson held his car keys up and pressed a button. The lights of his Lexus flashed. 'Hop in.'

'What now?'

'Get in the car, and I'll tell you.'

Tom climbed in the passenger seat. Henrickson yanked the car around in a tight circle and took it fast onto the main road, passing Big Frank's and heading east.

Tom thought, but couldn't be sure, that he saw Connolly watching them from the windows of the bar.

'Jim, where are we going?'

'To talk to someone,' the man said. 'Someone who knows a lot more than they've been letting on.'

★ ★ ★

The man said nothing else on the half-hour journey. Tom knew where they were going long before the car turned onto the lonely road that led up into the development no one had wanted. Henrickson parked on the windy, empty road,

359

five yards from the gateway to the Anders property. He left the engine running but killed the lights. Darkness fell like a stone.

'Wait here.'

Tom watched as the other man got out of the car and walked up ahead. By the time Henrickson was past the wooden sign it was hard to make him out. Ten minutes later he came back.

'Somebody's home this time,' he said. His face looked cold and hard and there was wet ice in his hair. 'Or isn't hiding well enough to remember to turn out all the lights.'

He pulled the car forward and through the gate. Drove slowly down the track between the trees.

'You haven't put your headlights back on.'

'That's right.'

As they took the penultimate bend the lake became visible, frigid in straggly moonlight. It looked flat and eldritch, proud that nothing had changed for it, ever, that it had always been this way. Then Tom could see the dark shape of the cabin, huddled in the trees, with two small, dim rectangles of yellow light.

Henrickson pulled the car over, turned off the engine. Sat a moment, watching the house.

'Okay,' he said. 'Let's go. Shut your door quietly.'

'Look, Jim,' Tom said. 'We can't do this now. We should have called ahead. We can't just turn up. Two guys appearing at her door, it's going to scare her to death.'

Henrickson turned to him then, and did

something with his mouth. It wasn't a grin. It wasn't a smile, even. It was similar enough to the things he had been doing with it all along, however, and it made Tom wonder, with a low, quiet dismay, whether any of them had been grins after all.

'Get out,' the man said.

Tom climbed out into the cold, squinting against the sleet. He shut his door silently, looking over at the cabin. If Henrickson was right, this woman had lied to make him look foolish. At least once, maybe twice. Of course Connolly was going to believe her instead of him, especially as he evidently hated the mere idea of Bigfoot. And through her lies, this woman had destroyed his story. She'd taken away the only thing that could make his life take him back.

If it took a little surprise in the evening to undo that, maybe it was okay.

He turned at the sound of Henrickson opening the trunk of the car. The man pulled a large rucksack out and looped it over his back in one smooth movement. Then he leaned in again, reaching with both arms. When he straightened once more, Tom gaped at him.

'What the fuck is that?'

It was a stupid question. It was obvious what the man had slipped over his shoulder. It was a rifle. It was also obvious that the shorter, blunter thing he had in his hand was a large-calibre handgun. Neither looked like the sort of thing you saw in hunting stores. They looked like the kind of weapon you saw on the news, with plumes of smoke in the distance behind.

Henrickson closed the trunk. 'The forest can be dangerous,' he said.

'It certainly is now,' Tom said. 'Jesus. Look, can we leave those things in the car?'

The other man had turned and was walking towards the cabin. Suddenly very unsure about what was happening, Tom hurried after him. By the time he caught up, Henrickson had already rapped on the front door. They waited. Henrickson was just raising his hand again when he stopped, head cocked. Tom hadn't heard anything.

There was the sound of two bolts being pulled, and then the door opened.

Patrice Anders stood inside. Beyond was a small, cosy room. She looked a little older than Tom remembered, and smaller. But she didn't look afraid, or even much surprised.

'Good evening, Mr Kozelek,' she said. 'Who's your friend?'

'You know who I am,' Henrickson said.

'No,' she said, 'I don't. But I know why you're here.'

'That should make things easy.'

She shrugged. 'It does for me. I'm not telling you anything.'

'You will,' Henrickson said. There was something off about his voice. He walked straight past the woman and into the cabin, eyes raking the walls and surfaces. He yanked the phone out of the wall socket. He found the woman's cell, knocked it to the floor and stood on it.

'Jim,' Tom said, aghast. 'This isn't the way to go about this.'

'Go about what?' the old woman said. She was trying to seem unperturbed, but her voice was constricted and her face pinched. 'What do you think he's here for?'

'He's a reporter,' Tom said, stepping inside. 'He wants to write a story about what I saw. That's all.'

Patrice looked at him. 'God, you're dumb,' she said.

'What do you mean?' he snapped. He was tired of feeling that everyone understood things except him.

'He's not here to write. He's a hunter. He's here to kill.'

'Kill what?'

'Bear, I assume. Only thing we've got in these woods.'

Tom looked at Henrickson, and had to concede that his friend didn't look like a reporter any more. Partly it was the guns, partly the way he was yanking open the cupboards that lined the back wall of the room, rifling through the contents as though the fact they were someone else's possessions was of absolutely no moment. 'Jim, tell me this isn't true.'

'Ms Anders is dissembling, but otherwise she and I are in total agreement,' Henrickson said, without turning. 'On both my intentions and your intelligence. Aha.' He pulled out a thick bundle of rope and threw it to Tom. 'Tie her hands behind her back.'

'You're kidding me,' Tom said. 'I'm not doing that.'

The butt of Henrickson's rifle whipped round in a short, clipped arc that ended with Tom's face. He didn't even see it coming.

He crashed backwards into a kitchen unit, slipped on the rug, dropped to the floor. He was dimly aware of Henrickson stepping over him and kicking the front door shut; then of him grabbing the old woman by the hair. He shook his head, to try to clear it. It felt like someone had hammered a screwdriver up each side of his nose.

'You may as well do it now,' he heard the woman saying, through a fog. 'Because I'm not going to help you.'

Henrickson's response was a blow that sent her across the couch. Then he was standing over Tom, holding the rope.

'We're going to find this thing,' he told him, quietly. 'And I am going to do what I came to do.'

Tom stared up at him, feeling blood pouring out of his nose and knowing why Henrickson's voice sounded different. His accent had gone, the folksy lilt and the backwoods terms. Now he had the voice of a stranger. Tom felt as if he had never been in a room with this man before, and that anyone who had heard this voice would be likely to remember it, and remember it the rest of their life. His voice said that he knew you. That he knew you, and all about you, and all about everybody else too.

'You're going to help me because otherwise I

will make you kill her, and I don't think you'll enjoy doing that.'

All Tom could do was shake his head.

'You'll do it,' Henrickson said. 'After all, it won't be the first time. Different circumstances, I'll admit.'

'Shut up,' Tom said. The woman was staring at him now.

'Tom's already on the board,' Henrickson told her. 'Used to be a partner in a design firm down in LA. Everything in place — cute car, cute family, regular fuckfest with one of the cute little designer girls driving the big-screen Apple Macs. One night they work late in the office and have a drink on the way home and round the corner from her apartment Tom slides a red light — can't be *too* late back, not again — and a Porsche smacks into the passenger side. The girl dies looking like modern art. So does the little boy Tom didn't know she was carrying inside. Tom's just under the limit, and fortunately the Porsche driver is completely shit-faced. So Tom walks.'

'You think so?' Tom shouted. He pushed himself to his feet. He swiped his sleeve under his nose, viciously, not caring how much it hurt. 'You really think I walked from it?'

'You're alive, they're dead,' Henrickson said. 'You do the math.'

Tom started to move, but the man knew about the thought before he did. A quick movement, and the barrel of his handgun was planted squarely in the middle of Patrice's forehead.

'I'll make you kill her and then when we're

done I'll set you free,' Henrickson said. 'You couldn't kill yourself last time. I doubt you'll be able to again. I'll let you flail for a year or two, and then I'll come find you and put you out of your misery. Maybe. Or we can find this thing and we will photograph it and then it will escape, so far as anyone else knows. Everything will be good. You will attain the distinction and purpose you now know can't be found in a young woman's pants. Sarah might even take you back.'

'How do you know all this?'

'Because he's not human,' the old woman said, quietly.

Henrickson laughed shortly. 'Tom — are you going to tie her fucking hands, or what?'

Tom looked at Patrice. One side of her face was red, but her eyes were clear and locked on his.

'Don't,' she said. 'Not for me. For them.'

But he looked away, and when the bundle of rope hit his chest this time, he caught it.

24

'Ward, be still, for God's sake.'

'It hurts.'

'Well, just, be cool.'

'Screw that. Cool is for teenagers. I'm old enough to admit it hurts like a motherfuck.'

I was sitting on the passenger seat with my feet outside. Nina was crouched outside the car dabbing at my shoulder with a cloth soaked in disinfectant. I had no idea where we were except that we were in the parking lot of a gas station just outside a small town whose name we didn't know.

'It's clean,' she said. 'I think.'

I glanced across at my shoulder and saw a ragged tear across the deltoid muscle. It was bleeding still, but less than it had been for most of the fifty miles from Fresno. It hurt a *lot*, even though I'd eaten a fistful of the strongest pain pills we could find in the market where we'd bought the cloth and disinfectant. It hurt like I was eight years old and a bully was repeatedly smacking a fist into my shoulder, so hard and so fast that the impacts blurred into one long, keening ache.

Nina was looking up at me. She looked young and worried and as if she hoped she had done something well enough; also as if she hoped I wasn't going to keep whining for much longer. I realized the dent in my shoulder was nothing compared to the hit she'd taken up at The Halls. I also knew I should just be thankful the bullet hadn't landed about nine inches to the right.

'Thank you,' I said. 'It does feel better.'

'Liar,' she said. She stood and looked over the roof of the car at the station, where a man with a beard was standing in the window. 'We're being watched.'

'It's just the till monkey. Wondering if we're going to buy gas or what. It's okay. Not everyone is out to get us.'

'Attractive theory,' she said. 'You got any proof?'

'Not really.'

'What are we going to do?'

'You're going to have to call someone,' I said. 'Tell them about Monroe.'

'They'll know already,' she said, glumly. 'He'll have had ID on him.'

'I don't mean the fact,' I said. 'I mean what happened. And what it means.'

'We don't know,' she said. 'Not for sure.'

'Yeah we do.'

'I didn't see the man who came out of The Knights and killed the cop. I'm just going on the witness statements.'

'I know. But he sure sounded a lot like the man who just tried to kill us. Down to the clothes.'

'It's a very general description. The wage slave in there probably doesn't look so different.'

'I don't mean just physically similar. I also mean the kind of man who will walk into a restaurant and keep shooting — in front of

368

witnesses — even when three people are shooting back. Don't split the atom. I don't think we need to look for two people here.'

'So who is he? You've got something on your mind again and I really wish you'd just tell me what it is.'

'We need to keep driving,' I said. 'Not just because we need to get ourselves as far from that disaster as possible. Also because there's a woman we have to see tonight and it's a long way.'

'Where?'

'North. Get my bag for me. I've got the address.'

★   ★   ★

Mrs Campbell wasn't home.

This time I called ahead, long before we approached San Francisco. There was no answer, and no machine. It's funny how quickly you get used to the idea that houses have a memory, and liaise with strangers, and will pass on a message for you. This house wasn't there to help. So we just drove up there instead. Nina meanwhile continued to refuse to call the FBI in LA. They would either know about Monroe, or would do soon. She didn't feel inclined to trust them either way. I thought this was wrong, that declaring our position and innocence as early as possible made sense. There might be one strange person wandering the halls of justice: it didn't mean the whole organization was riddled. I couldn't convince her. In the end we stopped

369

discussing it. The more time I spent with Nina, the more I got the sense that there were inner defences — a whole castle, with a moat and a keep and probably boiling oil in reserve too — that it would be hard or impossible to bust through.

The ache in my shoulder was manageable so long as I kept gobbling painkillers. More of a problem was that it started to tighten up. By the time we were at the outskirts of San Francisco it felt like it had been sewn on by someone who hadn't bothered learning how it was supposed to work inside the cloth. This kept me on map-reading duty, which was probably a good division of labour. Nina drove well. Her sense of direction wasn't so hot; the inconveniences of three-dimensional space seemed to irritate her. I wouldn't want to see her in a Humvee. I suspect she'd just drive straight through anything in the way.

'Why now?' she said, eventually. 'Why wait three months before pouring it on? Okay, you were AWOL and hard to find. But they could have clipped me and John right away.'

'Assume regrouping time, I guess, after The Halls got blown up.'

'But that can't have been all of them up there. If they're as powerful as we think, there must be more. Do we really think the guy I saw with Monroe was one of them?'

'I do,' I said. 'And that scares me.'

'Me too. But it makes it even harder to believe that they couldn't have had us killed.'

'They sure as hell tried, tonight.'

'Yes. But why not sooner?'

'You work for the FBI. If you turn up in a dumpster, questions are going be asked. Questions that wouldn't go away. I could see Monroe turning it into a crusade.'

'For the good of the department, of course. But I'm still dead.'

'These people take a long view. The cabin we found near Yakima says they've been at this kind of thing a long time. They were going to let us sweat on the grounds we were no real danger, and clear us up when the opportunity arose. Then everything went wide immediately after John capped this Ferillo person. He must have got hold of some huge great stick and pushed it right into their nest. They obviously had someone surveilling him after his daughter disappeared, taped him coming out of DeLong's house. Evidently they decided to let it go, maybe DeLong was overdue for retirement anyhow, but now John's done something big enough for them to dust it off. John's the key to this.'

'If he doesn't call soon I'm going to kill him myself.'

'Cool,' I said. 'I'll help.'

It was nine o'clock by the time we were getting close. I called again. Still no response. Either she wasn't answering the phone for reasons of her own, or she wasn't home. First didn't make much sense. Second worried me.

Nina parked right outside a house that showed a single light, over the door. We got out and looked at the house.

'Nobody home, Ward.'

371

'Maybe.'

I walked up the steps and rang on the bell. It jangled inside. No lights came on. Nobody came to the door.

'I don't like this,' I said. 'Old people don't get out much. They're always home.'

'Maybe we should talk to the neighbours.'

I looked down at myself, then at her. Her blouse had a decent-sized splash of blood on it. The arm of my jacket was hanging on by a string and looked dark and blotched under the streetlight. 'Yeah, right.'

'I see your point,' she said. 'So what do we do now?'

I got out an ATM card which still didn't work, but which I'd never had the heart to throw away.

'Oh great,' she said.

She turned and watched the nearby windows while I worked the card into the frame of Mrs Campbell's door.

Five minutes later we'd confirmed she wasn't home. I had been half convinced we'd find her with an axe in her head. All the rooms were empty, however, and tidy.

'So she's out,' Nina said. 'Maybe she's just got more of a social life than you.'

We sat and waited until half past nine. Then Nina sat some more, while I paced around. Finally this took me out into the hallway, where I saw something I hadn't seen in a while. A telephone table. One of those pieces of furniture designed to hold a phone, and someone using it, back in the days when being able to speak to people from afar was still something of a big deal. Next to the phone itself was a small notebook covered in a floral fabric.

A personal telephone book.

I picked it up and riffled through to the letter 'D'. No names I recognized. Then, realizing I would probably have done the same, I looked under the letter 'M' instead.

There it was.

I picked up the phone and dialled. It was late. Mrs Campbell had told me Muriel had kids, but I hadn't gathered what age. Probably I was going to get an earful even assuming she answered the phone.

'Dupree household.'

'Is that Muriel?'

'Who is this?'

'My name's Ward Hopkins. We met a few . . . '

'I remember who you are. How did you get my number?'

'I'm in Mrs Campbell's house. It's in her book.'

'What the hell are you doing there?'

'I need to speak to her urgently. I came to see her. She wasn't home. I got worried and thought I should check inside.'

'Why would you be worried? Do you know something I don't?'

'Muriel, could you just tell me: do you know where she is?'

There was a pause, and then she said, 'Wait there.'

The sound of the phone became muffled. I heard her voice talking, but couldn't make out any of the words. Then it became clear again.

'She says she'll talk to you,' Muriel said, making it clear she thought this was a mistake. 'You'd better come over.'

★ ★ ★

It was a twenty-minute drive across town. Muriel Dupree didn't look at all welcoming when she opened her door, but she did eventually step aside. She looked at Nina suspiciously.

'Who's she?'

'A friend,' I said.

'She know she's got blood on her shirt?'

'Yes,' Nina said. 'It's been a long day. Ward has it on him too.'

'He's a man. What do you expect?'

Mrs Dupree's house was tidy and airy and one of the nicest decorated I'd seen in a while. Plain and simple, the house of someone who both lived and valued an orderly life. She led us down a hallway into the back, where a wide kitchen gave onto a sitting area. Mrs Campbell was in a chair right next to the electric fire. She looked more frail than I remembered.

'If you don't mind me asking,' I said, 'what are you doing here?'

'Any reason she shouldn't be?'

I glanced at Muriel and realized Mrs Campbell meant a great deal to her. Also that, beneath the screw-you exterior, there was something else. Concern, certainly. Fear, perhaps.

I sat on the end of the couch. 'Mrs Campbell,' I said. 'There's something I have to ask you . . .'

'I know,' she said. 'So why don't you go ahead?'

' . . . but why are you here?'

'Funny things been happening,' Muriel said. 'Joan had been hearing strange sounds outside her house in the night. Where she lives, that's not unknown. But then some man came to the door and asks her a lot of questions.'

'When was this?'

'The day after you came,' Mrs Campbell said. 'It's okay, Muriel. I'll talk to him.'

'What did this man look like?'

'Your height. A little broader across the shoulders.'

I looked at Nina. 'John. I hope so, at least. He's a detective. He'd have been able to find out an old employee list.'

'He knew I'd worked there, that's for sure. I didn't know the answers to his questions, though. He went away. He was polite. But he didn't seem like a man who would treat everyone that way.'

'What did he ask you about?'

'Same thing you're about to. But I know the answers now.'

'When we spoke before, you told me about a family who had taken Paul in. The one in which the woman had a dog that died in strange circumstances.'

'I remember.'

'Was their name Jones?'

Nina's head jerked around to stare at me.

'No,' Mrs Campbell said. 'It was Wallace. Jones was the other family. The one who let him

375

go when they had a baby girl.'

I felt dizzy. 'How come you remember this now?'

'She had me find out,' Muriel said, quietly. 'After you'd gone, she called me up. First I thought she was going to be angry with me for putting you in touch with her. But she wasn't.'

'I asked Muriel to do a little detective work on my behalf,' the old woman said. 'Track down a couple of my old colleagues, people who had been there back then. Found one in Florida, of course, baking herself to alligator hide. Other one in Maine. Moved back to be close to family, then the kids died ahead of her. That's life, I guess. With three sets of memories, we could put it together.' She bit her lip. 'So tell me. What has happened?'

'Paul has killed both of them,' I said. 'Jessica Jones was found dead in a motel four days ago, down in Los Angeles. Katelyn Wallace yesterday morning.'

'Where?'

'Up north. East of Seattle. He murdered them and left erased hard disks in their bodies. This seems to be something about undoing the past, wiping a life clean, maybe even some kind of purification thing.'

'Oh my God,' the old woman said. Her hands were shaking. Muriel reached across and gently put her hand on top of them.

'Jessica and Katelyn were children in his foster families?' Nina said. 'He killed them just because of that?'

'They were families that tried to take him in

for good, actually tried to give him a home. Something about him made it impossible. He evidently needs someone to blame. He's wiping his disk clean. He's . . . Mrs Campbell, do you have any idea where Katelyn Wallace's parents live now?'

'They're dead,' Muriel said. 'Natural causes, five years ago. Well, kind of natural. Nature, anyhow. They were on a sail boat that sank out in the Bay. Nobody seemed to think there was anything weird about it.'

'What about the Joneses?' I asked.

'Don't know anything about them.'

'LAPD had local cops looking for them down in Monterey,' Nina said. 'I told you. They had an address but there was nobody home. The neighbours said they hadn't seen them in six weeks. The assumption was they were on vacation.'

'Maybe they are,' I said, but I was thinking of two people, of about the right age, whose bodies I had seen on a desolate, isolated plain five hundred miles north of where I was sitting. Whom John had photographed, and might possibly have been able to trace — if he'd subsequently made progress in an investigation he'd chosen to keep secret from Nina and me. I wasn't sure enough to say anything. It was equally possible that John really had been in Florida, had talked to the old woman's other friend, and traced the background that way.

Nina was looking at me. 'How did you know, Ward?'

'I didn't,' I said, distracted. 'I just wondered

why the killer took a picture of Jessica's parents. If you're going to take a souvenir, a typical talisman, it's generally something closer to the victim. A body part, perhaps, a piece of clothing. Instead he took a picture that wasn't even of the victim. Monroe said there'd been an attempt to locate her months ago; doesn't that sound more like tracing someone, rather than a serial murder MO? And assume the person who killed Jessica *is* different from the man who killed the cop. What's the cop-killer's motivation? It can only be to up the ante on Jessica's killer. You got a dead woman in a dusty motel, the cops can only spare so much time even if she's pretty and has got a hard disk in her mouth. If you've got that *plus* a policeman being capped in broad daylight — then suddenly you've got a full-on task force and a homicide lieutenant and a Bureau SAC competing for screen time — with a SAC who's already been called with a tip-off.'

'But what says it's the Upright Man who killed Jessica?'

'Nina, how much do you need? You've just heard Mrs Campbell confirm the only possible connection between two women killed in the same way. It's Paul.'

'Yes. But how did you know that before you got here?'

'I didn't. I was just . . . As soon as the guy tried to kill us in Fresno, and it seemed possible it could be the same man as in LA, then how else do you put it together?'

'About a million other ways, Ward. Okay, the shooter is working for the Straw Men. Maybe.

378

Okay, he's trying to draw attention to a murderer. Perhaps. But how did you get from there to your brother being the killer? How was that the only solution?'

I didn't understand what she was getting at. 'Because . . . because I assume that if they're trying to get someone caught it can only be someone they can't get to by themselves. It can only be someone who is so out there, who is sufficiently dangerous and autonomous and outside standard human rules that they need the help of the regular law to try to catch him.'

'But why do they want him caught? He's *one of them*. He supplied them with people to kill and he helped them blow up buildings and organize shootings. Why . . . '

'Because he also did things — killing my parents, and abducting Zandt's daughter — which brought four dedicated people looking for them with guns. He got their lawyers killed. He got their multi-million-dollar nest in Montana blown to dust. And who knows what else he's doing now? If Paul turns on you, or you cast him out, I'll bet you're going to fucking know about it.'

Suddenly I realized that the two older women were staring at us, and that we'd been shouting. I tried to speak more calmly. 'Nina, I don't see the problem here. You've just heard what . . . '

'Ward, for God's sake — *it could be John.*'

I stared at her, suddenly winded. 'What do you mean?'

'Who do we *know* the Straw Men want hurt? John. Who's incriminated in the video they supplied? John. Who's murdered a man who can only be something to do with them? What's to say it wasn't *John* who killed these women?'

'Because . . . why on earth would he do that?'

'They were part of the Upright Man's life. You know what your brother did to him. He took Karen. He killed her but he didn't even do it fast. He disappeared her and only proved she was dead when he arranged her bones as a trail to lead John into a trap where he meant to kill him too. He took John's life and destroyed it. What do you think John's going to stop at in his revenge?'

I opened my mouth. Shut it again.

Nina stood. She was furious, as angry as I'd ever seen anyone.

'Fuck you, Ward. I'm going to wait in the car.'

She strode out of the house, slamming the door hard on the way. I turned to the two women, who were looking at me like a pair of interested cats.

'Thank you,' I said. 'I have to go.' I heard the sound of a child calling out from upstairs.

'Oh, shoot,' Muriel said. 'There goes the night.'

I was at the door before Mrs Campbell spoke. 'You know, you never even asked me what I thought you would want to know.'

I turned. 'What are you talking about?'

'I don't know anything about catching people,' she said, 'but I figured you'd want to know where he went last.'

'When?' I said, without a clue what she was talking about, half expecting to hear the sound of the car as Nina drove away.

'Back then. The family that took him,' she said. 'My friend in Florida was the case worker. She said the family moved up to Washington because the woman's mother was getting old and not so good at looking after herself. Last Dianne heard of them was a year after they moved. The husband had taken off with some young girl he met in a bar.'

'Did she remember a name?'

'She did. She remembered it because it was kind of like that dead guitarist who'd been so big a few years before. Dianne was into all that, back then. Spelled differently, though.'

I shook my head. 'Who?'

'The name was Henrickson,' she said. 'They lived in a place called Snowcalm, something like that, up near the Cascades.'

⋆ ⋆ ⋆

Nina drove to the airport in a silence that was murderous and dark. I tried to talk to her but she was like a ghost driver, caught in some time to the side or in the past. So nobody said anything, and I sat thinking about John Zandt, and what he might or might not be capable of. I remembered too something he'd said when we had our meeting outside the hotel in San Francisco, something that hadn't made much sense at the time:

Sometimes you have to go back a way to do what you need to get done.

I could see a meaning for that now.

381

Nina parked in the lot and we got out. She marched straight towards the stairway and I followed, struggling with my bag.

'Nina,' I said, loudly. My voice bounced off dirty concrete and came back flat and dull.

She turned right round and smacked me in the face. I was caught so much by surprise that I staggered backwards. She closed in, slapping me, and then again, shouting something I couldn't make out.

I tried to hold up my left hand to ward her off, but the pain this caused in my shoulder was enough to make the movement awkward and incomplete. I saw her notice this, make to punch me again anyway — to actually hit me right on the shoulder — and then pull back at the last moment.

Instead she glared at me, with eyes so green and bright it was as though I'd never seen them before.

'Don't you ever do that again,' she shouted. 'Don't you *ever* keep anything from me.'

'Nina, I didn't know whether . . . '

'I don't care. Just don't. Don't treat me like whatever you choose to tell me is enough, like I'm some fucking . . . chick who just gets what she's given. John did that and if I ever see him again I'm going to break his fucking nose.'

'Fine, but don't take it out on . . . '

' . . . on poor you. In two days I've been suspended, my ex has started killing people, God knows how many, and I've seen my boss shot to death in front of my eyes. I've still got his blood all over my shirt, as people keep pointing out. So

382

don't you, don't you dare . . . '

She stopped shouting, blinked twice, rapidly, and I realized her eyes looked brighter not just because I was so close to them, but also because they were full. I took a risk and put a hand on her shoulder. She shrugged it off viciously, and suddenly her eyes were dry again.

'Nina, I'm sorry. Look . . . I'm just not used to having to say things. I've spent three months in a void and was not the world's best socialized person even before that. My whole life I've relied on the comfort of strangers, room service and barmen. I'm just not used to having someone around to listen or give a damn.'

'I'm not saying I give a damn. I'm just saying don't lie to me. Don't hide things from me. Ever.'

'Okay,' I said. 'I understand.' I did, too, or thought I did. John had cut her deep. Right now I was his surrogate. Given how angry she was, I thought he was lucky to be somewhere else.

She took a step back from me, put her hands on her hips. Looked away and breathed out in one harsh, long exhalation. 'Did I hurt your shoulder?'

'Least of my problems,' I said. 'My face feels like I ran into a wall. When you slap someone, they stay slapped.'

She looked back up at me, head cocked. 'Right. You know that about me now. So don't make me do it again.'

'I'll try.'

'Don't just try. Anyone can try. I need you to be better than that.'

383

'Okay,' I said, seriously. 'Trust me. I won't do it again.'

'Good,' she said, and cracked a smile that was briefer than a flap of a bird's wings but still made the hair rise on the back of my neck. 'Because remember — I've also got a gun.'

She turned briskly and started walking to the stairs.

'Christ,' I said. 'You really aren't like the other girls.'

'Oh, I am,' she said, and now I couldn't tell whether she was joking or not. 'You men just have no idea.'

★   ★   ★

We made the last flight up to Seattle, but only just. By the time we were out the other side and in a rental, it was midnight. With a map and a pair of burgers from a Spinner's in Tacoma we were good to go, though by then neither of us was moving fast.

I drove, trying to keep my arm from seizing completely, and also leaving Nina free to do what we'd finally agreed on the flight. She still wouldn't talk to the FBI — for all she knew, the man who'd sat in the boardroom with Monroe might still be in town, and on her case — but there was one person she was prepared to try.

She called Doug Olbrich. They spoke for five minutes. I was sufficiently busy dealing with Seattle-Tacoma's freeway system to not get much of what was said, though at least some of the conversation sounded positive.

She finished the call, stared into space for a moment, then rapped her hand on the dashboard — tap tap — as she had the day before, but this time not seeming so pissed.

'What's the score?'

'It could be worse,' she said. 'Monroe isn't dead.'

'You're joking.'

'Nope. Fucker's still alive. Astounding. He evidently has *far* more balls than I gave him credit for. He's got five holes in him and has been in surgery for six straight hours. He's very sick. They're saying he's got a twenty percent chance at best. But he's not dead yet.'

I felt appallingly guilty for having abandoned Monroe, for having assumed he was as good as gone.

'You did the right thing pulling me out,' Nina said. 'Without that I probably wouldn't be here.'

'There's more bad news. I can hear it.'

'Doug went up to my place to try to find me. Someone's taken it apart. Smashed it up and stolen all my files.' She shrugged, and sounded weary rather than sad. 'You were right, Ward. It was time to leave.'

'I'm sorry.'

'Whatever,' she said, tightly. 'The Gary Johnson thing is getting very heavy. It turns out this lawyer in Louisiana has a *lot* of money behind him, and a powerful following wind.'

'Really. I wonder where that's coming from.'

'Indeed. Monroe's in a hard place even if he lives. You know how these things go. Once someone lifts up that kind of rock, they have to find *something* underneath to justify lifting it in the first place. I know I didn't miss a beat with the Johnson case, but what's to say Monroe didn't cut a corner somewhere? He wanted that ball down. It's how he made SAC.'

She stopped and sat quietly for a little while. I let her be until I was safely out onto 18, with 90 in sight, and I had a cigarette in my hand.

'You didn't tell him what we know,' I said then.

'Think we know.'

'Whatever. You didn't tell.'

'No,' she said, quietly. 'Does that make me a bad person?'

I laughed, but then realized she wasn't smiling. I glanced at her a moment, thinking she was hard to get to the bottom of. 'In the eyes of the law, yes. In a withholding-of-evidence kind of way. Which is a jail-sentence kind of thing.'

She nodded, but said nothing.

'Come on, Nina,' I said. 'The deal cuts both ways.'

'I know,' she said. 'So here it is. I didn't tell him because I don't think there's anyone other than us going to see this through to where it needs to go.'

'And where is that?'

'There's a place for men who stick things in women's heads, and it isn't jail.'

'You don't mean that.'

'Right at this minute I do. Even if it's John. And I also didn't tell Doug because he mentioned something in passing and after he said it I just couldn't seem to . . . ' She turned to me, and finally smiled. 'You got some miles in you yet?'

'I guess so. How many do you need?'

'The car that Monroe mentioned, the one that was clocked passing through Snoqualmie the night before Katelyn's body was found?'

'What about it?'

'Three hours ago a local sheriff ran a check on it. It bounced because it's a rental and there was no felony involved, but Doug noted it as logged and said someone might get around to a look-see tomorrow, if it's a slow day. The shout came from about another fifty miles into the mountains after Snoqualmie. I think we should be there first.'

'So where are we heading, exactly?'

She looked at the map briefly, then stabbed her finger in a spot that seemed to be right in the middle of the mountains.

'This place. Sheffer.'

★   ★   ★

At about one a.m. Nina drifted off to sleep, head lolling on the rest but arms folded tight in front. I listened to her breathing as I sped us east along 90. The landscape was way too dark to make out clearly, but some vestigial organ in my body or head clocked the steadily increasing altitude. Every now and then a car sped the other way, some other traveller on some other journey.

We climbed higher, and I dropped back to fifty, and then forty, as the road became more twisty. It was getting very cold, too, misty ghosts

387

hanging in the trees that pressed the road, illuminated by sodium lights and a moon that kept swapping places with clouds way up above. I pulled over at one point, to get a clearer fix on where I was headed. Nina shifted, but didn't wake, and I set off again as gently as I could.

Just over the crest of the mountains I took an exit onto a smaller, local road, which signposted Sheffer ten miles ahead. After feeling as if the mountains and trees were a mere backdrop, I quickly felt like an intruder among them instead.

Sheffer was small, and closed. It was quarter of three in the morning. I pulled slowly down the main street, feeling like an alien invader who'd picked exactly the right time to make his move. I passed a market, a bar, a couple of diners. Then I saw there was a sign for a motel, right at the other end.

I pulled into the lot and pulled around in a big, slow loop to park up. There was no light on in the office. Out of season, a town this small, I didn't see there being a night bell. It was looking like a couple of cold, stiff hours in my seat.

I turned the engine off and opened the door, slipping out quickly before too much mountain chill could enter the car. My intention was to have a final cigarette before trying to get some sleep.

As I stood, sucking it down, I suddenly realized four cars were parked on the other side of the lot. Of course — there always are, in motel lots. But we were looking for one in particular.

I didn't know the licence we were after. Nina hadn't told me and I probably wouldn't have remembered it anyhow. And would it really just be parked outside a motel?

I walked across to the first of the cars, and peered in through the window. The back seat was full of vacation junk: spare fleece jackets, trail maps, and a selection of brightly coloured objects designed to forestall questions as to whether we were there yet.

The next was ten yards further on. It was very cold, and I'd finished my cigarette. I considered leaving it. Instead I walked over. It didn't look like something anyone would rent. It was big and rusty and covered with mud. But I leaned down to look in anyway.

I heard a quiet footstep at the last second, and started to turn.

Then my head was full of stars, which rapidly turned black.

25

Something red, like a light across a harbour in the dead of night. A sound, quiet, like the rustle of water on a shoreline — the kind of noise the world makes to itself when it thinks there's no one around to hear. Drowsy comfort, for a moment, before two types of pain came in like two long screws being slowly tightened. The ache in my shoulder. Another in the back and side of my head.

I jerked my head up, opened my eyes a little wider. I realized the red glow was a bedside clock. It took a moment to focus on the numbers properly. They said it was just after five a.m. The room was deadly quiet, the kind of silence where you think you can hear the carpet. It smelled of motel.

I was sitting in a chair, it seemed, slumped over. My head still seemed to be floating in cushioning ether, thoughts tottering forward like over-ambitious toddlers. I tried to sit up properly, and found I couldn't. This scared me until I realized it was because my feet and wrists were tied to the chair's front legs. Then it scared me in a different way.

I gave up trying to move and turned my head instead. A pain ripped down from my temple straight to my shoulder, and it was all I could do not to cry out. There was probably no reason why I shouldn't have. There's just something about finding yourself tied to a chair in a dark room. You tend not to want to attract any more attention than you've already received.

I waited a moment, while small flashing lights faded in front of my eyes. Then I tried again, more slowly this time. The room was very dark indeed, the darkness you can only get a long way from a city's ambient light. There was just enough glow for my heart to thud heavily when I saw someone was standing by the window.

My lips separated with an audible click, but I didn't speak. Couldn't, maybe. I kept my head rigid and my eyes open wide and saw that the shape by the window wasn't standing after all, but sitting cross-legged on a desk.

Finally I managed to speak: 'Paul?'

'Of course not,' a voice said, immediately. 'You think you'd be alive if it was?'

At that moment I mentally gave up hope. Just like that. How the man from the restaurant in Fresno had found us, I had no idea. But I knew I wouldn't be walking away a second time. Not tied to a chair. I wondered where Nina was, and hoped she was alive, or if not, that I'd never know.

There was a rustling sound, and I realized it was the same noise I'd heard while fighting to regain consciousness. It was caused by the man's thick coat, as he slid forward off the desk.

He took the four steps between us, stood a moment looking down. Then squatted to bring his face close to mine.

'Hello, Ward.'

'You fucker.'
It was John Zandt.

★ ★ ★

He sat on the end of the bed, facing me, but made no movement towards untying the ropes.

'Where's Nina?'

'In the next room. Tied just like you, and with a Do Not Disturb sign on the door.'

'She will shout when she wakes. She will shout like you won't believe.'

'Not gagged as she is. And if you even take a deep breath I'll hit you so hard you won't wake up for a week, or maybe ever.'

'What are you doing, John? What is *wrong* with you?'

'Nothing,' he said. 'I'm just not having you screwing things up.'

'Screwing *what* up? Your murder spree?'

'Who do you think I've killed?'

'Peter Ferillo, for one.'

He sniffed. 'Yes. I did kill him.'

'And who else?'

'Why do you think there's someone else?'

'Otherwise why would you ask? Did you kill the women? Did you kill Jessica and Katelyn to get back at Paul?'

'Stop calling him that. He doesn't deserve a name.'

'He's got one. Get used to it. Did you kill them or not?'

'You really think I'd kill a woman?'

'What's the difference? Why is it okay to kill a

man? You start making distinctions like that and there's not so big a distance between you and Paul. You hit the Ferillo girl hard enough to give her concussion. Where's that lie on your new moral spectrum?'

'That wasn't planned. I knew what I was going to have to do to make Ferillo talk, and I was just too wired. I put her somewhere she'd be found quickly.'

'You're a prince. And once he'd talked, he had to die, right?'

'Yes. Once I'd found out that while he was in LA he helped organize the transportation of young girls to killers. He may have thought they were just going to be trained up to be whores — that's what he claimed. But you know what? That's enough.'

I could see in John's face that he either wasn't able or wasn't prepared to revisit Ferillo's death at his hands. 'John, untie me. For God's sake.'

He shook his head. 'Not going to happen. You'll get in the way. You're just not up to it.'

'Screw you.'

Suddenly his finger was in my face. 'Were you last time? With a clear shot? I'm sorry — did I miss that? Did you kill the man who dismembered my daughter, when he was right there in front of you?'

I couldn't answer that. I knew I hadn't. 'He's here, isn't he?'

'Yes,' John said. 'He's here looking for something because he believes it's going to make everything okay.'

'He screwed up. Is that it? He's not the bad

guys' poster psycho any more. They've exiled him and now they want him dead.'

'You're not stupid, I'll admit that.'

'Tell me, John. I've got a right to know. And either untie me or get me a drink. It's freezing in here.'

He walked through into the bathroom. A couple of clinks in the darkness, and then he reappeared with a small glass with two inches of amber fluid in it. I opened my mouth and he tipped it in. It made me cough hard, but warmth flooded through my chest.

He stepped back, walked over to the window. Watched the parking lot for a while.

'He's not staying here, surely?'

'He was, along with some guy he's with. I got here mid-evening and he wasn't here any more. But he's still around.'

'How do you know?'

'Because he's insane. He thinks he's found a magic masterstroke that's going to make the world in his image.'

'What? What is it?'

He shook his head. 'You won't believe it.'

'You know the dead women were from foster families when he was a kid?'

'Yes. I traced people who'd worked on his case. I talked to the old woman in San Francisco. I put two and six together.'

'Why Ferillo?'

'He was a front for the Straw Men, one of many all over the country. They arranged for him to walk from prosecution four years ago. I don't think he even understood what they're into, but

394

he was party to them laundering money through his restaurant. The apartment he died in belonged to a man called George Dravecky. Dravecky is a property developer and a very rich man. He didn't own a house up at The Halls but he put in the original application. He bankrolled the start-up costs. He's one of them.'

'How did you find that out?'

'I'm good at what I do.'

'You're no longer a cop and you obviously refused to involve Nina. So where's your in to information sources?'

'Guy I used to work with in LAPD. In the old days he had a habit of reallocating an occasional bag of pharmaceutical evidence for personal use. No big deal, but he's straight and more senior now and wouldn't want it widely known. He does what I ask.'

'Doug Olbrich, by any chance?'

John smiled briefly. It wasn't a nice sight. 'Not stupid at all.'

'No. Just prone to trust the wrong people, especially ones I thought were friends. Does Olbrich know about the rest of it?'

'No. He's just a cop.'

'Did you get to Dravecky?'

'Yes. He confirmed things I'd already begun to work out. You have no idea what we're up against.'

'I think I do.'

'No, you really don't. I mentioned Roanoke to see if it sparked anything. I watched your face for some sign that you'd got anywhere by yourself, and I saw nothing. How can that be, Ward? What have you been *doing* all this time?'

'Trying to stay alive.'

'Hiding, you mean. For *what*? Once you know about these people, there's no way back. You can't just sit and watch television and jerk off. There's no happy families, no walks along the beach, no normal life. There's nothing to do and nowhere to go.'

'John, what is it that you think you know?'

'The Indians didn't kill the settlers at Roanoke, Ward. The Straw Men did.'

I stared at him. '*What*?'

'The Croatoans knew all about it. They told the next group of settlers that 'another tribe' did it, that another tribe had killed the fifteen left behind from the second expedition. That other tribe was the Straw Men. Ancestors to them, anyway, trying to wipe out other Europeans before they could get a foothold in a country that had been quietly theirs for a long, long time. They took out the next expedition too, except they kept some of the women and children — guess why. They did the same with the Spanish and with everyone else, whatever chance they got. That's why the word 'Croatoan' was on that cabin. Then it was a blatant attempt to pass the blame: now it's come to mean 'we were here' or 'this is our place'.'

'The Straw Men were here back in the 1500s? Get real.'

'They were here long before that. They got here first, Ward. They stole America from the locals four thousand years before anyone else even knew it was here. You ever hear of a place called Oak Island?'

I shook my head. He wanted to tell, and I wanted to hear. But most of all I wanted him to keep talking, in case his voice made it through to the next room, and Nina was awake, and could hear I was still alive.

'It's a tiny rock off Nova Scotia. In 1795 a guy called McGinnis discovered an old shaft covered by flagstones made of rock you don't find in the area. Since then hundreds of people have tried to find what's at the bottom. When they dug it in 1859 the thing flooded because there was a clever second tunnel which led out to the sea. They're still trying. They've gone down through six oak platforms, down and down to two hundred feet without hitting the bottom. Nobody knows who put it there, they've guessed at everything from privateers to Vikings to the Knights Templar.'

'So who was it?'

'The Straw Men. The pit is nearly a thousand years old. It was one of the places they stashed money once they realized they couldn't keep the continent to themselves for much longer.'

'But who *are* they?'

'No one, and everyone. They came from all over the world at different times. Phoenicians, Romans, Irish, ancient Egyptians, Portuguese, Norse. The Romans conquered half the world, moved tens of thousands of men across whole continents — you really think some of them couldn't make a few hundred-mile hops up around the North Atlantic? They came in

397

handfuls, people who didn't want to live with the new rules of the world, who didn't want any part of the way it was going, especially after Christianity started screwing things for the old beliefs. There are signs of them all over the country, pieces of suppressed evidence. Western artefacts in the wrong strata, ancient Chinese coins in the North West, folk tales of natives speaking English or Welsh, a hidden Egyptian shrine in the Grand Canyon, old Celtic Ogham script carved into rocks in New England, megaliths in New Hampshire, legends of red-haired Indians in Oregon. The New World has always attracted those who didn't like the old one, who thought it was getting tainted with the virus of modern civilization — and gradually the groups came into contact and worked together. Every now and then a story would leak back — the journey of St Brendan, or the Piri Reis map, showing sections of the world we now claim we didn't know about back then — but it was always quashed. The Straw Men wanted the place to themselves, their own private country and kingdom and lair — not least because it was making them rich.'

'How, precisely?'

'Copper. Starting from 3000 BC, half a million tons of copper was mined out of the upper peninsula in Michigan. Five thousand mines, stretching one hundred and fifty miles, with work taking place over the course of a thousand years.'

'I've never heard anything about that.'

'Strange, huh? Despite the fact they left

behind millions of tools and thousands of holes. Where did five hundred thousand tons of copper go? It was exported around the world, and it's what first made the Straw Men rich — and gave them the power to keep the place secret. When anyone here gave them trouble, they simply took them out. They took out the Anasazi when it looked like their civilization was getting too advanced. They wiped out Roanoke. They nearly did the same with Jamestown. They just picked off as many of the pioneers as they could. In the middle of the diary of Patrick Breen, a member of the Donner party, there's this weird reference where he says in the entry for Friday 18th: 'Saw no strangers to day from any of the shantys'. What strangers? Through the rest of the diary, there's no mention of these 'strangers'. What were they doing out there, out in a place so remote that the original party was dying left and right and — interestingly — starting to eat each other? Who *were* they?'

'Straw Men, presumably, according to you.'

'Yes. They were here before us. They had always been here. People knew, occasionally came into contact with them, but it didn't fit in with our genesis myths for the country we've become and so gradually mention of them died out.'

'And they just gave up?'

'Of course not. But you can't fight an influx of millions of sane people, and there's never been many of the Straw Men. They faded into the shadows, did their business the quiet way. I think they have connections with the neo-Conservatives now, but I'm never going to prove it. They make their money and do the things they like to do, the kind of things we're not supposed to do any more, and every now and then they create an atrocity just to keep their hand in and honour the gods. It's their way.'

'Murder isn't a belief system.'

'Yes it is, Ward. That's *exactly* what it is. We all did it. These days we only ever kill out of hate, or through greed, or as a punishment, but for a hundred thousand years our species believed in a kind of killing that was to do with life and hope.'

'Which was what?'

'Sacrifice. We sacrificed animals, and we sacrificed each other. Sacrifice is killing for magic purpose, and serial murder is a misplaced version of this instinct. They're turning teenage girls and lost boys into symbols of the 'gods' — perfect, unattainable, cruel — and their whole MO is a curdled version of an ancient ritual.'

'I don't get it.'

'*Every step is the same*. They make preparations, choose a victim; they take the victim off to a secret place, then wash/feed/attempt to communicate with them — honouring before sacrifice. They may have sex with them, too, and partly this is an attempt to mate with these gods but it's also because sexual dysfunction is the only thing strong enough to pull modern man down through civilization back to these elemental, innate impulses. Then they sacrifice them or 'kill' them, to use another word. Sometimes they'll eat parts, to take on their power. They'll

400

often keep a piece of the victim or their clothes, much like a bear's pelt or a wolf's tooth, putting it in a special place, keeping it with them to keep the dead alive. Does this not sound *familiar* to you?'

'Yes,' I admitted. 'It does.'

'Then they'll bury the remainder, returning it to the earth, or they distribute it — and dismemberment was a common feature of sacrifice too, breaking the body down to parts. They will be dormant for a while then, until the cycle starts again — until the music of the spheres tells them it's time for another sacrifice.'

'But serial killers are not priests.'

'No. They're fucking *lunatics*, and so there will come a point at which the cycle starts to speed up. Most killers know they are wrong, deep down. They understand they're at the beck and call of a neurotic dysfunction they try to rationalize but can't understand. They speed up in the end because they give up giving up. But the Straw Men *do* believe that this is acceptable. That's the difference. They believe what they're doing is more than okay, that it's essential, that it's what put our species where it is. They believe that if you kill the right thing at the right time, everything will be well. It's the original magic act. They've stuck with an ancient belief system that says *killing is right.*'

He stopped talking. His jaw was thrust forward belligerently, and his whole body vibrated with an unwillingness to see the world any other way. I looked back at him, not knowing what to say. I didn't know how to tell him that a

401

little knowledge is a dangerous thing, or that not everything he had read on the internet was true, or that the willingness to fit any piece of information into a predetermined plan was a sign of mania. I didn't know how to tell him that if he believed everything he'd told me, he'd lost his mind. You don't want to use any of those words, when you've been tied to a chair by a man with a gun.

'Did you get all that from Dravecky?'

'Some of the history. He also confirmed that the view amongst some of the 'tribe' — he used that actual word — was that the Upright Man had become a liability, and he told me what he's doing here. A sacrifice that hasn't been made in a long, long time.'

'Does Paul think the Straw Men will take him back if he pulls it off?'

'I doubt he cares. He's off on his own thing. This is a guy who thinks even the Straw Men are going soft.'

'Where's Dravecky now?'

'In the Columbia River.'

'Great. You're the man. Tell me, John: did you kill the women or not?'

'No.'

The word was said immediately and simply. I still didn't know what to think. 'So what is Paul doing up here?'

John shook his head. 'You don't believe what I've told you,' he said. 'And I don't care.' He stood and took something from his pocket. It was a thick piece of cloth, about two feet long.

'Don't put that — '

But with one quick movement the gag was on. He yanked it tight. Then he came round and squatted in front of me, looked deep into my eyes. I hadn't even noticed that, while he'd been talking, the drapes had started to lighten. Dawn was on the way. In the murky light I could make out the sharp blue of his irises, the dark circle in the centre. Beyond that, I couldn't go.

'Stay out of my way, Ward,' he said. 'Him being dead is a lot more important to me than you being alive.'

He checked the knots, straightened and then laughed. 'You want to know the kicker? Forty years ago they believed the country was going to liberal ruin. That called for the ultimate. The sacrifice of the king. November 22nd, 1963.'

I just looked at him. He winked. 'They killed JFK.'

Then he went to the door, stepped out into dark blue-black, and was gone.

26

During the night the man with the guns sat bolt upright in a chair in front of the door. The other man, Kozelek, tried to talk to him on two occasions, and got nowhere, after which he seemed to give up. He sat slumped in another chair, staring into space for a while. Then he poked around in the kitchen until he found a bottle of wine. He drank it in twenty minutes flat, and fell asleep. His dreams did not look good. He said a woman's name twice.

Patrice meanwhile lay on her side on the couch. With her hands tied behind her back, there wasn't much else she could do. For a while she had kept her eyes open. When she realized this would do little to prevent any harm befalling her, she let them close. She didn't sleep, however. Sleep didn't come anywhere near.

They set off at first light. The man with the guns, Henrickson, made her walk in the front. Kozelek staggered along behind her. Partly it looked like hangover, partly a problem with one ankle. Mainly it seemed like he had given up in general.

Henrickson walked in the back. Every now and then she glanced that way to check where he was. Though the night had finally brought new snow underfoot, after the rain and sleet, he seemed to be able to move with very little sound.

She led them up around the north shore of the

lake. There seemed little point in not doing so, little point in not taking him where he thought he wanted to go. It was much further than he realized, it wouldn't get him what he wanted — and might have other advantages.

As they passed the second cabin she glanced up, and saw her reflection in the dusty window. She smiled, just in case something of Bill still lingered there, and in case she didn't come back.

★ ★ ★

'I hope you're not screwing me around,' Henrickson said.

Tom stopped, glad for an excuse to rest. Two straight hours' walking, all of it uphill, had taken him to the brink. The sky, at first a pale and searing blue up between the trees, had gradually turned dark and mottled, clouds arriving like clumps of dropped clay. His head felt bad, and — wretched though he felt — he couldn't help appreciating the parallel with the first time he'd returned to the place they were headed for, brain cracked wide. Of course he hadn't planned it this way. He'd just wanted to be asleep, and getting drunk had done that. He wanted to be asleep now, too. Asleep, or far away. His absurd belief that somehow he was going to be able to get away with everything, that his find was going to heal his life, had disappeared.

Henrickson stood right in front of the old woman. 'You told the cops this place was an hour's walk from the edge of your land. Unless

405

you own a State Park, that's beginning to look far-fetched.'

'I lied,' she said, simply.

'How much further is it?'

'Quite a ways.'

'You can try to get us lost,' Henrickson said. 'I could see that might look like a good plan. But I can out-walk the two of you put together, and will be going long after you both collapse. Sure, you'll have stopped me finding the place today. But I know it's here to be found now, and so I'll stay. I'll find it sooner or later, and I'll find them, and all that will have happened is that the two of you will have died and I'll have lost a little time.'

'What's the difference?' Tom said. 'If you're just going to shoot it, kill this amazing thing, who cares whether it's today or next week?'

'What exactly do you think is out there?' Patrice asked, looking at him curiously.

'You know,' Tom said.

She shrugged. 'All I know about is bears. Just some animals been living out here a long, long time, and deserve to be left alone.'

Tom looked at Henrickson.

He didn't say anything, just nodded ahead.

So they walked some more. After a time Tom began walking level with the old woman. He started talking, and she seemed to listen. He told her about his walk in the woods, and what had brought him there, and in the end he found his mouth telling her the thing no one else knew. It came out slowly, but it wouldn't stop. He told her how he had turned to see the girl in the passenger seat of his car, how broken she was,

406

and how hard she still fought to stay alive. He told her about the problems with the accounts of the company he had worked for, discrepancies which would almost certainly come to light sooner or later. Restaurants are expensive, as are gifts, and Rachel's tastes had not been cheap. It is hard to run an affair without financial implications, especially if it's your wife who checks the card and bank statements. Sarah would have spotted the spending even if all had come from withdrawals of cash. The company's accounts were more complex, and there was a chance it might go unnoticed. But there was a chance it would not, and Tom knew that because of what had happened his name would be on the top of any list. The really screwed-up thing, he admitted, was that the guilt he felt over this was actually more acute than at Rachel's death. Of course he should not have been having an affair with her — but she was very pretty, and once he'd started it was hard to stop. He should not have tried to get across the intersection that night — the arrival of the Porsche and its drunk driver, however, had been completely out of his hands. The theft of the money had not. He had stood there, made the decision and worked out the method. He had done the thing of his own volition, knowing it was wrong. Everyone makes mistakes, and he could categorize just about everything else that way. Very human errors. Not the stealing. He had started, deliberately, and then he couldn't stop. The chance to tell Sarah about it had come and gone in the week following the accident. Not telling her had either been a second crime or doubled the magnitude of the first, he wasn't sure which. He crossed that road. He was now trapped on the other side.

The old woman listened, and didn't say a great deal. Telling her made him feel a little better, but not much, and he realized the only thing that would make a real difference was telling Sarah. The crime against the company was the stealing; the crime against her was lying. The latter was far worse. He decided that tonight, regardless of what they did or did not find this afternoon, he was going to phone home. She had loved him once, and maybe she did still. At the very least she would tell him what to do, and that might be as much absolution as he could expect.

Eventually, at a time Tom's beleaguered guts told him was past midday, they got where they were going.

★　★　★

They had been cresting a rise for a long time. Tom had absolutely no idea of where they were by now. For a time he had believed that Henrickson might be right, that the woman was simply trying to get them lost. But he watched her carefully and saw she never seemed to hesitate, even for a moment, the beat required to decide which wrong way to go. Progress had been slow but constant. She had turned this way and that, taken them around some features and over others. For a woman of her age, she was surprisingly fit. She winced occasionally, however, and twice slipped and fell quickly on her side, unable to use her hands to halt her fall; and gradually she began to get slower, and to tire.

Then she stopped. She was panting. She indicated with her head.

'It's down there.'

Henrickson walked past her and up to the edge of the gully. He looked down for a few moments, and then beckoned to Tom.

'That the place?'

Tom walked up and stood with him, looking down into the stream bed. At first it looked just like any of the others they'd passed through. Then he picked out the little area where he'd sat in the dark, then returned to the next morning. Still less than a week ago, but it felt like an eternity. As if this was some place he was bound to come back to, over and over.

'Yeah,' he said. 'That's where it happened.' That defining moment, before which everything seemed grey and indistinct.

'Good,' Henrickson said. He turned away from the edge and walked back to Patrice. 'Thank you, ma'am.'

'What was the big deal, anyway?' Tom said. 'Why did you want to come back here? Or was that just part of pretending to be something you're not?'

'Not at all,' the man said. 'Follow me.'

He turned and started walking up the edge of the gully. They followed. After five minutes Henrickson started cutting left again, through the trees clustered around the lip of the drop. In another few minutes he stopped.

Tom stared. The man had led them to the trunk which had fallen across the gully.

'Ms Anders — would you tell Tom what we've got here?'

'A fallen tree,' she said.

Henrickson shook his head, walked the last few yards to the edge, and then stepped up onto the tree. He examined the end, and then walked straight across to the other side, as if the trunk was ten feet wide.

'Both ends have been worked,' the man said, squatting down to examine the wood. 'And branches along the trunk trimmed off. It's also been pulled about twenty degrees round from the angle it fell. I'm astonished you didn't notice, Tom.'

'I wasn't well,' Tom said. This was true, but in all honesty he couldn't believe he'd missed it either. Once you'd seen it, it was so obvious.

'You can cross the river down the way for the time being,' Henrickson said, 'but come the spring it's a long, long walk in either direction. This is a bridge, and it was manufactured. Some of our forest friends put it together. Consciousness solidified. We are here, but we want to be over there. So we build a simple machine. There's your proof, Tom. Told you it would be worth the walk.'

'How do you know it wasn't just some guy? Or something left from logging?'

'Because I know this area has never been felled, and that it's unlikely a human would do the job with stone tools.' He looked at Patrice.

410

'Just a fallen tree, right?'

'That's all I see. Think perhaps you're seeing something in your head, not what's actually there in front of your eyes. Lots of people are like that.'

Henrickson walked back over the bridge, and one last time, he grinned. He looked up the gully.

'Have it your own way. But let's walk a little more. See what we find.'

They walked another ten minutes, keeping close to the edge of the gully. The sides grew steeper and deeper, and the stream grew in width and sound, swollen by waterfalls, winter-thin but relentless.

Finally they got to the top of the ridge, and Tom gasped.

Beneath their feet the ground fell away. To the left the river suddenly dropped out into space, to tumble helplessly into a large rocky bowl two hundred feet below. The forest stretched out in front, a craggy carpet of white-crusted green, limitless, towards Canada and beyond. Way up above was the thin, fading trail of a jet, across the remaining narrow band of clear sky. That was the only work of man you could see. Otherwise it was if we had never been here. Tom watched as cloud slowly filled the gap, until the sky was all over grey, then tilted his head back to look back over the forest.

'It's beautiful,' he said.

'Imagine when this was all there was,' Henrickson said, quietly, standing beside him. 'When nobody else was here.' Tom could only shake his head again, faced with the world as it was before words. He kept on shaking it, slowly, feeling his eyes fill up with water. He didn't know why.

'I want to thank you, Tom,' Henrickson added, and suddenly his accent was backwoods again, and he was the person Tom had thought he'd come to know. 'You tried real hard, my friend, and it's not been an easy time for you, I know. You know the weirdest thing? I've actually enjoyed having someone to talk to.'

Tom's head, shaking still, and then nodding. He looked up, saw the blurry shape of the old woman, hands still behind her back. She smiled at him, sadly, then looked away.

And then Henrickson put his hand on Tom's shoulder and pushed him over the edge.

There was a feeling of tilt, the hollow wrongness of knowing nothing was beneath, as if he was back on the bridge he had found all by himself, and the voice in his head had not been there to help him. Then the weightlessness of pure free fall, fast and brief, before he started hitting things. The collisions were not rustles or slides this time, but brief, bone-cracking impacts that spun and twisted him into a rag doll. Another momentary unbroken plummet, and then he landed like a dropped glass.

★   ★   ★

Two hundred feet nearer heaven, Patrice glared dully at the man.

'Did you have to do that?'

'Yes. I don't expect you to understand.'

'You going to shove me over too?'

'One human is enough. And you've got a job to do.'

'This place is all I know and I can't go any further. You want a bear, you're going to have to go find one by yourself.'

The man shook his head. 'If it comes to it, I'll make you tell me where they live. But for the time being we're going back down to the stream, where Tom saw his 'bear', and we're going to sit and wait.'

'You think they're just going to wander by?'

'No. But they mean a lot to you, which makes me think you might mean something to them. When they know you're there, they may choose to visit.'

'Like I'm some big mother bear? Right. My own kids haven't visited in eighteen months.'

'Patrice, you're beginning to piss me off with this denial.'

'They'll know I'm not alone.'

'Of course they will. Especially when I start doing things to you. On short acquaintance I already suspect you'll be good at keeping quiet, but they'll hear your discomfort in other ways. And they'll come.'

She looked at the ground, dismayed.

'I thought someone would come,' she said, eventually. 'But I thought it would just be a hunter. Some asshole who wanted to make his fortune or get on the *Tonight Show*. But you're not one of those.'

'No,' he said. 'I'm not.'

'So what are you?'

'My name is Paul,' he said. 'Sometimes I'm called the Upright Man. I'm just doing what needs to be done.'

* * *

Tom lay wedged between two big rocks, hidden beneath a mossy overhang thirty feet above the ground. He tried to make a sound, but heard only a liquid bubbling. His body was bent around and smashed, clothes torn and blood-stained, and something appalling had happened to his left leg. Cold water ran over his feet and his outstretched left hand, but he couldn't feel it. Though his skull was broken, and his cheekbone, his eyes still saw, and his right arm still worked, a little.

Over the next twenty minutes he managed only one thing. He worked his cell phone out of his jacket pocket. He navigated laboriously to the text messaging facility, and, with a thumb that alternatively tremored and stalled, he got as far as:

i saw bigfoot. i lov

Then he died. There was no signal anyway. His body was never found.

27

I had slept for a little while. Incredible, you might think, but just as the guilty will sometimes nod off in a holding cell, the spastic tension of their lives momentarily resolved into an incarceration they can no longer flee, so you're largely absolved of action when you're securely tied to a chair.

Once I woke, I couldn't get back there. It was worse being awake. It left me free to think, and also to attempt to escape. I tried rocking the chair, using my back to pull the legs off the floor. When a rash movement nearly tipped the whole lot straight over forward — gateway to a smashed face and broken neck — I stopped. Screw that. I'm not Jackie Chan.

Doing nothing was worst of all. I watched the curtain get lighter still, heard the sounds of a world waking up outside: gravel under tyres, distant half-second bursts of laughter, clangs and tweets and coughs. I felt a pain in my lower back gradually get more and more acute, and my shoulder begin to glow like fire. I stared at the bedside clock and yearned for each number to increment by just one unit — sometimes I thought it must have broken, it took so long — but when they did, nothing changed.

It was a long, long wait until 12.51, when Nina finally kicked the door down, accompanied by two men I'd never seen before.

415

'He sure as hell looked like you,' the big one admitted. I had been told he was called Sheriff Connolly. The other one was called Phil and he was young and game and sandy-haired. 'But I can see you're not the same.'

'His name is Paul.'

'Mr Kozelek was overheard calling him Jim.'

'He may be using the name Henrickson.'

Connolly nodded, slowly. 'Yes, that would be him.'

Phil's eyes were like saucers. 'He's a *serial* killer?'

'Oh yes. And then some.'

We were in the police station. We had coffee. My hands were still numb and I had problems holding the cup. Nina wasn't faring any better. The motel maid had found her tied up, and fetched the police before thinking to untie her. Her face was pale and she looked exhausted and thin. I wanted to find John Zandt and punch his head more than once, and not just for the previous night.

In a half-hour we had given the cops a very limited account of what had happened and what we knew. In this version it had been the Upright Man who had tied us up, rather than John. Nina had made it clear she was a Federal agent, and managed to dissuade the head cop from calling it in. For now. A lady doctor with a nice smile had looked us over and put a bandage over the open stripe across my shoulder, and then gone away. My eyes felt dry and scratchy and wide, and the

416

light in the room seemed very bright.

Phil shook his head. 'Holy crap.'

'So what's he doing here in Sheffer?' Connolly said. 'And where has he gone?'

'I don't know,' I said. 'But . . . ' I glanced at Nina. 'He said some weird things last night. Things about sacrifice. He seems to be on some kind of weird purification thing. He's already murdered everyone from his past, though, so I can't think who might be next on the list. Unless it's something to do with the people he used to work for.'

Connolly was looking right over my shoulder, a strange look on his face.

'Mr Kozelek spent some time in the woods,' he said. 'He came back dishevelled, claiming he'd seen something.'

'What kind of thing?' Nina asked.

'Said he'd seen a Bigfoot.'

I was surprised into a laugh. 'Right.'

Connolly smiled tightly. 'Exactly. It was a bear, of course. But this brother of yours spent a lot of time with Mr Kozelek, and I can't see why he'd do that unless Kozelek's claim was of interest to him. Can you think of any reason why that might be?'

I couldn't. I shook my head.

Connolly looked away, bit his lip. 'Phil. Give Mrs Anders a call for me, would you?'

'Why . . . '

'Just do it. Number's 3849.'

The younger policeman grabbed a phone and punched in the number. Let it ring for a while, and shook his head. 'No answer.'

417

'Try her cell.' He reeled off that number too. Phil tried it, waited, and again shook his head. The sheriff bit his lip thoughtfully. 'You seen her around town this morning?'

'No.'

'Me neither.' Connolly stood up. 'And I mentioned her name last night. I think we'd better go take a look-see. Phil — get some coats and gloves for these people. See if we got any boots in the right size, too.'

'Sure.'

'Also go to the cabinet and get us some guns.'

'Which ones?'

Connolly looked at me, and I nodded.

'The big ones.'

We walked quickly out to the lot behind the station to find it had started to rain. Neither policeman seemed to notice. If you live in the NW, rain is evidently business as usual. Connolly pointed us to one vehicle, and his deputy to another.

'Don't be trying to get there first,' he told him. 'Just stick behind me, you hear?'

Nina and I climbed into the back seat. Connolly got in the front, and closed the door. He started the engine, then turned in his seat to look back at us.

'Funny thing,' he said. 'I saw Henrickson and Kozelek leave town around eight thirty last night, which is when I ran his registration. Checked in the motel lot later. No sign of the car. But then you get here in the small hours, and he's around to tie you people up.'

We didn't say anything.

418

Connolly sighed. 'That's what I thought. This other guy. He going to be a problem to us?'

'I don't know,' I said.

'He with you or with them?'

'He's with nobody.'

'Everything else you told me was true?'

Nina replied. 'Mostly.'

Connolly faced front and put the car in gear. 'Great. I am so glad you people came to town.'

He pulled quickly around the lot and onto the wet blacktop of the main road; waited for his deputy to catch up, and then sped off up the road. Later I heard that two minutes after the patrol cars set off, a woman in Izzy's coffee shop saw a car come around from the back of a bar called Big Frank's, and follow us out of town.

★   ★   ★

I spent the next fifteen minutes trying to rub feeling back into my hands. Nina did the same. I wanted to tell her more of what John had said, but it didn't seem the right time. Connolly took us fast along a road that had very few other cars on it. Though it was only a little after two, the sky was trying hard to make it look later. The rain stopped, but not in a good way. It was getting colder.

We took a turn-off just past a coffee hut, onto a narrow road that didn't seem to have a name. We'd only been on it thirty seconds when the deputy's voice came crackling over the radio.

'Chief,' he said, 'you missed the turn. Cascade Falls is back up . . .'

419

'Just keep your eyes on the road and follow me,' Connolly said. 'We're going a different way.'

He kept driving for a lot longer than I expected. From what I gathered the woman we were going to visit had lived in a development not too far off the main road. This road didn't look like it was going anywhere. After twenty minutes it narrowed to a single lane and he dropped speed because of the snow still on it. Tall trees grew right up to the sides, and there were no little signs saying the local Kiwanis were proudly sponsoring the road's upkeep. Still he kept driving. I glanced through the rear windshield once in a while and saw the deputy doggedly hanging on our tail. He kept a decent stopping distance but was still close enough for me to make out the puzzlement in his face.

Then Connolly slowed, for no reason I could see. He was peering out to the right. I glanced at Nina.

'Sheriff — are you sure you know where you're going?'

'I am,' he said. 'Matter of fact, we're here.'

He killed the engine and climbed out. When Nina and I were standing by the side of the road, the place we were in seemed even more remote. Bushes and trees stopped you from being able to see very far on either side, and the ground was carpeted with unbroken snow. The road petered out completely about fifty yards ahead.

Phil had parked right behind us. 'Chief, where are we?'

'End of the old service road,' he said. He

pointed into the trees over my shoulder. 'You see?'

If you looked hard, you could just make out the shape of a ruined building, hidden amongst trees about ten yards away.

'Okay,' I said. 'Why?'

Connolly slung his gun over his back and started walking.

'I talked to Mrs Anders couple nights ago,' he said. 'And she told me she'd not been truthful when she said where she'd found Mr Kozelek's stuff. She thought he didn't seem like a man quite in his right mind, and didn't want him going back out there again. She gave me an indication of where it was. If Henrickson's got her, which I guess he has, then he'll make her take him there.'

'Is it close?'

'No,' he said, turning off the road and heading into the forest. I saw there was an area ahead where the trees were thinner on the ground, and looked a little younger. An old logging road, I guessed, now overgrown. 'Not as such. This will get us some of the way. Then it's a hard walk.'

★ ★ ★

So far as Nina and I were concerned the walking got hard pretty much immediately. We just seemed to go up and up. After an hour there was no longer any sign we were on a track. I didn't really notice it go. The trees around us were huge and thick now, and the way was steep. I'm no kind of hiker, as I'd told Zandt, and was finding

421

it tough. With the snow on the ground it was difficult to tell what was underneath. Sometimes it was rocks, sometimes you'd step somewhere that looked dependable and without warning find yourself up to your knees. It started getting darker, partly because of the wall-to-wall cloud. It still wasn't raining. It had been cold when we started out, but I soon began to look back on that as a halcyon period of balmy comfort. If Kozelek had spent two days out in this, I was amazed he'd come back alive. I was also amazed at the dedication of the pioneers who'd forged roads across this landscape. The thing about us is we always want to be on the other side. We bring our saws and trucks and sweat and make it so. Turn your back, though, and it comes creeping home again, and it creeps fast.

'You okay?'

'More or less,' I said. Nina and I were walking together, a couple yards back from the two cops. 'You?'

'I guess. Unbelievably cold.'

And tired, and hungry. I called out, 'Are we nearly there yet?'

'No,' he said, without turning. 'About halfway.'

'Fuck,' Nina said, quietly. 'I hate the outdoors. It sucks.'

We kept on walking. I quietly told Nina more of what John had said the night before. She concurred that it sounded as though he'd lost his mind. It's funny, though. First time you hear something, it sounds outlandish and broken and like it doesn't make sense. But once it's been in your head a while it's as if the other thoughts in there wriggle out of the way to give it some room. The stuff about serial murder and a curdled sacrificial instinct was easiest to accommodate. As a theory it made as much sense as any. I found it harder to believe that any anomalous rumour about my country could be laid at the feet of the Straw Men. There were lots of things about them which took them outside the realm of the explicable, however. So who knew?

After a while we stopped talking, mainly because we ran out of breath. Phil looked to be struggling too, but Connolly kept up an even pace. It was loud, the sound of four pairs of boots in the snow, four rhythms of panting breath. The combination of tiredness, sleeplessness and the semi-constant white in front of my eyes began to have a hypnotic effect. I stopped thinking, seeing only the next step, which rock to head for; feeling the rises and dips and smelling pine needles and bark in the shockingly clean air. My face began to lose elasticity, feeling numb when I rubbed it, and when I blinked there was a flash in front of my eyes. I stumbled every once in a while, and Nina did too.

'Stop.'

When Connolly spoke it was low and quiet and intent.

I was pulled out of a reverie; I jerked my head up and stopped dead. 'What? Are we there?'

He turned around to face us, but didn't reply. Just squinted into the forest back the way we'd come, over to our left. After the walking, the silence was very loud, and my ears sang.

'What did you hear?' Nina asked.

Connolly was silent for another twenty seconds. 'Nothing,' he said, eventually. 'Thought I saw something. Looked back to see if you two were bearing up and I thought I saw a shadow back there, about forty yards over to the side.'

'Lot of shadows,' I said. 'It's getting dark.'

'Maybe,' he said. He looked at his deputy. 'Our friends here know another party who might be interested in Henrickson. Seems possible he might be in these parts too.'

'Oh yes?' Phil said, suspiciously. 'And who's that?'

'An ex-cop. The Upright Man fucked up his life pretty bad,' Nina said. She tramped a couple of yards in the direction Connolly was looking, also peering hard between the trees. 'He wants him as much as we do.'

'Is this guy dangerous?'

I nodded. 'But not to us, I hope.'

Suddenly Nina called out, startling the rest of us.

'John!' she shouted. 'John — are you there?'

Four pairs of eyes open wide, watching the spaces between the trees. Nothing seemed to move.

She tried again. 'If you're there, John, come up here. We want him too. Do this the right way. Come with us.'

Nothing stirred. Nina shook her head.

'Just shadows,' she said. She frowned, then looked up. 'Oh Jesus, great. Now it's starting to snow.'

She was right. Tiny little flakes of white had

424

begun to spiral down.

'Wish you hadn't done that,' Connolly said. 'Sound travels a long way out here. I wouldn't want this guy to know we're coming.'

'I'm familiar with the way sound travels,' she said. 'He'll already know someone's coming. Right, Ward?'

'Yes. And I've got to warn you, Sheriff, it won't make any difference. He won't run, he won't hide. He'll just do what he was going to do.'

The cop reached across his shoulder and pulled his shotgun over into his hands. He stood with it in the port arms position and looked down at me. Though Connolly was ten, fifteen years younger than he'd been, there was something of my father in his eyes: a cool appraisal, and a sense of not really understanding the concept of backing down.

'Okay,' he said. 'Then that's the way it will be.'

The wind was picking up now, and snow swirled around his face.

28

Patrice was colder than she had ever been before in her life. The man had let her put a coat on before leaving the cabin, and for most of the journey she wished she hadn't. When you're moving, a coat is no use to you: it's the parts it doesn't cover, the face and hands — especially hands tied behind you — which get the coldest. All a coat does is sweat you up. But for the two hours they'd now been sitting, waiting, she'd been very grateful for it. Probably dead without it, she knew. Her nose had run a little, and the water had frozen into little icicles in her nose. She'd asked if he could retie her hands in front, so she could keep them warmer, but he'd said no. She knew why. Her arms and shoulders were beginning to hurt. A lot. This was the start of what she knew he would do if he didn't get what he'd come for by sitting still. He thought this would make some difference to what happened here. She thought he was wrong.

The snow began to come down just after four o'clock. The light had begun to die and though some of the flakes sparkled as they fell, others looked like tiny floating shadows. She knew that some of the locals regarded snow as a cross to bear. She didn't. Even after three years, to her it still seemed like magic. It made her sad, sometimes, bringing memories of Bill, and the children when they were much younger; but nobody said all magic was of a happy kind.

The man had seated her close to the steep wall of the gully, which was something. At least she only got the wind from one direction. Meanwhile he sat up on the low bank on the other side of the stream, with his gun on his lap, in utter silence. If he was cold, he didn't show it.

The snow had been falling for maybe twenty minutes, and getting harder, when she saw him suddenly look up. He listened for a moment.

'Hear something?'

'Long distance away,' he said.

'I really have no idea what you're talking about, you know. Tom saw a bear. That's it. I led you out here because you're a very bad man and I think it would be best if you froze to death somewhere you'll never be found.'

'Maybe,' he said. 'I could see you doing that.' He smiled. 'I like you. You remind me of someone.'

'Your mother?'

'No,' he said. 'Not her.'

'Is she still alive?'

He said nothing, and she knew suddenly and with certainty that this man's mother was dead, not buried in a conventional place, and that he knew where the bones lay.

'Were you an only child?'

Henrickson's head swivelled towards her.

She shrugged. 'I'm just moving my mouth to keep my face from freezing solid.' This was true. In teaching she had also discovered that, very occasionally, you could get through to a child by just talking and talking at them. This man wasn't

427

a child, she knew that. He was a psychopath. Perhaps they worked the same. 'Hey — and maybe they'll hear us. Come see what we're talking about. So were you, or not?'

'I became one,' he said, without emotion. 'I had three mothers. All of them are now dead, which gave me strength. I was born in a forest, my father killed my mother, and then people came and killed him too. They kept me and my brother for a while, and then they kept him and got rid of me. People tried to make me live in places, but I didn't, until in the end I lived with my final mother not far from here.'

'Did she treat you badly?'

'Patrice, I am so far beyond pop psychology you wouldn't believe.'

'So who do I remind you of?'

'The woman who was my grandmother for a while.'

Patrice supposed that was something like a compliment, for what that was worth. 'Why do you want to do this?'

'Killing is what animals do. Carnivores kill to eat. Wild dogs kill the young of other wild dogs. Flies lay their eggs in the flesh of dying mammals. They don't care and neither should we. Arab slave traders in Zanzibar would throw sick men and women into the waters of the bay, so as not to pay duty on goods they couldn't sell. Russian peasants in Siberia sold human body parts in the killing winters of the 1920s. We are the animal that will invent flying machines and then crash them into buildings full of our own kind. We are the ones that will rigorously attempt

428

genocide. Humans are animals and we kill and we destroy.'

'I'd like to hear you sounding more like you thought these were bad things.'

'It's neither bad nor good. It's merely the truth. Our species walked into Europe, where beings had lived for hundreds of thousands of years, and within a few millennia it was ours. How do you think that happened?'

'We were better adapted.'

'In one way only. Our advantage was the willingness to kill other human-like creatures. We killed the Neanderthals until we ran out of them and then we started on each other. We don't respect animals like hyenas and vultures, scavengers. We glorify lions, tigers, sharks: animals with fresh blood around their maws. The fact we have words and thumbs and delusions of spiritual grandeur makes no difference. There is no evil. There is no good. There is only behaviour, and this is ours.'

'So go kill someone already. You obviously have before, right?'

He didn't answer, which was somehow worse. Frozen though she was, Patrice felt the flesh on her neck crawl. She knew she was with someone who did not understand what others understood. 'So go kill some other *human*. There's millions of us. Why not go kill some more of them?'

'Because it's time to do this.'

'So say the voices, right?'

'No one has done this for many lifetimes. They've killed other things. Symbols of power, women, babies. They're all just standing in for the wild man, the real sacrifice.'

'For God's sake — and just how is that supposed to work?'

'Because it does.'

'You kill something, and somehow that retunes the music of the spheres? You really *believe* that?'

'It's true, and if you'd been born only a few hundred years ago you'd know it. But we forget. Everyone, even those who should know better. Now we believe in flossing instead. We believe it matters which long-distance operator we choose. We try not to tread on the cracks.'

'You're insane,' she said.

'I don't think so.' His eyes were sharp in the gathering gloom. 'And your opinion is of no interest to me.'

'Don't tell me anything else then. I don't want to hear it.'

'Fine. But you should know this. The grandmother I mentioned?'

She swallowed.

'I killed her. We were helping her down the stairs, and I gave her a nudge before I even realized the idea had come into my head. I was twelve years old. I know it's what she really wanted. She died fast and well. If your friends don't show up soon, you're going to die too. But it's going to be very, very slow. People ten thousand miles away will turn in their sleep.'

Without even realizing she was doing it, Patrice had scrunched herself a foot further away from the man, which was as far as she could go. She still felt far too close. She had sometimes thought, over the last couple of years, that she was ready for death. She didn't want to play his game, but without Bill there wasn't a great deal to keep her here and maybe it was time to dance with the Man. Huddled in the snow with someone who seemed both less and more than human, she now knew that wasn't true. When you met the Man himself, you realized that to dance with him would never be something heroic or meaningful. It would just make you dead. She didn't want to join their silent ranks.

She wondered what to say next. It was snowing harder now, and nearly full dark, and she was trapped in the forest, hands tied, with a lunatic.

She decided to say nothing at all.

★ ★ ★

Suddenly he stood.

He looked up at the top of the gully wall behind her. Then turned and stared behind him. His head was cocked, his mouth open very slightly. He stepped over the stream, vaulted to the top of the gully wall as if making a single step.

'They're coming,' he said.

He didn't seem pleased. Patrice wasn't even sure who he was talking about. He stood there a moment, as if smelling the wind, and then disappeared like the moon passing behind cloud.

Patrice thought about running, but her legs had gone dead and she knew there was nowhere to go. Instead she curled up small, closed her eyes, and thought of Verona.

431

29

This time we all heard it.

A brittle snapping sound, not close. It was sharp enough to cut through the swelling wind and the hot, ragged sound of breathing in my head. Connolly turned quickly.

'Get down.'

Nina put her hand on my back and pushed. The two of us broke sideways, bent over. Tried to run, but ended up in a fast stumbling shamble through foot-deep snow. We split behind two trees, close by a six-foot outcrop of rock, guns now in our hands.

We watched as Connolly and his deputy backed towards us, rifles in shooting position. Phil's voice was low and cracked a little, but his backward steps were measured and tight. 'You see him?'

Connolly shook his head; kept his gun moving in a smooth, thirty-degree arc.

They made it round to our side of the outcrop. When they were in place I glanced behind us — it's not always easy to divine sound direction in the woods, and I've seen all those movies. I couldn't make out much. The land rose darkly, more trees, rocks, bushes, snow. The contrasts turned everything into one of those Escher drawings where different interpretations flip back and forth before your eyes, and then coalesce into muddy I-don't-know. Nothing was moving that I could see.

I looked ahead again. Nothing was moving there either, except for falling snow. All of us turned our heads, slowly, nothing but eyes and ears. Seconds came and went.

The moment burst. The tension in my legs began to slacken off. My right hand, ungloved, felt cold and useless. I swapped the gun to the left and rubbed my right under my armpit, wincing as the shoulder took the strain of the abrupt movement. I felt better when I had the gun in the right hand again, even though it felt like the heavy metal might just freeze right to it.

'It's not John out there,' I said. 'Surely.'

'No. We're close now. It's the Upright Man.'

'So what now?' Phil whispered.

'We keep going,' Connolly said. He revealed a small device hidden in the palm of his hand. I'd wondered how he was keeping track of where we were in the dark. He thumbed a button and a tiny screen lit up for a moment, then went off. 'Can only be three, four hundred yards ahead.'

'He must have heard us coming.'

'There's four of us and one of him,' Nina said. 'He's not going to come right at us. He's going to wait until we split up, or move without thinking. Then he'll take us one at a time.'

Connolly nodded. 'So how do you want to do it?'

'Stay tight. You think it's directly ahead?'

'Pretty much.'

'So let's move up around this side, come up

left, go at it from the side. What are we headed
for exactly?'

'It's a gully. We've come at it from the top. The
land's gentler to the north, where we are, steeper
the other side. Banks flatten out to the right, get
a lot higher out to the east.'

Nina looked at me. 'What do you think: pull
round right, try and come up the course?'

'Sounds good to me.'

'Let's do it.'

★   ★   ★

We moved more slowly now, and took our
breaths quietly. Suddenly I was seeing every
piece of wood sticking up out of the snow,
making sure I went nowhere near it. We moved
tightly together, in a rough square, six feet apart,
each keeping watchful eyes on our own
quadrant.

Connolly kept us bearing left. The ground
started to rise sharply into a craggy ridge and I
had to use my hand to steady myself against the
rocks as we climbed. I felt dog tired, brain
wiped, my head fuzzy. My foot slipped on wet
rock and I cracked my knee but barely noticed.
Most of me hurt in one way or another. When I
made the top I turned at the waist and reached
down; Nina grabbed my hand and pulled herself
up.

The forest floor curved down away on both
sides, as if we were making our way along some
huge animal's spine. We slipped amongst the
trees, crouched low, barely breathing now.

Suddenly a howling wind whipped in, swirling up at us from the miles of forest below. It came with a cold that was like a nail hammered into both ears, and it shook the branches all around us.

'Jesus,' Nina whispered.

The sound went on and on, a vast shivering wrapped around a frigid shriek. It felt like an object, hard to push against, and perhaps one of us straightened up a little, maybe even more than one. Just enough.

There was a flat *crack* and a grunt and I saw Connolly turn with a jerk and fall over on his back.

I was dimly aware of Nina and Phil moving fast around me, taking cover behind trees. I threw myself forward on the ground and pulled myself up level with the sheriff.

Connolly's face was tight. 'I'm okay,' he said.

I pulled the front of his coat and saw a dark blotch swelling over the lower left side of his chest. I put his hand over the wound, pressed it down tight. He was breathing deep and steady. He was tough.

I looked down and saw Nina crouched three yards away, arms locked, pointing her gun back down the way we'd come. The deputy squatted with his back to a tree. The wind was fading to a tidal roar.

'Phil, come up here,' I said. He stood. There were two more flat cracking sounds. 'Keep DOWN!'

He dropped flat on his stomach and crawled quickly up to me, combat-style. Nina fired two rounds in the direction of the noise.

'Shit, Chief,' Phil said, when he saw the blood.

'Stay with him,' I said.

I scooted along to Nina. 'You see him?'

She shook her head. 'Too dark. He could have been tracking us for a half-hour, waiting until it got like this.'

'From the direction Connolly was hit, the shot had to come from somewhere over there,' I said, pointing down and right. 'He's trying to come around us.' I glanced up at the rock face behind. 'I'm going to head up that crest there, loop back down, try and do the same to him. You see anything move, shoot at it. Knock yourself out.'

'Be careful,' she said.

'I'll try.' I started to move but she grabbed my arm. I looked at her cold, white face. 'Okay,' I said. 'I'll do better than that.'

I waved at Phil, indicated what I was going to do. He nodded, and turned so his rifle was pointing the same way as Nina's gun.

Then I clambered quickly up the rocks. As I reached the top there was another cracking sound from below, followed quickly by two more shots from Nina. I heard her swear, then start to reload.

I crawled ten yards and then lay flat on my stomach, looked down. The mountainside cut away sharply here, cold and empty. There was nothing to lock onto below, no pattern to recognize. The shapes of trunk and branch and rock were endless and random and as soon as you moved your eyes you lost track of where you were. All you could do was take it steadily, move

436

your head slowly . . .

I saw him.

The glimpse was so faint it could have been just a shadow, a fleeting artefact imagined out of the darkness and the drifting snow. But then I saw it again, and I knew I'd seen him move.

He was about thirty yards away, just where we'd thought he'd be.

I crawled a few feet further along the ridge until I was masked by a small stand of trees. Got up onto my knee and one foot. Looked ahead, and judged it. If he hadn't seen me get into this position, I could probably make it. I could sprint from behind this stand, head quickly out right and down, making for a pair of big, thick trees I could see ahead. Reckon on emptying my gun on the way. Assuming I made it there without being cut down, reload in the cover of the trees, ready for stage two. Then it would be him and me, close quarters, and I would just have to make sure it was me who remained upright.

One against one, there was no reason it couldn't go my way. Maybe. I put my hand in the right-hand pocket of the thick coat, to check the clips were where I thought. They were. My heart was beating hard, knowing this was one of those moments when you just have to go, when planning is less important than speed and belief.

I edged a little further right — slowly, four feet, five — and that was going to have to be enough; I was teetering to go, leaning forward into the run. I took a final checking glance to the side.

Someone was standing there.

It was a young woman. She was ten feet away, on higher ground. She was wearing floral pyjamas, and had bare feet. She stood between two trees, half in shadow; snow spiralled down around her and I saw some of it land on her shoulders and in her long hair. I could just make out her eyes, the lines of her cheekbones.

It was Jessica Jones.

'Careful,' she said. 'There are many.'

Then she was gone.

I was off-balance in readiness to run forward, and instead fell back against the rock. I froze there for a moment, blinking fast, staring up at where she'd been. I looked left, right. She'd vanished.

I quickly scrabbled up to where I thought I'd seen her standing. There was no one there, but the snow on the ground was messed up. I thought I saw something that could have been a footprint, maybe even two of them, but they were far too big.

I suddenly couldn't do what I'd been going to. I headed back, slid back over the ridge and scooted up to Nina in a crouch. She stared. 'What the fuck?'

'I think there's more than one of them,' I said, avoiding her eyes.

'*What?* How do you know? Who's with him?'

'I don't know.'

'So what did you see? What happened to you, Ward?'

I didn't answer, couldn't. I didn't know what to tell her. Instead I scooted halfway to where Phil was holding his position next to the sheriff.

'How's he looking?'

'I'm fine,' Connolly said. He didn't look it. 'I don't need baby sitting. Just go take this asshole down.'

'There's at least two of them,' I said. 'So, Phil, we are going to need you back down here.'

Phil glanced down at his boss, who nodded curtly. 'Just don't get yourself killed,' Connolly muttered. 'Day's gone enough to hell without me having to talk to your mother.'

Phil came back with me in a half-crouch. 'I thought I smelled something weird just then,' he said. 'Did you smell anything?'

'No,' I said. 'What kind of weird?'

He just shook his head.

When we got back to Nina she was looking at me hard. 'What is it, Ward? What happened up there? You look strange.'

'Nothing. I just got a feeling. Now . . . '

Then it came. A shot from up and to the left.

'Shit,' she said. 'You were right.'

'He's got someone with him?' Phil said. 'Who?'

'I don't . . . ' For a second the ludicrous idea of John and Paul joining forces crossed my mind. Of course not. So who . . .

Then the thinking was over, because a man was running up the hill towards us like a fleet shadow, firing as he came.

Nina and I fired at the same time. Both of us missed. Phil threw himself in a roll and bumped hard against a tree. Dodged around to fire, but hesitated a beat too long. I stood straight up and pulled the trigger twice.

439

The man did something like a spinning hop and dropped to the ground. I fired twice more at him, heard a grunt. Nina slipped off around the back, gun ready, stepping sideways.

'Nina, hold here,' I said. 'Phil, come with me.' She looked up, signed OK.

I pointed Phil back up along the ridge. Ran behind him in a crouch, the two of us splitting to go around Connolly. A series of clapping sounds echoed up to us from the original shooter's position.

'Shit,' Phil said. 'I thought you just *got* that guy.'

'There's three of them, then,' I said. 'Jesus Christ.'

We held tight and still for a moment. Looked ahead. The forest seemed yet darker and thicker up there. I was shivering and felt odd. My neck tickled and I whipped my head to the left and thought I saw someone running through the trees about twenty yards away; but it couldn't have been, because again it looked like they were wearing nothing more than pyjamas, and that would be madness out in a place like this when it was so cold and dark. I was exhausted, amped up and making patterns in the shadows, projecting pictures that made no sense. I needed to be careful. I dropped my head and took a couple of deep breaths.

I looked up again when there was a single crack out front, and something whined through the air right between our heads to spang off the rock behind. Phil and I returned fire.

Then I heard Nina start shooting down below us.

'Christ,' I said, panicky. 'Phil — hold position there. Take that guy out if you can. I'm going back.'

'I'm on it,' Phil said. He went down on his stomach again and squirted quickly forward along the ground. I got the sense he'd watched a few war movies in his time. That was cool by me.

I straightened up more than I should have and went stumble-running back down towards where Nina was supposed to be. I couldn't see any sign of her, but I could hear firing in the trees over to the left. I passed the first man's body on the ground and saw his face: cold, lean, hard. I didn't recognize him.

There were more shots ahead, harder to hear as the wind spiralled up into voice once more. I ran down to where I could hear the sound of shooting. I couldn't tell if it was one gun firing or two.

I dropped down off a rock outcrop and nearly pulled my ankle apart, but kept upright by a hair. I hit a thicker layer of snow and struggled through it, legs impeded, slugging through it like frozen treacle.

Finally pulled up out of it onto rockier ground. The shooting had stopped but I couldn't see anyone.

'Nina?'

No reply. I turned in a full circle, started to run in the direction I thought I had seen her go.

I'd got ten feet and was picking up speed when suddenly I had nothing in my lungs and I

441

was lying on my back with snow in my ears and a rock sticking in my spine.

Someone stepped out from behind a tree. Then there was a foot pressing down hard on my chest. I was struggling to breathe, badly winded, pain lancing up my back in shooting bursts. I howled without even meaning to. The foot pressed down harder and a face appeared three feet above mine.

Short hair, round glasses.

The shooter from the diner in Fresno. He placed the cold barrel of a shotgun in the middle of my forehead. Leaned on it hard.

'Hello, fucker,' he said.

★   ★   ★

Nina was fifty yards away. She'd heard something running through the trees, something that seemed not to be slowed by the rocks and snow and unpredictable, ragged ground. That had to be Paul, she thought. Never mind who he'd got with him, these guys they didn't know about, had never met, but who wanted to kill them anyway, she believed the only person who could move like that in these conditions had to be the Upright Man.

So she'd headed down the slope after the sound, firing indiscriminately, and caught a brief glimpse of something moving below. But after a few minutes she stopped, winded, and could see or hear nothing more.

Then she heard the sound of a shout behind her.

'Ward,' she said, and then she was scrambling back up the bank. Slipped, cracked her face against the rock.

She kept going.

★ ★ ★

The man pressed the barrel harder into my head.

'So you're the brother,' he said. 'You were lucky in the diner. Not so lucky tonight. Seems like you don't have what he has. Just another amateur.'

I coughed. I couldn't do much else.

'He's going to die tonight too,' the guy added, grinding the barrel still harder. 'Thanks to your friend.'

'Who?'

'This guy Zandt. How do you think we knew where to come? He cut a deal.'

'He didn't kill Dravecky?'

'The boss is alive and well. Course, your friend thinks he's going to be walking away from this. He couldn't be more wrong.'

He stood on my chest harder for a moment. His eyes twinkled behind the small circles of glass. His enjoyment of the fact I couldn't breathe was evident.

'So adios, shithead. Time be moving on.'

I could see his finger slowly tightening on the trigger of the shotgun, felt the ground beneath me flatten as it became a slab.

I closed my eyes. I didn't want this man's face to be the last thing I saw.

There was the sound of a gunshot, close. Then

443

two more, quickly afterwards.

I opened my eyes just as the man fell over backwards. Turned my head. Nina came hurtling into view.

She dropped to one knee by my side. 'Are you okay?' She had blood dribbling down one cheek.

I groggily pushed myself up onto my elbows. I was okay in the sense I could move, and could tell everything hurt a lot, which presumably meant my back wasn't broken and I was free to go.

'What happened to your face?'

'Don't fuss. What was he saying? Was he saying something about John? I thought I heard his name.'

'No. They're after Paul.'

She grabbed my arm and helped me up. I staggered, lurching, barely able to stand upright. Got my balance, took deep sucking breaths, hands on my knees.

When I straightened I saw Nina standing over the other guy.

I heard three shots from some distance ahead. Nina didn't move.

'Nina . . . '

'Wait a minute,' she said.

The man on the ground was trying to sit upright. He had blood coming out of his thigh and the base of his neck. Nina had evidently remembered he might still be wearing a vest. He was moving slowly but like he could keep it up.

Nina kicked him in the side.

'That's for Monroe,' she said, voice tight and

low and hard. 'He's an asshole, but he's my asshole.'

'He's dirty,' the man said. His voice was little more than a wheeze.

'Who isn't?' Nina's face was pinched. 'And if you'd already tipped him off, why the *hell* did you kill the cop?'

'Insurance. Monroe didn't do anything the first time.'

'The cop's name was Steve Ryan.'

'Whatever.' He grinned. 'Just doing my job.'

'Right,' Nina said. She nodded, once. Turned away.

Then turned back and shot him in the head.

Leaned down low and said to him: 'That's from his wife.'

30

Patrice had been huddled in a ball for perhaps ten minutes when she heard the sound of running up above, something or someone pushing through the bushes at the lip of the gully. She debated what to do. Doing nothing at all had the most immediate appeal. Ultimately everyone truly believes that if you stay real still, and don't peek, the monsters won't see you.

But she decided she had to know.

She lifted her head and saw Death leaping back down into the stream bed. He stood irresolute for a moment, in the middle of the water, appearing to have forgotten she was there. She could see him weighing up choices.

Then he loped up the river, and faded behind a pair of big trees. He hadn't gone far though, she knew.

★ ★ ★

I felt through the man's coat and took all the shells I could. Then I realized I didn't want to use this man's weapon, and dropped them on his chest.

'Something happened up there,' I said.

'Shit,' Nina said. 'Yes. I heard the shots.'

We hurriedly climbed back up the way we'd come. It was cold and the wind still moaned and shook and I felt a very long way from home. I was limping now, and the outrageous pain round the back of my right side said some ribs had been cracked. We'd come further than I realized. It was five minutes before I saw Nina stiffen and go still, and I looked up to see someone standing up ahead, near the top of the ridge.

'Don't shoot.' It was Phil. 'Jesus,' he said. 'Are you guys okay? What happened to you?'

'We got one,' I said. 'What about you?'

He shook his head, turned and started walking quickly back up to Connolly's position. We followed.

'I went up after him,' he said. 'Couldn't find him. Then he started shooting from somewhere, damned near took my head off. I fired back and took cover behind a big rock and tried to get around the other side but I came up against a big drop and thought 'Damn — that's the end of that.' I got nowhere to go, and . . . '

He looked ashamed for a moment. 'Maybe I could have taken a shot a little earlier. But I didn't. I never tried to kill a man before. So I half stood up, thinking I've got to work out some route to get back the other way, and that's when I see this other guy.'

'What other guy?'

'I don't know. He came from nowhere. I saw him for like a single second. He does this — ' Phil mimed someone bringing a rifle up to his shoulder ' — and he fired before it was even in position. One shot. Bang, just like that. I ducked like I was falling down. Don't hear anything else for a couple minutes. So I finally stuck my head up to see. The guy with the gun has vanished.

447

There's this dead body lying about thirty feet to the side of me.'

'You didn't shoot him?'

'No, I just told you. But somebody sure as hell did. I went and looked at the body. One hole, plumb in the middle of his forehead, like someone painted a target there. So who the hell was *that* guy? What the hell is going *on* out here?'

'Must be John,' I said.

Nina shook her head. 'John's a city boy. I don't see him being able to creep up on one of these guys and drop them with a single shot. Far as I know he's never used a hunting rifle in his life.'

'So who?'

'The Upright Man,' she said. 'Got to be. These other guys came out here to kill him, not us.'

'I don't buy it. He'd let them kill us first.'

'You're his brother, Ward.'

I didn't see what difference that made.

When we got to Connolly we found him standing. Leaning against a tree, but upright.

'Christ, Sheriff, sit back down.'

'I'm okay,' he said.

'Sir, with respect, you're really not,' Nina said. 'You're bleeding like a stuck pig.'

The big man looked down, saw the thick dark stains which had started to spread down his pants. 'That's true. So we'd better be quick.'

He reached in his coat pocket again and pulled out his GPS. His hand was shaking, but not too much. A quick flash of the screen, and then he nodded ahead and down to the right.

'Might as well go straight at it now,' he said.

We went onwards through the trees. We passed the body of the other gunman, lying on his back on the ground. Phil was right. The man who killed him knew how to shoot.

The ground levelled out a little after a while, curved up towards ridges on both sides, as if we were entering a wide half-tunnel lined with trees and shadow: some long-ago watercourse, I guessed, or even more ancient glacial scrape. The wind wound itself up again, pulled at us, and we moved forward a little faster, hoping it would cover the sound of our feet.

Connolly stumbled, stopped; he pitched forward and fell. I bent down to him but he shook his head slowly.

'Go,' he said.

I pulled my coat off and dropped it over him.

And on we went. The bushes were thick, huge balls of frigid, spiky cotton wool. Something shrieked way over to the left. I think it was the wind. The lowest branches of the trees whipped back and forth, on and on, endlessly, as if shaken by lunatic hands.

Nina put her arm out, stopped. 'There.'

I peered. Sixty yards ahead you could make out that trunks gave way to a black void.

The edge of the gully. It had to be.

Phil whispered. 'We just going to go straight in there?'

'No,' Nina said. 'You go wide right. I'll go ahead. Ward, you come in from the left. First sighting, shoot, then shout loud.'

We nodded. Phil cut away quickly, pushing through the undergrowth as quietly as he could.

Nina pointed a warning finger at me, an inch from my face, then she was off, straight ahead. I turned ninety degrees and headed along the side of the slope as quickly as I could.

It was all okay, I told myself, until I heard the sound of a shot.

After that it was in the lap of the gods. I hoped they were paying attention, and bore no grudge.

★ ★ ★

Nina began to slow it down, get quiet. Five minutes of hard-fought forward progress had got her maybe thirty yards. Glancing right showed her a faint shadow, heading up around the side of this rough, high valley. Phil. He disappeared from view after a few moments, presumably behind trees or down into lower ground. She couldn't see Ward to her right. The ground was tough and steep in that direction. He was going to have to go very wide. She hoped none of them got lost. She hoped they weren't all going to die. Not out here, where it was so cold.

It was dark as hell too. The trees gave her only one way forward now, but the bushes made it hard to follow. She ducked under a sloping trunk, leant drunkenly against trees that were still alive. Beneath the sound of the wind she could hear water ahead, a lonely, splashy chuckle. It's strange how just from the sound you can tell the water will be bone-chilling cold.

She pushed forward, carefully, one foot out in front. She tried to slide it but the snow and tangles made it impossible. Had to keep lifting

450

her feet, small, cautious steps.

Then: *pop* — she heard the sound of a shot.

She turned her head quickly. Where had it come from? Please not left, unless . . .

She heard a shout then, muffled and indistinct. This came from the right, she was sure. It had to be Phil. He'd got something.

She threw caution aside and pushed forward, hard. She had to get down there quickly now. She hoped Ward had heard the sounds too. He'd come fast, she knew he would.

She held her gun out straight in front, ducked her head against the clutching undergrowth, trying to tune out the scratching branches with their cold, wet, stinging slaps, and shoving forward as hard and fast as she could. It was like fighting through spiny cobwebs. She turned sideways, trying to slip past gnarled vegetation that held like a fence. Heard another shout and realized that probably meant trouble and stopped being careful enough.

Four more steps and then she fell.

★   ★   ★

I'd gone too far. Way too far. I judged a good distance to start with but then each time I tried to pull back down towards the gully, something was in the way. Trees, upright and fallen. Nursery logs too awkward to clamber over. Rock outcrops in looming, slippery piles, suddenly splitting into slopping chasms I couldn't jump and had to go around. I kept being forced further and further to the left, along an increasingly narrow ridge that wasn't going anywhere I wanted to be.

I abandoned it in the end, swearing breathlessly, and cut back even further up the slope until I crossed a saddle of rock and at least had a clear run for a while. I still couldn't seem to cut back down, however, and time was stretching out. This was taking too long. I wished it was light. I wished Nina had called in the Feds or the army or the Girl Scouts. All we had at our back was two cops and one of those was curled shivering around the base of a tree sixty yards back.

Finally I seemed to be making a little headway, scrabbling hectically along a stretch of unencumbered rock, towards a break at the top where I thought I could get over.

Then I heard the sound of a shot.

And maybe a shout, a couple seconds afterwards, but I wasn't sure.

I slipped the gun into my pocket and grabbed at the rocks in front of me. I was going over them, come what may.

I hauled myself up and over and slip-slid down the other side and saw some clearer ground ahead. At last.

I hit the ground and ran and ran.

⋆　⋆　⋆

She fell fast, trying to grab at things, losing the gun. The fall was noisy and fast but felt longer; then she collided stomach-first with something hard and was swung around it so fast her head

452

spun. She landed on the ground on her side like a bag of logs dropped out of a plane.

She sat up immediately, head rolling, and pulled forward before she was even sure where she was. When she was on hands and knees she looked left and right, back and forth, trying to spot the gun.

She saw she was in some dark and rocky place and the water was much closer now.

But where was the gun?

She hoped it wasn't caught up above her, wedged in some crevice or root. She wanted it now. She wanted it badly.

She crawled forward, feeling out with her hands. Her head was still liquid and rocking from the fall and she was finding it hard to lock herself in space. There was cold gravel under her hands. Wet. Sharp. Her eyes were lost in blackness. It was hard to differentiate: hard to see what was what. Was that thing ahead just more darkness, or was it a wall of rock?

There was something that sounded like groaning, over on the right. Not close. She couldn't see anything up there. *Groaning can't be good. Unless it's him. Unless Phil got him. Or unless it's just the wind. If it's not the wind or the Upright Man, then it's not good.*

Am I even sure that was Phil's direction? What if it was where Ward was? Am I near the gully? Is this it?

Where's the gun? Where's the fucking, fucking gun?

She saw something ahead, pale but not snow. She looked harder and made out what it was. An old woman, scrunched up small in a big coat. She was sitting on the other side of a low wide stream, her back tight against high rock.

She was staring at Nina, eyes wide, unblinking, not making a sound. Her head and shoulders were covered in snow, like a statue in an overgrown graveyard way off the beaten track.

The woman's shape and position finally gave Nina a visual reference, a key to understanding the space. She was near the bottom of a gully — *the* gully, it must be — with steep walls but a fairly flat bottom maybe fifteen feet across, narrowing rapidly to both sides.

She blinked to lock it in her head, then looked for the gun again: forcing herself to do it slowly this time, as if it didn't matter a bit, as if it was just an earring she'd dropped back in Malibu and the cab wasn't due for a quarter-hour and the night's big question was whether to have an entrée or two appetizers or maybe just a big bucket of wine.

There it was. Thank God.

Nina scrambled over to the stream, picked her gun out of the shallows. Shook it, changed clips. She ran in a low crouch to the other side of the gully and dropped down on her haunches next to the woman. She spoke very quietly, trying to control her breath, to keep it steady.

'Are you Patrice Anders?'

The woman kept staring at her. She had ice in her eyelashes. She was two steps away from a Popsicle. Her head seemed to move, a little. Was that a nod?

Nina shook her shoulder gently. 'Ma'am?'

'Yes,' she said, loudly.

'Shh. Is someone with you? Is he still here?' More quietly: 'He's here. Somewhere.'

'Who? This guy Tom, or is it Henrickson?'

'Him. That's not his real name.'

'Actually, it is.' Nina squatted down beside her, looked back the way the woman's head was facing. She couldn't see anything except the rock sides of the watercourse, levelling out a little up on the left side.

Then she heard the sound of pain again.

'Don't move,' she said. Then she realized why the woman's posture looked so weird. He'd tied her hands behind her back. She fumbled at the knot with her own numb fingers. The rope was part frozen with ice and it seemed to take forever to start it loosening. She finally got it undone. The woman slowly, slowly pulled her hands around in front, as if afraid her arms would shatter.

'Still don't move,' Nina said. 'Seriously.'

She slipped around the bush shield and kept low as she made her way along the side of the gully. She wasn't going to let go of her gun, not ever again, but she kept slipping on the wet rocks with only one hand to steady herself. She grabbed at the branch stumps, tried to pull herself along, and it worked but wasn't very fast. Small rivulets of water turned her hands to ice. It took her long minutes to go fifty feet upstream, every step a bad adventure.

She hoped Ward was coming. She really, really hoped so.

Up ahead the walls were only six to eight feet

455

high. She could see something lying sprawled at the bottom.

It was Phil.

He was alive, but holding his thigh very tightly with both hands, his body twisting in a slow roll. He was trying so hard not to make a noise, eyes bulging like white marbles with the pain, but another groan escaped when he saw her.

'Shot me,' he said, like a wheezy cough. 'Henrickson. Took my gun.' With a jerk of his head he indicated back the way she'd come, along the stream bed.

Nina looked behind him instead, scanning the tops of the gully walls. The fact he'd gone the way Phil indicated meant nothing. He could be back up the top there now.

Or she could be, in fact . . . She quickly considered going upriver past the deputy, trying to clamber up one of the walls, getting back on higher ground, above all this, and hoping the Upright Man came back down below. Make him the fish in the barrel instead of her.

But she knew she wouldn't be able to climb while holding a gun, and also that her back was a very wide target for someone who knew how to kill.

'Keep holding the wound,' she said, and crept back the other way.

She stayed away from the walls this time and went straight down the middle through the stream, the water nearly up to her knees, cold as anything she'd ever felt. Cold and loud: lapping, rushing water and more of that howling wind, the drifting curtain of the endless snow.

She couldn't turn and look around because the bed of the stream was too loose and unpredictable underfoot. So she maintained a straight course down the centre line, squinting ahead, trying to spot the Anders woman so she'd know how close she was to where she'd started. She thought about shouting in case Ward could hear, but the Upright Man could be a lot closer, and she realized with painful clarity what a stupid idea the 'shoot and shout' plan had been and wished someone else had made that decision instead of her.

She still couldn't see the woman yet and that freaked her and she started pushing ahead more quickly.

Then out of the corner of her eye she saw someone standing on the left side of the gully. In a space of time too small to measure, she saw he had a rifle locked in his shoulder and so she knew it wasn't Ward — and with a speed that bypassed her conscious mind altogether she swivelled and lifted her hands and fired three times.

Two of the sounds disappeared in handclaps. The last returned a dry, rustling slap. The shape slipped, came sliding down the low slope of the gully.

She ran up through the water, the cold forgotten, everything tangential and of no interest except the man on the ground in front of her. She kept her gun pointed at him, edging closer until she was ten feet away.

Once was never enough. She should shoot him again.

Her trigger finger was tightening when he pushed himself upwards and showed his face.

'Oh Christ,' she said, aghast. 'John . . . '

Then there was the sound of someone landing lightly behind her. The gun was knocked out of her hand and an arm wrapped tight around her neck and a cold circle of metal pressed into her temple.

'Hello, Agent Baynam,' said a voice. '*Excellent work.*'

31

I nearly ran off the end of the world.

If I hadn't grabbed out at the last minute with my left hand, it would have happened. I would have gotten right up to that high rocky place and taken one long step too many and just gone sailing into forever night. As it was my stomach bowed outwards, hanging out over space, and I got a horrifying split-second glimpse of a huge drop, and felt the branch bend, and heard clearly the roar of water landing somewhere a very, very long way beneath me.

I pulled myself back and turned my back on the drop quickly, desperate and terrified. My lungs were crying, aching as if full of ground glass. My lungs hated me a lot.

I lurched over and saw that, yes, I'd made it to the gully — but it couldn't be anywhere near the right place. It was forty feet across here and had sides so steep and deep they looked like they'd been made with a single violent sweep from a giant's axe.

Yet this must be the right gully.

So I had to go back.

I kept a couple of yards back from the edge and shoved through the bushes. The trees were a little smaller here but that didn't help much: all it meant was the undergrowth had room to expand and really get into its stride. Before long I was drifting further away from the gully again, forced back up the way I'd come.

I kept struggling forward, running when I could, but always fighting against the tide. I was beginning to think I was going to have to go all the way back around when I stopped dead in my tracks.

I had been looking through the ranks of trees between me and the ravine, and I thought I saw something, a glimpse of something at the gully edge. I pushed my way over towards the spot, knowing the gap would still be too wide.

But when I got there I understood what I'd seen.

There was a big tree trunk lying across the gully. It had fallen plumb across, in fact. It looked bizarrely like an actual bridge, and it was hard not to see it as an invitation. The other side was much more open.

I pushed my way through to the end of the log, kicked it. It was solid. The bank on the other side looked like it would give me a clear run back down to where I was supposed to be, or at least a lot nearer than I was now.

Assuming I could get ten feet or so over a nasty drop down to cold and jagged rocks, across a trunk four inches deep in snow.

Screw that. I'd be no use to anyone with a smashed skull. I turned away.

Then I heard three more shots. Something that sounded like Nina's voice, making a noise that was not a cry of triumph.

I jumped up onto the log. Took a deep breath.

I didn't know what else to do but take it at a run.

Patrice watched what was happening in front of her. She had seen Henrickson drop down into the river like a piece of film run backwards. She'd never seen someone so unlikely to stumble or fall. In one smooth movement he'd disarmed the woman and put a gun to her head.

He knocked the other man's rifle into the water with his foot, then pulled the woman back a few yards, until they were standing in the middle of the stream bed.

The man on the ground looked in pain but was trying not to show it. Patrice knew it was that way with men. Except sometimes, when they whined like hell. Even Bill had. Cancer will kick the grit out of most anyone.

'How did you get here, John?'

'Dravecky,' the man told him, not without satisfaction. 'Even the psychopaths of the world want rid of you. You're the outcast's outcast. You've got nowhere to go.'

'There's always somewhere,' Henrickson said. 'Finding Dravecky and killing him will be item one. Item two will be his NSA buddy down in LA. You run into him yet, Nina?'

'Yes.'

'Thought you might. Don't worry. They're a lot less important than they think.'

Patrice saw the man on the ground move suddenly, and then he had a gun in his hand. But Henrickson had moved at the same time, back two more yards, and now he had the woman

461

right in front of him; his body behind hers, his head behind hers.

'What are you going to do, John? You going to shoot her to get to me?'

Patrice watched the woman's face and knew she didn't actually know what the man would do. The woman tried to move, to give him a shot at something that wasn't part of her own body, but the man behind her was graceful and quick.

'What's more important to you? Getting a bullet in me for Karen's sake, and killing your agent friend in the process? Maybe I should just save you the decision and kill her right away.'

The man on the ground had pulled himself upright. The hand holding the gun out didn't look too steady.

'You shoot her and I'll shoot you,' he said.

Patrice thought he had not a chance in hell of getting the guy, even if he showed him an inch. She knew Henrickson thought this too, and knew also that might not stop the man trying.

Then she realized: he hasn't looked at me.

Henrickson hadn't done so much as glance her way since he'd been back in the gully. She didn't think that meant he'd forgotten about her. She guessed he was a man who'd know how much small change he had in his pockets to the nearest cent, assuming something like him even had a need for small change. But maybe she wasn't the first thing on his mind.

Could she do it? Could she leap forward, throw herself either at him or somewhere near? Just throw him off balance enough to let the guy with the gun take his shot?

462

She didn't know for sure. But she thought she could try.

She slowly unfolded her arms. They hurt like someone was pushing hot wire into her bones. She tried to move her feet and not much happened, but that didn't matter. She didn't need to actually get to him. She just needed a moment of surprise.

She pushed herself forward.

She didn't move. She pushed again. She couldn't move. It was like something was holding her back. She was so frozen in place, her legs so locked, that . . .

No. Something *was* holding her back.

She swivelled her eyes. Something had its hands on her shoulders. She slowly turned her head.

Tom Kozelek was crouched behind her. He smelt warm and strange. He was gently gripping her shoulders with big hands, holding her back, stopping her from moving.

Be safe, he said, in her head. *A man comes.*

Then he let go of her and melted back away, and was gone. She thought she heard a quiet sloshing sound in the water behind.

But she still couldn't move. It had just been her frozen legs, after all.

★   ★   ★

I made it three quarters of the way across and then my foot slipped. It slipped like I'd stepped onto ice while wearing shoes made of ice. I threw both my hands forward and prayed.

I crashed into the top with bushes in both hands. I hauled myself up, hands and feet scrabbling like a dog's. I pulled up through rocks and roots and snow — and then something I could stand on.

I ran. My lungs didn't hurt any more, nor my ribs or back or shoulder. My feet found every step as if I was running across a flat field of mown grass; bushes melted back like misty dreams and the trees yielded up a path that had always been there, as if the mountains had long ago shaped themselves to provide it. I couldn't see much through the falling white, but I knew where I had to be — if I could get there fast enough.

I had to dodge upwards briefly, but only for fifty yards. Then I carved back right and round, and straight at the lip of the gully I could now see. I ran fast and low, not caring about noise. It was too late to worry about that or anything else.

At the top I slid up to a tree and pushed myself to the side, dropping into a crouch. I put a fresh clip in my gun. Took a breath and stood up.

'Hey, Ward,' said a voice from below. 'I waited for you.'

I took a half step forward, then a half step back nearer to the tree. I looked down into the gully. I saw someone lying on the ground down at the bottom of the gully wall below me, gun pointing straight ahead. At first I thought it was Paul, then I saw it was John, and realized it hadn't been him who'd called out to me.

Maybe thirty feet away was Nina, on a

diagonal up the river. She was standing in a very odd way, right in the middle of the water. Then I saw this was because a man's arm was around her neck and there was a gun held up to her head. It was Paul.

'Let her go,' I shouted.

'Not until I drop her.'

'I'll shoot.'

'I don't think so. John can't and neither will you.'

I saw he was right. He'd positioned himself with his back to the opposite side of the gully. With John and me on the same side, neither of us could take a shot without hitting Nina first.

I looked at her. 'Do it, Ward,' she said.

I took a step back nearer cover. Paul fired and I thought he'd killed Nina and my heart tried to stop but I realized he'd shot at me instead when the bullet sang through the wind right past my face. The gun was immediately back in place at Nina's temple.

'Yes, do it,' he said. 'Come on, your turn.'

'Ward, for God's sake *shoot him*!' John shouted.

'I don't have the angle.' I didn't know what to do. I tried moving up the bank a little, but Paul could see me. He altered his position just enough, still keeping himself shielded from both John and me.

'What are you going to do?' I shouted. 'Back up all the way to Seattle? It's a long fucking hike, I've got to warn you.'

He just laughed.

It was just a game. He'd known I was coming.

465

He'd waited. He wanted it to be one of us who did this, goaded to the point of making a horrible mistake.

If not, he'd do it himself without blinking and then it would be him against me and a man who was lying on the ground as if he'd been shot. I didn't feel very positive towards John right then but I couldn't do something that would get his head blown off.

John took a shot.

He missed. The Upright Man took another step back, pulling Nina with him.

I glanced up the gully and saw that if he killed her now and ran straight upstream, he could be away before I got anywhere near him. I knew time was running out.

He was going to kill Nina and get away.

Her eyes were on me still. I felt her tell me that this was a time where I had to do what I thought was the best thing, and see how it panned out.

I took a step back the way I'd come, letting my arms drop for a moment. My hands were getting cold. My head was cold too, sharp and empty and full of one simple decision.

All I could see was Nina's face.

Then something moved in the very corner of my vision, right at the top of the far side of the gully. Not quite at the edge, a little way back. I saw something moving, very low.

I stood up straight.

'Fuck you, Paul,' I said. 'I'm not doing this for you.'

'Whatever,' he said. He looked me right in the eyes, pushed the gun harder into the side of

466

Nina's head. 'I'll do it for you.'

The shape on the other side slipped a little closer, now nearly up to the edge of the wall. I kept looking at Paul, not letting my eyes flicker at all.

'Ward, shoot him. Or I will.'

'John — don't you do anything.'

I waited a beat. Then quickly moved to my left. I shouted, 'Now!'

Paul swung around and stepped back to keep Nina between him and me.

Connolly fired. He picked his shot and planted a single round in the top of Paul's shoulder, from his vantage slumped up on the other side of the gully.

Paul swung around, gun out, and for a precious moment it was him I could see, just him, with nothing in the way. I fired three times. Shoulder, arm, leg.

He turned clumsily, and tried to keep hold of Nina but she shoved out and kicked back at him, managed to wrench herself out of his grasp. Tried to run but only got a few yards before falling.

By then I was scrambling down the wall. I fired again on the way down, hit real body mass this time and he was thrown back against the wall, gun flying out of his hand.

I quickly got between him and John. I wasn't sure that would make a difference. But John didn't shoot.

I crossed the river. I walked through the cold, flowing water to the other side. I stopped six feet short.

Raised my arm. Pointed my gun down at him. Paul lay sprawled against the bottom of the wall. He was broken and bleeding heavily. It was hard to believe who he was.

He looked up at me.

His face was so like my own.

Cannon Beach

Four days later we took a tip from Patrice. We drove down to Portland and then struck out due west along Route 6. It rained all the way down through Washington, and it rained as we drove to the coast through the Tillamook State Forest. It's a fine forest. It has many trees. It didn't use to. It was logged for decades and then in 1933 a massive fire, the Tillamook Burn, cut a swathe right through the middle. By the end of it more than three hundred thousand acres of old-growth timber was gone, and it's said that hot ashes fell on ships five hundred miles down the coast. But the fire was put out, eventually, and more trees were planted. By some strange quirk of fate, the forest burned again in '39, '45 and '51, like a returning six-year curse. So people went out and planted a bunch more seeds: garden clubs, scouts, civic groups all spent their weekends out there doing good. Now it just looks like a regular forest. Unless you knew what had happened to it, you'd think it had always been that way. We're like that. Sometimes.

It didn't really occur to either of us to pull over and take a walk. Wouldn't have even if it hadn't been so wet. We had seen enough trees for a while.

★ ★ ★

Nina wouldn't let me shoot him.

I was going to. I really was. I didn't see what else made sense. He was the man who had killed my parents and pulled apart my life. He had killed the daughter of the man who lay on the other side of the gully, his eyes burning holes in my back. He had killed people whose names I would never learn, who might always go unaccounted for. I didn't know whether John was right to hate me for not shooting him the last time. But I thought he would be right if I didn't do it now.

She came up behind me. Didn't say anything, or try to physically stay my hand. I just felt her standing there, close enough to feel the warmth of her breath on my neck. I watched the man beneath me try to move, hands slipping feebly against the rocks like two small, pale creatures near the end of their lives. I don't know what it is with the mad, but they've certainly got force of will. Maybe it's not having the checks and balances the rest of us have, or perhaps I'm kidding myself: maybe their minds are simply clearer, unclouded with the anxieties and morality that the rest of us are swaddled with. Force of will wasn't enough for him now, however. He couldn't move, and he had no gun, and he wasn't going to be hurting anyone.

I could still shoot him, I knew. Nobody there would blame me for it. Connolly was watching from the top of the gully. His face looked waxy and I could hear his breathing from where I stood, but the end of his rifle was steady enough. He looked like he might take another shot if I didn't. I knew what John wanted. I didn't know Phil's position at that stage: he seemed a nice guy and not prone to hurt people, but — given that the Upright Man had shot him in the leg and held his head under the water for a spell — I suspect he'd have been with the hawks on this one.

In the end I let my arm drop.

'Useless fucker,' John muttered. Nina walked over to him, dropped to a crouch, and said something quietly in his ear. She kept talking a little while, then took the gun from his hand.

She came and stood with it trained on the Upright Man while I helped Connolly down the side of the gully. He looked dreadful but no worse than I felt. Any man who could make it alone to the gully from where we'd left him was not going to be giving up the ghost easily.

He limped down with me to where Nina said Phil was lying. He tried to help, but in the end it was mainly me who half carried his deputy up to where the others were. There was a lot of noise involved. I propped him up against the far wall, opposite Paul. Connolly sank down next to Phil, his gun firmly trained on Paul.

I didn't know what was going to happen next. It was still snowing. It had slackened off a little, but didn't look like stopping. We were stuck way out in the middle of nowhere. Neither Phil nor Connolly were going to be able to go home under their own steam, and the sheriff's radio wasn't getting anything. John looked more fit: judging by his coat, Nina's shot had not done much more than take a chunk out of his arm. He

471

wouldn't say anything to me, though. He wouldn't even look me in the eyes.

Nina went and fetched the old lady. I hadn't even realized she was there. She looked about as cold as I can imagine anyone could look without actually being discovered in permafrost astride a woolly mammoth. They talked for a few moments, and then Nina went over to Connolly and asked him for his GPS device.

'You won't need that,' the old woman said. 'I know the way.'

Nina put it in her pocket anyway. She came over to me, rubbed my arm for a moment, then took off her coat and gave it to me.

Then she and the old woman started to walk up the river.

'I'll come with you,' John said. He hauled himself up onto his feet.

'We're fine, thanks,' Nina said.

'Maybe. But there are bears around here. I saw one earlier. Saw something, anyway.'

Nina looked at me. I shrugged. I found myself a big, flat rock a couple of yards away from Paul, and watched them go.

Two things happened in the night that I didn't understand.

The first was minor. I realized Phil and Connolly were talking to each other, voices low, and turned to listen.

I heard Phil say: 'You've always known, haven't you?'

'I was with your uncle that night,' Connolly said. He looked like he was about to say more, but then glanced my way and saw I was listening.

He winked at Phil, shook his head. They didn't talk any more after that.

After an hour or so they went to sleep. I didn't know whether that was a good idea, but they were leaning close together, as warm as they were going to get. I couldn't keep them both awake through the night. Felt so tired I couldn't guarantee I could manage it myself. Both were breathing loudly. I'd just have to keep track of that.

My head felt like a stone balanced on another stone. I felt like I had been running for three months and reached the end of the track, to find there was no tape there, just more of the same. Paul seemed to be unconscious now, but he was shivering hard. It occurred to me that I still had a gun in my hand. It also struck me as unlikely that Nina knew exactly how many holes he had in him. One more would most likely go unnoticed. Maybe the key to finding that finish line lay in my right hand. Perhaps shooting Paul was the only thing that was going to end anything for me.

I got up quietly, moved a little closer.

One shot.

The others would wake up, but I could say he moved.

I knew why Nina had stopped me. I thought she didn't want me to commit murder in cold blood. I thought also that she believed that the relatives of the people we knew the Upright Man had killed — the families of the girls who had disappeared in LA two years before, and any others he might eventually be tied to — had a

473

right to more than hearing some backwoods execution had taken place, out of sight, miles away. I knew that this belief was a big part of what had kept her in her job down the years, kept her trying to put bad people away in face of the evidence that others just popped up to take their place. We had kept The Halls secret, admittedly, but then we'd had no captive in our hands.

In the end, it was neither of those things that made me lower the gun. If I'm honest, I don't know what it was.

I stood up, took off Nina's coat. I laid it over Paul's body, tucked it in around the sides. His face was pure white, lips turning blue.

I found I was crying.

I found myself sitting down close to his head. I found myself pulling it onto my lap, where it would be warmer, and putting my arm around the other side.

I don't know why. I don't understand it. I knew how many people he had killed. I knew he would have killed Nina, and John, and me. But it's what happened.

Connolly woke after a while, but said nothing. I slept then, slumped awkwardly back against the gully wall, a sleep ridged with shivered cramps. I slept until I was woken by a heavy sound above, and a different kind of wind.

I opened my eyes to see Connolly and Phil standing up, supporting each other; white-lit, looking up to heaven as the stretcher was slowly lowered from the helicopter.

I was the last to be winched up, the last to

leave that cold place. My head was splitting, and I was so tired I could barely see straight. As I was pulled spiralling up into the noise and wind and billowing snow, it was all I could do to hang on.

I looked down once, ill-advisedly, and for a strange moment, in a sweep of light, I thought I saw a small group of figures down there, in the gully, standing watching me as I was pulled into the sky. I blinked, tried to make out detail, but it was as if it wasn't there to be seen.

Then a swirl of snow blotted the ground out for good, and hands were pulling me into a flying metal machine.

★   ★   ★

Once we hit the ocean we turned right and headed north up the coast road. You're not allowed to own the coast in Oregon, and so it looks wild and old and like a place strange things might happen. Yes, a while back people used to find lumps of beeswax in the sand, and further inland, several tons in total; some looked like they had symbols on them, I gather, and a few could have been ancient Chinese. I knew this much of what Zandt had told me was true, at least, but I didn't believe much of the rest of it. Patterns are just patterns. They don't necessarily describe anything real.

We didn't know where John was now. That night he'd limped back most of the way with Patrice and Nina, not saying anything. I guess he'd been helping them out, watching their backs. A penance. Something. But when they were getting close to civilization, he disappeared. Nina called back into the forest for ten minutes, but he never called back.

That's the thing about that man, as Nina said later: he just *will not* return your calls.

I didn't tell her what the man with the round glasses had told me about John, and what he had done. He had probably been telling the truth, but I didn't think it changed things a great deal. I also thought it possible that Dravecky might get another visit from him soon. I thought John should never have killed Peter Ferillo. He had crossed a bad river in doing so, and would never come back to our side.

The remaining drive up the coast took about forty minutes. For most of this Nina sat with her feet up on the dash, looking out to sea. Just past Nehalem, her phone rang. She looked at the screen, took the call.

'Doug,' she said, when it was over.

'And?'

'He didn't die.'

'Who?'

'Either of them. The heroic Charles Monroe is progressing in leaps and bounds, by the sound of it. I seriously misjudged that man.'

'No you didn't,' I said. 'He's just not ready for a curtain call.'

It was good news, anyhow. Between Monroe and Doug things could be put back in place. Nina had been foot-stamping pissed to discover Doug had been dealing with John behind her back, but that was nothing in the face of the advantages it had for us. We had already been

476

erased from what happened in the forests north of Sheffer. That was organized with Connolly before anyone else got involved. As far as any law up there was concerned, we blew town right after the doctor had treated my shoulder. Only Connolly and his deputy went into the forest. One of the guys in the chopper was Connolly's nephew, so they'd play ball. Connolly had our guns, to fix ballistics on the dead shooters and Paul. A handgun found in the car the Straw Men's shooters had used would likely tie the glasses-wearing killer to the shooting of Charles Monroe. Patrice Anders would corroborate Connolly's story. She's a tough old bird. I got the sense she and the sheriff had some business in common that wasn't being spoken about, something they took responsibility for. I do also wonder how he knew exactly where to head for in the forest. Whatever. Let people have their secrets, I say.

'Where is Paul?'

'A secure hospital in LA. The physicians there are scratching their heads on how he pulled through.'

'God looks after children, drunks, and the criminally insane.'

Nina smiled. 'I think what's really healing Monroe is knowing he's got the guy he thinks of as the Delivery Boy, broken up to hell and stashed in a hospital with armed guards on all sides. Charles finally gets that case solved, and his problems are going to fade.'

'Which means you're okay, too, right?'

'We'll see.'

Her voice was quiet. I checked the road, then glanced at her. 'What?' I said. 'What's wrong?'

She shook her head. 'Nothing, really. Doug just told me something about a girl called Jean I interviewed last week. Two nights ago she went to a party up at some big house on Mulholland Drive. She's in hospital now with cigarette burns and a broken jaw.'

She stared through the windshield at the road ahead, looking sad and tired. 'Why are we like this?'

I didn't have an answer for her.

★ ★ ★

We got into Cannon Beach just before five. Drove slowly through the town, which isn't much more than a few rows of nice wooden beach houses, a main road with a market and a couple of arty mini-malls. It was dark and still raining and off-season quiet, but at the north end of town we found a place called Dunes that looked okay and was displaying a lit sign saying Vacancy. Judging by the empty lot, we had most of the place to ourselves.

We got a couple of rooms and turned in.

My room was on the third floor. It was big and had a wood fire on one wall. The whole of the far end was glass, pretty much, looking out to sea. I couldn't see anything but darkness, but I sat at the table there anyway, and drank a little beer. On impulse I got out my laptop — Bobby's laptop — and plugged the phone cable in the wall socket. I found myself kicking up a web browser, and typing in an address.

A few seconds later it was on my screen. Jessica's website. It was still there. The web guy evidently hadn't bothered to take the site down yet. Might never bother: a few megs up on a server somewhere, who's going to notice? It would join all the other stuff, the ephemeral memories, the words and pictures on the web. Was it immortality? No. Like the man said: immortality is about not dying. It was something, however, both better and worse than nothing.

There was a welcome page with Jessica's bright, smiling face. A link to the webcam page itself, which was dead. Another page where she had written about her hobbies — song writing, which I guess made sense of the guitar — and a few pages of specimen stills. Only one of these was semi-nude, and I flicked past it. It was the others that spoke. Pictures of a young woman, going about her life, watching her television and reading her magazines. The way she really had been, still there: something more than the cold body in the tray of a cabinet in an LA morgue. I still found it hard to rid my head of the idea that I'd seen her in the forest, but I knew it was just a trick of the mind.

I did a little hacking and got past the browser, into the folder on the server itself. Copied the contents down onto my own computer. To keep them safe, I guess, in case the guy did ever get around to cleaning out. When I'd finished I noticed there was a text file amongst them. I opened it up. It was short, a few brief diary entries she'd evidently decided not to link to from the site. The Feds would have had it all along, and there was certainly nothing there that would have helped. The last entry was dated three days before she died. It was about some guy called Don, who she thought maybe liked her a little, wondering whether she should call him sometime.

I closed Bobby's laptop and thought of him for a while, in his silent place deep inside my head. It's where they all go to: the cemeteries in our heads. Back there, behind your eyes, where you can't see them whichever way you turn. But the things they did, the people they were, it's all still true. It doesn't have to be lonely in there. You can visit, from time to time.

★   ★   ★

The next morning I got up late. It had stopped raining but the wind was back in force. Out of my window I could now see a long stretch of beach — grey sand, grey water, grey sky — between craggy cliffs.

A while later Nina knocked on my door. 'You up for a walk?'

'What — because it's such a lovely day?'

We wandered the empty streets, grabbed a coffee or two, sniggered at bad art. Spent a few hours down on the sands, alone in all the world, sometimes together, sometimes apart. We watched big rough waves crash down and around the rocks, cheered brave birds as they wheeled hectically in the stormy chaos above. In the mid-afternoon the wind got so fierce and strong that you could stand with your arms out-stretched and lean into it, trusting it to hold you up. So we did, as sand whirled around us and the world spun.

When it began to rain again we found a place half sheltered at the foot of high rocks and sat, a little distance apart, and watched the sea. I realized then why we respond to the sound of the waves, and the falling of rain, and wind in the trees. Because they are meaningless. They are nothing to do with us. They are outside our control. They remind us of a time, very early in our lives, when we did not understand the noises around us but simply accepted them in our ears; and so they provide blessed relief from our continual needy attempts to change our world in magic deed or endless thought. Meaningless sound, which we love against the anxiety of action, of pattern-making, of seeking to compre-hend and change. As soon as we picked up something and used it for a purpose, we were both made and damned. Tool-making gave us the world, and lost us our minds.

For an hour we did nothing, two people on the edge of the world, with our backs to it all. When it got dark we went back to the hotel. I took a shower, changed my clothes, then went around the wooden walkway to knock on Nina's door.

'Hey,' she said.

'You want to go get a drink?'

She raised an eyebrow. 'Is this like, a date, or something?'

'No,' I said. 'It is not.'

A couple of streets away we found a place called Red's Tavern where you could sit and drink strong beers they made upstairs. After a while the bar began to fill with locals, and eventually a pick-up band coalesced down the far end. A couple of guitars, a lap steel, a violin and washboard; people sat and played for a while, wandering off and back as the whim took them. The lamps were low and warm and I realized, for the first time, that the woman opposite me had auburn lights in her hair. We listened to the music the band made, and we clapped and sang along when everybody else did, and we watched the barmaids dance and laugh behind the counter as they filled pitchers with beer as clean as stream water, and I finally got myself a bowl of chilli and it was not bad at all.

The band was still playing, but more quietly, when we left them to it. We walked back to the hotel, bought a bottle of wine from the market on the way. We lit the fire in my room and split the window open a little, so we could hear the sound of the waves and the crackling of the wood at the same time. We sat on the floor with our backs to the end of the bed, and we talked for a long time, talked until it was late and yet didn't feel late at all.

We kept putting wood on the fire because we didn't want it to burn down, and in the end the room was dark and warm enough and didn't need any more words.

She made the first move.

She's like that.

We do hope that you have enjoyed reading this large print book.

Did you know that all of our titles are available for purchase?

We publish a wide range of high quality large print books including:
Romances, Mysteries, Classics
General Fiction
Non Fiction and Westerns

Special interest titles available in large print are:
The Little Oxford Dictionary
Music Book
Song Book
Hymn Book
Service Book

Also available from us courtesy of Oxford University Press:
Young Readers' Dictionary
(large print edition)
Young Readers' Thesaurus
(large print edition)

For further information or a free brochure, please contact us at:
Ulverscroft Large Print Books Ltd.,
The Green, Bradgate Road, Anstey,
Leicester, LE7 7FU, England.
Tel: (00 44) 0116 236 4325
Fax: (00 44) 0116 234 0205

Other titles published by
The House of Ulverscroft:

THE STRAW MEN

Michael Marshall

Sarah tries to struggle, but the man holds her. The scream never makes it out of her throat . . . Sarah is the fifth girl to be abducted by this maniac. Her long hair will be hacked off and she will be tortured. She has about a week to live . . . Former LA homicide detective John Zandt has an inside track on the perpetrator — his own daughter was one of his victims. But the key to Sarah's whereabouts lies with Ward Hopkins, a man with a past so secret not even he knows about it. As he investigates his past, Ward finds himself drawn into the sinister world of the Straw Men — and into the desperate race to find Sarah, before her time runs out . . .

APHRODITE'S SMILE

Stuart Harrison

When Robert French travels to the tranquil Greek island of Ithaca after his archaeologist father goes missing, he meets Alex, a young woman in search of her roots and the truth about her grandmother's exile from the island sixty years earlier. Gradually, it seems possible that there is a link between an ancient treasure that Robert's father spent many years searching for and the tragic events surrounding Alex's grandmother during the Second World War. Then, suddenly, Alex vanishes and Robert is embroiled in a desperate search — for the woman and for the solution that had evaded his father. To find the truth he must come to understand his own past . . .

A PLACE OF SAFETY

Natasha Cooper

Barrister Trish Maguire needs all the time she can find to help her young half-brother adjust to life after the violent death of his mother. Sir Henry Buxford, an influential acquaintance, has other ideas. He asks Trish to investigate one of his private charities, a magnificent art collection that has been lost for most of the twentieth century. Trish's research takes her not only into the heart of an engrossing love story, but also the agonizing reality of life in the trenches of the First World War. She soon discovers a web of deceit that has spanned the decades since, catching all kinds of people in its filaments.

Physics and Chemistry in Space
Volume 1

Edited by
J. G. Roederer, Denver and J. Zähringer, Heidelberg

J. A. Jacobs

Geomagnetic Micropulsations

With 81 figures

Springer-Verlag New York Heidelberg Berlin 1970

J. A. Jacobs

Killam Memorial Professor of Science
The University of Alberta, Edmonton, Canada

Preface

The subject of geomagnetic micropulsations has developed extremely rapidly and it is difficult to know when is an appropriate time to pause and assess the sum total of our knowledge—both observational and theoretical. There has in recent years been a tremendous increase in both the quantity and quality of data and also many theoretical advances in our understanding of the phenomenon. Undoubtedly there will be further progress in both areas but it seems worthwhile now to review both our knowledge and our ignorance. This book was essentially completed by the end of April 1969 and tries to give a summary of the subject up to that time.

The Earth is enclosed in the magnetosphere, a hollow carved out of the solar wind by the Earth's magnetic field. Above the ionosphere there is a very tenuous thermal plasma of partially ionized hydrogen in diffusive equilibrium with magnetic and gravitational forces, and energetic protons and electrons that constitute the trapped Van Allen radiation belts. Throughout this anisotropic and inhomogeneous plasma, natural and man-made electromagnetic energy propagates in a wide variety of modes and frequency bands. This book is concerned with that class of natural signals called geomagnetic micropulsations—short period (usually of the order of seconds or minutes) fluctuations of the Earth's magnetic field. They are transitory variations of small amplitude (usually less than one part in 10^4 of the Earth's main magnetic field) and leave no lasting effects on the Earth's field. One of the most exciting aspects of the subject is the very real possibility of using them as natural probes for remote sensing of the magnetosphere.

In the development and application of plasma physics to micropulsations only a cold, two-component plasma will be considered. Undoubtedly this is inadequate to properly describe conditions in the magnetosphere. However in our present uncertain state of knowledge, I do not believe that a more sophisticated detailed treatment of plasma physics is warranted in a book on micropulsations. I believe that the time will soon come however when homogeneous models in cosmic electrodynamics will be inadequate to describe the data, and that the essential properties of cosmic plasma will only be understood by models which take into account strong, inhomogeneous small-scale structures.

In this book I have not tried to anticipate this trend and have kept the mathematics and physical models as simple as possible.

Cgs—Gaussian units are used throughout. Although there is much in favor of using MKS units, I feel that much would be lost if the units were not Gauss units.

February 1970   J. A. Jacobs

Contents

1 The Earth's Magnetic Field

1.1 Introduction

Geomagnetic micropulsations are short period (usually of the order of seconds or minutes) fluctuations of the Earth's magnetic field. They are transitory variations of small amplitude (usually less than one part in 10^4 of the Earth's main field) and leave no permanent effect on the field. Like longer period disturbances such as magnetic storms they are of solar origin, in contrast to the Earth's main field and secular variation which are of internal origin.

At its strongest near the poles the Earth's magnetic field is several hundred times weaker than that between the poles of a toy horseshoe magnet — being less than one gauss (Γ). Thus in geomagnetism we are measuring extremely small magnetic fields and a more convenient unit is the gamma (γ), defined as $10^{-5}\ \Gamma$.* In 1 600 William Gilbert published the results of his investigations on the variation in direction of the magnetic force over the surface of a piece of the naturally magnetized mineral lodestone which he had cut in the shape of a sphere. He found that the variation of the inclination was in agreement with what was then known about the Earth's magnetic field, and he came to the conclusion that the Earth behaved substantially as a uniformly magnetized sphere, its magnetic field being due to causes within the Earth and not from any external agency as was supposed at that time. In 1839 Gauss showed by a spherical harmonic analysis that the field of a uniformly magnetized sphere, which is the same as that of a geocentric dipole, is an excellent first approximation to the Earth's magnetic field. The geomagnetic poles, i. e. the points where the axis of the geocentric dipole which best approximates the Earth's field meets the surface of the Earth, are situated approximately at 78.8° N, 70.0° W, 78.8° S, 110° E. The geomagnetic axis is thus inclined at about 11° to the Earth's geographical axis.

---

* Strictly speaking the unit of magnetic field is the oersted, the gauss being reserved for magnetic induction, and some geophysicists define the gamma in terms of the oersted. However the distinction is somewhat pedantic in geophysical applications since the permeability of air is virtually one in cgs units. In accord with most of the geophysical literature the term gauss has been retained in both contexts.

1.2 Transient Magnetic Variations

The range of the spectrum of variations in the Earth's magnetic field is enormous extending from a fraction of a second to more than 30 million years (see Table 1.1). The causes of the longer period changes such as the secular variation are internal: fluctuations with periods less than a few days are of external origin.

Table 1.1. *Spectrum of geomagnetic phenomena*

Period Seconds	Years	Origin	Comments
10^{17}	$3 \cdot 10^9$	?	?
10^{16}			
10^{15}	$3 \cdot 10^7$	Internal and Dipolar	Dipole Reversals
10^{14}			
10^{13}			
10^{12}			
10^{11}			
10^{10}	300	Internal, Non-dipolar	Secular variation
10^{9}	30		
10^{8}			
10^{7}			
10^{6}	$3 \cdot 10^{-2}$	External	Magnetic Storms
10^{5}	$3 \cdot 10^{-3}$	External	Diurnal Variation
10^{4}			
10^{3}			
10^{2}			
10^{1}		External	Micropulsations
10^{0}			
10^{-1}		External	Sub-acoustic

The records from any magnetic observatory show that on some days all three components exhibit smooth and regular variations, while on other days they are disturbed and show irregular fluctuations. At each observatory a figure K between 0 and 9 is assigned to describe the magnetic conditions for each period of three Greenwich hours 0–3, 3–6, etc. K indices are a measure, for an interval of 3 hr, of the intensity of magnetic disturbance as shown on the magnetograms of an observatory. Thus they incorporate also any local effects such as the systematic diurnal variations in geomagnetic activity. There is, therefore, a need for an abstract of the individual K indices to express world-wide features of geomagnetic disturbances over a 3-hr period. An average of all individual K indices would not be satisfactory, owing to the inadequate geographical distribution of magnetic observatories. Thus a new index

K_p has been designed to measure "planetary" variations in magnetic activity. It is based on "standardized" indices which have been freed as far as possible from local features. K_p indices are given to thirds as follows: The intensity interval 1.5 to 2.5 for example, is divided equally into three thirds designated as $2-$, $2o$, and $2+$. This provides 28 grades of K_p from $0o, 0+, 1-, 1o, 1+, ..., 8+, 9-, 9o$.

The definition of K_p was chosen so that the whole range of geomagnetic activity from the quietest conditions to the most intense storm could be expressed by a single digit and an affix. This was achieved by a quasi-logarithmic relation between the amplitudes of disturbance in the 3 hr interval and K_p. In order to obtain a linear scale, K_p may be converted into a 3 hr equivalent planetary amplitude, a_p, by means of Table 1.2. At a standard station in about $50°$ geomagnetic latitude, a_p may be thought of as the range of the most disturbed of the three field components expressed in the unit 2γ, e.g. the range in a 3 hr interval with $K = 4+$ is 2×32, i.e. 64γ. The average of the eight a_p values for a day is called A_p.

In general day to day changes in the intensity of any disturbance follow a similar pattern over a wide area; similarly, quiet conditions are usually widespread. Most days show some magnetic disturbance, but except in periods of very violent activity, it is found that the disturbance D is superposed on a regular daily variation—called the solar daily variation S. S is seen in its pure form on quiet days when it is denoted by S_q. Each magnetic element is affected in a characteristic way by each of the variations S and D. For a detailed study of transient magnetic phenomena results must be obtained from a number of observatories widely distributed geographically. The type and range of variation also vary throughout the year, showing a seasonal change and the range and incidence of D also vary from year to year.

Table 1.2. *Relation between K_p and a_p magnetic indices*

K_p	$0o$	$0+$	$1-$	$1o$	$1+$	$2-$	$2o$	$2+$	$3-$	$3o$	$3+$	$4-$	$4o$	$4+$
a_p	0	2	3	4	5	6	7	9	12	15	18	22	27	32

K_p	$5-$	$5o$	$5+$	$6-$	$6o$	$6+$	$7-$	$7o$	$7+$	$8-$	$8o$	$8+$	$9-$	$9o$
a_p	39	48	56	67	80	94	111	132	154	179	207	236	300	400

It is found that the intensity of magnetic disturbances increases from low to high latitudes up to about magnetic latitude $65°$, the latitude of the auroral zones. Within these zones the intensity, although con-

1*

siderable, decreases slightly towards the magnetic poles. Magnetograms
are seldom completely undisturbed in high latitudes. Intense magnetic
storms usually commence suddenly at almost the same instant (to
within $\frac{1}{2}$ min) all over the Earth although the records of individual
storms differ greatly among themselves. In middle and lower latitudes,
the horizontal intensity H rises to a maximum within an hour or two
of the commencement and remains above its initial value for a period
of 2–6 hours. This is called the initial phase. H then decreases, attaining
after several hours a minimum which is much more below the initial

Fig. 1.1.   Example of a magnetic storm of moderate intensity at different latitudes.
(After M. Sugiura and J. P. Heppner)

undisturbed value than the maximum was above it. This is called the main phase, and is followed by a gradual recovery which may last for several days. The main phase generally lasts from 12 to 14 hours and tends to be noisy. Often large positive and negative excursions with amplitudes of the order of hundreds of gammas and periods of about $\frac{1}{2}$ hour occur. The greater the storm, the more rapid is the development of these phases. Fig. 1.1 shows the striking difference in the storm time variations in low latitudes (Honolulu) and those in the auroral zone (College, Alaska). On crossing the auroral zone towards the magnetic pole the characteristics of storm time variations undergo a further transition to yet another type peculiar to the polar cap (see Godhavn, Fig. 1.1).

In addition to large scale magnetic storms there are disturbances of much shorter duration such as polar magnetic substorms and bays. Abrupt impulsive changes (sudden impulses) may also occur and are often observed simultaneously all over the world and have also been detected in the magnetosphere. Variations with periods roughly from 0.1 sec to 10 min are grouped together and called geomagnetic micropulsations—their morphology is considered in detail in the next chapter.

1.3 The Magnetosphere

From direct observation of interplanetary space we now know that there exists a continuous flow of ionized gas or plasma out from the sun. This gas, which flows radially outwards, has been called the solar wind. In a series of papers beginning in 1957 on the investigation of the expansion of the solar corona into interplanetary space, E. N. Parker developed a magneto-hydrodynamic theory of the solar wind (see Parker, 1963). An essentially static situation had been considered for many years to represent the steady state interplanetary medium into which transient tongues of plasma were ejected following solar activity thereby leading to magnetic storms. Parker showed that the only reasonable model of the interplanetary medium utilizing all available information on coronal temperatures and densities was of necessity hydrodynamic and, most important, supersonic. The theory predicted that velocities of 400–1000 km/sec would be observed at the orbit of the Earth. Since then the investigation of interplanetary space by artificial satellites and space probes has confirmed the model of the solar wind as developed by Parker. Satellites have shown that the interplanetary medium in the vicinity of the Earth is not just empty space but instead is filled with a highly tenuous plasma which is being continuously blown radially out from the sun at speeds averaging 300–500 km/sec. The wind is very "gusty", however, showing fluctuations in energy, energy spread, and density in times of the order of hours. The solar plasma consists primarily of ionized hydrogen (protons and electrons) and is electrically neutral. The density is of the order of 10 ions/cm^3. Imbedded in the solar wind is an interplanetary magnetic field whose strength is of the order of 5γ during quiet solar periods but increases to many times this value during periods of high solar activity. Its energy density is much smaller (aproximately 1 per cent of that of the solar wind), and it is thus carried along by the solar wind.

Plasmas and magnetic fields tend to confine one another. If a streaming plasma encounters a magnetic object such as a magnetized sphere, the plasma will confine the magnetic field to a limited region around the object. The object in turn will tend to exclude the plasma thus creating a hole or cavity. The size of the cavity is determined by the energy density of the streaming plasma and the degree of magnetization of the object. In addition, if the velocity of the plasma is great enough to be highly supersonic, i.e. if the velocity is much greater than the Alfvén velocity in that medium, a detached shock wave may be produced in a region ahead of the cavity boundary. This is analogous to the formation of the detached shock front of an aerodynamic object travelling at hypersonic speed (above about Mach 5). The analogy however is by no means perfect. In aerodynamics the shock wave results from collisions of particles and is about one mean free path thick. In the solar wind a Coulomb collision mean free path (approximately 10^{14} cm) is so large that collisions play no part in the observed shock wave. This collisionless shock is produced by the action of the magnetic field and the characteristic dimension is the cyclotron radius, not the mean free path. A 1-kev proton in the interplanetary magnetic field of 5γ at IAU has a cyclotron radius of about 1000 km.

S. Chapman and V. C. A. Ferraro had predicted in 1931 the confinement of the Earth's magnetic field inside an elongated cavity during magnetic storms. The continual presence of such a cavity has been experimentally verified by many satellite observations. The region inside the cavity is called the *magnetosphere* and the boundary the *magnetopause*. The region between the magnetopause and the shock wave is referred to as the *magnetosheath* or *transition region*. Outside this transition region, i.e. beyond the shock wave, conditions are characteristic of the interplanetary medium and the presence of the magnetized Earth has little or no effect.

The dimensions of the cavity depend on the intensity of the solar wind although large changes in the solar wind intensity produce comparatively small changes in the size of the cavity. The distance from the centre of the Earth to the magnetopause in the solar direction is around 10

Earth radii (R_e) although distances less than 8 R_e and greater than 13 R_e have occasionally been observed. The shock wave is located several R_e beyond this distance. At 90° to the solar direction both the magnetopause and shock wave are observed to flare out to distances about 30–50 per cent greater than in the sub-solar direction. In the anti-solar direction the cavity extends out to very large distances, very likely as far as the moon ($\simeq 60\ R_e$) or farther. No definite closure of the magneto-spheric tail has yet been observed by satellites.

Fig. 1.2 shows magnetic field data observed by Explorer 12. The magnitude of the field is plotted as a function of radial distance together with the theoretical dipole field. The direction of the field as measured

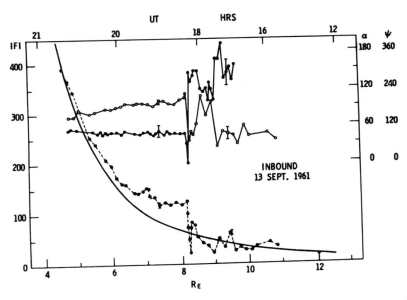

Fig. 1.2. Magnetic field data from Explorer 12 showing an abrupt change in the field at 8.2 R_e. This change, the magnetopause, is the outer limit of the geo-magnetic field. (After L. J. Cahill and P. G. Amazeen)

by the spacecraft coordinates α and ψ (angles relating the field direction to the spin axis of the satellite) is also plotted. Out to 8 R_e the direction and magnitude of the field show little fluctuations but in the region of 6–8 R_e the magnitude is almost twice the dipole field. At 8.2 R_e the field magnitude suddenly decreases and the direction of the field simul-taneously changes. Beyond this point the field is much more disordered.

These results are typical of all the early Explorer 12 passes, both inbound and outbound. The closest approach to the boundary was $8.2\,R_e$ (on the pass shown in Fig. 1.2). More typically it was about $10\,R_e$ near the noon meridian, although there was considerable movement of the magnetopause from day to day. The thickness of the magnetopause appears to be quite small, of the order of 100 km or less. Fig. 1.3 shows

Fig. 1.3. The location of the magnetopause and bow shock as determined by the magnetometer on Imp I. Shown for comparison are the theoretically expected locations. (After N. F. Ness)

the location of the magnetopause and bow shock as determined by the magnetometer on board the Imp 1 satellite (Explorer 18), which was launched in November, 1963. The figure also shows, for comparison, theoretical estimates of the boundary positions. Proceeding outwards on orbit 11 (see Fig. 1.4) at $13.6\,R_e$ the magnetopause was encountered as indicated by the sharp change in magnitude and direction of the field. Then at $20\,R_e$ a second change occurred, the field suddenly becoming steady at about 5γ in a relatively constant direction. Upstream of the shock the flow is quiet and steady but behind the shock it is disturbed and turbulent.

From the Imp 1 data it appears that in the region beyond 8 or $10\,R_e$ near the midnight meridian the field is very nearly in the solar or anti-

Fig. 1.4.   Magnetic field data from Orbit 11 of Explorer 18 (Imp *I*). The magneto-pause is at 13.6 R_e. The second transition at 20 R_e to an ordered field outside is the location of the bow shock wave. (After N. F. Ness, C. S. Scearce and J. B. Seek)

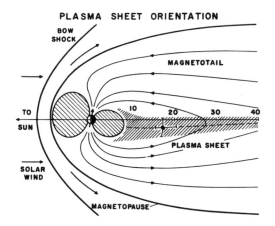

Fig. 1.5.   Approximate configuration of the magnetosphere in the solar magneto-spheric noon-midnight meridional plane for a 12° tilt of the magnetic dipole axis. The point shows the Vela determination of the plasma sheet center at 17 R_e. The direction of the solar wind is assumed to be along the sun-earth line. (After S. J. Bame et al.)

solar direction. The component of the field perpendicular to the sun–earth line is usually an order of magnitude or so less than the parallel component. These early results have been confirmed by more recent satellite data — e.g. from Explorer 33. Another unusual feature from the Imp data is the existence of a *neutral sheet* in the tail (see Fig. 1.5) separating those regions where the field is pointing away from the sun from those where the field points back towards the sun. This transition is rather sudden. The sheet appears to be quite thin (about 600 km or less). The intensity of the magnetic field sharply decreases inside the sheet to a small fraction of its value in the adjacent regions of the magnetotail. The abrupt change of the vector of magnetic field indicates the existence of a strong electric current flowing in the sheet perpendicular to the magnetic lines of force.

Another distinctive feature of the magnetosphere is the *plasmapause*, which is a three dimensional field aligned boundary that divides the closed field line portion of the Earth's magnetosphere into two physically distinct regions. The boundary is asymmetric — for moderately disturbed days ($K_p = 2$–4) there is a broad minimum in geocentric radius near

Fig. 1.6.   Equatorial radius of the plasmapause vs local time. (After D. L. Carpenter)

dawn, and near the dusk meridian there is a bulge with equatorial radius $1-2\ R_e$ larger than that of the dawn minimum (see the dark curve of Fig. 1.6 which was obtained by D. L. Carpenter (1966) from whistler observations at Eights, Antarctica). The mean equatorial radius of the plasmapause is typically about $4\ R_e$, but may vary from about $7\ R_e$ during extremely quiet periods to $2-3\ R_e$ during great storms. Carpenter found two basic types of drift motions of the plasma inside the boundary. The first is a slow "breathing" motion during which the plasmapause may be thought of as fixed in space with the plasma inside approximately co-rotating with the Earth and also drifting inward and outward in conformity with the asymmetries of the boundary. The other type of motion is of short duration $(1 \sim 2\ \mathrm{hr})$ and involves changes in the boundary itself. At such a time the plasmapause and the dense plasma within it move radially at speeds of the order of $0.4\ R_e/\mathrm{hr}$—such motions usually take place during polar substorms and occur on the night side of the Earth near the longitude where the substorm is observed.

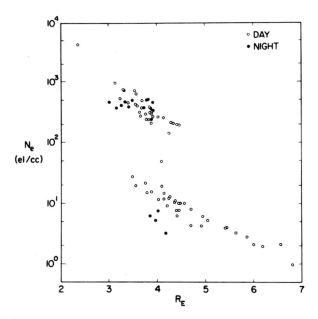

Fig. 1.7.   Scatter plot of day and nighttime data on equatorial density vs. geocentric distance in Earth radii. (After J. J. Angerami and D. L. Carpenter)

At the plasmapause there is an abrupt change in plasma density, equatorial values of the electron density changing by a factor of 10–100 (from $\simeq 100/\mathrm{cm}^3$ to $1/\mathrm{cm}^3$) within a distance of less than $0.15\ R_e$. Satellite

VLF experiments suggest that the change may be far more abrupt, possibly of the order of a few km. In the tenuous outer region the density decreases approximately as R^{-4}. In the plasmasphere the density distribution along the field lines is in approximate agreement with a diffusive equilibrium model which gives a much less rapid decrease than the R^{-4} model (J. J. Angerami and D. L. Carpenter, 1966). A summary of the variation in electron density across the "knee" based on whistler data is shown in Fig. 1.7.

1.4 Conjugacy

Two points on the Earth's surface linked by a geomagnetic field line are called conjugate points. Information about certain magnetospheric processes can propagate along field lines and may be detected on the ground at, or near, the points at which the field line intersects the lower ionosphere or the Earth's surface. This information may be carried by charged particles such as energetic electrons or protons, low energy photoelectrons or plasma, or by waves, such as very low frequency electromagnetic waves ducted through the magnetospheric plasma along field lines or magnetohydrodynamic undulations of the field lines themselves. Sets of conjugate points have been computed by various authors using field expansions for sources located inside the Earth.

Conjugacy at high latitudes is determined not only by the Earth's internal magnetic field, but also by external sources such as ring currents, magnetospheric boundary currents, and currents in the neutral sheet of the Earth's magnetic tail. These external sources significantly modify the conjugacy of points above approximately 60° magnetic latitude, i.e., where $L > 4$—the effect increasing very sharply with increasing latitude*. Conjugate point calculations using the internal field alone become meaningless above about 65° magnetic latitude. Models of the magnetosphere which take these external sources into account have usually assumed north-south symmetry, with the incident solar wind perpendicular to the magnetic dipole axis. Under this assumption, none of the existing models of external sources (boundary currents, ring currents, or tail currents) can alter the conjugacy at any latitude. To determine magnetospheric effects and to predict seasonal or diurnal changes in conjugacy, this north-south symmetry must be removed.

---

* For a pure dipole field the parameter L is the maximum radial distance of a line of force from the dipole, and is measured in Earth radii R_e. For the physical significance of L see C. E. McIlwain (1961); for further information on magnetic coordinates see E. C. Stone (1963), C. E. McIlwain (1966).

G. D. Mead (1967) has carried out field line calculations in an asymmetric magnetosphere distorted by the solar wind, making reasonable assumptions as to the expected orientation of external current sources. He found that in the northern winter the south conjugate point moves equatorwards (at noon and midnight) and the north conjugate point moves polewards. The magnitude of the effect is largest at noon (± 150 km at $L=7$, ± 25 km at $L=4$) and smallest at midnight (± 50 km at $L=7$, ± 10 km at $L=4$). At dawn and dusk there are also changes in longitude.

There are three classes of conjugate-point phenomena, depending on whether the source is located on or around the equator, at or near one of the end points of the field line, or at the ends of open field lines which come close together in the neutral sheet. J. G. Roederer (1967) has divided each of these classes into three types—point conjugacy when the source is well localized in space, shell conjugacy when the source is centered around the equatorial region of a magnetic shell and area or gross conjugacy when the source occupies an extended but finite region in the magnetosphere.

Although conjugate points have in common the field line which links them, they differ in many physical aspects. Thus, in general, the B-value at both points will be different, leading, for instance, to differences in mirror point altitudes of particles. Again the local time and the season will in general be different at the two points. Finally in many cases of conjugate point phenomena the information does not travel exactly along a field line—charged particles may drift appreciably and ray paths of unducted waves may depart considerably from a field line.

References

No attempt is made to give comprehensive references to the very wide field covered in this chapter. In recent years there have been many excellent books written on all branches of Upper Atmospheric Physics—some of a review nature and some on specialized topics. It is impossible to give a complete list, but some are listed below:

Space Research. Proceedings of International Space Science Symposium. North Holland Publishing Co., published yearly since 1960.

Satellite Environment Handbook (Ed. F.S. Johnson), Stanford University Press 1961.

Geophysics and the Earth's Environment, Gordon and Breach 1963.

Natural Electromagnetic Phenomena below 30 kc/s (Ed. D. F. Bleil), Plenum Press 1964.

Physics of the Earth's upper atmosphere (Ed. C. O. Hines, I. Paghis, T. R. Hartz, and J. A. Feyer), Prentice Hall 1965.

Introduction to Space Science (Ed. W. H. Hess), Gordon and Breach 1965.

Solar-Terrestrial Physics (Ed. J. W. King and W. S. Newman), Academic Press 1967.

Physics of Geomagnetic Phenomena (Ed. S. Matsushita and W. H. Campbell), International Geophysics Series Vol. 11, Academic Press 1967.

Alfvén, H., Fälthammar, C. G.: Cosmical electrodynamics. Oxford: University Press 1963.

Chamberlain, J. W.: Physics of the aurora and airglow. International Geophysics Series Vol. 2, Academic Press 1961.

Davies, K.: Ionospheric radio propagation. National Bureau of Standards, Monograph **80**, 1965. U.S. Department of Commerce.

Dungey, J. H.: Cosmic electrodynamics. Cambridge: University Press 1958.

Ratcliffe, J. A.: Physics of the upper atmosphere. Academic Press 1960.

Special references in Chapter 1

Angerami, J. J., Carpenter, D. L.: Whistler studies of the plasmapause in the magnetosphere 2. *Electron density and total tube electron content near the knee in magnetospheric ionization.* J. Geophys. Res. **71**, 711—725 (1966).

Carpenter, D. L.: Whistler studies of the plasmapause in the magnetosphere 1. *Temporal variations in the position of the knee and some evidence on plasma motions near the knee.* J. Geophys. Res. **71**, 693—709 (1966).

McIlwain, C. E.: Coordinates for mapping the distribution of magnetically trapped particles. J. Geophys. Res. **66**, 3681—3691 (1961).

— Radiation trapped in the Earth's magnetic field. Reidel Publ. Co. 1966 (Magnetic coordinates pp. 45—61).

Mead, G. D.: Calculations of high latitude conjugate points in a model magnetosphere. *Conjugate Point Symposium.* Colorado: Boulder 1967.

Parker, E. N.: Interplanetary dynamical processes. *Interscience Monographs in Physics and Astronomy.* Vol. VIII, Interscience Publ. 1963.

Roederer, J. G.: Conjugate point phenomena. *IQSY-COSPAR Symposium.* London 1967.

Stone, E. C.: The physical significance and application of L, B_0 and R_0 to geomagnetically trapped particles. J. Geophys. Res. **68**, 4157—4166 (1963).

2 The Morphology of Geomagnetic Micropulsations

2.1 Introduction

Geomagnetic micropulsations are fluctuations of the Earth's magnetic field whose amplitudes range from a fraction of a gamma to, on rare occasions, as much as a few tens of gammas. Periods range from about 0.1 sec to 10 min. Most work has been done in the lower frequency end of this range, very little being known at the higher frequencies from 3 to 10 Hz. In recent years, mainly as a result of the greatly increased number of continuous observations that are being made, certain definite types of micropulsations have been recognized and some systematic classification has been attempted. The great increase in the amount of data obtained during and since the International Geophysical Year (IGY) has only served to show that in some cases the earlier classification was too simple and that in reality there exist many more different types or variations of the earlier, broader classification. This classification divided micropulsations into three categories, pc's, pt's and pg's, which will be defined later.

The International Association of Geomagnetism and Aeronomy (IAGA), one of the associations of the International Union of Geodesy and Geophysics (IUGG) established a Committee on Rapid Magnetic Variations and Earth Currents. This committee met at Copenhagen in April 1957, and tabled a number of resolutions which were reported at the eleventh General Assembly of the IUGG which was held in Toronto later that year (September 3rd–14th). The resolutions included a description of the different types of geomagnetic micropulsations and general comments on the manner in which they should be reported by all observatories. Beginning January 1958, quarterly reports containing observational data on rapid variations have been published by IAGA. Also, following checking by all observatories, rapid variation data are published annually in the IAGA Bulletin No. 12 Series. In 1958 the IAGA Committee on Rapid Magnetic Variations and Earth Currents published a provisional atlas with examples of the different types of phenomena.

Pulsations of the Earth's electromagnetic field may be observed in a number of ways:

(i) by direct recording of the magnetic elements with high-sensitivity variometers and rapid run recorders;

(ii) by recording the time derivative of the magnetic elements (induction magnetograph);

(iii) by recording Earth currents.

The frequency response in each case will be different, and care must be taken in comparing results obtained by different means. No description will be given here of the experimental methods of measuring rapid changes in the electromagnetic field—excellent review articles have been given in the Annals of the IGY (1957) and by K. Whitham (1960), J. E. Lokken (1964), H. J. Duffus (1966), L. R. Alldredge (1967), and J. P. Heppner (1967).

It is impossible to review all the work that has been done in the field of geomagnetic micropulsations. A detailed bibliography of the early work up to 1956 has been given by Y. Kato and T. Watanabe (1957). Since then a number of important review articles have appeared (J. A. Jacobs and K. O. Westphal, 1964; V. A. Troitskaya, 1964, 1967; T. Saito, 1964a; W. H. Campbell, 1967 and Y. Kato, 1967).

2.2 Classification of Micropulsations

An important problem in the investigation of micropulsations is the description and classification of the observed types of oscillations and of the conditions under which they are generated. Three essentially independent principles of classification have been suggested:

(1) Classification based on morphological properties (periods, amplitudes, time of occurrence, etc.);

(2) Correlative classification (based on connection with other types of phenomena—magnetic storms, aurora, VLF emissions, etc.);

(3) Genetical classification (based on the mechanism of generation).

Because the origin of micropulsations is not known with any certainty, the genetical classification, which in other circumstances would be the best, cannot serve as a basis for a general classification. The correlative principle, unfortunately, also cannot be used, because a clearly expressed correlation is not observed for all types of pulsations. This is the reason why a classification based on a morphological description has been adopted.

The old classification divided micropulsations into three categories defined as follows:

(i) pc (continuous pulsations). A series of pulsations lasting for many hours with periods usually in the range from 10 to 60 sec and amplitudes of the order of $\frac{1}{10}\gamma$. The maximum occurrence frequency is during the morning hours.

(ii) pt (pulsations trains). These appear as several series of oscillations, each series usually lasting from 10 to 20 min, the whole phenomenon lasting for not more than about 1 hr. They are well damped with longer periods than pc's (40 sec to a few min.) and usually of greater amplitude (of the order of 0.5 γ). The maximum occurrence frequency is before midnight. pt's often precede or accompany a bay* disturbance.

(iii) pg (giant pulsations). A series of pulsations of large amplitude (up to a few tens of gammas) appearing only in or near the auroral zones. The period is longer than that of pc's (up to several min), and the duration is of the order of an hour or more.

At the 13th General Assembly of the IUGG held in Berkeley, California, August 1963, the question of the notation and classification of geomagnetic micropulsations was considered in some detail by IAGA. A small sub-committee consisting of J. A. Jacobs, Y. Kato, S. Matsushita and V. A. Troitskaya was set up to submit recommendations (1964) which are presented below.

From experimental knowledge, particularly that obtained since the IGY, it has been recognized that micropulsations may be divided into two main classes—those of a regular and mainly continuous character and those with an irregular pattern. The first class covers the whole range of micropulsations with periods from about 0.2 to 600 sec. They may be divided into sub-groups depending on their period but it is extremely difficult to decide where the boundaries should be drawn. A purely mathematical division may be made, based perhaps on a logarithmic scale, or a division may be based on their physical and morphological properties. The second approach was adopted and Table 2.1 gives the proposed classification and notation.

Table 2.1.

Notation	Period Range (sec.)
Pc 1	0.2— 5
Pc 2	5 — 10
Pc 3	10 — 45
Pc 4	45 —150
Pc 5	150 —600

* The magnetic elements sometimes undergo quite large deviations even on magnetically quiet days. In such cases they generally show a fairly rapid increase (or decrease) and, after attaining their maximum departure, regain their normal values, the whole phenomenon, called a bay, lasting an hour or two.

The boundaries may have to be changed later as a result of further knowledge and special attention must be paid in future investigations to micropulsations in these boundary regions, and to those falling in the class designated Pc 2. This sub-group of regular pulsations falls between the classes formerly called PP and the lower boundary of those designated Pc's. Their properties have been but little investigated but they do not seem to be physically related to those micropulsations in classes Pc 1 and Pc 3.

The second main class of micropulsations is characterized by their irregular form, their close connection with disturbances of the magnetic field, and their correlation with upper atmospheric phenomena. It was suggested that this class be divided into two sub-groups covering the frequency ranges shown in Table 2.2.

Table 2.2.

Notation	Period Range (sec)
Pi 1	1— 40
Pi 2	40—150

Thus Pi 2 corresponds to what was formerly called Pt and Pi 1 to the higher frequency components which are often superimposed. Usually the period of Pi 1 is quite small, seldom exceeding 20 sec. These two sub-groups form the microstructure of magnetic bays and similar disturbances during magnetic storms.

In any decisions on notation and classification, some compromise is inevitable. Since the physical processes involved are not completely understood, it is pointless to introduce a highly sophisticated scheme. Moreover a balance must be kept between the needs of the research worker and the observatories who have to report the phenomena. In this respect it is desirable that the notation be kept as simple as possible. It is for this reason that the symbol Pc was retained. It was also suggested that some observatories may prefer to use the symbol Pt as before and use Pi for the shorter period irregular oscillations. If they adopt this method of reporting then $Pi \equiv Pi\,1$ and $Pt \equiv Pi\,2$. The above classification will, of course, have to be improved upon as observational knowledge increases. T. Saito (1964) and R. V. Shchepetnov (1969) in particular have made further suggestions in this regard. Table 2.3 (after B. Hultquist, 1966) gives a brief summary of the different classifications that have been suggested.

2.3 Continuous Pulsations (Pc 1)

In recent years Pc 1's, hydromagnetic emissions, or pulsations of pearl
type (PP) as they have variously been called, have attracted the attention
of many investigators (detailed accounts have been given by W. H. Campbell and E. C. Stiltner (1965), J. A. Dawson (1965), and L. Tepley (1965).
The characteristics of these pulsations show that they are an important
source of information on plasma instabilities that may develop in the
outer regions of the radiation belts, and are a useful indicator of the
state of the magnetosphere. (This will be discussed in more detail in
Chapter 6.)

Pc 1 pulsations are regular sinusoidal oscillations with periods
mainly from 0.3 to 4 sec. These pulsations may occur in the form of
separate bursts (individual pearls), gradually developing into a series
of pulsations lasting from tens of min to hours (see Fig. 2.1). They may

Fig. 2.1. Example of Pc 1's (pearls) recorded at four stations simultaneously.
(After J. E. Lokken, J. A. Shand, and C. S. Wright, DREP photograph 2751)

Table 2.3

Notation	Period (sec)	Duration	Amplitude	Max. occurrence L.T.	Polarization	Characteristics
Pc 1	0.2– 5		$<10^{-3}-\sim 1\gamma$		Elliptical, right- or left-handed (left is more common)	Modulated with a period of a few min
Benioff's Type A	0.3– 2.5					
Benioff's Type B	3 – 8					
Troitskaya's PP	0.3– 4	From a few min up to several hours		Night in middle lat. More evenly in high lat.		
Hydromagnetic emissions (Tepley & Wentworth)	0.1– 2.5	Several min	$5\cdot 10^{-3}\gamma$			
Pc 2	5 – 10					
Benioff's Type B	3 – 8					
Pc 3	10 – 45					
Pc (Pc-I of Saito)	10 – 40	Several hours	$\sim 0.1\gamma$	Morning	Elliptical or linear	
Pc 4	45 –150					
Pc° (Pc-II of Saito)	60 –~120	Several hours	$\sim 1\gamma$	Daytime	Elliptical	
Pc 5	150 –600					
Lpc (of Jacobs and Sinno) (Pc-III of Saito)	120 –420		Tens of γ		Sometimes linear Elliptical	
pg (giant pulsations)	one to several minutes		Several tens of γ		Elliptical	
πpg (Kerguelen)	50 –200	Exist most of the time	$<20\gamma$	Noon	Elliptical always to the left	Occur in trains
Pi 1	1 – 40					
Troitskaya's SIP	1 – 15	Min to tens of min	$\sim 1\gamma$	Night	Elliptical	
Noise bursts (Tepley & Wentworth)	0.1– 2.5					
IPDP (intervals of pulsations diminishing by period; Troitskaya)						
Pi 2	2 – 10					
	40 –150					
Pt (pulsation trains)	40 –150	10–20 min	$\sim\frac{1}{2}\gamma$	Just before midnight	Elliptic, right handed before midnight, left handed after midnight	Series of damped pulsation trains of total duration $\leqslant 1$ hour

also occur in the form of characteristic consecutive groups of pulsations with sharply varying frequency (IPDP's or solar whistlers, which will be discussed later).

The rapid increase in our knowledge of Pc 1's has been largely brought about by frequency/time analyses (sonagrams) from a large network of stations. Such investigations have revealed a fine structure in the signals. The types of fine structure observed vary greatly and range from horizontal "structured" elements (rising tones) i.e. with constant frequency in each "pearl", to almost vertical ones; occasionally they are inclined to the left relative to the time axis, i.e. they exhibit falling

Fig. 2.2. Typical fine structure of Pc 1's observed simultaneously at Borok and Kerguelen. The fine structure (rising tones) can be clearly seen. (After V. A. Troitskaya)

tones. Some emissions consist of very narrow bands displaced in time, which can be confused with the simple rising structured elements of the usual series. (Examples of sonagrams are shown in Fig. 2.2.)

It is difficult to obtain quantitative information from sonagram records, the output medium of which is sensitized paper with relative blackness proportional to the signal strength at a particular frequency and time. J. F. Kenney et al. (1967) have developed a simple modification of the standard technique replacing the sensitized paper with an oscilloscope and camera. Since a change in the horizontal or vertical deflection sensitivity of the oscilloscope will allow expansion of the output record to any desired amount, the frequency and time resolution of the signal will be limited only by the filter characteristics of the sonagraph, not by the size of the output record. The increased resolution makes possible the separation of signals when more than one event is occurring: it is impossible to resolve the fine structure of complicated events with conventional sonagram techniques. Fig. 2.3a is another example of a sonagram of a Pc 1 event, and Fig. 2.3b is an expansion of a portion of the record illustrating the improved character of the data resolution obtained by Kenney et al. Such detailed resolution permits the separation of signals when more than one event is occurring. Fig. 2.4 shows the unsmoothed power spectra of the elements in the Pc 1 event shown in Fig. 2.3a, b.

The bandwidth of Pc 1's lies, as a rule in the frequency range 0.1–0.5 Hz and the rate of frequency rise is of the order of 0.1 Hz/min. It should be emphasized that series which have a stable repetitive structure are, in general, typical of a quiet magnetosphere. For the disturbed magnetosphere an irregular scattering of structured elements with different slopes of frequency rise is typical. These elements are superimposed on a background of intense noise, usually rising in frequency (see Fig. 2.5). Investigations at high latitudes and at the polar caps have shown that the fine structure typical for the Pc 1 series is more characteristic for pul-

Fig. 2.3a.   Sonagram of a Pc 1 observed at Tulalip, Washington. (After J. F. Kenney, H. B. Knaflich and H. B. Liemohn)

ut
17 January 1967

Fig. 2.3 b.   An expansion of a portion of the Pc 1 record shown in Fig. 2.3 a
to illustrate the improved character of the data resolution. (After J. F. Kenney,
H. B. Knaflich and H. B. Liemohn)

sations with periods less than 3 sec (E. T. Matveeva and V. A. Troitskaya,
1965; R. R. Heacock, 1966). Pulsations with periods from 3 to 8 sec,
which predominate at high latitudes do not always show this property.
   An analysis of Pc 1 periods at middle- and highlatitude stations
shows that pulsations with periods less than 2 sec are most common,
the longer period pulsations being more characteristic of high-latitude
stations. Thus recordings of Pc 1's at two auroral zone stations, College,
Alaska and Sodankyla, Finland (64°6 N and 63°8 N geomagnetic latitude)
and one sub auroral station, Nurmijaarvi, Finland (57°8 N) by R. R.
Heacock et al. (1968) show a marked latitude variation in the mid frequency of structured Pc 1 events—the average frequency of structured
Pc 1's at Nurmijaarvi, the lower latitude station being significantly

Fig. 2.4.   The unsmoothed power spectra of the elements in the Pc 1 event shown in Fig. 2.3 a, b. (After J. F. Kenney, H. B. Knaflich and H. B. Liemohn)

Fig. 2.5.   Typical sonagram of a disturbed period observed at Kerguelen. Isolated structured elements are superimposed on a background of noise. (After R. Gendrin, M. Gokhberg, S. Lacourly and V. A. Troitskaya)

higher than that for the auroral zone stations even after allowance for differences in K_p are made. Moreover structured Pc 1 events recorded at one of the Finnish stations in the summer months were usually not received at the other in spite of a latitude separation of only 6°. There is also a wide spread in frequencies for nighttime occurrences: the existence of a latitude frequency relation within this Pc 1 source region is important, since some theoretical mechanisms involve ion cyclotron instabilities (see Chapter 4). and the ion cyclotron frequency increases inwards in the magnetosphere's equatorial plane. Some other mechanisms, for example, hydromagnetic whistlers (J. A. Jacobs and T. Watanabe, 1967) do not require this latitude variation in source frequency if a simple broad-band initiating impulse is postulated. The sharp decrease in observed Pc 1's with small periods (which is confirmed by observations at many stations) raises the question of spectrum cutoff and the critical frequency of Pc 1's at different geomagnetic latitudes. The sunlit ionosphere is practically opaque to pulsations with periods less than 1 sec—periods of about 0.3 sec for middle-latitude stations appear to be the limit.

One of the main physical characteristics of Pc 1's is the repetition period, T, of structured elements in the Pc 1 series. This period is a function of the frequency of the Pc 1 oscillations, $1/t$. The product $T \times 1/t$ remains approximately constant—i.e. if the frequency $1/t$ falls, the period of repetition becomes greater (R. R. Heacock and V. P. Hessler, 1962; J. H. Pope, 1965). Experimentally determined relations between these quantities are: $60 \sec < (T/t) < 140 \sec$ (L. R. Tepley, 1965) or $T = 86 t_{average}$ sec (W. H. Campbell and E. C. Stiltner, 1965). J. F. Kenney and H. B. Knaflich (1967) have shown, however, that although the general trend is for the spacing T to be inversely proportional to the frequency, in an individual pearl the spacing is usually directly proportional to the frequency.

The existence of a distinct period of repetition for structured elements (rising tones) in the Pc 1 series has been used by many authors as the starting point for a theory of their origin (see Chapter 4). This parameter has been connected, for example, with the bouncing of charged particles along magnetic field lines, the particle drift around the earth, as well as with the propagation of hydromagnetic (hm) wave packets along field lines. The repetition period of structured elements has been interpreted by many authors as the time needed for an hm wave packet to travel from one hemisphere to the other and back. Structure doubling of Pc 1 series (i. e. a reduction of the repetition period T to about one half) is sometimes observed. Such structure doubling was first noted at two equatorial stations by L. R. Tepley in 1964 (see Fig. 2.6). It is interpreted as the superposition, at the place of observation of signals arriving from both hemispheres; this can, of course, account for some of the observed scattering.

The repetition period, T, has been found to be the same for stations located at conjugate points in the southern and northern hemispheres. However, bursts of oscillations (on amplitude/time records) and, consequently, separate structured elements (on frequency/time records) occur approximately in antiphase at conjugate points (K. Yanagihara, 1963; L. R. Tepley, 1965). It is important to determine whether the structured elements are precisely in antiphase at conjugate points or

Fig. 2.6.   Example of structure doubling of Pc 1's. At Canton Island (geomagnetic latitude 5.1° S), the spacing between structured elements is about one half that at Kauai (21.7° N) and Tongatapu (24.0° S). (After L. R. Tepley)

whether their repetition period is asymmetrically divided between the stations. In the latter case this would signify that the propagation time from one hemisphere to the other is not the same as that in the opposite direction.

The present evidence on this subject is not unanimous. For the low-latitude stations Palo Alto and Tongatapu this shift appears to be symmetrical (L. R. Tepley and R. K. Landshoff, 1966). Using similar spectrographic techniques on records from the near conjugate pair Borok and Kerguelen Island ($L \simeq 3.27$), V. A. Troitskaya, R. Gendrin and R. Stefant (1964) reported a phase shift noticeably different from 180°. They measured the occurrence times of signals at a certain fixed frequency (0.68 Hz) and found that the signal was delayed on the average by 98.0 ± 3.2 sec from Kerguelen to Borok and by 67.0 ± 2.5 sec from Borok to Kerguelen. However the absolute precision in time measurements in that experiment was of the order of 20 sec (R. Gendrin and V. A. Troitskaya, 1965). A. H. Borsoukov and M. C. Ponsot (1964) also reported an off 180° phase shift for an hm emission event on 17 Feb. 1964 received at the same pair of stations. The correlation functions of the envelopes of the horizontal component of the magnetic signals at the two stations indicated that the hm signal appeared 70 sec later in Kerguelen than in Borok while the repetition period was 120 sec. J. O. Annexstad and C. R. Wilson (1968) also found that the phase shift between the conjugate pair of stations, Kotzebue, Alaska and Macquarie Island ($L \simeq 5.23$) was not always 180°.

The quantity T depends on the length of the magnetic field line, on the velocity of propagation of hm waves along the line (and consequently on the distribution of plasma concentration) and on the intensity of the magnetic field: observations of the variability of T may, therefore yield information about changes in these parameters.

A very typical characteristic of Pc 1 series of oscillations is a tendency for them to recur on consecutive days, approximately at the same hours, or to disappear for days and even weeks. This characteristic has been well established and has been emphasized by many workers. In this respect the character of Pc 1 excitation differs significantly from that of the excitation of other groups of continuous pulsations which recur regularly day after day.

The characteristics of Pc 1's undergo large changes during the solar cycle—in duration, average amplitude, and number. There are very few Pc 1's on quiet and moderately disturbed days during years of solar maximum. Thus even very sensitive installations at Borok failed to record a single Pc 1 during the whole month of December 1957. On the other hand, intensive series of pearls with diminishing periods during the main phase of magnetic storms (IPDP's) are characteristic of years of solar maximum. The mean duration of Pc 1's at Borok increased by about a factor of two from 1957 to 1961 and the mean-annual amplitude by almost 1.5 times from 1957 to 1960.

An analysis of one of the longest series of Pc 1 observations for the mid-latitude stations Alma-Ata and Borok (E. T. Matveeva and V. A. Troitskaya, 1965) showed that the maximum number of Pc 1 events occurs during the years between maximum and minimum solar activity. This regular behaviour is also typical for other mid-latitude stations. Thus during the current solar cycle, maximum occurrence was observed in 1961, exceeding that in 1958 (sunspot maximum) by about 7 times.

For stations located in or near the auroral zone, preliminary data from Lovozero indicate that the maximum of the curve is shifted towards later years (1962–1964). The longest duration of Pc 1 series has also been observed in the years between maximum and minimum solar activity.

The diurnal variation of Pc 1's has been analysed for an extensive network of stations. All distributions are similar, broad curves being obtained at high latitudes with maxima around midday and in the after-

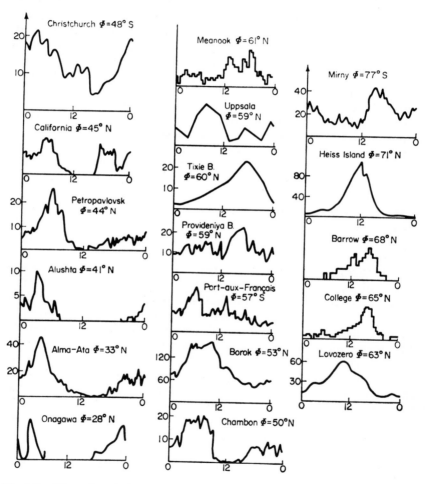

Fig. 2.7.   Diurnal variation of Pc 1's for a worldwide network of stations. The abscissae show local time and the ordinates the number of events. (After V. A. Troitskaya)

noon, and much narrower ones at middle and low latitudes, with maxima during the night and early morning hours (see Fig. 2.7). A diurnal variation in mid-frequency has been found by W. H. Campbell and E. C. Stiltner (1965), higher frequencies occurring at post midnight hours and lower ones near early afternoon. The seasonal variation of Pc 1's is not clearly defined. This is due in part to the fact that only a few stations have carried out sufficiently long series of observations and because of the sharp changes in Pc 1 occurrence during the solar cycle. An analysis of the data for Borok (the most complete for Pc 1 data) indicates that the maximum occurrence of Pc 1 ($T \leqslant 3$ sec) falls mainly in the fall and winter months. At the polar caps a summer maximum for oscillations with $T \simeq 4-6$ sec is observed. In the auroral zones the maximum number of Pc 1's seems to occur at the equinoxes. Investigations of the occurrence of Pc 1 over the Earth's surface and of the character of their amplitude

Fig. 2.8. 'Cultured pearl' technique for measurement of inter- and intrahemisphere fine-structure phase shift. The sonagrams at the upper left show broad-band hm emissions observed simultaneously at Palo Alto and Tongatapu. The sonagrams at the upper right show the corresponding narrow-band hm emissions produced in the laboratory by passing the broad-band emissions through a narrow-band filter. The chart records at the bottom of the figure show waveforms (cultured pearls) of the narrow-band emissions for the time periods indicated, as well as the broad-band Tongatapu waveform. Comparison of the waveform records clearly shows the 180° phase shift between Palo Alto and Tongatapu. In addition, comparison of the Tongatapu narrow and broad-band waveforms shows the broadening and time delay introduced by the filter. (After R. C. Wentworth, L. R. Tepley, and K. D. Amundsen)

changes with latitude indicate that they are most frequently excited in subauroral and auroral regions. From preliminary data it seems that during the solar cycle the location of the zone of maximum occurrence changes its position. In the northern hemisphere it is located further south during the years of solar maximum and during solar minimum it moves northward.

Recently an elegant technique for producing "cultured pearls", i.e. narrow-band filtering of a natural Pc 1 series has been proposed (L.R. Tepley and R. K. Landshoff, 1966; Wentworth et al., 1966) (Fig. 2.8). This technique enables comparisons to be made of separate pearls at different stations, not only for the narrow-band natural series, but for many more complicated series. A comparison of the times of occurrence of individual pearls shows that the oscillations propagate from high to low latitudes with velocities around 900 km/sec. The same order of magnitude for the velocity of propagation of narrow-band natural series was obtained at the USSR stations Sogra-Ashkhabad (L. N. Baransky et al., 1967).

The polarization of narrow-band Pc 1's, consisting of a single series of structured elements, is opposite at magnetically conjugate points, which is the case for the propagation of a definite mode of hm waves (see Chapter 3). Agreement has not been reached on the predominant direction of rotation in each hemisphere. Some data indicate that both directions of rotation are possible (R. Gendrin et al., 1966 a, b), although there is evidence that a counterclockwise direction of rotation predominates in the northern hemisphere (W. H. Campbell and E. C. Stiltner, 1965). In the case of a complicated overlapping series of pulsations comprising several series of structured elements the simultaneous propagation of wave packets with different polarization along the field line is possible (see Fig. 2.9). From an analysis of the records from many stations, the preferred direction of the major axis of the polarization ellipse is the N–S direction, which can be interpreted as additional evidence for the longitudinal propagation of Pc 1 pulsations. Data relating to the disturbed magnetosphere (R. Gendrin et al., 1966 c) show that the polarization of Pc 1 oscillations in the structured elements of an IPDP occurring simultaneously at magnetically conjugate points differs from that observed for normal Pc 1's during quiet conditions in that the direction of rotation in both hemispheres for these simultaneous Pc 1 bursts is the same. This suggests a simultaneous generation of two wave packets with left- and right-hand polarization propagating in opposite directions.

It is now well known that regular long series of Pc 1 pulsations are characteristic of the quiet and weakly disturbed state of the magnetosphere—at K-indices which do not exceed 1–2 (e.g. R. R. Heacock and V. P. Hessler, 1963, showed that more than 50 per cent of Pc 1's occur when $Kp<2$). Thus slowly developing Pc 1 series should not be considered as a fine structure of some other macroscopic slow-field variations, but rather as a special undisturbed state of the magnetosphere. During magnetic disturbance, however, the character of the excitation of Pc 1 pulsations changes (L.R. Tepley, 1964; V.A. Troitskaya and R. Gendrin, 1966). In this case the separate, irregularly scattered structured elements of Pc 1's are, as a rule, observed against a suddenly

Fig. 2.9. Sonagram from the conjugate pair of stations Kerguelen and Sogra. Between 1505 and 1605 there appears to be two frequency bands. The numbers give the percentage of time that the sense of rotation is positive or negative during a 3 min interval. When the sense of rotation was constant during a 3 min interval at one station it was also constant at the other. At each station left and right hand polarizations occurred with comparable probabilities. (After R. Gendrin, M. Gokhberg, S. Lacourly and V.A. Troitskaya)

increased level of background noise. Often the noise level systematically increases with frequency, forming a characteristic rising tail. In this case the amplitude/time records, after an intense burst of pulsations of the Pi 1 type, show a series of Pc 1 pulsations of diminishing period; this effect constitutes the end of an IPDP sequence (V.A. Troitskaya and M.V. Melnikova, 1959; V.A. Troitskaya and R. Gendrin, 1966). This

32 The Morphology of Geomagnetic Micropulsations

characteristic sequence of disturbances appears to be the same as the so-called "gurglers" (L. R. Tepley, 1964) and pulsations storms (E. Selzer, 1964).

In the Pc 1 category, there are several types of micropulsations other than hm emissions—one such type has been named continuous sub-ELF emissions by L. R. Tepley and K. D. Amundsen (1965) (see Fig. 2.10).

Fig. 2.10. Example of continuous emissions. They differ from Pc 1's by the lack of fine structure, by significantly greater duration and by smaller amplitudes. Note the different appearance of the bands at the different stations and the simultaneous appearance of three bands at Kauai in the interval 0800—1300. (After L. R. Tepley and K. D. Amundsen)

This type of micropulsation seems to be the same as the 4-sec band micropulsations of R. R. Heacock (1966). Continuous sub-ELF emissions look similar to hm emissions on magnetograms, since both of them appear as continuous oscillations. There are several differences between the two phenomena, however. Whereas hm emissions fall mostly in the Pc 1 frequency range, frequencies of continuous sub-ELF emissions cover both Pc 1 as well as Pc 2 ranges. On the average, hm emissions have a frequency higher than continuous sub-ELF emissions. Hm emissions take place when the general magnetic activity represented by the Kp index is low. On the other hand, continuous sub-ELF emissions at College, Alaska, are more likely to take place when the general magnetic activity is higher. In contrast to the discrete structure of hm emission signals on spectrograms, continuous sub-ELF emissions show no such structures. Their sonagram shows several bands occurring simultaneously with a slowly varying central frequency. Their mean frequency rises towards dawn and then falls off sharply (see Fig. 2.10).

Despite these differences in observational characteristics, careful investigation is needed to answer the question as to whether or not the two types of micropulsations are essentially different in their mechanisms of generation and propagation. In this respect, L.R. Tepley and K.D. Amundsen (1965) observed that a continuous sub-ELF emission event may appear to turn into a fine-structured hm emission and vice versa. From observations at the four Lockheed stations (Palo Alto, Kauai, Canton Island and Tongatapu) they found that continuous sub-ELF emissions were never observed at Canton Island, an equatorial station. At the three other stations, they occurred only during the night hours. The signal spectrum of an event differs from one station to another —the spectra are not necessarily identical even at the conjugate pair Kauai and Tongatapu.

2.4 Continuous Pulsations (Pc 2/3, Pc 4, and Pc 5)

A common feature of all the above groups is the continuity of their regimen, and an important property of all is the absence of fine structure and of any connection with other upper atmospheric phenomena which may be due to particle injection during the Pc occurrence.

A clear dependence of Pc-periods on planetary magnetic activity has been discovered. There exists a range of Kp-values for which the excitation of all Pc-types may occur. Conversely for some values of Kp some types of Pc's are never seen. Fig. 2.11 shows that Pc 4's are observed at the smallest Kp values ($\sim 0-2.5$): most cases of Pc 3 occur in the range of $1 < Kp < 3.5$, and the number falls off sharply for Kp equal to 5 or more. Finally, for very disturbed magnetic fields, only Pc's with small periods ($T \sim 8-15$ sec) are observed. For studying any diurnal changes of the period of Pc's, it is essential to take into account the dependence on magnetic activity. It is better to measure periods for hours of the day with the same Kp ratio, even for different days, than to determine periods without taking into account their dependence on Kp. Discrepancies in the literature may perhaps be due to this dependence.

The dependence of continuous pulsations on magnetic activity is also reflected in their occurrence frequency during the solar cycle. Whereas around solar maximum all Pc groups have an almost equal probability (Pc 2: 35%; Pc 3: 30%; Pc 4: 35%), around sunspot minimum the picture is very different. At Borok the number of Pc 4's

increased to 57%, that of Pc 2's was reduced to 7% while the number
of Pc 3's remained approximately the same. Such a change in the Pc
spectrum is closely related to the redistribution of Kp indices which
occurred during the same period. It is also interesting to note that,
according to data obtained by T. Saito (1964b) which coincide with
those of the USSR observatories (O.V. Bolshakova, 1965), the mean
periods of Pc 4 and Pc 5 decrease from sunspot maximum to sunspot
minimum.

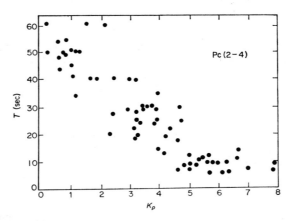

Fig. 2.11.   Dependence of Pc 2—4 periods on K_p at Borok. (After V. A. Troitskaya)

The amplitudes of most continuous pulsations, as well as irregular
pulsations, increase with latitude, sometimes sharply by an order of
magnitude when approaching the auroral zones (J. R. Heirtzler, 1964,
1965). The character of this dependence can, however, change considerably
from case to case. For instance, on some occasions the amplitude remains
approximately constant (H. Voelker, 1965) while on others its change
may depend on the level of magnetic activity and on other factors.
The amplitudes of Pc 2's and Pc 3's increase with a rise in the Kp index.
The dependence of the amplitude of Pc 4's on Kp is more complicated,
however, and there are instances when the Pc 4 amplitude actually
decreases with an increase in Kp. Maximum amplitudes of Pc 2/3's and
Pc 4's occur in the auroral zones.
        Different authors using different methods of investigation have
reached contradictory conclusions on the question of the change in
period of continuous pulsations with latitude ϕ. Thus one of the principal
criteria for distinguishing on the Earth's surface between guided and
unguided oscillations viz the character of the changes in pulsation

period with latitude for that part of the spectrum most frequently excited (Pc 2 – Pc 5), still proves uncertain (see also Chapter 5). An increase of period with latitude was found by T. Obayashi and J. A. Jacobs (1958), their experimental results agreeing with theory according to which the period is inversely proportional to $\cos^2 \phi$. Obayashi and Jacobs found that this relation held not only for Pc's but also for Pi 2 pulsations. Results for Pc 5 were also obtained by A. I. Ol' (1963) for the latitude range 60.5° N–71.5° N. The data show a similar dependence of the period on the cosine of the latitude, but the periods have greater values than those found by Obayashi and Jacobs at the same latitude, and they increase more rapidly with latitude. O. V. Bolshakova and K. Y. Zybin found that the periods of the most stable pulsations at each of five stations within the latitude range 23° N–64° N, had the same latitude dependence as that found by Obayashi and Jacobs. On the other hand investigations by R. A. Duncan (1961) and G. R. A. Ellis (1960) using data from three stations in the latitude range 29° S–52° S gave contradictory results. A definite increase in period with latitude was obtained by M. Siebert (1964) and H. Voelker (1965) from simultaneous observations with identical equipment at several points within the rather narrow latitude range 48.9° N–58.5° N for a special class of pulsations—those of Pse type (i.e. single-effect pulsations). V. A. Troitskaya (1967) investigated the latitude-dependent characteristics of pulsations for almost 100 events observed simultaneously at the stations Lovozero, Borok and Alushta. In the Pc 3–4 range she found examples showing both an increase and a decrease of period with latitude. Care must be taken however when comparing statistically obtained mean periods when no account has been taken of magnetic activity, diurnal and seasonal changes, etc.

In the northern hemisphere micropulsations of Pc 2–5 type exhibit predominantly counterclockwise rotation during the morning and clockwise rotation in the evening. Pulsations appearing simultaneously at conjugate points show different directions of rotation. The longitudinal plane dividing the hemispheres with different signs of rotation is slightly displaced however from the midday-midnight meridian towards the day side during the morning, and towards the night side in the evening.

2.4.1 Continuous Pc 2/3 Oscillations

The observed signal amplitudes of Pc 2/3 oscillations are usually under 0.5γ and typical periods are from about 5 to 30 sec. The duration of recorded signals seems to be simply related to the sensitivity of the detector. The average period undergoes a diurnal variation, although there is not complete agreement amongst investigators, which may be partly explained by observations being made at different Kp values. J. G. Linford (1969) found a slight diurnal U-type variation and a seasonal change (see Fig. 2.12) consistent with the period being determined by the radius of the magnetosphere in the local time meridian of the site. The wave form is more irregular and the duration shorter at night.

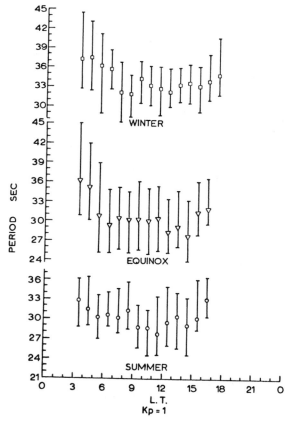

Fig. 2.12. Diurnal variation of period for Pc 3's observed at Awarua (New Zealand) for different seasons when $K_p=1$. The median and the quartiles are presented so that 50 per cent of all readings are within the error bars in the diagrams. (After J. G. Linford)

These pulsations are typically dayside phenomena maximizing around noon (see Fig. 2.13). J. A. Jacobs and K. Sinno (1960a) found a small additional universal time factor in the occurrence time for northern hemisphere data, the number of occurrences being greater when the north geomagnetic pole was at about 1 600–1 700 LMT. The diurnal varia-

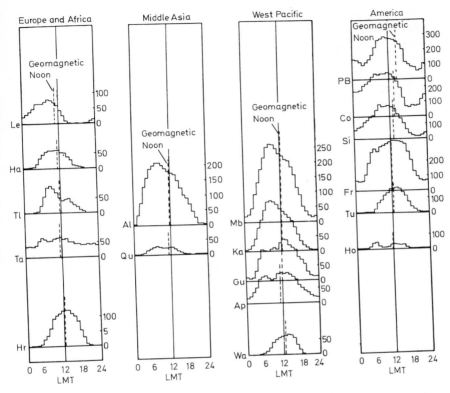

Fig. 2.13. Diurnal occurrence frequencies of Pc 2, 3's at various observatories arranged in longitudinal groups illustrating the mid-day maximum. (After J. A. Jacobs and K. Sinno)

tion of Pc's in the equatorial regions has rather specific peculiarities. R. Hutton (1962, 1965) found three maxima with the main maximum during the evening (1800–2000 LMT), a peculiarity which is as yet unexplained (see Fig. 2.14).

The vertical field component is generally less than the horizontal. T. Terada (1917) reported a rather regular increase in this amplitude ratio with increasing period. The major direction of the horizontal disturbing vector, although typically north–south, undergoes a diurnal variation at most latitudes and, with this change, a reversal of the polarization sense occurs. A semi-diurnal variation in the direction and polarization has generally been found—during the daytime maximum occurrence period a counterclockwise polarization sense predominates in the northern hemisphere. Fam Van-chi et al. (1968) investigated Pc 3 oscillations at the conjugate pair of stations Sogra and Kerguelen and found that they were excited synchronously, the form and period of the pulsations being the same at both points. The amplitudes at the two conjugate points were also of the same order of magnitude. They also confirmed the diurnal pattern of the polarization—counterclockwise in the northern hemisphere and clockwise in the southern during the

Fig. 2.14. Diurnal variation of frequency of occurence of regular pulsations Pc 3 at Legon (5° 38′ N). Solid curve telluric pulsations, dotted curve magnetic pulsations. (After R. Hutton)

morning. The direction of rotation changed in both hemispheres in the afternoon. In middle latitudes about 95 per cent of the curves described by the disturbance vector have a non linear form and about 75 per cent have a ratio of minor to major ellipse axis less than 0.5.

The seasonal variation of Pc 3's has been studied in many regions by many observers. All investigations indicate that the minimum of this Pc activity occurs during the winter months. The curve of maximum occurrence varies from year to year, from summer to the equinoxes or shows a flat maximum during the summer and both equinoxes. Differences in equipment and different methods of data processing probably account for the different shapes of Pc 3 seasonal variations. T. Saito, (1962) has suggested that the shift of the seasonal maximum is due to $F-2$ control of Pc. There is no general agreement about the seasonal change of Pc 3 periods. Investigations in the Soviet Union however have shown that Pc 3 periods in summer are about 15–20 sec and in winter about 25–30 sec. This question requires special investigation at a number of stations, in which particular attention is given to the state of magnetic activity. There appears to be a 27 day (solar rotation) recurrence tendency for pulsations with periods between about 5 and 50 sec which is related to changes in Kp—the characteristic frequency of Pc 2/3's increasing with increasing Kp. The incidence of these pulsations also increases during the initial phase of magnetic storms. K. Yanagihara (1960) found an eleven year solar cycle variation in activity roughly paralleling changes in sunspot number; a shift in the seasonal pattern also follows the solar cycle.

2.4.2 *Continuous* Pc 4 *Oscillations*

Typical amplitudes of Pc 4's in high latitudes are from 5 to 20 γ. The signals usually last from 10 min to several hours averaging about one hour. They often rise slowly to a maximum amplitude that is long sustained and then fade away. At middle and low latitudes a daytime occurrence pattern with a midday maximum is found. The pattern at auroral zone stations in the Antarctic is similar to that for stations in the northern auroral zone with a maximum around 0300–0600 LMT, changing to the noon hours at lower latitudes (T. Sato 1965). At middle latitudes Pc 4 periods tend to be somewhat shorter during the daytime than at night; at high latitudes the evening periods are slightly shorter than the morning ones. For both Pc 4's and Pc 5's the larger amplitude events typically have longer periods. Like Pc 2/3's the amplitudes of Pc 4's show an auroral zone enhancement. The frequency of occurrence of Pc 4's increases with a decrease of solar activity although their amplitude remains almost constant throughout a solar cycle. On the other hand the frequency of occurrence of Pc 3's does not change much throughout a solar cycle whereas their amplitude decreases sharply with decreasing solar activity. Thus Pc 4's are much more dominant than Pc 3's during the quietest solar conditions.

Large events seem to have a greater longitudinal extent although at high latitudes most events are confined to a region of about 1000 km. Oscillations similar in amplitude and period often appear simultaneously at conjugate stations (see Fig. 2.15 which shows Pc 4's recorded at Byrd, Antarctica and Great Whale River, Canada). T. J. Herron (1965) has studied the phase variations of pulsations at stations separated by a few 100 km in the northeastern U.S.A. He found an apparent increase in phase velocity with decreasing period from about 10 km/sec for

150 sec periods to 50 km/sec for 50 sec periods. An exact evaluation of this result is difficult because of the unknown effect of geological structures and the possible self-interference pattern of some signal sources. Herron also found an approximate east-west symmetry in the sense of phase lag about the 1000–1100 local time meridian with the station nearer the dark hemisphere leading in phase.

Fig. 2.15.   Pc 4's recorded at the conjugate auroral zone stations of Great Whale River, Canada and Byrd, Antarctica. (After J. A. Jacobs and C. S. Wright—DREP photograph 4192–5 B)

At equatorial and auroral latitudes signals occur most frequently during the equinoctial months with secondary summer enhancements and a winter minimum (about $\frac{1}{3}$ as many as in the equinoctial months). An interesting feature of Pc seasonal variations is the change in their period. Pc 4 and Pc 5 periods are shorter in summer (Pc 4, 40 sec; Pc 5, 400 sec) than in winter (Pc 4, 70 sec; Pc 5, 450 sec). No special relationships with Kp or the 27 day solar rotation period have been found for Pc 4's. At all latitudes their occurrence seems to be connected with the solar cycle—more activity in years of sunspot minimum than maximum and more in times of decreasing than increasing sunspot number.

2.4.3 *Continuous* Pc 5 *Oscillations*

This class of pulsations with the longest period (3–9 min) may have extremely large amplitudes reaching several hundred gammas. In the older terminology they were called "giant pulsations" pg. A group of Pc 5's lasts from 10 min to several hours—morning events seem to continue longer than those in the afternoon. Their form is quite sinusoidal, often damped with some distortion appearing with increasing magnetic activity (see Fig. 2.16). Near the northern auroral zone the

Fig. 2.16.   Pc 5 oscillations at the conjugate auroral zone stations of Great Whale River, Canada and Byrd, Antarctica. The oscillations are of about 4 min period and lasted for several hours. (After J. A. Jacobs and C. S. Wright—DREP photograph 4159–3 B)

occurrence follows a semi-diurnal pattern with maxima around 0600 and 1800 LMT. These maxima show a systematic variation in relative intensity in winter and summer, the times of the maxima shifting towards midday in the summer. Data for 1958 from Byrd and Syowa in the Antarctic however indicate only a morning maximum. Both a single midday maximum and semi-diurnal peaks in amplitude are reported occasionally for middle latitudes. Periods tend to be somewhat shorter during the morning peak activity hours, and longer at the June than at the December solstice.

There is a broad latitude distribution of Pc 5's including a rapid decrease in amplitude with distance from the auroral zone and a clear equatorial enhancement. N. Matuura (1961) found that the component of the disturbance parallel to the main field of the Earth had comparable amplitudes at the auroral zone and the equator. He also found a systematic diurnal change in the relative amplitudes at various latitudes, as well as a clear equatorial enhancement of midday signals at Koror with respect to those at Honolulu and Kakioka. Such an enhancement in the equatorial region would be expected from an ionospheric current system. The maximum occurrence frequency is at about $67-70°$ geomagnetic latitude and decreases to about $\frac{1}{5}$ at $80°$ and $50°$. The narrowness in the diurnal maximum indicates a rather limited longitudinal extent for a typical event. Thus A. L. Ol' (1963) found that out of 142 events at Cape Chelyuskin (longitude $104°\ 17'$ E), 114 at Dixon Island ($80°\ 33'$ E) and 59 at Wellen ($169°\ 50'$ W) only 20 were simultaneous at the first two stations and only 7 at the first and third. P. Obertz and O. M. Raspopov (1968) also found that the region of excitation of Pc 5's is localized in space, in agreement with the idea of a "centre" of Pc 5 activity (see E. Kaneda et al. (1964) who determined a Pc 5 centre based on maximum amplitude). The characteristic longitudinal dimension of the centre is about $60°$, the amplitude of Pc 5's decreasing by an order of magnitude over half this distance. In contrast the latitudinal extent of the region of Pc 5 excitation does not exceed a few degrees. Obertz and Raspopov also found a dependence of Pc 5 period on the location of the Pc 5 centre. The period of the pulsations in each individual occurrence is constant over the entire region of excitation but its value depends on the geomagnetic latitude at which the Pc 5's reach their maximum amplitude i.e. on the Pc 5 centre.

The vertical component is generally the smallest at most latitudes: the horizontal component usually has an elliptical polarization. In individual events an appreciable phase shift can appear at latitudes about $50°$. In particular oscillations that occur on the poleward side of the auroral zone can differ in wave form and phase from those at lower latitudes. There is a shift in the sense of polarization from counter-clockwise in the morning hours to clockwise in the evening hours in the northern hemisphere. The transition period is often less than an hour and occurs typically around 1100 local geomagnetic time. The principal axis of polarization is perpendicular to the direction of the line of force of the Earth's main field. Studies at pairs of conjugate stations show similar signals, the rotation sense of the horizontal disturbance vector with respect to the magnetic line of force joining the two stations being the same.

A 27 day recurrence tendency for Pc 5's is occasionally reported but is not very clear. The average periods in active sun years are greater than those during quiet years by a factor of about 1.5. A correlation between Pc 5's and the Kp index is not strong—Pc 5's seem to be absent on both very quiet and on strongly disturbed days. They generally occur during the subsidence period several days after moderate magnetic disturbances.

Y. Kato and T. Saito (1964) have compared seasonal and yearly changes in Pc 4,5 period with upper atmospheric plasma density variations, as reflected by satellite drag, VLF whistler dispersion, critical frequencies of the E and $F2$ ionosphere, and sun–earth distance. Fig. 2.17 illustrates some of these striking parallel changes with decreasing sunspot number.

Fig. 2.17.   Secular and annual changes of Pc 4,5 period and concurrent magnetospheric and ionospheric phenomena. (After Y. Kato and T. Saito)

Satellite probe experiments have also shown magnetospheric oscillations above 100 sec period occurring simultaneously with field changes observed at the Earth's surface. J. G. Keys (1965) has studied pulsating radar echoes from the auroral zone *E* region south of New Zealand. The occurrence times, independence of *Kp*, typical period, and variation of period with latitude all match Pc 5 event characteristics. Coincident with the radar pulsation onsets, changes in the character of the magnetic record were observed at Macquarie Island. E. Kanada et al. (1964) found that the position of the centre of Pc 5 activity corresponded to the region

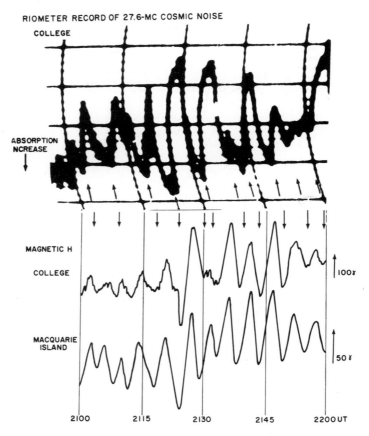

Fig. 2.18.   Cosmic noise absorption at College, Alaska and Pc 5 micropulsations at College and Macquarie Island. (After T. Sato)

returning auroral radar echoes. Fig. 2.18 illustrates one of the many cases of simultaneous *D* region ionospheric absorption of 27.6 Mc cosmic radio noise at College which were found to pulsate in unison with the magnetic records.

2.5 Pulsations with Irregular Forms

Irregular pulsations (Pi 1 and Pi 2), in the general frequency range from about 2.0 to 0.005 Hz have been shown to have a close relationship with other upper atmospheric auroral zone phenomena. The sudden appearances of large amplitude pulsations in this category have been called micropulsation storms (W. H. Campbell and S. Matsushita, 1962) and pulsation sudden commencements, pse (Y. Kato et al. 1956). They are typically a part of polar magnetic substorms (S. Akasofu and S. Chapman, 1963). The irregular form of the pulsations is found both in the individual oscillations and the amplitude envelope of the event (see Fig. 2.19). Spectral analyses of Pi's display a rather broad band of frequencies. Higher frequency components seem to be less common at lower latitudes and tend to fade more quickly than lower frequencies following large amplitude onsets. There seems to be a fair probability of enhanced activity twenty-four hours after the commencement of a large storm. The equinoxes are often times of large activity and the summer months relatively quiet.

Fig. 2.19.   Irregular pulsations at the conjugate auroral zone stations of Great Whale River, Canada and Byrd, Antarctica. Fluctuations are very similar at the two stations. The sudden onset of activity about 0240 Z is simultaneous at the two stations. (After J. A. Jacobs and C. S. Wright—DREP photograph 4178 B)

2.5.1 *Irregular Pulsations* Pi 1

These oscillations form, as a rule, the microstructure of slow electro-magnetic field disturbances, observed during the main phase of magnetic storms. They are a part of the microstructure of isolated bays and pulsation trains Pt. A connection with auroral intensity variations, bursts of X-rays, and absorption of cosmic noise has also been established. The connection of these oscillations to definite slow magnetic field disturbances, and the peculiarities and sequence of the development, define a family of genetically connected disturbances of the electromagnetic field (Fig. 2.20).

Fig. 2.20.   Family of genetically related disturbances. (After V. A. Troitskaya)

The scheme implies independent development, in the electromagnetic field, of oscillations to the right of the preceeding member of the family. Thus, Pc 1's may be observed on the records without analogs in the slower variations; on the other hand they may be the final phase of the microstructure of a very intensive bay during a magnetic storm.

Pi 1's may also appear on a background of almost quiet magnetic field, even in the auroral zones. While Pc 1's and Pi 1's are sometimes recorded simultaneously with slow disturbances, and sometimes as independent field disturbances, pt-type pulsations are always accompanied by disturbances of either Pi 1 type or of both Pi 1 + Pc 1. The most complete development of the disturbed field microstructure is expressed in an IPDP (intervals of pulsations with diminishing periods).

Pi 1's have an irregular form; their periods, as a rule are less than 15 sec (mainly 6–10 sec). Their amplitudes have maximum values in the auroral zones, and their intensity decreases sharply with latitude. W. H. Campbell and S. Matsushita (1962) found that their intensity is on the average 10 times greater at College (Alaska) than in California. Pi 1's are observed mainly early in the morning and late at night. V. A.

Troitskaya et al. (1962) found two maxima in their distribution. The first is connected with those Pi 1's which form the fine structure of slow disturbances and the second reflects Pi 1 excitation mainly against the background of a comparatively quiet field (see Fig. 2.21).

Fig. 2.21. Diurnal variation of Pi 1's at Lovozero (1957—1959). Those observed during disturbed periods are shown by the broken line, and those during quiet periods by the solid line. (after V. A. Troitskaya, L. V. Alperovich and N. V. Giorgio)

The most characteristic variation of Pi 1's during the solar cycle is the decrease in their number from years of solar maximum to solar minimum. For example, an analysis of the storms of 1957–1959 and of 1962–1963 shows a decrease in duration by a factor of 8–10 in the period close to minimum solar activity. In addition Pi 1 activity shows a distinct dependence on the Kp-index, increasing with increasing Kp.

2.5.2 Irregular Pulsations Pi 2

Pi 2's may occur against a quiet background as one or several series of oscillations, or they may coincide with the beginning of a bay. They are observed in all regions—sometimes the longitudinal extent over which they can be traced exceeding 100°. The most characteristic feature of Pi 2's (distinguishing them for instance, from Pc 4's) is their short

duration and the superposition of Pi 1's which may be followed on occasions by Pc 1's. J.A. Jacobs and K. Sinno (1960b) divided Pi 2's into
two groups, those occurring before a negative bay in the auroral zone
(Pt⁻) and those occurring either before a positive bay or against a
quiet field (Pt⁺). Maximum amplitudes are observed in the auroral
zones for the first group and near geomagnetic latitude 50° for the second
(Fig. 2.22 a, b).

Fig. 2.22. Amplitude dependence of Pi 2's on latitude a Pt⁻, b Pt⁺. (After J. A.
Jacobs and K. Sinno).

As in the case of auroral and geomagnetic bay activity, Pi 2 micropulsations have a maximum occurrence frequency around local midnight.
However, like Pc's, the maxima of the diurnal variations at different
stations show some longitudinal scattering. The relationship between
the occurrence of Pi 2's and planetary magnetic activity is not clear.
K. Yanagihara (1959) presented evidence that while auroral and geomagnetic bay activity increase towards sunspot maximum, Pi 2 activity
in low latitude regions decreases. On the other hand he found that the

probability of occurrence of a Pi 2 increases with increasing Kp index (K. Yanagihara, 1960). At the same time, Pi 1 activity increases towards sunspot maximum, suggesting either that Pi 1's and Pi 2's have different source mechanisms or that they have different modes of propagation over the Earth's surface.

T. Saito and S. Matsushita (1968) examined rapid run magnetograms of more than 6000 Pi 2 events associated with bay disturbances at Onagawa, Japan and Fredericksburg, Virginia, for the period 1956–1966 in a study of solar cycle effects. They confirmed that the yearly occurrence frequency of medium and small amplitude Pi 2's, as well as large ones, showed an inverse relation with solar activity. They also found clear maxima during the equinoctial months in sunspot declining and minimum years corresponding to the same seasonal behavior in the A_p magnetic index (cf T. Saito, 1965). There were also more Pi 2's in the fall than in the spring equinoxes and the local time of the maximum occurrence of Pi 2's changed from year to year between 2200–0100 LMT. They also found some evidence for a recurrence tendency—the recurrence period changing from about 29 days at the beginning of the solar cycle (sunspot maximum) to about 26 days at the end of the solar cycle. The same variation in recurrence period is found for A_p suggesting that the occurrence of Pi 2's depends on the solar wind coming from solar M regions. The solar active regions as expressed by sunspots, plages etc. shift gradually from about 40° heliographic latitude at the beginning of the solar cycle to about 5° at the end. Also the rotation period of the sun is about 29 days near 40° heliographic latitude and about 26 days near 5°. This suggests that the solar M regions, as well as the solar active regions gradually shift from about 40° heliographic latitude at the beginning of the solar cycle to about 5° at the end. The solar wind may then blow towards the Earth's magnetosphere most effectively at the end of the solar cycle, since the solar M region approaches closest to the sun–Earth line at that time. This may explain why both the occurrence frequency and the recurrence tendency of Pi 2's reach their maxima near the end of the solar cycle. T. Saito and S. Matsushita also found that the period of a Pi 2 associated with a large bay disturbance is shorter than that associated with a small bay—there is also a variation in the Pi 2 period from year to year with a minimum between years of solar maximum and solar minimum activity.

G. Rostoker (1967a) has shown that Pi 2's may be considered to consist of two separate contributions; the initial kick that is a broadband effect and the actual damped oscillation. Sometimes the initial kick may occur but insufficient energy is imparted to the mechanism of generation to cause an oscillation to take place. Such kicks often appear prior to an auroral breakup, and Rostoker refers to these occurrences as "one pulse effects". Spectral analysis of Pi 2 trains bears out this picture. G. Rostoker (1967b) found that, exclusive of Pi 1 activity, a Pi 2 may contain anywhere from one to several frequency components (see Figs. 2.23, 2.24). None of the frequency components in the spectra he obtained were present prior to the initiation of the Pi 2 event.

Fig. 2.23.   Example of a single frequency Pi 2 event. (After G. Rostoker)

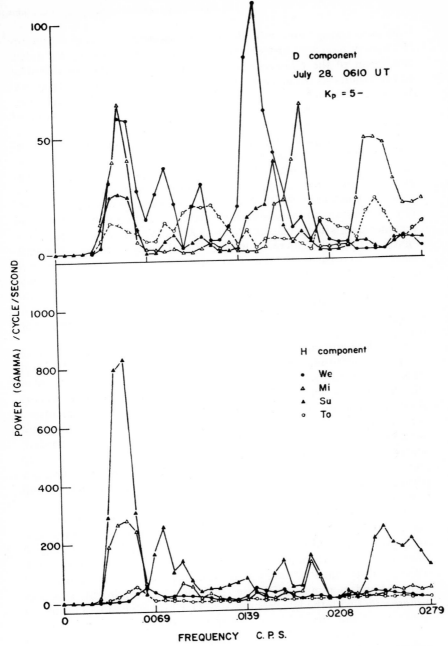

Fig. 2.24. Example of a Pi 2 event containing several frequency components. (After G. Rostoker)

Rostoker also found that the number of frequency components in a Pi 2 event increased approximately linearly with increasing Kp index, reminiscent of the relationship obtained by K. Yanagihara (1960) of the probability of occurrence of a Pi 2 as a function of the Kp index. The frequencies measured in each event were usually not harmonics of a fundamental frequency and thus each frequency may be thought of as having a separate generation from one another.

V. A. Troitskaya (1964) has presented evidence that the period of a Pi 2 decreases with increasing Kp index; however, this conclusion is a result of the assignment of a single frequency to a Pi 2 event by visual analysis of chart recordings. With the aid of power spectra of 18 Pi 2 events, G. Rostoker (1967b) showed that the minimum period in a Pi 2 event decreases with increasing Kp, whereas the maximum period in an event increases with increasing Kp up to $Kp \simeq 2\circ$, after which it decreases slightly with further increase in Kp. Visual analysis of the 18 events reveals a decrease in dominant apparent period with increasing Kp, in accordance with the results of Troitskaya. Rostoker's results indicate that the period of a given Pi 2 event does not change with latitude for a single event, but F. Eleman (1966) has shown that the average period of many Pi 2's at a given station is longer the closer the observing station is to the auroral zone.

M. L. T. Kannangara and P. C. B. Fernando (1969) carried out an analysis of nighttime Pi 2 micropulsations recorded at Colombo, over an uninterrupted period of one year from October 17, 1964, to October 16, 1965. They found that Pi 2 events were most prominent, especially about midnight, during the equinoxes and that their occurrence increased almost linearly with Kp up to a Kp level of at least 5. The dominant periodicity of Pi 2 events showed a definite Kp dependence, the median shifting smoothly from a value of about 100 sec at the $Kp=0$ level to about 45 sec at the $Kp=5$ level. Pi 2 oscillations tended to have longer periods when they occurred at or immediately before midnight, and to have shorter periods when they occurred before dawn.

It is generally agreed that Pi 2's are polarized in the horizontal plane in mid- and low-latitude regions, although there is usually a relatively strong vertical component in the vicinity of the auroral zone of an event. The results obtained at low-latitude stations by Y. Kato et al. (1956) indicate that Pi 2's are polarized in a clockwise sense before local midnight and in an anti-clockwise sense after local midnight. This is in disagreement with the later results of A. D. Christoffel and J. G. Linford (1966) who found that Pi 2's are polarized predominantly, although not always, in a clockwise sense in mid-latitude regions in the southern hemisphere. G. Rostoker (1967a) showed that the polarization of Pi 2's in mid-latitude regions in the northern hemisphere is predominantly in the anticlockwise sense, although cases of clockwise rotation are observed on occasion. He found that the sense of polarization does not depend on the position of the observing station relative to local midnight but that its geographical location relative to the source of the Pi 2 directly influences the polarization characteristics.

2.5.3 *Other Forms of* Pi *Activity*

L. R. Tepley (1966) has found that other types of signals may be observed, particularly during stormy periods, which are less regular in appearance than the continuous emissions but are more regular than noise bursts (Pi 1). Tepley refers to these signals as storm time emissions since all events observed so far have occurred during magnetically disturbed periods, often in conjunction with magnetic bays. Less formally he has called such signals, gurglers, since when monitored aurally on time compressed magnetic tape with a speed-up factor of 1 000–2 000, the signals are characterized by a sound similar to bubbles being blown under water. Occasionally, rising frequency structural elements are superimposed on Pi emissions and a composite signal may be placed in the transition category, gurgler-Pi 1. Transition signals are characterized aurally by bubbly sounds similar to those made by gurglers. The occurrence times of gurglers and gurgler-Pi 1 transition signals at Palo Alto, California, show a strong maximum around 2000 L.M.T. (0400 UT). W. J. Helms and J. P. Turtle (1964) found an almost identical occurrence curve for impulsive high frequency micropulsations recorded at Byrd Station and reported a strong intensification of visual auroral activity with each micropulsation burst.

R. Gendrin and S. Lacourly (1968) have distinguished five different types of Pi's in the frequency range 0.1–3 Hz, the two most important being SIP's and IPDP's.

(i) Continuous Noise. On sonagrams a continuous broad band noise often appears, the frequency of which is centered around 0.2–0.3 Hz. This noise has been noticed by other workers and L. R. Tepley and K. D. Amundsen (1965) found that it tended generally to have a broader frequency band during the night than during the day. The upper frequency increases during the evening hours and decreases during the morning hours (see Fig. 2.25). There does not seem to be any connection with the degree of magnetic activity.

(ii) Short irregular pulsations (SIP). In a noise burst, a train of short period micropulsations is often seen. R. Gendrin et al. (1966 d) have called them SIP's. SIP's seem to be a typical Pi-1 type of micropulsation and have been investigated in some detail at the Sogra-Kerguelen pair of stations. An SIP lasts only for several min and tends to be repeated

Fig. 2.25. Sonagrams of continuous noise at Kerguelen showing that the upper frequency increases during the evening hours and decreases during the morning hours. (After R. Gendrin and S. Lacourly)

a few times with a time interval of 10–20 min (see Fig. 2.26). They take place only in the beginning stages of geomagnetic bays accompanying long period (20–60 sec) irregular micropulsations. The onset of an SIP is simultaneous at Sogra and Kerguelen within ± 5 sec although the spectral contents of simultaneous SIP's are not identical. They are related to particle precipitation events and appear simultaneously over a wide area.

Fig. 2.26.   Sonagrams of SIP's at the two conjugate stations, Kerguelen and Sogra showing the impulsive nature, repetitive structure and simultaneity at the two stations. (After R. Gendrin, B. Kazak, G. Laurent and O. Raspopov)

(iii) **Irregular pulsations of diminishing period** (IPDP). These consist of a more or less narrow frequency band whose mean frequency increases fairly rapidly (typically from 0.5 to 1.5 Hz in 30 min). Superimposed on this noise appears some randomly scattered elements of higher intensity (see Fig. 2.5). This kind of event has often been noticed and given different names (e. g. gurglers (L. R. Tepley and K. Amundson, 1964), sweepers (R. R. Heacock, 1967 a). R. Gendrin et al. (1967) have published a very detailed study on IPDP's. They have identical spectra at conjugate points, the structured elements arriving simultaneously at both ends of the line of force. They generally occur between about 1700–0100 LMT (see Fig. 2.27) and seem to appear in a rather restricted longitudinal range and between geomagnetic latitudes 50–65°. Unlike "continuous noise",

Fig. 2.27. Diurnal variation of the occurre rate of IPDP's observed at Seattle, Washington. (After J. F. Kenney, H. B. Knaflich and H. B. Liemohn)

IPDP's are observed during days of high magnetic activity ($20 < \Sigma Kp < 35$) and often appear at the time of a negative bay. They are related to visual aurora and, on occasion, the spectrum of the luminosity of the aurora resembles that of the magnetic intensity. The increase of frequency during an IPDP often occurs at the same time as the appearance of auroral sporadic E. Satellite measurements show that there is a decrease in the flux of low energy (50–150 Kev) trapped electrons at the time of an IPDP. There is also a diminution in the size of the outer Van Allen radiation belt and an increase in the magnetic field measured in the tail of the magnetosphere at the time of occurrence of an IPDP (see also Chapter 6). It has been suggested that IPDP's are generated in the equatorial plane by a wave particle interaction with low energy $(10 \sim 100 \text{ Kev})$ protons on the evening side of the Earth at $\sim 5-6$ Earth radii. During the disconnection of the lines of force which accompanies such a precipitation, there is an inward motion of the instability region thus leading to an increase in the emitted frequency.

(iv) **Irregular pulsations of increasing period (IPIP)**. Such events have been detected recently. They are a daytime phenomenon and do not occur very frequently but can be distinguished from the continuous noise.

(v) **Auroral irregular pulsations (AIP)**. Near the auroral zone and during auroral disturbances a characteristic type of noise is observed, consisting of a continuous broad band signal of long duration. It is often preceeded by SIP bursts.

R. R. Heacock (1967b) distinguishes two subtypes of Pi. The first subtype are midnight Pi bursts. He finds (1966) that most weak impulsive noise bursts occurring on summer nights show an enhancement in the 2–6 sec period range. There seems to be an annual variation in the midfrequency of an enhancement with the lowest value occurring in summer —the midfrequency varying from approximately 0.2 Hz in daytime in summer to 0.3–1.0 Hz during dark nights in fall and winter. Bursts tend to be seen clearly on the records only when $Kp \leqslant 3$. At times of high Kp, bursts seem to be superimposed on other Pi activity and cannot be clearly distinguished. Sudden commencements (ssc's) and sudden impulses that occur during the nighttime at College, Alaska, rarely coincide with the onset of micropulsation bursts (although ssc's that occur at College during the daytime usually coincide with the onset of micropulsation events).

In addition to impulsive bursts, the records of Pi activity at College contain events which have a continuous nonimpulsive character, designated by R. R. Heacock as Pi(c). A subclass (elementary Pi(c)) are simple isolated events characterized by the auroral electrojet being nearly stationary just north of College. These events are characterized by simultaneous negative bays in the magnetic H and Z components. R. R. Heacock found that every elementary Pi(c) event which began in the interval 2300–0200 LMT was inaugurated with at least one Pi burst. Pi(c) can occur any time of the day, but are most intense in early morning near 0400 LMT. At high Kp values, Pi occurrence is increasingly dominated by Pi(c).

A general summary of the morphological properties of geomagnetic micropulsations is given in Table 2.4. (after V.A. Troitskaya and A.V. Gul'elmi, 1967).

Table 2.4. *General characteristics of geomagnetic micropulsations (after V. A. Troitskaya*

Classification (1963)	Period (sec)	Additional characteristics and namens	Average amplitude (γ)	Characteristic of the spectrum
Pc 1	0.2–5	Pearls. According to recent investigations they consist of two groups: $T<2$ sec and $T>2$ sec	0.05–0.1	Signals in a narrow band frequency range with periodic structure on sonograms
Pc 2 Pc 3 Pc 4	5–10 10–45 45–150	Continuous pulsations pc	0.1–1	Relatively regular pulsations with distinct mean period
Pc 5	150–600	pg (giant pulsations)	1–10	Relatively regular pulsations
Pi 1	1–40	Noise bursts	0.01–0.1	Wide band emission. Bursts of wide band emissions
IPDP	1–40 (1–10 for the regular part)	Gurglers Pi 1 + Pc 1	0.01–0.1	Wide band emissions with growing average frequency, and with separate, superimposed, structured elements (pearls)
Pi 2	40–150	Pulsation trains (pt) According to recent investigations they have periods up to 250 sec	1–5	Separate trains or series of oscillation trains

and A. V. Gul'elmi)

Time of occurrence	Character of planetary distribution	Connection with different types of magnetic activity
Daytime in auroral zone: night and early morning hours in middle latitudes	Antiphase relation for the envelope of the series in opposite hemispheres; the global character in one hemisphere depends on the period of Pc 1 and the state of SMIG	Increase of Pc-1 activity 1–2 hours before, and 4–7 days after a magnetic storm
Daytime	Global on the dayside, sometimes global for the whole earth; the modulation of amplitude—global	Decrease of period with increasing magnetic activity
Morning and evening hours	Local in latitude and not greatly extended in longitude; strong correlation of conjugate points; dependence of the period on latitude	Most typical for moderate magnetic activity
Night and early morning hours	Maximum in the auroral zone. Observed also in low and middle latitudes	Close correlation with aurora and connected with phenomena occurring simultaneously with aurora; X-ray bursts, etc.
Evening hours	Maximum in subauroral zone. Observed also in middle and low latitudes	Occur during the main phase of magnetic storms; coincide with aurora in low latitudes, and drastic changes of intensity in the radiation belts
Evening and night hours	On the night hemisphere in general, often over the whole globe	Occur on the initial phase of bays. Periods decrease with increasing magnetic activity. The greatest periods correspond to quiet days with $Kp=0$

References

Akasofu, S., Chapman, S.: The enhancement of the equatorial electrojet during polar magnetic sub-storms. J. Geophys. Res. **68**, 2375—2382 (1963).

Alldredge, L. R.: Instruments and geomagnetic stations. *Physics of Geomagnetic Phenomena*. (Ed. S. Matsushita and W. H. Campbell), Acad. Press pp. 29—66 (1967).

Ann. IGY, IV, Pt V, Geomagnetism Part **II**, 247—329 (1957).

Annexstad, J. O., Wilson, C. R.: Pc 1 fine structure phase shift at high latitude conjugate points. J. Geophys. Res. **73**, 3063—3065 (1968).

Baransky, L. N., Kazak, B. N., Geller, L. A.: Propagation velocity of Pc 1 waves in the electromagnetic field of the Earth. Dokl. Akad. Nauk SSSR No 1, **85**, 1967.

Bolshakova, O. V.: Continuous pulsations and dynamics of magnetosphere. Diss. Moscow, 1965.

Borsoukov, A. M., Ponsot, M. C.: Caractéristiques essentielles de la structure des oscillations en perles dans des régions géomagnétiquement conjugées. Ann. Géophys. **20**, 473—479 (1964).

Campbell, W. H.: Geomagnetic pulsations. *Physics of Geomagnetic Phenomena*. (Ed. S. Matsushita and W. H. Campbell), Acad. Press pp. 821—909 (1967).

— Matsushita, S.: Auroral zone geomagnetic micropulsations with periods of 5 to 30 seconds. J. Geophys. Res. **67**, 555—573 (1962).

— Stiltner, E. C.: Some characteristics of geomagnetic pulsations at frequencies near 1 c/s. J. Res. NBS, Radio Sci. **69 D**, 1117—1132 (1965).

Christoffel, A. D., Linford, J. G.: Diurnal properties of the horizontal geomagnetic micropulsation field in New Zealand. J. Geophys. Res. **71**, 891—897 (1966).

Dawson, J. A.: Geomagnetic micropulsations with emphasis placed on the properties of and interpretation of pearls. Ph. D. Thesis, Univ. Alaska 1965.

Duffus, H. J.: Techniques for measuring high frequency components of the geomagnetic field. *Methods and Techniques in Geophysics*. (Ed. S. K. Runcorn), Vol. 11, 81—121, Inter-Science Publ. 1966.

Duncan, R. A.: Some studies of geomagnetic micropulsations. J. Geophys. Res. **66**, 2087—2094 (1961).

Eleman, F.: Studies of giant pulsations, continuous pulsations and pulsation trains in the geomagnetic field. Arkiv. Geofys. **5**, 231—282 (1967).

Ellis, G. R. A.: Geomagnetic micropulsations. Aust. J. Phys. **13**, 625—632 (1960).

Fam Van-chi, Yanovskiy, B. M., Kovtun, A. A., Raspopov, O. M., Troitskaya, V. A., Schlich, R.: Investigation of type Pc 3 geomagnetic pulsations at magnetically conjugate points. Geomag. Aeron **VIII**, 94—97 (1968).

Gendrin, R., Troitskaya, V. A.: Preliminary results of a micropulsation experiment at conjugate points. J. Res. NBS Radio Sci. **69 D**, 1107—1116 (1965).

— Gokhberg, M., Lacourly, S., Troitskaya, V. A.: Étude en deux stations magnétiquement conjugées de la polarization des oscillations hydromagnétiques de type Pc 1. C. R. Acad. Sci. **262**, 786—789 (1966a).

— Lacourly, S., Gokhberg, M., Malevskaya, O., Troitskaya, V. A.: Polarization des oscillations hydromagnétiques de type Pc 1 observées en deux stations géomagnétiquement conjugées. Ann. Géophys. **22**, 329—337 (1966b).

— Gokhberg, M., Lacourly, S., Troitskaya, V. A.: Apparition simultanée de pulsations magnétiques d'ultrabasse fréquence en phase en deux points conjugées. C. R. Acad. Sci. **262**, 845—848 (1966c).

— Kazak, B., Laurent, G., Raspopov, O.: Caractéristiques nouvelles de certaines oscillations hydromagnétiques irrégulières. C. R. Acad. Sci. **263**, 841—843 (1966d).

— Lacourly, S., Troitskaya, V. A., Gokhberg, M., Shepetnov, R. V.: Caractéristiques des pulsations irrégulières de période décroissante (IPDP) et leurs relations avec les variations du flux des particules piégées dans la magnétosphère. Plan. Space Sci. **15**, 1239—1259 (1967).

— — Irregular micropulsations and their relations with the far magnetospheric perturbations. Ann. Géophys. **24**, 267—273 (1968).

Heacock, R. R.: The 4-second summertime micropulsation band at College. J. Geophys. Res. **71**, 2763—2775 (1966).

— Evening micropulsation events with a rising mid-frequency characteristic. J. Geophys. Res. **72**, 399—408 (1967 a).

— Two sub-types of type Pi micropulsations. J. Geophys. Res. **72**, 3905—3917 (1967 b).

— Hessler, V. P.: Pearl-type telluric current micropulsations at College. J. Geophys. Res. **67**, 3985—3995 (1962).

— — Telluric current micropulsation bursts. J. Geophys. Res. **68**, 953—954 (1963).

— — Sucksdorff, C., Kivinen, M. Kataja, E.: Variations in Pc 1 frequency with latitude. Nature **217**, 153—155 (1968).

Heirtzler, J. R.: A summary of the observed characteristics of geomagnetic micropulsations. *Natural Electromagnetic Phenomena below* 30 kc/s. (Ed. D. F. Bleil), Plenum Press pp. 351—372 (1964).

— Regular oscillations with periods of 5 sec to 7 min: the experimental approach. Rep. No. 8815 NBS, Boulder, Colorado 1965.

Helms, W. J., Turtle, J. P.: A cooperative report on the correlation between auroral, magnetic and ELF phenomena at Byrd Station, Antarctica. Stanford Elect. Lab. Tech. Rept. No. 3408-2 (1964).

Heppner, J. P.: Satellite and rocket observations. *Physics of Geomagnetic Phenomena.* (Ed. S. Matsushita and W. H. Campbell), Acad. Press. pp. 935—1036 (1967).

Herron, T. J.: Phase characteristics of geomagnetic micropulsations. J. Geophys. Res. **71**, 871—889 (1966).

Hultquist, B.: Plasma waves in the frequency range 0.001—10 cps in the Earth's magnetosphere and ionosphere. Space Sci. Rev. **5**, 599—695 (1966).

Hutton, R.: Equatorial micropulsations. J. Phys. Soc. Japan **17**, Suppl. **A-11**, 20—23 (1962).

— Equatorial effects. J. Res. NBS, Radio Sci. **69 D**, 1169—1177 (1965).

Jacobs, J. A., Sinno, K.: Occurrence frequency of geomagnetic pulsations, Pc. J. Geophys. Res. **65**, 107—133 (1960 a).

— — World-wide characteristics of geomagnetic micropulsations. Geophys. J. **3**, 333—353 (1960 b).

— Westphal, K. O.: Geomagnetic micropulsations. Physics and Chemistry of the Earth **5**, 157—224 (1964).

— Kato, Y., Matsushita, S., Troitskaya, V. A.: Classification of geomagnetic micropulsations. J. Geophys. Res. **69**, 180—181 (1964).

— Watanabe, T.: Theoretical notes on whistlers and periodic emissions in the hydromagnetic regime, Planet. Space Sci. **15**, 799—809 (1967).

Kaneda, E., Kokubun, S., Oguti, T., Nagata, T.: Auroral radar echoes associated with Pc 5. Rept. Ionos. Space Res. Japan **XVIII**, 165—172 (1964).

Kannangara, M. L. T., Fernando, P. C. B.: Nighttime equatorial Pi 2 micropulsations. J. Geophys. Res. **74**, 844—852 (1969).

Kato, Y.: Report of Working Group IV-10 Micropulsations Pc 1, Pc 2, Pi 1, Pi 2. IAGA Bull. **25**, 91—100 (1967).

— Watanabe, T.: A survey of observational knowledge of the geomagnetic pulsation. Sci. Rep. Tohoku Univ. Ser. 5, Geophys. **8**, 157—185 (1957).

— Ossaka, J., Watanabe, T., Okuda, M., Tamao, T.: Investigation on the magnetic disturbance by the induction magnetograph, V, on the rapid pulsation psc. Sci. Rept. Tohoku Univ., Ser. 5, Geophys. 7, 136—146 (1956).

— Saito, T.: Secular and annual variation in the periods of Pc 4 and Pc 5. Rept. Ionos. Space Res. Japan XVIII, 183—187 (1964).

Kenney, J. F., Knaflich, H. B.: A systematic study of structured micropulsations. J. Geophys. Res. 72, 2857—2869 (1967).

— Deaton, T. K., Miller, J. E.: Improved displays for measuring power spectra of complex non stationary signals. Rev. Sci. Instr. 38, 665—667 (1967).

Keys, J. G.: Pulsating auroral radar echoes and their possible hydromagnetic association. J. Atmos. Terr. Phys. 27, 385—393 (1965).

Linford, J. G.: Ph. D. thesis. Victoria Univ. Wellington, New Zealand 1969.

Lokken, J. E.: Instrumentation for receiving electromagnetic noise below 3,000 cps. Natural Electromagnetic Phenomena below 30 kc/s. (Ed. D. F. Bleil), Plenum Press, pp. 373—428 (1964).

Matuura, N.: Characteristics of large amplitude geomagnetic pulsations. Rept. Ionos. Space Res. Japan 15, 192—214 (1961).

Matveeva, E. T., Troitskaya, V. A.: Investigations of pearltype pulsations for the years 1957—1964. Rep. Inst. Phys. Earth, Moscow 1965.

Obayashi, T., Jacobs, J. A.: Geomagnetic pulsations and the Earth's outer atmosphere. Geophys. J. 1, 53—63 (1958).

Obertz, P., Raspopov, O. M.: Study of the spatial characteristics of type Pc 5 geomagnetic pulsations. Geomag. Aeron. VIII, 424—427 (1968).

Ol', A. I.: Long period gigantic geomagnetic field pulsations. Geomag. Aeron 3, 90—95 (1963).

Pope, J. H.: Dynamic spectral characteristics of micropulsation pearls. J. Geophys. Res. 70, 3595—3603 (1965).

Rostoker, G.: The polarization characteristics of Pi 2 micropulsations and their relation to the determination of possible source mechanisms for the production of nighttime impulsive micropulsation activity. Can. J. Phys. 45, 1319—1335 (1967a).

— The frequency spectrum of Pi 2 micropulsation activity and its relationship to planetary magnetic activity. J. Geophys. Res. 72, 2032—2039 (1967b).

Saito, T.: Statistical studies on three types of geomagnetic continuous pulsations, Pt I. Sci. Rept. Tohoku Univ. Ser. 5, Geophys. 14, 81—106 (1962).

— Mechanisms of geomagnetic continuous pulsations and physical states of the exosphere. J. Geomag. Geoelect. XVI, 115—151 (1964a).

— Annual and semi-annual variations in the exospheric plasma densities deduced from pc 4 and pc 5. Rep. Ionos. Space Res. Japan XVIII, 197—212 (1964b).

— A new index of geomagnetic pulsation and its relation to solar M region, Pt 3, Annual variation and latitudinal dependence of M regions. Rept. Ionos. Res. Japan 19, 30—46 (1965).

— Matsushita, S.: Solar cycle effects on geomagnetic Pi 2 pulsations. J. Geophys. Res. 73, 267—286 (1968).

Sato, T.: Long period geomagnetic oscillations in southern high latitudes. Geomag. Aeron. 4, Antarctic Res. Ser. (Ed. A. H. Waynick), Amer. Geophys. Union 173—188 (1965).

Shchepetnov, R. V.: Classification of Pi 2 pulsations Geomag. i. Aeron.

Siebert, M.: Geomagnetic pulsations with latitude dependent periods and their relation to the structure of the magnetosphere. Planet. Space Sci. 12, 137—147 (1964).

Smith, H. W.: Some observations and characteristics of type Pc 1 geomagnetic micropulsations. J. Geophys. Res. 69, 1875—1881 (1964).

Tepley, L. R.: Low latitude observations of fine structured hydromagnetic emissions. J. Geophys. Res. **69**, 2273—2290 (1964).
— Regular oscillations near 1 c/s observed at middle and low latitudes. J. Res. NBS, Radio Sci. **69 D**, 1089—1105 (1965).
— Recent investigations of hydromagnetic emissions, Pt 1 Experimental observations. J. Geomag. Geoelect. **18**, 227—256 (1966).
— Amundsen, K. D.: Notes on sub ELF emissions observed during magnetic storms. J. Geophys. Res. **69**, 3749—3754 (1964).
— — Observations of continuous sub ELF emissions in the frequency range 0.2 to 1.0 cycles per second. J. Geophys. Res. **70**, 234—239 (1965).
— Landshoff, R. K.: Wave guide theory for ionospheric propagation of hydromagnetic emissions. J. Geophys. Res. **71**, 1499—1504 (1966).
Terada, T.: On the rapid periodic variations of terrestrial magnetism. J. Coll. Sci., Tokyo Imperial Univ. **37**, Art. 9, 1—85 (1917).
Troitskaya, V. A.: Rapid variations of the electromagnetic field of the Earth. Research in Geophysics Vol. 1. pp. 485—532, M. I. T. Press 1964.
— Micropulsations and the state of the magnetosphere. *Solar-Terrestrial Physics.* (Ed. J. W. King and W. S. Newman), pp. 213—274, Acad. Press 1967.
— Melnikova, M. V.: On the characteristic intervals of pulsations diminishing by periods (10—1 sec) in the electromagnetic field of the earth and their relation to phenomena in the upper atmosphere. Dok. Akad. Nauk. **128**, 917 (1959).
— Alperovich, L. V., Giorgio, N. V.: On the relation between short-period pulsations of the electromagnetic field of the earth and aurora. Izv. Akad. Nauk. SSSR., Geophys. Ser. **2**, 262—270 (1962).
— Gendrin, R., Stefant, R.: Observations en points conjugées de haute latitude des emissions hydromagnétiques structurées. C. R. Acad. Sci. **259**, 1175—1178 (1964).
— — Caractéristiques nouvelles der IPDP du champ magnétique terrestre. Inter-Union Symp. Solar Terrestrial Physics, Belgrade, 1966.
— Gul'elmi, A. V.: Geomagnetic micropulsations and diagnostics of the magnetosphere. Space Sci. Rev. **7**, 689—768 (1967).
Voelker, H.: On the latitude dependence of Pc-type micropulsations: results of observations on a north-south profile through Europe. Rep. No. 8815 NBS, Boulder, Colorado 1965.
Wentworth, R. C., Tepley, L. R., Amundsen, K. D., Heacock, R. R.: Intra- and interhemisphere differences in occurrence times of hydromagnetic emissions. J. Geophys. Res. **71**, 1492—1498 (1966).
Whitham, K.: Measurement of the geomagnetic elements. *Methods and Techniques in Geophysics.* (Ed. S. K. Runcorn), Wiley (Interscience) pp. 104—167 (1960).
Yanagihara, K.: Some characters of geomagnetic pulsation pt and accompanied oscillation spt. J. Geomag. Geoelect. **10**, 172—176 (1959).
— Geomagnetic pulsations in middle latitudes, morphology and its interpretation. Mem. Kakioka Mag. Obs. **9/2**, 15—74 (1960).
— Geomagnetic micropulsations with periods from 0.03 to 10 seconds in the auroral zones with special reference to conjugate point studies. J. Geophys. Rev. **68**, 3383—3397 (1963).

3 Magneto-Hydrodynamic Waves

3.1 Alfvén Waves

Electromagnetic waves cannot propagate in rigid conductors. However, H. Alfvén showed in 1942 that in a steady magnetic field waves of low enough frequency can propagate in fluids of high electrical conductivity. Since such waves are attenuated by electrical resistance—the attenuation per wave length being proportioned to the resistivity divided by the wave length—they are difficult to observe on a small scale. For strong interaction between electromagnetic and hydrodynamic phenomena, S. Lundquist (1952) obtained the criterion

$$(3.1) \qquad\qquad BL\sigma\rho^{-\frac{1}{2}} \gg 1$$

where L is the linear dimension of a liquid conductor, of density ρ, and conductivity σ in the presence of a magnetic field B. It can easily be seen that under normal laboratory conditions, this condition is not satisfied and magneto-hydrodynamic effects are not observed. Thus for mercury with $L = 10$ cm, and $B = 1\,000\,\Gamma$, the value of the left-hand side is 10^{-1}. The situation, however, is very different in problems of cosmic physics. Because of the enormous dimensions involved in such cases the criterion (3.1) is easily satisfied and considerable interaction between electromagnetic and hydrodynamic phenomena can be expected. Many attempts have been made in recent years to explain geomagnetic micropulsations in terms of magnetohydrodynamic wave action. For a perfectly conducting inviscid, incompressible fluid of density ρ permeated by a uniform magnetic field $\boldsymbol{B}_0$, it can be shown that a small disturbance can propagate in the direction of the magnetic field with a velocity V_A given by

$$(3.2) \qquad\qquad V_A = (4\pi\rho)^{-\frac{1}{2}} B_0 .$$

V_A is called the Alfvén velocity. If the disturbance varies as $\exp i(\boldsymbol{k}\cdot\boldsymbol{r} - \omega t)$ where $\boldsymbol{k}$ is the propagation vector and ω the angular frequency, it is easy to obtain, under the same assumptions, the dispersion equation

$$(3.3) \qquad\qquad \omega = k V_A \cos\theta$$

where θ is the angle between $\boldsymbol{k}$ and $\boldsymbol{B}_0$. The phase velocity $V_A \cos\theta$ is equivalent to motion of the phase fronts in the direction $\boldsymbol{B}_0$ with speed V_A.

The restriction to plane waves makes the Alfvén wave transverse i.e. the local fluid velocity v is perpendicular to k and the disturbance field b is perpendicular to B_0. When the effects of plasma pressure are taken into account, additional modes appear.

If the disturbance in the pressure is isotropic and proportional to the disturbance in density, the transverse mode is unaffected but two compressional waves (a fast and a slow mode) are set up in addition. The phase velocities $V = \omega/k$ of these two magneto-sonic or magneto-acoustic waves are given by the roots of the quadratic equation

$$(3.4) \qquad V^4 - V^2(V_A^2 + V_S^2) + V_A^2 V_S^2 \cos^2\theta = 0$$

where $V_S = (dp/d\rho)^{\frac{1}{2}}$ is the speed of sound. Thus

$$(3.5) \qquad V^2 = \tfrac{1}{2}\{V_A^2 + V_S^2 \pm (V_A^4 + V_S^4 - 2V_A^2 V_S^2 \cos 2\theta)^{\frac{1}{2}}\}.$$

If $\theta = 0$, the roots of equation (3.4) are $\pm V_S$ and $\pm V_A$ so that the motion is a superposition of a pure Alfvén wave and a pure acoustic wave both travelling in the direction of the magnetic field. When $\theta = \pi/2$, the roots of equation (3.4) are zero and $\pm \sqrt{V_S^2 + V_A^2}$ and thus there is only one mode, in which the waves are propagated at right angles to the magnetic field with speed $\sqrt{V_S^2 + V_A^2}$.

The above assumptions on the pressure variation will not, however, be realized in the magnetosphere, where the major contribution to the pressure comes from energetic protons ($\sim 10^9\ °K$). The speed of these protons is comparable to the maximum value of V_A in the magnetosphere so that transport of the disturbance by particles may be important —the disturbance in the particles at one place being affected by the disturbance field everywhere. Also for the thermal particles ($1000\ °K \sim 2000\ °K$) collisions will not have time to remove the anisotropy of the velocity distribution due to anisotropic compression, so that the perturbations in pressure parallel and perpendicular to B_0 will, in general, be different.

3.2 The Equations of Small Hydromagnetic Oscillations

In order to relate the phenomena of electrodynamics and hydrodynamics, Maxwell's equations and the basic equations of hydrodynamics are used. The resulting equations are exceedingly complex and, in general, exact solutions cannot be obtained. In special applications, some simplifications are possible which under certain conditions lead to solutions. It follows from a consideration of the orders of magnitude of the quantities involved that in problems of cosmic physics displacement currents are negligible in comparison with the conduction current.

Therefore Maxwell's first equation is simply

(3.6) $$\text{curl}\,\boldsymbol{B} = \frac{4\pi}{c}\,\boldsymbol{j}$$

where $\boldsymbol{B}$ is the magnetic field strength and $\boldsymbol{j}$ the current density. In addition $\boldsymbol{B}$ and $\boldsymbol{j}$ satisfy the equations

(3.7) $$\text{div}\,\boldsymbol{B} = 0 \text{ and div}\,\boldsymbol{j} = 0\,.$$

Maxwell's second equation which connects the electric field intensity $\boldsymbol{E}$ with the change of magnetic flux $\boldsymbol{B}$ is

(3.8) $$\text{curl}\,\boldsymbol{E} = \frac{-1}{c}\,\frac{\partial \boldsymbol{B}}{\partial t}\,.$$

Ohm's law for a medium moving with velocity $\boldsymbol{v}$ is

(3.9) $$\boldsymbol{j} = \sigma\left(\boldsymbol{E} + \frac{\boldsymbol{v}}{c} \times \boldsymbol{B}\right).$$

Considering the outer atmosphere as a perfect conductor ($\sigma \to \infty$) this becomes

(3.10) $$\boldsymbol{E} = \frac{-\boldsymbol{v}}{c} \times \boldsymbol{B}\,.$$

The basic equation of hydrodynamics can be written in the form

(3.11) $$\rho\frac{d\boldsymbol{v}}{dt} = \boldsymbol{C} + \boldsymbol{j} \times \boldsymbol{B}/c$$

where ρ is the density, $\boldsymbol{v}$ the velocity, and $\boldsymbol{C}$ the sum of all external, non-magnetic forces. The term $\boldsymbol{j} \times \boldsymbol{B}/c$ is the mechanical force exerted by the magnetic field $\boldsymbol{B}$ on a volume element carrying the current density $\boldsymbol{j}$. d/dt is the mobile operator defined as

(3.12) $$\frac{d}{dt} = \frac{\partial}{\partial t} + \boldsymbol{v}\cdot\text{grad}\,.$$

Considering the medium to be incompressible, equation (3.11) is supplemented by

(3.13) $$\text{div}\,\boldsymbol{v} = 0\,.$$

This assumption has been reviewed by A. Lehnert (1956).

J. W. Dungey (1954a, b) has shown that for Alfvén waves in the outer atmosphere the effects of viscosity, which is usually the most important cause of attenuation, can be neglected when considering long-period oscillations in the presence of the Earth's magnetic field.

Since the magnetic pressure gradient due to the disturbance is small compared with the magnetic force, equation (3.11) reduces to

$$(3.14) \qquad \rho \frac{d\boldsymbol{v}}{dt} = \boldsymbol{j} \times \boldsymbol{B}/c .$$

These are the basic equations which have been applied to the problem of micropulsations.

From equations (3.6) and (3.14)

$$(3.15) \qquad \rho \frac{d\boldsymbol{v}}{dt} = \frac{-1}{4\pi} \boldsymbol{B} \times \operatorname{curl} \boldsymbol{B} .$$

Considering $\boldsymbol{B}$ as the sum of a constant dipole field $\boldsymbol{B}_0$ and a small disturbance $\boldsymbol{b}$ introduced through the motion of the medium where $|\boldsymbol{B}_0| \gg |\boldsymbol{b}|$ and assuming that $|\partial v/\partial t| \gg |(\boldsymbol{v} \cdot \operatorname{grad})\boldsymbol{v}|$, equation (3.15) becomes

$$(3.16) \qquad 4\pi \rho \frac{\partial \boldsymbol{v}}{\partial t} = - \boldsymbol{B}_0 \times \operatorname{curl} \boldsymbol{b} .$$

Taking the vector product of the time derivative of this equation with $\boldsymbol{B} = \boldsymbol{B}_0 + \boldsymbol{b} \simeq \boldsymbol{B}_0$ it follows that

$$4\pi \rho \left(\frac{\partial^2 \boldsymbol{v}}{\partial t^2} \times \boldsymbol{B} \right) = - \boldsymbol{B}_0 \times (\operatorname{curl} \dot{\boldsymbol{b}}) \times \boldsymbol{B}_0$$

which, using equations (3.10) and (3.8), may be further written as

$$(3.17) \qquad -4\pi \rho \frac{\partial^2 \boldsymbol{E}}{\partial t^2} = \boldsymbol{B}_0 \times (\operatorname{curl} \operatorname{curl} \boldsymbol{E}) \times \boldsymbol{B}_0 .$$

This is the general wave equation for Alfvén waves in a non-uniform magnetic field when the pressure gradient is omitted. J. W. Dungey (1954a, b), using spherical polar coordinates (R, θ, ϕ) with $\boldsymbol{B}_0 = (B_R, B_\theta, 0)$, showed that two modes may be excited—poloidal and toroidal oscillations which in general will be coupled. This system will have eigenperiods corresponding to eigenfunctions which must satisfy certain boundary conditions.

The equation governing poloidal oscillations is

$$
\left\{ \frac{4\pi \rho}{B_0^2} \frac{\partial^2}{\partial t^2} - \frac{\partial^2}{\partial R^2} - R^{-2} \sin\theta \frac{\partial}{\partial \theta} (\sin\theta)^{-1} \frac{\partial}{\partial \theta} \right\} (R \sin\theta \, E_\phi)
$$

$$(3.18)$$

$$
= \sin\theta \left\{ B_R \frac{\partial}{\partial \theta} - B_\theta R \frac{\partial}{\partial R} \right\} (R \sin\theta)^{-1} \frac{\partial v_\phi}{\partial \phi} .
$$

The right-hand side of this equation shows that poloidal oscillations are connected with toroidal oscillations (v_ϕ) of the outer atmosphere.

The equation governing toroidal oscillations is

$$\left\{ 4\pi\rho\frac{\partial^2}{\partial t^2} - \frac{1}{(R\sin\theta)^2}\left[(\boldsymbol{B}_0\cdot\nabla)(R\sin\theta)^2(\boldsymbol{B}_0\cdot\nabla) + B_0^2\frac{\partial^2}{\partial\phi^2} \right] \right\}\left(\frac{v_\phi}{R\sin\theta} \right)$$

(3.19)

$$= \frac{1}{(R\sin\theta)^3}\left(\frac{B_R}{R}\frac{\partial}{\partial\theta} - B_\theta\frac{\partial}{\partial R} \right)\left(R\sin\theta\frac{\partial E_\phi}{\partial\phi} \right).$$

(3.18) and (3.19) are the two basic equations which together with the boundary conditions describe the behaviour of the outer atmosphere due to a disturbance. However, the equations are far too complicated to be of much use in studying geomagnetic micropulsations, and some simplifying assumptions must be made.

Assuming axial symmetry, i.e. $\partial/\partial\phi = 0$, the equation of poloidal oscillations takes the form

(3.20) $$\left\{ \frac{4\pi\rho}{B_0^2}\frac{\partial^2}{\partial t^2} - \frac{\partial^2}{\partial R^2} - R^{-2}\sin\theta\frac{\partial}{\partial\theta}(\sin\theta)^{-1}\frac{\partial}{\partial\theta} \right\}(R\sin\theta\, E_\phi) = 0$$

and that of toroidal oscillations becomes

(3.21) $$\left\{ 4\pi\rho\frac{\partial^2}{\partial t^2} - (R\sin\theta)^{-2}\left[(\boldsymbol{B}_0\cdot\nabla)(R\sin\theta)^2(\boldsymbol{B}_0\cdot\nabla) \right] \right\}\left(\frac{v_\phi}{R\sin\theta} \right) = 0.$$

The assumption $\partial/\partial\phi = 0$ implies a decoupling of the two modes of hydromagnetic oscillations and the disturbance may then be considered to occur in phase over the whole earth. It follows that equation (3.20) for poloidal oscillations governs the following set of quantities

$$(0; 0; E_\phi); (b_R; b_\theta; 0); (v_R; v_\theta; 0).$$

The remaining set

$$(E_R; E_\theta; 0); (0; 0; b_\phi); (0; 0; v_\phi)$$

are governed by equation (3.21) for toroidal oscillations.

In the equation for toroidal oscillations (3.21), the only spatial derivatives which occur are those in the operator $(\boldsymbol{B}_0\cdot\nabla)$ operating on the function v_ϕ; this can be interpreted as the derivative of v_ϕ in the direction of $\boldsymbol{B}_0$. Thus the equation can be interpreted as a wave equation where the disturbance propagates along a line of force. Choosing for $\boldsymbol{B}_0$ a dipole field, the equation represents the wave equation governing the time-space relationship of a disturbance which propagates along the magnetic lines of force of the dipole. It is in this sense that one speaks of oscillations of the lines of force. K. O. Westphal and J. A. Jacobs (1962) have derived the equations of small hydromagnetic oscillations in cylindrical coordinates with the main magnetic field lying in the plane perpendicular to the axis of the cylinder. Since the structure of the equations in this system is somewhat simpler than those in spherical polar coordinates (3.18) and (3.19), they were able to obtain the eigen periods of toroidal oscillations as a function of latitude without making any approximations. With the aid of a computer they were also able to extend the calculations to the case of a non-uniform plasma density distribution and also for a compressed dipole field. These will be discussed later in Chapter 5. Theoretical studies of propagation properties have also provided more realistic estimates of poloidal and toroidal mode periods (R. L. Carovillano and H. R. Radoski, 1967), better justification for field line guidance of Alfvén waves in the magnetosphere (J. A. Fejer and H. F. Lee, 1967), and a comprehensive treatment of transmission, mode coupling and guidance in the ionosphere (C. Greifinger and P. S. Greifinger). These will be discussed in more detail in later chapters.

3.3 The Dispersion Relation

An effect neglected by the use of equation (3.10) is the Hall electric field (caused by the difference in mass of electrons and positive ions). This becomes important when the wave frequency is comparable to the gyro frequency of the ions and causes dispersion. Consider now a cold, homogeneous plasma consisting of ions and electrons immersed in a uniform static magnetic field B_0. On the zero-temperature assumption the ions and electrons are motionless in the unperturbed state. Thus one essential quality which distinguishes a plasma from an ordinary gas viz, the almost free streaming of the particles is absent in this cold plasma model. On the other hand, the inertial effects of the ions and electrons are retained and all the important resonances appear. In spite of its limitations the cold plasma model gives a reasonably accurate description of the small amplitude perturbations which occur in a hot plasma.

In the cold plasma model each particle oscillates about a fixed position in space under the influence of the electromagnetic field of the wave. All dissipative effects (including collisions) are neglected as are forces which are quadratic in the particle velocities. In the unperturbed state of the plasma, the coefficients of the stress tensor are all zero—in the perturbed state, only small amplitude motions of the particles are considered. Moreover, the strength of the oscillating magnetic fields induced by currents in the plasma remains small compared to the strength of the static magnetic field.

If all first order field quantities vary as $\exp i(\mathbf{k} \cdot \mathbf{r} - \omega t)$, the dispersion relation may be written (T. H. Stix, 1962),

$$(3.22) \qquad \tan^2 \theta = -\frac{P(n^2 - R)(n^2 - L)}{(Sn^2 - RL)(n^2 - P)}$$

where

$$(3.23) \qquad R = 1 - \sum_k \frac{\Omega_k^2}{\omega^2} \left(\frac{\omega}{\omega + \varepsilon_k \omega_k} \right),$$

$$(3.24) \qquad L = 1 - \sum_k \frac{\Omega_k^2}{\omega^2} \left(\frac{\omega}{\omega - \varepsilon_k \omega_k} \right),$$

$$(3.25) \qquad P = 1 - \sum_k \frac{\Omega_k^2}{\omega^2}$$

and

$$(3.26) \qquad S = \tfrac{1}{2}(R + L).$$

ω_k is the cyclotron frequency for particles of the k-th type, i.e.

$$(3.27) \qquad \omega_k = \left| \frac{Z_k e B_0}{m_k c} \right|$$

and Ω_k is the plasma frequency defined by the equation

$$(3.28) \qquad \Omega_k^2 = \frac{4\pi n_k Z_k^2 e^2}{m_k}.$$

n_k is the number density of particles of mass m_k with charge of magnitude $Z_k e$. The sign of the charge, ± 1, is given by ε_k. $\mathbf{n}$ is the dimensionless vector which has the direction of the propagation vector $\mathbf{k}$ and the magnitude of the refractive index i.e.

$$(3.29) \qquad \mathbf{n} = \frac{c}{\omega} \mathbf{k}.$$

The magnitude $n = |\mathbf{n}|$ is thus the ratio of the velocity of light c to the phase velocity. Finally θ is the angle between $\mathbf{B}_0$ and $\mathbf{n}$. It follows from equation (3.22) that the dispersion relation for propagation at $\theta = 0$ (i.e. along $\mathbf{B}_0$) reduces to

$$(3.30) \qquad P = 0, \quad n_R^2 = R, \quad n_L^2 = L.$$

For propagation at $\theta = \pi/2$ (transverse to $\mathbf{B}_0$),

$$(3.31) \qquad n_x^2 = \frac{RL}{S} = \frac{2RL}{R + L}, \quad n_0^2 = P.$$

The symbols R, L, x and 0 stand for right, left, extraordinary and ordinary.

A number of simplifications arise if we consider a plasma formed of electrons with ions of a single charge-to-mass ratio. In this case we have the charge neutrality relation viz $n_i Z_i = n_e$ and in addition a number of terms may be neglected because of the very large ion to electron mass ratio. Further approximations and simplification of the dispersion equation can be made depending upon the frequency range of interest. In the magnetosphere at a distance of $L = 5.6$, $B_0 \simeq 170\gamma$ and the electron gyrofrequency

$$\omega_e = \frac{B_0 e}{m_e c} \text{ rad/sec} \simeq 4.8 \times 10^3 \text{ Hz}.$$

The proton gyrofrequency

$$\omega_i = \left(\frac{m_e}{m_i}\right) \omega_e \simeq 2.6 \text{ Hz}.$$

Again the electron plasma frequency is given by the equation

$$\Omega_e^2 = 4\pi n_e e^2 / m_e$$

so that taking $n_e \simeq 10 \text{ cm}^{-1}$, we have $\Omega_e \simeq 2.8 \times 10^4 \text{ Hz}$ and the proton gyrofrequency

$$\Omega_i = \left(\frac{m_e}{m_i}\right)^{\frac{1}{2}} \Omega_e \simeq 6.5 \times 10^2 \text{ Hz}.$$

Thus at $L = 5.6$, we have $\Omega_e > \omega_e > \Omega_i \gg \omega_i$.

3.4 Theories of Pc Oscillations

The observed magnetic activity at the Earth's surface reflects the nature of the source of the disturbance and is modified by the hydromagnetic (hm) properties of the Earth's magnetosphere and outer atmosphere and also by the Earth's crust. M. J. Davidson and J. R. Heirtzler (1968) studied the spatial coherence of geomagnetic rapid variations by computing the auto and cross spectra of time variations of the total intensity for a number of pairs of stations. The stations were set up in the northeastern United States and were separated by distances of up to 550 km in the north–south and east–west directions. On the basis of power density spectra they divided geomagnetic variations into two major components—a background component (because it appears to be always present) and the other component, micropulsation activity.

The background component appears to be due to turbulence in the Sq current system since the spectrum amplitude is related to the strength of Sq, the cross-station coherence is high and the relative phase undergoes a change of sign at the edges of the Sq current system. The second component includes the regular sinusoidal variations which appear as spectrum peaks rising above the background component. When two or more pulsation bands occur simultaneously they are incoherent with one another and incoherent with the background component. It would thus appear that independent excitation mechanisms must exist for the background component and for simultaneous pulsations in different period ranges. The micropulsations also have measurable phase differences between stations. At the mid band of the pulsation activity the relative phase angle is not zero, although the slope of relative phase versus frequency is small—suggesting that the mid-band energy has arrived nearly simultaneously at the two stations, even though the relative phase may be as great as 120°. M. J. Davidson and J. R. Heirtzler suggest that the simplest model that would produce such an effect is a local eddy in a near vertical plane that is rotating or precessing about a vertical axis. With this type of model the relative phase would be a function of source configuration, source height and station separation. It is also conceivable that purely local and independent sources could produce cross spectra results similar to those observed by Davidson and Heirtzler.

According to modern ideas, micropulsations are caused by hm waves which can be generated on the boundary of the magnetosphere and within it (e. g. during the injection of plasma). These waves propagate in the magnetosphere both along the lines of force (toroidal pulsations) and across the lines of force (poloidal pulsations). In their general form the equations of hm waves in the magnetosphere have not yet been solved. To simplify the problem, toroidal and poloidal oscillations are usually treated separately.

The change in the type of polarization which is observed at different latitudes (e.g. the transition from elliptical to linear polarization) may possibly be explained by the transformation, under certain conditions, of poloidal waves into toroidal waves due to the coupling of these two oscillations, which has not been taken into account. If the change of periods and polarization with latitude are known, it is possible to determine the distance in the equatorial plane at which this transformation of hm waves takes place.

On reaching the lower limit of the ionosphere hm waves are transformed into electromagnetic waves which are observed on the surface of the Earth as pulsations of the magnetic field and earth currents. Davidson and Heirtzler point out, however, that the fundamental and low order modes would produce in phase variations over large parts of the Earth's surface. Higher mode solutions on the other hand, which are equivalent to wave guide or cavity resonance theories are capable of producing the required large apparent phase velocities across the surface of the Earth. Theoretical research has shown that, for hm waves, the magnetosphere behaves as a layered inhomogeneous medium, whose coefficient of refraction changes with altitude. At a height of about 2000–3000 km the vertical gradient of the refractive index increases rapidly. The existence of such a region causes the formation of cavities dividing the magnetosphere into two parts. In each of them, under the influence of a disturbing agent, resonant oscillations can originate which may be observed on the Earth's surface as micropulsations. The periods of these pulsations characterize the dimensions of the cavities; their intensity and modulation depend on the activity of the primary source and on its structure. The sunlit ionosphere is practically opaque to pulsations with periods less than 1 sec. It is probable therefore, that we observe a cutoff of the pulsation spectrum at frequencies of 3–5 Hz. Besides this type of excitation, short-period pulsations may be set up during the injection of plasma into the ionosphere. In this case the region of generation is in the immediate vicinity of the Earth, and the characteristics of such pulsations are, to a great extent, connected with the properties and structure of the plasma clouds.

Using theoretical models, regular pulsations of the electromagnetic field of the Earth covering the whole spectral range may be explained by resonance excitations in the cavities of the magnetosphere. It must not be forgotten however that the frequency characteristics of the system (the outer boundary of the magnetosphere—the lower limit of the ionosphere) are changing and are considerably influenced by many factors (the pressure of the solar wind which squeezes the magnetosphere and determines its dimensions, the distribution of plasma within the magnetosphere, the presence of additional sources of disturbances in the magnetosphere, etc.). Thus, even with one type of input disturbance of the system, various phenomena may be observed on the Earth's surface due to changes in the transient characteristics of the system.

Theoretical investigations of micropulsations are hindered by some of their characteristics. Thus wave lengths in the low-frequency end of their spectrum (Pc 3–Pc 5, Pi 2) are comparable with the dimensions of the magnetosphere, and a solution of the problem requires numerical methods. At the other end of the frequency range (Pc 1), wavelengths are significantly smaller than the linear dimensions of the magnetosphere, so that methods of geometrical optics can be used in studying their propagation. Even in this case, however, at low altitudes (<2 to 3000 km), such methods are no longer applicable. Again the physical conditions in different parts of the magnetosphere are quite different. Above the ionosphere (i.e. higher than about 500 km), the number of collisions between particles is small and consequently the absorption (and amplification) of waves is determined only by kinetic effects. In the ionosphere on the other hand the number of collisions between ions and electrons and with neutral particles is large, causing dissipation of hm waves arriving from outer space. In the far regions of the magnetosphere the frequencies of the shortest period pulsations (Pc 1) become comparable with the gyro-frequencies of ions leading to dispersion effects. We thus have to deal with a medium, whose electrodynamic parameters change in space in a complicated manner and moreover depend on the frequency and direction of wave propagation. It is generally agreed that micropulsations are produced as a result of different types of plasma instabilities in the magnetosphere or on its boundary. The conditions of generation and growth of small disturbances can be investigated in detail by a linear approximation. However, the determination of the amplitudes of stationary oscillations requires a non-linear theory.

3.5 Transmission of Hydromagnetic Waves Through the Ionosphere and Magnetosphere

C. E. Prince and F. X. Bostick (1964) have analysed the steady state frequency response of certain model ionospheres to the passage of transverse plane waves at micropulsation frequencies. Other authors (e.g. W. E. Francis and R. Karplus, 1960; J. A. Jacobs and T. Watanabe, 1962) had carried out similar investigations but the more general equations including neutral particles and collisions were not used and longitudinal propagation (i.e. the wave normal at 0° with respect to the magnetic field) was assumed. Prince and Bostick assumed that the Earth's magnetic field is dipolar and considered a wave front normally incident at the equatorial point. Thus they assume that various waves are generated at a distant boundary by streaming solar particles and that these waves propagate across field lines to the Earth's surface, which they assumed to be perfectly reflecting at the extremely low frequencies considered. From the attenuation and phase constants for plane waves in a partly ionized magneto-ionic medium they calculated the resultant surface magnetic field for discrete, constant amplitude, input signals at the outer boundary.

Their results show that the simple formula for the Alfvén wave velocity used by other authors in considering propagation along field lines cannot be used below a height of about 800 km. The Alfvén formula can be used, however, for a fully ionized gas but not for a gas with many neutral particles. The slope and fine structure of the calculated spectra based on the conductivity tensor seem fairly reasonable for daytime

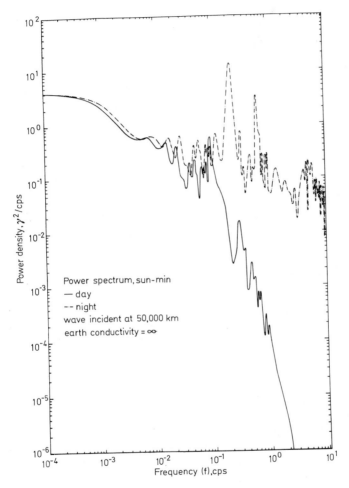

Fig. 3.1. Computed power spectrum for sunspot minimum conditions. (After C. E. Prince, Jr., and F. X. Bostick, Jr.)

conditons (see Fig. 3.1). R. A. Santirocco and D. G. Parker obtained Pc power spectra from Bermuda with a smoothed slope of −20 db/decade with many fine structured peaks superimposed from 0.002

to about 1 Hz. Since their data are for a midlatitude region, precise agreement with a model dealing with equatorial regions cannot be expected. Other workers have shown spectra with large peaks near 0.05 or 0.1 Hz. It should be pointed out however that the theoretical spectra of Prince and Bostick do not imply that certain particular frequencies and peaks are actually present, since the calculations assume equal input for *all* frequencies. Their calculated spectra support the suggestion of J. A. Jacobs and T. Watanabe (1962) that a filtering action of the region between the bottom of the ionosphere and the region of maximum Alfvén velocity around 2000 km explains not only "pearl" type oscillations, mostly nighttime phenomena, but also daytime Pc oscillations in the period range 20–30 sec, lower frequencies being permitted by the use of the more complete propagation equations including collisional effects. (Ion-neutral particle collisions control the attenuation of the spectra to a great degree and also the relative amplitudes of the resonant peaks.)

The low frequency transmission characteristics of the lower ionosphere have been investigated by W. E. Francis and R. Karplus (1960) and by E. C. Field (1963). Francis and Karplus, making certain simplifying assumptions, numerically integrated the differential equations for the propagation of hm disturbances in the ionosphere using empirical ionospheric properties chosen to correspond to the daytime at sunspot maximum. Their numerical results showed that the ionosphere is essentially transparent for angular frequencies somewhat less than one rad/sec. Field used empirical ionospheric properties to calculate an altitude dependent complex index of refraction for the ionosphere. He then approximated the ionosphere by two layers, the upper of which has a real index of refraction and the lower a complex index of refraction, and calculated the resulting transmission coefficient. Field's results are substantially in agreement with those of Francis and Karplus; neither investigation however revealed any prominent resonances in the transmission coefficient.

C. Greifinger and P. Greifinger (1965) have also calculated the transmission and reflection coefficients of the lower ionosphere, using essentially the same model as Francis and Karplus but with some additional simplifications which make possible an analytic rather than a numerical solution. They considered the case of a plane wave propagating in the vertical direction in the presence of a uniform magnetic field which is also in the vertical direction. Their model is thus strictly only applicable to the polar and auroral regions. The charged particle density is assumed to be constant throughout the ionosphere and the neutral particle density to vary exponentially with altitude. Much of the simplification results from the properties of the ionosphere in the region of interest (80–500 km) viz,

$$(3.32) \quad \begin{cases} \text{(a)} \quad \omega_e \sim 10^6 & \text{rad/sec}, \\ \text{(b)} \quad 10^2 < v_e < 10^5 & \text{rad/sec}, \\ \text{(c)} \quad \omega_i \sim 10^2 & \text{rad/sec}, \\ \text{(d)} \quad 10^{-2} < v_i < 10^4 & \text{rad/sec} \end{cases}$$

where ω_e and ω_i are the electron and ion gyro frequencies and v_e and v_i the collision frequencies of electrons and ions with neutral particles respectively.

For the polar propagation of hm waves in the frequency regime below about 1 Hz they showed that the ionosphere consists of three essentially distinct regions which are characterized by the relative magnitudes of the three frequencies v_i, ω_i and ω (the angular frequency of the disturbance). These regions are

(a) Hall region. This is the region in which the inequality $\omega \ll \omega_i < v_i$ is satisfied, i.e. where the collision frequency is the dominant frequency. It lies therefore between about 80 and 130 km. The boundaries of this region are independent of ω provided that $\omega \ll \omega_i$.

(b) Transition region. This region is defined by the inequality $\omega < v_i < \omega_i$, and lies between about 130 and 350 km, the location of the upper boundary depending on the frequency ω.

(c) Alfvén region. This is the region in which the inequality $v_i < \omega \ll \omega_i$ is satisfied. It lies therefore above about 350 km and is assumed to be semi-infinite in extent. In it the disturbance propagates as a pure Alfvén wave.

The actual functional form of the frequency enters only in the transition region. For both L and R modes of propagation the Alfvén region is a lossless and non dispersive medium. On the other hand the Hall region appears quite different for the two modes. For the L mode, the index of refraction is real and the mode thus propagates without attenuation (although with dispersion). For the R mode, the index of refraction is purely imaginary and the mode is thus evanescent. Because of this, the transmission coefficient for the R mode drops off very rapidly with frequency and it is mainly the L mode that gets through the ionosphere. In the transition region the index of refraction of both modes is complex so that in this region each mode undergoes both attenuation and dispersion.

C. Greifinger and P. Greifinger linearized the hydrodynamic and electromagnetic equations and showed that, with the approximations valid for low frequency waves, the resulting system reduces to a second order wave equation. A steady state solution of this equation was obtained from which transmission and reflection coefficients were calculated. The transmission coefficient was found to exhibit a pronounced resonance at a frequency of 0.015 Hz for daytime conditions, with an upward shift in frequency from day to night and from sunspot maximum to sunspot minimum. This resonance is in the frequency range of Pc oscillations which they therefore explained by the filtering action of the lower ionosphere. This resonance does not appear in the work of W. E. Francis and R. Karplus (1960) because they did not consider low enough frequencies, nor in the work of E. C. Field (1963) who was concerned only with an average transmission coefficient and not with its dependence on frequency.

The assumption of a constant Alfvén speed throughout a semi-infinite ionosphere treats the upper ionosphere as a lossless, non dispersive medium (or transmission line). However in fact the Alfvén speed increases with altitude in the region between about 200 and 2000 km and may thus be expected to modify signals which are generated at altitudes of 2000 km or more. (See e.g. J. A. Jacobs and T. Watanabe (1962), E. C. Field (1963) and C. E. Prince and F. X. Bostick (1964) who found resonances in the transmission coefficient of the upper atmosphere. The lowest resonance occurs at a frequency of about 0.1 Hz.) Thus for disturbances originating at 2000 km or more (and in the frequency range below about 1 Hz) the ionosphere below 2000 km appears very much like two separate filters. The upper filter has a transmission resonance at about 0.1 Hz and the lower filter a transmission resonance at about 0.015 Hz. The combined transmission coefficient is essentially the product of the separate transmission coefficients.

In a later paper E. C. Field and C. Greifinger (1965) extended their investigation of the transmission of geomagnetic micropulsations to a height of about 2000 km, i. e. they included the lower exosphere as well. In the lower exosphere the propagation is determined solely by the behaviour of the Alfvén speed V_A provided that the periods are short enough so that collision effects are small at heights greater than about 500 km — this requirement restricts the treatment to periods less than about 100 sec. V_A is relatively constant between the bottom of the ionosphere (some 80 km above the Earth's surface) and, depending on the local time and sunspot conditions, an altitude of some 400–500 km. This height is taken to be the top of the ionosphere. In the lower exosphere, the region between the ionosphere and some 1 500–2 000 km (again depending on the time and sunspot activity) V_A exhibits a dependence which is well fitted by a height-increasing exponential. Above the lower exosphere V_A again becomes quite uniform and was taken as constant.

C. Greifinger and P. Greifinger had shown in their earlier paper that, by taking the origin at that height where $v_i = |\omega_i|$ and choosing the coordinate system so that increasing Z corresponds to decreasing altitude, it is possible to write

$$(3.33) \qquad v_i = |\omega_i| e^{Z/\zeta}$$

where ζ is a local scale height of the order of 10 km. In order for this representation to be valid, it is only necessary for v_i to have the form of equation (3.33) within a few tens of kilometers on either side of the origin. This corresponds to the actual physical situation.

Fig. 3.2.   Schematic model of the ionosphere and lower exosphere. (After E. C. Field and C. Greifinger)

For $\omega_i = 175$ rad/sec, equation (3.33) places the origin some 130 km above the ground. Thus, their propagation model, which is shown schematically in Fig. 3.2, is described by equation (3.33) and the following formulae;

$$Z = 130 \qquad \text{(perfectly reflecting ground)},$$
$$130 \geqslant Z \geqslant 50 \qquad \text{(earth-ionosphere cavity)},$$
$$(3.34) \quad 50 \geqslant Z \geqslant Z_2, \ V_A = V_0 \qquad \text{(ionosphere)},$$
$$(3.35) \quad Z_2 \geqslant Z \geqslant Z_3, \ V_A = V_2 e^{-(Z-Z_2)/\lambda} \qquad \text{(lower exosphere)},$$
$$(3.36) \quad Z \leqslant Z_3, \ V_A = V_3 = V_2 e^{-(Z_3-Z_2)/\lambda} \qquad \text{(exosphere)}.$$

Z is measured in km and λ is the scale height associated with the Alfvén speed in the lower exosphere. The behavior of V_A at the level Z_2 depends on local time. The data indicate that under daytime conditions $V_0 = V_2$

and V_A is continuous, but has a discontinuous derivative. At night, however, the depletion of ionization in the ionosphere causes $V_0 \gg V_2$ and the ionosphere-exosphere boundary is best characterized by a rather severe discontinuity in Alfvén speed. At the level Z_3, it is reasonable to take V_A to be continuous, with a discontinuous derivative at all times.

E. C. Field and C. Greifinger obtained the transmission and reflection coefficients for a number of model ionospheres and lower exospheres.

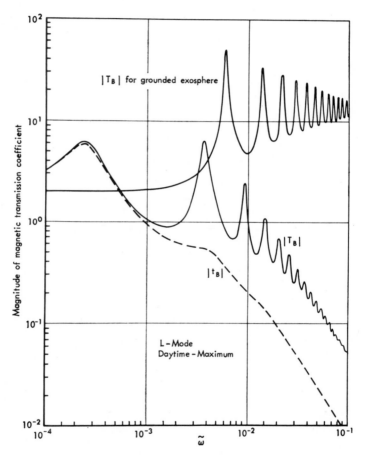

Fig. 3.3. Magnitude of the composite magnetic transmission coefficient $|T_B|$ for the L mode as a function of frequency for daytime sunspot maximum conditions showing a prominent double resonance. The transmission coefficient for the grounded exosphere model of J. A. Jacobs and T. Watanabe (1962) and the ionospheric transmission coefficient $|t_b|$ are shown for comparison. (After E. C. Field and C. Greifinger)

They found that the daytime resonant structure of the transmitted signal is governed primarily by the L mode. This would imply, at least for high latitudes, that the polarization of the daytime signals near the resonant frequencies should be nearly circular. The main conclusion drawn in their earlier paper is unaffected by the inclusion of the lower exosphere. In particular the daytime Pc 4 resonance, which has a period of many tens of sec and which is clearly due to the filtering action of the ionosphere, remains intact. However, the inclusion of the lower exosphere introduces a series of higher frequency resonances falling in the lower Pc 3 to Pc 1 range (see Fig. 3.3). These peaks, which are clearly exospheric in origin, are a modified version of those predicted by J.A. Jacobs and T. Watanabe (1962). One of the most striking features of the daytime models is that the first exospheric resonance is comparable in magnitude with that due to the ionosphere. This pronounced double peak in the daytime spectrum is in good qualitative agreement with the two prominent

Fig. 3.4.   Magnitude of the composite transmission coefficient $|T_B|$ for the L mode as a function of frequency for nighttime sunspot maximum conditions. The composite transmission coefficient for a uniform exosphere $|T_B(\lambda=\infty)|$ and the ionospheric transmission coefficient $|t_b|$ are shown for comparison. (After E. C. Field and C. Greifinger)

daytime bands observed by several workers. The magnitude of the higher frequency exospheric Pc 1 and Pc 2 daytime resonances falls off rapidly with increasing frequency owing to the opacity of the daytime ionosphere. The nighttime transmission coefficients differ both qualitatively and quantitatively from those obtained for daytime conditions. One major difference is that the L mode ionospheric Pc 4 resonance, which was prominent in the daytime, vanishes (see Fig. 3.4). Finally and of equal importance the first few R mode resonances are nearly identical in size and location to those of the L mode: this is a consequence of the relative transparency of the nighttime ionosphere.

In a final paper, E. C. Field and C. Greifinger (1966) extended their work to the case when the geomagnetic field is horizontal rather than vertical, i.e. they considered equatorial propagation. The approach used was basically the same as that in the previous papers. The horizontal orientation of the equatorial geomagnetic field causes the ionospheric part of the propagation to differ substantially from that found in the earlier papers for the case of vertical propagation. Also micropulsations are quite heavily damped in the entire region below the Alfvén region. This is quite different from the polar case where the lefthand polarized mode was shown to encounter an essentially lossless "Hall region" in the lower ionosphere.

The daytime composite transmission coefficient falls off very rapidly with increasing frequency and exhibits a series of rather small resonances (see Fig. 3.5). The ionospheric transmission coefficient has no resonances in the frequency range considered. The computed peaks in the transmitted signal are therefore due to filtering in the lower exosphere. The daytime polar transmission coefficients (for the left-hand polarized mode) had a much more pronounced resonance structure: the ionospheric coefficient had a strong peak in the Pc 4 range and the composite coefficient fell off with frequency much more slowly (cf Figs. 3.3 and 3.5). The nighttime composite transmission coefficient (for equatorial propagation) exhibits quite strong resonances and it generally has a much larger amplitude than the daytime one. This is due to the transparency of the ionosphere produced by the nighttime depletion of ionization in the ionosphere. The ionospheric transmission coefficient again has no resonances, indicating that the resonances in the composite transmission coefficient are exospheric in origin.

A. K. Sen (1968 a, b) has shown that the effect of the long inhomogeneous transmission path from the ionosphere to the boundary of the magnetosphere, which was neglected by J. A. Jacobs and T. Watanabe (1962), C. Greifinger and P. Greifinger (1965) and E. C. Field and C. Greifinger (1965) is of profound importance in determining the spectrum of micropulsations. Although C. E. Prince and F. X. Bostick (1964) considered numerically the entire transmission path, they, as well as the above authors, did not consider the crucial effect of variations in the lengths of the various parts of the path. Sen (1965) had shown earlier that substantial portions of the magnetospheric boundary are unstable under all conditions of the solar wind. G. Atkinson and T. Watanabe (1966) used this idea as the basis of a mechanism for the generation of

Fig. 3.5. Magnitude of the composite transmission coefficient $|T_B|$ and of the ionospheric transmission coefficient $|t_b|$ as a function of frequency for daytime sunspot minimum conditions. (After E. C. Field and C. Greifinger)

long period micropulsations (see Chapter 5). They were also able to account for the polarization characteristics of Pc 5's. Sen suggests that hm surface waves generated by this instability may leave the magnetospheric boundary along lines of force of the geomagnetic field and travel towards the surface of the Earth as micropulsations.

The inclusion of the transmission path in the outer magnetosphere yields important new features. Sen found that the transmission of micropulsations is extremely sensitive to the variation in the various path lengths encountered in the propagation from the boundary of the magnetosphere to the surface of the Earth. As the distance of the magnetospheric boundary varies with different solar wind conditions the path length in the outer magnetosphere will be subject to considerable variation. Sen showed that as little as one per cent variation in this path length will completely annihilate a resonance in the transmission. Hence resonances in the lower exosphere and ionosphere, or even in the outer exosphere, may not necessarily imply the reception of micropulsations at those frequencies at the surface of the Earth. Sen also showed that some resonances are more sensitive to this "detuning" than others and hence their occurrence is less probable.

Sen set up the propagation problem by analogy with an electromagnetic wave transmission line. For the analogy to exist we must consider the one dimensional propagation of plane transverse waves. The two parameters which characterize a transmission line are the propagation constant and the intrinsic impedance (i. e. the ratio of the electric to the magnetic field). Although the transmission coefficient below the ionosphere is unity it cannot be neglected because its impedance will influence all the transmission coefficients. Sen found that all the resonances of the middle and lower exosphere are completely masked in the overall transmission due to the effect of the path in the outer magnetosphere. The relative maxima of the overall transmission at the resonances of all the sections below the outer magnetosphere have very small amplitudes and these will not be present in the micropulsation signals received at the surface of the Earth. The only relative maxima of the overall transmission which have large amplitudes are those of the resonances of the outer magnetospheric path. Their periods are approximately 935, 311, 134, 103 and 71 sec which are much longer than the lowest period resonances found in all other theoretical work. Their amplitudes are also much larger than those calculated by other authors. Less likely resonances due to the path in the lower exosphere and upper ionosphere were found to have time periods of approximately 39, 14, 9, 7 and 4 sec.

The physical reason for the extreme sensitivity of the overall transmission on the variation of the path length in the outer magnetosphere can be explained in terms of the highly tuned nature of each section of the transmission line acting as a filter. The "band width" of such a sharp resonance of any section is very small: the path length variation equivalent to this band width is consequently small. Therefore a slight variation of path length in the outer magnetosphere can detune a resonance of the lower exosphere and ionosphere, especially since these resonances are of relatively shorter periods and the corresponding wave lengths and band lengths are shorter.

The amplitude spectrum of micropulsation signals observed at the surface of the Earth is essentially determined by the resonances of the transmission path. On the other hand the power spectral density depends both on the squared amplitude of transmission and the occurrence probability, which is a function of the sensitivity of the overall transmission on the variation of the path length in the outer magnetosphere. In a later paper (1968 b), Sen showed that the occurrence probability of micropulsations with periods of 2.5, 6, 11 and especially 20 sec should be much higher than others. The peaks corresponding to these periods are so sharp as to suggest almost single frequency sinusoidal signals which are a characteristic of micropulsation reception. Because of the much higher occurrence probability, Sen predicts spectral lines or peaks at these periods in the power spectrum of micropulsations. This is in striking agreement with M. J. Davidson (1964) who found the first group of spectral peaks at ~ 5 and 10 sec and a second group at 17–70 sec. Sen also showed that certain slight statistical variations in the transmission path will have a profound influence on the power spectral density causing it to be very different from the squared magnitude of the transmission coefficient. Hence comparisons between theoretical transmission resonances and observed spectral peaks can be somewhat misleading. All that can be expected at transmission resonances is a measure of the relative prevalence, but not necessarily spectral peaks.

Micropulsations may also be the result of transient disturbances of the geomagnetic field. The characteristics of micropulsations due to such transient causes will however differ from those of Sen's steady state theory in two important respects. Firstly the spectrum of the transient source will influence the spectrum of the received signal much more strongly than is the case in the steady state theory or the common assumption of white noise at source. Secondly the manner in which the transfer function of the transmission path influences the spectrum of the received signal. Thus in a steady state theory the frequencies of the received signal are the same as those of the source—only the magnitudes and phases of the various spectral components are altered by the transfer function of the transmission path. In a transient situation the frequencies of the received signal are determined both by the spectral content of the source and the transfer function, i.e. the frequencies of the received signal contain the frequencies of the transient disturbance as well as the natural modes of the transmission path. The natural modes of the transmission path play a significant role in the steady state theory, only because they are highly discriminating pass bands of the effective filtering action of the transmission path and the source was considered to be discrete, dense and essentially uniform.

References

There have been many books written on plasma physics during the last few years, and no attempt will be made to give a comprehensive bibliography. Three older books on magnetohydrodynamics of special interest to the physics of the upper atmosphere are

Alfvén, H., Fälthammar, C.-G.: Cosmical Electrodynamics. 2nd Ed. Oxford: Univ. Press 1963.
Cowling, T. G.: Magnetohydrodynamics. Interscience 1957.
Dungey, J. W.: Cosmic Electrodynamics. Cambridge: Univ. Press 1958.
J. W. Dungey has also contributed to the following two publications
Geophysics—The Earth's environment. (Ed. C. DeWitt, J. Hieblot, and A. Lebeau.) Gordon and Breach 1963: *The structure of the exosphere or adventures in velocity space.* pp. 505—550.
Physics of Geomagnetic Phenomena. (Ed. S. Matsushita and W. H. Campbell.) Academic Press, 1967: *Hydromagnetic waves.* pp. 913—934.

Special references in Chapter 3

Alfvén, H.: On the existence of electromagnetic-hydromagnetic waves. Arkiv. f. Mat. **29**B No. 2, 1942.
Atkinson, G., Watanabe, T.: Surface waves on the magnetospheric boundary as a possible origin of long period geomagnetic micropulsations. Earth Plan. Sci. Letters **1**, 89—91 (1966).
Carovillano, R. L., Radoski, H. R.: Latitude dependent plasmasphere oscillations. Phys. Fluids **10**, 225—229 (1967).
Davidson, M. J.: Average diurnal characteristics of geomagnetic power spectrums in the period range 4.5 to 1000 seconds. J. Geophys. Res. **69**, 5116—5119 (1964).
— Heirtzler, J. R.: Spatial coherence of geomagnetic rapid variations. J. Geophys. Res. **73**, 2143—2162 (1968).
Dungey, J. W.: The propagation of Alfvén waves through the ionosphere. Penn. State Univ. Ionos. Res. Lab. Sci. Rept. No. 57, 1954a.
— Electrodynamics of the outer atmosphere. Penn. State Univ. Ionos. Res. Lab. Sci. Rept. No. 69, 1954b.
Fejer, J. A., Lee, H. F.: Guided propagation of Alfvén waves in the magnetosphere. J. Plasma Phys. **1**, 387—406 (1967).
Field, E. C.: Hydromagnetic signals in the ionosphere. Rand Corp. Rept. RM-3830-PR, Sept. 1963.
— Greifinger, C.: Transmission of geomagnetic micropulsations through the ionosphere and lower exosphere. J. Geophys. Res. **70**, 4885—4899 (1965).
— — Equatorial transmission of geomagnetic micropulsations through the ionosphere and lower exosphere. J. Geophys. Res. **71**, 3223—3232 (1966).
Francis, W. E., Karplus, R.: Hydromagnetic waves in the ionosphere. J. Geophys. Res. **65**, 3593—3600 (1960).
Greifinger, C., Greifinger, P.: Transmission of micropulsations through the lower ionosphere. J. Geophys. Res. **70**, 2217—2231 (1965).
— — Theory of hydromagnetic propagation in the ionosphere waveguide. J. Geophys. Res. **73**, 7473—7490 (1968).
Jacobs, J. A., Watanabe, T.: Propagation of hydromagnetic waves in the lower exosphere and the origin of short period geomagnetic micropulsations. J. Atmos. Terr. Phys. **24**, 413—434 (1962).
Lehnert, A.: Magnetohydrodynamic waves in the ionosphere and their application to giant pulsations. Tellus **VIII**, 241—251 (1956).
Lundquist, S.: Studies in magneto-hydrodynamics. Ark. Fsyik. **5**, 297—347 (1952).

Prince, C. E., Jr., Bostick, F. X., Jr.: Ionospheric transmission of transversely propagated plane waves at micropulsation frequencies and theoretical power spectrums. J. Geophys. Res. **69**, 3213—3234 (1964).

Sen, A. K.: Stability of the magnetospheric boundary. Planet. Space Sci. **13**, 131—141 (1965).

— A theory of geomagnetic micropulsations I. J. Geomag. Geoelect. **20**, 225—243 (1968a).

— A theory of geomagnetic micropulsations II. J. Geomag. Geoelect. **20**, 245—261 (1968b).

Santirocco, R. A., Parker, D. G.: The polarization and power spectrums of Pc micropulsations in Bermuda. J. Geophys. Res. **68**, 5545—5558 (1963).

Stix, T. H.: The theory of plasma waves. McGraw-Hill 1962.

Westphal, K. O., Jacobs, J. A.: Oscillations of the Earth's outer atmosphere and micropulsations. Geophys. J. **6**, 360—376 (1962).

4 Theories of the Origin of Pc 1 Pulsations

4.1 Introduction

One model of Pc 1 pulsations is that they are the result of oscillations of bunches of monochromatic particles trapped by the Earth's magnetic field. In this case the period of Pc 1's is that of the oscillations of the bunch from one conjugate point to the other, and their amplitude is determined by the density and energy of the charged particles in the group, by the height of the mirror points and by the absorption of hydromagnetic (hm) waves in the ionosphere. The basis for such a view is the morphological features of Pc 1's and their connection with other upper atmospheric phenomena. It is further suggested that the spacing

Table 4.1. *Data for* Pc 1 *Oscillations (after R. C. Wentworth and L. R. Tepley, 1962)*

Station	Palo Alto	Victoria	Uppsala	Reykjavik
Geomagnetic latitude	45°	55°	60°	70°
Full length of arc ($\times 10^{-9}$ cm)	5.71	9.42	12.2	22.4
Energy of electrons for 1 Hz oscillations (kev)	9.25	25.2	48.6	260
Electron drift velocity for 1 Hz oscillations ($\times 10^{-5}$ rad/sec)	3.32	12.0	27.0	142
Maximum frequency of oscillations (Hz)	5.25	3.18	2.46	1.34
Maximum frequency of oscillations for a point 500 km distant (Hz)	7.8	4.6	3.6	2.1
Maximum observed frequency of hydromagnetic emissions (Hz)	5	3	3	2

between successive "pearls" is the drift time of the particles around the Earth. R. C. Wentworth and L. R. Tepley (1962) assumed the particle bunches to consist of energetic electrons and Table 4.1 shows their calculated and the observed data for Pc 1's. The mirror points of the particle bunches are thought to be situated above the *F*-2 layer of the ionosphere. As the ionosphere has high conductivity, the arrival of a diamagnetic bunch of particles at the mirror point cannot be recorded directly at the surface of the Earth. The disturbance must reach the E-layer as a hm wave. Propagation through the ionosphere reduces the disturbance because of absorption due to joule heating. Calculations of the absorption of hm waves in the ionosphere show that in the daytime, especially in years of maximum solar activity, the ionosphere is practically opaque even for 1 Hz waves. Absorption of Pc 1's is not very large at night. Another consequence of the above theory is the dependence of the period of the observed oscillations on latitude—the average Pc 1 period increasing monotonically with latitude. This is not definitely confirmed although longer period Pc 1's tend to occur at higher latitudes. Wentworth and Tepley based their theory on their interpretation of the auroral electron bremsstrahlung events which occur with Pi activity but extend into the same frequency range as Pc 1 emissions. Their predicted signal polarization and occurrence with solar-terrestrial ionospheric disturbances do not agree with observations. Later R. Gendrin (1963) proposed a fast *proton* bunch model. Both this model and the fast *electron* bunch model of Wentworth and Tepley associate the period of Pc 1's with the bounce period of the particles along the field line joining the conjugate mirror points. These models, however, cannot explain the 180° phase shift of Pc 1 amplitudes between conjugate points since the interhemisphere phase shift of the rapidly oscillating particles is negligible.

To overcome this difficulty J.A. Jacobs and T. Watanabe (1963) proposed a slow proton bunch model in which the proton bounce period is associated with the repetition period of the structured elements in the Pc 1 series. This model attributes the Pc 1 period to hm resonance in the lower magnetosphere. Later J.A. Jacobs and T. Watanabe (1964) and T. Obayashi (1965) proposed that a wave packet bounces along the geomagnetic field line between conjugate points. In this model the period of the Pc 1 oscillations and the repetition period of the structured elements correspond to the period of the hm wave and the bounce period of the wave packet respectively. Because of wave dispersion during the course of bouncing, the dynamic spectrum of this model should have the fan shaped structure observed.

The generation of oscillations in both the Pc 1 and Pi 1 frequency ranges by hm resonance in the lower exosphere and ionosphere has been discussed by G.J.F. MacDonald (1961) and J.A. Jacobs and T. Watanabe (1963). Calculations for a number of models have shown that such a resonance can occur, for instance, at a frequency around 0.27 Hz (E.C. Field and C. Greifinger, 1965). Jacobs and Watanabe proposed that bunches of protons bouncing between hemispheres on geomagnetic field lines generate standing hm waves in a resonant trap between the ionosphere and a height of about 2000 km, where there exists a maximum in the Alfvén velocity.

A simple example is sufficient to understand intuitively how the region of lower velocity in the lower exosphere affects the intensity of waves observed at the Earth's surface. The example concerns the propagation of an Alfvén wave through two layers of a hm medium which are situated above a metallic layer of extremely high electrical conductivity (Fig. 4.1).

Fig. 4.1.

Assuming that the external magnetic field is uniform and normal to every layer, the intensity of the magnetic field (associated with the Alfvén wave) at the Earth's surface of the metallic layer is given by

$$2 \times \frac{\text{magnetic field intensity of the incident Alfvén wave}}{\sqrt{\left[\left(1 - \dfrac{V_1}{V_2}\right)^2 \cos^2\left(\dfrac{\omega L}{V_1}\right) + \left(\dfrac{V_1}{V_2}\right)^2\right]}}$$

where L = the thickness of the intermediate layer,
        V_1 = the Alfvén velocity in the intermediate layer,
        V_2 = the Alfvén velocity in the upper layer (it is assumed
               that $V_2 > V_1$) and
        ω = the angular frequency of the wave.
The above equation shows that the observed intensity becomes a maximum at the frequencies given by

$$\frac{\omega L}{V_1} = \frac{\pi}{2} + n\pi \qquad (n = 1, 2 \ldots)$$

the maximum value being $2V_2/V_1 \times$ incident wave's intensity. On the other hand, it becomes a minimum at the frequencies given by

$$\frac{\omega L}{V_1} = n\pi \qquad (n = 1, 2 \ldots).$$

The lowest frequency ω_0 (longest period T_0) among those modes in which the observed intensity becomes a maximum, is given by

$$\omega_0 = \frac{\pi}{2} \cdot \frac{V_1}{L},$$

i.e.

$$T_0 = \frac{4L}{V_1}$$

which means that the fundamental (favoured) mode is such that the thickness of the layer is one quarter of a wavelength.

Fig. 4.2.   Distribution of the Alfvén velocity against height—daytime, maximum sunspot activity. (After J. A. Jacobs and T. Watanabe)

In the lower exosphere, the Alfvén velocity increases from about 10^7 to 10^9 cm/sec, the average velocity being 10^8 cm/sec. Taking the thickness of the intermediate layer to be 2000 km, the fundamental period is 8 sec. This preliminary calculation shows that such a model is encouraging. The two-layer model is, of course, far too simple for the actual distribution of the Alfvén velocity, and J. A. Jacobs and

T. Watanabe in 1962 used a six-layer model, i.e. the distribution of the actual Alfvén velocity was approximated by a stepwise distribution as shown in Fig. 4.2. They put forward a theory of Pc 1 micropulsations in which hm activity originates in outer space (several Earth radii distant) and is propagated to limited areas in the polar or auroral regions along magnetic lines of force. The lower exosphere, below an altitude of about 2000 km where the Alfvén velocity has a very steep gradient, selectively amplifies the intensity of waves of certain frequencies. Secondary hm waves are then emitted from the region(s) of incidence of the primary waves and propagated to lower latitudes where they are observed as micropulsations. Jacobs and Watanabe suggested that these secondary waves are trapped in the region between the ionosphere and the layer of maximum Alfvén velocity, the wave energy leaking from the trapping region through the ionosphere being observed as geomagnetic micropulsations at the Earth's surface. However a regular longitudinal drift of the observed excitation due to the expected precessional drift of the bouncing protons is not clearly observed. Also the resonance conditions at conjugate points should vary considerably, which is not always observed to be the case. However, the results of investigations at high latitudes (R. R. Heacock, 1966) of oscillations with periods around 4 sec, which agree with those obtained by the USSR network of stations (E. T. Matveeva and V. A. Troitskaya, 1965) show that the characteristics of these pulsations may perhaps be attributed to resonance oscillations in the cavity formed between the ionosphere and the layer at which the Alfvén velocity is a maximum.

Theoretical investigations (see Sec. 4.5) have shown that the distribution of Pc 1's over the Earth's surface probably involves the propagation of hm waves from high to low latitudes in a low altitude waveguide centered on the F_2 region (R. N. Manchester, 1966, 1968; L. R. Tepley and R. K. Landshoff, 1966). An interesting conclusion from the investigations of Manchester is the establishment of a waveguide cut-off for the propagation of Pc 1's with periods greater than about 2 sec. This may explain the reason for the observed relative predominance of short-period Pc 1's at low latitudes. The fact that these oscillations at middle and low latitudes occur mainly at night may be attributed to waveguide absorption which is greater during the day than during the night.

The global distribution of Pc 1's is closely affected by the role the ionosphere plays in the propagation of these oscillations. It would appear, however, that the influence of the ionosphere is largely masked by other factors, above all by variations in source intensity. For middle latitudes at night, the mean amplitude of these Pc 1 oscillations above the ionosphere which are still observable at the surface of the Earth is only 4 mγ. During the day, however, amplitudes of Pc 1's above the ionosphere must exceed 50–100 mγ to be observable (R. C. Wentworth, 1964 a, b), This means that all Pc 1 occurrences during the night can probably be detected, whereas during the day most of them may be lost.

J. F. Kenney and H. B. Knaflich (1967) have found a seasonal variation in the diurnal occurrence of pearls, but not necessarily in the diurnal pattern of emission frequency and bandwidth. They based their conclusions on data obtained at Tulalip (near Seattle, Washington). Their results are shown in Fig. 4.3—the most notable feature is a strong midday maximum in winter. As is expected from the diurnal pattern of emission frequency the average mid-frequency in winter is low because that is characteristic for the time of day when most of the pearls are received at Tulalip. This is consistent with the generation of pearls at high latitudes. In summer more nighttime pearls are received so the average frequency is higher. Consequently the seasonal variation in average frequency is merely a reflection of the seasonal variation in diurnal occurrence probability together with the strong diurnal variation in emission frequency—it does not necessarily reflect any seasonal variation in exospheric parameters. Kenney and Knaflich also found that there was almost as much difference between the same seasons in different years as between different seasons in the same year. Thus other factors such as solar activity exert a control over the diurnal variation of emission frequency and bandwidth that is strong enough to mask most of any seasonal variation.

The experimentally observed properties of Pc 1's have led several authors to conclude that these oscillations may be generated by streams of protons moving at speeds greater than the velocity of Alfvén waves (see Sec. 4.3). The emission occurs at the frequency corresponding to that of cyclotron instability, the time of growth of the instability being proportional to the ratio of the magnetic to the kinetic pressure. The experimentally observed characteristics of the emission frequency, period of repetition and bandwidth place severe limitations on the region where the instability can occur. Estimates of the proton energy necessary to explain the observed characteristics of Pc 1 pulsations show that for energies of 200–500 keV the region of generation must be located at a distance of $L \sim 4$. Protons of such energies can be identified with those reported by L. R. Davis and J. M. Williamson (1963); the maximum flux occurs at distances near $L \sim 3.5$. Pc 1 pulsations can also be excited by protons of lower energy (several tens of keV); in this case the region of excitation would be located further away from the surface of the Earth, approximately at a distance of $5 \sim 7 L$. The effectiveness of low-energy protons in creating an instability is greater because the time for the development of the instability is proportional to the ratio of the density of the protons to that of the surrounding plasma, which is greater

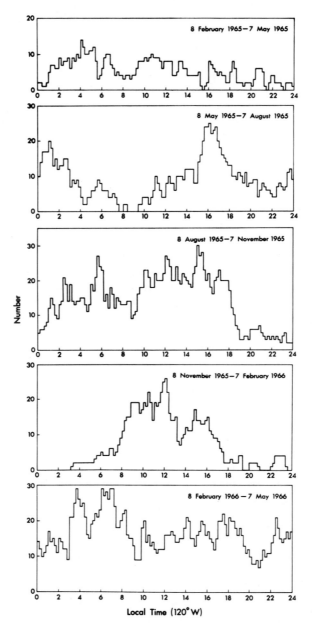

Fig. 4.3.   Seasonal histograms of Pc 1 occurrence at Tulalip, Washington. (After J. F. Kenney and H. B. Knaflich)

for low-energy protons (J. M. Cornwall, 1966). It is interesting that the above estimates suggest that the region of Pc 1 generation is approximately at the same distance from the Earth as the plasmapause, the sharp boundary of thermal plasma concentration (D. L. Carpenter, 1966).

As already mentioned it has been suggested that Pc 1 emissions arise from wave packets oscillating along field lines between conjugate points. Owing to dispersion the wave packet will spread, the low frequency components travelling more quickly than the high-frequency ones, so that the signal observed on the Earth's surface will be a rising tone. This phenomenon is similar to whistlers, but differs from them as regards polarization and dispersion characteristics (the high frequencies of Pc 1's propagating at lower velocities, which is opposite to that in the case of whistlers).

J. M. Cornwall (1966), obtained the critical frequency ω of a wave above which frequencies are attenuated, and below which they are amplified. His result is

$$\frac{\omega}{\omega_i} \sim 0.5\text{--}0.6$$

where ω_i is the equatorial ion gyrofrequency. This means that the excitation of emissions occurs at frequencies $\simeq \frac{1}{2}\omega_i$ which is in good agreement with the analysis of observed Pc 1 characteristics (R. C. Wentworth, 1966).

For those Pc 1's with structured elements consisting of successive "rising tones" with diminishing slope ("hydromagnetic whistlers") a method has been proposed by T. Watanabe (1965) for the determination of the plasma concentration in the outer regions of the magnetosphere (see also Sec. 6.3.). By using the change in the dispersion from one element of the Pc 1 series to the next, and the general characteristics of the series $(1/t, T)$ the magnetic field line along which the wave packets propagate can be determined, and the integrated plasma density along the field line estimated as well as the energy of the protons that amplify the emission in the region of interaction which is suggested to be the equatorial zone. Such an analysis has been carried out by R. C. Wentworth (1966) for 20 cases of emissions recorded at Palo Alto. His results show that Pc 1 hm whistlers are generated and amplified along field lines that cross the equatorial plane at distances corresponding to $L \sim 4.5\text{--}6$. The energy of the protons involved in the interaction is about $5-20\,\text{keV}$ (for the component parallel to the field). The plasma concentration determined by this method exhibits an abrupt fall approximately in the same region as that discovered by whistlers (the plasmapause, D. L. Carpenter, 1966).

One of the most typical features of Pc 1's is the absence of dispersion in successive structured elements of the series, the rising tones usually exhibiting a constant slope relative to the time axis. This type of Pc 1 fine structure has been called "periodic hydromagnetic emissions" (see Sec. 4.4). Just as in hm whistlers each signal is the echo of the pre-ceeding one, so in periodic emissions each successive burst is generated by the previous packet. It is suggested that the mechanism of generation in this case is also a cyclotron instability which arises from the interaction of 1–10 keV protons with the ambient plasma. J. A. Jacobs and T. Wata-nabe (1967) have explained the rise of signal frequency with increasing amplitude, as observed on some records, and the finite duration and peculiarities of the Pc 1 fine structure as the result of non-linear effects in the cyclotron instability.

A. K. Sen (1968) has extended his theory of micropulsations (see Sec. 3.5) to include Pc 1 oscillations. The primary pearl signal of 1–4 sec-period is produced in the same manner as that which he proposed for other types of micropulsations—this later (1968) paper suggests a modulation mechanism of the primary signal. Sen proposes that during the sudden commencement of a magnetic storm the boundary of the magnetosphere will be set in oscillatory motion under the impulsive impact of the enhanced solar wind. The oscillations will be transverse to the boundary and hence of magnetosonic type. Sen shows that the characteristic periods of the oscillations are much longer than the 1–4 sec period of the primary signal of the pearls. The long period oscillations of the boundary perpendicular to itself cause a periodic variation of the path length traversed by the micropulsations in the outer magneto-sphere. The lenght of this path will thus vary sinusoidally in time much more slowly compared to the frequency of the primary signal of the micropulsations. Hence the transmission coefficient will be a slowly varying function of time and the signal received at the Earth's surface will be amplitude modulated with a period long compared to its own.

Sen further shows that the slightest variation in the path length in the outer magnetosphere can completely annihilate the resonance of the transmission and that the period t of the primary pearl signal received at the Earth should be near $2.5 \sim 6$ sec. Even then if the amplitude of the boundary oscillation is less than 50 km (for $t \sim 2.5$ sec) or 42 km ($t \sim 6$ sec), there may be negligible or no modulation. Also the modulating signal produced by the slowly varying transmission coefficient in the outer magnetosphere is very much sharper than a sine wave, yielding repetitive spikes or pulses of oscillations—which is quite often observed to be the case.

The most likely explanation of Pc 1 emissions involves a wave amplification by a transfer of energy from particles in the magnetosphere. The resonance takes place at some fraction of the gyrofrequency due to Doppler shifting and the repetition period is indicative of the latitudinal bounce time of a field-guided energy packet. Many authors have shown that protons, not electrons, are the most reasonable source for this interaction. The general trend from all data is for the repetition period to be inversely proportional to the frequency and that low frequency emissions are produced at high latitudes and high frequency emissions at low latitudes. Whether or not a particular station detects an emission will depend on whether an exciting source is present and whether or not the proper ionospheric conditions exist for ducting of the radiation from the field line to the site without absorption. Since College, Alaska has a strong daytime maximum and Palo Alto, California, a nighttime maximum with little seasonal variation, it appears that the exciting source has a diurnal variation in latitude. This gives rise to a locus of points of most probable emission with high latitude on the day side of the Earth and low latitude on the night side (see Fig. 4.4). A particular station may see either type of emission depending on the ionospheric conditions that exist between source and site. J. F. Kenney and H. B. Knaflich (1967) have suggested the term "pearl oval" analogous to "auroral oval" to describe the locus of points of maximum occurrence. Ionospheric ducting away from the oval will be large and will be a function of local time, season, magnetic disturbance etc. If the average frequency increases with K_p as indicated by many observers this would be consistent with the idea of an equatorial motion of the pearl oval with large K_p—a similar effect has been noted by S.-I. Akasofu (1966) for the auroral oval.

If the spacing between structured elements is determined by the latitudinal bounce time of the wave packet the increase in spacing with frequency, which is normally noted in an individual pearl, agrees with the idea that the magnetosphere is a dispersive medium. When pearls occur on different L shells each could separately display the charac-

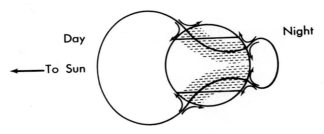

Fig. 4.4. Diurnal variation of Pc 1 ("pearl") zone location. Ionosphere ducting away from the pearl zone is indicated by the arrows. (After J. F. Kenney and H. B. Knaflich)

teristics of propagation through a dispersive medium, although collectively the opposite trend would be noted. The pearl occurring on the lower L shell will have a smaller spacing as well as a higher mid-frequency if the pearl frequency is a relatively fixed fraction of the minimum ion gyrofrequency along its path. Hence the overall trend as well as the structure of the individual pearl is satisfied by the idea of pearls being generated on different field lines in a dispersive medium. The particles responsible for a particular pearl event do not occupy a large volume of L space, but are more probably confined to a thin lamina with many eigen frequencies being excited both on and off the equator by particles of different energies and pitch angles.

4.2 The Structure of the Frequency Spectrum of Pc 1's

Several authors, e. g. R. C. Wentworth and L. R. Tepley (1962), R. R. Heacock (1963), R. Gendrin (1963), J. A. Jacobs and T. Watanabe (1963) have tried to interpret the characteristic structure of the dynamic spectrum of Pc 1's as the magnetic effect of a bunch of charged particles trapped in the magnetic field of the Earth. T. Obayashi (1965) suggested an alternative explanation—that the sequence of rising tones is an expression of dispersion in the propagation of a hm wave packet guided by a magnetic line of force of the Earth's field in a manner similar to the falling tones of atmospheric whistlers. The same suggestion was made later by J. E. Lokken (1963) who called the rising tones "micropulsation whistlers". Of the two modes of waves propagated in a magneto-active plasma along an external magnetic field, one mode (right-handed), which has a cut-off frequency near the electron gyrofrequency, is propagated faster at higher frequencies. Whistlers are propagated in this mode. The other mode (left-handed), which has a cut-off frequency near the ion gyrofrequency, is propagated slower at higher frequencies. The dispersion to be expected for this mode of waves is opposite to that in the case of the former mode.

Fig. 4.5 (J. A. Jacobs and T. Watanabe, 1964) shows a family of surfaces of refractive index n for the two modes of waves propagating in a homogeneous plasma permeated by an external uniform magnetic field. If the positive y direction is that of the external magnetic field, a radius vector from the origin O to any point P gives the value of the refractive index, n, of a plane wave with the wave normal parallel to the direction OP. The intensity of the external magnetic field has been taken as 1.71×10^{-3} gauss which is the intensity of the dipole field of the Earth at the furthest point on a magnetic line of force intersecting the Earth's surface at a latitude of 65°. The electron density has been assumed to

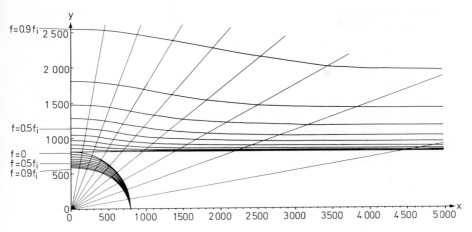

Fig. 4.5.   Surfaces of refractive index for waves in a homogeneous plasma permeated by an external magnetic field. (After J. A. Jacobs and T. Watanabe)

be $100/cm^3$. The straight line parallel to the x axis having an n value of 810 at $\theta=0$ corresponds to the limiting case of the two modes as the wave frequency tends to zero where θ is the angle between the wave normal and the external magnetic field. The nine curves above this line correspond to the cases where the frequency ω runs from $0.1\,\omega_i$ to $0.9\,\omega_i$ where the ion gyro-frequency $\omega_i=2.61$ Hz. In the limiting case as the angle θ tends to zero, these waves tend to the left-hand mode of waves propagating along the magnetic field. The n value is larger for higher frequencies, i.e. the phase velocity is smaller at higher frequencies as already mentioned. The circle with centre at the origin and an n value of 810 represents the limiting case for the other mode as ω tends to zero. The nine curves below the circle correspond to the cases when ω equals $0.1\,\omega_i$ to $0.9\,\omega_i$.

In the above method of representation of the refractive index, a normal to the surface of refractive index, which is axi-symmetric with respect to the y axis, drawn at a representative point P is parallel to the group velocity of a wave whose wave normal is parallel to OP (C. O. Hines, 1960). As pointed out by F. X. Bostick, Jr. (1963) it follows from this result that in the limiting case as ω tends to zero in the first mode, the wave energy is propagated only along the direction of the external magnetic field. Not only in this limiting case but also in all other cases, the wave energy is propagated more or less along the external magnetic field for this mode (left-hand). On the other hand, in the second (right-hand) mode the wave energy can be propagated more or less in all directions. This situation holds true not only at the furthest point on the

65° magnetic line of force but also at every point on it. It has been checked
at six points on the 65° line of force at latitudes from 10° to 60°.

It is thus reasonable to suppose that if a hm wave-packet is generated
somehow in the magnetosphere only the left-hand mode is likely to
be guided along a magnetic line of force and to echo between two magnetically conjugate points giving rise to a sequence of rising tones. One example
of a theoretical dynamic spectrum based upon this idea is shown in
Fig. 4.6 which may be compared with Fig. 2.2. It has been drawn (J. A.
Jacobs and T. Watanabe, 1964) by computing the travel time of a left-
hand hm wave between conjugate points on the 65° magnetic line of
force as a function of the wave frequency. The travel time is given by
$\int ds/V_g$ where V_g is the group velocity of a wave with a certain frequency
ω and the integration is carried out along the magnetic line of force
joining the two conjugate points. The wave normal of every component
wave was assumed to be parallel to the magnetic line of force for the
sake of simplicity. The number density of electrons in the magnetosphere,
which is assumed to consist of electrons and protons with equal densities
everywhere, was taken to be proportional to the intensity of the local
magnetic field of the Earth (the so-called gyro-frequency model of
R. L. Smith, 1961). The travel time in the ionosphere can be ignored.
The electron density at the furthest point on the magnetic line of force
was taken as $16/cm^3$ and the one hop travel time of a hm wave with an
extremely low frequency ($\omega \to 0$) is about 1 min. Fig. 4.6 shows what an
observer at the northern point of two conjugate points will see if a hm
wave packet is generated at the southern point.

Fig. 4.6. A theoretical Pc 1 spectrum to be compared with Fig. 2.2. (After J. A.
Jacobs and T. Watanabe)

4.3 The Cyclotron Instability Process and the Generation of Pc 1's

The cyclotron instability process sets up a circulary polarized electromagnetic wave (such as hm waves in a magneto-active plasma propagating in the direction of the external magnetic field) by resonance

between the wave and a stream of charged particles which run in the direction of propagation of the wave. The kinetic energy of the streaming particles is converted into the energy of the electromagnetic wave by resonance. Physical consideration of this kind of instability has been discussed by N. Brice (1964).

The resonance under consideration will take place, if the following two conditions are satisfied: when viewed from a reference system which moves with the same velocity as the particles (which are assumed to move with a uniform velocity), (1) the electric and magnetic vectors of the wave rotate in the same sense as the particles and (2) the angular frequency of rotation of the vectors is equal to the cyclotron frequency of the particles (I. Kimura, 1962; N. Brice, 1964).

The resonance frequency determined by the above two conditions may be obtained for each of the following four cases:

(a) Combination of a stream of ions (with positive charge) and an electromagnetic wave of electron resonance mode.

(b) Combination of a stream of ions and an electromagnetic wave of ion resonance mode.

(c) Combination of a stream of electrons and an electromagnetic wave of electron resonance mode.

(d) Combination of a stream of electrons and an electromagnetic wave of ion resonance mode.

Consider a circularly polarized electromagnetic wave with angular frequency ω and wave number k propagating along the external magnetic field. ω is taken positive: k is positive or negative according to whether the wave propagates in the same or opposite sense as the external magnetic field. Consider also a stream of charged particles of one kind with streaming velocity V_s, taken positive or negative according to whether the charged particles run in the same or opposite sense as the external magnetic field. The wave which is observed in the reference system moving with the same velocity as the streaming particles has an angular frequency $\omega' = \omega - kV_s$, which is different from the angular frequency ω observed from the system at rest due to the Doppler effect. Moreover, the polarization of the wave as viewed from the moving system is not necessarily the same as that from the system at rest, since the sign of ω' can be opposite to that of ω.

Consider, for instance, the resonance condition for an electromagnetic wave of the electron resonance mode. The condition for resonance with streaming electrons is given (case (c)) by

(4.1)
$$\omega_{ce} = \omega - kV_s$$

and the condition for resonance with streaming ions (case (a)) by

(4.2)
$$-\omega_{ci} = \omega - kV_s$$

with a minus sign on the left-hand side. Similarly, the resonance conditions for an ion resonance mode of wave with an electron stream (case (d)) and an ion stream (case (b)) are given by

(4.3) $-\omega_{ce} = \omega - kV_s$

and

(4.4) $\omega_{ci} = \omega - kV_s$.

The dispersion relation for propagation along the external magnetic field is given by equation (3.30) viz $n^2 = R, L$. From the definitions of R and L (equations (3.23) and (3.24)) this reduces to

(4.5) $$F(\omega, k) = \omega^2 - c^2 k^2 - \frac{\Omega_e^2 \omega}{\omega \mp \omega_e} - \frac{\Omega_i^2 \omega}{\omega \pm \omega_i} = 0.$$

The first term on the left hand side can be ignored in the following discussion. It arises from displacement currents in Maxwell's equations, and is negligible, at least for hm waves in the magnetosphere. The angular frequency ω is assumed to be positive so that

$$-\omega_e = \omega_{ce}(>0) \quad \text{and} \quad \omega_i = \omega_{ci}.$$

From equations (4.1) to (4.5) the streaming velocity, V_s, which satisfies the resonance condition can be determined as a function of the angular frequency ω for each of the four cases (a)–(d). The results are given in Fig. 4.7—those for cases (b) and (c) are drawn with dotted lines in order to show that the streaming velocity has the opposite sign to the phase velocity of the waves. In cases (a) and (d), the streaming velocities and phase velocities have the same sign. In equation (4.1) (for case (c)), kV_s must be negative for $\omega < \omega_{ce}$, implying that the streaming velocity V_s has the opposite sign to the phase velocity. In equation (4.3) (for case (d)), however, kV_s must be positive for $\omega < \omega_{ce}$.

Fig. 4.7 shows that, if the velocity of streaming protons is several times greater than the Alfvén velocity, V_A, the resonance frequencies in the hm frequency range ($\omega < \omega_{ci}$) are several fractions of the ion gyrofrequency for both modes of waves. The proton cyclotron frequency ω_{ci} at the furthermost point on a magnetic line of force which intersects the Earth's surface at 65° is about 16 rad/sec, and the wave frequency (not the angular frequency) at one half ω_{ci} is about 1.3 Hz, a typical Pc 1 frequency. A typical value of the Alfvén velocity at that point may be of the order of several hundred km/sec, and therefore a stream of protons with a velocity comparable to that of the solar wind during a magnetic disturbance can be in resonance with a typical Pc 1 hm wave. On the other hand, electrons must have an extremely high velocity, presumably relativistic, to meet the resonance condition.

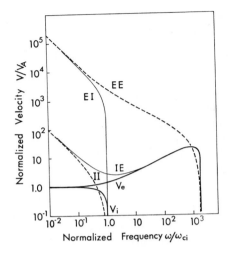

Fig. 4.7. Dispersion relations for electromagnetic waves in a magnetoactive plasma and conditions for cyclotron resonance. The velocities and angular frequencies are normalized with the Alfvén velocity V_A and the ion gyrofrequency ω_{ci}, respectively. The curves, V_e and V_i, represent the phase velocities of the electromagnetic waves of the electron resonance mode and the ion resonance mode for angular frequencies less than the electron cyclotron frequency. The curves IE, II, EE and EI represent the resonance-conditions for the four cases (a), (b), (c), and (d) respectively. (After J. A. Jacobs and T. Watanabe)

The problem of determining whether an electromagnetic wave is amplified or not at a resonance frequency is a difficult one. The starting point is the dispersion equation of the wave modified by the existence of a stream of charged particles. If the dispersion equation for the variables ω and k contains real coefficients only, the usual method to investigate the existence of an amplification process is to find, either a pair of conjugate complex k's for a certain real ω_0, or a pair of conjugate complex ω's for a certain real k_0. In the first approach, the existence of a pair of complex conjugates k's appears to show that there is one amplifying wave (the amplitude increasing with distance in the direction of wave propagation) and one evanescent wave. P. A. Sturrock (1958), however, has shown that such a casual interpretation is not necessarily justified. He has actually proved that the wave may be only evanescent even with the existence of a pair of complex conjugates k's and has provided a diagnostic method to determine whether the wave with a pair of complex conjugates k's is a true amplifying wave or only evanescent. He has also shown that the real amplifying wave, if it exists, is more specifically a travelling wave in which an amplifying signal moves with time and eventually departs from the place where it was initially generated.

His diagnostic method is to look at the behaviour of the locus of ω in the complex ω plane (called a Γ diagram) which is determined by the dispersion equation for changing k. In the second approach, the existence of a pair of complex conjugate ω's appears to show that there is one wave whose amplitude grows with time during propagation (a travelling amplifying wave) and one decaying with time. Sturrock has also shown that this usual interpretation of growing instabilities is not always justified. He has proved that there are two types of growing (in time) instabilities as indicated by the existence of a pair of conjugate complex ω's. One is a convective instability in which the region where the growing instability takes place moves in time and the instability is eventually removed from the place where the initial perturbation occurred. A convective instability is synonymous with a travelling amplifying wave. In the other type, which is a nonconvective instability, a disturbance whose amplitude grows with time remains near the place of the initial perturbation, although the disturbance may extend over an arbitrarily large region around the initial perturbation. This type of instability behaves as if it were a self-exciting oscillator rather than an amplifier. It is possible to distinguish between the two types of instability by drawing the locus of k in the complex k plane (called a Λ diagram) which is determined by the dispersion equation for changing ω.

J.A. Jacobs and T. Watanabe (1966) have investigated in some detail the cyclotron instability process. The dispersion equation (4.5) for an electromagnetic wave in a magneto active plasma is modified to take into account the effect of the stream of charged particles. The number densities of electrons n_e and ions n_i (assumed to be protons) in the background plasma are not equal because of the existence of the streaming particles since electrical neutrality is assumed everywhere. The electron and ion plasma frequencies in the background plasma must be calculated with these different values of n_e and n_i. The results of their calculations are given in Table 4.2. The existence of a perpendicular component of the velocity of the streaming particles is essential for nonconvective instabilities to occur (cases (b) and (c)).

In the hm frequency range, the ion resonance mode of waves is much more likely to be guided by the geomagnetic field than the electron resonance mode, and, for the ion resonance mode, the dispersion characteristic is as observed, viz lower frequency waves are propagated faster. The ion cyclotron mode grows in time because of cyclotron instability processes, either by a stream of electrons which flows in the propagation direction of the waves, or by a stream of ions which flows in the opposite direction. Electrons responsible for waves in the hm frequency range must have relativistic velocities. However protons, whose velocities are several times faster than the Alfvén velocity, can

Table 4.2. *Cyclotron instabilities in hm waves in the magnetosphere*

Mode of wave	Streaming particles	Case	Required velocity of the particle stream to cause instabilities at Pc 1 frequencies	Required direction of the particle stream with respect to the direction of propagation of the wave	Component of the velocity of the streaming particles perpendicular to the external magnetic field	Type of instability
Electron resonance	Protons	(a)	$\gtrsim 10^8$ cm/sec	Parallel	None	Convective
					Existing	No instability (evanescent wave)
	Electrons	(c)	Relativistic	Antiparallel	None	Nonconvective
					Existing	No instability (evanescent wave)
Ion resonance	Protons	(b)	$\gtrsim 10^8$ cm/sec	Antiparallel	None	Nonconvective
					Existing	No instability
	Electrons	(d)	Relativistic	Parallel	None	Convective
					Existing	

grow hm waves whose angular frequencies are several times smaller than the ion cyclotron frequency (see Fig. 4.7). The 'growing' process is different in the two cases. In the former case (electron stream), it is a convective instability, and, therefore, the effects of an instability which takes place in outer space will quite possibly be observed at the Earth's surface. However the growing instability in the latter case (ion stream) is nonconvective, and it is not immediately evident that an instability taking place in outer space has an observable effect at the Earth's surface.

D.R. Criswell (1969) has considered in some detail the amplification of hm waves in the magnetosphere assuming the mechanism to be cyclotron resonance between energetic protons and left hand polarized waves that form the wave packet. In his calculations he used a proton plasma distribution and a model of the differential energy distribution of the energetic protons consistent with all available observations. Fig. 4.8 shows the results of his calculations for a quiet-time plasmasphere (the region of high plasma density inside the plasmapause). The ordinate gives the total amplification A that a wave with a frequency ω will experience as it propagates along the magnetic field line through the 0600 local time meridian. The abscissa R is the geocentric distance of the intersection point of the field line with the geomagnetic equatorial plane. The parameter for the curves is the wave frequency ω (Hz).

Fig. 4.8. An amplification profile for the quiet time plasmasphere. (After D. R. Criswell)

There are at most two basic propagation regions inside the plasmasphere for 0.2–5 Hz left hand polarized hm waves. In the inner region, $A \gtrsim 1$ and amplification or at least undamped propagation occurs. In the outer region where $\omega/\omega_i \gtrsim 1$, hm waves will not propagate across the equatorial plane. Fig. 4.8 also shows that significant hm amplification in the plasmasphere is restricted to the frequency range from $0.2 \simeq 5$ Hz which is the range characteristic of Pc 1 emissions.

As K and K_p increase the plasmapause contracts earthward. R. R. Heacock (1966) found that at College (which is intersected by the $R \simeq 5.1$ field line) R_c, the distance to the field line associated with the plasmapause, will be below $R = 5.1$ as K_p increases. At times of very low magnetic activity he found that emissions with a 4 sec period ($\omega = 0.25$ Hz) constituted the lower frequency limit of those hm emissions that dominate College activity. As K_p increases the 4 sec period activity becomes less prominent and all but disappears when $K_p > 4$ (see Fig. 4.8). College activity is dominated by 0.5 Hz emissions and Fig. 4.8 indicates that maximum amplification along the $R = 5.1$ field line is for 0.5 Hz. Moreover the overall occurrence rate of Pc 1 activity falls to zero for $K > 6$ (when the plasmasphere is restricted to $R_c < 5.1$). It would thus appear that mid latitude activity is dominated by plasmasphere emissions. Fig. 4.8 is also in agreement with the observation that at higher latitudes the dominant emission period increases.

Criswell also evaluated amplification in the plasma trough (the magnetospheric region of low plasma density—its earthward boundary being the plasmapause). His results are consistent with the observation that plasma trough amplification is present. (An increase in the frequency of the dominant emission is found from Heiss Island (71° N) to Mirny (77° S) which could not have resulted from ducting of the plasmasphere emission to Mirny.) Observations indicate that the average frequency of the predominant emissions decreases from 1 to 0.25 Hz in going from 70–80°. These results are consistent with Criswell's calculations which indicate that the complete frequency range is amplified in the plasmasphere whereas plasma trough amplification is limited to the $0.3 \lesssim \omega \lesssim 1$ Hz range.

Criswell also calculated the dependence of the repetition period T of structured Pc 1 elements on emission mid-period t (see Sec. 2.3). His results for the plasmasphere are shown in Fig. 4.9. The curves are parameterized by the R value of each field line along the 0600 meridian. The heavy segment of each R curve delineates the range of the t value where $10 < A < A_{max}$, the dashed segments where $5 < A < 10$ and along the remainder of each R curve $1 < A < 5$. One would expect that the distribution of (t, T) values of pearl pulsations observed at mid latitude stations would be contained by the contours of maximum amplification

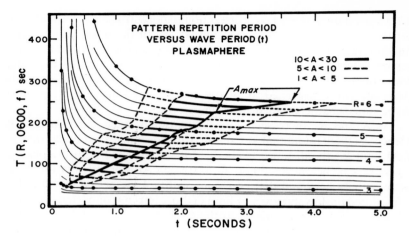

Fig. 4.9. The pattern repetition period T (sec.) versus the wave period t (sec.) for the plasmasphere. The curves are parameterized by the R value of each field line along the 0600 meridian. (After D. R. Criswell)

in Fig. 4.9 and this is indeed the case (see Fig. 4.10) which is based on data from College, Alaska ($R = 5.1$, $\lambda = 64.7°$ N), Chambon-La-Forêt, France ($R = 2.4$, $\lambda = 50°.4$ N) and Palo Alto, California ($R = 1.9$, $\lambda = 43.5°$ N). Criswell also found that the (t-T) region of significant plasma trough amplification is completely encompassed by the corresponding plasmasphere region unless $R_c < 3.6$.

Fig. 4.10. A scatter diagram of pattern repetition period (T) versus emission mid-period (t) with the amplification contours of Fig. 4.9 superposed. Low-latitude and mid-latitude emissions are presented. (After D. R. Criswell)

4.4 Sub Classes of Pc 1's—Non Linear Theories

As already pointed out geomagnetic micropulsation signals in the Pc 1 frequency range (0.2–5 Hz) often show a series of rising frequencies when displayed on a spectrogram. This type of signal is interpreted as a manifestation of dispersion in the propagation in the magnetosphere of a hm wave of the ion cyclotron mode, bouncing between a pair of magnetically conjugate areas under the guidance of the magnetic line of force connecting those areas. Such waves are believed to be generated by a cyclotron instability process caused by nonthermal and electrically charged particles, presumably protons, which are somehow injected into, or generated within, the magnetosphere. Such micropulsation signals have been called hm whistlers, micropulsation whistlers or simply hm emissions. However close examination of the spectrograms published in the literature seems to reveal the existence of at least two prototypes. The name hm whistler may be adequately reassigned to one of these, and implies that signals in this category are simply manifestations of the dispersion effect in their propagation as in the case of whistling atmospherics. The other type of signals, classed as periodic hm emissions, seems to be similar to periodic VLF emissions rather than whistling atmospherics. It is only for this type of signal that a cyclotron instability is suggested as the basic process involved.

Fig. 4.11.   An example of a hm whistler. (After L. P R. Tepley)

Fig. 4.11 is an example of a hm whistler. A hm whistler shows two characteristics on a spectrogram. The first is that the signal strength becomes systematically weaker as time passes. The second is that each individual signal is successively more inclined towards the time axis. This indicates dispersion in the propagation of an ion cyclotron mode of hm wave, the signals propagating in the magnetosphere faster (slower) for lower (higher) frequencies (see e.g. J. A. Jacobs and T. Watanabe, 1964).

Fig. 4.12.   An example of a periodic hm emission. (After R. W. E. McNicol and L. Johnson)

The series of signals in Fig. 4.12 shows different characteristics from those in Fig. 4.11 although they are similar in that the frequency of each individual signal increases with time. The first difference is that the strength of the signals in Fig. 4.12 becomes stronger with time and later decays gradually. Secondly, each individual signal does not follow the law of dispersion i.e. the signals run almost parallel to one another. Signals of this type form a class distinct from that of hm whistlers and have been termed periodic hm emissions. On occasion each individual signal successively tends to be more inclined towards the frequency axis. This trend in the frequency change with time is exactly opposite to that expected from the dispersion law.

The generation mechanism of periodic hm emissions seems to be analogous to that of periodic VLF emissions. The essential point of the presently accepted model of VLF emissions is to assume the existence of a region of instability somewhere on the ray path of an electromagnetic wave of the electron cyclotron (right hand polarization) mode which is propagated under the guidance of the magnetic field of the earth in the same way as whistling atmospherics (R. A. Helliwell, 1963; N. Brice, 1964). A new emission occurs each time the previous wave enters the region of instability having travelled along a magnetic line of force forwards, being bounced at a conjugate point, and travelling again backwards (see Fig. 4.13). The emission mechanism is supposed to be the cyclotron instability process caused by a cloud of nonthermal electrons. J. A. Jacobs and T. Watanabe (1967) suggested that if the mode of the electromagnetic wave is changed from the electron cyclotron (right hand polarization) to the ion cyclotron (left hand polarization) and the nonthermal electrons are replaced by a cloud of nonthermal ions the model holds for hm periodic emissions.

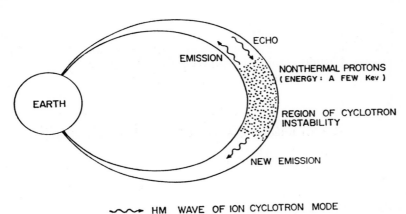

Fig. 4.13.   Model of periodic hm emissions. (After J. A. Jacobs and T. Watanabe)

Several problems concerning periodic hm emissions which have been raised by observations still remain unsolved on a linear theory. For example, why does the emission frequency of a hm emission increase with time, and why does not a hm emission last indefinitely? In other words, why does not the cyclotron instability continue indefinitely? If the instability process should continue indefinitely after being triggered once, a hm emission signal would appear as one (or several, if higher harmonics are generated) series of infinitely long line(s) on a spectrogram, instead of one (or several) series of signals of some finite duration or possibly dots.

It seems that dispersion alone cannot account for the increase in the emission frequency with time. Emission signals in Fig. 4.12 run almost parallel to one another and there are examples where each individual signal becomes more inclined towards the frequency axis as time passes. (This trend is more pronounced as the signal strength increases with time.) It seems probable that the emission frequency may change with time due to the emission mechanism itself. J. A. Jacobs and T. Watanabe (1967) have attempted to answer these two problems using a non-linear theory of cyclotron instability.

The dispersion equation (4.5) is obtained under two basic assumptions

(i) the temperature of both the electron gas and the proton gas of the plasma is zero and

(ii) the nonlinear terms in the collisionless Boltzmann equations for both the electron and proton gases are negligible. If the assumption (i) is replaced by the following condition (i') that the plasma includes nonthermal electrons and/or nonthermal protons in addition to the background zero temperature electron and proton gas, it can be proved that, in general, the amplitude of the magnetic field b of the wave is no longer a pure constant but changes gradually with time. T. Watanabe (1966) has shown that the rate of time change is given by

(4.6)
$$\frac{db}{dt} = \Gamma b.$$

The ratio of the number density of the nonthermal particles to that of the background plasma particles is assumed to be much smaller than 1. The coefficient Γ is positive under certain conditions, and, in this case, the wave amplitude grows with time. It is positive and maximum in the vicinity of a certain frequency satisfying the cyclotron resonance condition. In this sense, the process in which the amplitude b grows with time is called a cyclotron instability.

In deriving equation (4.6), the second assumption (ii) is still retained. If this assumption is lifted as well, Watanabe has shown that not only the amplitude b but also the phase constant θ changes with time gradually. This means that the effective frequency of the wave is not equal to the frequency ω determined by the dispersions equation (4.5). Although this may seem strange at first, it is understandable in view of the result that, in a system of nonlinear oscillations, the frequency is different from that given by the linearized approximation which is valid only for oscillations with an infinitesimal amplitude. A simple example of this is given by a pendulum whose period is constant, independent of amplitude, if it is sufficiently small. If the amplitude is large, however, the period depends on it, being longer for a larger amplitude. The difference between the period for a large amplitude and that in the limiting case for an infinitesimal amplitude (determined by linear theory) is not proportional to the amplitude itself but to its square (a nonlinear effect), ignoring higher order terms. The magnetic field, b, is governed by the differential equation of simple harmonic oscillations; if the effects of nonthermal particles as well as the nonlinear terms in the Boltzmann equations are taken into account, the differential equation for b is that of simple harmonic motion together with perturbation terms.

Thus the differential equation for the time change of the magnetic field b is analogous to that of large amplitude motion of a pendulum.

Watanabe has shown that the time rate of change of the effective frequency ω' is given by

(4.7)
$$\frac{d\omega'}{dt} = C\Gamma \left(\frac{b}{B_0}\right)^2 .$$

The coefficient C is a constant which is determined by the number densities of the nonthermal particles and of the background (zero temperature) plasma particles and also by ω, the frequency obtained in the linearized approximation. The coefficient C is positive for the ion cyclotron mode of hm waves, and therefore the effective frequency increases with time when the wave amplitude grows with time ($\Gamma > 0$). The rate of increase of the effective frequency can be calculated at a typical place in the magnetosphere. At a point in the geomagnetic equatorial plane with an L value of 5.6 the strength of the main magnetic field, B, is about 170γ. The strength of the perturbing magnetic field, b, may be taken as 0.5γ. The frequency ω in the linearized approximation is about one half the proton gyrofrequency at the point under consideration. The nonthermal particles may be assumed to be protons and the ratio of the number density of the nonthermal protons to the background plasma particles taken to be 10^{-2}. With these values for the parameters involved, the growth rate, Γ, is of the order of 10^{-1} sec^{-1} and the rate of change of the effective frequency is about 0.08 Hz per min, which is reasonable when compared with observed results. Thus equation (4.7) seems to give an answer to the first problem raised.

In assumption (i'), the background plasma gases are still assumed to be at zero temperature. If this assumption is lifted Watanabe has shown that equation (4.6) must be replaced by

(4.8)
$$\frac{db}{dt} = \Gamma b - A b^3 .$$

The coefficient Γ is the growth rate, although its algebraic expression is different from that in the case of a zero temperature background plasma. The second term on the right hand side introduces an attenuation or a nonlinear instability process according to whether A is positive or negative. In the case of a growing electrostatic wave in a nonthermal electron gas (the so-called two stream longitudinal instability), it can be proved that the electric field obeys a differential equation of the same form as equation (4.8). In that case it can be shown that the coefficient A can be positive, negative or zero. It is surmised, therefore, that this is also true in the present case. Although it has not been proved, it is believed that the coefficient A is in general positive. The reason for this

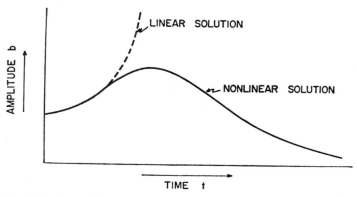

Fig. 4.14. Evolution of the signal strength on the non linear theory of cyclotron instabilities. The dotted curve shows the time change in the signal strength on the linear theory. (After J. A. Jacobs and T. Watanabe)

is that the coefficient A can be shown to depend on the distribution functions of the background plasma particles, but not on the nonthermal particles and that, in general, no instability seems to arise due to background plasma particles only unless their distribution functions in velocity space are unusual. If Γ is positive and constant, the magnetic field strength b tends to a constant value $(\Gamma/A)^{\frac{1}{2}}$. In fact, however, Γ is not constant. If Γ tends to zero as time passes, equation (4.8) shows that the magnetic field strength b also tends to zero after passing through a maximum (see Fig. 4.14). Kinetic energy of motion of the nonthermal protons in the direction perpendicular to the external magnetic field is essential to cause an instability ($\Gamma > 0$). Also the pitch angles of the particles must decrease on the average as the hm wave grows with time. It is therefore surmised that the growth rate Γ tends to zero as time passes. In the case of two stream longitudinal instability, it can be rigorously proved that the growth rate tends to zero as time passes and that the electric field strength follows the trend described. Although no exact proof has been obtained in the present case, it may hopefully be expected that this result also holds true. This is an important consequence of the nonlinear theory of cyclotron instabilities. According to the linear theory, the magnetic field strength b would have to increase indefinitely as an exponential function of time.

4.5 Propagation of Pc 1's to Lower Latitudes

A left-hand hm wave packet generated in the magnetosphere and guided to the Earth by a magnetic field line has been suggested as the mechanism responsible for Pc 1's by many other authors (R. L. Dowden, 1965; R. L.

Fig. 4.15. Typical profile for the right hand mode propagation constants. (After R. N. Manchester)

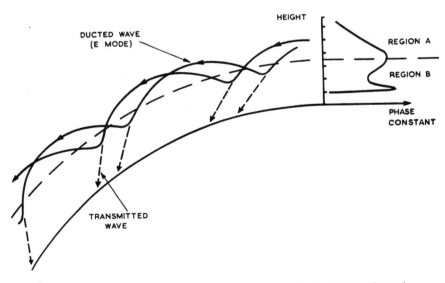

Fig. 4.16. Ray paths in the ionospheric duct. (After R. N. Manchester)

Dowden and M. W. Emery, 1965; T. Obayashi, 1965; R. C. Wentworth, 1966). Calculations show that this field line generally lies between L values of 4–10 corresponding to magnetic latitudes of 60–72°. Observations of these events (L. R. Tepley et al., 1965) show that they occur almost simultaneously over a latitude range extending from the auroral zone to the equator. The range of longitude over which an event is observed however appears to be restricted. This implies propagation of hm waves for a considerable distance in a north-south direction parallel to the surface of the Earth. The left-hand mode is strongly guided by the Earth's magnetic field, but the right-hand mode is isotropic. There is coupling between the left and right-hand modes especially in the lower ionosphere, so that micropulsation energy could be propagated across the magnetic field lines in the right-hand mode.

A typical profile for the right-hand mode propagation constants is shown in Fig. 4.15. This was obtained by R. N. Manchester (1966) using the relationships given by C. E. Prince et al. (1964). A propagation duct is formed by the bulge in the phase constant profile centered on the F-region electron-density maximum. The type of ray path to be expected in such a duct is illustrated in Fig. 4.16. As the walls of the duct are not perfect reflectors, the wave is attenuated as it propagates down the duct. A portion of the wave energy is transmitted through the ionosphere to the surface of the Earth where it may be detected as geomagnetic micropulsations. A. J. Dessler (1958) had suggested some years earlier that guided propagation of hm waves over large distances may take place in an ionospheric duct centered around the Alfvén speed minimum near the F_2 ionization peak.

Manchester (1966) has calculated the propagation constants in the ionosphere at middle latitudes for a range of frequencies in the Pc 1 category and for different local times. At 1200 LMT he found a rapid increase in the mode angle as the frequency decreases in the region of 0.5 Hz (the mode angle is the real part of the angle θ between the ray and the horizontal). As the mode angle increases i.e. as the frequency decreases, the imaginary part of θ, which represents the duct attenuation, increases. Thus the duct exhibits a low frequency cut-off at about 0.5 Hz, the attenuation becoming large below this frequency.

Manchester thus explains the experimental result that Pc 1's of frequency less than 0.5 Hz are seldom observed simultaneously at a number of stations, and he suggests that the observed variation of hm emission frequency with latitude is a propagation rather than a source effect. Fig. 4.17 shows the diurnal variation of the duct attenuation for a frequency of 3 Hz. At night the duct is very deep, and both the upper and lower walls are good reflectors so that the attenuation is less and the duct is very efficient at this time. During the day, especially for the

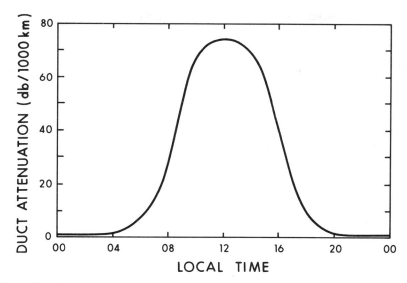

Fig. 4.17.   Diurnal variation of duct attenuation for a frquency of 3 Hz. (After R. N. Manchester)

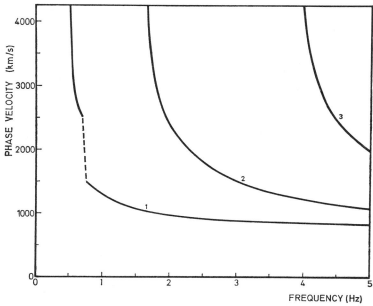

Fig. 4.18.   Phase velocity for propagation in the ionospheric duct as a function of frequency. (After R. N. Manchester)

lower wall, the reflectivity decreases and the duct attenuation becomes large. This would be sufficient to account for the low occurrence rate of Pc 1 events at middle latitudes at this time. Similar results have been obtained by L. R. Tepley and R. K. Landshoff (1966) and C. and P. S. Greifinger (1968), while in a later paper (1968) Manchester himself has refined his calculations. C. and P. S. Greifinger (1968) showed that attenuation, in any band, generally increases with frequency, being smallest at cut-off. Attenuation is not necessary for the existence of a cut-off—for nighttime sunspot minimum conditions, attenuation is entirely absent, but a cut-off exists. The cut-off is a consequence of the boundary conditions, not of the properties of the medium.

The results of Manchester's calculations for an ionospheric duct for nighttime conditions ($f_0 F_2 = 2.9$ MHz) are shown in Fig. 4.18 which is a plot of the phase velocity versus frequency for propagation towards the equator, showing that below 0.45 Hz there is no propagating mode. Below 0.7 Hz, the E layer is essentially transparent, and the duct includes all the ionosphere and the free space layer. Above this frequency the E layer forms the effective lower edge of the duct. For the ionosphere considered in his calculations, above 1.5 Hz there are two propagation

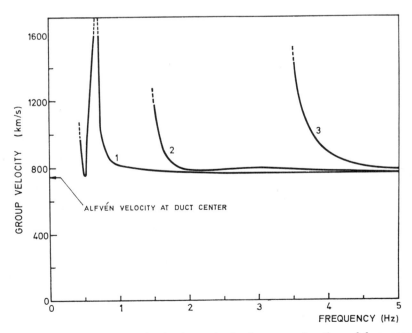

Fig. 4.19. Group velocity in the ionospheric duct as a function of frequency. (After R. N. Manchester)

modes, and above 3.4 Hz, there are three modes. At the cut-off frequencies 0.45, 1.5, and 3.4 Hz, the mode equation is satisfied for vertical propagation. These frequencies are therefore the resonant frequencies of the ionosphere–exosphere cavity (cf. J. A. Jacobs and T. Watanabe, 1962; E. C. Field and C. Greifinger, 1965).

In Fig. 4.19, the variation with frequency of the group velocity for propagation in the duct is shown. Except near the cut-off frequency for each mode, the group velocity is slightly larger than the Alfvén velocity at the duct center. The sharp peak in the curve at 0.7 Hz is associated with the phase velocity transition at the same frequency. For propagation away from the equator, the phase velocity discontinuity and group velocity peak are not present.

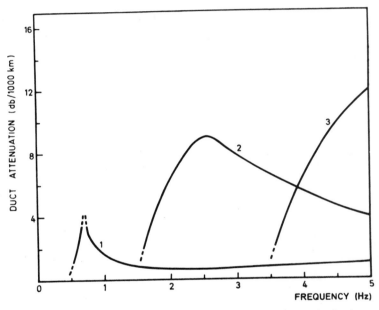

Fig. 4.20. Attenuation for waves propagating along the ionospheric duct as a function of frequency. (After R. N. Manchester)

The variation with frequency of the duct attenuation is shown in Fig. 4.20. Wave absorption in the E region is the principal source of attenuation; however, near the peak of the curves coupling between the right and left-hand modes in the lower ionosphere also contributes to the attenuation of the right-hand mode wave propagating along the duct.

For daytime conditions (when $f_0 F_2$ is larger) Manchester found that the cut-off frequencies are more closely spaced and that the cut-off frequency of the first mode is at a lower frequency. Variation of the various parameters with frequency is similar to that for the nighttime case. The Alfvén velocity at the duct center is lower and therefore, away from cut-off, phase and group velocities are lower. Owing to increased

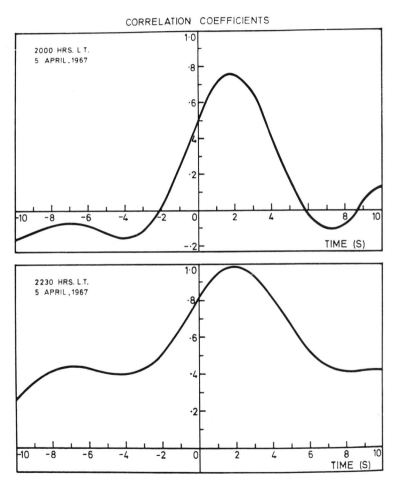

Fig. 4.21. Cross correlation curves obtained from the envelopes of bandpass filtered amplitude-time records from Hobart and Newcastle (Hobart before Newcastle). For the upper curve the event frequency is 0.61 Hz and for the lower curve it is 0.62 Hz. (After R. N. Manchester)

absorption in the E region, duct attenuation is generally larger during the day, especially for higher-order modes.

There have been a number of attempts to estimate the propagation velocity using the records from different stations. Thus R. C. Wentworth et al. (1966) found that the regularly spaced fine structured elements seen in Pc 1's were consistently received earlier at higher latitudes. Within an accuracy of ± 0.8 sec the average time delay between College, Alaska, and Kauai, Hawaii, was found to be 5.8 sec, and between Palo Alto, California, and Kauai, 3.2 sec. This leads to an average projected propagation velocity at sea-level of about 900 km/sec towards the equator which is of the order of the Alfvén wave velocity in the F region of the ionosphere. R. N. Manchester (1968) analysed seven months data of Pc 1's from two mid latitude stations in Australia (Newcastle and Hobart) situated approximately on the same magnetic meridian but separated in latitude by about 1200 km. Approximately the same amount of Pc 1 activity was observed at both stations and approximately half the total number of events were recorded simultaneously (events were considered simultaneous when activity had the same frequency-time structure at each station although relative amplitudes were often widely different). Manchester carried out a more detailed correlation analysis using bandpass filtered amplitude-time records—filtering is necessary to avoid beating effects caused by overlapping bands. Peak to peak amplitudes were measured at 1 sec intervals and crosscorrelation curves obtained—two examples are shown in Fig. 4.21. Except for a number of events the correlation curves were of this general shape (called by Manchester Type 1). It can be seen that the correlation is very high at a lag of approximately 2 sec.

For correlation curves such as those illustrated in Fig. 4.21, the lag at maximum correlation gives a measure of the time taken for the event to propagate between the two stations and hence gives the group velo-city. For all but two events the velocity was in the direction from Hobart to Newcastle, i.e. towards the equator. Manchester also found that the group velocity was approximately inversely proportional to $f_0 F_2$, and slightly larger than the Alfvén velocity at an altitude of 340 km. A number of events did not show the same type of correlation curve as those illustrated in Fig. 4.21. These events (called Type II) either had a broad maximum centered on approximately zero lag or two peaks located symmetrically about zero lag with one peak larger than the other. For those events with a double peaked curve the group velocity for propagation both towards and away from the equator is similar in magnitude to the Alfvén velocity at an altitude of 340 km. Manchester interprets these experimental results as propagation of hm waves in the ionospheric duct in a general north–south direction.

References

Akasofu, S.-I.: The auroral oval, the auroral sub-storm and their relations with the internal structure of the magnetosphere. Planet. Space Sci. **14**, 587—595 (1966).

Bostick, F. X., Jr.: Private communication 1963.

Brice, N.: Fundamentals of very low frequency emission generation mechanisms. J. Geophys. Res. **69**, 4515—4522 (1964).

— Discrete VLF emissions from the upper atmosphere. Stanford Electronics Lab. Tech. Rept. No. 3412-6, Stanford Univ. 1964.

Carpenter, D. L.: Whistler studies of the plasmapause in the magnetosphere 1. *Temporal variations in the position of the knee and some evidence on plasma motions near the knee.* J. Geophys. Res. **71**, 693—709 (1966).

Cornwall, J. M.: Micropulsations and the outer radiation zone. J. Geophys. Res. **71**, 2185—2199 (1966).

Criswell, D. R.: Pc 1 micropulsation activity and magnetospheric amplification of 0.2 to 5.0 Hz hydromagnetic waves. J. Geophys. Res. **74**, 205—224 (1969).

Davis, L. R., Williamson, J. M.: Space Research III. (Ed. W. Priester.) North Holland Publ. Co. 1963.

Dessler, A. J.: The propagation velocity of world wide sudden commencements of magnetic storms. J. Geophys. Res. **63**, 507—511 (1958).

Dowden, R. L.: Micropulsation mode propagations in the magnetosphere. Planet. Space Sci. **13**, 761—772 (1965).

— Emery, M. W.: The use of micropulsation whistlers in the study of the outer magnetosphere. Planet. Space Sci. **13**, 773—779 (1965).

Field, E. C., Greifinger, C.: Transmission of geomagnetic micropulsations through the ionosphere and lower exosphere. J. Geophys. Res. **70**, 4885—4899 (1965).

Gendrin, R.: Sur une théorie des pulsations rapides structurées du champ magnétique terrestre. Ann. Geophys. **19**, 197—214 (1963).

Greifinger, C., Greifinger, P. S.: Theory of hydromagnetic propagation in the ionospheric waveguide. J. Geophys. Res. **73**, 7473—7490 (1968).

Heacock, R. R.: Notes on pearl-type micropulsations. J. Geophys. Res. **68**, 589—591 (1963).

— The 4-second summertime micropulsation band at College. J. Geophys. Res. **71**, 2763—2775 (1966).

Helliwell, R. A.: Whistler-triggered periodic very low frequency emissions. J. Geophys. Res. **68**, 5387—5395 (1963).

Hines, C. O.: Internal atmospheric gravity waves at ionospheric heights. Can. J. Phys. **38**, 1441—1481 (1960).

Jacobs, J. A., Watanabe, T.: Propagation of hydromagnetic waves in the lower exosphere and the origin of shortperiod geomagnetic pulsations. J. Atmos. Terr. Phys. **24**, 413—434 (1962).

— — Trapped charged particles as the origin of short period geomagnetic pulsations. Planet. Space Sci. **11**, 869—878 (1963).

— — Micropulsation whistlers. J. Atmos. Terr. Phys. **26**, 825—829 (1964).

— — Amplification of hydromagnetic waves in the magnetosphere by a cyclotron instability process with application to the theory of hydromagnetic whistlers. J. Atmos. Terr. Phys. **28**, 235—253 (1966).

— — Theoretical notes on whistlers and periodic emissions in the hydromagnetic regime. Planet. Space Sci. **15**, 799—809 (1967).

Kenney, J. F., Knaflich, H. B.: A systematic study of structured micropulsations. J. Geophys. Res. **72**, 2857—2869 (1967).

References

Kimura, I.: Meeting on cosmic plasma physics. Inst. Plasma Phys., Nagoya Univ., Japan, 1962.

Lokken, J. E.: Private communication 1963.

MacDonald, G. J. F.: Spectrum of hydromagnetic waves in the exosphere. J. Geophys. Res. **66**, 3639—3670 (1961).

Manchester, R. N.: Propagation of Pc 1 micropulsations from high to low latitudes. J. Geophys. Res. **71**, 3749—3754 (1966).

— Correlation of Pc 1 micropulsations at spaced stations. J. Geophys. Res. **73**, 3549—3556 (1968).

Matveeva, E. T., Troitskaya, V. A.: Investigations of pearl type pulsations for the years 1957—1964. Rep. Inst. Phys. Earth, Moscow 1965.

Obayashi, T.: Hydromagnetic whistlers. J. Geophys. Res. **70**, 1069—1082 (1965).

Prince, C. E., Bostick, F. X., Jr., Smith, H. W.: A study of the transmission of plane hydromagnetic waves through the upper atmosphere. Elec. Eng. Res. Lab., Univ. Texas Rept. No. 134, 1964.

Sen, A. K.: Pearl time geomagnetic oscillations. J. Atmos. Terr. Phys. **30**, 439—451 (1968).

Smith, R. L.: Properties of the outer ionosphere deduced from nose whistlers. J. Geophys. Res. **66**, 3709—3716 (1961).

Sturrock, P. A.: Kinematics of growing waves. Phys. Rev. **112**, 1488—1503 (1958).

Tepley, L. R., Heacock, R. R., Fraser, B. J.: Hydromagnetic emissions (Pc 1) observed simultaneously in the auroral zone and at low latitudes. J. Geophys. Res. **70**, 2720—2725 (1965).

— Landshoff, R. K.: Waveguide theory for ionospheric propagation of hydromagnetic emissions. J. Geophys. Res. **71**, 1499—1504 (1966).

Watanabe, T.: Determination of the electron distribution in the magnetosphere using hydromagnetic whistlers. J. Geophys. Res. **70**, 5839—5848 (1965).

— Quasi linear theory of transverse plasma instabilities with applications to hydromagnetic emissions from the magnetosphere. Can. J. Phys. **44**, 815—835 (1966).

Wentworth, R. C.: Evidence for maximum production of hydromagnetic emissions above the afternoon hemisphere of the Earth, I, Extrapolation to the base of the exosphere. J. Geophys. Res. **69**, 2689—2698 (1964a).

— Evidence for maximum production of hydromagnetic emissions above the afternoon hemisphere of the Earth, II, Analysis of statistical studies. J. Geophys. Res. **69**, 2699—2705 (1964b).

— Recent investigations of hydromagnetic emissions. Part II. J. Geomag. Geoelect. **18**, 257—273 (1966).

— Tepley, L. R.: Hydromagnetic emissions, X-ray bursts and electron bunches, Part 2., Theoretical interpretation. J. Geophys. Res. **67**, 3335—3343 (1962).

— — Amundsen, K. D.: Intra-and inter hemisphere differences in occurrence times of hydromagnetic emissions. J. Geophys. Res. **71**, 1492—1498 (1966).

5 Theories of Pc 2—5 and Pi Oscillations

5.1 Introduction

Continuous pulsations (Pc 2–5) as well as irregular pulsations (Pi 2) can be explained in terms of Alfvén and magnetosonic waves by considering the propagation and transformation of these waves in the whole magnetospheric cavity, as well as in the resonators formed by the extremes of the Alfvén velocity distribution in the magnetosphere. Theoretical calculations of hm wave propagation in a cold plasma have so far treated poloidal and toroidal oscillations separately. The equations (3.18) and (3.19) formulated by J. W. Dungey (1954a, b) for the distribution of the magnetic field and for the plasma concentration in the magnetosphere remain, as yet, unsolved.

The auroral zone maxima, conjugate similarities, and the detection in space give convincing evidence of magnetospheric propagation of the signals. It is generally agreed that conditions are suitable for generative hm resonances in the upper atmosphere. T. Watanabe (1959) considered Pc 2–3's to be a result of hm resonances in the region above the Earth's surface below a "barrier" defined by the Alfvén phase velocity maximum at several thousand kilometers. Such oscillations must be poloidal. The observed inverted U-type diurnal change in period is assumed to be due to a change in the barrier altitude between day and night. One of the weakest points of this theory for Pc 2–3's is the discrepancy between the theoretical and observed resonant periods. A precise calculation of the resonant period is difficult, however, because values of the parameters involved vary greatly even within one wave length of the hm waves.

The lower exosphere and ionosphere also act as a filter for hm waves because of changes in dispersion due to neutral particles. Several workers have calculated the power spectra of geomagnetic micropulsations to be expected on the ground for the transmission of L mode hm waves through the lower exosphere and the ionosphere (see Sec. 3.5). In particular C. E. Prince et al. (1964) explained some of the Pc 2–3 power spectra, polarization, and diurnal changes by considering hm resonances in the region from 200–1000 km above the Earth's surface. Attenuation of Pc 2–5 hm waves by the ionosphere should be less than that for 0.5 Hz pulsations. C. Greifinger and P. Greifinger (1965) found a pronounced resonance in the transmission for waves in the Pc 4 range, which shifted to higher frequencies with the lower ion density at sunspot minimum and nighttime ionospheric conditions. Although this may be responsible for some of the pattern in the 11-year cycle in average periods (Fig. 2.17), the diurnal changes in Pc 2–3 and Pc 4 which are in opposition to each other and shift to shorter periods at lower latitudes are not so easily explained. In addition, the diurnal polarization pattern of Pc 5's is apparently not dependent on selective ionospheric modulation of the propagation modes.

5.2 Toroidal Osçillations

Continuous pulsations of Pc 5 type are usually described by toroidal oscillations propagating along field lines. In analogy to waves propagating along an elastic string, the period T of a hm wave along a geomagnetic line of force corresponding to co-latitude θ_0 is given by

(5.1)
$$T = 2 \int_{\theta_0} \frac{ds}{V}$$

the integration being along the line of force which cuts the Earth's surface at θ_0 (see Fig. 5.1). Assuming that the geomagnetic field is a centred dipole, the equation of a line of force is given by

(5.2)
$$R = R_0 \sin^2 \theta .$$

Since

(5.3)
$$B = \frac{M}{R^3} (1 + 3\cos^2 \theta)^{\frac{1}{2}}$$

where M is the magnetic dipole moment of the Earth and $V = B(4\pi\rho)^{-\frac{1}{2}}$ (see Sec. 3.1), it follows that

(5.4)
$$T = \frac{8\pi^{\frac{1}{2}} a^4}{M \sin^8 \theta_0} \int_{\theta_0}^{\pi/2} \rho^{\frac{1}{2}} \sin^7 \theta \, d\theta .$$

Thus T depends on the length of the field line and the plasma density in the magnetosphere. Since T can be observed in different latitudes θ_0 it is possible in principle to solve the integral equation (5.4) to determine the unknown function ρ. However a formal mathematical solution is complicated—it is easier to assume a particular mathematical form for the function ρ and calculate T by numerical integration. This concept of oscillating magnetic lines of force was first used by T. Obayashi and

J. A. Jacobs (1958) for computing the plasma density distribution of the outer atmosphere making use of the observed periods of micropulsations. To carry out the analysis, however, it was necessary to make an assumption about the functional relationship between height and plasma density.

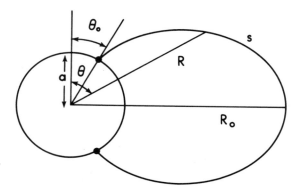

Fig. 5.1. Geometry of the geomagnetic lines of force. (After J. A. Jacobs and T. Obayashi)

The equation governing toroidal oscillations v_ϕ, under the simplifying assumption $\partial/\partial\phi = 0$, is (3.21) which, with v_ϕ depending on t through the factor $\exp(i\omega t)$, becomes

$$(5.5) \quad 4\pi\rho\omega^2 v_\phi + \frac{1}{R\sin\theta}(\boldsymbol{B}_0\cdot\nabla)(R\sin\theta)^2(\boldsymbol{B}_0\cdot\nabla)\left(\frac{v_\phi}{R\sin\theta}\right) = 0\,.$$

In equation (5.5) the only spatial derivatives which occur are those in the operator $(\boldsymbol{B}_0\cdot\nabla)$ operating on the function v_ϕ; this, however, can be interpreted as the derivative of v_ϕ in the direction of $\boldsymbol{B}_0$. Therefore the equation can be interpreted as a wave equation where the disturbance propagates along a line of force. Choosing for $\boldsymbol{B}_0$ a dipole field, the equation represents the wave equation governing the time-space relationship of a disturbance which propagates along the magnetic lines of force of the dipole. It is in this sense that one speaks of oscillations of the lines of force which, it must be emphasized, applies in a strict sense only to the case of an infinitely conducting medium.

Having obtained v_ϕ from equation (5.5), the components E_R and E_θ may be computed from equation (3.10). Because of axial symmetry, it follows from equation (3.8) that there is only a ϕ-component of $\boldsymbol{b}$. Hence equation (5.5) governs the following set of quantities:

$$(5.6) \qquad\qquad (0,0,v_\phi); \quad (E_R, E_\theta, 0); \quad (0,0,b_\phi)\,.$$

Since the operator

(5.7) $$(\boldsymbol{B}_0 \cdot \nabla) = B_R \frac{\partial}{\partial R} + \frac{B_\theta}{R} \frac{\partial}{\partial \theta} = \frac{-M}{R^4} \sin \theta \frac{d}{d\theta}$$

equation (5.5) becomes

(5.8) $$4\pi \rho \omega^2 v_\phi + \frac{M^2}{R^5} \frac{d}{d\theta} \left[\frac{\sin^3 \theta}{R^2} \frac{d}{d\theta} \left(\frac{v_\phi}{R \sin \theta} \right) \right] = 0 .$$

Selecting a particular line of force by introducing equation (5.2) into equation (5.8), we have

(5.9) $$4\pi \rho \omega^2 v_\phi + \frac{M^2}{R_0^8 \sin^{10} \theta} \frac{d}{d\theta} \left[\frac{1}{\sin \theta} \frac{d}{d\theta} \left(\frac{v_\phi}{\sin^3 \theta} \right) \right] = 0 .$$

It is obvious from this equation that toroidal oscillations exhibit a very strong latitudinal dependence. Assuming reflection at the surface of the earth the resonant frequencies for each line of force may be calculated. For the fundamental mode, $dv_\phi/d\theta = 0$ at $\theta = \pi/2$, and taking $\rho = 10^{-21}$ gm/cm^3, J. W. Dungey (1954a, b) obtained the following relation for the period T (in seconds) at co-latitude $\theta_0 \leqslant 60°$,

(5.10) $$T \simeq 0.6 \operatorname{cosec}^8 \theta_0 .$$

Numerical values are given in Table 5.1.

Table 5.1. *Fundamental periods T of toroidal oscillations at different co-latitudes* θ_0 *(normal dipole field, constant plasma density)*

θ_0	T
45°	10 sec
35°	54 sec
25°	11 min
20°	55 min

A different method of approach for obtaining the periods of the higher modes of oscillation has been adopted by Y. Kato and T. Watanabe (1956). In order to calculate the eigen values they used an asymptotic expression for the behaviour of the higher order modes (Courant and Hilbert, 1953). Taking the plasma density to be constant (equal to its value ρ_0 at the most distant point, $\theta = \pi/2$) they obtained the fundamental periods at four different co-latitudes for three different plasma densities

ρ_0. The results of their calculations are given in Table 5.2. Comparing their calculated values with the observed Pc 5 periods, they found fair agreement for $\theta_0 = 25°$ if ρ_0 is taken as 1.6 or 2.4×10^{-21} gm/cm³.

Table 5.2. *Fundamental periods T (sec) of toroidal oscillations at different co-latitudes θ_0 and plasma densities ρ_0 (normal dipole field)*

θ_0 \ ρ_0	0.8×10^{-21} gm/cm³	1.6×10^{-21} gm/cm³	2.4×10^{-21} gm/cm³
45°	6	9	11
35°	33	47	57
25°	381	538	659
20°	2071	2929	3585

An interesting approach to the solution of equation (5.9) has been taken by M. Siebert (1964). Choosing a special plasma density distribution he obtained for the solution closed formulae which, under the condition of perfect reflection at the surface of the earth, yield the eigenperiods of a particular line of force as a function of co-latitude θ_0 and of the plasma

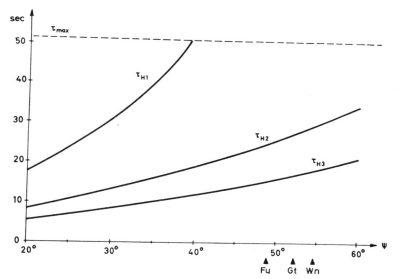

Fig. 5.2. Computed distribution of the periods of the first three symmetric eigen-oscillations in the H-component as a function of geomagnetic latitude under the assumption of a plasma distribution decreasing with height as R^{-8}. (After M. Siebert)

density at the Earth's surface. The results of his calculations under the assumption of a plasma distribution decreasing with height as R^{-8} are shown in Fig. 5.2.

Because of the complexity of equations (3.18) and (3.19) describing poloidal and toroidal oscillations in spherical polar coordinates, K. O. Westphal and J. A. Jacobs (1962) derived similar equations in cylindrical coordinates (r, θ, z) with the main magnetic field lying in the plane perpendicular to the axis of the cylinder. Considering only phenomena in the meridional plane i.e. assuming $\partial/\partial z = 0$ so that the two modes are decoupled the equations of poloidal and toroidal oscillations in cylindrical coordinates corresponding to equations (3.20) and (3.21) are respectively

(5.11)
$$\left\{ \frac{4\pi\rho}{B_0^2} \frac{\partial^2}{\partial t^2} - \frac{1}{r}\frac{\partial}{\partial r} - \frac{\partial^2}{\partial r^2} - \frac{1}{r^2}\frac{\partial^2}{\partial \theta^2} \right\} E_z = 0$$

and

(5.12)
$$\left\{ 4\pi\rho \frac{\partial^2}{\partial t^2} - (\mathbf{B}_0 \cdot \nabla)(\mathbf{B}_0 \cdot \nabla) \right\} v_z = 0.$$

Considering motion along a line of force given by equation (5.2) and time dependence to be of the form $\exp(i\omega t)$, and using equation (5.7) for the operator $(\mathbf{B}_0 \cdot \nabla)$, equation (5.12) for toroidal oscillations becomes

(5.13)
$$\frac{4\pi\rho R_0^8 \omega^2}{M^2} v_z + \frac{1}{\sin^7\theta} \frac{d}{d\theta}\left[\frac{1}{\sin^7\theta} \frac{dv_z}{d\theta} \right] = 0.$$

Hm waves with long periods are almost perfectly reflected when they hit the ionosphere. Taking this point to be at the surface of the Earth the boundary conditions are $v_z = 0$ at $\theta = \theta_0$ and $\theta = 180° - \theta_0$.

Changing the independent variable by putting

(5.14)
$$\sin^7\theta \, d\theta = dx$$

equation (5.13) becomes

(5.15)
$$\frac{d^2 v_z}{dx^2} + \frac{4\pi\rho R_0^8 \omega^2}{M^2} v_z = 0.$$

Assuming a constant plasma density distribution of 6.5×10^{-22} gm/cm^3, Westphal and Jacobs obtained the fundamental periods of toroidal oscillations (see Fig. 5.3). They also computed the periods using a variable plasma density distribution (A. J. Dessler, 1958)—the fundamental period is plotted as a function of θ_0 in Fig. 5.4. Westphal and Jacobs (1962) repeated the calculations for the case of a compressed dipole field, i. e. a dipole field confined to a spherical cavity. Fig. 5.5 shows their results for a constant plasma density distribution of 6.5×10^{-22} gm/cm^3, and for different values of α, the radius of the cavity expressed in units of the

Earth's radius. The eigenperiods were also computed for a variable plasma density distribution—the results for the fundamental period are given in Table 5.3.

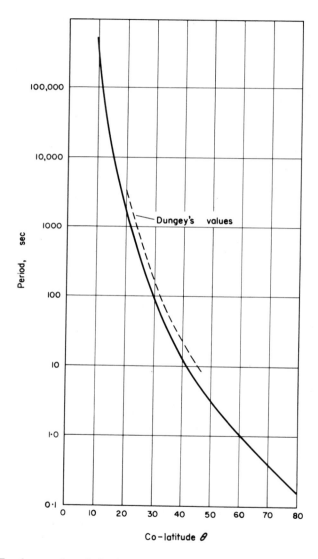

Fig. 5.3. Fundamental period of toroidal oscillations in the case of a normal dipole field and constant plasma density distribution. (After K. O. Westphal and J. A. Jacobs)

Table 5.3. *Fundamental periods T of toroidal oscillations at different co-latitudes* θ_0 *(compressed dipole field, variable plasma density)*

θ_0	$T_{(sec)}$
10°	111
20°	124
30°	252
40°	245
50°	159
60°	69
70°	46

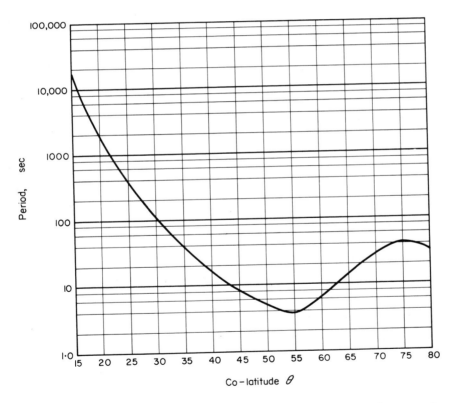

Fig. 5.4. Fundamental period of toroidal oscillations in the case of a normal dipole field and variable plasma density distribution. (After K. O. Westphal and J. A. Jacobs)

9*

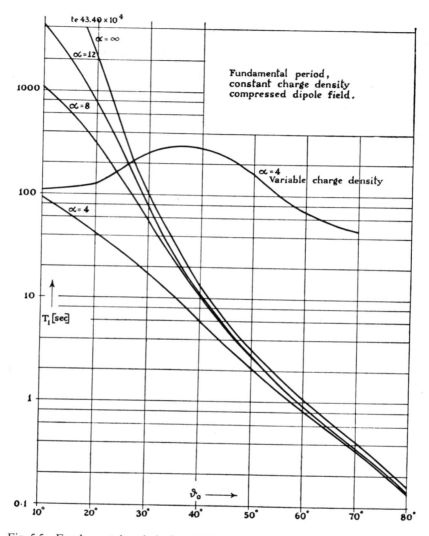

Fig. 5.5. Fundamental period of toroidal oscillations in the case of a compressed dipole field and constant plasma density distribution. (After K. O. Westphal and J. A. Jacobs)

The best agreement up to moderate latitudes is obtained for a normal dipole field and a variable plasma density distribution. Thus at Abbotsford, some 40 miles inland from Vancouver (latitude $\simeq 49°$ N, i.e. $\theta \simeq 41°$)

the characteristic period is just under 20 sec whereas Fig. 5.4 indicates a period of 18 sec. The main defect in this model is that in polar regions, i.e. as $\theta \to 0$, the period $\to \infty$. It was to correct this failing that the model of a compressed dipole field was introduced. Unfortunately the agreement between the observed and calculated values is not too satisfactory for middle and low latitudes. Apart from the fact that the model may not be appropriate, the discrepancy may be due to an incorrect plasma density distribution or to a wrong choice of α. Since the value of α is not critical in the range of co-latitudes under discussion (see Fig. 5.5) the major cause for the discrepancy probably lies in the plasma density distribution. At high latitudes, however, the agreement between experiment and theory is quite good for long period pulsations (LPc's, J. A. Jacobs and K. Sinno, 1960 b). A period of about 400 sec is observed at Point Barrow ($\theta \simeq 18°$). Fig. 5.5 gives the same result for $\alpha = 8$.

Unexplained by torsional oscillation theories is the reason why Pc 4 amplitudes are a maximum and the waveform most sinusoidal at latitude $\simeq 50°$ i.e. why field lines preferentially at $L \simeq 2.4$ should oscillate in this manner. Y. Kato and T. Tamao (1962) considered a source of hm waves (isotropic mode) located at a distance of about 10 Re in the equatorial plane. They suggested that perhaps the normal component propagates towards the Earth for a certain distance until it reaches a particular field line across which it cannot propagate. At this point there is conversion to the transverse mode and the wave propagates along the field line to the Earth. The distance to the conversion point depends on the period of the hm wave—a period of 70 sec would give a distance of $2 \sim 3$ Re. Their theory gives an explanation as to how toroidal oscillations of a field line can be set up deep in the magnetosphere, but again fails to explain why only selected field lines can oscillate.

In polar latitudes (higher than the auroral oval), toroidal oscillations of field lines cannot be expected to account for Pc 5's since field lines at these high latitudes may not be connected. The scarcity of Pc 5's in the polar regions is, of course, support for torsional oscillation models. The latitudes of maximum Pc 5 amplitudes are lower than those of the auroral oval i.e. the field lines joining points of maximum Pc 5 amplitude reach to $L \simeq 6$, inside the magnetopause, where hm perturbations are supposed to be greatest. Recently OGO and VELA satellites have observed a plasma sheet stretching across the tail of the magnetosphere and confined to within several Re of the neutral sheet. Since the plasma sheet will absorb hm waves, the largest amplitude hm waves should be observed, not in the outer magnetosphere, but in a region near the inner boundary of the plasma sheet i.e. the plasmapause. The observed latitudinal dependence of Pc 5 amplitudes may be related to this region.

5.3 The Excitation Mechanism of Pc 5's

G. Atkinson and T. Watanabe (1966) have investigated the excitation mechanism of Pc 5's, basing their ideas on the observed polarization of long period micropulsations. T. Nagata et al. (1963) observed that the end point of the disturbance vector of a Pc 5 micropulsation traced out a certain figure with time as the vector is projected on the Earth's surface. In the auroral regions where Pc 5's are seen with the greatest intensity and the probability of occurrence is largest, the figure is, in most cases, a fairly regular ellipse. The sense of rotation of the radius vector obeys the following laws

(i) In the northern auroral zone, it is counter clockwise on the morning side of the earth, and clockwise on the evening side.

(ii) The reversal of the sense takes place around 1 100–1 130 geomagnetic local time.

(iii) The sense of rotation in the southern auroral zone is reversed to that in the northern hemisphere.

A model for Pc 5's has been presented by T. Nagata et al. (1963) and S. Kokubun and T. Nagata (1965) based on the above polarization characteristics. In their model, magnetic lines of force in the equatorial plane are forced by the solar wind to move in circular or elliptical orbits (see Fig. 5.6). Such a motion in the equatorial region is propagated as a transverse hm wave along the magnetic lines of force towards the Earth's surface. The laws of polarization mentioned above are explained if it is assumed that the field lines follow their elliptical path in the left-hand sense on the morning side, and in the right-hand sense on the evening side, with respect to the magnetic field direction.

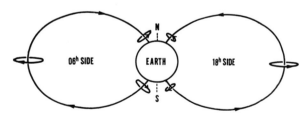

Fig. 5.6. Model showing the polarization of long period geomagnetic micropulsations (viewed from the sun). (After T. Nagata, S. Kokubun and T. Iijima)

Atkinson and Watanabe suggest that this motion is a result of a surface wave at the boundary between the magnetosphere and interplanetary space. The existence of surface waves as a generation mechanism of geomagnetic micropulsations was first suggested by J. W. Dungey (1955).

Assume that there is a surface wave on the boundary of the magnetosphere. A fluid element in the equatorial plane beneath the boundary will have a rotational motion similar to that of the fluid motion associated with a wave on a free surface in a uniform gravitational field (see Fig. 5.7). If the surface propagates westward on the morning side and eastward on the evening side, the sense of rotation of fluid elements beneath the magnetospheric boundary and in the equatorial plane is just that required by the model in Fig. 5.6.

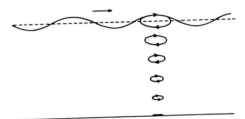

Fig. 5.7. Motion of fluid elements in a free surface wave

The generation of a surface wave in the magnetopause by the solar wind is expected to arise from a hm instability of the Kelvin-Helmholtz type. Whether or not the magnetopause is unstable in this sense has been a matter of controversy. A theory of hm Kelvin-Helmholtz instabilities has been given by J. W. Dungey (1955) and E. N. Parker (1958), the conclusion being that the magnetopause can be unstable. In their theories, no magnetic field was assumed to exist on one side of the interface—the discovery of the interplanetary magnetic field necessitates a theory that considers magnetic fields on both sides of the boundary. Much theoretical work has been done on this problem including allowance for the compressibility of the media. Applying these results to the magnetopause, A. K. Sen (1965) concluded that substantial portions of the dayside magnetospheric boundary are unstable under all conditions of the solar wind. On the other hand A. J. Dessler and J. A. Fejer (1963) contend that the magnetopause is stable. They found that the condition for stability is satisfied, using two sets of satellite-observed values (which were obtained on the daylight side of the magnetospheric boundary) for the parameters involved. As observational evidence in favour of stability, A. J. Dessler (1961) drew attention to the fact that after the onset of a sudden commencement (ssc) of a geomagnetic storm, the magnetic field observed on the earth's surface sometimes remains undisturbed for a few hours or even longer, although it is disturbed at other times. Sen (1965) attributes this apparently self-contradictory observation to one of his theoretical findings that the stability is critically dependent on the angle between the magnetic fields on both sides of the magnetopause. As the angle approaches 90°, the magnetopause rapidly tends to become more stable. An important result regarding magnetic activity after the onset of a ssc is the observation by C. R. Wilson and M. Sugiura (1961) that, in about 80 per cent of all cases, geomagnetic micropulsations with periods from 2.5 to 10 min (Pc 5's) take place at College, Alaska at the time of a ssc and continue for 10 min to a few hours. Satellite observations (IMP 1) show magnetic field fluctuations of the order of 10 γ at the magnetopause on the sunlit hemisphere (N. F. Ness, 1964). It seems likely that this is the result of waves in this region.

V. L. Patel (1965) also found examples of elliptically polarized waves in the magnetosphere using Explorer XII magnetometer results. They had amplitudes of the order of 10γ and periods in the range 100–200 sec. In two instances they were observed by the satellite and a ground station with comparable amplitudes and periods. He lists eight observations between 0650 and 1 200 local time. All four observations before 1045 have the required polarization, adding support to the surface wave theory.

5.4 Theories of Pi's

The morphological features of Pi 1's and their connection with aurora and X-ray bursts confirm the idea that their excitation is caused by the injection of charged particles (probably electrons with energies of tens of kev) into the high atmosphere. These injections result in auroral excitation, X-ray occurrence, and in the development of current systems in the ionosphere which are responsible for bays. Simultaneously with Pi 1 development, Pi 2's are observed in the magnetic field. The primary reason for all these disturbances is probably the interaction of the solar wind with the geomagnetic field in the equatorial plane at a great distance from the earth. Because of this interaction, the pitch angles of trapped particles are redistributed and symmetrical dumping of particles into the ionospheres of both polar caps takes place (W. H. Campbell and M. H. Rees, 1961). These ideas are confirmed by the simultaneity of auroral excitation and their development at conjugate points (R. N. de Witt, 1964). They are also confirmed by the excitation characteristics of the family of connected disturbances (Fig. 2.20). The conjugacy of bay disturbances is well known; for Pi 1's it is seen even better since their almost simultaneous excitation is confirmed to within several sec. The conjugacy of Pc 1's has been discussed in Chapter 2. However simultaneity and similarity of their series development is not, as a rule, distinctly seen. Pulsation periods are more stable for Pc 1's than for Pi 1's; this, together with differences in their development in magneto-conjugate regions, confirms their origin as an effect of oscillations of particle

Fig. 5.8. Bremsstrahlung event associated with 27.6 Mc/s cosmic noise absorption, geomagnetic pulsations and magnetic bays at College and Sitka, Alaska, June 28, 1960. The Pfotzev maximum in the X-ray data between 2230 and 2330 while the balloon is gaining altitude should be disregarded. (After W. H. Campbell and S. Matsushita)

bunches along magnetic lines of force. Thus the interaction of the solar wind with the geomagnetic field in the equatorial plane leads, on the one hand to the symmetrical dumping of charged particles into both hemispheres, and on the other to the development of pulsating currents in the lower ionosphere (E-layer). These pulsations are observed as Pi 1's.

A major source of Pi electromagnetic field fluctuations is an ionospheric current system perturbed by conductivity variations as a result of magnetospheric particle bombardment at higher latitudes. These pulsations appear at times of auroral electrojet enhancements as evidenced by bay disturbances on magnetograms (J. A. Jacobs and K. Sinno, 1960 b). (See Fig. 5.8 which illustrates the magnetic bay associated with a pulsation storm.) It appears that the current associated with Pi pulsation events is a typical auroral electrojet in the high conductivity (100 km) region of the ionosphere.

One of the most interesting results of recent years has been the discovery of the connection between Pi 1-excitation and X-ray bursts (C. D. Anger et al., 1963). Not only are comparable oscillation periods observed, but the beginnings of these two phenomena are often coincident (sometimes to within one min). The range of periods for which this correlation is observed is very wide. However the main period of 7–9 sec in X-ray bursts coincides with the most frequent characteristic Pi 1 period.

The existence of a connection between visual aurora and magnetic activity has been known for a number of years. The auroral luminosity fluctuations in the region of 5577 and 3914 Å have been found to be closely related both to micropulsations (W. H. Campbell and M. H. Rees, 1961) and to cosmic noise absorption (W. H. Campbell and H. Leinbach, 1961) (see Fig. 5.9 and 5.10). The average nightly variations of the luminosity and magnetic pulsations parallel each other except at the beginning of the night when luminosity pulsations are at a minimum and micropulsation amplitudes are significant, very likely because of Pc 2/3 events which may be mixed into the scaling. Since the luminosity maximum occurs in the region around 100 km it is reasonable to suppose that the major contribution to micropulsations also arises at these E-region heights. This is evidence that most irregular pulsations of the natural electromagnetic field in the frequency range 2.0 to 0.005 Hz which are associated with aurora have their source in perturbations of E-region current systems due to conductivity changes produced by bombarding auroral electrons. These perturbations may be communicated to lower latitudes as brief modifications in the ionospheric Sq current system (S. Akasofu and S. Chapman, 1963). Assuming micropulsation and total field magnetitudes of 3 and 60 γ, a 5 per cent variation in electron density would be sufficient to cause a typical perturbation of the electrojet

λ 3914
AURORA PULSATIONS

MAGNETIC FIELD
MICROPULSATIONS

Fig. 5.9. Corresponding pulsations of the aurora (3914 Å) and the north component of the magnetic field at stations separated by 30 miles near College, Alaska. (After W. H. Campbell)

necessary for micropulsations. E-region ionospheric variations of this magnitude are easily attained.

The implication of the results of G. Rostoker (1967) and A. D. Christoffel and J. G. Linford (1966) on the polarization characteristics of Pi 2's (see 2.5.2) is that at least the last part of their propagation may be dominated by the Alfvén mode of a hm wave propagating through the ionosphere in a direction parallel to the ambient field lines. However the fact that some clockwise pulsations are observed in the northern hemisphere and some anticlockwise pulsations in the southern hemisphere suggests that the mode of propagation of a Pi 2 is not a pure Alfvén wave.

The observed polarization characteristics indicate that Pi 2 micropulsations cannot be described by a simple equivalent current system such as that used to describe a bay. Such a current system provides an "in phase" relationship between the H and D components, which is not observed to be the case. Nor can a rotating line current such as that proposed by C. R. Wilson (1966) for Pc 4, Pc 5, and Pg-type micropulsations fully describe the source mechanism for Pi 2's, since, for anticlockwise rotation of the current system, all pulsations in the northern hemisphere should be polarized in an anticlockwise sense,

Fig. 5.10. Simultaneous recordings of magnetic field micropulsations, 3914Å auroral luminosity variations, and 27.6 Mc/s riometer-measured ionospheric absorption of cosmic noise. (After W. H. Campbell)

which is not the case. The appearance on occasion of a clockwise rotation at a station, while the sense of polarization at other stations for the same event is anticlockwise, together with the fact that the dominant sense of rotation is anticlockwise in the northern hemisphere and clockwise in the southern hemisphere, suggests that the disturbance is subject to propagation effects. Hence in mid-latitude regions Pi 2's may be considered to propagate as a wave rather than being the effect of an ionospheric current system.

Although Pi 2 micropulsations as a whole seem to be unrelated to the bay-type equivalent current system, the initial kick on the magnetogram appears to be strongly correlated with the polarity of the accom-

panying bay. In general, the direction of the initial kick of either component on the micropulsation record has the same sign as the polarity
of the corresponding component of the bay. This effect is strongest
in the *D* component, although it is also prominent in the *H* component.

It is suggested that the initial kick of a Pi 2 micropulsation may
be represented by an equivalent overhead current system in the manner
shown by J.A. Jacobs and K. Sinno (1960b) (see Fig. 5.11). Although

Fig. 5.11.   Equivalent overhead current system for Pi 2's associated with a negative
bay in the auroral zone at 0936 UT, Dec. 26, 1957. Electric current between successive lines is 5×10^3 amp. (After J. A. Jacobs and K. Sinno)

Pi 2's have synchronous wave forms at different stations, it is not easy
to draw the contours on account of the complexity of the wave form,
especially near the auroral zones. For simplicity the direction of the
current contours and magnetic arrows shown in Fig. 5.11 are drawn for
the maximum amplitude of the oscillation which fluctuates with the

period of the Pi 2's. The current is set up in the Hall region of the ionosphere because the ambient ionospheric particles cannot respond rapidly
enough to the first hm impulse generated in the breakup. The contours
for the Pi 2 current system resemble the well known bay current systems
which have been drawn by H. C. Silsbee and E. H. Vestine (1942), although
the Pi 2's have only one intense current vortex centre on the night side,
located at about latitude 50–60° in the sub-auroral zone.

Y. Kato and T. Tamao (1962) proposed that hm waves generated by
sudden proton precipitation set up an ionospheric current system as
evidenced by the observed distribution of the initial movement of the
Pi 2 vector. The fact that Pi 2 periods decrease with increasing K_p
(see Sec. 2.5.2 for a more detailed discussion) has been attributed to the
more compressed state of the closed magnetosphere on the night side
of the Earth (V. A. Troitskaya and A. V. Gul'elmi, 1967; T. Saito, and
S. Matsushita, 1968), or to the smaller L value of the plasmapause at
the time of larger K_p (T. Hirasawa and T. Nagata, 1966). The observed
result that Pi 2 periods in auroral latitudes are similar to those in lower
latitudes has been interpreted, partly as an effect of an ionospheric
return current induced by hm waves (Y. Kato and T. Tamao, 1962),
and partly as an effect of poloidal oscillations of the closed magnetosphere (T. Saito and S. Matsushita, 1968).

T. Hirasawa and T. Nagata (1966) suggested that Pi 2's are different
from Pi bursts in the auroral electrojet region and that they are essentially
lower latitude events caused by transient surface waves on the plasmapause excited by plasma instabilities in the tail. They based their theory
on the results of a detailed spectral analysis of all types of geomagnetic
micropulsations. They found that at Kakioka Pi 2's often transform
to sinusoidal Pc 4 pulsations, and that the diurnal variation of Pi 2
periods is similar to that of Pc 4 periods. Also sinusoidal Pi 2's, like
Pc 4's, are observed most frequently around latitude 50° while the waveform of Pi's is irregular at higher latitudes. Finally both Pi 2's and Pc 4's
are observed more frequently during sunspot minimum than during
sunspot maximum years. They explain this inverse relationship between
sunspot cycle activity and Pi 2 occurrence frequency by the formation
of a sharper plasmapause during sunspot minimum years. Alternatively
J. A. Jacobs and K. Sinno (1960 b) suggested the development of a barrier
in the Alfvén phase velocity profile against altitude in years of sunspot
maximum thereby inhibiting hm waves: T. Saito and S. Matsushita
(1968) suggested that the inverse relationship may be due to the approach
of the solar wind to the Earth's orbital plane during sunspot minimum
years (see also Sec. 2.5.2).

The initial hm impulse arriving in the auroral zone from the tail
region of the magnetosphere is broadband, containing periods ranging

from those of a Pi to a bay. Near the source all the frequency components arrive at approximately the same time and thus the leading edge of the bay near the source is very steep. The dispersive effect of the ionosphere on the propagation to lower latitudes, however, causes the higher frequencies to arrive at a field point earlier than the lower frequencies. This effect results in a spreading on the time axis of the impulse, and the leading edge of the bay becomes less steep the farther it is observed from the source. In this respect, the bay and initial pulse of the Pi 2 may be regarded as part of the response of the ionosphere to a hm impulse generated in the magnetosphere. S. H. Ward (1963) has endeavored to find the transfer function of the magnetosphere, i.e. how the incoming solar plasma generates hm disturbances which, when modified by the ionosphere, are received on the surface of the earth.

G. Rostoker (1967) suggested that Pi 2's originate as eigen oscillations on auroral zone field lines, although the initial movement is probably due to a current system set up in the ionosphere as an impulse response to the influx of energy from the tail of the magnetosphere. That part of the Pi 2 generated by the eigen oscillations of the field lines is thought to propagate through the E-region of the ionosphere, and the observed polarization at a field point is determined by the screening effect of the ionosphere over that point. T. J. Herron (1966) observed sizeable phase shifts (of the order of seconds) in the appearance of micropulsations at stations separated by hundreds of kilometers along an east–west line. From Herron's results, the relationship between the projected velocity of propagation of the disturbance and its period appears to be hyperbolic in nature. G. Rostoker (1965) showed that Pi 2 micropulsations can be described by a weak coupling of fluid and electromagnetic disturbances in which the electromagnetic contribution is dominant. Any variation in the values of the parameters which may occur in the course of propagation of the waves over the Earth's surface may cause one or other of the coupled modes to become dominant. Thus alterations in ionospheric conductivity caused by the precipitation of auroral particles will cause the waves to acquire irregular phase velocities during the course of their propagation from the source of the pulsations to the field points. In the case of pulsating auroras particularly, different phase shifts between two stations would be expected for different sets of peaks in a chain of pulsations. G. Rostoker observed this to be the case for the horizontal components of Pi 2's observed at Vancouver, British Columbia, and Ralston, Alberta.

Pc theories are quite different from Pi theories. Pc theories generally depend on some kind of resonance to achieve the narrow band effect. Although a number of sources for broadband geomagnetic noise have been suggested, including auroral electrojets and the action of the solar wind at the surface of the magnetosphere, the only detailed Pi theory is that of A. Nishida (1964). Nishida showed that the presence of a passing electron beam through the magnetospheric plasma modifies the character of hm waves in such a way that an instability takes place. The situation is reminiscent of the hm instability due to runaway electrons encountered in Project Matterhorn (J. Dawson and I. B. Bernstein, 1958). With adequately chosen parameters for the beam and the ambient plasma, Nishida estimated the range of the period of growing waves generated in the magnetosphere and found close agreement with that of a pulsation burst. As the bombardment of the ionosphere by the electron beam continues, the electrical conductivity of the ionosphere would be enhanced and hm waves incident from above would be shielded to an increasing degree. This might be the explanation of why pulsation bursts are observed only in the early stages of the development of a magnetic bay. It might also explain why the longer period part of the burst lasts for a longer time.

Nishida suggests two mechanisms as possible causes of Pi 1's and Pi 2's in middle and low latitudes. The first is the oblique propagation of unstable hm waves to lower latitudes. The second is the leakage of the screening current that flows in the auroral zone when the pulsation burst passes through the ionosphere to lower latitudes. The occurrence of Pi 2's is less frequent in solar active years than in quiet years, although the activity of Pi 1's is higher in solar active years. Because the ionospheric conductivity is higher and the degree of ionospheric screening and the intensity of the screening current is also higher in solar active years, it might be possible to account for Pi 2's by oblique propagation and for Pi 1's by the leakage of the screening current. The ionospheric conductivity, however, is also different in the two hemispheres, especially away from the equinoxes. Hence although the generation of Pi events may be conjugate, stations in opposite hemispheres can easily receive different signals.

O. M. Raspopov (1968) has examined possible resonances of hm waves on the night side of the magnetosphere as an excitation mechanism for Pi 2's. Because of the presence of the neutral sheet in the tail of the magnetosphere there are three possible cavities where resonance conditions may exist for hm waves along magnetic lines of force (a) an internal cavity bounded by magnetic lines of force unaffected by the neutral sheet (b) a central cavity between the beginning of the neutral sheet and the boundary of the internal cavity. In this region the magnetic lines of force are continuous but are influenced by the neutral sheet in their central part (c) an external cavity beyond the first two containing broken lines of force.

Since Pi 2 amplitudes, periods and form are the same at conjugate points, resonance in the central or inner cavities is indicated. Raspopov favours the central cavity as the region of excitation basing his conclusions on the morphology of Pi 2's observed at four stations between geomagnetic latitudes $53-63°$ from $1964-1966$ and on observations at the conjugate pair of stations, Sogra and Kerguelen. In the central cavity the magnetic field decreases because of the proximity of the neutral sheet in the central part, leading to a decrease in the velocity of Alfvén waves. The conditions are favourable for the excitation of the fundamental harmonic of standing Alfvén waves and of waves with nodes in the central part and at ends of lines of force. The field decreases most in the central part of a line of force and thus the conditions for resonance will be most favourable in the vicinity of the midnight part of the magnetosphere and this probably explains the maximum in the frequency of occurrence of Pi 2's at that time. Raspopov also interprets Pc 5 pulsations as a manifestation of Alfvén resonance with a period equal to the first harmonic of standing waves in the inner cavity of the nighttime portion of the magnetosphere.

References

Akasofu, S., Chapman, S.: The enhancement of the equatorial electrojet during polar magnetic substorms. J. Geophys. Res. **68**, 2375—2387 (1963).

Anger, C. D., Barcus, J. R., Brown, R. R., Evans, D. S.: Auroral zone X-ray pulsations in the 1—15 sec period range. J. Geophys. Res. **68**, 1023—1030 (1963).

Atkinson, G., Watanabe, T.: Surface waves in the magnetospheric boundary as a possible origin of long period geomagnetic micropulsations. *Earth Planet. Sci. Letters* **1**, 89—91 (1966).

Campbell, W. H., Leinbach, H.: Ionospheric absorption at times of auroral and magnetic pulsations. J. Geophys. Res. **66**, 25—34 (1961).

— Rees, M. H.: A study of auroral coruscations. J. Geophys. Res. **66**, 41—55 (1961).

Christoffel, A. D., Linford, J. G.: Diurnal properties of the horizontal geomagnetic micropulsation field in New Zealand. J. Geophys. Res. **71**, 891—897 (1966).

Courant, R., Hilbert, D.: Methods of Mathematical Physics. Vol. 1, p. 414, Interscience Publ. 1953.

Dawson, J., Bernstein, I. B.: Hydromagnetic instabilities caused by runaway electrons. Controlled Thermonuclear Conference, 360—365 (U. S. Atomic Energy Commission) 1958.

Dessler, A. J.: The propagation velocity of world-wide sudden commencements of magnetic storms. J. Geophys. Res. **63**, 405—408 (1958).

— The stability of the interface between the solar wind and the geomagnetic field. J. Geophys. Res. **66**, 3587—3590 (1961).

— Fejer, J. A.: Interpretation of the K_P index and M-region geomagnetic storms. Planet. Space Sci. **11**, 505—511 (1963).

De Witt, R. N.: The occurrence of aurora in geomagnetically conjugate areas. J. Geophys. Res. **67**, 1347—1355 (1962).

Dungey, J. W.: The propagation of Alfvén waves through the ionosphere. Penn. State Univ. Ionos. Res. Lab. Sci. Rept. No. 57 (1954a).
— Electrodynamics of the outer atmosphere. Penn. State Univ. Ionos. Res. Lab. Sci. Rept. No. 69 (1954b).
— Electrodynamics of the outer atmosphere, in: *The Physics of the Ionosphere.* 1954 Cambridge Conference (Phys. Soc. London 1955).
Greifinger, C., Greifinger, P.: Transmission of micropulsations through the lower atmosphere. J. Geophys. Res. **70**, 2217—2231 (1965).
Herron, T. J.: Phase characteristics of geomagnetic micropulsations. J. Geophys. Res. **71**, 871—889 (1966).
Hirasawa, T., Nagata, T.: Spectral analysis of geomagnetic pulsations from 0.5 to 100 sec in period for the quiet sun condition. Pure and Appl. Geophys. **65**, 102—124 (1966).
Jacobs, J. A., Sinno, K.: Occurrence frequency of geomagnetic pulsations, Pc. J. Geophys. Res. **65**, 107—113 (1960a).
— — World wide charactersistics of geomagnetic micropulsations. Geophys. J. **3**, 333—353 (1960b).
Kato, Y., Watanabe, T.: Further study on the cause of giant pulsations. Sci. Rept. Tohoku Univ. Ser. **5**, Geophys. **8**, 1—10 (1956).
— Tamao, T.: Hydromagnetic waves in the Earth's exosphere and geomagnetic pulsations. J. Phys. Soc. Japan 17, Suppl. **A-11**, 39—43 (1962).
Kokubun, S., Nagata, T.: Geomagnetic pulsation Pc 5 in and near the auroral zones. Rept. Ionos. Space Res. Japan **19**, 158—175 (1965).
Nagata, T., Kokubun, S., Iijima, T.: Geomagnetically conjugate relationships of giant pulsations at Syowa Base, Antarctica and Rejkjavik, Iceland. J. Geophys. Res. **68**, 4621—4625 (1963).
Ness, N. F., Scearce, S. C., Seek, J. B.: Initial results of the Imp *I* magnetic field experiment. J. Geophys. Res. **69**, 3531—3569 (1964).
Nishida, A.: Theory of irregular magnetic micropulsations associated with a magnetic bay. J. Geophys. Res. **69**, 947—954 (1964).
Obayashi, T., Jacobs, J. A.: Geomagnetic pulsations and the Earth's outer atmosphere. Geophys. J. **1**, 53—63 (1958).
Parker, E. N.: Interaction of the solar wind with the geomagnetic field. Phys. Fluids **1**, 171—187 (1958).
Patel, V. L.: Low frequency hydromagnetic waves in the magnetosphere: Explorer XII. Planet. Space Sci. **13**, 488 (1965).
Prince, C. E., Bostick, F. X., Jr., Smith, H. W.: A study of the transmission of plane hydromagnetic waves through the upper atmosphere. Elec. Eng. Res. Lab. Univ. Texas, Rept. 134 (1964).
Raspopov, O. M.: Possible excitation mechanism of type Pi 2 geomagnetic field pulsations. Geomag. i. Aeron. **VIII**, 257—260 (1968).
Rostoker, G.: Propagation of Pi 2 micropulsations through the ionosphere. J. Geophys. Res. **70**, 4388—4390 (1965).
— The polarization characteristics of Pi 2 micropulsations and their relation to the determination of possible source mechanisms for the production of nighttime impulsive micropulsation activity. Can. J. Phys. **45**, 1319—1335 (1967).
Saito, T., Matsushita, S.: Solar-cycle effects on geomagnetic Pi 2 pulsations. J. Geophys. Res. **73**, 267—286 (1968).
Sen, A. K.: Stability of the magnetospheric boundary. Planet. Space Sci. **13**, 131—141 (1965).

Siebert, M.: Geomagnetic pulsations with latitude-dependent periods and their relation to the structure of the magnetosphere. Planet. Space Sci. **12**, 137—147 (1964).

Silsbee, H. C., Vestine, E. H.: Geomagnetic bays, their frequency and current systems. Terr. Mag. **47**, 195—208 (1942).

Troitskaya, V. A., Gul'elmi, A. V.: Geomagnetic micropulsations and diagnostics of the magnetosphere. Space Sci. Rev. **7**, 689—768 (1967).

Ward, S. H.: Dynamics of the magnetosphere. J. Geophys. Res. **68**, 781—788 (1963).

Watanabe, T.: Hydromagnetic oscillation of the outer ionosphere and geomagnetic pulsation. J. Geomag. Geoelect. **X**, 195—202 (1959).

Westphal, K. O., Jacobs, J. A.: Oscillations of the Earth's outer atmosphere and micropulsations. Geophys. J. **6**, 360—376 (1962).

Wilson, C. R.: Conjugate three-dimensional polarization of high latitude micropulsations from a hydromagnetic wave—ionospheric current model. J. Geophys. Res. **71**, 3233—3249 (1966).

— Sugiura, M.: Hydromagnetic interpretation of sudden commencements of magnetic storms. J. Geophys. Res. **66**, 4097— 4111 (1961).

6 Micropulsations and the Diagnostics of the Magnetosphere

6.1 Introduction

Experimental and theoretical research indicates that short-period geo-magnetic micropulsations are a sensitive indirect means of determining changes in the state of the upper atmosphere. L. R. O. Storey (1953) found that the space between the outer boundary of the magnetic field and the ionosphere is filled with plasma so that any disturbance reaching the outer limit of that space can be transmitted to the Earth in the form of hm waves.

All data gathered on Pc's indicate that they are the result of hm poloidal and toroidal waves generated by the interaction of solar corpuscular streams with the magnetosphere. The periods of observed pulsations characterize the dimensions of the magnetosphere and of its resonant cavities. Also the dependence of the periods on latitude (for toroidal oscillations) determines the distance in the equatorial plane at which the interaction of the solar wind with the magnetosphere takes place. Again the intensity and modulation of the amplitudes of Pc's may be used to estimate the degree of irregularity of the structure of the solar corpuscular stream.

Observations of Pc 1's may be used to determine the plasma concentration and its changes in both the quiet and disturbed states of the magnetosphere. They can also be used for detecting the injection of charged particles into the outer regions of the magnetosphere, for discovering any anisotropy in the parameters of the particle population in the outer region, as well as for the determination of particle energy, concentration of helium ions, etc. (see e. g. T. Watanabe, 1965; J. M. Cornwall, 1966; V. A. Troitskaya and A. V. Gul'elmi, 1967a; R. C. Wentworth, 1966).

The family of continuous pulsations, Pc 2– Pc 5, and the longer period irregular pulsations (Pi 2) which are recorded practically every day on the Earth's surface carry information about the parameters of the solar wind, about its interaction with the Earth's magnetosphere and the consequent changes in the dimensions of the magnetosphere. During the transition from the quiet to the disturbed state of the magnetosphere a change of Pc pattern from one category to another occurs and there is also a change in the characteristics of Pi 2 excitation. The discovery of the "knee" or plasmapause in the magnetosphere (D. L. Carpenter, 1966) has important consequences in the calculation of resonance oscillations in the magnetosphere. It gives rise to an additional maximum in the Alfvén velocity profile, forming a resonating cavity which has periods close to those of Pc 3's (J. W. Dungey, 1963; L. O. Vanyan and K. Yu Zybin, 1966).

In recent years the excitation of oscillations in the magnetosphere has been discussed in relation to the impedance of the magnetosphere (S. H. Ward, 1963; C. E. Prince et al., 1965). The existence of a wide-band source on the boundary of the magnetosphere may explain the broad spectrum of oscillations excited at the Earth. It is, however, difficult to ascribe to this source the excitation of oscillations in one or two relativity narrow bands so often observed on the Earth, particulary during quiet periods (R. R. Heacock, 1966).

Fig. 6.1. Spectrum of the natural low frequency emissions in California. (After W. H. Campbell)

The spectrum of natural low frequency emissions observed in California is shown in Fig. 6.1. Geomagnetic micropulsations cover the frequency range from mHz to several Hz: in the range from about 1 to several kHz, low frequency (VLF) emissions propagate as electron-cyclotron waves with right hand polarization. This property could be used to help distinguish them from micropulsations which are attributed to ion-cyclotron hm waves. However in a medium with smoothly changing parameters, electron-cyclotron waves propagating in the direction of increasing magnetic field can generally be continuously transformed into fast magneto-acoustic waves, since in a two component plasma they form essentially the same branch of the dispersion curve. Ion-cyclotron waves have a left-hand polarization and form the other branch of the dispersion curve (see Fig. 6.2). Nevertheless some of their general properties are similar to those of electron-cyclotron waves.

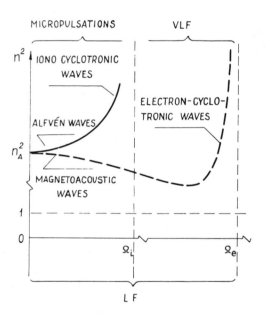

Fig. 6.2. Dispersion curves for low frequency waves in a cold magneto-active plasma (longitudinal propagation). (After V. A. Troitskaya and A. V. Gul'elmi)

Moreover, in a multicomponent plasma, waves of the one type can be transformed with change of polarization into waves of the other type in the regions of intersection of the dispersion curves (T. H. Stix, 1962). Finally, as N. M. Brice (1965) has pointed out, VLF emissions and micropulsations may both be generated by the same stream of energetic particles with the possibility of mutual transformation of waves as a result of non-linear processes.

6.2 Relationship Between Micropulsations, the Solar Wind and the Dimensions of the Magnetosphere

Since the frequency spectrum of Pc's is approximately the same for the whole Earth, an index of magnetic activity determined by Pc periods can give a more objective evaluation, less influenced by local factors than any other index, and would not have such a complex character as K_p. It is also possible that in order to obtain a planetary index based on Pc periods only a comparatively small number of stations would be needed.

By analysing many sporadic and recurrent storms and micropulsation behavior during both quiet and disturbed conditions, O. V. Bolshakova (1965) distinguished between different types of corpuscular streams, which correspond to different intensities of the solar wind, and cause continuous pulsations in the magnetosphere with different period ranges. Thus streams from chromospheric flares causing sporadic storms correspond to continuous pulsations Pc 2 (5–10 sec). Quasi-stationary streams from active regions on the sun, responsible for recurrent storms, cause Pc 3 pulsations (10–40 sec) while Pc 4 pulsations (in the 50–70 sec period range) are associated with the continuous emission from undisturbed solar regions, even during magnetically quiet days when $K_p = 0$.

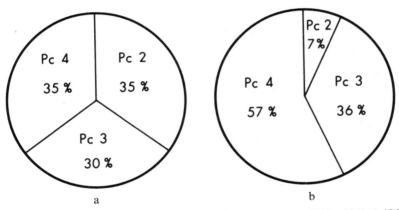

Fig. 6.3.   Pc activity at different stages in the solar cycle. a 1957—1959, b 1961 to 1962. (After V. A. Troitskaya, O. V. Bolshakova and R. V. Shchepetnov)

During maximum solar activity pulsations of all groups are observed with about equal probability, but during minimum activity longer period pulsations, Pc 4, dominate (see Fig. 6.3). This dependence of the Pc period on the level of magnetic activity allows us to use it as an index of the size of the magnetosphere. O. V. Bolshakova has also shown that during the initial phase of magnetic storms, when the dimensions of the magnetospheric cavity decrease, the period of stable Pc pulsations undergoes significant changes. Using Explorer 12 data she found that when the magnetopause was at a distance of 10 or more R_e, Pc 4 pulsations were more common. When the magnetosphere was compressed, Pc 2's and Pc 3's appeared, their period decreasing as the magnetopause approached the Earth. V. A. Troitskaya et al. (1966) suggested a power law relationship between the period T of stable pulsations and the radius R_m of the magnetosphere of the form $T \propto R_m^n$ with the value of $n \simeq 5$. Such a relationship was confirmed by data obtained from the Soviet satellites Elektron 2 and Elektron 4. In a later paper, V. L. Patel and R. N. Hastings (1969) analysed all the available IMP I and Explorer 12 data and obtained a value of 13 for the exponent n. It is possible that the value of n may vary with time depending on magnetic activity but a value as high as 13 seems rather improbable. Such an empirical relationship between T and R_m makes it possible to obtain information about the degree of compression of the magnetosphere by the solar wind from a knowledge of the period of continuous pulsations. An index of activity determined by Pc periods has an advantage over the K_p-index in that it reflects actual changes in the solar wind intensity and, therefore, has a more definite physical meaning compared with the standardised K_p-index.

Pc's are a characteristic feature of the electromagnetic field of the Earth which are regularly observed on records even when $K_p = 0$. As already mentioned the major variations observed when $K_p = 0$ are the continuous pulsations Pc 4 with periods from 50–90 sec. Thus the properties of Pc 4 pulsations reflect the characteristic peculiarities of the undisturbed solar wind. V. A. Troitskaya et al. (1967b) found that continuous pulsations occur in a definite period range depending on the velocity of the solar wind. Their amplitudes depend most probably on the energy spectrum of the solar stream. When Pc pulsations were not present on the records, the energy spectrum obtained by satellites was very narrow, single banded and the velocity of the solar wind was in the range 0–310 km/sec. With the appearance of Pc 4 pulsations the velocity increased somewhat, but did not exceed 450 km/sec. When the energy of the solar wind increased, the period of continuous pulsations decreased.

C. W. Snyder, M. Neugebauer and U. R. Rao (1963) have shown that the K_p index can be used as a measure of the solar wind velocity. The inverse dependence of Pc period on K_p means, therefore, that continuous pulsations can serve as a parameter characteristing the solar wind. However the relationship between the period of continuous pulsations T_{Pc} and K_p differs considerably from a functional type of dependence. Any value of K_p may correspond to several values of T_{Pc} sometimes over a rather wide range. V.A. Troitskaya (1967) obtained the empirical expression

$$(6.1) \qquad T_{Pc} = 58.3 - 8.25\,\bar{K}_p$$

where T_{Pc} is measured in seconds and $\bar{K}_p$ is the mean value of K_p for the time interval during which Pc's were observed. Each range of Pc periods (Pc 2, Pc 3, Pc 4), therefore tends to appear mostly in conjunction with a definite K_p index. The quiet state of the magnetosphere ($K_p = 0-1$) is characterized by continuous pulsations with $T \sim 50-90$ sec (Pc 4); a state of moderate disturbance is typically associated with Pc 3 pulsations, and the disturbed magnetosphere with Pc 2 and irregular pulsations Pi 1. Pc 5 pulsations usually appear when $K_p = 1-3$.

V.A. Troitskaya et al. (1967b) found that when the solar plasma velocity was within $300-500$ km/sec not a single case of Pc pulsations with periods up to 10 sec (the Pc 2 group) was observed. On the other hand 80 per cent of all cases of Pc 4 occurrence were observed in this velocity interval. For velocities up to 750 km/sec Pc 2's and Pc 3's were dominant while Pc 4's were practically absent. Since continuous pulsations are observed nearly every day, differing from day to day in period, intensity and character of regime, there is a real possibility of being able to characterize the degree of intensity of processes occurring on the boundary of the magnetosphere by establishing a sufficiently accurate quantitative relationship between Pc periods and solar wind velocity.

V.A. Troitskaya (1967) also obtained an empirical relation between the velocity of the solar wind v (km/sec) and T_{Pc} (sec) viz

$$(6.2) \qquad v = (850 \pm 15) - (9.5 \pm 0.8)\,T_{Pc}.$$

Combining equations (6.1) and (6.2) we obtain

$$(6.3) \qquad v \simeq 300 + 77\,\bar{K}_p.$$

This is in good agreement with the relation (equation (6.7)) obtained by C.W. Snyder et al. (1963). Substituting $8\,\bar{K}_p$ for ΣK_p, Snyder's result is

$$(6.4) \qquad v \simeq 330 + 68\,\bar{K}_p.$$

The difference between equations (6.3) and (6.4) is well within experimental error. When $\bar{K}_p = 5$, equation (6.3) gives $v = 685$ km/sec and equation (6.4) gives $v = 670$ km/sec.

The dominant period of a train of irregular Pi 2 pulsations also shows an inverse relationship with magnetic activity. This is in agreement with modern ideas about the dependence of Pi 2 periods on the size of the closed cavity on the night side of the magnetosphere. The size of this cavity in its turn is determined by the level of magnetic activity

and, finally, by the velocity of the solar wind which envelopes the magnetosphere of the Earth. Comparisons of solar wind velocities measured directly in space (Mariner 2, Pioneer 6, Venus 3) with values of Pi 2 periods
observed on the Earth have shown that large velocities correspond
to small Pi 2 periods, and vice versa. The analysis by K. I. Gringauz et al.
(1966) of low energy spectra of the solar wind obtained on Venus 3,
together with Pi 2 periods observed during the approach to the boundary
of the magnetosphere, indicates that, for solar wind spectra with dominant
low energy components (0–300 km/sec), Pi 2 periods in the range 120
to 150 sec are characteristic, while for spectra with the major components
in the intervals 300–415 and 415–510 km/sec, periods of 90 and 60 sec
respectively are more common. Since the characteristic solar wind
velocity near the Earth's orbit is ~ 500 km/sec, it should correspond
to typical Pi periods i.e. 60 sec. V. A. Troitskaya et al. (1967b) have
suggested a power law dependence for the relationship between Pi 2
periods and solar wind velocity of the form

(6.5) $v \alpha A T^{-\mu}$.

Present data indicate that $\mu \simeq 0.7$.

The period of continuous pulsations Pc can be regarded as an
index of the dimensions of the daytime resonator in the magnetosphere,
whereas the period of Pi 2's reflects changes in the dimensions of the
nighttime resonator. According to some theories, Pc's and Pi 2's represent
the same type of hm wave (poloidal mode) so that a comparison of their
periods may thus indicate the relative dimensions of the day and nighttime resonant cavities. A comparison of the inverse dependence between
the periods of continuous and irregular pulsations and the velocity of
the solar wind is shown in Fig. 6.4.

It must be emphasized that the regularities of behavior discussed
above were detected on the basis of records of "pure" continuous pulsations, i.e. records unaffected by the overlapping of pulsations of different periods. Special precautions must be taken in cases where overlapping periods occur if they are to be used for the determination of
magnetospheric parameters. The systematic behavior patterns suggest
however that micropulsations of the magnetic field are a sensitive
indicator of changes in the state of the magnetosphere. A study of the
behavior of continuous pulsations and the character of their amplitude
modulation enables processes at the boundary of the magnetosphere
to be continuously monitored.

T. Hirasawa et al. (1965, 1966) have also analysed the dynamic
spectra of geomagnetic micropulsations and found that in general they
are composed of several discrete frequency bands as well as continuous
white noise. They found that the frequency spectra of Pc pulsations in

Fig. 6.4. Dependence of micropulsation periods on the velocity of the solar wind. (After V. A. Troitskaya): a Continuous pulsations Pc, b Irregular pulsations Pi 2

the frequency range 5–100 mHz consist of two main bands—a 15 mHz band and a 35 mHz band, corresponding to Pc 4 and Pc 3 pulsations respectively. Both bands show a marked diurnal variation in their frequency—maximum in the early morning and minimum in the evening. They also found that the frequency of both the 15 and 35 mHz bands increased with increasing geomagnetic activity. Fig. 6.5 shows the dependence of the 15 mHz band upon ΣK_p. In general the width of each band is broadened and the range of the daily variation of frequency increased as geomagnetic activity increases. T. Nagata and H. Fukunishi (1968) found an approximate linear relationship between the maximum central frequency $\bar{f}$ and $\bar{K}_p$ or ΣK_p, provided that $\bar{K}_p \leqslant 4$ or $\Sigma K_p \leqslant 30$. Their empirical relationships are

Fig. 6.5. Dependence of the daily variation of frequency of the 15 mHz band on ΣK_p. The full line indicates the eigen-frequency of a standing Alfvén wave along the field line on the plasmapause based on Carpenter's model. (After T. Hirasawa and T. Nagata)

$$(6.6) \quad \begin{cases} \bar{f}\,(mHz) = 11 + 4.5\,\bar{K}_p & \text{(for the 15 mHz band)}, \\ \bar{f}\,(mHz) = 11 + 0.7\,\Sigma K_p & \text{(for the 15 mHz band)}, \\ \bar{f}\,(mHz) = 20 + 7\,\bar{K}_p & \text{(for the 35 mHz band)}. \end{cases}$$

As already mentioned approximate linear relationships have also been obtained between the velocity v(km/sec) of the solar wind and

ΣK_p or $\overline{K}_p$. Thus C. W. Snyder et al. (1963) using Mariner 2 data found that

(6.7) $$v = (330 \pm 17) + (8.44 \pm 0.74) \Sigma K_p$$

while J. W. Wilcox et al. (1964) using Imp-1 data obtained

(6.8) $$v = 250 + 23 \overline{K}_p.$$

Thus the eigen-frequency $\overline{f}$ may be correlated with the solar wind velocity v—such a correlation seems reasonable intuitively since a more compressed magnetosphere by a stronger solar wind should result in shorter period hm eigen-oscillations. Combining the above results Nagata and Fukunishi obtained for the 15 mHz band

(6.9) $$v \simeq 200 + 12 \, \overline{f}.$$

The time of occurrence of maximum frequency of both the 15 mHz and 35 mHz bands becomes earlier as magnetic activity increases. The maximum frequency occurs around noon under extremely quiet conditions and shifts towards dawn as geomagnetic activity increases. If the eigen-frequency of the bands is interpreted as hm standing waves along magnetic field lines on the plasmapause or between the ionosphere and the plasmapause or the magnetopause, the maximum frequency will correspond to the shortest geocentric distance of the boundary surface. D. L. Carpenter (1966) has shown that the geocentric distance of the plasmapause is greatest around 2000 LMT and shortest around 1600 LMT when the geomagnetic field is moderately disturbed ($K_p = 2 \sim 4$). T. Hirasawa and T. Nagata (1966) have shown that the daily variation curve of the 15 mHz frequency band on moderately disturbed days is in good agreement with a daily variation curve of the eigen-frequency of a standing Alfvén wave along the field lines in the plasmapause based on Carpenter's model. During quiet conditions there may be no interaction between the solar wind and the magnetospheric plasma. In such a case the solar wind pressure simply causes a compression of the magnetosphere (and the plasmapause) on the noon side, thus making the eigen-frequency of the standing hm waves in the plasmapause largest around noon.

T. Nagata and H. Fukunishi (1968) further suggest that the 35 mHz band is due to a standing modified Alfvén wave between the plasmapause and the ionosphere—they found that the eigen-frequency of the standing modified Alfvén wave is about three times that of the Alfvén wave in approximate agreement with the observed ratio of the 35 to the 15 mHz band. They thus ascribe the dependence of the eigen-frequencies of both

Table 6.1. *Diagnostics of the magnetosphere from micropulsation data*

Type of micropulsations	Interpretation		Diagnostics	
	Generation	Propagation	Parameters of the magneto-sphere	Method of Diagnostics
Pc 1 (Pearls)	Cyclotron instability of energetic protons	In the magnetosphere along the field lines (anisotropic mode): in the ionosphere parallel to the Earth's surface (isotropic-mode)	Plasma density and energy of resonant protons	Using data on the frequency and dispersion of signals
Pc 2 (Continuous Pc 3 pulsations) Pc 4	Turbulent pulsations on the boundary of the magnetosphere	Poloidal oscillations	Location of the boundary of the magnetosphere	Using the empirical relation $T \sim R^5$
Pc 5	Interaction of the solar wind with the magnetosphere on the morning and evening sides of the Earth	Toroidal oscillations	Plasma density	Using the dependence of the period of oscillations on latitude
Pi 1 (SIP) Noise bursts	Injections of charged particles in the ionosphere	Magneto-static variations due to changes in parameters of the auroral electrojet	Spectra of electron stream fluctuations in the auroral zone	Using the spectra of micropulsations
IPDP	Instability of the distribution of charged particles in the ring current	L or R-mode	Intensity changes in the radiation belts during magnetic storms	Using data on the frequency gradient in an IPDP, and the last attained frequency (empirical relation)
Pi 2 (Pulsation trains)	Impulsive processes in the neutral sheet in the tail of the magnetosphere	Toroidal oscillations	Location of the last closed field lines on the night side of the magnetosphere	Using data on periods of Pi 2 (empirical relation)

the 15 and 35 mHz bands on the K_p index to the interaction and deformation of the plasmapause caused by the intensified solar wind.

V. A. Troitskaya et al. (1966) also studied the relationship between intensity variations in the radiation belts and short period micropulsations. Using data from Elektron 1 they found that different types of pulsations correspond to different segments of the intensity variation curve. In particular they found a relation between IPDP's and the change in electron flux in the radiation belts—the greater the decrease of periods in an IPDP and the lower the minimum period of pulsations, the greater the decrease in the intensity of charged particles in the radiation belts. S. Lacourly and R. Gendrin (1967) have also reported that IPDP's appear when the outer boundary of the Van Allen belt approaches the Earth.

V. A. Troitskaya et al. (1966) also found, from an analysis of Elektron 1, 2 and 4 data, that a relationship existed between the period of stable Pc pulsations and the outer boundary of the Van Allen radiation belt (see Fig. 6.6). Since the variation of Pc periods corresponds both to a

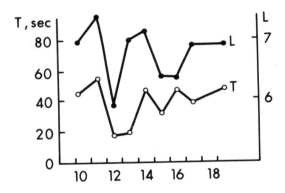

Fig. 6.6.   Variation in the position of the outer boundary of the Van Allen radiation belt and the corresponding average diurnal Pc period, February 1964. (After V. A. Troitskaya, O. V. Bolshakova, and E. T. Matveyeva)

change in the position of the magnetosphere boundary and the outer boundary of the Van Allen belt, they thus suggest that these two boundaries move synchronously. A summary of the diagnostics of the magnetosphere based on micropulsation data is given in Table 6.1 (after V. A. Troitskaya and A. V. Gul'elmi, 1967a).

6.3 Plasma Densities in the Magnetosphere Determined from Micropulsation Measurements

The dispersion of successive elements in a Pc 1 event is due to the frequency dependence of the group velocity of the wave packet which bounces back and forth between hemispheres along a field line. The dispersion of the signals depends primarily on the plasma density distribution along the field line and the L value of that field line. Thus measurements of experimental dispersion can be used to estimate the plasma density at various distances in the magnetosphere (H. B. Liemohn et al. 1967). Results are in reasonably good agreement with the independent determination of the exospheric plasma density from VLF whistler analyses.

The dispersion relation (left-hand mode) for propagation along the external magnetic field (cf. equation (4.5)) may be approximated by

$$(6.10) \qquad n^2 = \frac{c^2 k^2}{\omega^2} = 1 - \frac{\Omega_i^2}{\omega(\omega - \omega_i)} - \frac{\Omega_e^2}{\omega(\omega + \omega_e)}.$$

The geomagnetic field is assumed to be a dipole so that the field lines are given by $R = L \cos^2 \lambda$ where λ is the geomagnetic latitude. The plasma distribution is assumed to have the general form

$$(6.11) \qquad N = N_0(L) P(L, \lambda)$$

where $P(L, 0)$ is normalized to unity, so that N_0 is the equatorial density distribution.

The signals propagate along the field line with group velocity U of the form

$$(6.12) \qquad U = \frac{c}{n + \omega \dfrac{dn}{d\omega}} = \frac{c}{\sqrt{N_0}} \beta(\omega, P, B).$$

The time for the signal to propagate from one hemisphere to the other and return is given by

$$(6.13) \qquad t = \int_{path} \frac{ds}{U} = \sqrt{N_0}\, \tau(\omega, L)$$

where

$$(6.14) \qquad \tau = 4 \int_0^{\lambda_1} \frac{\partial s(L, \lambda)}{\partial \lambda} \cdot \frac{d\lambda}{c\, \beta(\omega, L, \lambda)}.$$

The integration along the path may be terminated at the surface of the Earth since the integrand is negligibly small at low altitudes i.e. the effect of the ionosphere on the total transit time is negligible. Although the parameters N_0 and L in equation (6.13) can be determined from two quantitative measurements, it is easier to eliminate N_0 by taking the logarithmic derivative of equation (6.13) viz

$$(6.15) \qquad \frac{1}{t}\frac{dt}{d\omega} = \frac{1}{\tau}\frac{\partial\tau}{\partial\omega}.$$

Plots of τ and $(1/\tau)(\partial\tau/\partial\omega)$ have been constructed by H. B. Liemohn et al. (1967) for the specific case of a dipole field B and a given plasma density distribution $P = f(R)$ along the path (see Fig. 6.7).

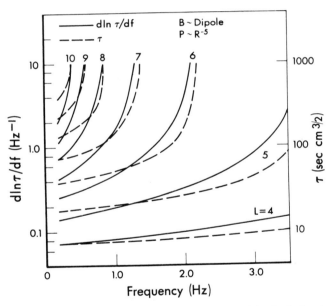

Fig. 6.7. Normalized dispersion function τ and its logarithmic derivative for the left hand mode. The geomagnetic field B is assumed to be a dipole and the plasma density distribution along the field line $P \sim R^{-5}$. (After H. B. Liemohn, J. F. Kenney and H. B. Knaflich)

Equation (6.15) can then be solved for L at some particular ω when t and $dt/d\omega$ have been measured; equation (6.13) then gives N_0. Fig. 6.8 shows the equatorial plasma density N_0 as a function of L for the case $P \alpha R^{-5}$. A strong diurnal anisotropy is found in the location of the excitation region, with nighttime emissions propagating on field lines intercepting the Earth at about 65° geomagnetic latitude, and daytime emissions on field lines at about 75°. Determination of N_0 from pearls which were detected either simultaneously or within a short time are connected by straight line segments (Fig. 6.8). It can be seen that pearls which are detected essentially at the same time may have a spread of L values greater than 1 Re but invariably occur on a very steep density gradient. This suggests that pearls may be generated primarily along the plasmapause. Liemohn et al. have also carried out calculations for a distorted dipole model of the geomagnetic field as proposed by G. D. Mead (1964). There is almost no difference in the L value obtained and hence the principal effect of the field distortion is to change the latitude where the field line intercepts the Earth's surface.

Fig. 6.8. The equatorial plasma density, $N_0(L)$, for the field line plasma density distribution $P \sim R^{-5}$. Determinations of N_0 from pearls which were detected either simultaneously or within a short time interval are connected by straight line segments. (After H. B. Liemohn, J. F. Kenney and H. B. Knaflich)

H. B. Knaflich and J. F. Kenney (1967) have applied the same methods to structured elements of IPDP events to locate their origin in the magnetosphere. The principal distinguishing feature of IPDP events is a characteristic broad-band noise which gradually increases in frequency over the lifetime of the event, usually about half an hour. Amplitude enhancements which are superimposed on the broad-band noise source occur quite frequently and give some structured appearance to the event. Unlike pearls, however, these amplitude enhancements do not have a simple repetitive structure but seem to occur more or less at random superimposed on the broad-band unstructured noise. R. Gendrin et al. (1966) showed that the structured elements are detected simultaneously at conjugate stations—again unlike pearls. If the IPDP signals are guided along geomagnetic field lines, this fact requires that the event be initiated in the magnetosphere in the equatorial plane.

In the case of IPDP's the structured elements are not repetitive and the actual half-hop propagation time, T, is unknown. However if it is assumed that the initiating mechanism is an impulsive event at the equator of the field line so that a range of frequencies is excited simultaneously by a broad-band pulse, it is possible to measure the dispersion, $dT/d\omega$, resulting from a traversal of the field line from the equator to the Earth's surface without knowing the actual time T. Knowing $dT/d\omega$, but not T, it is impossible to determine both L and N_0 as was done in the case of pearls. However it is possible to proceed if the reasonable assumption is made that the exospheric plasma density derived from pearl data may be applied to IPDP's. H. B. Knaflich and J. F. Kenney used the model $N_0(L)=4.47(10^4)L^{-5}$ and found that IPDP's are generated in a narrow range of solar magnetospheric longitude centered around 2000 LMT at L values between 6 and 13—considerably farther out in the magnetosphere than pearls.

The broad-band unstructured noise seems to originate in a zone of magnetic turbulence just outside the normal trapping regions so that the structured elements could be the dispersed signal resulting from a broad-band impulse. This could also be evidence for particle injection into the magnetosphere during times of increased magnetic activity, since there is a strong correlation between the occurrence of IPDP's and local magnetic K index. That part of the magnetosphere where turbulence exists is also the same region where the field lines cease to be closed and become transported to the region. Hence it is possible that the broad-band impulses that cause the amplitude enhancements are merely manifestations of the instabilities associated with opening and closing of field lines in a critical region.

Knaflich and Kenney suggest that the reason why the structured elements do not turn into repetitive bouncing wave packets is attenuation. H. B. Liemohn (1967) showed that for values of ω near the ion cyclotron cutoff frequency (which is the case for IPDP events) the signals are attenuated around the equator and amplified elsewhere along the path. Thus an impulsive signal near the equator is amplified as it propagates to the Earth's surface but the reflected signal is not amplified sufficiently before it encounters the strong equatorial attenuation.

    In general the magnitude of the plasma density obtained from the
dispersion analysis of Pc 1 events agrees quite well with the earlier
work using VLF whistlers. However the results from VLF measurements
indicate an abrupt drop in the density of one or two orders of magnitude
over a radial distance of $\simeq 0.1$ Re at about 4 Re. Evidence for this abrupt
drop in plasma density (the plasmapause) is not so evident in the micropulsation data which indicate that about 1 Re is needed for the plasma
density to drop by an order of magnitude.

    J. F. Kenney et al. (1968) pointed out that the discrepancies between
the VLF and micropulsation plasma density results are probably due
to different source mechanisms and propagation conditions for the two
types of waves. During the recovery phase of a magnetic storm when
most Pc 1 whistlers are observed, the magnetospheric plasma must also
be recovering to its pre-storm value and density distributions may be
obtained that are not typical of most times when VLF whistlers are
detected. Thus the density distributions determined by these two methods
may not necessarily be in conflict but may complement one another.

    T. Kitamura and J. A. Jacobs (1968) have given a new method for
determining the plasma density in the magnetosphere using long period
micropulsations. Such micropulsations are assumed to be caused by
resonant toroidal oscillations of field lines. They obtained a second
order differential equation for the azimuthal component b_ϕ of the
magnetic disturbance vector b. Two boundary values, b_0 and the
derivative $(db/ds)_0$ (where ds is an increment along a line of force), need
to be known at the starting point of the integration. Exact values of
the derivative (db/ds) are not obtainable unless simultaneous measurements of Pc 4 and Pc 5 micropulsations can be made from a number
of satellites fixed along a particular field line. However values may
be estimated approximately by converting the time axis on the magnetogram into distance assuming an average Alfvén velocity in the
lower magnetosphere. Eigen solutions have to satisfy one of two boundary
conditions in the equatorial plane viz either $b=0$ or $db/d\lambda=0$ (where
$\lambda=$ latitude). The former gives an odd mode of oscillation between
conjugate points with respect to the field line, and the latter an even
mode. Each mode could also have higher harmonic components.
Integrations were carried out assuming three different models of ionization distribution;

(1) *gyrofrequency model* (Smith 1961), $\rho=\rho_0 B$, where B is the local
magnetic field intensity;

(2) *thermal diffusive model* (Dungey 1954, Obayashi and Jacobs 1958,
Angerami and Thomas 1964), $\rho=\rho_0 \exp(\mu m g_0/k T R)$, where μ is the
ionization rate (in the fully ionized case $\mu=\frac{1}{2}$), m the mass of a proton,
g_0 the acceleration due to gravity at the Earth's surface, k Boltzmann's

Fig. 6.9a. Magnetospheric plasma density in the equatorial plane vs. period of geomagnetic micropulsations (Model 3, with $T=500°$K). Each family of curves consists of four curves corresponding to four different assumed Alfvén velocities (500, 1000, 2000, and 5000 km/sec) in the boundary value $(db/ds)_0$. *Odd mode.* (After T. Kitamura and J. A. Jacobs)

constant, T the average temperature in the magnetosphere and R radial distance;

(3) *a model based on Johnson (1959) and Smith (1961)*, $\rho = \rho_0 B \exp(\mu m g_0 / k T R)$ where the symbols are defined as above.

The plasma density of Model 3 with the assumption $T=500°$K was chosen as the most reasonable on comparison of the calculated amplitude in the equatorial plane with that observed by Explorer 12. Calculations were made for the case of the fundamental (odd mode, $b=0$ in the

Fig. 6.9b.   Magnetospheric plasma density in the equatorial plane vs. period of geomagnetic micropulsations (Model 3, with $T = 500\,°K$). Each family of curves consists of four curves corresponding to four different assumed Alfvén velocities (500, 1000, 2000, and 5000 km/sec) in the boundary value $(db/ds)_0$. *Even mode.* (After T. Kitamura and J. A. Jacobs)

equatorial plane) and the second harmonic (even mode, $db/d\lambda = 0$), since it is not possible to determine the mode definitely by observation. The last uncertain quantity, $(db/d\lambda)_0$, depends upon the Alfvén velocity assumed—calculations were carried out taking 500, 1000, 2000, and 5000 km/sec, for the average Alfvén velocity in the lower magnetosphere.

Calculated equatorial plasma densities plotted against period are shown in Fig. 6.9(a) (odd mode) and Fig. 6.9(b) (even mode). Each family of curves consists of four lines corresponding to the four dif-

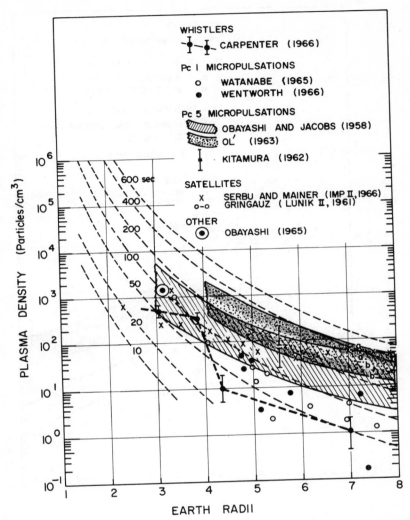

Fig. 6.10a. Comparison of magnetospheric plasma density in the equatorial plane with that obtained from other investigations. The plasma density (ordinate) is determined when micropulsation periods (dotted lines) and the *L* value (abscissa) at specific observation sites on the ground are given. *Odd mode.* (After T. Kitamura and J. A. Jacobs)

ferent Alfvén velocities assumed. It can be seen that at longer periods, values of the plasma density are almost independent of the assumed Alfvén velocity. Differences between plasma densities due to different

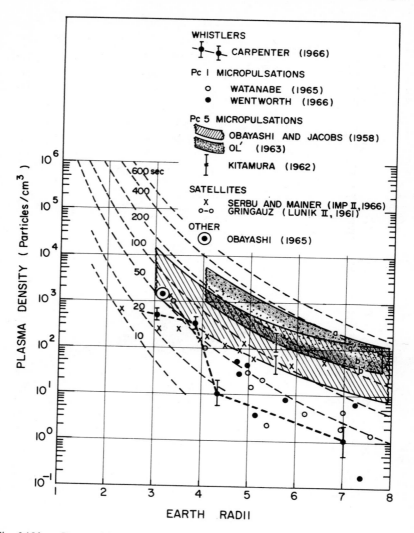

Fig. 6.10b. Comparison of magnetospheric plasma density in the equatorial plane with that obtained from other investigations. The plasma density (ordinate) is determined when micropulsation periods (dotted lines) and the L value (abscissa) at specific observation sites on the ground are given. *Even mode*. (After T. Kitamura and J. A. Jacobs)

assumed Alfvén velocities can be seen in each family of curves only at the lower Alfvén velocities. However relatively high Alfvén velocities (1000–5000 km/sec) are believed to exist in the lower magnetosphere and estimates may be made of the plasma density within the accuracy of present observations (particularly for periods longer than about 45 sec), in spite of the uncertainty of the boundary value $(db/d\lambda)_0$.

Fig. 6.10(a) and 6.10(b) show the plasma density derived by T. Kitamura and J. A. Jacobs together with values obtained from other measurements for comparison. In the figures the broken lines show the relation between the period which is expected to be observed at a specific location on the ground, and the plasma density in the equatorial plane of the field line which passes through that location. Good agreement with other measurements, particularly with observations by the Imp II satellite, is obtained. However the results from whistler investigations as well as those from shorter period micropulsations show lower values.

6.4 Micropulsations Observed in the Magnetosphere

Sudden commencements (ssc's) and sudden impulses (si's) tend to be world-wide and essentially simultaneous. A. Nishida and L. J. Cahill (1964) have shown from Explorer 12 data that the simultaneity extends throughout the magnetosphere and that positive and negative si's are related respectively to compression and expansion of the magnetospheric boundary. However to date few observations have been made by satellites of micropulsations—particularly on their relation with ground recordings, although there have been many measurements of the fluctuating field at the magnetopause. Observations of pulsations in the magnetic field inside the magnetosphere were carried out on board Pioneer I and V and Explorer 6 by means of two-component magnetometers (see e.g. C. P. Sonett et al. 1962; P. J. Coleman et al. 1960; D. L. Judge and P. J. Coleman, 1962).

Judge and Coleman observed both transverse Pc pulsations with periods of about 200 sec and longitudinal pulsations with periods of about 100 sec in the magnetosphere. The variations were damped with a time constant of about 500 sec. Similar measurements, but with total vector magnetometers, were made on board Explorer 12 by V. L. Patel and L. J. Cahill (1964) and V. L. Patel (1965). They observed transverse oscillations of 2–3 min period simultaneously both in the magnetosphere at a distance of 55000 km from the Earth and on the gound at the end of the magnetic field line. The wave needed a time of about $1\frac{1}{2}$ min to travel from the satellite to the ground. The amplitude of the variations was 6–8 γ in the magnetosphere and slightly less at the Earth's surface. In all of these cases the satellite was apparently in motion at rather high velocities relative to the plasma in which the waves were propagating at the time of their observation. The recorded oscillations seldom included more than a few cycles, and in most cases they could be described at best as quasi-sinusoidal.

K. I. Brody et al. (1966) observed magnetic fluctuations in the spectral range from 0.01–1000 Hz on the OGO 2 satellite at altitudes from 400–1500 km. Large changes in the intensity of magnetic activity (1 to 3 orders of magnitude) were observed in the vicinity of the auroral zones within a spectral range of 0.05–5 Hz. The enhanced activity, generally located between 67°–82° geomagnetic latitude, was in the form of bursts occurring within a range of 4°–12° great circle arc. The extent of the range, as well as its position, was found to be related to local time and to the Kp index. The bursts lasted for intervals of 3–20 sec, while the satellite was travelling 20–200 km. The beginnings and endings of the intervals were exceedingly sharp with rise and decay times of 1 sec or less. The structure of the signals appears to be similar to hm emissions.

E. W. Greenstadt et al. (1966) have reported on the structure and pulsations in the magnetosheath using data obtained from Vela 3A. They found that irregular fluctuations of the magneto-sheath occasionally give way to sections of record exhibiting periodicity or near periodicity, sometimes for many minutes. The periods of these quasi-sinusoidal oscillations are consistently confined to certain preferred ranges: 10–15 sec, 20–25 sec, 30–40 sec, and around 1 min; their amplitudes vary from just resolvable, at about 2γ peak-to-peak, to 50γ peak-to-peak. By far the most commonly observed range of periods is between 10 and 15 sec. Much work is necessary to establish whether or not a significant correlation exists between the effects observed in the magneto-sheath by Vela 3A and the commonly occurring pulsations observed at the surface of the Earth, let alone whether they have a physical connection. Many characteristics of Pc 2, Pc 3, and Pc 4, however, support the idea that they may have a common origin with the magneto-sheath effects detected by Vela. Additional support has been given by observations of long period (100 sec) hm waves (both linearly and elliptically polarized) in the magnetosphere. These waves, first reported by D. L. Judge and P. J. Coleman (1962) from Explorer 6 measurements, were again seen by Explorer 12 and 14 and correlated with surface records by V. L. Patel and L. J. Cahill (1964) and V. L. Patel (1965). The most outstanding distinction between magneto-sheath and surface observations is the brevity of pulse trains seen by Vela and the corresponding longevity of typical Pc events seen on the ground.

J. P. Heppner et al. (1967), in an initial study of the OGO-A fluxgate magnetometer measurements, reported two classes of field oscillations which are frequently observed at the bow shock front superimposed on the average shock structure—coherent circularly polarized waves with frequencies typically between 0.5 and 1.5 Hz in the satellite reference frame, and higher frequency fluctuations (>3 Hz) which are unresolved by the measurements and whose identity is not known. The coherent oscillations are identified as propagating in the whistler mode, existing in the form of wave packets of 4 to 6 cycles and usually showing a sharp upper frequency cutoff in the power spectra analysis.

A. J. Zmuda et al. (1966, 1967) have reported that transverse magnetic disturbances are regularly observed at a height of 1100 km in the auroral oval. The disturbance region exhibits a diurnal variation and during magnetically quiet conditions has a lower-latitude boundary at $76°$ at local noon and at $67°$ at local midnight. The boundary moves southward with increasing magnetic activity. The amplitude of the disturbance is normally about 100γ but variations as large as 560γ have been observed. W. D. Cummings and A. J. Dessler (1967) attribute the disturbances to a field aligned current system of magnitude around 10^5 amperes. With a few exceptions, disturbances at satellite altitudes correlate temporally with variations at the surface on the same line of force as the satellite disturbance.

W. D. Cummings et al. (1969) have detected low frequency transverse oscillations of the geomagnetic field on magnetically quiet days on records from the geostationary satellite ATS 1. This satellite is located at $150°$ W longitude and its nearly circular orbit has a mean radius of 6.6 Re. The geographic latitude was held at $0° \pm 0.5°$ during the period of the observations. The sensitivity of the magnetometer aboard the spacecraft was about 1γ and amplitudes up to 20γ peak-to-peak were recorded. The pulsations were observed only during magnetically quiet periods ($K_p < 3$) and chiefly between 0400–1600 LMT. The fluctuations were very nearly monochromatic and those with periods ranging from 50–300 sec were studied. The pulsation events lasted from 10–400 min and the period usually varied little during an event. A histogram for the periods showed two groups, one centered on 190 sec and the other on 102 sec. The oscillations were confined to a plane approximately perpendicular to the steady magnetic field. They were generally elliptically polarized in this plane, with the major axis of the polarization ellipse typically inclined eastward at an angle $\simeq 30°$ to the radially outward direction.

The longer period events occurred during very quiet conditions and never during local nighttime. W. D. Cummings et al. suggest that these pulsations are related to the "giant pulsations" pg observed on the ground near the auroral zones. In line with the observed localization of pg's, they suggest that quasi-transverse hm standing waves can occur for which the disturbance is concentrated near one line of force. When changes in the magnitude of the field are neglected, so that the disturbance is purely in direction, the hm equations for weak disturbances simplify so that only spatial variation along a field line is involved and normal modes can be calculated for a field line. Cummings et al. have carried out normal mode computations for the first six harmonics for several plasma density models. The Earth is considered a perfect conductor and the background magnetic field dipolar. The results of their analysis indicate that the observed transverse oscillations are the second harmonic of a standing Alfvén wave. (The odd harmonics have no magnetic disturbance at the equator. For pg's the phase relationships between conjugate points also require even modes.) The longer period ($\simeq 190$ sec) oscillations represent the standing wave when the plasmapause is beyond the geosynchronous orbit. In agreement with other observations the number density in the plasmasphere is $\simeq 100/cm^3$ and the distribution of plasma along the field line is roughly independent of geocentric distance. Also the equatorial geocentric distance to the plasmapause is > 6.6 Re only for very quiet conditions. The shorter period ($\simeq 102$ sec) oscillations represent standing waves when the plasmapause is inside the geosynchronous orbit. The predicted equatorial number density is $\simeq 10/cm^3$ which is somewhat higher than that previously observed. This was also found in other estimates of the plasma density using micropulsation data. However in agreement with previous observations the density along the field line in the plasma trough must decrease extremely rapidly with geocentric distance.

P. J. Coleman (1969) has also reported on fluctuations observed at ATS 1 during disturbed conditions. Abrupt changes in the D (eastward) component of the field sometimes occur between midnight and dawn LT early in the expansion phase of a substorm. On occasion these transients in D have been accompanied by quasi-sinusoidal fluctuations of roughly 3-sec period and about 0.5-γ amplitude in all components. These fluctuations at ATS 1 are probably associated with the 3-sec enhancement in noise bursts recorded at the Earth's surface. Irregular fluctuations of relatively large amplitude, primarily in the H component, have also been detected during the expansion phases of substorms. They occur at night and are probably associated with the irregular pulsations observed at the Earth's surface during substorm expansions. During the recovery phase of substorms, quasi-sinusoidal waves with periods of roughly 20 sec and amplitudes of about 0.5γ have been recorded at ATS 1 near 0600 LT. Fluctuations of roughly equal amplitude appear in all three components. The periods lie in the range associated with the irregular band-limited pulsations that usually occur at the Earth's surface between midnight and 1000 LT during substorm recoveries. Relatively large-amplitude compressional oscillations occur regularly during the main and recovery phases of geomagnetic storms in the late morning and afternoon. Their periods are from 2–15 min (with 4 to 5 min the most common) and their amplitudes are typically 8γ, extending up to 20γ. These long period oscillations are sometimes accompanied by transverse fluctuations with much higher frequencies (periods 5 sec and amplitudes $1-2\gamma$). Moreover they are amplitude modulated with amplitude maxima at the minima and maxima of the longer period oscillations.

J. P. Heppner et al. (1969) have carried out a preliminary examination of the distribution of micropulsations in the magnetosphere using rubidium magnetometer data from OGO 3 and OGO 5. The characteristics and distribution of Pc 3's show a broad dayside maximum, roughly independent of distance from the Earth, in striking agreement with the diurnal variation of the occurrence frequency of Pc 3's at the Earth's surface. The maximum in the occurrence between $L=5$ and 8 probably reflects an amplification rather than a source effect—this is again in agreement with surface observations, amplitudes in the band being greater at the corresponding surface latitudes ($\sim65°$) than at lower latitudes.

The distribution of pulsations in the 45-120 sec period range is similar to that of Pc 3's in having a maximum occurence on the dayside. The percentage of time is, however, lower and decreases greatly as distance from the Earth decreases indicating that the propagation and/or source of Pc 4 pulsations may be different from that of Pc 3's. The increase in Pc 4 amplitudes with increasing latitude is considerably more pronounced than that for Pc 3's—again in agreement with surface observations.

Pc 1's and Pc 2's have a similar statistical distribution in the magnetosphere which is completely different from that of longer period (10-120 sec) pulsations. The percentage of signals in the 0.8-10 sec range has a pronounced maximum near the magnetopause at the 0600 LMT meridian with high values extending tailward near the magnetopause. This distribution is similar in many respects to the magnetospheric distribution of incoherent irregularities which statistically support the observation that 0.8-10 sec pulsations are in general closely associated with other field irregularities, suggesting a local plasma instability origin. It is thus unlikely that statistical comparisons with surface observations can be meaningful.

J. P. Heppner et al. also found that quasi-periodic waves at Pc 3 frequencies and recurrent pulses separated in time by Pc 3 periods, frequently dominate large amplitude fluctuations in the magnetosheath on the sunward side of the cavity. In most cases the three components measured by fluxgate magnetometers simultaneously decrease and increase in intensity approximately in phase, suggesting that these waves are primarily compressional (i.e. magneto—acoustic mode). They speculate as to whether the frequent occurence of large amplitude dayside magneto-sheath fluctuations at Pc 3 periods is related to the prevalence of Pc 3 oscillations in the dayside magnetosphere. This would imply that the magnetopause acts as a source for Pc 3 pulsations observed within the magnetosphere and lends support to the suggestion that a Pc 3 activity index, based on surface observations, be derived for use as an indicator of activity taking place at the dayside magnetopause.

References

Angerami, J. J., Thomas, J. O.: Studies of planetary atmosphere Pt I. *The distribution of electrons and ions in the Earth's exosphere.* J. Geophys. Res. **69**, 4537 to 4560 (1964).

Bolshakova, O. V.: Micropulsations of the geomagnetic field and dynamics of the magnetosphere. Geomag. i Aeron. **5**, 675—679 (1965).

Brice, N. M.: Generation of very low frequency and hydromagnetic emissions. Nature **206**, 283—284 (1965).

Brody, K. I., Holzer, R. E., Smith, E. J.: Observations of magnetic fluctuations on the OGO 2 satellite. Trans. Amer. Geophys. Union **47**, 463 (1966).

Carpenter, D. L.: Whistler studies of the plasmapause in the magnetosphere 1. *Temporal variations in the position of the knee and some evidence on plasma motions near the knee.* J. Geophys. Res. **71**, 693—709 (1966).

Coleman, P. J., Sonett, C. P., Judge, D. L., Smith, E. J.: Some preliminary results of the Pioneer 5 magnetometer experiments. J. Geophys. Res. **65**, 1856—1857 (1960).

— Magnetic field variations at ATS 1 and on the Earth's surface. IAGA Scientific Assembly, Madrid 1969.

Cornwall, J. M.: Micropulsations and the outer radiation zone. J. Geophys. Res. **71**, 2185—2199 (1966).

Cummings, W. D., Dessler, A. J.: Field aligned currents in the magnetosphere. J. Geophys. Res. **72**, 1007—1013 (1967).

— O'Sullivan, R. J., Coleman, P. J., Jr.: Standing Alfvén waves in the magnetosphere. J. Geophys. Res. **74**, 778—793 (1969).

Dungey, J. W.: Electrodynamics of the outer atmosphere. Penn. State Univ. Ionos. Res. Lab. Sci. Rept. No. 69 (1954).

— The structure of the exosphere or adventures in velocity space, in Geophysics: The Earth's environment. (Eds. C. DeWitt et al.), 505—550, Gordon and Breach Sci. Publ. (1963).

Gendrin, R., Gokhberg, M., Lacourly, S., Troitskaya, V. A.: Apparition simultanée de pulsations magnétiques d'ultrabasse fréquence en phase en deux points conjugués. C. R. Acad. Sci. **262**, 845—848 (1966).

Greenstadt, E. W., Inouye, G. T., Green, I. M., Judge, D. L.: Vela 3 magnetograms at 18 Re, structure and pulsations in the magnetosheath. J. Geophys. Res. **72**, 3855—3876 (1967).

Gringauz, K. I.: The structure of the Earth's ionized gas envelope based on local charged particle concentrations measured in the USSR. Space Res. **11**, 574—592 (1961).

References

— Bezrukikh, V. V., Musatov, L. S.: Observations of the solar wind by Venus 3 probe. IUCSTP Symp. Belgrade 1966.

Heacock, R. R.: The 4-second summertime micropulsation band at College. J. Geophys. Res. **71**, 2763—2775 (1966).

Heppner, J. P., Sugiura, M., Skillman, T. L., Ledly, B. G., Campbell, M.: Ogo-A Magnetic field observations. J. Geophys. Res. **72**, 5417—5471 (1967).

— Ledley, B. G., Skillman, T. L., Sugiura, M.: A preliminary survey of the distribution of micropulsations in the magnetosphere from OGO's 3 and 5. Goddard Space Flight Center, X-612-69-429 (1969).

Hirasawa, T., Oguti, T., Nagata T.: Dynamic spectrum of geomagnetic pulsations at low latitudes. Rept. Ionos. Space Res. Japan **19**, 452—469 (1965).

— Nagata, T.: Spectral analysis of geomagnetic pulsations from 0.5 to 100 s in period for the quiet sun condition. Pure Appl. Geophys. **65**, 102—124 (1966).

Johnson, F. S.: The structure of the outer atmosphere including the ion distribution above the F2 maximum. Sci. Rept. LMSD-49719, Lockheed Missiles and Space Co. (1959).

Judge, D. L., Coleman, P. J., Jr.: Observations of low frequency hydromagnetic waves in the distant geomagnetic field: Explorer 6. J. Geophys. Res. **67**, 5071 to 5090 (1962).

Kenney, J. F., Knaflich, H. B., Liemohn, H. B.: Magnetospheric parameters determined from structured micropulsations. J. Geophys. Res. **73**, 6737—6749 (1968).

Kitamura, T.: Geomagnetic pulsations and the exosphere Part III. Ion Density distribution in the exosphere. Rept. Ionos. Space Res. Japan **19**, 1—9 (1965).

— Jacobs, J. A.: Determination of the magnetospheric plasma density by the use of long period geomagnetic micropulsations. J. Geomag. Geoelect. **20**, 33—44 (1968).

Knaflich, H. B., Kenney, J. F.: IPDP events and their generation in the magneto-sphere. Earth Plan. Sci. Letters **2**, 453—459 (1967).

Lacourly, S., Gendrin, R.: Apparition d'IPDP au cours des déplacements de la frontière extérieure des zones de Van Allen. C. R. Acad. Sci. **264**, 658—661 (1967).

Liemohn, H. B.: Cyclotron resonance amplification of VLF and ULF whistlers. J. Geophys. Res. **72**, 39—55 (1967).

— Kenney, J. F., Knaflich, H. B.: Proton densities in the magnetosphere from pearl dispersion measurements. Earth Plan. Sci. Letters **2**, 360—366 (1967).

Mead, G. D.: Deformation of the geomagnetic field by the solar wind. J. Geophys. Res. **69**, 1181—1195 (1964).

Nagata, T., Fukunishi, H.: Dependence on geomagnetic activity of magnetic pulsation frequency of pc-3 and pc-4 ranges. Geophys. J. **15**, 69—78 (1968).

Nishida, A., Cahill, L. J., Jr.: Sudden impulses in the magnetosphere observed by Explorer 12. J. Geophys. Res. **69**, 2243—2255 (1964).

Obayashi, T.: Ionospheric experiment using the orbiting geophysical observatory (OGO-A) at the Ionospheric Research Laboratory, Kyoto University. Rept. Ionos. Space Res. Japan **19**, 214—224 (1965).

— Jacobs, J. A.: Geomagnetic micropulsations and the Earth's outer atmosphere. Geophys. J. **1**, 53—62 (1958).

Ol', A. I.: Long period gigantic geomagnetic field pulsations. Geomag. i Aeron. **3**, 90—95 (1963).

Patel, V. L.: Low frequency hydromagnetic waves in the magnetosphere: Explorer 12. Plan. Space Sci. **13**, 485—506 (1965).

— A note on the propagation of hydromagnetic waves in the magnetosphere. Earth Planet. Sci. Letters **1**, 282—283 (1966).

— Cahill, L. J., Jr.: Evidence of hydromagnetic waves in the Earth's magnetosphere and of their propagation to the Earth's surface. Phys. Rev. Letters 12,
   213—215 (1964).
— Hastings, R. N.: Dependence of the micropulsation periods on the size of the
   magnetosphere. Planet. Space Sci. 17, 1432—1434 (1969).
Prince, C. E., Jr., Bostick, F. X., Jr., Smith, H. W.: Impulse response of the mag-
   netospheric column. J. Geophys. Res. 70, 4901—4908 (1965).
Serbu, G. P., Mainer, E. J. R.: Low energy electrons measured on Imp 2. J. Geo-
   phys. Res. 71, 3755—3766 (1966).
Smith, R. L.: Properties of the outer ionosphere deduced from nose whistlers.
   J. Geophys. Res. 66, 3709—3716 (1961).
Snyder, C. W., Neugebauer, M., Rao, U. R.: The solar wind velocity and its
   correlation with cosmic ray variations and with solar and geomagnetic activity.
   J. Geophys. Res. 68, 6361—6370 (1963).
Sonett, C. P., Sims, A. R., Abrams, I. J.: The distant geomagnetic field 1. In-
   finitesimal hydromagnetic waves. J. Geophys. Res. 67, 1191—1207 (1962).
Stix, T. H.: The theory of plasma waves. New York: McGraw Hill 1962.
Storey, L. R. O.: An investigation of whistling atmospherics. Phil. Trans. Roy. Soc.
   A 246, 113—141 (1953).
Troitskaya, V. A.: Micropulsations and the state of the magnetosphere. Solar
   Terrestrial Physics. (Eds. J. W. King and W. S. Newman) 213—274, Acad.
   Press 1967.
— Bolshakova, O. V., Matveyeva, E. T.: Rapid variations of the electromagnetic
   field as an indication of the state of the radiation belts and the geomagneto-
   sphere. Geomag. i. Aeron. 6, 393—398 (1966).
— Gul'elmi, A. V.: Geomagnetic micropulsations and diagnostics of the mag-
   netosphere. Space Sci. Rev. 7, 689—768 (1967a).
— Bolshakova, O. V., Shchepetnov, R. V.: On the possibility of introduction of the
   solar wind index W_{sw} with applications of properties of micropulsations of the
   electromagnetic field of the Earth. IUGG Assembly, Zurich (1967b).
Vanyan, L. L., Zybin, K. Yu.: Kosm. Issled. (Cosmic Research) 4, 11 (1966).
Ward, S. H.: Dynamics of the magnetosphere. J. Geophys. Res. 68, 781—788 (1963).
Watanabe, T.: Determination of the electron distribution in the magnetosphere
   using hydromagnetic whistlers. J. Geophys. Res. 70, 5839—5848 (1965).
Wentworth, R. C.: Recent investigations of hydromagnetic emissions Part II,
   Theoretical Interpretation. J. Geomag. Geoelect. 18, 257—273 (1966).
Wilcox, J. W., Schatten, K. H., Ness, N. F.: Influences of interplanetary magnetic
   field and plasma on geomagnetic activity during the quiet sun condition. J.
   Geophys. Res. 72, 19—26 (1964).
Zmuda, A. J., Martin, J. H., Heuring, F. T.: Transverse magnetic disturbances at
   1100 kilometers in the auroral region. J. Geophys. Res. 71, 5033—5045 (1966).
— Heuring, F. T., Martin, J. H.: Dayside magnetic disturbances at 1100 kilo-
   meters in the auroral oval. J. Geophys. Res. 72, 1115—1117 (1967).

Subject Index

Typesetting and printing: Zechnersche Buchdruckerei, Speyer
Bookbinding: Konrad Triltsch, Würzburg